Jack London had a wild and colorful youth on the waterfront of San Francisco, his native city. Born in 1876, he left school at the age of fourteen and worked in a cannery. By the time he was sixteen he had been both an oyster pirate and a member of the Fish Patrol in San Francisco Bay, and he later wrote about his experiences in *The Cruise of the Dazzler* (1902) and *Tales of the Fish Patrol* (1905). In 1893 he joined a sealing cruise, which took him as far as Japan. Returning to the United States, he traveled throughout the country. He was determined to become a writer and read voraciously. After a brief period of study at the University of California he joined the gold rush to the Klondike in 1897. He returned to San Francisco the following year and began writing his fabulous Northland Saga. His short stories of the Yukon were initially published in the *Overland Monthly* (1898) and the *Atlantic Monthly* (1899); in 1900 his first collection, *The Son of the Wolf*, appeared, bringing him national fame. In 1902 he went to London, where he studied the slum conditions of the East End and wrote *The People of the Abyss* (1903). In 1904 he reported on the Russo-Japanese War for the Hearst papers; during the following year he traveled the lecture circuit, delivering lectures at Harvard and Yale. From 1907 to 1909, he sailed the South Seas, recording his adventures in *The Cruise of the Snark* (1911). From 1910 until his death he devoted most of his extraliterary energies to building his celebrated Beauty Ranch in the Valley of the Moon. An extraordinarily disciplined and prolific writer, during a career that lasted less than twenty years, he produced more than four hundred nonfiction works, 200 stories, and twenty novels, including *The Call of the Wild* (1903), *The Sea-Wolf* (1904), *White Fang* (1906), *The Iron Heel* (1908), *Martin Eden* (1909), *Burning Daylight* (1910), *The Star Rover* (1915), and *The Little Lady of the Big House* (1916). After two extended visits to Hawaii, London died in 1916 at his home in Glen Ellen, California.

Born in Tuskahoma, Oklahoma, in 1928, Earle Labor is part Choctaw Indian. He received his A.B. and M.A. degrees from Southern Methodist University, where he was a member of the varsity track team and a champion weightlifter before graduating *magna cum laude*, Phi Beta Kappa. After serving as a recruit instructor for the U.S. Navy and assistant sales manager for Haggar Company, he earned his Ph.D. from the University of Wisconsin. In 1966, as a visiting professor at Utah State University, he taught the first course on Jack London ever offered in the United States;

in 1974, as a Fulbright lecturer at the University of Aarhus, Denmark, he presented the first Jack London course in Western Europe. During the past three decades he has published more than fifty articles and reviews on London, as well as seven books, including the Stanford editions of *The Letters of Jack London* (1988) and *The Complete Short Stories of Jack London* (1993). He is currently the Wilson Professor of American Literature and Director of the Jack London Research Center at Centenary College of Louisiana.

Each volume in The Viking Portable Library either presents a representative selection from the works of a single outstanding writer or offers a comprehensive anthology on a special subject. Averaging 700 pages in length and designed for compactness and readability, these books fill a need not met by other compilations. All are edited by distinguished authorities, who have written introductory essays and included much other helpful material.

*The Portable*

# JACK LONDON

*Edited by*

EARLE LABOR

PENGUIN BOOKS

PENGUIN BOOKS
Published by the Penguin Group
Penguin Books USA Inc., 375 Hudson Street,
New York, New York 10014, U.S.A.
Penguin Books Ltd, 27 Wrights Lane,
London W8 5TZ, England
Penguin Books Australia Ltd, Ringwood,
Victoria, Australia
Penguin Books Canada Ltd, 10 Alcorn Avenue,
Toronto, Ontario, Canada M4V 3B2
Penguin Books (N.Z.) Ltd, 182–190 Wairau Road,
Auckland 10, New Zealand

Penguin Books Ltd, Registered Offices:
Harmondsworth, Middlesex, England

First published in Penguin Books 1994

5 7 9 10 8 6

Grateful acknowledgment is made for permission to reprint "The
Water Baby" from On the Makaloa Mat, Macmillan, and selections
from The Letters of Jack London edited by Earle Labor, Robert C.
Leitz, III, and I. Milo Shepard, Stanford University Press. By permission
of the Trust of Irving Shepard, I. Milo Shepard, Trustee.

LIBRARY OF CONGRESS CATALOGING IN PUBLICATION DATA
London, Jack, 1876–1916.
[Selections. 1994]
The portable Jack London/ edited by Earle Labor.
p. cm.
Includes bibliographical references.
ISBN 0 14 01.7969 0
I. Labor, Earle, 1928– . II. Title.
PS3523.O46A6 1994
93-38740 813'.52—dc20

Printed in the United States of America
Set in Sabon

TO MY CHILDREN

*Royce Garrett Labor*
*Phillips Kirk Labor*
*Earle Kyle Labor*
*Isabel Labor Hamiter*

AND TO MY GRANDSONS

*Erik Owen Garrett Labor*
*Christian Jensen Hamiter*

# CONTENTS

## A SELECTION OF LETTERS

# INTRODUCTION

"ASK PEOPLE who know me today, what I am," Jack London wrote to Charmian Kittredge shortly after their romantic affair had begun in the summer of 1903. "A rough, savage fellow, they will say, who likes prizefights and brutalities, who has a clever turn of pen, a charlatan's smattering of art, and the inevitable deficiencies of the untrained, unrefined, self-made man which he strives with a fair measure of success to hide beneath an attitude of roughness and unconventionality. Do I endeavor to unconvince them? It's so much easier to leave their convictions alone."

And leave their convictions alone he did, as have the millions of his fans and common readers worldwide who were content merely to enjoy the adventures of his "rough, savage" literary heroes, while keeping the name of "Jack London" on the popular bookstands now for nearly a century.

Similar "convictions"—or, more accurately, "misconceptions"—on the part of our academic Establishment have led three generations of American critics to "ghettoize" (to use Leslie Fiedler's handy term) Jack London as a naturalist hack who managed to produce a handful of entertaining children's stories, mainly about Alaskan superdogs and wolves. Yet even a cursory reading of the full range of the works London produced during his remarkable twenty-year writing career—some two hundred stories, twenty novels, four hundred nonfiction pieces, and several thousand letters—leads to the inevitable realization that stereotyped labels like the "Dogmatist of Darwinism" and "Sideshow in the Naturalist Carnival" should be replaced by such more accurate titles as "Major American Author" and perhaps even, as some foreign critics have suggested, "America's Most Powerful Writer."

As early as 1914, for example, Georg Brandes singled out London as the best of the new twentieth-century American writers: "He is absolutely original," the Danish scholar remarked, "and his style is singularly forcible and free from all affectation." Anatole France praised London for possessing "that particular genius which perceives what is hidden from the common herd." Both George Orwell and Jorge Luis Borges thought well enough of London to edit collections of his stories, Orwell citing London's "aim at rousing pity and indignation" and Borges noting the literary bond between London and Hemingway. Russian critic Vil Bykov has compared London favorably with Tolstoy and Chekhov in their common pursuit of "the man of noble spirit," noting that, along with the essential vitality of London's works, it was this theme, more than his socialistic ideas, that made him the most popular foreign writer in the Soviet Union. "Healthy people better understand a healthy person," explains Bykov. "They believe in man and they tend toward that which is full of life. Jack London brought to the Russian reader a world full of romanticism and vigor, and the reader came to love him." And most recently, Beijing University professor Li Shuyan has asserted that "whatever happens in the critical world, London will go on enjoying the admiration of the Chinese readers. Martin Eden and the many heroes of London's stories of the North will always be an encouraging force to those who are fighting against adversities, and who believe the worth of man lies in doing, creating, and achieving."

The range of subjects treated in London's works is simply astonishing: adventure, agronomy, alcoholism, androgyny, animal training (and rights), architecture, assassination, astral projection, big business, boxing, bullfighting, crime, dreams (collective as well as individual), ecology, economics, ethics (particularly situational), evolution, fantasy, folklore, friendship, gambling, gold hunting, greed, hatred, hoboing, justice, labor, leprosy, love, loyalty, mental retardation, mythology, old age, penal reform, political corruption, poverty, psychology (both animal and human), racial exploitation, revenge, revolution, science, seafaring, slum living, socialism, spiritualism, starvation (not only physical but also emotional), stockbreeding, superstition, surfing (which he introduced to the American public), survival, war, wildlife, and the writing game.

Geographically, London's fictions range from the frozen-hearted Arctic wilderness to the noisome jungles of Melanesia; from the Polynesian paradises of Hawaii, Samoa, and Tahiti to the cooler islands off the coasts of Scotland and Ireland; from the blight and miseries of the modern industrial city to the purifying ambiance of the pastoral wilderness; from the blood-soaked bullrings of South America to the prelapsarian pastures of the Valley of the Moon and "All Gold Canyon."

London's works range in mood from the merciless doom of the White Silence to the heartrending gloom of the child laborer; from the pathos of old age to the irrepressible exuberance of youth; from romantic sentimentalism to materialistic cynicism; from joy to horror; from dreadful suspense to comic—and sometimes tragic—relief; from the raucous fun of the tall tale to the gentler humor of the "Drooling Ward." Perhaps most impressive is the range of irony: dramatic, situational, tragic, and—most notably—cosmic.

Thematically, his works move from the foolishness of pride, the ruthlessness of greed, the blindness of racial prejudice, and the senselessness of war, to the indomitability of the human spirit, the unfailing salvation of true comradeship, and the ageless wisdom of the Great Mother and the Water Baby.

Here, in truth, is Humanity's as well as God's plenty.

The extraordinary richness of London's works is rivaled by that of his of his personal experiences. Alfred Kazin has aptly remarked that "the greatest story Jack London ever wrote was the story he lived." London's personal story was surely the stuff of which legends —and myths—are made. An unwanted child born out of wedlock and into poverty, he spent much of his boyhood in circumstances of emotional as well as physical deprivation. He was a farmboy at the age of seven; city newsboy at ten; factory "work beast" at fourteen; self-confessed boozer, gang member, and oyster pirate at fifteen; able-bodied seaman and prize-winning author at seventeen; hobo and convict at eighteen; notorious "Boy Socialist" of Oakland at nineteen; Klondike argonaut at twenty-one; the "American Kipling" and "Bret Harte of the Frozen Northland" at twenty-four; internationally renowned author, social crusader, and war correspondent at twenty-eight; world traveler and adventurer at thirty-one; award-winning stockbreeder and scientific farmer at thirty-five; America's most celebrated writer-as-folk-hero by the time of his death at forty. London's fantastic rise from rags to riches, from saloon and gutter to salon and hall of fame, not only makes a great story, it also validates the American Dream of Success.

Impressive as was his spectacular career, it is his achieved performance as a literary artist upon which London's ultimate fame must rest. As Henry James might have described him, he was a person on whom nothing was lost and whose sensibility was responsive to all that he experienced. Surprisingly, perhaps, much of the raw experience that he transformed into literary art came to him secondhand, from what he heard and, more often, from what he read. His appetite not only for books but for virtually everything in print—newspapers, magazines, broadsides, and pamphlets—was voracious. He subscribed to several scores of periodicals, and his personal library exceeded fifteen thousand volumes. His characteristic method of composing a story was to begin by jotting down ideas on his notepad or even in the margins of newspapers and magazines when he came across what he considered a viable subject and plot. He would then spend several days "mulling" the story, and then begin writing—virtually without hesitation or revision—at his minimum thousand-words-a-day clip.

Notwithstanding his eclectic tastes and the extraordinary variety of his experiences, there is nevertheless a discernible pattern in London's literary carpet, central to which are two recurring questions and an underlying thematic antithesis: What is humanity's relationship to the natural world? and What is the individual's relationship to his/her fellow beings, animal as well as human? The thematic antithesis, from which derives the essential creative tension for his literary artistry, is the opposition of materialism *versus* spiritualism—that is, the tension between the logical and the scientific on the one hand and the irrational and mystical on the other. While he persistently denied the latter, professing throughout his life that he was "a materialistic monist," his art betrays him, time and again revealing him to be, in fact, a philosophical dualist whose approach to the truth was ultimately hermeneutical rather than epistemological. Moreover, his greatest work is informed by what C. G. Jung has called the "primordial vision," which manifests itself through archetypal imagery, indelibly marking London as a mythopoeic genius who often wrote better than he knew.

The tension between these conflicting thematic elements is apparent from the very outset in London's Northland fictions. At first glance, the stories in his Klondike saga would seem to be standard naturalistic fare: puny human beings pitted against the inexorable forces of a hostile universe, nature's dice loaded in favor of the species against the individual, who is doomed to suffer and die, violently and pitilessly. Yet there is a counterbalancing theme of human comradeship and compassion. Furthermore, London's presentation is scarcely that of the coldly scientific observer. As is the case with such other

literary naturalists as Frank Norris and Theodore Dreiser, we find in
London's work a pervading sense of mystical wonder in the face of
natural and cosmic force, as witnessed even in such early stories as
"The White Silence":

> The afternoon wore on, and with the awe, born of the White
> Silence, the voiceless travelers bent to their work. Nature has
> many tricks wherewith she convinces man of his finity,—the
> ceaseless flow of the tides, the fury of the storm, the shock
> of the earthquake, the long roll of heaven's artillery,—but
> the most tremendous, the most stupefying of all, is the passive
> phase of the White Silence. All movement ceases, the sky
> clears, the heavens are as brass; the slightest whisper seems
> sacrilege, and man becomes timid, affrighted at the sound of
> his own voice. Sole speck of life journeying across the ghostly
> wastes of a dead world, he trembles at his audacity, realizes
> that his is a maggot's life, nothing more. Strange thoughts
> arise unsummoned, and the mystery of all things strives for
> utterance. And the fear of death, of God, of the universe,
> comes over him,—the hope of the Resurrection and the Life,
> the yearning for immortality, the vain striving of the impris-
> oned essence,—it is then, if ever, man walks alone with God.

In the face of this awesome force, only the fittest stand a chance
of survival, and the only hope for survival is adaptability. Ostensibly,
this theme appears to be purely Darwinian; however, London's Northland Code demands not only physical but also intellectual and ethical
adaptability, the "strength of the strong" (as he would preach later in
his socialistic writings) being communal rather than individual, and
the greatest of all (as he would assert throughout his works) being the
salvational power of *agape*. This is the implicit theme of his first published story, "To the Man on Trail" (appropriately subtitled "A Klondike Christmas" when it appeared in *The Overland Monthly*), and the
explicit message of his exemplum "In a Far Country," where the real
test comes "in learning properly to shape [one's] attitude toward all
things, and especially toward his fellow man. For the courtesies of
ordinary life, he must substitute unselfishness, forbearance, and tolerance. Thus, and thus only, can he gain that pearl of great price,—
true comradeship."

Even London's canine protagonists are not entirely exempt from
this higher ethic. Buck, for example, before succumbing to the "Call

of the Wild," undergoes a spiritual transformation through his selfless devotion to John Thornton, and at the end of the novel he has completely transcended his naturalistic milieu to become the legendary "Ghost Dog" of the Northland. White Fang, the title character of London's "companion novel," in his transformation from killer wolf to ranch pet, is similarly redeemed by the loving ministry of Weedon Scott: "Human kindness was like a sun shining upon him, and he flourished like a flower planted in good soil."

The inevitable failure of the ego-centered, loveless individualist is London's major theme in both *The Sea-Wolf* and *Martin Eden*. "I believe life is a mess," declares Wolf Larsen; "the strong eat the weak that they may retain their strength. The lucky eat the most and move the longest, that is all." One of the most powerful characters in the naturalist canon, Larsen is nevertheless bound to fail—and ultimately to die, paralyzed and speechless—because he is inflexible in his ruthless materialism, and incapable of compassion or love. Martin Eden, a far more sympathetic character, is likewise doomed: "Being an individualist, being unaware of the needs of others, of the whole human collective need, [he] lived only for himself, fought only for himself, and, if you please, died for himself," London explained in a 1910 letter to Rev. Charles Brown. "[He] failed and died, in my parable . . . because of his lack of faith in man."

Unlike Martin Eden, London himself was redeemed from his own "long sickness" of pessimistic disillusionment because he found true love in Charmian Kittredge and because he lived and fought for something besides himself. "Love, socialism, the PEOPLE," he confessed in *John Barleycorn*, "were the things that cured and saved me." Humanitarian compassion and humanistic faith, coupled with a fierce resentment of social injustice, constituted the basis for London's socialist convictions. His compassion was poignantly articulated in *The People of the Abyss*. "Of all my books on the long shelf," he remarked near the end of his career, "I love most 'The People of the Abyss.' No other book of mine took so much of my young heart and tears as that study of the economic degradation of the poor." And he proclaimed even more clearly his humanistic faith in the preface to his *War of the Classes*:

> The capitalist must learn, first and for always, that socialism is based, not upon equality, but upon the inequality, of men. Next, he must learn that no new birth into spiritual purity is necessary before socialism becomes possible. He must learn

that socialism deals with what is, not with what ought to be; and that the material with which it deals is the "clay of the common road," the warm human, fallible and frail, sordid and petty, absurd and contradictory, even grotesque, and yet, withal, shot through with flashes and glimmerings of something finer and God-like, with here and there sweetnesses of service and unselfishness, desires for goodness, for renunciation and sacrifice, and with conscience, stern and awful, at times blazingly imperious, demanding the right,—the right, nothing more nor less than the right.

London's socialistic enthusiasm reached its most intense pitch in *The Iron Heel*. The hero of that celebrated apocalyptic novel, Ernest Everhard, is a fascinating composite of Walt Whitman, Eugene V. Debs, Jesus Christ, and Jack London in his socialist persona. "He was a poet. A singer of deeds," rhapsodizes his biographer/widow Avis Everhard, herself a composite of Elizabeth Barrett Browning, Emma Goldman, and Charmian Kittredge London. "And all his life he sang the song of man. And he did it out of sheer love of man, and for man he gave his life and was crucified." Less hagiographic but more artistically effective is "The Mexican," the last and one of the best of his socialist-inspired fictions. In this well-wrought parable the indomitable spirit of revolution is dramatically characterized through London's superb description of physical action rather than through gratuitous encomia. So well has London modulated his message that his allegory may also be read simply as a first-rate boxing story.

We may detect a notable decline in London's socialist interests during the last years of his life, and this decline is reflected in his works; but, contrary to received opinion, there is neither a consequent diminishing of his humanistic concerns nor a deterioration of his artistic energies. At least three common misconceptions have obscured a fair assessment of the work produced after 1909, the year he returned home from the *Snark* voyage and published his confessional *roman à clef, Martin Eden*: first, that with "his drift away from the working class and working class ideas in his last years," as Philip Foner has put it, "Jack London lost the inspiration and the ability to write valid literature"; second, that the *Snark* voyage, which he had been forced to abandon after being hospitalized in Australia with multiple tropical diseases contracted in the Solomon Islands, had robbed him not only of his physical health but also of his creative energies; and third, that—driven by ever-mounting financial pressures incurred by bad investments, the overly ambitious expansion of Beauty Ranch, the subsequent crop failures and deaths of prize livestock, and the tragic burning of Wolf House, his magnificent rock-and-redwood home "designed to stand a thousand years"—London catered to the most common tastes of the literary marketplace with an increasing amount of formulaic hackwork.

These misconceptions can be rectified merely by reading through London's post-*Snark* writings, which reveal him experimenting with totally new fictional subject matter and techniques, some of which were so alien to the contemporary demands of the marketplace that even the famous name of "Jack London" was not enough to guarantee the acceptance by the best-paying magazines of such stories as "Samuel," "War," and "Told in the Drooling Ward." In other words, the critical commonplace that London hated his profession (reinforced by his own public complaints about the drudgery of writing), that he wrote only for money (but, as Dr. Johnson quipped, "No man but a blockhead ever wrote except for money"), and that during the last third of his career he became increasingly cynical in pandering to the popular market—this indictment is refuted by the quality of the works themselves. In short, as D. H. Lawrence reminds us, "Never trust the artist—trust the tale."

What we discover in examining London's later tales—and novels—is a progressive shift from socialism, naturalism, and violent action toward pastoralism, spiritualism (most notably Jungian theory), and dialogue. Moreover, as such critics as Jeanne Campbell Reesman and Clarice Stasz have pointed out, there is a corresponding trend away from male-dominated toward female-dominated narratives. This trend is evident in examples like "Samuel" and "The Night-Born," both of which may be found in this edition, as well as in London's Sonoma novels: *Burning Daylight, The Valley of the Moon,* and *The Little Lady of the Big House.* In the first of these three, the hero, a Klondike bonanza king turned robber baron, is redeemed by the love of a woman who persuades him to renounce the savage world of big business for the gentler arcadian world of ranching. In the second, a young working-class couple whose lives have been blighted in the strike-torn city of Oakland undertake an odyssey that ultimately leads them into the Edenic Valley of the Moon; significantly, it is the woman who possesses the vision and who serves as the guiding force in their quest for salvation. *The Little Lady of the Big House* presents the agrarian dream on a grander scale but, by contrast, ends in tragedy because Dick Forrest, owner of a splendid ranch and husband of the protagonist, has become a sterile clockwork figure obsessed with scientific efficiency. Paula Forrest—childless, treated like a child and a "little lady" but never a like a woman—falls hopelessly in love with Dick's best friend, then at the novel's climax commits suicide as her only means of resolving the love triangle. London's message is clear: to be fully human and whole, we must conjoin the male principle (science, rationality, efficiency) with the female principle (affection, compassion, and the capacity for wonder). As Hawthorne would say, head must be balanced by heart. Or, in Jungian terms, man must embrace and nurture his anima—that feminine element in his psyche representing not only gentleness and agape but also the vitalizing, mysterious forces of Nature and the Unconscious. This is also the central theme of "The Night-Born," whose male protagonist spurns the free-spirited Lucy for the fool's gold of material wealth and decadent "man-meanness" of city life. And it is likewise "The Message" (as London originally titled his great story) of "The Red One," whose hero's quest for Truth projects that of his author/creator.

The tempering of London's tough-minded scientism and professed materialistic monism is evident in the growing inclination toward spiritualism throughout his later writings, a proclivity evidently nurtured by his agrarian dream—his vision of "making the land better for my having been," as he put it. Return to the Edenic valley and the restoration of Nature's abundance: these become symbols for spiritual restoration and rebirth. For example, Darrell Standing, the protagonist of *The Star Rover*, is a professor of agronomics sentenced to life imprisonment for killing a colleague in a fit of passion. While in San Quentin, he masters the art of astral projection, or "soul flight," which enables him to move freely in time and space. He dreams of being a peaceful farmer in his next life and at the end of the novel philosophizes that "Spirit alone endures and continues to build upon itself through successive and endless incarnations as it works upward toward the light."

London's fascination with the spiritual, rejected dogmatically in his earlier years, culminated with his discovery of Jung's ideas in the summer of 1916. "I tell you I am standing on the edge of a world so new, so terrible, so wonderful, that I am almost afraid to look over into it," he exclaimed to Charmian on reading Dr. Beatrice Hinkle's just-published edition of Jung's works. Fortunately, he was not too afraid to incorporate this new world into his fiction, and the stories he wrote during the remaining few months of his life reverberate with Jungian theory. "The Water Baby," the last story he ever wrote, is exemplary. Cast in the narrative mold of a dialogue between an ancient Hawaiian native named Kohokumu (meaning "tree of knowledge"), who claims the sea as his mother, and a young fishing partner named John Lakana (London's own Hawaiian name), who rejoins that such mythic stuff is nonsense, the tale is on one level an interior debate between the author's two conflicting selves: the skeptical materialist and the mythopoeic idealist. London's conscious mind obviously clung to his scientific skepticism even as his unconscious drew him inexorably toward the wonders of the new world. "But listen, O Young Wise One, to my elderly wisdom," advises Kohokumu:

> This I know: as I grow old I seek less for the truth from without me, and find more of the truth from within me. Why have I thought this thought of my return to my mother and my rebirth from my mother into the sun? You do not know. I do not know, save that, without whisper of man's voice or printed word, without prompting from otherwhere, this thought has arisen from within me, from the deeps of me that are as deep as the sea.

London's own *Weltanschauung* was surely undergoing a sea change into something rich and strange during the last months of his life. While we may regret that he did not live longer to share more of his new-found treasures, we must be grateful for the remarkable legacy he did manage to create for us.

# CHRONOLOGY

1876   Born January 12 in San Francisco, California, and named John Griffith Chaney by his mother, Flora Wellman, who had been deserted by her common-law husband, professional astrologer/lecturer William Henry Chaney, when she informed him of her pregnancy. On September 7 Flora Wellman Chaney marries Civil War veteran and widower John London; her child is renamed John Griffith London.

1878   To escape the diphtheria epidemic that has almost claimed Jack and his stepsister, Eliza, John London moves his family across San Francisco Bay to Oakland, where he manages a grocery store and sells to local markets the produce he grows.

1881   The Londons move to a twenty-acre farm in Alameda.

1882   JL begins schooling in Alameda.

1886   After living on farms in San Mateo County and in the Livermore Valley, the Londons buy a house in Oakland. JL is introduced to the world of books in the Oakland Public Library.

1891   Graduates from Cole Grammar School and begins working in Hickmott's Cannery. With $300 borrowed from his former wet nurse, "Aunt Jennie" Prentiss, he buys the sloop *Razzle-Dazzle* and becomes an oyster pirate on San Francisco Bay.

*1892*     Joins the California Fish Patrol in Benecia as a deputy patrolman.

*1893*     Serves as able-bodied seaman aboard sealing schooner *Sophia Sutherland* on eight-month (January–August) voyage to the Bering Sea via Hawaii, the Bonin Islands, and Japan. Upon returning to California, works in jute mill. "Story of a Typhoon Off the Coast of Japan" wins first prize ($25.00) in contest for young writers sponsored by the *San Francisco Call.*

*1894*     Works as coal heaver in local electric railway power plant. In April joins Kelly's Army, the western contingent of Coxey's Army of the Unemployed, in its protest march to Washington. In late May leaves the Army in Hannibal, Missouri, to tramp on his own. Heads east after visiting Chicago World's Fair grounds. Arrested for vagrancy in Niagara; returns to California after thirty days in Erie County Penitentiary.

*1895*     Attends Oakland High School, where he publishes short stories and articles in *The High School Aegis.* Falls in love with Mabel Applegarth, who will become the model for Ruth Morse in *Martin Eden.*

*1896*     Joins the Socialist Labor Party, achieving notoriety as the "Boy Socialist" of Oakland. Leaves high school and, after intensive cramming for entrance examinations, is admitted to University of California.

*1897*     Leaves university because of lack of funds. After unsuccessful writing efforts, takes job in laundry at Belmont Academy (where Frank Norris had been a student twelve years before). With brother-in-law, Captain James H. Shepard, journeys to Alaska in late July to join Klondike Gold Rush. Spends winter in cabin on Split-Up Island in Yukon Territory.

*1898*     Suffering from scurvy, rafts down Yukon River from Dawson to St. Michael on the Bering Sea (June 8); works his way home as coal stoker, arriving in Oakland in late July. Begins intense regimen to become a professional writer.

*1899*     "To the Man on Trail" published in Christmas issue of the *Overland Monthly.* "An Odyssey of the North" accepted by *Atlantic Monthly* (published in January 1900). In December meets Anna Strunsky.

1900    Meets Charmian Kittredge in March. On April 7 marries Bessie Maddern. Publishes first book, *The Son of the Wolf.*

1901    Daughter Joan born, January 15. JL commissioned by Hearst newspaper syndicate to cover Third National Bundes Shooting Festival, his first journalism assignment. Runs unsuccessfully for mayor of Oakland on the Socialist ticket. On December 27 George Brett, president of Macmillan Company, writes to solicit book-length mss. JL elected secretary of the Economic League (with Oakland Public Library Director Frederick Irons Bamford as president). Publishes *The God of His Fathers.*

1902    Begins friendship with poet George Sterling, model for Russ Brissenden in *Martin Eden.* On April 28 signs contract with Macmillan to publish *Children of the Frost.* Spends six weeks (August–September) in the East End of London composing *The People of the Abyss.* Second daughter, Bess (Becky), born, October 20. Publishes first novel, *A Daughter of the Snows,* as well as *Children of the Frost* and *The Cruise of the Dazzler.*

1903    Falls in love with Charmian Kittredge and separates from Bessie London. Publishes *The Kempton-Wace Letters* (co-authored with Anna Strunsky), *The Call of the Wild,* and *The People of the Abyss.*

1904    Reports on Russo-Japanese War in Korea and Manchuria for Hearst (January–June). Divorce suit filed by Bessie London, who names Anna Strunsky as co-respondent. Publishes *The Faith of Men* and *The Sea-Wolf.*

1905    Runs (again unsuccessfully) as Socialist candidate for mayor of Oakland. Moves to the Sonoma Valley town of Glen Ellen, where he purchases the 129-acre Hill Ranch, the beginning of 1500-acre "Beauty Ranch." In October starts socialist lecture tour throughout the Midwest and East, including Harvard. Granted divorce on November 18; marries Charmian Kittredge the following day in Chicago. Publishes *War of the Classes, The Game,* and *Tales of the Fish Patrol.*

1906    Resumes socialist lecture tour after honeymoon in Jamaica. After appearances at Carnegie Hall, Yale, and the Universities of Chicago and North Dakota, cancels lecture tour because of illness and returns to Glen Ellen in mid-February. Starts building the schooner *Snark* for projected seven-year voyage around the world. Reports San Francisco earthquake for *Collier's*, April 18. Publishes *Moon-Face and Other Stories*, *White Fang*, and *Scorn of Women*.

1907    After repeated delays, *Snark* sets sail from Oakland on April 23, bound for Hawaiian Islands; arrives at Pearl Harbor on May 20. Leaves Hawaii on October 7, sailing to Marquesas Islands and Tahiti. Publishes *Before Adam*, *Love of Life and Other Stories*, and *The Road*.

1908    Returns to Oakland from Tahiti to attend to financial affairs (mid-January). Resumes *Snark* voyage in April, sailing to Samoa, Fiji Islands, New Hebrides, Solomon Islands, and Australia. Hospitalized with multiple tropical ailments in Sydney, Australia, on November 29 and forced to abandon cruise. Publishes *The Iron Heel*.

1909    Returns to Glen Ellen, via Ecuador, Panama, and New Orleans, arriving home on July 24. Publishes *Martin Eden*.

1910    Hires Eliza London Shepard as ranch manager in February; expands Beauty Ranch to nearly 1,000 acres. Visits friends at the artists' colony in Carmel. Agrees to buy several story outlines from Sinclair Lewis at $5.00 apiece. Daughter Joy born June 19; dies June 21. JL reports Johnson-Jeffries fight in Reno, Nevada, July 4. Discusses plans to build "Wolf House" with architect Albert Farr. Publishes *Lost Face*, *Revolution and Other Essays*, *Burning Daylight*, and *Theft: A Play in Four Acts*.

1911    With Charmian and valet Nakata, spends summer driving four-horse wagon to Oregon and back. Departs on December 24 for two-month trip to New York. Publishes *When God Laughs and Other Stories*, *Adventure*, *The Cruise of the Snark*, and *South Sea Tales*.

1912    On March 1 sails from Baltimore with Charmian aboard the barque *Dirigo* for five-month voyage to Seattle around Cape Horn. Returns to Glen Ellen in early August. Signs five-year fiction contract with *Cosmopolitan*. Publishes *The House of Pride and Other Tales of Hawaii*, *A Son of the Sun*, and *Smoke Bellew*.

1913    Operated on for appendicitis, July 8; informed by surgeon that kidneys are diseased. "Wolf House" destroyed by fire, August 22. Attends Grauman's Imperial Theatre in San Francisco for premiere of Hobart Bosworth's *The Sea-Wolf*, first feature-length film produced in America, on October 5. Publishes *The Night-Born [and Other Stories]*, *The Abysmal Brute*, *John Barleycorn*, and *The Valley of the Moon*.

1914    On January 9 travels to New York to discuss business affairs. Leaves with Charmian, April 16, for Vera Cruz to report on Mexican Revolution for *Collier's*. Following attack of acute dysentery, returns to Glen Ellen in June. Publishes *The Strength of the Strong* and *The Mutiny of the Elsinore*.

1915    After severe rheumatism attack in February, sails to Hawaii hoping to improve health. Returns to Glen Ellen in July and sails back to Hawaii in December. Publishes *The Scarlet Plague* and *The Star Rover*.

1916    On March 7 resigns from Socialist party. Returns from Hawaii in late July. On September 3 visits California State Fair in Sacramento, where he is stricken again with rheumatism. Dies November 22 of "Uraemia following renal colic" (more probably stroke and heart failure). *The Acorn-Planter: A California Forest Play*, *The Little Lady of the Big House*, and *The Turtles of Tasman* are published.

*Posthumously published books:*

1917    *The Human Drift; Jerry of the Islands; Michael, Brother of Jerry.*

1918    *The Red One; Hearts of Three.*

1919    *On the Makaloa Mat.*

1922    *Dutch Courage and Other Stories.*

1963    *The Assassination Bureau, Ltd.*, based on plot by Sinclair Lewis and completed by Robert L. Fish (receives Edgar Award from Mystery Writers of America).

1965    *Letters from Jack London*, ed. King Hendricks and Irving Shepard.

1970    *Jack London Reports: War Correspondence, Sports Articles, and Miscellaneous Writings*, ed. King Hendricks and Irving Shepard.

1979    *No Mentor But Myself: A Collection of Articles, Essays, Reviews and Letters by Jack London, on Writing and Writers*, ed. Dale L. Walker; *Jack London on the Road: The Tramp Diary and Other Hobo Writings*, ed. Richard W. Etulain.

1983    *A Klondike Trilogy: Three Uncollected Stories*, ed. Earle Labor.

1988    *The Letters of Jack London*, ed. Earle Labor, Robert C. Leitz, III, and I. Milo Shepard.

1993    *The Complete Stories of Jack London*, ed. Earle Labor, Robert C. Leitz, III, and I. Milo Shepard.

# NOTE ON THE
# TEXTS AND SELECTIONS

IN MOST CASES I have used as texts for this volume the first editions
of London's books. When other texts are used (such as in the case of
"Things Alive," London's commentary on the attitudes of university
students, which appears here for the first time since its original publication in *The Yale Magazine*), the sources are indicated in footnotes.
My text for London's letters is the Stanford Edition (1988).

Now, an editorial apologia:

My original prospectus for this edition included nearly twice as
many selections as have been included here; however, realizing that
such a volume (or multivolume) would undercut the functional principle of "portability," I have chosen—often agonizingly—to cut rather
than undercut. I therefore ask the forbearance of those Jack London
fans and scholars who miss herein some of their own favorites.

I had originally planned, for instance, to include key excerpts from
such important confessional treatises as *Martin Eden* (the passionate
*bildungsroman* that first inspired me to consider London as a serious
literary artist more than forty years ago, when I was stationed at the
U.S. Naval Recruit Training Center in Bainbridge, Maryland); *John
Barleycorn* (particularly those passages in which London recollects his
early attempts to break into the literary marketplace); *The Road* (especially the section on his prison experiences); and *The Cruise of the
Snark*.

I had also wanted to include passages from several London novels:
the philosophical dialogue between Wolf Larsen, the incorrigible materialist, and Humphrey Van Weyden, the romantic idealist, as well as

the latter's androgynous observations concerning the lack of gender balance in the crewmembers' lives aboard the *Ghost*, in *The Sea-Wolf* (second only to *The Call of the Wild* in reader appeal, and more films—eight at latest count—have been made of this classic of the sea than of any other novel in our literature); *White Fang* (another popular classic, whose opening chapter represents some of the finest writing in American literary naturalism, and the closing section of which powerfully underscores London's faith in the healing effects of science enhanced by courage and love); *The Star Rover* (an astonishing *tour de force* rightly labeled by Leslie Fiedler as "one of America's greatest neglected novels"); London's plays (*e.g.*, his exposé of corruption in Washington politics in *Theft* and his celebration of the agrarian dream in *The Acorn-Planter*); and his three ranch novels: *Burning Daylight*, *The Valley of the Moon*, and *The Little Lady of the Big House*.

I can rationalize that all these book-length works are better read *in toto*, and several are, indeed, readily available in paperback editions. Unfortunately, this is not the usual case with the ranch novels and assuredly not with the plays, which exist at present only in extremely scarce first editions.

Among the stories I reluctantly omitted were such Klondike nuggets as "The White Silence"; "An Odyssey of the North" (which marked a major breakthrough in London's early career when it was accepted for publication in the great *Atlantic Monthly*); "The League of the Old Men" (which he considered one of his best); three noteworthy stories in which the central characters are heroic Indian women—"The Story of Jees Uck," "The Wit of Porportuk," and "Wonder of Woman"; and "Like Argus of the Ancient Times," London's sole intentionally Jungian Klondike fiction in which the gritty "ancient" hero, a vigorous incarnation of the Wise Old Man, not only endures but prevails over the rigors of the Northland winter and the ridicule of his Southland offspring. Also omitted with regret were "South of the Slot" (a whimsical blend of socialism and romance with a roguish twist of Jekyll and Hyde); London's notorious genocidal fantasy "The Unparalleled Invasion"; his tautly drawn, relentlessly naturalistic "Just Meat" (praised by George Orwell as London's best); his delightfully wry "The Princess" (featuring tropical tall tales told by three one-armed tramps); and more of the wonderful Hawaiian stories London wrote shortly before his death in 1916—*e.g.*, "On the Makaloa Mat," "Shin Bones," and "When Alice Told Her Soul." All of these are now accessible, of course, in the new Stanford Edition of London's complete stories.

Of London's nonfiction, I would like to have included more of his journalistic work, particularly his war correspondence and such moving essays as "Our Guiltless Scapegoats, the Stricken of Molokai" and "My Hawaiian Aloha." These may be found in *Jack London Reports.*

Finally, I was compelled to omit more than a dozen London letters but am comforted by the knowledge that these too are accessible—along with some fifteen hundred others—in the three-volume Stanford Edition (1988) of London's correspondence.

The task of inclusion has been much easier than that of exclusion, and my rationale has been simple: to present, as far as possible, a truly representative collection, one that gives the reader a fair sampling of London's extraordinarily diverse talents and subjects of interest.


# THE FICTIONS

Of the short stories, more than a third—ten of twenty-six—are Northland tales, but even among these the variety is remarkable. "To the Man on Trail" and "In a Far Country" are positive and negative examples of London's Northland Code, which is quite explicitly articulated in the opening paragraphs of the latter story. The little-known 1902 version of "To Build a Fire" is another exemplum—*i.e.*, a brief, vivid narrative intended to reinforce the weekly sermon preached to America's strenuous young manhood in the pages of *The Youth's Companion.* As London himself explains in a 1908 letter to R. W. Gilder, editor of the *Century Magazine,* this first version is radically different from the 1908 "To Build a Fire," which has become a world classic, translated into more languages than any other piece of short fiction in American literature. To compare the two versions is itself an instructive lesson in what distinguishes a great work of literary art from a good children's story. "The Law of Life," like the adult version of "To Build a Fire," is a little naturalistic gem. Especially praiseworthy is London's skillful use of point of view and interior monologue, as well as his use of the old moose as what T. S. Eliot would call an "objective correlative," in dramatizing the question that still haunts us: "What is the most ethical way of dealing with those once-honored old people who have become too heavy a burden on their families and on society?" "A Relic of the Pliocene" and "Nam-Bok, the Unveracious," while not as artistically deserving as some of the omitted stories, were selected to help illustrate the range of London's humor: the first being an incredible tall tale (underlaid with some subtly disturbing implications about the preservation of species), the second a lightly satiric Arctic variation on the theme of Plato's "The Cave."

"Moon-Face" cannot be ranked among London's masterpieces, but it is included because it shows Poe's influence and because it triggered charges that London had plagiarized a Frank Norris story (see his April 10, 1906, letter to the publisher of *McClure's Magazine*).

"Bâtard" and "Love of Life" are important in that London said he wrote *The Call of the Wild* "to redeem the species" after the demonic portrayal of his canine protagonist in the earlier story, and in that the latter story is consistently rated as a world classic. (In her memoirs Nadeszhda Krupskaya tells of how "greatly pleased" Lenin was when she read this story to him on his deathbed.)

"All Gold Canyon" and "The Apostate" are two of London's best, and, despite their totally different themes and settings, complement each other nicely. "All Gold Canyon" was the first of London's fictions to celebrate the pastoral wilderness, so vastly different from the frozen-hearted Northland wilderness (see his May 28, 1905, letter to Frederick Bamford). It is worthy noting that he mailed the story off to *Century Magazine* on June 8, 1905, the day after he bought his first ranch in the Valley of the Moon. The contrast between the canyon's salubrious atmosphere and the nightmare world of "The Apostate" is striking indeed. The latter, one of his most poignant stories, is obviously a semi-autobiographical recounting of London's own miserable experiences as a child laborer (note that the protagonist's name is "Johnny" and see the letters of November 30, 1898, to Mabel Applegarth, and January 31, 1900, to Houghton, Mifflin).

I have included four of the best, as well as most widely representative, of London's pre-Jungian Pacific tales. King Hendricks has ranked "The Chinago" above even "To Build a Fire": "I believe, from the point of view of the building of an atmosphere, the telling of a narrative, and the development of irony, that 'The Chinago' is the greatest story of London's career and one of the great stories of all time." Based upon an actual historical event, "Koolau the Leper" is one of London's most compelling stories, revealing the author's characteristic sympathy for the leper as well as for the underdog who battles heroically against overwhelming odds (*cf.* his letter of January 7, 1910, to the *Honolulu Advertiser*). Another view of leprosy, narrated with considerable dramatic irony, is "Good-by, Jack": to appreciate the powerful relevance of this story, we need merely to substitute for "leprosy" our own fearful responses to "AIDS." London's unlikeliest hero is portrayed in "Mauki," a chilling tale of poetic justice reminiscent of "Bâtard" in that the antagonist is hoist upon the grim petard of his own cruelty.

"The Strength of the Strong" is probably London's best-known —and most representative—socialist tale. In an August 30, 1909, letter to *Cosmopolitan,* he explained: "If you will remember, some time ago, Kipling made an attack on Socialism in the form of a parable . . . entitled 'Melissa,' in which he exploited his Jingoism and showed that a co-operation of individuals strong enough to overcome war meant the degeneration of said individuals. I have written 'The Strength of the Strong' as a reply to his attack." (Note London's epigraph to this story and also see his November 5, 1915, letter to Mary Austin.)

"Samuel" and the eight stories following it provide abundant evidence that London's creative powers were not in decline during his post-*Snark* years—and that he repeatedly wrote stories without appealing to the popular tastes of the contemporary marketplace (see his letters of March 17, 1914, to Ethan Cross and November 5, 1916, to Waldo Frank). Of all these, "Samuel" and "The Night-Born" are two of the most unusual, both dealing with strong women characters drawn from real life who transcend the naturalistic world to become figures of profound archetypal significance: the Great Mother in the character of Margaret Henan (St. Margaret being the patron saint of women in childbirth) and the Anima in the character of Lucy (spiritual enlightenment), who has been inspired by Thoreau. Her story, though composed before London discovered Jung, is a paradigm of the process of Self-realization Jung calls "individuation": successful in the case of Lucy and failed in the case of the man who rejects her, Trefethan, whose name is, appropriately, a combination of two Hebrew words meaning "unclean spokesman" (*cf.* London's September 30, 1903, letter to Charmian Kittredge).

"A Piece of Steak" and "The Mexican" are two great boxing stories; more than this, they are also allegories of "Youth *vs.* Age" and the "Spirit of Revolution," respectively. (In connection with the latter, see London's February 4, 1911, letter to the "Comrades of the Mexican Revolution," written shortly before this story.) "The Madness of John Harned," prompted by London's witnessing a bullfight in Quito, Ecuador, on his way home from the *Snark* cruise, is remarkable for its narrative point of view as well as for a dramatic intensity that preceded Hemingway's treatment of that subject by more than a decade.

"War" has been justly praised by Dale Walker as "a gem, a diamond which is virtually unknown today. . . . This is London's 148th short story, and he had written none better." It is indeed a little masterpiece ranking with the best of the war stories by Bierce, Crane, and Hemingway.

"Told in the Drooling Ward" is, quite simply, *sui generis*: nothing quite like it had ever been done before. In choosing as his central intelligence a feeble-minded narrator, London achieves humor without condescension and sympathy without sentimentality. "If London's story reminds us of almost nothing from the past," Don Graham has remarked, "in style, comedy, and realism it seems to foretell certain fictional experiments with the feeble-minded to come" in the works of such modern writers as Faulkner, Steinbeck, and Kesey. A testimonial to its realism may be found in a November 5, 1911, letter written to London by Dr. William J. G. Dawson, medical superintendent of the Sonoma State Home adjacent to the London Ranch: "I have read ["The Drooling Ward"] with a great deal of interest and find it in greater part to be true to life. The 'hero' of the story I think is our old inmate, Newton Dole" (Huntington Library Collection).

"The Red One," written in May 1916, is one of London's most haunting tales, clearly showing the influence of Conrad (see the June 4, 1915, letter to Conrad). Originally titled "The Message," it anticipates by more than a generation such modern science-fiction classics as Arthur C. Clarke's "The Sentinel," which inspired Stanley Kubrick's *2001: A Space Odyssey*. This fantastic tale has been highly praised by such outstanding science-fiction writers as Clarke himself and Philip José Farmer, and also by Dr. James Kirsch, founder of the Jungian Institute of Los Angeles, who calls London "one of the great mythmakers of mankind."

This mythopoeic genius is clearly evident in his last story, "The Water Baby," one of the half-dozen Hawaiian stories London composed after his discovery of Jung. But it is perhaps even more evident in *The Call of the Wild*, the greatest of his fictions and quite likely America's greatest "world novel." On the deeper level it is not really a novel at all but, as Maxwell Geismar has observed, "a beautiful prose poem, or *nouvelle*, of gold and death on the instinctual level . . . a handsome parable of the buried impulses." Of course these impulses are essentially human, not canine, and the call to which Buck responds is ultimately the universal music to which the human spirit reverberates in seeking to achieve total freedom. Moreover, the plot is informed by one of the most fundamental archetypal patterns, the Myth of the Hero. The call to adventure, departure, initiation, the perilous journey to what Joseph Campbell calls "the world navel" or mysterious life-center, transformation, and apotheosis—these are the characteristic "passages" of the monomyth, and all are delineated in Buck's progressive transformation from ranch pet into sled-dog in the naturalistic world and ultimately into legendary Ghost-Dog in the supernatural *urwelt* at the end of the seventh and final chapter.

# THE NONFICTION

Of London's more than four hundred published works of nonfiction, I have selected fifteen that I consider fairly representative.

"Typhoon off the Coast of Japan," originally titled "Story of a Typhoon off the Coast of Japan," has often been included in collections of London's short stories; however, I believe it may be more accurately classified as a nonfictional sketch, being the description of an actual experience and containing characters such as the bricklayer who were crewmembers aboard the *Sophia Sutherland*. It is not great literature, but it does show hints of the narrative and descriptive talents that would, as they matured, produce works of outstanding literary merit. The sketch is, in any event, a singular achievement for a seventeen-year-old working-class youth with only a grade-school education.

The four critical essays I have included—"On the Writer's Philosophy of Life," "First Aid to Rising Authors," "Getting into Print," and "The Terrible and Tragic in Fiction"—provide insights into the mindset of the turn-of-the-century literary marketplace as well as into London's literary principles. As Howard Lachtman observes in his foreword to Dale Walker's *No Mentor But Myself*, "London's public role, typically perceived as that of a daring man of action and swash-buckling freelancer of fortune, has often obscured the shrewd, disciplined, and methodical writer whose work helped to shape the myth. That elusive, authorial 'self' is by far the least known of all London identities." I might add that—also contrary to the impression London often gave that he hated writing and wrote only for the money—he was a dedicated professional with a strong sense of artistic integrity, as "On the Writer's Philosophy of Life" makes clear. Moreover, as Walker points out, "he was ever the available man," never refusing advice to the scores of young writers who sought it from him. The comments he makes in "First Aid to Rising Authors" and "Getting into Print" are representative of the advice he gave freely and often in his letters (see his letters of June 16, 1900, to Cloudesley Johns and April 1907, to the *Editor,* as well as "Eight Factors of Literary Success"). Apropos of "Getting into Print," I should perhaps explain that the five-dollar disappointment London recounts was the letter he received from the *Overland Monthly* on acceptance of "To the Man on Trail"—and that, because the magazine, despite its prestigious name, was in serious financial straits, he had difficulty collecting even that modest payment (an episode humorously fictionalized in *Martin Eden*). In connection with the steady stream of rejections London recollects, his Magazine Sales Records list more than six hundred rejections during the first five years of his career (see also his letters of November 27 and 30 to Mabel Applegarth).

London was not a prolific writer of literary essays and book reviews, principally because these paid less than fiction. I have included his reviews of Norris's *The Octopus* and Dana's *Two Years Before the Mast*, which lend some understanding to London's literary values as well as to the works he reviews (the latter review also contains a significant allusion to Melville, particularly to *Moby-Dick*, long before that author and his greatest novel were seriously regarded by the American critical establishment). I have omitted his review of Sinclair's *The Jungle* in favor of his enthusiastic "Dear Comrades" letter of December 1905.

"How I Became a Socialist" and "What Life Means to Me" are seminal autobiographical essays. The selections I have excerpted from *The People of the Abyss* give some sense of London's deep compassion for his fellow human beings. The section on the beautiful, doomed children is perhaps even more moving—and depressing—than his description of the working children's terrible plight in "The Apostate." The brief passage from his chapter on "The Carter and the Carpenter" should be read in connection with "Things Alive." The introduction to Sinclair's *Cry for Justice* is particularly notable for London's plea for service to humanity.

This sympathetic concern is manifest even in London's newspaper work. For example, beyond his vivid descriptions of the inferno that followed the great San Francisco Earthquake of 1906 (in "The Story of an Eye-Witness"), it is the unforgettable cameos of individual tragedy—the pathetic old cripple left with only his crutches after the fire has wiped out his home and all his possessions, the "cool and cheerful and hospitable" owner of the palatial Mark Hopkins residence who can only watch helplessly as the flames consume his mansion with all its beautiful, priceless contents—it is these human touches that serve to transform London's journalism into art.

The same human touches distinguish his sports writing. "Jack London was our first celebrity sportswriter," Lachtman points out in *Sporting Blood*, "the first to stake a claim on the sports world as a legitimate and worthwhile subject for writing, and the first to depict that world in the multiple forms (short story, novel, journalistic report, autobiographical essay) of his craft." Moreover, says Lachtman, "that world also engaged his humanitarian impulses as he attacked the exploitation of athletes, denounced the glorification of blood sport as public entertainment, championed the cause of underdogs who defied the venality of the sports mob, and satirized fans who demanded victory at any cost"—concerns as relevant to our own times as they were nearly a century ago to London's. In addition to stories like "A Piece of Steak," "The Madness of John Harned," and "The Mexican," I have included herein two reports from the series on the celebrated "fight of the century" London covered for the *New York Herald & Syndicate* in 1910. It was the media's fulsome promotion of this fight that valorized the "Great White Hope" slogan. Undefeated champion James J. Jeffries was forced out of retirement by popular demand as the one opponent considered capable of beating Jack Johnson, the first—and perhaps the greatest as well as the most hated—of the brilliant African-American boxers to hold the heavyweight crown. London's reports are of course first-rate sportswriting, but even more noteworthy are his comments about Johnson. In view of the prevalent and explicit racial attitudes of his times, his description of the black fighter as "a marvel of sensitiveness, sensibility, and perceptibility" is something of a marvel itself.

# THE LETTERS

Limiting my choices to fewer than thirty of the several thousand letters London wrote has been difficult, to say the least. My aim has been to choose those letters that not only give some revealing glimpses into London's complex personality and into his many-faceted career but that also relate, wherever expedient, to other selections in this volume. Even so, these few can scarcely reveal the rich contrarieties of London's person and persona. I can only hope that readers will find this portable edition a substantial text for better understanding—and appreciating—the real Jack London.

# ACKNOWLEDGMENTS

FOR THEIR CONSTANT SUPPORT as well as for their permission to include several important selections in this edition, I wish to express my sincere appreciation to the staff at the Huntington Library, the director and editors of the Stanford University Press, and the Trustees of the Estate of Irving Shepard—particularly to I. Milo Shepard.

A number of friends and scholars have been helpful in sharing their expertise and good sense as I have worked to put together a usable edition of London's selected works. I want especially to thank Lawrence Berkove, Harry Cook, Andrew Furer, Russ Kingman, Howard Lachtman, Robert Leitz, Joseph McElrath, Jeanne Reesman, Earl Wilcox, and Hensley Woodbridge.

I also wish to say how much I appreciate Michael Millman for granting Jack London the eminence of a place in the distinguished Viking Penguin Portable series.

Finally, I am deeply indebted to my administrative and faculty colleagues at Centenary for their continuing moral as well as fiscal support—and most especially to Patty Roberts, for her patience and hard work in preparing the manuscript for this edition.

EARLE LABOR
*Centenary College of Louisiana*

*The Portable*

# JACK LONDON

# Selected Stories

# TO THE MAN ON TRAIL

"Dump it in."

"But I say, Kid, is n't that going it a little too strong? Whiskey and alcohol's bad enough; but when it comes to brandy and pepper-sauce and"—

"Dump it in. Who's making this punch, anyway?" And Malemute Kid smiled benignantly through the clouds of steam. "By the time you've been in this country as long as I have, my son, and lived on rabbit-tracks and salmon-belly, you'll learn that Christmas comes only once per annum. And a Christmas without punch is sinking a hole to bedrock with nary a pay-streak."

"Stack up on that fer a high cyard," approved Big Jim Belden, who had come down from his claim on Mazy May to spend Christmas, and who, as every one knew, had been living the two months past on straight moosemeat. "Hain't fergot the *hooch* we-uns made on the Tanana, hev yeh?"

"Well, I guess yes. Boys, it would have done your hearts good to see that whole tribe fighting drunk—and all because of a glorious ferment of sugar and sour dough. That was before your time," Malemute Kid said as he turned to Stanley Prince, a young mining expert who had been in two years. "No white women in the country then, and Mason wanted to get married. Ruth's father was chief of the Tananas, and objected, like the rest of the tribe. Stiff? Why, I used my last pound of sugar; finest work in that line I ever did in my life. You should have seen the chase, down the river and across the portage."

"But the squaw?" asked Louis Savoy, the tall French-Canadian,

becoming interested; for he had heard of this wild deed, when at Forty
Mile the preceding winter.

Then Malemute Kid, who was a born raconteur, told the unvarnished tale of the Northland Lochinvar. More than one rough adventurer of the North felt his heartstrings draw closer, and experienced
vague yearnings for the sunnier pastures of the Southland, where life
promised something more than a barren struggle with cold and death.

"We struck the Yukon just behind the first ice-run," he concluded,
"and the tribe only a quarter of an hour behind. But that saved us;
for the second run broke the jam above and shut them out. When they
finally got into Nuklukyeto, the whole Post was ready for them. And
as to the foregathering, ask Father Roubeau here: he performed the
ceremony."

The Jesuit took the pipe from his lips, but could only express his
gratification with patriarchal smiles, while Protestant and Catholic vigorously applauded.

"By gar!" ejaculated Louis Savoy, who seemed overcome by the
romance of it. "La petite squaw; mon Mason brav. By gar!"

Then, as the first tin cups of punch went round, Bettles the Unquenchable sprang to his feet and struck up his favorite drinking
song:—

> *"There's Henry Ward Beecher*
> *And Sunday-school teachers,*
> *All drink of the sassafras root;*
> *But you bet all the same,*
> *If it had its right name,*
> *"It's the juice of the forbidden fruit."*

> *"Oh the juice of the forbidden fruit,"*

roared out the Bacchanalian chorus,—

> *"Oh the juice of the forbidden fruit;*
> *But you bet all the same,*
> *If it had its right name,*
> *It's the juice of the forbidden fruit."*

Malemute Kid's frightful concoction did its work; the men of the
camps and trails unbent in its genial glow, and jest and song and tales
of past adventure went round the board. Aliens from a dozen lands,

they toasted each and all. It was the Englishman, Prince, who pledged "Uncle Sam, the precocious infant of the New World;" the Yankee, Bettles, who drank to "The Queen, God bless her;" and together, Savoy and Meyers, the German trader, clanged their cups to Alsace and Lorraine.

Then Malemute Kid arose, cup in hand, and glanced at the greased-paper window, where the frost stood full three inches thick. "A health to the man on trail this night; may his grub hold out; may his dogs keep their legs; may his matches never miss fire."

Crack! Crack!—they heard the familiar music of the dogwhip, the whining howl of the Malemutes, and the crunch of a sled as it drew up to the cabin. Conversation languished while they waited the issue.

"An old-timer; cares for his dogs and then himself," whispered Malemute Kid to Prince, as they listened to the snapping jaws and the wolfish snarls and yelps of pain which proclaimed to their practiced ears that the stranger was beating back their dogs while he fed his own.

Then came the expected knock, sharp and confident, and the stranger entered. Dazzled by the light, he hesitated a moment at the door, giving to all a chance for scrutiny. He was a striking personage, and a most picturesque one, in his Arctic dress of wool and fur. Standing six foot two or three, with proportionate breadth of shoulders and depth of chest, his smooth-shaven face nipped by the cold to a gleaming pink, his long lashes and eyebrows white with ice, and the ear and neck flaps of his great wolfskin cap loosely raised, he seemed, of a verity, the Frost King, just stepped in out of the night. Clasped outside his mackinaw jacket, a beaded belt held two large Colt's revolvers and a hunting-knife, while he carried, in addition to the inevitable dog-whip, a smokeless rifle of the largest bore and latest pattern. As he came forward, for all his step was firm and elastic, they could see that fatigue bore heavily upon him.

An awkward silence had fallen, but his hearty "What cheer, my lads?" put them quickly at ease, and the next instant Malemute Kid and he had gripped hands. Though they had never met, each had heard of the other, and the recognition was mutual. A sweeping introduction and a mug of punch were forced upon him before he could explain his errand.

"How long since that basket-sled, with three men and eight dogs, passed?" he asked.

"An even two days ahead. Are you after them?"

"Yes; my team. Run them off under my very nose, the cusses. I've gained two days on them already,—pick them up on the next run."

"Reckon they'll show spunk?" asked Belden, in order to keep up the conversation, for Malemute Kid already had the coffee-pot on and was busily frying bacon and moosemeat.

The stranger significantly tapped his revolvers.

"When 'd yeh leave Dawson?"

"Twelve o'clock."

"Last night?"—as a matter of course.

"To-day."

A murmur of surprise passed round the circle. And well it might; for it was just midnight, and seventy-five miles of rough river trail was not to be sneered at for a twelve hours' run.

The talk soon became impersonal, however, harking back to the trails of childhood. As the young stranger ate of the rude fare, Malemute Kid attentively studied his face. Nor was he long in deciding that it was fair, honest, and open, and that he liked it. Still youthful, the lines had been firmly traced by toil and hardship. Though genial in conversation, and mild when at rest, the blue eyes gave promise of the hard steel-glitter which comes when called into action, especially against odds. The heavy jaw and squarecut chin demonstrated rugged pertinacity and indomitability. Nor, though the attributes of the lion were there, was there wanting the certain softness, the hint of womanliness, which bespoke the emotional nature.

"So thet's how me an' the ol' woman got spliced," said Belden, concluding the exciting tale of his courtship. " 'Here we be, dad,' sez she. 'An' may yeh be damned,' sez he to her, an' then to me, 'Jim, yeh—yeh git outen them good duds o' yourn; I want a right peart slice o' thet forty acre ploughed 'fore dinner.' An' then he turns on her an' sez, 'An' yeh, Sal; yeh sail inter them dishes.' An' then he sort o' sniffled an' kissed her. An' I was thet happy,—but he seen me an' roars out, 'Yeh, Jim!' An' yeh bet I dusted fer the barn."

"Any kids waiting for you back in the States?" asked the stranger.

"Nope; Sal died 'fore any come. Thet's why I'm here." Belden abstractedly began to light his pipe, which had failed to go out, and then brightened up with, "How 'bout yerself, stranger,—married man?"

For reply, he opened his watch, slipped it from the thong which served for a chain, and passed it over. Belden pricked up the slush-lamp, surveyed the inside of the case critically, and swearing admiringly to himself, handed it over to Louis Savoy. With numerous "By gars!" he finally surrendered it to Prince, and they noticed that his hands trembled and his eyes took on a peculiar softness. And so it passed from horny hand to horny hand—the pasted photograph of a woman, the clinging kind that such men fancy, with a babe at the breast. Those who had not yet seen the wonder were keen with curiosity; those who had, became silent and retrospective. They could face the pinch of famine, the grip of scurvy, or the quick death by field or flood; but the pictured semblance of a stranger woman and child made women and children of them all.

"Never have seen the youngster yet,—he's a boy, she says, and two years old," said the stranger as he received the treasure back. A lingering moment he gazed upon it, then snapped the case and turned away, but not quick enough to hide the restrained rush of tears.

Malemute Kid led him to a bunk and bade him turn in.

"Call me at four, sharp. Don't fail me," were his last words, and a moment later he was breathing in the heaviness of exhausted sleep.

"By Jove! he's a plucky chap," commented Prince. "Three hours' sleep after seventy-five miles with the dogs, and then the trail again. Who is he, Kid?"

"Jack Westondale. Been in going on three years, with nothing but the name of working like a horse, and any amount of bad luck to his credit. I never knew him, but Sitka Charley told me about him."

"It seems hard that a man with a sweet young wife like his should be putting in his years in this God-forsaken hole, where every year counts two on the outside."

"The trouble with him is clean grit and stubbornness. He's cleaned up twice with a stake, but lost it both times."

Here the conversation was broken off by an uproar from Bettles, for the effect had begun to wear away. And soon the bleak years of monotonous grub and deadening toil were being forgotten in rough merriment. Malemute Kid alone seemed unable to lose himself, and cast many an anxious look at his watch. Once he put on his mittens and beaver-skin cap, and leaving the cabin, fell to rummaging about in the cache.

Nor could he wait the hour designated; for he was fifteen minutes ahead of time in rousing his guest. The young giant had stiffened badly, and brisk rubbing was necessary to bring him to his feet. He tottered painfully out of the cabin, to find his dogs harnessed and everything ready for the start. The company wished him good luck and a short chase, while Father Roubeau, hurriedly blessing him, led the stampede for the cabin; and small wonder, for it is not good to face seventy-four degrees below zero with naked ears and hands.

Malemute Kid saw him to the main trail, and there, gripping his hand heartily, gave him advice.

"You'll find a hundred pounds of salmon-eggs on the sled," he said. "The dogs will go as far on that as with one hundred and fifty of fish, and you can't get dog-food at Pelly, as you probably expected." The stranger started, and his eyes flashed, but he did not interrupt. "You can't get an ounce of food for dog or man till you reach Five Fingers, and that's a stiff two hundred miles. Watch out for open water on the Thirty Mile River, and be sure you take the big cut-off above Le Barge."

"How did you know it? Surely the news can't be ahead of me already?"

"I don't know it; and what's more, I don't want to know it. But you never owned that team you're chasing. Sitka Charley sold it to them last spring. But he sized you up to me as square once, and I believe him. I've seen your face; I like it. And I've seen—why, damn you, hit the high places for salt water and that wife of yours, and"— Here the Kid unmittened and jerked out his sack.

"No; I don't need it," and the tears froze on his cheeks as he convulsively gripped Malemute Kid's hand.

"Then don't spare the dogs; cut them out of the traces as fast as they drop; buy them, and think they're cheap at ten dollars a pound. You can get them at Five Fingers, Little Salmon, and the Hootalinqua. And watch out for wet feet," was his parting advice. "Keep a-traveling up to twenty-five, but if it gets below that, build a fire and change your socks."

Fifteen minutes had barely elapsed when the jingle of bells announced new arrivals. The door opened, and a mounted policeman of the Northwest Territory entered, followed by two half-breed dog-drivers. Like Westondale, they were heavily armed and showed signs of fatigue. The half-breeds had been born to the trail, and bore it easily; but the young policeman was badly exhausted. Still, the dogged obstinacy of his race held him to the pace he had set, and would hold him till he dropped in his tracks.

"When did Westondale pull out?" he asked. "He stopped here, did n't he?" This was supererogatory, for the tracks told their own tale too well.

Malemute Kid had caught Belden's eye, and he, scenting the wind, replied evasively, "A right peart while back."

"Come, my man; speak up," the policeman admonished.

"Yeh seem to want him right smart. Hez he ben gittin' cantankerous down Dawson way?"

"Held up Harry McFarland's for forty thousand; exchanged it at the P. C. store for a check on Seattle; and who's to stop the cashing of it if we don't overtake him? When did he pull out?"

Every eye suppressed its excitement, for Malemute Kid had given the cue, and the young officer encountered wooden faces on every hand.

Striding over to Prince, he put the question to him. Though it hurt him, gazing into the frank, earnest face of his fellow countryman, he replied inconsequentially on the state of the trail.

Then he espied Father Roubeau, who could not lie. "A quarter of an hour ago," the priest answered; "but he had four hours' rest for himself and dogs."

"Fifteen minutes' start, and he's fresh! My God!" The poor fellow staggered back, half fainting from exhaustion and disappointment, murmuring something about the run from Dawson in ten hours and the dogs being played out.

Malemute Kid forced a mug of punch upon him; then he turned for the door, ordering the dog-drivers to follow. But the warmth and promise of rest were too tempting, and they objected strenuously. The Kid was conversant with their French patois, and followed it anxiously.

They swore that the dogs were gone up; that Siwash and Babette would have to be shot before the first mile was covered; that the rest were almost as bad; and that it would be better for all hands to rest up.

"Lend me five dogs?" he asked, turning to Malemute Kid.

But the Kid shook his head.

"I'll sign a check on Captain Constantine for five thousand,—here's my papers,—I'm authorized to draw at my own discretion."

Again the silent refusal.

"Then I'll requisition them in the name of the Queen."

Smiling incredulously, the Kid glanced at his well-stocked arsenal, and the Englishman, realizing his impotency, turned for the door. But the dog-drivers still objecting, he whirled upon them fiercely, calling them women and curs. The swart face of the older half-breed flushed angrily, as he drew himself up and promised in good, round terms that he would travel his leader off his legs, and would then be delighted to plant him in the snow.

The young officer—and it required his whole will—walked steadily to the door, exhibiting a freshness he did not possess. But they all knew and appreciated his proud effort; nor could he veil the twinges of agony that shot across his face. Covered with frost, the dogs were curled up in the snow, and it was almost impossible to get them to their feet. The poor brutes whined under the stinging lash, for the dog-drivers were angry and cruel; nor till Babette, the leader, was cut from the traces, could they break out the sled and get under way.

"A dirty scoundrel and a liar!" "By gar! him no good!" "A thief!" "Worse than an Indian!" It was evident that they were angry—first, at the way they had been deceived; and second, at the outraged ethics of the Northland, where honesty, above all, was man's prime jewel. "An' we gave the cuss a hand, after knowin' what he'd did." All eyes were turned accusingly upon Malemute Kid, who rose from the corner where he had been making Babette comfortable, and silently emptied the bowl for a final round of punch.

"It's a cold night, boys,—a bitter cold night," was the irrelevant commencement of his defense. "You've all traveled trail, and know what that stands for. Don't jump a dog when he's down. You've only heard one side. A whiter man than Jack Westondale never ate from the same pot nor stretched blanket with you or me. Last fall he gave his whole clean-up, forty thousand, to Joe Castrell, to buy in on Dominion. To-day he'd be a millionaire. But while he stayed behind at Circle City, taking care of his partner with the scurvy, what does Castrell do? Goes into McFarland's, jumps the limit, and drops the whole sack. Found him dead in the snow the next day. And poor Jack laying his plans to go out this winter to his wife and the boy he's never seen. You'll notice he took exactly what his partner lost,—forty thousand. Well, he's gone out; and what are you going to do about it?"

The Kid glanced round the circle of his judges, noted the softening of their faces, then raised his mug aloft. "So a health to the man on trail this night; may his grub hold out; may his dogs keep their legs; may his matches never miss fire. God prosper him; good luck go with him; and"—

"Confusion to the Mounted Police!" cried Bettles, to the crash of the empty cups.

# IN A FAR COUNTRY

WHEN A MAN journeys into a far country, he must be prepared to forget many of the things he has learned, and to acquire such customs as are inherent with existence in the new land; he must abandon the old ideals and the old gods, and oftentimes he must reverse the very codes by which his conduct has hitherto been shaped. To those who have the protean faculty of adaptability, the novelty of such change may even be a source of pleasure; but to those who happen to be hardened to the ruts in which they were created, the pressure of the altered environment is unbearable, and they chafe in body and in spirit under the new restrictions which they do not understand. This chafing is bound to act and react, producing divers evils and leading to various misfortunes. It were better for the man who cannot fit himself to the new groove to return to his own country; if he delay too long, he will surely die.

The man who turns his back upon the comforts of an elder civilization, to face the savage youth, the primordial simplicity of the North, may estimate success at an inverse ratio to the quantity and quality of his hopelessly fixed habits. He will soon discover, if he be a fit candidate, that the material habits are the less important. The exchange of such things as a dainty menu for rough fare, of the stiff leather shoe for the soft, shapeless moccasin, of the feather bed for a couch in the snow, is after all a very easy matter. But his pinch will come in learning properly to shape his mind's attitude toward all things, and especially toward his fellow man. For the courtesies of ordinary life, he must substitute unselfishness, forbearance, and tolerance. Thus, and thus only, can he gain that pearl of great price,—true comradeship. He must not say "Thank you;" he must mean it without opening his mouth, and prove it by responding in kind. In short, he must substitute the deed for the word, the spirit for the letter.

When the world rang with the tale of Arctic gold, and the lure of the North gripped the heartstrings of men, Carter Weatherbee threw up his snug clerkship, turned the half of his savings over to his wife, and with the remainder bought an outfit. There was no romance in his nature,—the bondage of commerce had crushed all that; he was simply tired of the ceaseless grind, and wished to risk great hazards in view of corresponding returns. Like many another fool, disdaining the old trails used by the Northland pioneers for a score of years, he hurried to Edmonton in the spring of the year; and there, unluckily for his soul's welfare, he allied himself with a party of men.

There was nothing unusual about this party, except its plans. Even its goal, like that of all other parties, was the Klondike. But the route it had mapped out to attain that goal took away the breath of the hardiest native, born and bred to the vicissitudes of the Northwest. Even Jacques Baptiste, born of a Chippewa woman and a renegade *voyageur* (having raised his first whimpers in a deerskin lodge north of the sixty-fifth parallel, and had the same hushed by blissful sucks of raw tallow), was surprised. Though he sold his services to them and agreed to travel even to the never-opening ice, he shook his head ominously whenever his advice was asked.

Percy Cuthfert's evil star must have been in the ascendant, for he, too, joined this company of argonauts. He was an ordinary man, with a bank account as deep as his culture, which is saying a good deal. He had no reason to embark on such a venture,—no reason in the world, save that he suffered from an abnormal development of sentimentality. He mistook this for the true spirit of romance and adventure. Many another man has done the like, and made as fatal a mistake.

The first break-up of spring found the party following the ice-run of Elk River. It was an imposing fleet, for the outfit was large, and they were accompanied by a disreputable contingent of half-breed *voyageurs* with their women and children. Day in and day out, they labored with the bateaux and canoes, fought mosquitoes and other kindred pests, or sweated and swore at the portages. Severe toil like this lays a man naked to the very roots of his soul, and ere Lake

Athabasca was lost in the south, each member of the party had hoisted his true colors.

The two shirks and chronic grumblers were Carter Weatherbee and Percy Cuthfert. The whole party complained less of its aches and pains than did either of them. Not once did they volunteer for the thousand and one petty duties of the camp. A bucket of water to be brought, an extra armful of wood to be chopped, the dishes to be washed and wiped, a search to be made through the outfit for some suddenly indispensable article,—and these two effete scions of civilization discovered sprains or blisters requiring instant attention. They were the first to turn in at night, with a score of tasks yet undone; the last to turn out in the morning, when the start should be in readiness before the breakfast was begun. They were the first to fall to at meal-time, the last to have a hand in the cooking; the first to dive for a slim delicacy, the last to discover they had added to their own another man's share. If they toiled at the oars, they slyly cut the water at each stroke and allowed the boat's momentum to float up the blade. They thought nobody noticed; but their comrades swore under their breaths and grew to hate them, while Jacques Baptiste sneered openly and damned them from morning till night. But Jacques Baptiste was no gentleman.

At the Great Slave, Hudson Bay dogs were purchased, and the fleet sank to the guards with its added burden of dried fish and pemmican. Then canoe and bateau answered to the swift current of the Mackenzie, and they plunged into the Great Barren Ground. Every likely-looking "feeder" was prospected, but the elusive "pay-dirt" danced ever to the north. At the Great Bear, overcome by the common dread of the Unknown Lands, their *voyageurs* began to desert, and Fort of Good Hope saw the last and bravest bending to the tow-lines as they bucked the current down which they had so treacherously glided. Jacques Baptiste alone remained. Had he not sworn to travel even to the never-opening ice?

The lying charts, compiled in main from hearsay, were now constantly consulted. And they felt the need of hurry, for the sun had already passed its northern solstice and was leading the winter south again. Skirting the shores of the bay, where the Mackenzie disembogues into the Arctic Ocean, they entered the mouth of the Little Peel River. Then began the arduous up-stream toil, and the two Incapables fared worse than ever. Tow-line and pole, paddle and tump-line, rapids and portages,—such tortures served to give the one a deep disgust for great hazards, and printed for the other a fiery text on the true romance of adventure. One day they waxed mutinous, and being vilely cursed by Jacques Baptiste, turned, as worms sometimes will. But the half-breed thrashed the twain, and sent them, bruised and bleeding, about their work. It was the first time either had been man-handled.

Abandoning their river craft at the headwaters of the Little Peel, they consumed the rest of the summer in the great portage over the Mackenzie watershed to the West Rat. This little stream fed the Porcupine, which in turn joined the Yukon where that mighty highway of the North countermarches on the Arctic Circle. But they had lost in the race with winter, and one day they tied their rafts to the thick eddy-ice and hurried their goods ashore. That night the river jammed and broke several times; the following morning it had fallen asleep for good.

"We can't be more'n four hundred miles from the Yukon," concluded Sloper, multiplying his thumb nails by the scale of the map. The council, in which the two Incapables had whined to excellent disadvantage, was drawing to a close.

"Hudson Bay Post, long time ago. No use um now." Jacques Baptiste's father had made the trip for the Fur Company in the old days, incidentally marking the trail with a couple of frozen toes.

"Sufferin' cracky!" cried another of the party. "No whites?"

"Nary white," Sloper sententiously affirmed; "but it's only five hundred more up the Yukon to Dawson. Call it a rough thousand from here."

Weatherbee and Cuthfert groaned in chorus.

"How long'll that take, Baptiste?"

The half-breed figured for a moment. "Workum like hell, no man play out, ten—twenty—forty—fifty days. Um babies come" (designating the Incapables), "no can tell. Mebbe when hell freeze over; mebbe not then."

The manufacture of snowshoes and moccasins ceased. Somebody called the name of an absent member, who came out of an ancient cabin at the edge of the camp-fire and joined them. The cabin was one of the many mysteries which lurk in the vast recesses of the North. Built when and by whom, no man could tell. Two graves in the open, piled high with stones, perhaps contained the secret of those early wanderers. But whose hand had piled the stones?

The moment had come. Jacques Baptiste paused in the fitting of a harness and pinned the struggling dog in the snow. The cook made mute protest for delay, threw a handful of bacon into a noisy pot of beans, then came to attention. Sloper rose to his feet. His body was a ludicrous contrast to the healthy physiques of the Incapables. Yellow and weak, fleeing from a South American feverhole, he had not broken his flight across the zones, and was still able to toil with men. His weight was probably ninety pounds, with the heavy hunting-knife thrown in, and his grizzled hair told of a prime which had ceased to be. The fresh young muscles of either Weatherbee or Cuthfert were equal to ten times the endeavor of his; yet he could walk them into the earth in a day's journey. And all this day he had whipped his stronger comrades into venturing a thousand miles of the stiffest hardship man can conceive. He was the incarnation of the unrest of his race, and the old Teutonic stubbornness, dashed with the quick grasp and action of the Yankee, held the flesh in the bondage of the spirit.

"All those in favor of going on with the dogs as soon as the ice sets, say ay."

"Ay!" rang out eight voices,—voices destined to string a trail of oaths along many a hundred miles of pain.

"Contrary minded?"

"No!" For the first time the Incapables were united without some compromise of personal interests.

"And what are you going to do about it?" Weatherbee added belligerently.

"Majority rule! Majority rule!" clamored the rest of the party.

"I know the expedition is liable to fall through if you don't come," Sloper replied sweetly; "but I guess, if we try real hard, we can manage to do without you. What do you say, boys?"

The sentiment was cheered to the echo.

"But I say, you know," Cuthfert ventured apprehensively; "what's a chap like me to do?"

"Ain't you coming with us?"

"No-o."

"Then do as you damn well please. We won't have nothing to say."

"Kind o' calkilate yuh might settle it with that canoodlin' pardner of yourn," suggested a heavy-going Westerner from the Dakotas, at the same time pointing out Weatherbee. "He'll be shore to ask yuh what yur a-goin' to do when it comes to cookin' an' gatherin' the wood."

"Then we'll consider it all arranged," concluded Sloper. "We'll pull out to-morrow, if we camp within five miles,—just to get everything in running order and remember if we've forgotten anything."

The sleds groaned by on their steel-shod runners, and the dogs strained low in the harnesses in which they were born to die. Jacques Baptiste paused by the side of Sloper to get a last glimpse of the cabin. The smoke curled up pathetically from the Yukon stovepipe. The two Incapables were watching them from the doorway.

Sloper laid his hand on the other's shoulder.

"Jacques Baptiste, did you ever hear of the Kilkenny cats?"

The half-breed shook his head.

"Well, my friend and good comrade, the Kilkenny cats fought till neither hide, nor hair, nor yowl, was left. You understand?—till nothing was left. Very good. Now, these two men don't like work. They won't work. We know that. They'll be all alone in that cabin all winter,—a might long, dark winter. Kilkenny cats,—well?"

The Frenchman in Baptiste shrugged his shoulders, but the Indian in him was silent. Nevertheless, it was an eloquent shrug, pregnant with prophecy.

Things prospered in the little cabin at first. The rough badinage of their comrades had made Weatherbee and Cuthfert conscious of the mutual responsibility which had devolved upon them; besides, there was not so much work after all for two healthy men. And the removal of the cruel whip-hand, or in other words the bulldozing half-breed, had brought with it a joyous reaction. At first, each strove to outdo the other, and they performed petty tasks with an unction which would have opened the eyes of their comrades who were now wearing out bodies and souls on the Long Trail.

All care was banished. The forest, which shouldered in upon them from three sides, was an inexhaustible woodyard. A few yards from their door slept the Porcupine, and a hole through its winter robe formed a bubbling spring of water, crystal clear and painfully cold. But they soon grew to find fault with even that. The hole would persist in freezing up, and thus gave them many a miserable hour of ice-chopping. The unknown builders of the cabin had extended the side-logs so as to support a cache at the rear. In this was stored the bulk of the party's provisions. Food there was, without stint, for three times the men who were fated to live upon it. But the most of it was of the kind which built up brawn and sinew, but did not tickle the palate.

True, there was sugar in plenty for two ordinary men; but these two were little else than children. They early discovered the virtues of hot water judiciously saturated with sugar, and they prodigally swam their flapjacks and soaked their crusts in the rich, white syrup. Then coffee and tea, and especially the dried fruits, made disastrous inroads upon it. The first words they had were over the sugar question. And it is a really serious thing when two men, wholly dependent upon each other for company, begin to quarrel.

Weatherbee loved to discourse blatantly on politics, while Cuthfert, who had been prone to clip his coupons and let the commonwealth jog on as best it might, either ignored the subject or delivered himself of startling epigrams. But the clerk was too obtuse to appreciate the clever shaping of thought, and this waste of ammunition irritated Cuthfert. He had been used to blinding people by his brilliancy, and it worked him quite a hardship, this loss of an audience. He felt personally aggrieved and unconsciously held his mutton-head companion responsible for it.

Save existence, they had nothing in common,—came in touch on no single point. Weatherbee was a clerk who had known naught but clerking all his life; Cuthfert was a master of arts, a dabbler in oils, and had written not a little. The one was a lower-class man who considered himself a gentleman, and the other was a gentleman who knew himself to be such. From this it may be remarked that a man can be a gentleman without possessing the first instinct of true comradeship. The clerk was as sensuous as the other was æsthetic, and his love adventures, told at great length and chiefly coined from his imagination, affected the supersensitive master of arts in the same way as so many whiffs of sewer gas. He deemed the clerk a filthy, uncultured brute, whose place was in the muck with the swine, and told him so; and he was reciprocally informed that he was a milk-and-water sissy and a cad. Weatherbee could not have defined "cad" for his life; but it satisfied its purpose, which after all seems the main point in life.

Weatherbee flatted every third note and sang such songs as "The Boston Burglar" and "The Handsome Cabin Boy," for hours at a time, while Cuthfert wept with rage, till he could stand it no longer and fled into the outer cold. But there was no escape. The intense frost could not be endured for long at a time, and the little cabin crowded them —beds, stove, table, and all—into a space of ten by twelve. The very presence of either became a personal affront to the other, and they lapsed into sullen silences which increased in length and strength as the days went by. Occasionally, the flash of an eye or the curl of a lip got the better of them, though they strove to wholly ignore each other during these mute periods. And a great wonder sprang up in the breast of each, as to how God had ever come to create the other.

With little to do, time became an intolerable burden to them. This naturally made them still lazier. They sank into a physical lethargy which there was no escaping, and which made them rebel at the performance of the smallest chore. One morning when it was his turn to cook the common breakfast, Weatherbee rolled out of his blankets, and to the snoring of his companion, lighted first the slush-lamp and then the fire. The kettles were frozen hard, and there was no water in the cabin with which to wash. But he did not mind that. Waiting for it to thaw, he sliced the bacon and plunged into the hateful task of bread-making. Cuthfert had been slyly watching through his half-closed lids. Consequently there was a scene, in which they fervently blessed each other, and agreed, thenceforth, that each do his own cooking. A week later, Cuthfert neglected his morning ablutions, but none the less complacently ate the meal which he had cooked. Weatherbee grinned. After that the foolish custom of washing passed out of their lives.

As the sugar-pile and other little luxuries dwindled, they began to be afraid they were not getting their proper shares, and in order that they might not be robbed, they fell to gorging themselves. The luxuries suffered in this gluttonous contest, as did also the men. In the absence of fresh vegetables and exercise, their blood became impoverished, and a loathsome, purplish rash crept over their bodies. Yet they refused to heed the warning. Next, their muscles and joints began to swell, the flesh turning black, while their mouths, gums, and lips took on the color of rich cream. Instead of being drawn together by their misery, each gloated over the other's symptoms as the scurvy took its course.

They lost all regard for personal appearance, and for that matter, common decency. The cabin became a pigpen, and never once were the beds made or fresh pine boughs laid underneath. Yet they could not keep to their blankets, as they would have wished; for the frost was inexorable, and the fire box consumed much fuel. The hair of their heads and faces grew long and shaggy, while their garments would have disgusted a ragpicker. But they did not care. They were sick, and there was no one to see; besides, it was very painful to move about.

To all this was added a new trouble,—the Fear of the North. This Fear was the joint child of the Great Cold and the Great Silence, and was born in the darkness of December, when the sun dipped below the southern horizon for good. It affected them according to their natures. Weatherbee fell prey to the grosser superstitions, and did his best to resurrect the spirits which slept in the forgotten graves. It was a fascinating thing, and in his dreams they came to him from out of the cold, and snuggled into his blankets, and told him of their toils and troubles ere they died. He shrank away from the clammy contact as they drew closer and twined their frozen limbs about him, and when they whispered in his ear of things to come, the cabin rang with his frightened shrieks. Cuthfert did not understand,—for they no longer spoke,—and when thus awakened he invariably grabbed for his revolver. Then he would sit up in bed, shivering nervously, with the weapon trained on the unconscious dreamer. Cuthfert deemed the man going mad, and so came to fear for his life.

His own malady assumed a less concrete form. The mysterious artisan who had laid the cabin, log by log, had pegged a windvane to the ridge-pole. Cuthfert noticed it always pointed south, and one day, irritated by its steadfastness of purpose, he turned it toward the east. He watched eagerly, but never a breath came by to disturb it. Then he turned the vane to the north, swearing never again to touch it till the wind did blow. But the air frightened him with its unearthly calm, and he often rose in the middle of the night to see if the vane had veered,—ten degrees would have satisfied him. But no, it poised above him as unchangeable as fate. His imagination ran riot, till it became to him a fetich. Sometimes he followed the path it pointed across the dismal dominions, and allowed his soul to become saturated with the Fear. He dwelt upon the unseen and the unknown till the burden of eternity appeared to be crushing him. Everything in the Northland had that crushing effect,—the absence of life and motion; the darkness; the infinite peace of the brooding land; the ghastly silence, which made the echo of each heart-beat a sacrilege; the solemn forest which seemed to guard an awful, inexpressible something, which neither word nor thought could compass.

The world he had so recently left, with its busy nations and great enterprises, seemed very far away. Recollections occasionally obtruded,—recollections of marts and galleries and crowded thoroughfares, of evening dress and social functions, of good men and dear women he had known,—but they were dim memories of a life he had lived long centuries agone, on some other planet. This phantasm was the Reality. Standing beneath the wind-vane, his eyes fixed on the polar skies, he could not bring himself to realize that the Southland really existed, that at that very moment it was a-roar with life and action. There was no Southland, no men being born of women, no giving and taking in marriage. Beyond his bleak sky-line there stretched vast solitudes, and beyond these still vaster solitudes. There were no lands of sunshine, heavy with the perfume of flowers. Such things were only old dreams of paradise. The sunlands of the West and the spicelands of the East, the smiling Arcadias and blissful Islands of the Blest,—ha! ha! His laughter split the void and shocked him with its unwonted sound. There was no sun. This was the Universe, dead and cold and dark, and he its only citizen. Weatherbee? At such moments Weatherbee did not count. He was a Caliban, a monstrous phantom, fettered to him for untold ages, the penalty of some forgotten crime.

He lived with Death among the dead, emasculated by the sense of his own insignificance, crushed by the passive mastery of the slumbering ages. The magnitude of all things appalled him. Everything partook of the superlative save himself,—the perfect cessation of wind and motion, the immensity of the snow-covered wilderness, the height of the sky and the depth of the silence. That wind-vane,—if it would only move. If a thunderbolt would fall, or the forest flare up in flame. The rolling up of the heavens as a scroll, the crash of Doom—anything, anything! But no, nothing moved; the Silence crowded in, and the Fear of the North laid icy fingers on his heart.

Once, like another Crusoe, by the edge of the river he came upon a track,—the faint tracery of a snowshoe rabbit on the delicate snow-crust. It was a revelation. There was life in the Northland. He would follow it, look upon it, gloat over it. He forgot his swollen muscles, plunging through the deep snow in an ecstasy of anticipation. The forest swallowed him up, and the brief midday twilight vanished; but he pursued his quest till exhausted nature asserted itself and laid him helpless in the snow. There he groaned and cursed his folly, and knew the track to be the fancy of his brain; and late that night he dragged himself into the cabin on hands and knees, his cheeks frozen and a strange numbness about his feet. Weatherbee grinned malevolently, but made no offer to help him. He thrust needles into his toes and thawed them out by the stove. A week later mortification set in.

But the clerk had his own troubles. The dead men came out of their graves more frequently now, and rarely left him, waking or sleeping. He grew to wait and dread their coming, never passing the twin cairns without a shudder. One night they came to him in his sleep and led him forth to an appointed task. Frightened into inarticulate horror, he awoke between the heaps of stones and fled wildly to the cabin. But he had lain there for some time, for his feet and cheeks were also frozen.

Sometimes he became frantic at their insistent presence, and danced about the cabin, cutting the empty air with an axe, and smashing everything within reach. During these ghostly encounters, Cuthfert huddled into his blankets and followed the madman about with a cocked revolver, ready to shoot him if he came too near. But, recovering from one of these spells, the clerk noticed the weapon trained upon him. His suspicions were aroused, and thenceforth he, too, lived in fear of his life. They watched each other closely after that, and faced about in startled fright whenever either passed behind the other's back. This apprehensiveness became a mania which controlled them even in their sleep. Through mutual fear they tacitly let the slush-lamp burn all night, and saw to a plentiful supply of bacon-grease before retiring. The slightest movement on the part of one was sufficient to arouse the other, and many a still watch their gazes countered as they shook beneath their blankets with fingers on the trigger-guards.

What with the Fear of the North, the mental strain, and the ravages of the disease, they lost all semblance of humanity, taking on the appearance of wild beasts, hunted and desperate. Their cheeks and noses, as an aftermath of the freezing, had turned black. Their frozen toes had begun to drop away at the first and second joints. Every movement brought pain, but the fire box was insatiable, wringing a ransom of torture from their miserable bodies. Day in, day out, it demanded its food,—a veritable pound of flesh,—and they dragged themselves into the forest to chop wood on their knees. Once, crawling thus in search of dry sticks, unknown to each other they entered a thicket from opposite sides. Suddenly, without warning, two peering death's-heads confronted each other. Suffering had so transformed them that recognition was impossible. They sprang to their feet, shrieking with terror, and dashed away on their mangled stumps; and falling at the cabin door, they clawed and scratched like demons till they discovered their mistake.

Occasionally they lapsed normal, and during one of these sane intervals, the chief bone of contention, the sugar, had been divided equally between them. They guarded their separate sacks, stored up in the cache, with jealous eyes; for there were but a few cupfuls left, and they were totally devoid of faith in each other. But one day Cuthfert made a mistake. Hardly able to move, sick with pain, with his head swimming and eyes blinded, he crept into the cache, sugar canister in hand, and mistook Weatherbee's sack for his own.

January had been born but a few days when this occurred. The sun had some time since passed its lowest southern declination, and at meridian now threw flaunting streaks of yellow light upon the northern sky. On the day following his mistake with the sugarbag, Cuthfert found himself feeling better, both in body and in spirit. As noontime drew near and the day brightened, he dragged himself outside to feast on the evanescent glow, which was to him an earnest of the sun's future intentions. Weatherbee was also feeling somewhat better, and crawled out beside him. They propped themselves in the snow beneath the moveless wind-vane, and waited.

The stillness of death was about them. In other climes, when nature falls into such moods, there is a subdued air of expectancy, a waiting for some small voice to take up the broken strain. Not so in the North. The two men had lived seeming æons in this ghostly peace. They could remember no song of the past; they could conjure no song of the future. This unearthly calm had always been,—the tranquil silence of eternity.

Their eyes were fixed upon the north. Unseen, behind their backs, behind the towering mountains to the south, the sun swept toward the zenith of another sky than theirs. Sole spectators of the mighty canvas, they watched the false dawn slowly grow. A faint flame began to glow and smoulder. It deepened in intensity, ringing the changes of reddish-yellow, purple, and saffron. So bright did it become that Cuthfert thought the sun must surely be behind it,—a miracle, the sun rising in the north! Suddenly, without warning and without fading, the canvas was swept clean. There was no color in the sky. The light had gone out of the day. They caught their breaths in half-sobs. But lo! the air was a-glint with particles of scintillating frost, and there, to the north, the wind-vane lay in vague outline on the snow. A shadow! A shadow! It was exactly midday. They jerked their heads hurriedly to the south. A golden rim peeped over the mountain's snowy shoulder, smiled upon them an instant, then dipped from sight again.

There were tears in their eyes as they sought each other. A strange softening came over them. They felt irresistibly drawn toward each other. The sun was coming back again. It would be with them tomorrow, and the next day, and the next. And it would stay longer every visit, and a time would come when it would ride their heaven day and night, never once dropping below the sky-line. There would be no night. The ice-locked winter would be broken; the winds would blow and the forests answer; the land would bathe in the blessed sunshine, and life renew. Hand in hand, they would quit this horrid dream and journey back to the Southland. They lurched blindly forward, and their hands met,—their poor maimed hands, swollen and distorted beneath their mittens.

But the promise was destined to remain unfulfilled. The Northland is the Northland, and men work out their souls by strange rules, which other men, who have not journeyed into far countries, cannot come to understand.

An hour later, Cuthfert put a pan of bread into the oven, and fell to speculating on what the surgeons could do with his feet when he got back. Home did not seem so very far away now. Weatherbee was rummaging in the cache. Of a sudden, he raised a whirlwind of blasphemy, which in turn ceased with startling abruptness. The other man had robbed his sugar-sack. Still, things might have happened differently, had not the two dead men come out from under the stones and hushed the hot words in his throat. They led him quite gently from the cache, which he forgot to close. That consummation was reached; that something they had whispered to him in his dreams was about to happen. They guided him gently, very gently, to the woodpile, where they put the axe in his hands. Then they helped him shove open the cabin door, and he felt sure they shut it after him,—at least he heard it slam and the latch fall sharply into place. And he knew they were waiting just without, waiting for him to do his task.

"Carter! I say, Carter!"

Percy Cuthfert was frightened at the look on the clerk's face, and he made haste to put the table between them.

Carter Weatherbee followed, without haste and without enthusiasm. There was neither pity nor passion in his face, but rather the patient, stolid look of one who has certain work to do and goes about it methodically.

"I say, what's the matter?"

The clerk dodged back, cutting off his retreat to the door, but never opening his mouth.

"I say, Carter, I say; let's talk. There's a good chap."

The master of arts was thinking rapidly, now, shaping a skillful flank movement on the bed where his Smith & Wesson lay. Keeping his eyes on the madman, he rolled backward on the bunk, at the same time clutching the pistol.

"Carter!"

The powder flashed full in Weatherbee's face, but he swung his weapon and leaped forward. The axe bit deeply at the base of the spine, and Percy Cuthfert felt all consciousness of his lower limbs leave him. Then the clerk fell heavily upon him, clutching him by the throat with feeble fingers. The sharp bite of the axe had caused Cuthfert to drop the pistol, and as his lungs panted for release, he fumbled aimlessly for it among the blankets. Then he remembered. He slid a hand up the clerk's belt to the sheath-knife; and they drew very close to each other in that last clinch.

Percy Cuthfert felt his strength leave him. The lower portion of his body was useless. The inert weight of Weatherbee crushed him,— crushed him and pinned him there like a bear under a trap. The cabin became filled with a familiar odor, and he knew the bread to be burning. Yet what did it matter? He would never need it. And there were all of six cupfuls of sugar in the cache,—if he had foreseen this he would not have been so saving the last several days. Would the wind-vane ever move? It might even be veering now. Why not? Had he not seen the sun to-day? He would go and see. No; it was impossible to move. He had not thought the clerk so heavy a man.

How quickly the cabin cooled! The fire must be out. The cold was forcing in. It must be below zero already, and the ice creeping up the inside of the door. He could not see it, but his past experience enabled him to gauge its progress by the cabin's temperature. The lower hinge must be white ere now. Would the tale of this ever reach the world? How would his friends take it? They would read it over their coffee, most likely, and talk it over at the clubs. He could see them very clearly. "Poor Old Cuthfert," they murmured; "not such a bad sort of a chap, after all." He smiled at their eulogies, and passed on in search of a Turkish bath. It was the same old crowd upon the streets. Strange, they did not notice his moosehide moccasins and tattered German socks! He would take a cab. And after the bath a shave would not be bad. No; he would eat first. Steak, and potatoes, and green things,—how fresh it all was! And what was that? Squares of honey, streaming liquid amber! But why did they bring so much? Ha! ha! he could never eat it all. Shine! Why certainly. He put his foot on the box. The bootblack looked curiously up at him, and he remembered his moosehide moccasins and went away hastily.

Hark! The wind-vane must be surely spinning. No; a mere singing in his ears. That was all,—a mere singing. The ice must have passed the latch by now. More likely the upper hinge was covered. Between the moss-chinked roof-poles, little points of frost began to appear. How slowly they grew! No; not so slowly. There was a new one, and there another. Two—three—four; they were coming too fast to count. There were two growing together. And there, a third had joined them. Why, there were no more spots. They had run together and formed a sheet.

Well, he would have company. If Gabriel ever broke the silence of the North, they would stand together, hand in hand, before the great White Throne. And God would judge them, God would judge them!

Then Percy Cuthfert closed his eyes and dropped off to sleep.

# THE LAW OF LIFE

OLD KOSKOOSH listened greedily. Though his sight had long since faded, his hearing was still acute, and the slightest sound penetrated to the glimmering intelligence which yet abode behind the withered forehead, but which no longer gazed forth upon the things of the world. Ah! that was Sit-cum-to-ha, shrilly anathematizing the dogs as she cuffed and beat them into the harnesses. Sit-cum-to-ha was his daughter's daughter, but she was too busy to waste a thought upon her broken grandfather, sitting alone there in the snow, forlorn and helpless. Camp must be broken. The long trail waited while the short day refused to linger. Life called her, and the duties of life, not death. And he was very close to death now.

The thought made the old man panicky for the moment, and he stretched forth a palsied hand which wandered tremblingly over the small heap of dry wood beside him. Reassured that it was indeed there, his hand returned to the shelter of his mangy furs, and he again fell to listening. The sulky crackling of half-frozen hides told him that the chief's moose-skin lodge had been struck, and even then was being rammed and jammed into portable compass. The chief was his son, stalwart and strong, head man of the tribesmen, and a mighty hunter. As the women toiled with the camp luggage, his voice rose, chiding them for their slowness. Old Koskoosh strained his ears. It was the last time he would hear that voice. There went Geehow's lodge! And Tusken's! Seven, eight, nine; only the shaman's could be still standing. There! They were at work upon it now. He could hear the shaman grunt as he piled it on the sled. A child whimpered, and a woman soothed it with soft, crooning gutturals. Little Koo-tee, the old man thought, a fretful child, and not overstrong. It would die soon, perhaps, and they would burn a hole through the frozen tundra and pile rocks above to keep the wolverines away. Well, what did it matter? A few years at best, and as many an empty belly as a full one. And in the end, Death waited, ever-hungry and hungriest of them all.

What was that? Oh, the men lashing the sleds and drawing tight the thongs. He listened, who would listen no more. The whip-lashes snarled and bit among the dogs. Hear them whine! How they hated the work and the trail! They were off! Sled after sled churned slowly away into the silence. They were gone. They had passed out of his life, and he faced the last bitter hour alone. No. The snow crunched beneath a moccasin; a man stood beside him; upon his head a hand rested gently. His son was good to do this thing. He remembered other old men whose sons had not waited after the tribe. But his son had. He wandered away into the past, till the young man's voice brought him back.

"Is it well with you?" he asked.

And the old man answered, "It is well."

"There be wood beside you," the younger man continued, "and the fire burns bright. The morning is gray, and the cold has broken. It will snow presently. Even now is it snowing."

"Ay, even now is it snowing."

"The tribesmen hurry. Their bales are heavy, and their bellies flat with lack of feasting. The trail is long and they travel fast. I go now. It is well?"

"It is well. I am as a last year's leaf, clinging lightly to the stem. The first breath that blows, and I fall. My voice is become like an old woman's. My eyes no longer show me the way of my feet, and my feet are heavy, and I am tired. It is well."

He bowed his head in content till the last noise of the complaining snow had died away, and he knew his son was beyond recall. Then his hand crept out in haste to the wood. It alone stood between him and the eternity that yawned in upon him. At last the measure of his life was a handful of fagots. One by one they would go to feed the fire, and just so, step by step, death would creep upon him. When the last stick had surrendered up its heat, the frost would begin to gather strength. First his feet would yield, then his hands; and the numbness would travel, slowly, from the extremities to the body. His head would fall forward upon his knees, and he would rest. It was easy. All men must die.

He did not complain. It was the way of life, and it was just. He had been born close to the earth, close to the earth had he lived, and the law thereof was not new to him. It was the law of all flesh. Nature was not kindly to the flesh. She had no concern for that concrete thing called the individual. Her interest lay in the species, the race. This was the deepest abstraction old Koskoosh's barbaric mind was capable of, but he grasped it firmly. He saw it exemplified in all life. The rise of the sap, the bursting greenness of the willow bud, the fall of the yellow leaf—in this alone was told the whole history. But one task did Nature set the individual. Did he not perform it, he died. Did he perform it, it was all the same, he died. Nature did not care; there were plenty who were obedient, and it was only the obedience in this matter, not the obedient, which lived and lived always. The tribe of Koskoosh was very old. The old men he had known when a boy, had known old men before them. Therefore it was true that the tribe lived, that it stood for the obedience of all its members, way down into the forgotten past, whose very resting-places were unremembered. They did not count; they were episodes. They had passed away like clouds from a summer sky. He also was an episode, and would pass away. Nature did not care. To life she set one task, gave one law. To perpetuate was the task of life, its law was death. A maiden was a good creature to look upon, full-breasted and strong, with spring to her step and light in her eyes. But her task was yet before her. The light in her eyes brightened, her step quickened, she was now bold with the young men, now timid, and she gave them of her own unrest. And ever she grew fairer and yet fairer to look upon, till some hunter, able no longer to withhold himself, took her to his lodge to cook and toil for him and to become the mother of his children. And with the coming of her offspring her looks left her. Her limbs dragged and shuffled, her eyes dimmed and bleared, and only the little children found joy against the withered cheek of the old squaw by the fire. Her task was done. But a little while, on the first pinch of famine or the first long trail, and she would be left, even as he had been left, in the snow, with a little pile of wood. Such was the law.

He placed a stick carefully upon the fire and resumed his meditations. It was the same everywhere, with all things. The mosquitoes vanished with the first frost. The little tree-squirrel crawled away to die. When age settled upon the rabbit it became slow and heavy, and could no longer outfoot its enemies. Even the big bald-face grew clumsy and blind and quarrelsome, in the end to be dragged down by a handful of yelping huskies. He remembered how he had abandoned his own father on an upper reach of the Klondike one winter, the winter before the missionary came with his talk-books and his box of medicines. Many a time had Koskoosh smacked his lips over the recollection of that box, though now his mouth refused to moisten. The "painkiller" had been especially good. But the missionary was a bother after all, for he brought no meat into the camp, and he ate heartily, and the hunters grumbled. But he chilled his lungs on the divide by the Mayo, and the dogs afterwards nosed the stones away and fought over his bones.

Koskoosh placed another stick on the fire and harked back deeper into the past. There was the time of the Great Famine, when the old men crouched empty-bellied to the fire, and let fall from their lips dim traditions of the ancient day when the Yukon ran wide open for three winters, and then lay frozen for three summers. He had lost his mother in that famine. In the summer the salmon run had failed, and the tribe looked forward to the winter and the coming of the caribou. Then the winter came, but with it there were no caribou. Never had the like been known, not even in the lives of the old men. But the caribou did not come, and it was the seventh year, and the rabbits had not replenished, and the dogs were naught but bundles of bones. And through the long darkness the children wailed and died, and the women, and the old men; and not one in ten of the tribe lived to meet the sun when it came back in the spring. That *was* a famine!

But he had seen times of plenty, too, when the meat spoiled on their hands, and the dogs were fat and worthless with overeating—times when they let the game go unkilled, and the women were fertile, and the lodges were cluttered with sprawling men-children and women-children. Then it was the men became high-stomached, and revived ancient quarrels, and crossed the divides to the south to kill the Pellys, and to the west that they might sit by the dead fires of the Tananas. He remembered, when a boy, during a time of plenty, when he saw a moose pulled down by the wolves. Zing-ha lay with him in the snow and watched—Zing-ha, who later became the craftiest of hunters, and who, in the end, fell through an air-hole on the Yukon. They found him, a month afterward, just as he had crawled halfway out and frozen stiff to the ice.

But the moose. Zing-ha and he had gone out that day to play at hunting after the manner of their fathers. On the bed of the creek they struck the fresh track of a moose, and with it the tracks of many wolves. "An old one," Zing-ha, who was quicker at reading the sign, said—"an old one who cannot keep up with the herd. The wolves

have cut him out from his brothers, and they will never leave him."
And it was so. It was their way. By day and by night, never resting,
snarling on his heels, snapping at his nose, they would stay by him to
the end. How Zing-ha and he felt the blood-lust quicken! The finish
would be a sight to see!

Eager-footed, they took the trail, and even he, Koskoosh, slow of
sight and an unversed tracker, could have followed it blind, it was so
wide. Hot were they on the heels of the chase, reading the grim tragedy, fresh-written, at every step. Now they came to where the moose
had made a stand. Thrice the length of a grown man's body, in every
direction, had the snow been stamped about and uptossed. In the midst
were the deep impressions of the splay-hoofed game, and all about,
everywhere, were the lighter footmarks of the wolves. Some, while
their brothers harried the kill, had lain to one side and rested. The
full-stretched impress of their bodies in the snow was as perfect as
though made the moment before. One wolf had been caught in a wild
lunge of the maddened victim and trampled to death. A few bones,
well picked, bore witness.

Again, they ceased the uplift of their snowshoes at a second stand.
Here the great animal had fought desperately. Twice had he been
dragged down, as the snow attested, and twice had he shaken his
assailants clear and gained footing once more. He had done his task
long since, but none the less was life dear to him. Zing-ha said it was
a strange thing, a moose once down to get free again; but this one
certainly had. The shaman would see signs and wonders in this when
they told him.

And yet again, they come to where the moose had made to mount
the bank and gain the timber. But his foes had laid on from behind,
till he reared and fell back upon them, crushing two deep into the
snow. It was plain the kill was at hand, for their brothers had left
them untouched. Two more stands were hurried past, brief in time-
length and very close together. The trail was red now, and the clean
stride of the great beast had grown short and slovenly. Then they heard
the first sounds of the battle—not the full-throated chorus of the chase,
but the short, snappy bark which spoke of close quarters and teeth to
flesh. Crawling up the wind, Zing-ha bellied it through the snow, and
with him crept he, Koskoosh, who was to be chief of the tribesmen in
the years to come. Together they shoved aside the under branches of
a young spruce and peered forth. It was the end they saw.

The picture, like all of youth's impressions, was still strong with
him, and his dim eyes watched the end played out as vividly as in that

far-off time. Koskoosh marvelled at this, for in the days which followed, when he was a leader of men and a head of councillors, he had done great deeds and made his name a curse in the mouths of the Pellys, to say naught of the strange white man he had killed, knife to knife, in open fight.

For long he pondered on the days of his youth, till the fire died down and the frost bit deeper. He replenished it with two sticks this time, and gauged his grip on life by what remained. If Sit-cum-to-ha had only remembered her grandfather, and gathered a larger armful, his hours would have been longer. It would have been easy. But she was ever a careless child, and honored not her ancestors from the time the Beaver, son of the son of Zing-ha, first cast eyes upon her. Well, what mattered it? Had he not done likewise in his own quick youth? For a while he listened to the silence. Perhaps the heart of his son might soften, and he would come back with the dogs to take his old father on with the tribe to where the caribou ran thick and the fat hung heavy upon them.

He strained his ears, his restless brain for the moment stilled. Not a stir, nothing. He alone took breath in the midst of the great silence. It was very lonely. Hark! What was that? A chill passed over his body. The familiar, long-drawn howl broke the void, and it was close at hand. Then on his darkened eyes was projected the vision of the moose—the old bull moose—the torn flanks and bloody sides, the riddled mane, and the great branching horns, down low and tossing to the last. He saw the flashing forms of gray, the gleaming eyes, the lolling tongues, the slavered fangs. And he saw the inexorable circle close in till it became a dark point in the midst of the stamped snow.

A cold muzzle thrust against his cheek, and at its touch his soul leaped back to the present. His hand shot into the fire and dragged out a burning fagot. Overcome for the nonce by his hereditary fear of man, the brute retreated, raising a prolonged call to his brothers; and greedily they answered, till a ring of crouching, jaw-slobbered gray was stretched round about. The old man listened to the drawing in of this circle. He waved his brand wildly, and sniffs turned to snarls; but the panting brutes refused to scatter. Now one wormed his chest forward, dragging his haunches after, now a second, now a third; but never a one drew back. Why should he cling to life? he asked, and dropped the blazing stick into the snow. It sizzled and went out. The circle grunted uneasily, but held its own. Again he saw the last stand of the old bull moose, and Koskoosh dropped his head wearily upon his knees. What did it matter after all? Was it not the law of life?

# A RELIC OF THE PLIOCENE

I WASH MY HANDS of him at the start. I cannot father his tales, nor will I be responsible for them. I make these preliminary reservations, observe, as a guard upon my own integrity. I possess a certain definite position in a small way, also a wife; and for the good name of the community that honors my existence with its approval, and for the sake of her posterity and mine, I cannot take the chances I once did, nor foster probabilities with the careless improvidence of youth. So, I repeat, I wash my hands of him, this Nimrod, this mighty hunter, this homely, blue-eyed, freckle-faced Thomas Stevens.

Having been honest to myself, and to whatever prospective olive branches my wife may be pleased to tender me, I can now afford to be generous. I shall not criticise the tales told me by Thomas Stevens, and, further, I shall withhold my judgment. If it be asked why, I can only add that judgment I have none. Long have I pondered, weighed, and balanced, but never have my conclusions been twice the same—forsooth! because Thomas Stevens is a greater man than I. If he have told truths, well and good; if untruths, still well and good. For who can prove? or who disprove? I eliminate myself from the proposition, while those of little faith may do as I have done—go find the said Thomas Stevens, and discuss to his face the various matters which, if fortune serve, I shall relate. As to where he may be found? The directions are simple: anywhere between 53 north latitude and the Pole, on the one hand; and, on the other, the likeliest hunting grounds that lie between the east coast of Siberia and farthermost Labrador. That he is there, somewhere, within that clearly defined territory, I pledge the word of an honorable man whose expectations entail straight speaking and right living.

Thomas Stevens may have toyed prodigiously with truth, but when we first met (it were well to mark this point), he wandered into my camp when I thought myself a thousand miles beyond the outermost post of civilization. At the sight of his human face, the first in weary months, I could have sprung forward and folded him in my arms (and I am not by any means a demonstrative man); but to him his visit seemed the most casual thing under the sun. He just strolled into the light of my camp, passed the time of day after the custom of men on beaten trails, threw my snowshoes the one way and a couple of dogs the other, and so made room for himself by the fire. Said he'd just dropped in to borrow a pinch of soda and to see if I had any decent tobacco. He plucked forth an ancient pipe, loaded it with painstaking care, and, without as much as by your leave, whacked half the tobacco of my pouch into his. Yes, the stuff was fairly good. He sighed with the contentment of the just, and literally absorbed the smoke from the crisping yellow flakes, and it did my smoker's heart good to behold him.

Hunter? Trapper? Prospector? He shrugged his shoulders No; just sort of knocking round a bit. Had come up from the Great Slave some time since, and was thinking of trapsing over into the Yukon country. The Factor of Koshim had spoken about the discoveries on the Klondike, and he was of a mind to run over for a peep. I noticed that he spoke of the Klondike in the archaic vernacular, calling it the Reindeer River—a conceited custom that the Old Timers employ against the *che-cha-quas* and all tenderfeet in general. But he did it so naïvely and as such a matter of course, that there was no sting, and I forgave him. He also had it in view, he said, before he crossed the divide into the Yukon, to make a little run up Fort o' Good Hope way.

Now Fort o' Good Hope is a far journey to the north, over and beyond the Circle, in a place where the feet of few men have trod; and when a nondescript ragamuffin comes in out of the night, from nowhere in particular, to sit by one's fire and discourse on such in terms of "trapsing" and "a little run," it is fair time to rouse up and shake off the dream. Wherefore I looked about me; saw the fly, and, underneath, the pine boughs spread for the sleeping furs; saw the grub sacks, the camera, the frosty breaths of the dogs circling on the edge of the light; and, above, a great streamer of the aurora bridging the zenith from southeast to northwest. I shivered. There is a magic in the Northland night, that steals in on one like fevers from malarial marshes.

You are clutched and downed before you are aware. Then I looked to the snowshoes, lying prone and crossed where he had flung them. Also I had an eye to my tobacco pouch. Half, at least, of its goodly store had vamosed. That settled it. Fancy had not tricked me after all.

Crazed with suffering, I thought, looking steadfastly at the man —one of those wild stampeders, strayed far from his bearings and wandering like a lost soul through great vastnesses and unknown deeps. Oh, well, let his moods slip on, until, mayhap, he gathers his tangled wits together. Who knows?—the mere sound of a fellow-creature's voice may bring all straight again.

So I led him on in talk, and soon I marvelled, for he talked of game and the ways thereof. He had killed the Siberian wolf of westernmost Alaska, and the chamois in the secret Rockies. He averred he knew the haunts where the last buffalo still roamed; that he had hung on the flanks of the caribou when they ran by the hundred thousand, and slept in the Great Barrens on the musk-ox's winter trail.

And I shifted my judgment accordingly (the first revision, but by no account the last), and deemed him a monumental effigy of truth. Why it was I know not, but the spirit moved me to repeat a tale told to me by a man who had dwelt in the land too long to know better. It was of the great bear that hugs the steep slopes of St. Elias, never descending to the levels of the gentler inclines. Now God so constituted this creature for its hillside habitat that the legs of one side are all of a foot longer than those of the other. This is mighty convenient, as will be readily admitted. So I hunted this rare beast in my own name, told it in the first person, present tense, painted the requisite locale, gave it the necessary garnishings and touches of verisimilitude, and looked to see the man stunned by the recital.

Not he. Had he doubted, I could have forgiven him. Had he objected, denying the dangers of such a hunt by virtue of the animal's inability to turn about and go the other way—had he done this, I say, I could have taken him by the hand for the true sportsman that he was. Not he. He sniffed, looked on me, and sniffed again; then gave my tobacco due praise, thrust one foot into my lap, and bade me examine the gear. It was a *mucluc* of the Innuit pattern, sewed together with sinew threads, and devoid of beads or furbelows. But it was the skin itself that was remarkable. In that it was all of half an inch thick, it reminded me of walrus-hide; but there the resemblance ceased, for no walrus ever bore so marvellous a growth of hair. On the side and ankles this hair was well-nigh worn away, what of friction with underbrush and snow; but around the top and down the more sheltered back it was coarse, dirty black, and very thick. I parted it with difficulty and looked beneath for the fine fur that is common with northern animals, but found it in this case to be absent. This, however, was compensated for by the length. Indeed, the tufts that had survived wear and tear measured all of seven or eight inches.

I looked up into the man's face, and he pulled his foot down and asked, "Find hide like that on your St. Elias bear?"

I shook my head. "Nor on any other creature of land or sea," I answered candidly. The thickness of it, and the length of the hair, puzzled me.

"That," he said, and said without the slightest hint of impressiveness, "that came from a mammoth."

"Nonsense!" I exclaimed, for I could not forbear the protest of my unbelief. "The mammoth, my dear sir, long ago vanished from the earth. We know it once existed by the fossil remains that we have unearthed, and by a frozen carcass that the Siberian sun saw fit to melt from out the bosom of a glacier; but we also know that no living specimen exists. Our explorers—"

At this word he broke in impatiently. "Your explorers? Pish! A weakly breed. Let us hear no more of them. But tell me, O man, what you may know of the mammoth and his ways."

Beyond contradiction, this was leading to a yarn; so I baited my hook by ransacking my memory for whatever data I possessed on the subject in hand. To begin with, I emphasized that the animal was prehistoric, and marshalled all my facts in support of this. I mentioned the Siberian sand bars that abounded with ancient mammoth bones; spoke of the large quantities of fossil ivory purchased from the Innuits by the Alaska Commercial Company; and acknowledged having myself mined six- and eight-foot tusks from the pay gravel of the Klondike creeks. "All fossils," I concluded, "found in the midst of débris deposited through countless ages."

"I remember when I was a kid," Thomas Stevens sniffed (he had a most confounded way of sniffing), "that I saw a petrified watermelon. Hence, though mistaken persons sometimes delude themselves into thinking that they are really raising or eating them, there are no such things as extant watermelons."

"But the question of food," I objected, ignoring his point, which was puerile and without bearing. "The soil must bring forth vegetable life in lavish abundance to support so monstrous creations. Nowhere in the North is the soil so prolific. Ergo, the mammoth cannot exist."

"I pardon your ignorance concerning many matters of this Northland, for you are a young man and have travelled little; but, at the same time, I am inclined to agree with you on one thing. The mammoth no longer exists. How do I know? I killed the last one with my own right arm."

Thus spake Nimrod, the Mighty Hunter. I threw a stick of firewood at the dogs and bade them quit their unholy howling, and waited. Undoubtedly this liar of singular felicity would open his mouth and requite me for my St. Elias bear.

"It was this way," he at last began, after the appropriate silence had intervened. "I was in camp one day—"

"Where?" I interrupted.

He waved his hand vaguely in the direction of the northeast, where stretched a terra incognita into which vastness few men have strayed and fewer emerged. "I was in camp one day with Klooch. Klooch was as handsome a little *kamooks* as ever whined betwixt the traces or shoved nose into a camp kettle. Her father was a full-blood Malemute from Russian Pastilik on Bering Sea, and I bred her, and with understanding, out of a clean-legged bitch of the Hudson Bay stock. I tell you, O man, she was a corker combination. And now, on this day I have in mind, she was brought to pup through a pure wild wolf of the woods—gray, and long of limb, with big lungs and no end of staying powers. Say! Was there ever the like? It was a new breed of dog I had started, and I could look forward to big things.

"As I have said, she was brought neatly to pup, and safely delivered. I was squatting on my hams over the litter—seven sturdy, blind little beggars—when from behind came a bray of trumpets and crash of brass. There was a rush, like the wind-squall that kicks the heels of the rain, and I was midway to my feet when knocked flat on my face. At the same instant I heard Klooch sigh, very much as a man does when you've planted your fist in his belly. You can stake your sack I lay quiet, but I twisted my head around and saw a huge bulk swaying above me. Then the blue sky flashed into view and I got to my feet. A hairy mountain of flesh was just disappearing in the underbrush on the edge of the open. I caught a rear-end glimpse, with a stiff tail, as big in girth as my body, standing out straight behind. The next second only a tremendous hole remained in the thicket, though I could still hear the sounds as of a tornado dying quickly away, underbrush ripping and tearing, and trees snapping and crashing.

"I cast about for my rifle. It had been lying on the ground with the muzzle against a log; but now the stock was smashed, the barrel out of line, and the working-gear in a thousand bits. Then I looked for the slut, and—and what do you suppose?"

I shook my head.

"May my soul burn in a thousand hells if there was anything left of her! Klooch, the seven sturdy, blind little beggars—gone, all gone. Where she had stretched was a slimy, bloody depression in the soft earth, all of a yard in diameter, and around the edges a few scattered hairs."

I measured three feet on the snow, threw about it a circle, and glanced at Nimrod.

"The beast was thirty long and twenty high," he answered, "and its tusks scaled over six times three feet. I couldn't believe, myself, at the time, for all that it had just happened. But if my senses had played me, there was the broken gun and the hole in the brush. And there was—or, rather, there was not—Klooch and the pups. O man, it makes me hot all over now when I think of it. Klooch! Another Eve! The mother of a new race! And a rampaging, ranting, old bull mammoth, like a second flood, wiping them, root and branch, off the face of the earth! Do you wonder that the blood-soaked earth cried out to high God? Or that I grabbed the hand-axe and took the trail?"

"The hand-axe?" I exclaimed, startled out of myself by the picture. "The hand-axe, and a big bull mammoth, thirty feet long, twenty feet—"

Nimrod joined me in my merriment, chuckling gleefully. "Wouldn't it kill you?" he cried. "Wasn't it a beaver's dream? Many's the time I've laughed about it since, but at the time it was no laughing matter, I was that danged mad, what of the gun and Klooch. Think of it, O man! A brand-new, unclassified, uncopyrighted breed, and wiped out before ever it opened its eyes or took out its intention papers! Well, so be it. Life's full of disappointments, and rightly so. Meat is best after a famine, and a bed soft after a hard trail.

"As I was saying, I took out after the beast with the hand-axe, and hung to its heels down the valley; but when he circled back toward the head, I was left winded at the lower end. Speaking of grub, I might as well stop long enough to explain a couple of points. Up thereabouts, in the midst of the mountains, is an almighty curious formation. There is no end of little valleys, each like the other much as peas in a pod, and all neatly tucked away with straight, rocky walls rising on all sides. And at the lower ends are always small openings where the drainage or glaciers must have broken out. The only way in is through these mouths, and they are all small, and some smaller than others. As to grub—you've slushed around on the rain-soaked islands of the Alaskan coast down Sitka way, most likely, seeing as you're a traveller. And you know how stuff grows there—big, and juicy, and jungly. Well, that's the way it was with those valleys. Thick, rich soil, with ferns and grasses and such things in patches higher than your head. Rain three days out of four during the summer months; and food in them for a thousand mammoths, to say nothing of small game for man.

"But to get back. Down at the lower end of the valley I got winded and gave over. I began to speculate, for when my wind left me my dander got hotter and hotter, and I knew I'd never know peace of mind till I dined on roasted mammoth-foot. And I knew, also, that that stood for *skookum mamook puka-puk*—excuse Chinook, I mean there was a big fight coming. Now the mouth of my valley was very narrow, and the walls steep. High up on one side was one of those big pivot rocks, or balancing rocks, as some call them, weighing all of a couple of hundred tons. Just the thing. I hit back for camp, keeping an eye open so the bull couldn't slip past, and got my ammunition. It wasn't worth anything with the rifle smashed; so I opened the shells, planted the powder under the rock, and touched it off with slow fuse. Wasn't much of a charge, but the old boulder tilted up lazily and dropped down into place, with just space enough to let the creek drain nicely. Now I had him."

"But how did you have him?" I queried. "Who ever heard of a man killing a mammoth with a hand-axe? And, for that matter, with anything else?"

"O man, have I not told you I was mad?" Nimrod replied, with a slight manifestation of sensitiveness. "Mad clean through, what of Klooch and the gun? Also, was I not a hunter? And was this not new and most unusual game? A hand-axe? Pish! I did not need it. Listen, and you shall hear of a hunt, such as might have happened in the youth of the world when caveman rounded up the kill with hand-axe of stone. Such would have served me as well. Now is it not a fact that man can outwalk the dog or horse? That he can wear them out with the intelligence of his endurance?"

I nodded.

"Well?"

The light broke in on me, and I bade him continue.

"My valley was perhaps five miles around. The mouth was closed.

There was no way to get out. A timid beast was that bull mammoth, and I had him at my mercy. I got on his heels again, hollered like a fiend, pelted him with cobbles, and raced him around the valley three times before I knocked off for supper. Don't you see? A race-course! A man and a mammoth! A hippodrome, with sun, moon, and stars to referee!

"It took me two months to do it, but I did it. And that's no beaver dream. Round and round I ran him, me travelling on the inner circle, eating jerked meat and salmon berries on the run, and snatching winks of sleep between. Of course, he'd get desperate at times and turn. Then I'd head for soft ground where the creek spread out, and lay anathema upon him and his ancestry, and dare him to come on. But he was too wise to bog in a mud puddle. Once he pinned me in against the walls, and I crawled back into a deep crevice and waited. Whenever he felt for me with his trunk, I'd belt him with the hand-axe till he pulled out, shrieking fit to split my ear drums, he was that mad. He knew he had me and didn't have me, and it near drove him wild. But he was no man's fool. He knew he was safe as long as I stayed in the crevice, and he made up his mind to keep me there. And he was dead right, only he hadn't figured on the commissary. There was neither grub nor water around that spot, so on the face of it he couldn't keep up the siege. He'd stand before the opening for hours, keeping an eye on me and flapping mosquitoes away with his big blanket ears. Then the thirst would come on him and he'd ramp round and roar till the earth shook, calling me every name he could lay tongue to. This was to frighten me, of course; and when he thought I was sufficiently impressed, he'd back away softly and try to make a sneak for the creek. Sometimes I'd let him get almost there—only a couple of hundred yards away it was—when out I'd pop and back he'd come, lumbering along like the old landslide he was. After I'd done this a few times, and he'd figured it out, he changed his tactics. Grasped the time element, you see. Without a word of warning, away he'd go, tearing for the water like mad, scheming to get there and back before I ran away. Finally, after cursing me most horribly, he raised the siege and deliberately stalked off to the water hole.

"That was the only time he penned me,—three days of it,—but after that the hippodrome never stopped. Round, and round, and round, like a six days' go-as-I-please, for he never pleased. My clothes went to rags and tatters, but I never stopped to mend, till at last I ran naked as a son of earth, with nothing but the old hand-axe in one hand and a cobble in the other. In fact, I never stopped, save for peeps of sleep in the crannies and ledges of the cliffs. As for the bull, he got perceptibly thinner and thinner—must have lost several tons at least —and as nervous as a schoolmarm on the wrong side of matrimony. When I'd come up with him and yell, or lam him with a rock at long range, he'd jump like a skittish colt and tremble all over. Then he'd pull out on the run, tail and trunk waving stiff, head over one shoulder and wicked eyes blazing, and the way he'd swear at me was something dreadful. A most immoral beast he was, a murderer, and a blasphemer.

"But toward the end he quit all this, and fell to whimpering and crying like a baby. His spirit broke and he became a quivering jelly-mountain of misery. He'd get attacks of palpitation of the heart, and stagger around like a drunken man, and fall down and bark his shins. And then he'd cry, but always on the run. O man, the gods themselves would have wept with him, and you yourself or any other man. It was pitiful, and there was so much of it, but I only hardened my heart and hit up the pace. At last I wore him clean out, and he lay down, broken-winded, broken-hearted, hungry, and thirsty. When I found he wouldn't budge, I hamstrung him, and spent the better part of the day wading into him with the hand-axe, he a sniffing and sobbing till I worked in far enough to shut him off. Thirty feet long he was, and twenty high, and a man could sling a hammock between his tusks and sleep comfortably. Barring the fact that I had run most of the juices out of him, he was fair eating, and his four feet, alone, roasted whole, would have lasted a man a twelvemonth. I spent the winter there myself."

"And where is this valley?" I asked.

He waved his hand in the direction of the northeast, and said: "Your tobacco is very good. I carry a fair share of it in my pouch, but I shall carry the recollection of it until I die. In token of my appreciation, and in return for the moccasins on your own feet, I will present to you these *muclucs*. They commemorate Klooch and the seven blind little beggars. They are also souvenirs of an unparalleled event in history, namely, the destruction of the oldest breed of animal on earth, and the youngest. And their chief virtue lies in that they will never wear out."

Having effected the exchange, he knocked the ashes from his pipe, gripped my hand good night, and wandered off through the snow. Concerning this tale, for which I have already disclaimed responsibility, I would recommend those of little faith to make a visit to the Smithsonian Institute. If they bring the requisite credentials and do not come in vacation time, they will undoubtedly gain an audience with Professor Dolvidson. The *muclucs* are in his possession, and he will verify, not the manner in which they were obtained, but the material of which they are composed. When he states that they are made from the skin of the mammoth, the scientific world accepts his verdict. What more would you have?

# NAM-BOK THE UNVERACIOUS

"A BIDARKA, is it not so? Look! a bidarka, and one man who drives clumsily with a paddle!"

Old Bask-Wah-Wan rose to her knees, trembling with weakness and eagerness, and gazed out over the sea.

"Nam-Bok was ever clumsy at the paddle," she maundered reminiscently, shading the sun from her eyes and staring across the silver-spilled water. "Nam-Bok was ever clumsy. I remember . . ."

But the women and children laughed loudly, and there was a gentle mockery in their laughter, and her voice dwindled till her lips moved without sound.

Koogah lifted his grizzled head from his bone-carving and followed the path of her eyes. Except when wide yaws took it off its course, a bidarka was heading in for the beach. Its occupant was paddling with more strength than dexterity, and made his approach along the zigzag line of most resistance. Koogah's head dropped to his work again, and on the ivory tusk between his knees he scratched the dorsal fin of a fish the like of which never swam in the sea.

"It is doubtless the man from the next village," he said finally, "come to consult with me about the marking of things on bone. And the man is a clumsy man. He will never know how."

"It is Nam-Bok," old Bask-Wah-Wan repeated. "Should I not know my son?" she demanded shrilly. "I say, and I say again, it is Nam-Bok."

"And so thou hast said these many summers," one of the women chided softly. "Ever when the ice passed out of the sea hast thou sat and watched through the long day, saying at each chance canoe, 'This is Nam-Bok.' Nam-Bok is dead, O Bask-Wah-Wan, and the dead do not come back. It cannot be that the dead come back."

"Nam-Bok!" the old woman cried, so loud and clear that the whole village was startled and looked at her.

She struggled to her feet and tottered down the sand. She stumbled over a baby lying in the sun, and the mother hushed its crying and hurled harsh words after the old woman, who took no notice. The children ran down the beach in advance of her, and as the man in the bidarka drew closer, nearly capsizing with one of his ill-directed strokes, the women followed. Koogah dropped his walrus tusk and went also, leaning heavily upon his staff, and after him loitered the men in twos and threes.

The bidarka turned broadside and the ripple of surf threatened to swamp it, only a naked boy ran into the water and pulled the bow high up on the sand. The man stood up and sent a questing glance along the line of villagers. A rainbow sweater, dirty and the worse for wear, clung loosely to his broad shoulders, and a red cotton handkerchief was knotted in sailor fashion about his throat. A fisherman's tam-o'-shanter on his close-clipped head, and dungaree trousers and heavy brogans, completed his outfit.

But he was none the less a striking personage to these simple fisherfolk of the great Yukon Delta, who, all their lives, had stared out on Bering Sea and in that time seen but two white men,—the census enumerator and a lost Jesuit priest. They were a poor people, with neither gold in the ground nor valuable furs in hand, so the whites had passed them afar. Also, the Yukon, through the thousands of years, had shoaled that portion of the sea with the detritus of Alaska till vessels grounded out of sight of land. So the sodden coast, with its long inside reaches and huge mud-land archipelagoes, was avoided by the ships of men, and the fisherfolk knew not that such things were.

Koogah, the Bone-Scratcher, retreated backward in sudden haste, tripping over his staff and falling to the ground. "Nam-Bok!" he cried, as he scrambled wildly for footing. "Nam-Bok, who was blown off to sea, come back!"

The men and women shrank away, and the children scuttled off between their legs. Only Opee-Kwan was brave, as befitted the head man of the village. He strode forward and gazed long and earnestly at the new-comer.

"It *is* Nam-Bok," he said at last, and at the conviction in his voice the women wailed apprehensively and drew farther away.

The lips of the stranger moved indecisively, and his brown throat writhed and wrestled with unspoken words.

"La la, it is Nam-Bok," Bask-Wah-Wan croaked, peering up into his face. "Ever did I say Nam-Bok would come back."

"Ay, it is Nam-Bok come back." This time it was Nam-Bok himself who spoke, putting a leg over the side of the bidarka and standing with one foot afloat and one ashore. Again his throat writhed and wrestled as he grappled after forgotten words. And when the words came forth they were strange of sound and a spluttering of the lips accompanied the gutturals. "Greeting, O brothers," he said, "brothers of old time before I went away with the off-shore wind."

He stepped out with both feet on the sand, and Opee-Kwan waved him back.

"Thou art dead, Nam-Bok," he said.

Nam-Bok laughed. "I am fat."

"Dead men are not fat," Opee-Kwan confessed. "Thou hast fared well, but it is strange. No man may mate with the off-shore wind and come back on the heels of the years."

"I have come back," Nam-Bok answered simply.

"Mayhap thou art a shadow, then, a passing shadow of the Nam-Bok that was. Shadows come back."

"I am hungry. Shadows do not eat."

But Opee-Kwan doubted, and brushed his hand across his brow in sore puzzlement. Nam-Bok was likewise puzzled, and as he looked up and down the line found no welcome in the eyes of the fisherfolk. The men and women whispered together. The children stole timidly back among their elders, and bristling dogs fawned up to him and sniffed suspiciously.

"I bore thee, Nam-Bok, and I gave thee suck when thou wast little," Bask-Wah-Wan whimpered, drawing closer; "and shadow though thou be, or no shadow, I will give thee to eat now."

Nam-Bok made to come to her, but a growl of fear and menace warned him back. He said something in a strange tongue which sounded like "Goddam," and added, "No shadow am I, but a man."

"Who may know concerning the things of mystery?" Opee-Kwan demanded, half of himself and half of his tribespeople. "We are, and in a breath we are not. If the man may become shadow, may not the shadow become man? Nam-Bok was, but is not. This we know, but we do not know if this be Nam-Bok or the shadow of Nam-Bok."

Nam-Bok cleared his throat and made answer. "In the old time long ago, thy father's father, Opee-Kwan, went away and came back on the heels of the years. Nor was a place by the fire denied him. It is said . . ." He paused significantly, and they hung on his utterance. "It is said," he repeated, driving his point home with deliberation, "that Sipsip, his *klooch*, bore him two sons after he came back."

"But he had no doings with the off-shore wind," Opee-Kwan retorted. "He went away into the heart of the land, and it is in the nature of things that a man may go on and on into the land."

"And likewise the sea. But that is neither here nor there. It is said . . . that thy father's father told strange tales of the things he saw."

"Ay, strange tales he told."

"I, too, have strange tales to tell," Nam-Bok stated insidiously. And, as they wavered, "And presents likewise."

He pulled from the bidarka a shawl, marvellous of texture and color, and flung it about his mother's shoulders. The women voiced a collective sigh of admiration, and old Bask-Wah-Wan ruffled the gay material and patted it and crooned in childish joy.

"He has tales to tell," Koogah muttered. "And presents," a woman seconded.

And Opee-Kwan knew that his people were eager, and further, he was aware himself of an itching curiosity concerning those untold tales. "The fishing has been good," he said judiciously, "and we have oil in plenty. So come, Nam-Bok, let us feast."

Two of the men hoisted the bidarka on their shoulders and carried it up to the fire. Nam-Bok walked by the side of Opee-Kwan, and the villagers followed after, save those of the women who lingered a moment to lay caressing fingers on the shawl.

There was little talk while the feast went on, though many and curious were the glances stolen at the son of Bask-Wah-Wan. This embarrassed him—not because he was modest of spirit, however, but for the fact that the stench of the seal-oil had robbed him of his appetite, and that he keenly desired to conceal his feelings on the subject.

"Eat; thou art hungry," Opee-Kwan commanded, and Nam-Bok shut both his eyes and shoved his fist into the big pot of putrid fish.

"La la, be not ashamed. The seal were many this year, and strong men are ever hungry." And Bask-Wah-Wan sopped a particularly offensive chunk of salmon into the oil and passed it fondly and dripping to her son.

In despair, when premonitory symptoms warned him that his stomach was not so strong as of old, he filled his pipe and struck up a smoke. The people fed on noisily and watched. Few of them could boast of intimate acquaintance with the precious weed, though now and again small quantities and abominable qualities were obtained in trade from the Eskimos to the northward. Koogah, sitting next to him, indicated that he was not averse to taking a draw, and between two mouthfuls, with the oil thick on his lips, sucked away at the amber stem. And thereupon Nam-Bok held his stomach with a shaky hand and declined the proffered return. Koogah could keep the pipe, he said, for he had intended so to honor him from the first. And the people licked their fingers and approved of his liberality.

Opee-Kwan rose to his feet. "And now, O Nam-Bok, the feast is ended, and we would listen concerning the strange things you have seen."

The fisherfolk applauded with their hands, and gathering about them their work, prepared to listen. The men were busy fashioning spears and carving on ivory, while the women scraped the fat from the hides of the hair seal and made them pliable or sewed muclucs with threads of sinew. Nam-Bok's eyes roved over the scene, but there was not the charm about it that his recollection had warranted him to expect. During the years of his wandering he had looked forward to just this scene, and now that it had come he was disappointed. It was a bare and meagre life, he deemed, and not to be compared to the one to which he had become used. Still, he would open their eyes a bit, and his own eyes sparkled at the thought.

"Brothers," he began, with the smug complacency of a man about to relate the big things he has done, "it was late summer of many summers back, with much such weather as this promises to be, when I went away. You all remember the day, when the gulls flew low, and the wind blew strong from the land, and I could not hold my bidarka against it. I tied the covering of the bidarka about me so that no water could get in, and all of the night I fought with the storm. And in the morning there was no land,—only the sea,—and the off-shore wind held me close in its arms and bore me along. Three such nights whitened into dawn and showed me no land, and the off-shore wind would not let me go.

"And when the fourth day came, I was as a madman. I could not dip my paddle for want of food; and my head went round and round, what of the thirst that was upon me. But the sea was no longer angry, and the soft south wind was blowing, and as I looked about me I saw a sight that made me think I was indeed mad."

Nam-Bok paused to pick away a sliver of salmon lodged between his teeth, and the men and women, with idle hands and heads craned forward, waited.

"It was a canoe, a big canoe. If all the canoes I have ever seen were made into one canoe, it would not be so large."

There were exclamations of doubt, and Koogah, whose years were many, shook his head.

"If each bidarka were as a grain of sand," Nam-Bok defiantly continued, "and if there were as many bidarkas as there be grains of sand in this beach, still would they not make so big a canoe as this I saw on the morning of the fourth day. It was a very big canoe, and it was called a *schooner*. I saw this thing of wonder, this great schooner, coming after me, and on it I saw men—"

"Hold, O Nam-Bok!" Opee-Kwan broke in. "What manner of men were they?—big men?"

"Nay, mere men like you and me."

"Did the big canoe come fast?"

"Ay."

"The sides were tall, the men short." Opee-Kwan stated the premises with conviction. "And did these men dip with long paddles?"

Nam-Bok grinned. "There were no paddles," he said.

Mouths remained open, and a long silence dropped down. Opee-Kwan borrowed Koogah's pipe for a couple of contemplative sucks. One of the younger women giggled nervously and drew upon herself angry eyes.

"There were no paddles?" Opee-Kwan asked softly, returning the pipe.

"The south wind was behind," Nam-Bok explained.

"But the wind-drift is slow."

"The schooner had wings—thus." He sketched a diagram of masts and sails in the sand, and the men crowded around and studied it. The wind was blowing briskly, and for more graphic elucidation he seized the corners of his mother's shawl and spread them out till it bellied like a sail. Bask-Wah-Wan scolded and struggled, but was blown down the beach for a score of feet and left breathless and stranded in a heap of driftwood. The men uttered sage grunts of comprehension, but Koogah suddenly tossed back his hoary head.

"Ho! Ho!" he laughed. "A foolish thing, this big canoe! A most foolish thing! The plaything of the wind! Wheresoever the wind goes, it goes too. No man who journeys therein may name the landing beach, for always he goes with the wind, and the wind goes everywhere, but no man knows where."

"It is so," Opee-Kwan supplemented gravely. "With the wind the going is easy, but against the wind a man striveth hard; and for that they had no paddles these men on the big canoe did not strive at all."

"Small need to strive," Nam-Bok cried angrily. "The schooner went likewise against the wind."

"And what said you made the sch—sch—schooner go?" Koogah asked, tripping craftily over the strange word.

"The wind," was the impatient response.

"Then the wind made the sch—sch—schooner go against the wind." Old Koogah dropped an open leer to Opee-Kwan, and, the laughter growing around him, continued: "The wind blows from the south and blows the schooner south. The wind blows against the wind. The wind blows one way and the other at the same time. It is very simple. We understand, Nam-Bok. We clearly understand."

"Thou art a fool!"

"Truth falls from thy lips," Koogah answered meekly. "I was over-long in understanding, and the thing was simple."

But Nam-Bok's face was dark, and he said rapid words which they had never heard before. Bone-scratching and skin-scraping were resumed, but he shut his lips tightly on the tongue that could not be believed.

"This sch—sch—schooner," Koogah imperturbably asked; "it was made of a big tree?"

"It was made of many trees," Nam-Bok snapped shortly. "It was very big."

He lapsed into sullen silence again, and Opee-Kwan nudged Koogah, who shook his head with slow amazement and murmured, "It is very strange."

Nam-bok took the bait. "That is nothing," he said airily; "you should see the *steamer*. As the grain of sand is to the bidarka, as the bidarka is to the schooner, so the schooner is to the steamer. Further, the steamer is made of iron. It is all iron."

"Nay, nay, Nam-Bok," cried the head man; "how can that be? Always iron goes to the bottom. For behold, I received an iron knife in trade from the head man of the next village, and yesterday the iron knife slipped from my fingers and went down, down, into the sea. To all things there be law. Never was there one thing outside the law. This we know. And, moreover, we know that things of a kind have the one law, and that all iron has the one law. So unsay thy words, Nam-Bok, that we may yet honor thee."

"It is so," Nam-Bok persisted. "The steamer is all iron and does not sink."

"Nay, nay; this cannot be."

"With my own eyes I saw it."

"It is not in the nature of things."

"But tell me, Nam-Bok," Koogah interrupted, for fear the tale would go no farther, "tell me the manner of these men in finding their way across the sea when there is no land by which to steer."

"The sun points out the path."

"But how?"

"At midday the head man of the schooner takes a thing through which his eye looks at the sun, and then he makes the sun climb down out of the sky to the edge of the earth."

"Now this be evil medicine!" cried Opee-Kwan, aghast at the sacrilege. The men held up their hands in horror, and the women moaned. "This be evil medicine. It is not good to misdirect the great sun which drives away the night and gives us the seal, the salmon, and warm weather."

"What if it be evil medicine?" Nam-Bok demanded truculently. "I, too, have looked through the thing at the sun and made the sun climb down out of the sky."

Those who were nearest drew away from him hurriedly, and a woman covered the face of a child at her breast so that his eye might not fall upon it.

"But on the morning of the fourth day, O Nam-Bok," Koogah suggested; "on the morning of the fourth day when the sch—sch—schooner came after thee?"

"I had little strength left in me and could not run away. So I was taken on board and water was poured down my throat and good food given me. Twice, my brothers, you have seen a white man. These men were all white and as many as have I fingers and toes. And when I saw they were full of kindness, I took heart, and I resolved to bring away with me report of all that I saw. And they taught me the work they did, and gave me good food and a place to sleep.

"And day after day we went over the sea, and each day the head man drew the sun down out of the sky and made it tell where we were. And when the waves were kind, we hunted the fur seal and I marvelled much, for always did they fling the meat and the fat away and save only the skin."

Opee-Kwan's mouth was twitching violently, and he was about to make denunciation of such waste when Koogah kicked him to be still.

"After a weary time, when the sun was gone and the bite of the frost come into the air, the head man pointed the nose of the schooner south. South and east we travelled for days upon days, with never the land in sight, and we were near to the village from which hailed the men—"

"How did they know they were near?" Opee-Kwan, unable to contain himself longer, demanded. "There was no land to see."

Nam-Bok glowered on him wrathfully. "Did I not say the head man brought the sun down out of the sky?"

Koogah interposed, and Nam-Bok went on.

"As I say, when we were near to that village a great storm blew up, and in the night we were helpless and knew not where we were—"

"Thou hast just said the head man knew—"

"Oh, peace, Opee-Kwan! Thou art a fool and cannot understand. As I say, we were helpless in the night, when I heard, above the roar of the storm, the sound of the sea on the beach. And next we struck with a mighty crash and I was in the water, swimming. It was a rock-bound coast, with one patch of beach in many miles, and the law was that I should dig my hands into the sand and draw myself clear of the surf. The other men must have pounded against the rocks, for none of them came ashore but the head man, and him I knew only by the ring on his finger.

"When day came, there being nothing of the schooner, I turned my face to the land and journeyed into it that I might get food and look upon the faces of the people. And when I came to a house I was taken in and given to eat, for I had learned their speech, and the white men are ever kindly. And it was a house bigger than all the houses built by us and our fathers before us."

"It was a mighty house," Koogah said, masking his unbelief with wonder.

"And many trees went into the making of such a house," Opee-Kwan added, taking the cue.

"That is nothing." Nam-Bok shrugged his shoulders in belittling fashion. "As our houses are to that house, so that house was to the houses I was yet to see."

"And they are not big men?"

"Nay; mere men like you and me," Nam-Bok answered. "I had cut a stick that I might walk in comfort, and remembering that I was to bring report to you, my brothers, I cut a notch in the stick for each person who lived in that house. And I stayed there many days, and worked, for which they gave me *money*—a thing of which you know nothing, but which is very good.

"And one day I departed from that place to go farther into

the land. And as I walked I met many people, and I cut smaller notches in the stick, that there might be room for all. Then I came upon a strange thing. On the ground before me was a bar of iron, as big in thickness as my arm, and a long step away was another bar of iron—"

"Then wert thou a rich man," Opee-Kwan asserted; "for iron be worth more than anything else in the world. It would have made many knives."

"Nay, it was not mine."

"It was a find, and a find be lawful."

"Not so; the white men had placed it there. And further, these bars were so long that no man could carry them away—so long that as far as I could see there was no end to them."

"Nam-Bok, that is very much iron," Opee-Kwan cautioned.

"Ay, it was hard to believe with my own eyes upon it; but I could not gainsay my eyes. And as I looked I heard . . ." He turned abruptly upon the head man. "Opee-Kwan, thou hast heard the sea-lion bellow in his anger. Make it plain in thy mind of as many sea-lions as there be waves to the sea, and make it plain that all these sea-lions be made into one sea-lion, and as that one sea-lion would bellow so bellowed the thing I heard."

The fisherfolk cried aloud in astonishment, and Opee-Kwan's jaw lowered and remained lowered.

"And in the distance I saw a monster like unto a thousand whales. It was one-eyed, and vomited smoke, and it snorted with exceeding loudness. I was afraid and ran with shaking legs along the path between the bars. But it came with the speed of the wind, this monster, and I leaped the iron bars with its breath hot on my face . . ."

Opee-Kwan gained control of his jaw again. "And—and then, O Nam-Bok?"

"Then it came by on the bars, and harmed me not; and when my legs could hold me up again it was gone from sight. And it is a very common thing in that country. Even the women and children are not afraid. Men make them to do work, these monsters."

"As we make our dogs do work?" Koogah asked, with sceptic twinkle in his eye.

"Ay, as we make our dogs do work."

"And how do they breed these—these things?" Opee-Kwan questioned.

"They breed not at all. Men fashion them cunningly of iron, and feed them with stone, and give them water to drink. The stone becomes fire, and the water becomes steam, and the steam of the water is the breath of their nostrils, and—"

"There, there, O Nam-Bok," Opee-Kwan interrupted. "Tell us of other wonders. We grow tired of this which we may not understand."

"You do not understand?" Nam-Bok asked despairingly.

"Nay, we do not understand," the men and women wailed back. "We cannot understand."

Nam-Bok thought of a combined harvester, and of the machines wherein visions of living men were to be seen, and of the machines from which came the voices of men, and he knew his people could never understand.

"Dare I say I rode this iron monster through the land?" he asked bitterly.

Opee-Kwan threw up his hands, palms outward, in open incredulity. "Say on; say anything. We listen."

"Then did I ride the iron monster, for which I gave money—"

"Thou saidst it was fed with stone."

"And likewise, thou fool, I said money was a thing of which you know nothing. As I say, I rode the monster through the land, and through many villages, until I came to a big village on a salt arm of the sea. And the houses shoved their roofs among the stars in the sky, and the clouds drifted by them, and everywhere was much smoke. And the roar of that village was like the roar of the sea in storm, and the people were so many that I flung away my stick and no longer remembered the notches upon it."

"Hadst thou made small notches," Koogah reproved, "thou mightst have brought report."

Nam-Bok whirled upon him in anger. "Had I made small notches! Listen, Koogah, thou scratcher of bone! If I had made small notches, neither the stick, nor twenty sticks, could have borne them—nay, not all the driftwood of all the beaches between this village and the next. And if all of you, the women and children as well, were twenty times as many, and if you had twenty hands each, and in each hand a stick and a knife, still the notches could not be cut for the people I saw, so many were they and so fast did they come and go."

"There cannot be so many people in all the world," Opee-Kwan objected, for he was stunned and his mind could not grasp such magnitude of numbers.

"What dost thou know of all the world and how large it is?" Nam-Bok demanded.

"But there cannot be so many people in one place."

"Who art thou to say what can be and what cannot be?"

"It stands to reason there cannot be so many people in one place. Their canoes would clutter the sea till there was no room. And they could empty the sea each day of its fish, and they would not all be fed."

"So it would seem," Nam-Bok made final answer; "yet it was so. With my own eyes I saw, and flung my stick away." He yawned heavily and rose to his feet. "I have paddled far. The day has been long, and I am tired. Now I will sleep, and to-morrow we will have further talk upon the things I have seen."

Bask-Wah-Wan, hobbling fearfully in advance, proud indeed, yet awed by her wonderful son, led him to her igloo and stowed him away among the greasy, ill-smelling furs. But the men lingered by the fire, and a council was held wherein was there much whispering and low-voiced discussion.

An hour passed, and a second, and Nam-Bok slept, and the talk went on. The evening sun dipped toward the northwest, and at eleven at night was nearly due north. Then it was that the head man and the bone-scratcher separated themselves from the council and aroused Nam-Bok. He blinked up into their faces and turned on his side to sleep again. Opee-Kwan gripped him by the arm and kindly but firmly shook his senses back into him.

"Come, Nam-Bok, arise!" he commanded. "It be time."

"Another feast?" Nam-Bok cried. "Nay, I am not hungry. Go on with the eating and let me sleep."

"Time to be gone!" Koogah thundered.

But Opee-Kwan spoke more softly. "Thou wast bidarka-mate with me when we were boys," he said. "Together we first chased the seal and drew the salmon from the traps. And thou didst drag me back to life, Nam-Bok, when the sea closed over me and I was sucked down to the black rocks. Together we hungered and bore the chill of the frost, and together we crawled beneath the one fur and lay close to each other. And because of these things, and the kindness in which I stood to thee, it grieves me sore that thou shouldst return such a remarkable liar. We cannot understand, and our heads be dizzy with the things thou hast spoken. It is not good, and there has been much talk in the council. Wherefore we send thee away, that our heads may remain clear and strong and be not troubled by the unaccountable things."

"These things thou speakest of be shadows," Koogah took up the strain. "From the shadow-world thou hast brought them, and to the shadow-world thou must return them. Thy bidarka be ready, and the tribespeople wait. They may not sleep until thou art gone."

Nam-Bok was perplexed, but hearkened to the voice of the head man.

"If thou art Nam-Bok," Opee-Kwan was saying, "thou art a fearful and most wonderful liar; if thou art the shadow of Nam-Bok, then thou speakest of shadows, concerning which it is not good that living men have knowledge. This great village thou hast spoken of we deem the village of shadows. Therein flutter the souls of the dead; for the dead be many and the living few. The dead do not come back. Never have the dead come back—save thou with thy wonder-tales. It is not meet that the dead come back, and should we permit it, great trouble may be our portion."

Nam-Bok knew his people well and was aware that the voice of the council was supreme. So he allowed himself to be led down to the water's edge, where he was put aboard his bidarka and a paddle thrust into his hand. A stray wild-fowl honked somewhere to seaward, and the surf broke limply and hollowly on the sand. A dim twilight brooded over land and water, and in the north the sun smouldered, vague and troubled, and draped about with blood-red mists. The gulls were flying low. The off-shore wind blew keen and chill, and the black-massed clouds behind it gave promise of bitter weather.

"Out of the sea thou camest," Opee-Kwan chanted oracularly, "and back into the sea thou goest. Thus is balance achieved and all things brought to law."

Bask-Wah-Wan limped to the froth-mark and cried, "I bless thee, Nam-Bok, for that thou remembered me."

But Koogah, shoving Nam-Bok clear of the beach, tore the shawl from her shoulders and flung it into the bidarka.

"It is cold in the long nights," she wailed; "and the frost is prone to nip old bones."

"The thing is a shadow," the bone-scratcher answered, "and shadows cannot keep thee warm."

Nam-Bok stood up that his voice might carry. "O Bask-Wah-Wan, mother that bore me!" he called. "Listen to the words of Nam-Bok, thy son. There be room in his bidarka for two, and he would that thou camest with him. For his journey is to where there are fish and oil in plenty. There the frost comes not, and life is easy, and the things of iron do the work of men. Wilt thou come, O Bask-Wah-Wan?"

She debated a moment, while the bidarka drifted swiftly from her, then raised her voice to a quavering treble. "I am old, Nam-Bok, and soon I shall pass down among the shadows. But I have no wish to go before my time. I am old, Nam-Bok, and I am afraid."

A shaft of light shot across the dim-lit sea and wrapped boat and man in a splendor of red and gold. Then a hush fell upon the fisherfolk, and only was heard the moan of the off-shore wind and the cries of the gulls flying low in the air.

# TO BUILD A FIRE (1902)

FOR LAND TRAVEL or seafaring, the world over, a companion is usually considered desirable. In the Klondike, as Tom Vincent found out, such a companion is absolutely essential. But he found it out, not by precept, but through bitter experience.

"Never travel alone," is a precept of the north. He had heard it many times and laughed; for he was a strapping young fellow, big-boned and big-muscled, with faith in himself and in the strength of his head and hands.

It was on a bleak January day when the experience came that taught him respect for the frost, and for the wisdom of the men who had battled with it.

He had left Calumet Camp on the Yukon with a light pack on his back, to go up Paul Creek to the divide between it and Cherry Creek, where his party was prospecting and hunting moose.

The frost was sixty degrees below zero, and he had thirty miles of lonely trail to cover, but he did not mind. In fact, he enjoyed it, swinging along through the silence, his blood pounding warmly through his veins, and his mind carefree and happy. For he and his comrades were certain they had struck "pay" up there on the Cherry Creek Divide; and, further, he was returning to them from Dawson with cheery home letters from the States.

At seven o'clock, when he turned the heels of his moccasins toward Calumet Camp, it was still black night. And when day broke at half past nine he had made the four-mile cut-off across the flats and was six miles up Paul Creek. The trail, which had seen little travel, followed the bed of the creek, and there was no possibility of his getting lost. He had gone to Dawson by way of Cherry Creek and Indian River, so Paul Creek was new and strange. By half past eleven he was at the forks, which had been described to him, and he knew he had covered fifteen miles, half the distance.

He knew that in the nature of things the trail was bound to grow worse from there on, and thought that, considering the good time he had made, he merited lunch. Casting off his pack and taking a seat on a fallen tree, he unmittened his right hand, reached inside his shirt next to the skin, and fished out a couple of biscuits sandwiched with sliced bacon and wrapped in a handkerchief—the only way they could be carried without freezing solid.

He had barely chewed the first mouthful when his numbing fingers warned him to put his mitten on again. This he did, not without surprise at the bitter swiftness with which the frost bit in. Undoubtedly it was the coldest snap he had ever experienced, he thought.

He spat upon the snow,—a favorite northland trick,—and the sharp crackle of the instantly congealed spittle startled him. The spirit thermometer at Calumet had registered sixty below when he left, but he was certain it had grown much colder, how much colder he could not imagine.

Half of the first biscuit was yet untouched, but he could feel himself beginning to chill—a thing most unusual for him. This would never do, he decided, and slipping the pack-straps across his shoulders, he leaped to his feet and ran briskly up the trail.

A few minutes of this made him warm again, and he settled down to a steady stride, munching the biscuits as he went along. The moisture that exhaled with his breath crusted his lips and mustache with pendent ice and formed a miniature glacier on his chin. Now and again sensation forsook his nose and cheeks, and he rubbed them till they burned with the returning blood.

Most men wore nose-straps; his partners did, but he had scorned such "feminine contraptions," and till now had never felt the need of them. Now he did feel the need, for he was rubbing constantly.

Nevertheless he was aware of a thrill of joy, of exultation. He was doing something, achieving something, mastering the elements. Once he laughed aloud in sheer strength of life, and with his clenched fist defied the frost. He was its master. What he did he did in spite of it. It could not stop him. He was going on to the Cherry Creek Divide.

Strong as were the elements, he was stronger. At such times animals crawled away into their holes and remained in hiding. But he did not hide. He was out in it, facing it, fighting it. He was a man, a master of things.

In such fashion, rejoicing proudly, he tramped on. After half an hour he rounded a bend, where the creek ran close to the mountainside, and came upon one of the most insignificant-appearing but most formidable dangers in northern travel.

The creek itself was frozen solid to its rocky bottom, but from the mountain came the outflow of several springs. These springs never froze, and the only effect of the severest cold snaps was to lessen their discharge. Protected from the frost by the blanket of snow, the water of these springs seeped down into the creek, and, on top of the creek ice, formed shallow pools.

The surface of these pools, in turn, took on a skin of ice which grew thicker and thicker, until the water overran, and so formed a second ice-skinned pool above the first.

Thus at the bottom was the solid creek ice, then probably six to eight inches of water, then a thin ice-skin, then another six inches of water and another ice-skin. And on top of this last skin was about an inch of recent snow to make the trap complete.

To Tom Vincent's eye the unbroken snow surface gave no warning of the lurking danger. As the crust was thicker at the edge, he was well toward the middle before he broke through.

In itself it was a very insignificant mishap,—a man does not drown in twelve inches of water,—but in its consequences as serious an accident as could possibly befall him.

At the instant he broke through he felt the cold water strike his feet and ankles, and with half a dozen lunges he made the bank. He was quite cool and collected. The thing to do, and the only thing to do, was to build a fire. For another precept of the north runs: *Travel with wet socks down to twenty below zero; after that build a fire.* And it was three times twenty below and colder, and he knew it.

He knew, further, that great care must be exercised; that with failure at the first attempt, the chance was made greater for failure at the second attempt. In short, he knew that there must be no failure. The moment before a strong, exulting man, boastful of his mastery of the elements, he was now fighting for his life against those same elements—such was the difference caused by the injection of a quart of water into a northland traveller's calculations.

In a clump of pines on the rim of the bank the spring high-water had lodged many twigs and small branches. Thoroughly dried by the summer sun, they now waited the match.

It is impossible to build a fire with heavy Alaskan mittens on one's hands, so Vincent bared his, gathered a sufficient number of twigs, and knocking the snow from them, knelt down to kindle his fire. From an inside pocket he drew out his matches and a strip of thin birch bark. The matches were of the Klondike kind, sulphur matches, one hundred in a bunch.

He noticed how quickly his fingers had chilled as he separated one match from the bunch and scratched it on his trousers. The birch bark, like the dryest of paper, burst into bright flame. This he carefully fed with the smallest twigs and finest débris, cherishing the flame with the utmost care. It did not do to hurry things, as he well knew, and although his fingers were now quite stiff, he did not hurry.

After the first quick, biting sensation of cold, his feet had ached with a heavy, dull ache and were rapidly growing numb. But the fire, although a very young one, was now a success, and he knew that a little snow, briskly rubbed, would speedily cure his feet.

But at the moment he was adding the first thick twigs to the fire a grievous thing happened. The pine boughs above his head were burdened with a four months' snowfall, and so finely adjusted were the burdens that his slight movements in collecting the twigs had been sufficient to disturb the balance.

The snow from the topmost bough was the first to fall, striking and dislodging the snow on the boughs beneath. And all this snow, accumulating as it fell, smote Tom Vincent's head and shoulders and blotted out his fire.

He still kept his presence of mind, for he knew how great his danger was. He started at once to rebuild the fire, but his fingers were now so cold that he could not bend them, and he was forced to pick up each twig and splinter between the tips of the fingers of either hand.

When he came to the match he encountered great difficulty in separating one from the bunch. This he succeeded in managing, however, and also, by a great effort, in clutching the match between his thumb and forefinger. But in scratching it, he dropped it in the snow and could not pick it up again.

He stood up, desperate. He could not feel even his weight on his feet, although the ankles were aching painfully. Putting on his mittens, he stepped to one side, so that the snow would not fall upon the new fire he was to build, and beat his hands violently against a tree-trunk.

This enabled him to separate and strike a second match and to set fire to the remaining fragment of birch bark. But his body had now begun to chill and he was shivering, so that when he tried to add the first twigs his hand shook and the tiny flame was quenched.

The frost had beaten him. His hands were worthless. But he had the foresight to drop the bunch of matches into his widemouthed outside pocket before he slipped on his mittens in despair, and started to run up the trail. One cannot run the frost out of wet feet at sixty below and colder, however, as he quickly discovered.

He came round a sharp turn of the creek to where he could look ahead for a mile. But there was no help, no sign of help, only the white trees and the white hills, the quiet cold and the brazen silence! If only he had a comrade whose feet were not freezing, he thought, only such a comrade to start the fire that could save him!

Then his eyes chanced upon another high-water lodgment of twigs and leaves and branches. If he could strike a match, all might yet be well. With stiff fingers which he could not bend, he got out a bunch of matches, but found it impossible to separate them.

He sat down and awkwardly shuffled the bunch about on his knees, until he got it resting on his palm with the sulphur ends projecting, somewhat in the manner the blade of a hunting-knife would project when clutched in the fist.

But his fingers stood straight out. They could not clutch. This he overcame by pressing the wrist of the other hand against them, and so forcing them down upon the bunch. Time and again, holding thus by both hands, he scratched the bunch on his leg and finally ignited it. But the flame burned into the flesh of his hand, and he involuntarily relaxed his hold. The bunch fell into the snow, and while he tried vainly to pick it up, sizzled and went out.

Again he ran, by this time badly frightened. His feet were utterly devoid of sensation. He stubbed his toes once on a buried log, but beyond pitching him into the snow and wrenching his back, it gave him no feelings.

His fingers were helpless and his wrists were beginning to grow numb. His nose and cheeks he knew were freezing, but they did not count. It was his feet and hands that were to save him, if he was to be saved.

He recollected being told of a camp of moose-hunters somewhere above the forks of Paul Creek. He must be somewhere near it, he thought, and if he could find it he yet might be saved. Five minutes later he came upon it, lone and deserted, with drifted snow sprinkled inside the pine-bough shelter in which the hunters had slept. He sank down, sobbing. All was over. In an hour at best, in that terrific temperature, he would be an icy corpse.

But the love of life was strong in him, and he sprang again to his feet. He was thinking quickly. What if the matches did burn his hands? Burned hands were better than dead hands. No hands at all were better than death. He floundered along the trail till he came upon another high-water lodgment. There were twigs and branches, leaves and grasses, all dry and waiting the fire.

Again he sat down and shuffled the bunch of matches on his knees, got it into place on his palm, with the wrist of his other hand forced the nerveless fingers down against the bunch, and with the wrist kept them there. At the second scratch the bunch caught fire, and he knew that if he could stand the pain he was saved. He choked with the sulphur fumes, and the blue flame licked the flesh of his hands.

At first he could not feel it, but it burned quickly in through the frosted surface. The odor of the burning flesh—his flesh—was strong in his nostrils. He writhed about in his torment, yet held on. He set his teeth and swayed back and forth, until the clear white flame of the burning match shot up, and he had applied that flame to the leaves and grasses.

An anxious five minutes followed, but the fire gained steadily. Then he set to work to save himself. Heroic measures were necessary, such was his extremity, and he took them.

Alternately rubbing his hands with snow and thrusting them into the flames, and now and again beating them against the hard trees, he restored their circulation sufficiently for them to be of use to him. With his hunting-knife he slashed the straps from his pack, unrolled his blanket, and got out dry socks and foot-gear.

Then he cut away his moccasins and bared his feet. But while he had taken liberties with his hands, he kept his feet fairly away from the fire and rubbed them with snow. He rubbed till his hands grew numb, when he would cover his feet with the blanket, warm his hands by the fire, and return to the rubbing.

For three hours he worked, till the worst effects of the freezing had been counteracted. All that night he stayed by the fire, and it was late the next day when he limped pitifully into the camp on the Cherry Creek Divide.

In a month's time he was able to be about on his feet, although the toes were destined always after that to be very sensitive to frost. But the scars on his hands he knows he will carry to the grave. And—"*Never travel alone!*" he now lays down the precept of the north.

# MOON-FACE

JOHN CLAVERHOUSE was a moon-faced man. You know the kind, cheek-bones wide apart, chin and forehead melting into the cheeks to complete the perfect round, and the nose, broad and pudgy, equidistant from the circumference, flattened against the very centre of the face like a dough-ball upon the ceiling. Perhaps that is why I hated him, for truly he had become an offence to my eyes, and I believed the earth to be cumbered with his presence. Perhaps my mother may have been superstitious of the moon and looked upon it over the wrong shoulder at the wrong time.

Be that as it may, I hated John Claverhouse. Not that he had done me what society would consider a wrong or an ill turn. Far from it. The evil was of a deeper, subtler sort; so elusive, so intangible, as to defy clear, definite analysis in words. We all experience such things at some period in our lives. For the first time we see a certain individual, one who the very instant before we did not dream existed; and yet, at the first moment of meeting, we say: "I do not like that man." Why do we not like him? Ah, we do not know why; we know only that we do not. We have taken a dislike, that is all. And so I with John Claverhouse.

What right had such a man to be happy? Yet he was an optimist. He was always gleeful and laughing. All things were always all right, curse him! Ah! how it grated on my soul that he should be so happy! Other men could laugh, and it did not bother me. I even used to laugh myself—before I met John Claverhouse.

But his laugh! It irritated me, maddened me, as nothing else under the sun could irritate or madden me. It haunted me, gripped hold of me, and would not let me go. It was a huge, Gargantuan laugh. Waking or sleeping it was always with me, whirring and jarring across my heart-strings like an enormous rasp. At break of day it came whooping across the fields to spoil my pleasant morning revery. Under the aching noonday glare, when the green things drooped and the birds withdrew to the depths of the forest, and all nature drowsed, his great "Ha! ha!" and "Ho! ho!" rose up to the sky and challenged the sun. And at black midnight, from the lonely cross-roads where he turned from town into his own place, came his plaguey cachinnations to rouse me from my sleep and make me writhe and clench my nails into my palms.

I went forth privily in the night-time, and turned his cattle into his fields, and in the morning heard his whooping laugh as he drove them out again. "It is nothing," he said; "the poor, dumb beasties are not to be blamed for straying into fatter pastures."

He had a dog he called "Mars," a big, splendid brute, part deer-hound and part blood-hound, and resembling both. Mars was a great delight to him, and they were always together. But I bided my time, and one day, when opportunity was ripe, lured the animal away and settled for him with strychnine and beefsteak. It made positively no impression on John Claverhouse. His laugh was as hearty and frequent as ever, and his face as much like the full moon as it always had been.

Then I set fire to his haystacks and his barn. But the next morning, being Sunday, he went forth blithe and cheerful.

"Where are you going?" I asked him, as he went by the cross-roads.

"Trout," he said, and his face beamed like a full moon. "I just dote on trout."

Was there ever such an impossible man! His whole harvest had gone up in his haystacks and barn. It was uninsured, I knew. And yet, in the face of famine and the rigorous winter, he went out gayly in quest of a mess of trout, forsooth, because he "doted" on them! Had gloom but rested, no matter how lightly, on his brow, or had his bovine countenance grown long and serious and less like the moon, or had he removed that smile but once from off his face, I am sure I could have forgiven him for existing. But no, he grew only more cheerful under misfortune.

I insulted him. He looked at me in slow and smiling surprise.

"I fight you? Why?" he asked slowly. And then he laughed. "You are so funny! Ho! ho! You'll be the death of me! He! he! he! Oh! Ho ho! ho!"

What would you? It was past endurance. By the blood of Judas, how I hated him! Then there was that name—Claverhouse! What a name! Wasn't it absurd? Claverhouse! Merciful heaven, *why* Claverhouse? Again and again I asked myself that question. I should not have minded Smith, or Brown, or Jones—but *Claverhouse*! I leave it to you. Repeat it to yourself—Claverhouse. Just listen to the ridiculous sound of it—Claverhouse! Should a man live with such a name? I ask of you. "No," you say. And "No" said I.

But I bethought me of his mortgage. What of his crops and barn destroyed, I knew he would be unable to meet it. So I got a shrewd, close-mouthed, tight-fisted money-lender to get the mortgage transferred to him. I did not appear, but through this agent I forced the foreclosure, and but few days (no more, believe me, than the law allowed) were given John Claverhouse to remove his goods and chattels from the premises. Then I strolled down to see how he took it, for he had lived there upward of twenty years. But he met me with his saucer-eyes twinkling, and the light glowing and spreading in his face till it was as a full-risen moon.

"Ha! ha! ha!" he laughed. "The funniest tike, that youngster of mine! Did you ever hear the like? Let me tell you. He was down playing by the edge of the river when a piece of the bank caved in and splashed him. 'O papa!' he cried; 'a great big puddle flewed up and hit me.'"

He stopped and waited for me to join him in his infernal glee.

"I don't see any laugh in it," I said shortly, and I know my face went sour.

He regarded me with wonderment, and then came the damnable light, glowing and spreading, as I have described it, till his face shone soft and warm, like the summer moon, and then the laugh—"Ha! ha! That's funny! You don't see it, eh? He! he! Ho! ho! ho! He doesn't see it! Why, look here. You know a puddle—"

But I turned on my heel and left him. That was the last. I could stand it no longer. The thing must end right there, I thought, curse him! The earth should be quit of him. And as I went over the hill, I could hear his monstrous laugh reverberating against the sky.

Now, I pride myself on doing things neatly, and when I resolved to kill John Claverhouse I had it in mind to do so in such fashion that I should not look back upon it and feel ashamed. I hate bungling, and

I hate brutality. To me there is something repugnant in merely striking a man with one's naked fist—faugh! it is sickening! So, to shoot, or stab, or club John Claverhouse (oh, that name!) did not appeal to me. And not only was I impelled to do it neatly and artistically, but also in such manner that not the slightest possible suspicion could be directed against me.

To this end I bent my intellect, and, after a week of profound incubation, I hatched the scheme. Then I set to work. I bought a water spaniel bitch, five months old, and devoted my whole attention to her training. Had any one spied upon me, they would have remarked that this training consisted entirely of one thing—*retrieving*. I taught the dog, which I called "Bellona," to fetch sticks I threw into the water, and not only to fetch, but to fetch at once, without mouthing or playing with them. The point was that she was to stop for nothing, but to deliver the stick in all haste. I made a practice of running away and leaving her to chase me, with the stick in her mouth, till she caught me. She was a bright animal, and took to the game with such eagerness that I was soon content.

After that, at the first casual opportunity, I presented Bellona to John Claverhouse. I knew what I was about, for I was aware of a little weakness of his, and of a little private sinning of which he was regularly and inveterately guilty.

"No," he said, when I placed the end of the rope in his hand. "No, you don't mean it." And his mouth opened wide and he grinned all over his damnable moon-face.

"I—I kind of thought, somehow, you didn't like me," he explained. "Wasn't it funny for me to make such a mistake?" And at the thought he held his sides with laughter.

"What is her name?" he managed to ask between paroxysms.

"Bellona," I said.

"He! he!" he tittered. "What a funny name!"

I gritted my teeth, for his mirth put them on edge, and snapped out between them, "She was the wife of Mars, you know."

Then the light of the full moon began to suffuse his face, until he exploded with: "That was my other dog. Well, I guess she's a widow now. Oh! Ho! ho! E! he! he! Ho!" he whooped after me, and I turned and fled swiftly over the hill.

The week passed by, and on Saturday evening I said to him, "You go away Monday, don't you?"

He nodded his head and grinned.

"Then you won't have another chance to get a mess of those trout you just 'dote' on."

But he did not notice the sneer. "Oh, I don't know," he chuckled. "I'm going up to-morrow to try pretty hard."

Thus was assurance made doubly sure, and I went back to my house hugging myself with rapture.

Early next morning I saw him go by with a dip-net and gunny-sack, and Bellona trotting at his heels. I knew where he was bound, and cut out by the back pasture and climbed through the underbrush to the top of the mountain. Keeping carefully out of sight, I followed the crest along for a couple of miles to a natural amphitheatre in the hills, where the little river raced down out of a gorge and stopped for breath in a large and placid rock-bound pool. That was the spot! I sat down on the croup of the mountain, where I could see all that occurred, and lighted my pipe.

Ere many minutes had passed, John Claverhouse came plodding up the bed of the stream. Bellona was ambling about him, and they were in high feather, her short, snappy barks mingling with his deeper chest-notes. Arrived at the pool, he threw down the dip-net and sack, and drew from his hip-pocket what looked like a large, fat candle. But I knew it to be a stick of "giant"; for such was his method of catching trout. He dynamited them. He attached the fuse by wrapping the "giant" tightly in a piece of cotton. Then he ignited the fuse and tossed the explosive into the pool.

Like a flash, Bellona was into the pool after it. I could have shrieked aloud for joy. Claverhouse yelled at her, but without avail. He pelted her with clods and rocks, but she swam steadily on till she got the stick of "giant" in her mouth, when she whirled about and headed for shore. Then, for the first time, he realized his danger, and started to run. As foreseen and planned by me, she made the bank and took out after him. Oh, I tell you, it was great! As I have said, the pool lay in a sort of amphitheatre. Above and below, the stream could be crossed on stepping-stones. And around and around, up and down and across the stones, raced Claverhouse and Bellona. I could never have believed that such an ungainly man could run so fast. But run he did, Bellona hot-footed after him, and gaining. And then, just as she caught up, he in full stride, and she leaping with nose at his knee, there was a sudden flash, a burst of smoke, a terrific detonation, and where man and dog had been the instant before there was naught to be seen but a big hole in the ground.

"Death from accident while engaged in illegal fishing." That was the verdict of the coroner's jury; and that is why I pride myself on the neat and artistic way in which I finished off John Claverhouse. There was no bungling, no brutality; nothing of which to be ashamed in the whole transaction, as I am sure you will agree. No more does his infernal laugh go echoing among the hills, and no more does his fat moon-face rise up to vex me. My days are peaceful now, and my night's sleep deep.

# BÂTARD

BÂTARD was a devil. This was recognized throughout the Northland. "Hell's Spawn" he was called by many men, but his master, Black Leclère, chose for him the shameful name "Bâtard." Now Black Leclère was also a devil, and the twain were well matched. There is a saying that when two devils come together, hell is to pay. This is to be expected, and this certainly was to be expected when Bâtard and Black Leclère came together. The first time they met, Bâtard was a part-grown puppy, lean and hungry, with bitter eyes; and they met with snap and snarl, and wicked looks, for Leclère's upper lip had a wolfish way of lifting and showing the white, cruel teeth. And it lifted then, and his eyes glinted viciously, as he reached for Bâtard and dragged him out from the squirming litter. It was certain that they divined each other, for on the instant Bâtard had buried his puppy fangs in Leclère's hand, and Leclère, thumb and finger, was coolly choking his young life out of him.

"*Sacredam*," the Frenchman said softly, flirting the quick blood from his bitten hand and gazing down on the little puppy choking and gasping in the snow.

Leclère turned to John Hamlin, storekeeper of the Sixty Mile Post. "Dat fo' w'at Ah lak heem. 'Ow moch, eh, you, *M'sieu'*? 'Ow moch? Ah buy heem, now; Ah buy heem queek."

And because he hated him with an exceeding bitter hate, Leclère bought Bâtard and gave him his shameful name. And for five years the twain adventured across the Northland, from St. Michael's and the Yukon delta to the head-reaches of the Pelly and even so far as the Peace River, Athabasca, and the Great Slave. And they acquired a reputation for uncompromising wickedness, the like of which never before attached itself to man and dog.

Bâtard did not know his father,—hence his name,—but, as John Hamlin knew, his father was a great gray timber wolf. But the mother of Bâtard, as he dimly remembered her, was a snarling, bickering, obscene husky,* full-fronted and heavy-chested, with a malign eye, a cat-like grip on life, and a genius for trickery and evil. There was neither faith nor trust in her. Her treachery alone could be relied upon, and her wild-wood amours attested her general depravity. Much of evil and much of strength were there in these, Bâtard's progenitors, and, bone and flesh of their bone and flesh, he had inherited it all. And then came Black Leclère, to lay his heavy hand on the bit of pulsating puppy life, to press and prod and mould till it became a big bristling beast, acute in knavery, overspilling with hate, sinister, malignant, diabolical. With a proper master Bâtard might have made an ordinary, fairly efficient sled-dog. He never got the chance: Leclère but confirmed him in his congenital iniquity.

The history of Bâtard and Leclère is a history of war—of five cruel, relentless years, of which their first meeting is fit summary. To begin with, it was Leclère's fault, for he hated with understanding and intelligence, while the long-legged, ungainly puppy hated only blindly, instinctively, without reason or method. At first there were no refinements of cruelty (these were to come later), but simple beatings and crude brutalities. In one of these Bâtard had an ear injured. He never regained control of the riven muscles, and ever after the ear drooped limply down to keep keen the memory of his tormentor. And he never forgot.

His puppyhood was a period of foolish rebellion. He was always worsted, but he fought back because it was his nature to fight back. And he was unconquerable. Yelping shrilly from the pain of lash and club, he none the less contrived always to throw in the defiant snarl, the bitter vindictive menace of his soul which fetched without fail more blows and beatings. But his was his mother's tenacious grip on life. Nothing could kill him. He flourished under misfortune, grew fat with famine, and out of his terrible struggle for life developed a preternat-

---

* Editor's note: The text of the first edition reads "was snarling, bickering, obscene, husky"—but it is clear from the context that Bâtard's mother was a sled-dog or "husky."

ural intelligence. His were the stealth and cunning of the husky, his mother, and the fierceness and valor of the wolf, his father.

Possibly it was because of his father that he never wailed. His puppy yelps passed with his lanky legs, so that he became grim and taciturn, quick to strike, slow to warn. He answered curse with snarl, and blow with snap, grinning the while his implacable hatred; but never again, under the extremest agony, did Leclère bring from him the cry of fear nor of pain. This unconquerableness but fanned Leclère's wrath and stirred him to greater deviltries.

Did Leclère give Bâtard half a fish and to his mates whole ones, Bâtard went forth to rob other dogs of their fish. Also he robbed cachés and expressed himself in a thousand rogueries, till he became a terror to all dogs and masters of dogs. Did Leclère beat Bâtard and fondle Babette,—Babette who was not half the worker he was,—why, Bâtard threw her down in the snow and broke her hind leg in his heavy jaws, so that Leclère was forced to shoot her. Likewise, in bloody battles, Bâtard mastered all his team-mates, set them the law of trail and forage, and made them live to the law he set.

In five years he heard but one kind word, received but one soft stroke of a hand, and then he did not know what manner of things they were. He leaped like the untamed thing he was, and his jaws were together in a flash. It was the missionary at Sunrise, a newcomer in the country, who spoke the kind word and gave the soft stroke of the hand. And for six months after, he wrote no letters home to the States, and the surgeon at McQuestion travelled two hundred miles on the ice to save him from blood-poisoning.

Men and dogs looked askance at Bâtard when he drifted into their camps and posts. The men greeted him with feet threateningly lifted for the kick, the dogs with bristling manes and bared fangs. Once a man did kick Bâtard, and Bâtard, with quick wolf snap, closed his jaws like a steel trap on the man's calf and crunched down to the bone. Whereat the man was determined to have his life, only Black Leclère, with ominous eyes and naked hunting-knife, stepped in between. The killing of Bâtard—ah, *sacredam, that* was a pleasure Leclère reserved for himself. Some day it would happen, or else—bah! who was to know? Anyway, the problem would be solved.

For they had become problems to each other. The very breath each drew was a challenge and a menace to the other. Their hate bound them together as love could never bind. Leclère was bent on the coming of the day when Bâtard should wilt in spirit and cringe and whimper at his feet. And Bâtard—Leclère knew what was in Bâtard's mind, and more than once had read it in Bâtard's eyes. And so clearly had he read, that when Bâtard was at his back, he made it a point to glance often over his shoulder.

Men marvelled when Leclère refused large money for the dog. "Some day you'll kill him and be out his price," said John Hamlin once, when Bâtard lay panting in the snow where Leclère had kicked him, and no one knew whether his ribs were broken, and no one dared look to see.

"Dat," said Leclère, dryly, "dat is my biz'ness, *M'sieu'*."

And the men marvelled that Bâtard did not run away. They did not understand. But Leclère understood. He was a man who lived much in the open, beyond the sound of human tongue, and he had learned the voices of wind and storm, the sigh of night, the whisper of dawn, the clash of day. In a dim way he could hear the green things growing, the running of the sap, the bursting of the bud. And he knew the subtle speech of the things that moved, of the rabbit in the snare, the moody raven beating the air with hollow wing, the baldface shuffling under the moon, the wolf like a gray shadow gliding betwixt the twilight and the dark. And to him Bâtard spoke clear and direct. Full well he understood why Bâtard did not run away, and he looked more often over his shoulder.

When in anger, Bâtard was not nice to look upon, and more than once had he leapt for Leclère's throat, to be stretched quivering and senseless in the snow, by the butt of the ever ready dogwhip. And so Bâtard learned to bide his time. When he reached his full strength and prime of youth, he thought the time had come. He was broad-chested, powerfully muscled, of far more than ordinary size, and his neck from head to shoulders was a mass of bristling hair—to all appearances a full-blooded wolf. Leclère was lying asleep in his furs when Bâtard deemed the time to be ripe. He crept upon him stealthily, head low to earth and lone ear laid back, with a feline softness of tread. Bâtard breathed gently, very gently, and not till he was close at hand did he raise his head. He paused for a moment, and looked at the bronzed bull throat, naked and knotty, and swelling to a deep and steady pulse. The slaver dripped down his fangs and slid off his tongue at the sight, and in that moment he remembered his drooping ear, his uncounted blows and prodigious wrongs, and without a sound sprang on the sleeping man.

Leclère awoke to the pang of the fangs in his throat, and, perfect animal that he was, he awoke clear-headed and with full comprehension. He closed on Bâtard's windpipe with both his hands, and rolled out of his furs to get his weight uppermost. But the thousands of Bâtard's ancestors had clung at the throats of unnumbered moose and caribou and dragged them down, and the wisdom of those ancestors was his. When Leclère's weight came on top of him, he drove his hind legs upward and in, and clawed down chest and abdomen, ripping and tearing through skin and muscle. And when he felt the man's body wince above him and lift, he worried and shook at the man's throat. His team-mates closed around in a snarling circle, and Bâtard, with failing breath and fading sense, knew that their jaws were hungry for him. But that did not matter—it was the man, the man above him, and he ripped and clawed, and shook and worried, to the last ounce of his strength. But Leclère choked him with both his hands, till Bâtard's chest heaved and writhed for the air denied, and his eyes glazed and set, and his jaws slowly loosened, and his tongue protruded black and swollen.

"Eh? *Bon,* you devil!" Leclère gurgled, mouth and throat clogged with his own blood, as he shoved the dizzy dog from him.

And then Leclère cursed the other dogs off as they fell upon Bâtard. They drew back into a wider circle, squatting alertly on their haunches and licking their chops, the hair on every neck bristling and erect.

Bâtard recovered quickly, and at sound of Leclère's voice, tottered to his feet and swayed weakly back and forth.

"A-h-ah! You beeg devil!" Leclère spluttered. "Ah fix you; Ah fix you plentee, by *Gar!*"

Bâtard, the air biting into his exhausted lungs like wine, flashed full into the man's face, his jaws missing and coming together with a metallic clip. They rolled over and over on the snow, Leclère striking madly with his fists. Then they separated, face to face, and circled back and forth before each other. Leclère could have drawn his knife. His rifle was at his feet. But the beast in him was up and raging. He would do the thing with his hands—and his teeth. Bâtard sprang in, but Leclère knocked him over with a blow of the fist, fell upon him, and buried his teeth to the bone in the dog's shoulder.

It was a primordial setting and a primordial scene, such as might have been in the savage youth of the world. An open space in a dark forest, a ring of grinning wolf-dogs, and in the centre two beasts, locked in combat, snapping and snarling, raging madly about, panting, sobbing, cursing, straining, wild with passion, in a fury of murder, ripping and tearing and clawing in elemental brutishness.

But Leclère caught Bâtard behind the ear, with a blow from his fist, knocking him over, and, for the instant, stunning him. Then Leclère leaped upon him with his feet, and sprang up and down, striving to grind him into the earth. Both Bâtard's hind legs were broken ere Leclère ceased that he might catch breath.

"A-a-ah! A-a-ah!" he screamed, incapable of speech, shaking his fist, through sheer impotence of throat and larynx.

But Bâtard was indomitable. He lay there in a helpless welter, his lip feebly lifting and writhing to the snarl he had not the strength to utter. Leclère kicked him, and the tired jaws closed on the ankle, but could not break the skin.

Then Leclère picked up the whip and proceeded almost to cut him to pieces, at each stroke of the lash crying: "Dis taim Ah break you! Eh? By *Gar!* Ah break you!"

In the end, exhausted, fainting from loss of blood, he crumpled up and fell by his victim, and when the wolf-dogs closed in to take their vengeance, with his last consciousness dragged his body on top Bâtard to shield him from their fangs.

This occurred not far from Sunrise, and the missionary, opening the door to Leclère a few hours later, was surprised to note the absence of Bâtard from the team. Nor did his surprise lessen when Leclère threw back the robes from the sled, gathered Bâtard into his arms, and staggered across the threshold. It happened that the surgeon of McQuestion, who was something of a gadabout, was up on a gossip, and between them they proceeded to repair Leclère.

"*Merci, non,*" said he. "Do you fix firs' de dog. To die? *Non.* Eet is not good. Becos' heem Ah mus' yet break. Dat fo' w'at he mus' not die."

The surgeon called it a marvel, the missionary a miracle, that Leclère pulled through at all; and so weakened was he, that in the spring the fever got him, and he went on his back again. Bâtard had been in even worse plight, but his grip on life prevailed, and the bones of his hind legs knit, and his organs righted themselves, during the several weeks he lay strapped to the floor. And by the time Leclère, finally convalescent, sallow and shaky, took the sun by the cabin door, Bâtard had reasserted his supremacy among his kind, and brought not only his own team-mates but the missionary's dogs into subjection.

He moved never a muscle, nor twitched a hair, when, for the first time, Leclère tottered out on the missionary's arm, and sank down slowly and with infinite caution on the three-legged stool.

"*Bon!*" he said. "*Bon!* De good sun!" And he stretched out his wasted hands and washed them in the warmth.

Then his gaze fell on the dog, and the old light blazed back in his eyes. He touched the missionary lightly on the arm. "*Mon père,* dat is one beeg devil, dat Bâtard. You will bring me one pistol, so, dat Ah drink de sun in peace."

And thenceforth for many days he sat in the sun before the cabin door. He never dozed, and the pistol lay always across his knees. Bâtard had a way, the first thing each day, of looking for the weapon in its wonted place. At sight of it he would lift his lip faintly in token that he understood, and Leclère would lift his own lip in an answering grin. One day the missionary took note of the trick.

"Bless me!" he said. "I really believe the brute comprehends."

Leclère laughed softly. "Look you, *mon père.* Dat w'at Ah now spik, to dat does he lissen."

As if in confirmation, Bâtard just perceptibly wriggled his lone ear up to catch the sound.

"Ah say 'keel.' "

Bâtard growled deep down in his throat, the hair bristled along his neck, and every muscle went tense and expectant.

"Ah lift de gun, so, like dat." And suiting action to word, he sighted the pistol at Bâtard.

Bâtard, with a single leap, sideways, landed around the corner of the cabin out of sight.

"Bless me!" he repeated at intervals.

Leclère grinned proudly.

"But why does he not run away?"

The Frenchman's shoulders went up in the racial shrug that means all things from total ignorance to infinite understanding.

"Then why do you not kill him?"

Again the shoulders went up.

"*Mon père,*" he said after a pause, "de taim is not yet. He is one beeg devil. Some taim Ah break heem, so, an' so, all to leetle bits. Hey? Some taim. *Bon!*"

A day came when Leclère gathered his dogs together and floated down in a bateau to Forty Mile, and on to the Porcupine, where he took a commission from the P. C. Company, and went exploring for the better part of a year. After that he poled up the Koyokuk to deserted Arctic City, and later came drifting back, from camp to camp, along the Yukon. And during the long months Bâtard was well lessoned. He learned many tortures, and, notably, the torture of hunger, the torture of thirst, the torture of fire, and, worst of all, the torture of music.

Like the rest of his kind, he did not enjoy music. It gave him exquisite anguish, racking him nerve by nerve, and ripping apart every fibre of his being. It made him howl, long and wolf-like, as when the wolves bay the stars on frosty nights. He could not help howling. It was his one weakness in the contest with Leclère, and it was his shame. Leclère, on the other hand, passionately loved music—as passionately as he loved strong drink. And when his soul clamored for expression, it usually uttered itself in one or the other of the two ways, and more usually in both ways. And when he had drunk, his brain a-lilt with unsung song and the devil in him aroused and rampant, his soul found its supreme utterance in torturing Bâtard.

"Now we will haf a leetle museek," he would say. "Eh? W'at you t'ink, Bâtard?"

It was only an old and battered harmonica, tenderly treasured and patiently repaired; but it was the best that money could buy, and out of its silver reeds he drew weird vagrant airs that men had never heard before. Then Bâtard, dumb of throat, with teeth tight clenched, would back away, inch by inch, to the farthest cabin corner. And Leclère, playing, playing, a stout club tucked under his arm, followed the animal up, inch by inch, step by step, till there was no further retreat.

At first Bâtard would crowd himself into the smallest possible space, grovelling close to the floor; but as the music came nearer and nearer, he was forced to uprear, his back jammed into the logs, his fore legs fanning the air as though to beat off the rippling waves of sound. He still kept his teeth together, but severe muscular contractions attacked his body, strange twitchings and jerkings, till he was all a-quiver and writhing in silent torment. As he lost control, his jaws spasmodically wrenched apart, and deep throaty vibrations issued forth, too low in the register of sound for human ear to catch. And then, nostrils distended, eyes dilated, hair bristling in helpless rage, arose the long wolf howl. It came with a slurring rush upward, swelling to a great heart-breaking burst of sound, and dying away in sadly cadenced woe—then the next rush upward, octave upon octave; the bursting heart; and the infinite sorrow and misery, fainting, fading, falling, and dying slowly away.

It was fit for hell. And Leclère, with fiendish ken, seemed to divine each particular nerve and heartstring, and with long wails and tremblings and sobbing minors to make it yield up its last shred of grief. It was frightful, and for twenty-four hours after, Bâtard was nervous and unstrung, starting at common sounds, tripping over his own shadow, but, withal, vicious and masterful with his team-mates. Nor did he show signs of a breaking spirit. Rather did he grow more grim and taciturn, biding his time with an inscrutable patience that began to puzzle and weigh upon Leclère. The dog would lie in the firelight, motionless, for hours, gazing straight before him at Leclère, and hating him with his bitter eyes.

Often the man felt that he had bucked against the very essence of life—the unconquerable essence that swept the hawk down out of the sky like a feathered thunderbolt, that drove the great gray goose across the zones, that hurled the spawning salmon through two thousand miles of boiling Yukon flood. At such times he felt impelled to express his own unconquerable essence; and with strong drink, wild music, and Bâtard, he indulged in vast orgies, wherein he pitted his puny strength in the face of things, and challenged all that was, and had been, and was yet to be.

"Dere is somet'ing dere," he affirmed, when the rhythmed vagaries of his mind touched the secret chords of Bâtard's being and brought forth the long lugubrious howl. "Ah pool eet out wid bot' my han's, so, an' so. Ha! Ha! Eet is fonee! Eet is ver' fonee! De priest chant, de womans pray, de mans swear, de leetle bird go *peep-peep,* Bâtard, heem go *yow-yow*—an' eet is all de ver' same t'ing. Ha! Ha!"

Father Gautier, a worthy priest, once reproved him with instances of concrete perdition. He never reproved him again.

"Eet may be so, *mon père,*" he made answer. "An' Ah t'ink Ah go troo hell a-snappin', lak de hemlock troo de fire. Eh, *mon père?*"

But all bad things come to an end as well as good, and so with Black Leclère. On the summer low water, in a poling boat, he left McDougall for Sunrise. He left McDougall in company with Timothy Brown, and arrived at Sunrise by himself. Further, it was known that they had quarrelled just previous to pulling out; for the *Lizzie,* a wheezy ten-ton sternwheeler, twenty-four hours behind, beat Leclère in by three days. And when he did get in, it was with a clean-drilled bullet-hole through his shoulder muscle, and a tale of ambush and murder.

A strike had been made at Sunrise, and things had changed considerably. With the infusion of several hundred gold-seekers, a deal of whiskey, and half a dozen equipped gamblers, the missionary had seen the page of his years of labor with the Indians wiped clean. When the squaws became preoccupied with cooking beans and keeping the fire going for the wifeless miners, and the bucks with swapping their warm furs for black bottles and broken timepieces, he took to his bed, said "bless me" several times, and departed to his final accounting in a rough-hewn, oblong box. Whereupon the gamblers moved their roulette and faro tables into the mission house, and the click of chips and clink of glasses went up from dawn till dark and to dawn again.

Now Timothy Brown was well beloved among these adventurers of the north. The one thing against him was his quick temper and ready fist,—a little thing, for which his kind heart and forgiving hand more than atoned. On the other hand, there was nothing to atone for Black Leclère. He was "black," as more than one remembered deed bore witness, while he was as well hated as the other was beloved. So the men of Sunrise put an antiseptic dressing on his shoulder and haled him before Judge Lynch.

It was a simple affair. He had quarrelled with Timothy Brown at McDougall. With Timothy Brown he had left McDougall. Without Timothy Brown he had arrived at Sunrise. Considered in the light of his evilness, the unanimous conclusion was that he had killed Timothy Brown. On the other hand, Leclère acknowledged their facts, but challenged their conclusion, and gave his own explanation. Twenty miles out of Sunrise he and Timothy Brown were poling the boat along the rocky shore. From that shore two rifle-shots rang out. Timothy Brown pitched out of the boat and went down bubbling red, and that was the last of Timothy Brown. He, Leclère, pitched into the bottom of the boat with a stinging shoulder. He lay very quiet, peeping at the shore. After a time two Indians stuck up their heads and came out to the water's edge, carrying between them a birch-bark canoe. As they launched it, Leclère let fly. He potted one, who went over the side after the manner of Timothy Brown. The other dropped into the bottom of the canoe, and then canoe and poling boat went down the stream in a drifting battle. After that they hung up on a split current, and the canoe passed on one side of an island, the poling boat on the other. That was the last of the canoe, and he came on into Sunrise. Yes, from the way the Indian in the canoe jumped, he was sure he had potted him. That was all.

This explanation was not deemed adequate. They gave him ten hours' grace while the *Lizzie* steamed down to investigate. Ten hours later she came wheezing back to Sunrise. There had been nothing to investigate. No evidence had been found to back up his statements. They told him to make his will, for he possessed a fifty-thousand-dollar Sunrise claim, and they were a law-abiding as well as a law-giving breed.

Leclère shrugged his shoulders. "Bot one t'ing," he said; "a leetle, w'at you call, favor—a leetle favor, dat is eet. I gif my feefty t'ousan' dollair to de church. I gif my husky dog, Bâtard, to de devil. De leetle favor? Firs' you hang heem, an' den you hang me. Eet is good, eh?"

Good it was, they agreed, that Hell's Spawn should break trail for his master across the last divide, and the court was adjourned down to the river bank, where a big spruce tree stood by itself. Slackwater Charley put a hangman's knot in the end of a hauling-line, and the noose was slipped over Leclère's head and pulled tight around his neck. His hands were tied behind his back, and he was assisted to the tcp of a cracker box. Then the running end of the line was passed over an overhanging branch, drawn taut, and made fast. To kick the box out from under would leave him dancing on the air.

"Now for the dog," said Webster Shaw, sometime mining engineer. "You'll have to rope him, Slackwater."

Leclère grinned. Slackwater took a chew of tobacco, rove a running noose, and proceeded leisurely to coil a few turns in his hand. He paused once or twice to brush particularly offensive mosquitoes from off his face. Everybody was brushing mosquitoes, except Leclère, about whose head a small cloud was visible. Even Bâtard, lying full-stretched on the ground, with his fore paws rubbed the pests away from eyes and mouth.

But while Slackwater waited for Bâtard to lift his head, a faint call came down the quiet air, and a man was seen waving his arms and running across the flat from Sunrise. It was the storekeeper.

"C-call 'er off, boys," he panted, as he came in among them.

"Little Sandy and Bernadotte's jes' got in," he explained with returning breath. "Landed down below an' come up by the short cut. Got the Beaver with 'm. Picked 'm up in his canoe, stuck in a back channel, with a couple of bullet holes in 'm. Other buck was Klok-Kutz, the one that knocked spots out of his squaw and dusted."

"Eh? W'at Ah say? Eh?" Leclère cried exultantly. "Dat de one fo' sure! Ah know. Ah spik true."

"The thing to do is teach these damned Siwashes a little manners," spoke Webster Shaw. "They're getting fat and sassy, and we'll have to bring them down a peg. Round in all the bucks and string up the Beaver for an object lesson. That's the programme. Come on and let's see what he's got to say for himself."

"Heh, M'sieu'!" Leclère called, as the crowd began to melt away through the twilight in the direction of Sunrise. "Ah lak ver' moch to see de fon."

"Oh, we'll turn you loose when we come back," Webster Shaw shouted over his shoulder. "In the meantime meditate on your sins and the ways of providence. It will do you good, so be grateful."

As is the way with men who are accustomed to great hazards, whose nerves are healthy and trained to patience, so it was with Leclère, who settled himself to the long wait—which is to say that he reconciled his mind to it. There was no settling of the body, for the taut rope forced him to stand rigidly erect. The least relaxation of the leg muscles pressed the rough-fibred noose into his neck, while the upright position caused him much pain in his wounded shoulder. He projected his under lip and expelled his breath upward along his face to blow the mosquitoes away from his eyes. But the situation had its compensation. To be snatched from the maw of death was well worth a little bodily suffering, only it was unfortunate that he should miss the hanging of the Beaver.

And so he mused, till his eyes chanced to fall upon Bâtard, head between fore paws and stretched on the ground asleep. And then Leclère ceased to muse. He studied the animal closely, striving to sense if the sleep were real or feigned. Bâtard's sides were heaving regularly, but Leclère felt that the breath came and went a shade too quickly; also he felt that there was a vigilance or alertness to every hair that belied unshackling sleep. He would have given his Sunrise claim to be assured that the dog was not awake, and once, when one of his joints cracked, he looked quickly and guiltily at Bâtard to see if he roused. He did not rouse then, but a few minutes later he got up slowly and lazily, stretched, and looked carefully about him.

"*Sacredam,*" said Leclère, under his breath.

Assured that no one was in sight or hearing, Bâtard sat down, curled his upper lip almost into a smile, looked up at Leclère, and licked his chops.

"Ah see my feenish," the man said, and laughed sardonically aloud.

Bâtard came nearer, the useless ear wabbling, the good ear cocked forward with devilish comprehension. He thrust his head on one side quizzically, and advanced with mincing, playful steps. He rubbed his body gently against the box till it shook and shook again. Leclère teetered carefully to maintain his equilibrium.

"Bâtard," he said calmly, "look out. Ah keel you."

Bâtard snarled at the word, and shook the box with greater force. Then he upreared, and with his fore paws threw his weight against it higher up. Leclère kicked out with one foot, but the rope bit into his neck and checked so abruptly as nearly to overbalance him.

"Hi, ya! *Chook! Mush-on!*" he screamed.

Bâtard retreated, for twenty feet or so, with a fiendish levity in his bearing that Leclère could not mistake. He remembered the dog often breaking the scum of ice on the water hole, by lifting up and throwing his weight upon it; and, remembering, he understood what he now had in mind. Bâtard faced about and paused. He showed his white teeth in a grin, which Leclère answered; and then hurled his body through the air, in full charge, straight for the box.

Fifteen minutes later, Slackwater Charley and Webster Shaw, returning, caught a glimpse of a ghostly pendulum swinging back and forth in the dim light. As they hurriedly drew in closer, they made out the man's inert body, and a live thing that clung to it, and shook and worried, and gave to it the swaying motion.

"Hi, ya! *Chook!* you Spawn of Hell," yelled Webster Shaw.

But Bâtard glared at him, and snarled threateningly, without loosing his jaws.

Slackwater Charley got out his revolver, but his hand was shaking, as with a chill, and he fumbled.

"Here, you take it," he said, passing the weapon over.

Webster Shaw laughed shortly, drew a sight between the gleaming eyes, and pressed the trigger. Bâtard's body twitched with the shock, threshed the ground spasmodically for a moment, and went suddenly limp. But his teeth still held fast locked.

# LOVE OF LIFE

*"This out of all will remain—*
*They have lived and have tossed:*
*So much of the game will be gain,*
*Though the gold of the dice has been lost."*

THEY LIMPED PAINFULLY down the bank, and once the foremost of the two men staggered among the rough-strewn rocks. They were tired and weak, and their faces had the drawn expression of patience which comes of hardship long endured. They were heavily burdened with blanket packs which were strapped to their shoulders. Head-straps, passing across the forehead, helped support these packs. Each man carried a rifle. They walked in a stooped posture, the shoulders well forward, the head still farther forward, the eyes bent upon the ground.

"I wish we had just about two of them cartridges that's layin' in that cache of ourn," said the second man.

His voice was utterly and drearily expressionless. He spoke without enthusiasm; and the first man, limping into the milky stream that foamed over the rocks, vouchsafed no reply.

The other man followed at his heels. They did not remove their foot-gear, though the water was icy cold—so cold that their ankles ached and their feet went numb. In places the water dashed against their knees, and both men staggered for footing.

The man who followed slipped on a smooth boulder, nearly fell, but recovered himself with a violent effort, at the same time uttering a sharp exclamation of pain. He seemed faint and dizzy and put out his free hand while he reeled, as though seeking support against the air. When he had steadied himself he stepped forward, but reeled again and nearly fell. Then he stood still and looked at the other man, who had never turned his head.

The man stood still for fully a minute, as though debating with himself. Then he called out:

"I say, Bill, I've sprained my ankle."

Bill staggered on through the milky water. He did not look around. The man watched him go, and though his face was expressionless as ever, his eyes were like the eyes of a wounded deer.

The other man limped up the farther bank and continued straight on without looking back. The man in the stream watched him. His lips trembled a little, so that the rough thatch of brown hair which covered them was visibly agitated. His tongue even strayed out to moisten them.

"Bill!" he cried out.

It was the pleading cry of a strong man in distress, but Bill's head did not turn. The man watched him go, limping grotesquely and lurching forward with stammering gait up the slow slope toward the soft sky-line of the low-lying hill. He watched him go till he passed over the crest and disappeared. Then he turned his gaze and slowly took in the circle of the world that remained to him now that Bill was gone.

Near the horizon the sun was smouldering dimly, almost obscured by formless mists and vapors, which gave an impression of mass and density without outline or tangibility. The man pulled out his watch, the while resting his weight on one leg. It was four o'clock, and as the season was near the last of July or first of August,—he did not know the precise date within a week or two,—he knew that the sun roughly marked the northwest. He looked to the south and knew that somewhere beyond those bleak hills lay the Great Bear Lake; also, he knew that in that direction the Arctic Circle cut its forbidding way across the Canadian Barrens. This stream in which he stood was a feeder to the Coppermine River, which in turn flowed north and emptied into Coronation Gulf and the Arctic Ocean. He had never been there, but he had seen it, once, on a Hudson Bay Company chart.

Again his gaze completed the circle of the world about him. It was not a heartening spectacle. Everywhere was soft sky-line. The hills were all low-lying. There were no trees, no shrubs, no grasses—naught but a tremendous and terrible desolation that sent fear swiftly dawning into his eyes.

"Bill!" he whispered, once and twice; "Bill!"

He cowered in the midst of the milky water, as though the vastness were pressing in upon him with overwhelming force, brutally crushing him with its complacent awfulness. He began to shake as

with an ague-fit, till the gun fell from his hand with a splash. This
served to rouse him. He fought with his fear and pulled himself together, groping in the water and recovering the weapon. He hitched
his pack farther over on his left shoulder, so as to take a portion of
its weight from off the injured ankle. Then he proceeded, slowly and
carefully, wincing with pain, to the bank.

He did not stop. With a desperation that was madness, unmindful
of the pain, he hurried up the slope to the crest of the hill over which
his comrade had disappeared—more grotesque and comical by far
than that limping, jerking comrade. But at the crest he saw a shallow
valley, empty of life. He fought with his fear again, overcame it,
hitched the pack still farther over on his left shoulder, and lurched on
down the slope.

The bottom of the valley was soggy with water, which the thick
moss held, spongelike, close to the surface. This water squirted out
from under his feet at every step, and each time he lifted a foot the
action culminated in a sucking sound as the wet moss reluctantly released its grip. He picked his way from muskeg to muskeg, and followed the other man's footsteps along and across the rocky ledges
which thrust like islets through the sea of moss.

Though alone, he was not lost. Farther on he knew he would
come to where dead spruce and fir, very small and weazened, bordered
the shore of a little lake, the *titchin-nichilie,* in the tongue of the country, the "land of little sticks." And into that lake flowed a small stream,
the water of which was not milky. There was rush-grass on that
stream—this he remembered well—but no timber, and he would follow it till its first trickle ceased at a divide. He would cross this divide
to the first trickle of another stream, flowing to the west, which he
would follow until it emptied into the river Dease, and here he would
find a cache under an upturned canoe and piled over with many rocks.
And in this cache would be ammunition for his empty gun, fish-hooks
and lines, a small net—all the utilities for the killing and snaring of
food. Also, he would find flour,—not much,—a piece of bacon, and
some beans.

Bill would be waiting for him there, and they would paddle away
south down the Dease to the Great Bear Lake. And south across the
lake they would go, ever south, till they gained the Mackenzie. And
south, still south, they would go, while the winter raced vainly after
them, and the ice formed in the eddies, and the days grew chill and
crisp, south to some warm Hudson Bay Company post, where timber
grew tall and generous and there was grub without end.

These were the thoughts of the man as he strove onward. But hard as he strove with his body, he strove equally hard with his mind, trying to think that Bill had not deserted him, that Bill would surely wait for him at the cache. He was compelled to think this thought, or else there would not be any use to strive, and he would have lain down and died. And as the dim ball of the sun sank slowly into the northwest he covered every inch—and many times—of his and Bill's flight south before the downcoming winter. And he conned the grub of the cache and the grub of the Hudson Bay Company post over and over again. He had not eaten for two days; for a far longer time he had not had all he wanted to eat. Often he stooped and picked pale muskeg berries, put them into his mouth, and chewed and swallowed them. A muskeg berry is a bit of seed enclosed in a bit of water. In the mouth the water melts away and the seed chews sharp and bitter. The man knew there was no nourishment in the berries, but he chewed them patiently with a hope greater than knowledge and defying experience.

At nine o'clock he stubbed his toe on a rocky ledge, and from sheer weariness and weakness staggered and fell. He lay for some time, without movement, on his side. Then he slipped out of the pack-straps and clumsily dragged himself into a sitting posture. It was not yet dark, and in the lingering twilight he groped about among the rocks for shreds of dry moss. When he had gathered a heap he built a fire,—a smouldering, smudgy fire,—and put a tin pot of water on to boil.

He unwrapped his pack and the first thing he did was to count his matches. There were sixty-seven. He counted them three times to make sure. He divided them into several portions, wrapping them in oil paper, disposing of one bunch in his empty tobacco pouch, of another bunch in the inside band of his battered hat, of a third bunch under his shirt on the chest. This accomplished, a panic came upon him, and he unwrapped them all and counted them again. There were still sixty-seven.

He dried his wet foot-gear by the fire. The moccasins were in soggy shreds. The blanket socks were worn through in places, and his feet were raw and bleeding. His ankle was throbbing, and he gave it an examination. It had swollen to the size of his knee. He tore a long strip from one of his two blankets and bound the ankle tightly. He tore other strips and bound them about his feet to serve for both moccasins and socks. Then he drank the pot of water, steaming hot, wound his watch, and crawled between his blankets.

He slept like a dead man. The brief darkness around midnight came and went. The sun arose in the northeast—at least the day dawned in that quarter, for the sun was hidden by gray clouds.

At six o'clock he awoke, quietly lying on his back. He gazed straight up into the gray sky and knew that he was hungry. As he rolled over on his elbow he was startled by a loud snort, and saw a bull caribou regarding him with alert curiosity. The animal was not more than fifty feet away, and instantly into the man's mind leaped the vision and the savor of a caribou steak sizzling and frying over a fire. Mechanically he reached for the empty gun, drew a bead, and pulled the trigger. The bull snorted and leaped away, his hoofs rattling and clattering as he fled across the ledges.

The man cursed and flung the empty gun from him. He groaned aloud as he started to drag himself to his feet. It was a slow and arduous task. His joints were like rusty hinges. They worked harshly in their sockets, with much friction, and each bending or unbending was accomplished only through a sheer exertion of will. When he finally gained his feet, another minute or so was consumed in straightening up, so that he could stand erect as a man should stand.

He crawled up a small knoll and surveyed the prospect. There were no trees, no bushes, nothing but a gray sea of moss scarcely diversified by gray rocks, gray lakelets, and gray streamlets. The sky was gray. There was no sun nor hint of sun. He had no idea of north, and he had forgotten the way he had come to this spot the night before. But he was not lost. He knew that. Soon he would come to the land of the little sticks. He felt that it lay off to the left somewhere, not far—possibly just over the next low hill.

He went back to put his pack into shape for travelling. He assured himself of the existence of his three separate parcels of matches, though he did not stop to count them. But he did linger, debating, over a squat moose-hide sack. It was not large. He could hide it under his two hands. He knew that it weighed fifteen pounds,—as much as all the rest of the pack,—and it worried him. He finally set it to one side and proceeded to roll the pack. He paused to gaze at the squat moose-hide sack. He picked it up hastily with a defiant glance about him, as though the desolation were trying to rob him of it; and when he rose to his feet to stagger on into the day, it was included in the pack on his back.

He bore away to the left, stopping now and again to eat muskeg berries. His ankle had stiffened, his limp was more pronounced, but the pain of it was as nothing compared with the pain of his stomach.

The hunger pangs were sharp. They gnawed and gnawed until he could not keep his mind steady on the course he must pursue to gain the land of little sticks. The muskeg berries did not allay this gnawing, while they made his tongue and the roof of his mouth sore with their irritating bite.

He came upon a valley where rock ptarmigan rose on whirring wings from the ledges and muskegs. Ker—ker—ker was the cry they made. He threw stones at them, but could not hit them. He placed his pack on the ground and stalked them as a cat stalks a sparrow. The sharp rocks cut through his pants' legs till his knees left a trail of blood; but the hurt was lost in the hurt of his hunger. He squirmed over the wet moss, saturating his clothes and chilling his body; but he was not aware of it, so great was his fever for food. And always the ptarmigan rose, whirring, before him, till their ker—ker—ker became a mock to him, and he cursed them and cried aloud at them with their own cry.

Once he crawled upon one that must have been asleep. He did not see it till it shot up in his face from its rocky nook. He made a clutch as startled as was the rise of the ptarmigan, and there remained in his hand three tail-feathers. As he watched its flight he hated it, as though it had done him some terrible wrong. Then he returned and shouldered his pack.

As the day wore along he came into valleys or swales where game was more plentiful. A band of caribou passed by, twenty and odd animals, tantalizingly within rifle range. He felt a wild desire to run after them, a certitude that he could run them down. A black fox came toward him, carrying a ptarmigan in his mouth. The man shouted. It was a fearful cry, but the fox, leaping away in fright, did not drop the ptarmigan.

Late in the afternoon he followed a stream, milky with lime, which ran through sparse patches of rush-grass. Grasping these rushes firmly near the root, he pulled up what resembled a young onion-sprout no larger than a shingle-nail. It was tender, and his teeth sank into it with a crunch that promised deliciously of food. But its fibers were tough. It was composed of stringy filaments saturated with water, like the berries, and devoid of nourishment. He threw off his pack and went into the rush-grass on hands and knees, crunching and munching, like some bovine creature.

He was very weary and often wished to rest—to lie down and sleep; but he was continually driven on—not so much by his desire to gain the land of little sticks as by his hunger. He searched little ponds for frogs and dug up the earth with his nails for worms, though he knew in spite that neither frogs nor worms existed so far north.

He looked into every pool of water vainly, until, as the long twilight came on, he discovered a solitary fish, the size of a minnow, in such a pool. He plunged his arm in up to the shoulder, but it eluded him. He reached for it with both hands and stirred up the milky mud at the bottom. In his excitement he fell in, wetting himself to the waist. Then the water was too muddy to admit of his seeing the fish, and he was compelled to wait until the sediment had settled.

The pursuit was renewed, till the water was again muddied. But he could not wait. He unstrapped the tin bucket and began to bale the pool. He baled wildly at first, splashing himself and flinging the water so short a distance that it ran back into the pool. He worked more carefully, striving to be cool, though his heart was pounding against his chest and his hands were trembling. At the end of half an hour the pool was nearly dry. Not a cupful of water remained. And there was no fish. He found a hidden crevice among the stones through which it had escaped to the adjoining and larger pool—a pool which he could not empty in a night and a day. Had he known of the crevice, he could have closed it with a rock at the beginning and the fish would have been his.

Thus he thought, and crumpled up and sank down upon the wet earth. At first he cried softly to himself, then he cried loudly to the pitiless desolation that ringed him around; and for a long time after he was shaken by great dry sobs.

He built a fire and warmed himself by drinking quarts of hot water, and made camp on a rocky ledge in the same fashion he had the night before. The last thing he did was to see that his matches were dry and to wind his watch. The blankets were wet and clammy. His ankle pulsed with pain. But he knew only that he was hungry, and through his restless sleep he dreamed of feasts and banquets and of food served and spread in all imaginable ways.

He awoke chilled and sick. There was no sun. The gray of earth and sky had become deeper, more profound. A raw wind was blowing, and the first flurries of snow were whitening the hilltops. The air about him thickened and grew white while he made a fire and boiled more water. It was wet snow, half rain, and the flakes were large and soggy. At first they melted as soon as they came in contact with the earth, but ever more fell, covering the ground, putting out the fire, spoiling his supply of moss-fuel.

This was a signal for him to strap on his pack and stumble onward, he knew not where. He was not concerned with the land of little
sticks, nor with Bill and the cache under the upturned canoe by the
river Dease. He was mastered by the verb "to eat." He was hunger-
mad. He took no heed of the course he pursued, so long as that course
led him through the swale bottoms. He felt his way through the wet
snow to the watery muskeg berries, and went by feel as he pulled up
the rush-grass by the roots. But it was tasteless stuff and did not satisfy. He found a weed that tasted sour and he ate all he could find of
it, which was not much, for it was a creeping growth, easily hidden
under the several inches of snow.

He had no fire that night, nor hot water, and crawled under his
blanket to sleep the broken hunger-sleep. The snow turned into a cold
rain. He awakened many times to feel it falling on his upturned face.
Day came—a gray day and no sun. It had ceased raining. The keenness
of his hunger had departed. Sensibility, as far as concerned the yearning for food, had been exhausted. There was a dull, heavy ache in his
stomach, but it did not bother him so much. He was more rational,
and once more he was chiefly interested in the land of little sticks and
the cache by the river Dease.

He ripped the remnant of one of his blankets into strips and
bound his bleeding feet. Also, he recinched the injured ankle and prepared himself for a day of travel. When he came to his pack, he paused
long over the squat moose-hide sack, but in the end it went with him.

The snow had melted under the rain, and only the hilltops showed
white. The sun came out, and he succeeded in locating the points of
the compass, though he knew now that he was lost. Perhaps, in his
previous days' wanderings, he had edged away too far to the left. He
now bore off to the right to counteract the possible deviation from his
true course.

Though the hunger pangs were no longer so exquisite, he realized
that he was weak. He was compelled to pause for frequent rests, when
he attacked the muskeg berries and rush-grass patches. His tongue felt
dry and large, as though covered with a fine hairy growth, and it tasted
bitter in his mouth. His heart gave him a great deal of trouble. When
he had travelled a few minutes it would begin a remorseless thump,
thump, thump, and then leap up and away in a painful flutter of beats
that choked him and made him go faint and dizzy.

In the middle of the day he found two minnows in a large pool.
It was impossible to bale it, but he was calmer now and managed to
catch them in his tin bucket. They were no longer than his little finger,

but he was not particularly hungry. The dull ache in his stomach had been growing duller and fainter. It seemed almost that his stomach was dozing. He ate the fish raw, masticating with painstaking care, for the eating was an act of pure reason. While he had no desire to eat, he knew that he must eat to live.

In the evening he caught three more minnows, eating two and saving the third for breakfast. The sun had dried stray shreds of moss, and he was able to warm himself with hot water. He had not covered more than ten miles that day; and the next day, travelling whenever his heart permitted him, he covered no more than five miles. But his stomach did not give him the slightest uneasiness. It had gone to sleep. He was in a strange country, too, and the caribou were growing more plentiful, also the wolves. Often their yelps drifted across the desolation, and once he saw three of them slinking away before his path.

Another night; and in the morning, being more rational, he untied the leather string that fastened the squat moose-hide sack. From its open mouth poured a yellow stream of coarse gold-dust and nuggets. He roughly divided the gold in halves, caching one half on a prominent ledge, wrapped in a piece of blanket, and returning the other half to the sack. He also began to use strips of the one remaining blanket for his feet. He still clung to his gun, for there were cartridges in that cache by the river Dease.

This was a day of fog, and this day hunger awoke in him again. He was very weak and was afflicted with a giddiness which at times blinded him. It was no uncommon thing now for him to stumble and fall; and stumbling once, he fell squarely into a ptarmigan nest. There were four newly hatched chicks, a day old—little specks of pulsating life no more than a mouthful; and he ate them ravenously, thrusting them alive into his mouth and crunching them like egg-shells between his teeth. The mother ptarmigan beat about him with great outcry. He used his gun as a club with which to knock her over, but she dodged out of reach. He threw stones at her and with one chance shot broke a wing. Then she fluttered away, running, trailing the broken wing, with him in pursuit.

The little chicks had no more than whetted his appetite. He hopped and bobbed clumsily along on his injured ankle, throwing stones and screaming hoarsely at times; at other times hopping and bobbing silently along, picking himself up grimly and patiently when he fell, or rubbing his eyes with his hand when the giddiness threatened to overpower him.

The chase led him across swampy ground in the bottom of the

valley, and he came upon footprints in the soggy moss. They were not his own—he could see that. They must be Bill's. But he could not stop, for the mother ptarmigan was running on. He would catch her first, then he would return and investigate.

He exhausted the mother ptarmigan; but he exhausted himself. She lay panting on her side. He lay panting on his side, a dozen feet away, unable to crawl to her. And as he recovered she recovered, fluttering out of reach as his hungry hand went out to her. The chase was resumed. Night settled down and she escaped. He stumbled from weakness and pitched head foremost on his face, cutting his cheek, his pack upon his back. He did not move for a long while; then he rolled over on his side, wound his watch, and lay there until morning.

Another day of fog. Half of his last blanket had gone into foot-wrappings. He failed to pick up Bill's trail. It did not matter. His hunger was driving him too compellingly—only—only he wondered if Bill, too, were lost. By midday the irk of his pack became too oppressive. Again he divided the gold, this time merely spilling half of it on the ground. In the afternoon he threw the rest of it away, there remaining to him only the half-blanket, the tin bucket, and the rifle.

An hallucination began to trouble him. He felt confident that one cartridge remained to him. It was in the chamber of the rifle and he had overlooked it. On the other hand, he knew all the time that the chamber was empty. But the hallucination persisted. He fought it off for hours, then threw his rifle open and was confronted with emptiness. The disappointment was as bitter as though he had really expected to find the cartridge.

He plodded on for half an hour, when the hallucination arose again. Again he fought it, and still it persisted, till for very relief he opened his rifle to unconvince himself. At times his mind wandered farther afield, and he plodded on, a mere automaton, strange conceits and whimsicalities gnawing at his brain like worms. But these excursions out of the real were of brief duration, for ever the pangs of the hunger-bite called him back. He was jerked back abruptly once from such an excursion by a sight that caused him nearly to faint. He reeled and swayed, doddering like a drunken man to keep from falling. Before him stood a horse. A horse! He could not believe his eyes. A thick mist was in them, intershot with sparkling points of light. He rubbed his eyes savagely to clear his vision, and beheld, not a horse, but a great brown bear. The animal was studying him with bellicose curiosity.

The man had brought his gun halfway to his shoulder before he realized. He lowered it and drew his hunting-knife from its beaded sheath at his hip. Before him was meat and life. He ran his thumb along the edge of his knife. It was sharp. The point was sharp. He would fling himself upon the bear and kill it. But his heart began its warning thump, thump, thump. Then followed the wild upward leap and tattoo of flutters, the pressing as of an iron band about his forehead, the creeping of the dizziness into his brain.

His desperate courage was evicted by a great surge of fear. In his weakness, what if the animal attacked him? He drew himself up to his most imposing stature, gripping the knife and staring hard at the bear. The bear advanced clumsily a couple of steps, reared up, and gave vent to a tentative growl. If the man ran, he would run after him; but the man did not run. He was animated now with the courage of fear. He, too, growled, savagely, terribly, voicing the fear that is to life germane and that lies twisted about life's deepest roots.

The bear edged away to one side, growling menacingly, himself appalled by this mysterious creature that appeared upright and unafraid. But the man did not move. He stood like a statue till the danger was past, when he yielded to a fit of trembling and sank down into the wet moss.

He pulled himself together and went on, afraid now in a new way. It was not the fear that he should die passively from lack of food, but that he should be destroyed violently before starvation had exhausted the last particle of the endeavor in him that made toward surviving. There were the wolves. Back and forth across the desolation drifted their howls, weaving the very air into a fabric of menace that was so tangible that he found himself, arms in the air, pressing it back from him as it might be the walls of a wind-blown tent.

Now and again the wolves, in packs of two and three, crossed his path. But they sheered clear of him. They were not in sufficient numbers, and besides they were hunting the caribou, which did not battle, while this strange creature that walked erect might scratch and bite.

In the late afternoon he came upon scattered bones where the wolves had made a kill. The débris had been a caribou calf an hour before, squawking and running and very much alive. He contemplated the bones, clean-picked and polished, pink with the cell-life in them which had not yet died. Could it possibly be that he might be that ere the day was done! Such was life, eh? A vain and fleeting thing. It was only life that pained. There was no hurt in death. To die was to sleep. It meant cessation, rest. Then why was he not content to die?

But he did not moralize long. He was squatting in the moss, a bone in his mouth, sucking at the shreds of life that still dyed it faintly pink. The sweet meaty taste, thin and elusive almost as a memory, maddened him. He closed his jaws on the bones and crunched. Sometimes it was the bone that broke, sometimes his teeth. Then he crushed the bones between rocks, pounded them to a pulp, and swallowed them. He pounded his fingers, too, in his haste, and yet found a moment in which to feel surprise at the fact that his fingers did not hurt much when caught under the descending rock.

Came frightful days of snow and rain. He did not know when he made camp, when he broke camp. He travelled in the night as much as in the day. He rested wherever he fell, crawled on whenever the dying life in him flickered up and burned less dimly. He, as a man, no longer strove. It was the life in him, unwilling to die, that drove him on. He did not suffer. His nerves had become blunted, numb, while his mind was filled with weird visions and delicious dreams.

But ever he sucked and chewed on the crushed bones of the caribou calf, the least remnants of which he had gathered up and carried with him. He crossed no more hills or divides, but automatically followed a large stream which flowed through a wide and shallow valley. He did not see this stream nor this valley. He saw nothing save visions. Soul and body walked or crawled side by side, yet apart, so slender was the thread that bound them.

He awoke in his right mind, lying on his back on a rocky ledge. The sun was shining bright and warm. Afar off he heard the squawking of caribou calves. He was aware of vague memories of rain and wind and snow, but whether he had been beaten by the storm for two days or two weeks he did not know.

For some time he lay without movement, the genial sunshine pouring upon him and saturating his miserable body with its warmth. A fine day, he thought. Perhaps he could manage to locate himself. By a painful effort he rolled over on his side. Below him flowed a wide and sluggish river. Its unfamiliarity puzzled him. Slowly he followed it with his eyes, winding in wide sweeps among the bleak, bare hills, bleaker and barer and lower-lying than any hills he had yet encountered. Slowly, deliberately, without excitement or more than the most casual interest, he followed the course of the strange stream toward the sky-line and saw it emptying into a bright and shining sea. He was still unexcited. Most unusual, he thought, a vision or a mirage—more likely a vision, a trick of his disordered mind. He was confirmed in this by sight of a ship lying at anchor in the midst of the shining sea. He closed his eyes for a while, then opened them. Strange how the vision persisted! Yet not strange. He knew there were no seas or ships in the heart of the barren lands, just as he had known there was no cartridge in the empty rifle.

He heard a snuffle behind him—a half-choking gasp or cough. Very slowly, because of his exceeding weakness and stiffness, he rolled over on his other side. He could see nothing near at hand, but he waited patiently. Again came the snuffle and cough, and outlined between two jagged rocks not a score of feet away he made out the gray head of a wolf. The sharp ears were not pricked so sharply as he had seen them on other wolves; the eyes were bleared and bloodshot, the head seemed to droop limply and forlornly. The animal blinked continually in the sunshine. It seemed sick. As he looked it snuffled and coughed again.

This, at least, was real, he thought, and turned on the other side so that he might see the reality of the world which had been veiled from him before by the vision. But the sea still shone in the distance and the ship was plainly discernible. Was it reality, after all? He closed his eyes for a long while and thought, and then it came to him. He had been making north by east, away from the Dease Divide and into the Coppermine Valley. This wide and sluggish river was the Coppermine. That shining sea was the Arctic Ocean. That ship was a whaler, strayed east, far east, from the mouth of the Mackenzie, and it was lying at anchor in Coronation Gulf. He remembered the Hudson Bay Company chart he had seen long ago, and it was all clear and reasonable to him.

He sat up and turned his attention to immediate affairs. He had worn through the blanket-wrappings, and his feet were shapeless lumps of raw meat. His last blanket was gone. Rifle and knife were both missing. He had lost his hat somewhere, with the bunch of matches in the band, but the matches against his chest were safe and dry inside the tobacco pouch and oil paper. He looked at his watch. It marked eleven o'clock and was still running. Evidently he had kept it wound.

He was calm and collected. Though extremely weak, he had no sensation of pain. He was not hungry. The thought of food was not even pleasant to him, and whatever he did was done by his reason alone. He ripped off his pants' legs to the knees and bound them about his feet. Somehow he had succeeded in retaining the tin bucket. He would have some hot water before he began what he foresaw was to be a terrible journey to the ship.

His movements were slow. He shook as with a palsy. When he

started to collect dry moss, he found he could not rise to his feet. He tried again and again, then contented himself with crawling about on hands and knees. Once he crawled near to the sick wolf. The animal dragged itself reluctantly out of his way, licking its chops with a tongue which seemed hardly to have the strength to curl. The man noticed that the tongue was not the customary healthy red. It was a yellowish brown and seemed coated with a rough and half-dry mucus.

After he had drunk a quart of hot water the man found he was able to stand, and even to walk as well as a dying man might be supposed to walk. Every minute or so he was compelled to rest. His steps were feeble and uncertain, just as the wolf's that trailed him were feeble and uncertain; and that night, when the shining sea was blotted out by blackness, he knew he was nearer to it by no more than four miles.

Throughout the night he heard the cough of the sick wolf, and now and then the squawking of the caribou calves. There was life all around him, but it was strong life, very much alive and well, and he knew the sick wolf clung to the sick man's trail in the hope that the man would die first. In the morning, on opening his eyes, he beheld it regarding him with a wistful and hungry stare. It stood crouched, with tail between its legs, like a miserable and woe-begone dog. It shivered in the chill morning wind, and grinned dispiritedly when the man spoke to it in a voice that achieved no more than a hoarse whisper.

The sun rose brightly, and all morning the man tottered and fell toward the ship on the shining sea. The weather was perfect. It was the brief Indian Summer of the high latitudes. It might last a week. To-morrow or next day it might be gone.

In the afternoon the man came upon a trail. It was of another man, who did not walk, but who dragged himself on all fours. The man thought it might be Bill, but he thought in a dull, uninterested way. He had no curiosity. In fact, sensation and emotion had left him. He was no longer susceptible to pain. Stomach and nerves had gone to sleep. Yet the life that was in him drove him on. He was very weary, but it refused to die. It was because it refused to die that he still ate muskeg berries and minnows, drank his hot water, and kept a wary eye on the sick wolf.

He followed the trail of the other man who dragged himself along, and soon came to the end of it—a few fresh-picked bones where the soggy moss was marked by the foot-pads of many wolves. He saw a squat moose-hide sack, mate to his own, which had been torn by sharp teeth. He picked it up, though its weight was almost too much for his feeble fingers. Bill had carried it to the last. Ha! ha! He would have the laugh on Bill. He would survive and carry it to the ship in the shining sea. His mirth was hoarse and ghastly, like a raven's croak, and the sick wolf joined him, howling lugubriously. The man ceased suddenly. How could he have the laugh on Bill if that were Bill; if those bones, so pinky-white and clean, were Bill?

He turned away. Well, Bill had deserted him; but he would not take the gold, nor would he suck Bill's bones. Bill would have, though, had it been the other way around, he mused as he staggered on.

He came to a pool of water. Stooping over in quest of minnows, he jerked his head back as though he had been stung. He had caught sight of his reflected face. So horrible was it that sensibility awoke long enough to be shocked. There were three minnows in the pool, which was too large to drain; and after several ineffectual attempts to catch them in the tin bucket he forbore. He was afraid, because of his great weakness, that he might fall in and drown. It was for this reason that he did not trust himself to the river astride one of the many drift-logs which lined its sand-spits.

That day he decreased the distance between him and the ship by three miles; the next day by two—for he was crawling now as Bill had crawled; and the end of the fifth day found the ship still seven miles away and him unable to make even a mile a day. Still the Indian Summer held on, and he continued to crawl and faint, turn and turn about; and ever the sick wolf coughed and wheezed at his heels. His knees had become raw meat like his feet, and though he padded them with the shirt from his back it was a red track he left behind him on the moss and stones. Once, glancing back, he saw the wolf licking hungrily his bleeding trail, and he saw sharply what his own end might be—unless—unless he could get the wolf. Then began as grim a tragedy of existence as was ever played—a sick man that crawled, a sick wolf that limped, two creatures dragging their dying carcasses across the desolation and hunting each other's lives.

Had it been a well wolf, it would not have mattered so much to the man; but the thought of going to feed the maw of that loathsome and all but dead thing was repugnant to him. He was finicky. His mind had begun to wander again, and to be perplexed by hallucinations, while his lucid intervals grew rarer and shorter.

He was awakened once from a faint by a wheeze close in his ear. The wolf leaped lamely back, losing its footing and falling in its weakness. It was ludicrous, but he was not amused. Nor was he even afraid. He was too far gone for that. But his mind was for the moment clear, and he lay and considered. The ship was no more than four miles away. He could see it quite distinctly when he rubbed the mists out of his eyes, and he could see the white sail of a small boat cutting the water of the shining sea. But he could never crawl those four miles. He knew that, and was very calm in the knowledge. He knew that he could not crawl half a mile. And yet he wanted to live. It was unreasonable that he should die after all he had undergone. Fate asked too much of him. And, dying, he declined to die. It was stark madness, perhaps, but in the very grip of Death he defied Death and refused to die.

He closed his eyes and composed himself with infinite precaution. He steeled himself to keep above the suffocating languor that lapped like a rising tide through all the wells of his being. It was very like a sea, this deadly languor, that rose and rose and drowned his consciousness bit by bit. Sometimes he was all but submerged, swimming through oblivion with a faltering stroke; and again, by some strange alchemy of soul, he would find another shred of will and strike out more strongly.

Without movement he lay on his back, and he could hear, slowly drawing near and nearer, the wheezing intake and output of the sick wolf's breath. It drew closer, ever closer, through an infinitude of time, and he did not move. It was at his ear. The harsh dry tongue grated like sandpaper against his cheek. His hands shot out—or at least he willed them to shoot out. The fingers were curved like talons, but they closed on empty air. Swiftness and certitude require strength, and the man had not this strength.

The patience of the wolf was terrible. The man's patience was no less terrible. For half a day he lay motionless, fighting off unconsciousness and waiting for the thing that was to feed upon him and upon which he wished to feed. Sometimes the languid sea rose over him and he dreamed long dreams; but ever through it all, waking and dreaming, he waited for the wheezing breath and the harsh caress of the tongue.

He did not hear the breath, and he slipped slowly from some dream to the feel of the tongue along his hand. He waited. The fangs pressed softly; the pressure increased; the wolf was exerting its last strength in an effort to sink teeth in the food for which it had waited so long. But the man had waited long, and the lacerated hand closed on the jaw. Slowly, while the wolf struggled feebly and the hand clutched feebly, the other hand crept across to a grip. Five minutes later the whole weight of the man's body was on top of the wolf. The hands had not sufficient strength to choke the wolf, but the face of the man was pressed close to the throat of the wolf and the mouth of the man was full of hair. At the end of half an hour the man was aware of a warm trickle in his throat. It was not pleasant. It was like molten lead being forced into his stomach, and it was forced by his will alone. Later the man rolled over on his back and slept.

There were some members of a scientific expedition on the whale-ship *Bedford*. From the deck they remarked a strange object on the shore. It was moving down the beach toward the water. They were unable to classify it, and, being scientific men, they climbed into the whale-boat alongside and went ashore to see. And they saw something that was alive but which could hardly be called a man. It was blind, unconscious. It squirmed along the ground like some monstrous worm. Most of its efforts were ineffectual, but it was persistent, and it writhed and twisted and went ahead perhaps a score of feet an hour.

Three weeks afterward the man lay in a bunk on the whale-ship *Bedford,* and with tears streaming down his wasted cheeks told who he was and what he had undergone. He also babbled incoherently of his mother, of sunny Southern California, and a home among the orange groves and flowers.

The days were not many after that when he sat at table with the scientific men and ship's officers. He gloated over the spectacle of so much food, watching it anxiously as it went into the mouths of others. With the disappearance of each mouthful an expression of deep regret came into his eyes. He was quite sane, yet he hated those men at mealtime. He was haunted by a fear that the food would not last. He inquired of the cook, the cabinboy, the captain, concerning the food stores. They reassured him countless times; but he could not believe them, and pried cunningly about the lazarette to see with his own eyes.

It was noticed that the man was getting fat. He grew stouter with each day. The scientific men shook their heads and theorized. They limited the man at his meals, but still his girth increased and he swelled prodigiously under his shirt.

The sailors grinned. They knew. And when the scientific men set a watch on the man, they knew too. They saw him slouch for'ard after breakfast, and, like a mendicant, with outstretched palm, accost a sailor. The sailor grinned and passed him a fragment of sea biscuit. He clutched it avariciously, looked at it as a miser looks at gold, and thrust it into his shirt bosom. Similar were the donations from other grinning sailors.

The scientific men were discreet. They let him alone. But they privily examined his bunk. It was lined with hardtack; the mattress was stuffed with hardtack; every nook and cranny was filled with hardtack. Yet he was sane. He was taking precautions against another possible famine—that was all. He would recover from it, the scientific men said; and he did, ere the *Bedford*'s anchor rumbled down in San Francisco Bay.

# ALL GOLD CANYON

IT WAS THE GREEN HEART of the canyon, where the walls swerved back from the rigid plan and relieved their harshness of line by making a little sheltered nook and filling it to the brim with sweetness and roundness and softness. Here all things rested. Even the narrow stream ceased its turbulent down-rush long enough to form a quiet pool. Knee-deep in the water, with drooping head and half-shut eyes, drowsed a red-coated, many-antlered buck.

On one side, beginning at the very lip of the pool, was a tiny meadow, a cool, resilient surface of green that extended to the base of the frowning wall. Beyond the pool a gentle slope of earth ran up and up to meet the opposing wall. Fine grass covered the slope—grass that was spangled with flowers, with here and there patches of color, orange and purple and golden. Below, the canyon was shut in. There was no view. The walls leaned together abruptly and the canyon ended in a chaos of rocks, moss-covered and hidden by a green screen of vines and creepers and boughs of trees. Up the canyon rose far hills and peaks, the big foot-hills, pine-covered and remote. And far beyond, like clouds upon the border of the sky, towered minarets of white, where the Sierra's eternal snows flashed austerely the blazes of the sun.

There was no dust in the canyon. The leaves and flowers were clean and virginal. The grass was young velvet. Over the pool three cottonwoods sent their snowy fluffs fluttering down the quiet air. On the slope the blossoms of the wine-wooded manzanita filled the air with springtime odors, while the leaves, wise with experience, were already beginning their vertical twist against the coming aridity of summer. In the open spaces on the slope, beyond the farthest shadow-reach of the manzanita, poised the mariposa lilies, like so many flights of jewelled moths suddenly arrested and on the verge of trembling into flight again. Here and there that woods harlequin, the madrone, permitting itself to be caught in the act of changing its pea-green trunk to madder-red, breathed its fragrance into the air from great clusters of waxen bells. Creamy white were these bells, shaped like lilies-of-the-valley, with the sweetness of perfume that is of the springtime.

There was not a sigh of wind. The air was drowsy with its weight of perfume. It was a sweetness that would have been cloying had the air been heavy and humid. But the air was sharp and thin. It was as starlight transmuted into atmosphere, shot through and warmed by sunshine, and flower-drenched with sweetness.

An occasional butterfly drifted in and out through the patches of light and shade. And from all about rose the low and sleepy hum of mountain bees—feasting Sybarites that jostled one another good-naturedly at the board, nor found time for rough discourtesy. So quietly did the little stream drip and ripple its way through the canyon that it spoke only in faint and occasional gurgles. The voice of the stream was as a drowsy whisper, ever interrupted by dozings and silences, ever lifted again in the awakenings.

The motion of all things was a drifting in the heart of the canyon. Sunshine and butterflies drifted in and out among the trees. The hum of the bees and the whisper of the stream were a drifting of sound. And the drifting sound and drifting color seemed to weave together in the making of a delicate and intangible fabric which was the spirit of the place. It was a spirit of peace that was not of death, but of smooth-pulsing life, of quietude that was not silence, of movement that was not action, of repose that was quick with existence without being violent with struggle and travail. The spirit of the place was the spirit of the peace of the living, somnolent with the easement and content of prosperity, and undisturbed by rumors of far wars.

The red-coated, many-antlered buck acknowledged the lordship of the spirit of the place and dozed knee-deep in the cool, shaded pool. There seemed no flies to vex him and he was languid with rest. Sometimes his ears moved when the stream awoke and whispered; but they moved lazily, with foreknowledge that it was merely the stream grown garrulous at discovery that it had slept.

But there came a time when the buck's ears lifted and tensed with swift eagerness for sound. His head was turned down the canyon. His sensitive, quivering nostrils scented the air. His eyes could not pierce the green screen through which the stream rippled away, but to his ears came the voice of a man. It was a steady, monotonous, singsong voice. Once the buck heard the harsh clash of metal upon rock. At the sound he snorted with a sudden start that jerked him through the air from water to meadow, and his feet sank into the young velvet, while he pricked his ears and again scented the air. Then he stole across the tiny meadow, pausing once and again to listen, and faded away out of the canyon like a wraith, soft-footed and without sound.

The clash of steel-shod soles against the rocks began to be heard, and the man's voice grew louder. It was raised in a sort of chant and became distinct with nearness, so that the words could be heard:

> *"Tu'n around an' tu'n yo' face*
> *Untoe them sweet hills of grace*
> *(D' pow'rs of sin yo' am scornin'!).*
> *Look about an' look aroun',*
> *Fling yo' sin-pack on d' groun'*
> *(Yo' will meet wid d' Lord in d' mornin'!)."*

A sound of scrambling accompanied the song, and the spirit of the place fled away on the heels of the red-coated buck. The green screen was burst asunder, and a man peered out at the meadow and the pool and the sloping side-hill. He was a deliberate sort of man. He took in the scene with one embracing glance, then ran his eyes over the details to verify the general impression. Then, and not until then, did he open his mouth in vivid and solemn approval:

"Smoke of life an' snakes of purgatory! Will you just look at that! Wood an' water an' grass an' a side-hill! A pocket-hunter's delight an' a cayuse's paradise! Cool green for tired eyes! Pink pills for pale people ain't in it. A secret pasture for prospectors and a resting-place for tired burros, by damn!"

He was a sandy-complexioned man in whose face geniality and humor seemed the salient characteristics. It was a mobile face, quick-changing to inward mood and thought. Thinking was in him a visible process. Ideas chased across his face like wind-flaws across the surface of a lake. His hair, sparse and unkempt of growth, was as indeterminate and colorless as his complexion. It would seem that all the color of his frame had gone into his eyes, for they were startlingly blue. Also, they were laughing and merry eyes, within them much of the naïveté and wonder of the child; and yet, in an unassertive way, they contained much of calm self-reliance and strength of purpose founded upon self-experience and experience of the world.

From out the screen of vines and creepers he flung ahead of him a miner's pick and shovel and gold-pan. Then he crawled out himself into the open. He was clad in faded overalls and black cotton shirt, with hobnailed brogans on his feet, and on his head a hat whose shape-lessness and stains advertised the rough usage of wind and rain and sun and camp-smoke. He stood erect, seeing wide-eyed the secrecy of the scene and sensuously inhaling the warm, sweet breath of the canyon-garden through nostrils that dilated and quivered with delight. His eyes narrowed to laughing slits of blue, his face wreathed itself in joy, and his mouth curled in a smile as he cried aloud:

"Jumping dandelions and happy hollyhocks, but that smells good to me! Talk about your attar o' roses an' cologne factories! They ain't in it!"

He had the habit of soliloquy. His quick-changing facial expres-sions might tell every thought and mood, but the tongue, perforce, ran hard after, repeating, like a second Boswell.

The man lay down on the lip of the pool and drank long and deep of its water. "Tastes good to me," he murmured, lifting his head and gazing across the pool at the side-hill, while he wiped his mouth with the back of his hand. The side-hill attracted his attention. Still lying on his stomach, he studied the hill formation long and carefully. It was a practised eye that travelled up the slope to the crumbling canyon-wall and back and down again to the edge of the pool. He scrambled to his feet and favored the side-hill with a second survey.

"Looks good to me," he concluded, picking up his pick and shovel and gold-pan.

He crossed the stream below the pool, stepping agilely from stone to stone. Where the side-hill touched the water he dug up a shovelful of dirt and put it into the gold-pan. He squatted down, holding the pan in his two hands, and partly immersing it in the stream. Then he imparted to the pan a deft circular motion that sent the water sluicing in and out through the dirt and gravel. The larger and the lighter particles worked to the surface, and these, by a skilful dipping move-ment of the pan, he spilled out and over the edge. Occasionally, to expedite matters, he rested the pan and with his fingers raked out the large pebbles and pieces of rock.

The contents of the pan diminished rapidly until only fine dirt and the smallest bits of gravel remained. At this stage he began to work very deliberately and carefully. It was fine washing, and he washed fine and finer, with a keen scrutiny and delicate and fastidious touch. At last the pan seemed empty of everything but water; but with a quick semicircular flirt that sent the water flying over the shallow rim into the stream, he disclosed a layer of black sand on the bottom of the pan. So thin was this layer that it was like a streak of paint. He examined it closely. In the midst of it was a tiny golden speck. He dribbled a little water in over the depressed edge of the pan. With a quick flirt he sent the water sluicing across the bottom, turning the grains of black sand over and over. A second tiny golden speck rewarded his effort.

The washing had now become very fine—fine beyond all need of ordinary placer-mining. He worked the black sand, a small portion at a time, up the shallow rim of the pan. Each small portion he examined sharply, so that his eyes saw every grain of it before he allowed it to slide over the edge and away. Jealously, bit by bit, he let the black sand slip away. A golden speck, no larger than a pin-point, appeared on the rim, and by his manipulation of the water it returned to the bottom of the pan. And in such fashion another speck was disclosed, and another. Great was his care of them. Like a shepherd he herded his flock of golden specks so that not one should be lost. At last, of the pan of dirt nothing remained but his golden herd. He counted it, and then, after all his labor, sent it flying out of the pan with one final swirl of water.

But his blue eyes were shining with desire as he rose to his feet. "Seven," he muttered aloud, asserting the sum of the specks for which he had toiled so hard and which he had so wantonly thrown away. "Seven," he repeated, with the emphasis of one trying to impress a number on his memory.

He stood still a long while, surveying the hill-side. In his eyes was a curiosity, new-aroused and burning. There was an exultance about his bearing and a keenness like that of a hunting animal catching the fresh scent of game.

He moved down the stream a few steps and took a second panful of dirt.

Again came the careful washing, the jealous herding of the golden specks, and the wantonness with which he sent them flying into the stream when he had counted their number.

"Five," he muttered, and repeated, "five."

He could not forbear another survey of the hill before filling the pan farther down the stream. His golden herds diminished. "Four, three, two, two, one," were his memory-tabulations as he moved down the stream. When but one speck of gold rewarded his washing, he stopped and built a fire of dry twigs. Into this he thrust the gold-pan and burned it till it was blue-black. He held up the pan and examined it critically. Then he nodded approbation. Against such a color-background he could defy the tiniest yellow speck to elude him.

Still moving down the stream, he panned again. A single speck was his reward. A third pan contained no gold at all. Not satisfied with this, he panned three times again, taking his shovels of dirt within a foot of one another. Each pan proved empty of gold, and the fact, instead of discouraging him, seemed to give him satisfaction. His elation increased with each barren washing, until he arose, exclaiming jubilantly:

"If it ain't the real thing, may God knock off my head with sour apples!"

Returning to where he had started operations, he began to pan up the stream. At first his golden herds increased—increased prodigiously. "Fourteen, eighteen, twenty-one, twenty-six," ran his memory tabulations. Just above the pool he struck his richest pan—thirty-five colors.

"Almost enough to save," he remarked regretfully as he allowed the water to sweep them away.

The sun climbed to the top of the sky. The man worked on. Pan by pan, he went up the stream, the tally of results steadily decreasing.

"It's just booful, the way it peters out," he exulted when a shovelful of dirt contained no more than a single speck of gold.

And when no specks at all were found in several pans, he straightened up and favored the hillside with a confident glance.

"Ah, ha! Mr. Pocket!" he cried out, as though to an auditor hidden somewhere above him beneath the surface of the slope. "Ah, ha! Mr. Pocket! I'm a-comin', I'm a-comin', an' I'm shorely gwine to get yer! You heah me, Mr. Pocket? I'm gwine to get yer as shore as punkins ain't cauliflowers!"

He turned and flung a measuring glance at the sun poised above him in the azure of the cloudless sky. Then he went down the canyon, following the line of shovel-holes he had made in filling the pans. He crossed the stream below the pool and disappeared through the green screen. There was little opportunity for the spirit of the place to return with its quietude and repose, for the man's voice, raised in ragtime song, still dominated the canyon with possession.

After a time, with a greater clashing of steel-shod feet on rock, he returned. The green screen was tremendously agitated. It surged back and forth in the throes of a struggle. There was a loud grating and clanging of metal. The man's voice leaped to a higher pitch and was sharp with imperativeness. A large body plunged and panted. There was a snapping and ripping and rending, and amid a shower of falling leaves a horse burst through the screen. On its back was a pack, and from this trailed broken vines and torn creepers. The animal gazed with astonished eyes at the scene into which it had been precipitated, then dropped its head to the grass and began contentedly to graze. A second horse scrambled into view, slipping once on the mossy rocks and regaining equilibrium when its hoofs sank into the yielding surface of the meadow. It was riderless, though on its back was a high-horned Mexican saddle, scarred and discolored by long usage.

The man brought up the rear. He threw off pack and saddle, with an eye to camp location, and gave the animals their freedom to graze. He unpacked his food and got out frying-pan and coffee-pot. He gathered an armful of dry wood, and with a few stones made a place for his fire.

"My!" he said, "but I've got an appetite. I could scoff iron-filings an' horseshoe nails an' thank you kindly, ma'am, for a second helpin'."

He straightened up, and, while he reached for matches in the pocket of his overalls, his eyes travelled across the pool to the side-hill. His fingers had clutched the match-box, but they relaxed their hold and the hand came out empty. The man wavered perceptibly. He looked at his preparations for cooking and he looked at the hill.

"Guess I'll take another whack at her," he concluded, starting to cross the stream.

"They ain't no sense in it, I know," he mumbled apologetically. "But keepin' grub back an hour ain't goin' to hurt none, I reckon."

A few feet back from his first line of test-pans he started a second line. The sun dropped down the western sky, the shadows lengthened, but the man worked on. He began a third line of test-pans. He was cross-cutting the hillside, line by line, as he ascended. The centre of each line produced the richest pans, while the ends came where no colors showed in the pan. And as he ascended the hill-side the lines grew perceptibly shorter. The regularity with which their length diminished served to indicate that somewhere up the slope the last line would be so short as to have scarcely length at all, and that beyond could come only a point. The design was growing into an inverted "V." The converging sides of this "V" marked the boundaries of the gold-bearing dirt.

The apex of the "V" was evidently the man's goal. Often he ran his eye along the converging sides and on up the hill, trying to divine the apex, the point where the gold-bearing dirt must cease. Here resided "Mr. Pocket"—for so the man familiarly addressed the imaginary point above him on the slope, crying out:

"Come down out o' that, Mr. Pocket! Be right smart an' agreeable, an' come down!"

"All right," he would add later, in a voice resigned to determination. "All right, Mr. Pocket. It's plain to me I got to come right up an' snatch you out bald-headed. An' I'll do it! I'll do it!" he would threaten still later.

Each pan he carried down to the water to wash, and as he went higher up the hill the pans grew richer, until he began to save the gold in an empty baking-powder can which he carried carelessly in his hip-pocket. So engrossed was he in his toil that he did not notice the long twilight of oncoming night. It was not until he tried vainly to see the gold colors in the bottom of the pan that he realized the passage of time. He straightened up abruptly. An expression of whimsical wonderment and awe overspread his face as he drawled:

"Gosh darn my buttons! if I didn't plumb forget dinner!"

He stumbled across the stream in the darkness and lighted his long-delayed fire. Flapjacks and bacon and warmed-over beans constituted his supper. Then he smoked a pipe by the smouldering coals, listening to the night noises and watching the moonlight stream through the canyon. After that he unrolled his bed, took off his heavy shoes, and pulled the blankets up to his chin. His face showed white in the moonlight, like the face of a corpse. But it was a corpse that knew its resurrection, for the man rose suddenly on one elbow and gazed across at his hillside.

"Good night, Mr. Pocket," he called sleepily. "Good night."

He slept through the early gray of morning until the direct rays of the sun smote his closed eyelids, when he awoke with a start and looked about him until he had established the continuity of his existence and identified his present self with the days previously lived.

To dress, he had merely to buckle on his shoes. He glanced at his fireplace and at his hillside, wavered, but fought down the temptation and started the fire.

"Keep yer shirt on, Bill; keep yer shirt on," he admonished himself. "What's the good of rushin'? No use in gettin' all het up an' sweaty. Mr. Pocket'll wait for you. He ain't a-runnin' away before you can get yer breakfast. Now, what you want, Bill, is something fresh in yer bill o' fare. So it's up to you to go an' get it."

He cut a short pole at the water's edge and drew from one of his pockets a bit of line and a draggled fly that had once been a royal coachman.

"Mebbe they'll bite in the early morning," he muttered, as he made his first cast into the pool. And a moment later he was gleefully crying: "What'd I tell you, eh? What'd I tell you?"

He had no reel, nor any inclination to waste time, and by main strength, and swiftly, he drew out of the water a flashing ten-inch trout. Three more, caught in rapid succession, furnished his breakfast. When he came to the stepping-stones on his way to his hillside, he was struck by a sudden thought, and paused.

"I'd just better take a hike down-stream a ways," he said. "There's no tellin' what cuss may be snoopin' around."

But he crossed over on the stones, and with a "I really oughter take that hike," the need of the precaution passed out of his mind and he fell to work.

At nightfall he straightened up. The small of his back was stiff from stooping toil, and as he put his hand behind him to soothe the protesting muscles, he said:

"Now what d'ye think of that, by damn? I clean forgot my dinner again! If I don't watch out, I'll sure be degeneratin' into a two-meal-a-day crank."

"Pockets is the damnedest things I ever see for makin' a man absent-minded," he communed that night, as he crawled into his blankets. Nor did he forget to call up the hillside, "Good night, Mr. Pocket! Good night!"

Rising with the sun, and snatching a hasty breakfast, he was early at work. A fever seemed to be growing in him, nor did the increasing richness of the test-pans allay this fever. There was a flush in his cheek other than that made by the heat of the sun, and he was oblivious to fatigue and the passage of time. When he filled a pan with dirt, he ran down the hill to wash it; nor could he forbear running up the hill again, panting and stumbling profanely, to refill the pan.

He was now a hundred yards from the water, and the inverted "V" was assuming definite proportions. The width of the pay-dirt steadily decreased, and the man extended in his mind's eye the sides of the "V" to their meeting-place far up the hill. This was his goal, the apex of the "V," and he panned many times to locate it.

"Just about two yards above that manzanita bush an' a yard to the right," he finally concluded.

Then the temptation seized him. "As plain as the nose on your face," he said, as he abandoned his laborious cross-cutting and climbed to the indicated apex. He filled a pan and carried it down the hill to wash. It contained no trace of gold. He dug deep, and he dug shallow, filling and washing a dozen pans, and was unrewarded even by the tiniest golden speck. He was enraged at having yielded to the temptation, and cursed himself blasphemously and pridelessly. Then he went down the hill and took up the cross-cutting.

"Slow an' certain, Bill; slow an' certain," he crooned. "Short-cuts to fortune ain't in your line, an' it's about time you know it. Get wise, Bill; get wise. Slow an' certain's the only hand you can play; so go to it, an' keep to it, too."

As the cross-cuts decreased, showing that the sides of the "V" were converging, the depth of the "V" increased. The gold-trace was dipping into the hill. It was only at thirty inches beneath the surface that he could get colors in his pan. The dirt he found at twenty-five inches from the surface, and at thirty-five inches, yielded barren pans. At the base of the "V," by the water's edge, he had found the gold colors at the grass roots. The higher he went up the hill, the deeper the gold dipped. To dig a hole three feet deep in order to get one test-pan was a task of no mean magnitude; while between the man and the apex intervened an untold number of such holes to be dug. "An' there's no tellin' how much deeper it'll pitch," he sighed, in a moment's pause, while his fingers soothed his aching back.

Feverish with desire, with aching back and stiffening muscles, with pick and shovel gouging and mauling the soft brown earth, the man toiled up the hill. Before him was the smooth slope, spangled with flowers and made sweet with their breath. Behind him was devastation. It looked like some terrible eruption breaking out on the smooth skin of the hill. His slow progress was like that of a slug, befouling beauty with a monstrous trail.

Though the dipping gold-trace increased the man's work, he found consolation in the increasing richness of the pans. Twenty cents, thirty cents, fifty cents, sixty cents, were the values of the gold found in the pans, and at nightfall he washed his banner pan, which gave him a dollar's worth of gold-dust from a shovelful of dirt.

"I'll just bet it's my luck to have some inquisitive cuss come buttin' in here on my pasture," he mumbled sleepily that night as he pulled the blankets up to his chin.

Suddenly he sat upright. "Bill!" he called sharply. "Now, listen to me, Bill; d'ye hear! It's up to you, to-morrow mornin', to mosey round an' see what you can see. Understand? To-morrow morning, an' don't you forget it!"

He yawned and glanced across at his side-hill. "Good night, Mr. Pocket," he called.

In the morning he stole a march on the sun, for he had finished breakfast when its first rays caught him, and he was climbing the wall of the canyon where it crumbled away and gave footing. From the outlook at the top he found himself in the midst of loneliness. As far as he could see, chain after chain of mountains heaved themselves into his vision. To the east his eyes, leaping the miles between range and range and between many ranges, brought up at last against the white-peaked Sierras—the main crest, where the backbone of the Western world reared itself against the sky. To the north and south he could see more distinctly the cross-systems that broke through the main trend of the sea of mountains. To the west the ranges fell away, one behind the other, diminishing and fading into the gentle foothills that, in turn, descended into the great valley which he could not see.

And in all that mighty sweep of earth he saw no sign of man nor of the handiwork of man—save only the torn bosom of the hillside at his feet. The man looked long and carefully. Once, far down his own canyon, he thought he saw in the air a faint hint of smoke. He looked again and decided that it was the purple haze of the hills made dark by a convolution of the canyon wall at its back.

"Hey, you, Mr. Pocket!" he called down into the canyon. "Stand out from under! I'm a-comin', Mr. Pocket! I'm a-comin'!"

The heavy brogans on the man's feet made him appear clumsy-footed, but he swung down from the giddy height as lightly and airily as a mountain goat. A rock, turning under his foot on the edge of the precipice, did not disconcert him. He seemed to know the precise time required for the turn to culminate in disaster, and in the meantime he utilized the false footing itself for the momentary earth-contact necessary to carry him on into safety. Where the earth sloped so steeply that it was impossible to stand for a second upright, the man did not hesitate. His foot pressed the impossible surface for but a fraction of the fatal second and gave him the bound that carried him onward. Again, where even the fraction of a second's footing was out of the question, he would swing his body past by a moment's hand-grip on a jutting knob of rock, a crevice, or a precariously rooted shrub. At last, with a wild leap and yell, he exchanged the face of the wall for an earth-slide and finished the descent in the midst of several tons of sliding earth and gravel.

His first pan of the morning washed out over two dollars in coarse gold. It was from the centre of the "V." To either side the diminution in the values of the pans was swift. His lines of cross-cutting holes were growing very short. The converging sides of the inverted "V" were only a few yards apart. Their meeting-point was only a few yards above him. But the pay-streak was dipping deeper and deeper into the earth. By early afternoon he was sinking the test-holes five feet before the pans could show the gold-trace.

For that matter, the gold-trace had become something more than a trace; it was a placer mine in itself, and the man resolved to come back after he had found the pocket and work over the ground. But the increasing richness of the pans began to worry him. By late afternoon the worth of the pans had grown to three and four dollars. The man scratched his head perplexedly and looked a few feet up the hill at the manzanita bush that marked approximately the apex of the "V." He nodded his head and said oracularly:

"It's one o' two things, Bill; one o' two things. Either Mr. Pocket's spilled himself all out an' down the hill, or else Mr. Pocket's that damned rich you maybe won't be able to carry him all away with you. And that'd be hell, wouldn't it, now?" He chuckled at contemplation of so pleasant a dilemma.

Nightfall found him by the edge of the stream, his eyes wrestling with the gathering darkness over the washing of a five-dollar pan.

"Wisht I had an electric light to go on working," he said.

He found sleep difficult that night. Many times he composed himself and closed his eyes for slumber to overtake him; but his blood pounded with too strong desire, and as many times his eyes opened and he murmured wearily, "Wisht it was sun-up."

Sleep came to him in the end, but his eyes were open with the first paling of the stars, and the gray of dawn caught him with breakfast finished and climbing the hillside in the direction of the secret abiding-place of Mr. Pocket.

The first cross-cut the man made, there was space for only three holes, so narrow had become the paystreak and so close was he to the fountainhead of the golden stream he had been following for four days.

"Be ca'm, Bill; be ca'm," he admonished himself, as he broke ground for the final hole where the sides of the "V" had at last come together in a point.

"I've got the almighty cinch on you, Mr. Pocket, an' you can't lose me," he said many times as he sank the hole deeper and deeper.

Four feet, five feet, six feet, he dug his way down into the earth. The digging grew harder. His pick grated on broken rock. He examined the rock. "Rotten quartz," was his conclusion as, with the shovel, he cleared the bottom of the hole of loose dirt. He attacked the crumbling quartz with the pick, bursting the disintegrating rock asunder with every stroke.

He thrust his shovel into the loose mass. His eye caught a gleam of yellow. He dropped the shovel and squatted suddenly on his heels. As a farmer rubs the clinging earth from fresh-dug potatoes, so the man, a piece of rotten quartz held in both hands, rubbed the dirt away.

"Sufferin' Sardanopolis!" he cried. "Lumps an' chunks of it! Lumps an' chunks of it!"

It was only half rock he held in his hand. The other half was virgin gold. He dropped it into his pan and examined another piece. Little yellow was to be seen, but with his strong fingers he crumbled the rotten quartz away till both hands were filled with glowing yellow. He rubbed the dirt away from fragment after fragment, tossing them into the gold-pan. It was a treasure-hole. So much had the quartz rotted away that there was less of it than there was of gold. Now and again he found a piece to which no rock clung—a piece that was all gold. A chunk, where the pick had laid open the heart of the gold, glittered like a handful of yellow jewels, and he cocked his head at it and slowly turned it around and over to observe the rich play of the light upon it.

"Talk about yer Too Much Gold diggin's!" the man snorted contemptuously. "Why, this diggin' 'd make it look like thirty cents. This diggin' is All Gold. An' right here an' now I name this yere canyon 'All Gold Canyon,' b' gosh!"

Still squatting on his heels, he continued examining the fragments and tossing them into the pan. Suddenly there came to him a premonition of danger. It seemed a shadow had fallen upon him. But there was no shadow. His heart had given a great jump up into his throat and was choking him. Then his blood slowly chilled and he felt the sweat of his shirt cold against his flesh.

He did not spring up nor look around. He did not move. He was considering the nature of the premonition he had received, trying to locate the source of the mysterious force that had warned him, striving to sense the imperative presence of the unseen thing that threatened him. There is an aura of things hostile, made manifest by messengers too refined for the senses to know; and this aura he felt, but knew not how he felt it. His was the feeling as when a cloud passes over the sun. It seemed that between him and life had passed something dark and smothering and menacing; a gloom, as it were, that swallowed up life and made for death—his death.

Every force of his being impelled him to spring up and confront the unseen danger, but his soul dominated the panic, and he remained squatting on his heels, in his hands a chunk of gold. He did not dare to look around, but he knew by now that there was something behind him and above him. He made believe to be interested in the gold in his hand. He examined it critically, turned it over and over, and rubbed the dirt from it. And all the time he knew that something behind him was looking at the gold over his shoulder.

Still feigning interest in the chunk of gold in his hand, he listened intently and he heard the breathing of the thing behind him. His eyes searched the ground in front of him for a weapon, but they saw only the uprooted gold, worthless to him now in his extremity. There was his pick, a handy weapon on occasion; but this was not such an occasion. The man realized his predicament. He was in a narrow hole that was seven feet deep. His head did not come to the surface of the ground. He was in a trap.

He remained squatting on his heels. He was quite cool and collected; but his mind, considering every factor, showed him only his helplessness. He continued rubbing the dirt from the quartz fragments and throwing the gold into the pan. There was nothing else for him to do. Yet he knew that he would have to rise up, sooner or later, and face the danger that breathed at his back. The minutes passed, and with the passage of each minute he knew that by so much he was nearer the time when he must stand up, or else—and his wet shirt went cold against his flesh again at the thought—or else he might receive death as he stooped there over his treasure.

Still he squatted on his heels, rubbing dirt from gold and debating in just what manner he should rise up. He might rise up with a rush and claw his way out of the hole to meet whatever threatened on the even footing above ground. Or he might rise up slowly and carelessly, and feign casually to discover the thing that breathed at his back. His instinct and every fighting fibre of his body favored the mad, clawing rush to the surface. His intellect, and the craft thereof, favored the slow and cautious meeting with the thing that menaced and which he could not see. And while he debated, a loud, crashing noise burst on his ear. At the same instant he received a stunning blow on the left side of the back, and from the point of impact felt a rush of flame through his flesh. He sprang up in the air, but halfway to his feet collapsed. His body crumpled in like a leaf withered in sudden heat, and he came down, his chest across his pan of gold, his face in the dirt and rock, his legs tangled and twisted because of the restricted space at the bottom of the hole. His legs twitched convulsively several times. His body was shaken as with a mighty ague. There was a slow expansion of the lungs, accompanied by a deep sigh. Then the air was slowly, very slowly, exhaled, and his body as slowly flattened itself down into inertness.

Above, revolver in hand, a man was peering down over the edge of the hole. He peered for a long time at the prone and motionless body beneath him. After a while the stranger sat down on the edge of the hole so that he could see into it, and rested the revolver on his knee. Reaching his hand into a pocket, he drew out a wisp of brown paper. Into this he dropped a few crumbs of tobacco. The combination became a cigarette, brown and squat, with the ends turned in. Not once did he take his eyes from the body at the bottom of the hole. He lighted the cigarette and drew its smoke into his lungs with a caressing intake of the breath. He smoked slowly. Once the cigarette went out and he relighted it. And all the while he studied the body beneath him.

In the end he tossed the cigarette stub away and rose to his feet. He moved to the edge of the hole. Spanning it, a hand resting on each edge, and with the revolver still in the right hand, he muscled his body down into the hole. While his feet were yet a yard from the bottom he released his hands and dropped down.

At the instant his feet struck bottom he saw the pocket-miner's arm leap out, and his own legs knew a swift, jerking grip that overthrew him. In the nature of the jump his revolver-hand was above his head. Swiftly as the grip had flashed about his legs, just as swiftly he brought the revolver down. He was still in the air, his fall in process of completion, when he pulled the trigger. The explosion was deafening in the confined space. The smoke filled the hole so that he could see nothing. He struck the bottom on his back, and like a cat's the pocket-miner's body was on top of him. Even as the miner's body passed on top, the stranger crooked in his right arm to fire; and even in that instant the miner, with a quick thrust of elbow, struck his wrist. The muzzle was thrown up and the bullet thudded into the dirt of the side of the hole.

The next instant the stranger felt the miner's hand grip his wrist. The struggle was now for the revolver. Each man strove to turn it against the other's body. The smoke in the hole was clearing. The stranger, lying on his back, was beginning to see dimly. But suddenly he was blinded by a handful of dirt deliberately flung into his eyes by his antagonist. In that moment of shock his grip on the revolver was broken. In the next moment he felt a smashing darkness descend upon his brain, and in the midst of the darkness even the darkness ceased.

But the pocket-miner fired again and again, until the revolver was empty. Then he tossed it from him and, breathing heavily, sat down on the dead man's legs.

The miner was sobbing and struggling for breath. "Measly skunk!" he panted; "a-campin' on my trail an' lettin' me do the work, an' then shootin' me in the back!"

He was half crying from anger and exhaustion. He peered at the face of the dead man. It was sprinkled with loose dirt and gravel, and it was difficult to distinguish the features.

"Never laid eyes on him before," the miner concluded his scrutiny. "Just a common an' ordinary thief, damn him! An' he shot me in the back! He shot me in the back!"

He opened his shirt and felt himself, front and back, on his left side.

"Went clean through, and no harm done!" he cried jubilantly. "I'll bet he aimed all right all right; but he drew the gun over when he pulled the trigger—the cuss! But I fixed 'm! Oh, I fixed 'm!"

His fingers were investigating the bullet-hole in his side, and a shade of regret passed over his face. "It's goin' to be stiffer'n hell," he said. "An' it's up to me to get mended an' get out o' here."

He crawled out of the hole and went down the hill to his camp. Half an hour later he returned, leading his pack-horse. His open shirt disclosed the rude bandages with which he had dressed his wound. He was slow and awkward with his left-hand movements, but that did not prevent his using the arm.

The bight of the pack-rope under the dead man's shoulders enabled him to heave the body out of the hole. Then he set to work gathering up his gold. He worked steadily for several hours, pausing often to rest his stiffening shoulder and to exclaim:

"He shot me in the back, the measly skunk! He shot me in the back!"

When his treasure was quite cleaned up and wrapped securely into a number of blanket-covered parcels, he made an estimate of its value.

"Four hundred pounds, or I'm a Hottentot," he concluded. "Say two hundred in quartz an' dirt—that leaves two hundred pounds of gold. Bill! Wake up! Two hundred pounds of gold! Forty thousand dollars! An' it's yourn—all yourn!"

He scratched his head delightedly and his fingers blundered into an unfamiliar groove. They quested along it for several inches. It was a crease through his scalp where the second bullet had ploughed.

He walked angrily over to the dead man.

"You would, would you?" he bullied. "You would, eh? Well, I fixed you good an' plenty, an' I'll give you decent burial, too. That's more'n you'd have done for me."

He dragged the body to the edge of the hole and toppled it in. It struck the bottom with a dull crash, on its side, the face twisted up to the light. The miner peered down at it.

"An' you shot me in the back!" he said accusingly.

With pick and shovel he filled the hole. Then he loaded the gold on his horse. It was too great a load for the animal, and when he had gained his camp he transferred part of it to his saddle-horse. Even so, he was compelled to abandon a portion of his outfit—pick and shovel and gold-pan, extra food and cooking utensils, and divers odds and ends.

The sun was at the zenith when the man forced the horses at the screen of vines and creepers. To climb the huge boulders the animals were compelled to uprear and struggle blindly through the tangled mass of vegetation. Once the saddle-horse fell heavily and the man removed the pack to get the animal on its feet. After it started on its way again the man thrust his head out from among the leaves and peered up at the hillside.

"The measly skunk!" he said, and disappeared.

There was a ripping and tearing of vines and boughs. The trees surged back and forth, marking the passage of the animals through the midst of them. There was a clashing of steel-shod hoofs on stone, and now and again an oath or a sharp cry of command. Then the voice of the man was raised in song:—

> "Tu'n around an' tu'n yo' face
> Untoe them sweet hills of grace
> (D' pow'rs of sin yo' am scornin'!).
> Look about an' look aroun',
> Fling yo' sin-pack on d' groun'
> (Yo' will meet wid d' Lord in d' mornin'!)."

The song grew faint and fainter, and through the silence crept back the spirit of the place. The stream once more drowsed and whispered; the hum of the mountain bees rose sleepily. Down through the perfume-weighted air fluttered the snowy fluffs of the cottonwoods. The butterflies drifted in and out among the trees, and over all blazed the quiet sunshine. Only remained the hoof-marks in the meadow and the torn hillside to mark the boisterous trail of the life that had broken the peace of the place and passed on.

# THE APOSTATE

*Now I wake me up to work;*
*I pray the Lord I may not shirk.*
*If I should die before the night,*
*I pray the Lord my work's all right.*
                                    *Amen.*

"IF YOU DON'T GIT UP, Johnny, I won't give you a bite to eat!"

The threat had no effect on the boy. He clung stubbornly to sleep, fighting for its oblivion as the dreamer fights for his dream. The boy's hands loosely clenched themselves, and he made feeble, spasmodic blows at the air. These blows were intended for his mother, but she betrayed practised familiarity in avoiding them as she shook him roughly by the shoulder.

"Lemme 'lone!"

It was a cry that began, muffled, in the deeps of sleep, that swiftly rushed upward, like a wail, into passionate belligerence, and that died away and sank down into an inarticulate whine. It was a bestial cry, as of a soul in torment, filled with infinite protest and pain.

But she did not mind. She was a sad-eyed, tired-faced woman, and she had grown used to this task, which she repeated every day of her life. She got a grip on the bed-clothes and tried to strip them down; but the boy, ceasing his punching, clung to them desperately. In a huddle, at the foot of the bed, he still remained covered. Then she tried dragging the bedding to the floor. The boy opposed her. She braced herself. Hers was the superior weight, and the boy and bedding gave, the former instinctively following the latter in order to shelter against the chill of the room that bit into his body.

As he toppled on the edge of the bed it seemed that he must fall head-first to the floor. But consciousness fluttered up in him. He righted himself and for a moment perilously balanced. Then he struck the floor on his feet. On the instant his mother seized him by the shoulders and shook him. Again his fists struck out, this time with more force and directness. At the same time his eyes opened. She released him. He was awake.

"All right," he mumbled.

She caught up the lamp and hurried out, leaving him in darkness.

"You'll be docked," she warned back to him.

He did not mind the darkness. When he had got into his clothes, he went out into the kitchen. His tread was very heavy for so thin and light a boy. His legs dragged with their own weight, which seemed unreasonable because they were such skinny legs. He drew a broken-bottomed chair to the table.

"Johnny!" his mother called sharply.

He arose as sharply from the chair, and, without a word, went to the sink. It was a greasy, filthy sink. A smell came up from the outlet. He took no notice of it. That a sink should smell was to him part of the natural order, just as it was a part of the natural order that the soap should be grimy with dish-water and hard to lather. Nor did he try very hard to make it lather. Several splashes of the cold water from the running faucet completed the function. He did not wash his teeth. For that matter he had never seen a tooth-brush, nor did he know that there existed beings in the world who were guilty of so great a foolishness as tooth washing.

"You might wash yourself wunst a day without bein' told," his mother complained.

She was holding a broken lid on the pot as she poured two cups of coffee. He made no remark, for this was a standing quarrel between them, and the one thing upon which his mother was hard as adamant. "Wunst" a day it was compulsory that he should wash his face. He dried himself on a greasy towel, damp and dirty and ragged, that left his face covered with shreds of lint.

"I wish we didn't live so far away," she said, as he sat down. "I try to do the best I can. You know that. But a dollar on the rent is such a savin', an' we've more room here. You know that."

He scarcely followed her. He had heard it all before, many times. The range of her thought was limited, and she was ever harking back to the hardship worked upon them by living so far from the mills.

"A dollar means more grub," he remarked sententiously. "I'd sooner do the walkin' an' git the grub."

He ate hurriedly, half chewing the bread and washing the un-masticated chunks down with coffee. The hot and muddy liquid went by the name of coffee. Johnny thought it was coffee—and excellent coffee. That was one of the few of life's illusions that remained to him. He had never drunk real coffee in his life.

In addition to the bread, there was a small piece of cold pork. His mother refilled his cup with coffee. As he was finishing the bread, he began to watch if more was forthcoming. She intercepted his questioning glance.

"Now, don't be hoggish, Johnny," was her comment. "You've had your share. Your brothers an' sisters are smaller'n you."

He did not answer the rebuke. He was not much of a talker. Also, he ceased his hungry glancing for more. He was uncomplaining, with a patience that was as terrible as the school in which it had been learned. He finished his coffee, wiped his mouth on the back of his hand, and started to rise.

"Wait a second," she said hastily. "I guess the loaf kin stand you another slice—a thin un."

There was legerdemain in her actions. With all the seeming of cutting a slice from the loaf for him, she put loaf and slice back in the bread box and conveyed to him one of her own two slices. She believed she had deceived him, but he had noted her sleight-of-hand. Nevertheless, he took the bread shamelessly. He had a philosophy that his mother, what of her chronic sickliness, was not much of an eater anyway.

She saw that he was chewing the bread dry, and reached over and emptied her coffee cup into his.

"Don't set good somehow on my stomach this morning," she explained.

A distant whistle, prolonged and shrieking, brought both of them to their feet. She glanced at the tin alarm-clock on the shelf. The hands stood at half-past five. The rest of the factory world was just arousing from sleep. She drew a shawl about her shoulders, and on her head put a dingy hat, shapeless and ancient.

"We've got to run," she said, turning the wick of the lamp and blowing down the chimney.

They groped their way out and down the stairs. It was clear and cold, and Johnny shivered at the first contact with the outside air. The stars had not yet begun to pale in the sky, and the city lay in blackness. Both Johnny and his mother shuffled their feet as they walked. There was no ambition in the leg muscles to swing the feet clear of the ground.

After fifteen silent minutes, his mother turned off to the right.

"Don't be late," was her final warning from out of the dark that was swallowing her up.

He made no response, steadily keeping on his way. In the factory quarter, doors were opening everywhere, and he was soon one of a multitude that pressed onward through the dark. As he entered the factory gate the whistle blew again. He glanced at the east. Across a ragged sky-line of housetops a pale light was beginning to creep. This much he saw of the day as he turned his back upon it and joined his work gang.

He took his place in one of many long rows of machines. Before him, above a bin filled with small bobbins, were large bobbins revolving rapidly. Upon these he wound the jute-twine of the small bobbins. The work was simple. All that was required was celerity. The small bobbins were emptied so rapidly, and there were so many large bobbins that did the emptying, that there were no idle moments.

He worked mechanically. When a small bobbin ran out, he used his left hand for a brake, stopping the large bobbin and at the same time, with thumb and forefinger, catching the flying end of twine. Also, at the same time, with his right hand, he caught up the loose twine-end of a small bobbin. These various acts with both hands were performed simultaneously and swiftly. Then there would come a flash of his hands as he looped the weaver's knot and released the bobbin. There was nothing difficult about weaver's knots. He once boasted he could tie them in his sleep. And for that matter, he sometimes did, toiling centuries long in a single night at tying an endless succession of weaver's knots.

Some of the boys shirked, wasting time and machinery by not replacing the small bobbins when they ran out. And there was an overseer to prevent this. He caught Johnny's neighbor at the trick, and boxed his ears.

"Look at Johnny there—why ain't you like him?" the overseer wrathfully demanded.

Johnny's bobbins were running full blast, but he did not thrill at the indirect praise. There had been a time . . . but that was long ago, very long ago. His apathetic face was expressionless as he listened to himself being held up as a shining example. He was the perfect worker. He knew that. He had been told so, often. It was a commonplace, and besides it didn't seem to mean anything to him any more. From the perfect worker he had evolved into the perfect machine. When his work went wrong, it was with him as with the machine, due to faulty material. It would have been as possible for a perfect nail-die to cut imperfect nails as for him to make a mistake.

And small wonder. There had never been a time when he had not been in intimate relationship with machines. Machinery had almost been bred into him, and at any rate he had been brought up on it. Twelve years before, there had been a small flutter of excitement in the loom room of this very mill. Johnny's mother had fainted. They stretched her out on the floor in the midst of the shrieking machines. A couple of elderly women were called from their looms. The foreman assisted. And in a few minutes there was one more soul in the loom room than had entered by the doors. It was Johnny, born with the pounding, crashing roar of the looms in his ears, drawing with his first breath the warm, moist air that was thick with flying lint. He had coughed that first day in order to rid his lungs of the lint; and for the same reason he had coughed ever since.

The boy alongside of Johnny whimpered and sniffed. The boy's face was convulsed with hatred for the overseer who kept a threatening eye on him from a distance; but every bobbin was running full. The boy yelled terrible oaths into the whirling bobbins before him; but the sound did not carry half a dozen feet, the roaring of the room holding it in and containing it like a wall.

Of all this Johnny took no notice. He had a way of accepting things. Besides, things grow monotonous by repetition, and this particular happening he had witnessed many times. It seemed to him as useless to oppose the overseer as to defy the will of a machine. Machines were made to go in certain ways and to perform certain tasks. It was the same with the overseer.

But at eleven o'clock there was excitement in the room. In an apparently occult way the excitement instantly permeated everywhere. The one-legged boy who worked on the other side of Johnny bobbed swiftly across the floor to a bin truck that stood empty. Into this he dived out of sight, crutch and all. The superintendent of the mill was coming along, accompanied by a young man. He was well dressed and wore a starched shirt—a gentleman, in Johnny's classification of men, and also, "the Inspector."

He looked sharply at the boys as he passed along. Sometimes he stopped and asked questions. When he did so, he was compelled to shout at the top of his lungs, at which moments his face was ludicrously contorted with the strain of making himself heard. His quick eye noted the empty machine alongside of Johnny's, but he said nothing. Johnny also caught his eye, and he stopped abruptly. He caught Johnny by the arm to draw him back a step from the machine; but with an exclamation of surprise he released the arm.

"Pretty skinny," the superintendent laughed anxiously.

"Pipe stems," was the answer. "Look at those legs. The boy's got the rickets—incipient, but he's got them. If epilepsy doesn't get him in the end, it will be because tuberculosis gets him first."

Johnny listened, but did not understand. Furthermore he was not interested in future ills. There was an immediate and more serious ill that threatened him in the form of the inspector.

"Now, my boy, I want you to tell me the truth," the inspector said, or shouted, bending close to the boy's ear to make him hear. "How old are you?"

"Fourteen," Johnny lied, and he lied with the full force of his lungs. So loudly did he lie that it started him off in a dry, hacking cough that lifted the lint which had been settling in his lungs all morning.

"Looks sixteen at least," said the superintendent.

"Or sixty," snapped the inspector.

"He's always looked that way."

"How long?" asked the inspector, quickly.

"For years. Never gets a bit older."

"Or younger, I dare say. I suppose he's worked here all those years?"

"Off and on—but that was before the new law was passed," the superintendent hastened to add.

"Machine idle?" the inspector asked, pointing at the unoccupied machine beside Johnny's, in which the part-filled bobbins were flying like mad.

"Looks that way." The superintendent motioned the overseer to him and shouted in his ear and pointed at the machine. "Machine's idle," he reported back to the inspector.

They passed on, and Johnny returned to his work, relieved in that the ill had been averted. But the one-legged boy was not so fortunate. The sharp-eyed inspector haled him out at arm's length from the bin truck. His lips were quivering, and his face had all the expression of one upon whom was fallen profound and irremediable disaster. The overseer looked astounded, as though for the first time he had laid eyes on the boy, while the superintendent's face expressed shock and displeasure.

"I know him," the inspector said. "He's twelve years old. I've had him discharged from three factories inside the year. This makes the fourth."

He turned to the one-legged boy. "You promised me, word and honor, that you'd go to school."

The one-legged boy burst into tears. "Please, Mr. Inspector, two babies died on us, and we're awful poor."

"What makes you cough that way?" the inspector demanded, as though charging him with crime.

And as in denial of guilt, the one-legged boy replied: "It ain't nothin'. I jes' caught a cold last week, Mr. Inspector, that's all."

In the end the one-legged boy went out of the room with the inspector, the latter accompanied by the anxious and protesting superintendent. After that monotony settled down again. The long morning and the longer afternoon wore away and the whistle blew for quitting time. Darkness had already fallen when Johnny passed out through the factory gate. In the interval the sun had made a golden ladder of the sky, flooded the world with its gracious warmth, and dropped down and disappeared in the west behind a ragged sky-line of housetops.

Supper was the family meal of the day—the one meal at which Johnny encountered his younger brothers and sisters. It partook of the nature of an encounter, to him, for he was very old, while they were distressingly young. He had no patience with their excessive and amazing juvenility. He did not understand it. His own childhood was too far behind him. He was like an old and irritable man, annoyed by the turbulence of their young spirits that was to him arrant silliness. He glowered silently over his food, finding compensation in the thought that they would soon have to go to work. That would take the edge off of them and make them sedate and dignified—like him. Thus it was, after the fashion of the human, that Johnny made of himself a yardstick with which to measure the universe.

During the meal, his mother explained in various ways and with infinite repetition that she was trying to do the best she could; so that it was with relief, the scant meal ended, that Johnny shoved back his chair and arose. He debated for a moment between bed and the front door, and finally went out the latter. He did not go far. He sat down on the stoop, his knees drawn up and his narrow shoulders drooping forward, his elbows on his knees and the palms of his hands supporting his chin.

As he sat there, he did no thinking. He was just resting. So far as his mind was concerned, it was asleep. His brothers and sisters came out, and with other children played noisily about him. An electric globe on the corner lighted their frolics. He was peevish and irritable, that they knew; but the spirit of adventure lured them into teasing him. They joined hands before him, and, keeping time with their bodies, chanted in his face weird and uncomplimentary doggerel. At first he snarled curses at them—curses he had learned from the lips of various foremen. Finding this futile, and remembering his dignity, he relapsed into dogged silence.

His brother Will, next to him in age, having just passed his tenth birthday, was the ring-leader. Johnny did not possess particularly kindly feelings toward him. His life had early been embittered by continual giving over and giving way to Will. He had a definite feeling that Will was greatly in his debt and was ungrateful about it. In his own playtime, far back in the dim past, he had been robbed of a large part of that playtime by being compelled to take care of Will. Will was a baby then, and then, as now, their mother had spent her days in the mills. To Johnny had fallen the part of little father and little mother as well.

Will seemed to show the benefit of the giving over and the giving way. He was well-built, fairly rugged, as tall as his elder brother and even heavier. It was as though the life-blood of the one had been diverted into the other's veins. And in spirits it was the same. Johnny was jaded, worn out, without resilience, while his younger brother seemed bursting and spilling over with exuberance.

The mocking chant rose louder and louder. Will leaned closer as he danced, thrusting out his tongue. Johnny's left arm shot out and caught the other around the neck. At the same time he rapped his bony fist to the other's nose. It was a pathetically bony fist, but that it was sharp to hurt was evidenced by the squeal of pain it produced. The other children were uttering frightened cries, while Johnny's sister, Jennie, had dashed into the house.

He thrust Will from him, kicked him savagely on the shins, then reached for him and slammed him face downward in the dirt. Nor did he release him till the face had been rubbed into the dirt several times. Then the mother arrived, an anæmic whirlwind of solicitude and maternal wrath.

"Why can't he leave me alone?" was Johnny's reply to her upbraiding. "Can't he see I'm tired?"

"I'm as big as you," Will raged in her arms, his face a mess of tears, dirt, and blood. "I'm as big as you now, an' I'm goin' to git bigger. Then I'll lick you—see if I don't."

"You ought to be to work, seein' how big you are," Johnny snarled. "That's what's the matter with you. You ought to be to work. An' it's up to your ma to put you to work."

"But he's too young," she protested. "He's only a little boy."

"I was younger'n him when I started to work."

Johnny's mouth was open, further to express the sense of unfairness that he felt, but the mouth closed with a snap. He turned gloomily on his heel and stalked into the house and to bed. The door of his room was open to let in warmth from the kitchen. As he undressed in the semi-darkness he could hear his mother talking with a neighbor woman who had dropped in. His mother was crying, and her speech was punctuated with spiritless sniffles.

"I can't make out what's gittin' into Johnny," he could hear her say. "He didn't used to be this way. He was a patient little angel."

"An' he *is* a good boy," she hastened to defend. "He's worked faithful, an' he did go to work too young. But it wasn't my fault. I do the best I can, I'm sure."

Prolonged sniffling from the kitchen, and Johnny murmured to himself as his eyelids closed down, "You betcher life I've worked faithful."

The next morning he was torn bodily by his mother from the grip of sleep. Then came the meagre breakfast, the tramp through the dark, and the pale glimpse of day across the housetops as he turned his back on it and went in through the factory gate. It was another day, of all the days, and all the days were alike.

And yet there had been variety in his life—at the times he changed from one job to another, or was taken sick. When he was six, he was little mother and father to Will and the other children still younger. At seven he went into the mills—winding bobbins. When he was eight, he got work in another mill. His new job was marvellously easy. All he had to do was to sit down with a little stick in his hand and guide a stream of cloth that flowed past him. This stream of cloth came out of the maw of a machine, passed over a hot roller, and went on its way elsewhere. But he sat always in the one place, beyond the reach of daylight, a gas-jet flaring over him, himself part of the mechanism.

He was very happy at that job, in spite of the moist heat, for he was still young and in possession of dreams and illusions. And wonderful dreams he dreamed as he watched the steaming cloth streaming endlessly by. But there was no exercise about the work, no call upon his mind, and he dreamed less and less, while his mind grew torpid and drowsy. Nevertheless, he earned two dollars a week, and two dollars represented the difference between acute starvation and chronic underfeeding.

But when he was nine, he lost his job. Measles was the cause of it. After he recovered, he got work in a glass factory. The pay was better, and the work demanded skill. It was piece-work, and the more skilful he was, the bigger wages he earned. Here was incentive. And under this incentive he developed into a remarkable worker.

It was simple work, the tying of glass stoppers into small bottles. At his waist he carried a bundle of twine. He held the bottles between his knees so that he might work with both hands. Thus, in a sitting position and bending over his own knees, his narrow shoulders grew humped and his chest was contracted for ten hours each day. This was not good for the lungs, but he tied three hundred dozen bottles a day.

The superintendent was very proud of him, and brought visitors to look at him. In ten hours three hundred dozen bottles passed through his hands. This meant that he had attained machine-like perfection. All waste movements were eliminated. Every motion of his thin arms, every movement of a muscle in the thin fingers, was swift and accurate. He worked at high tension, and the result was that he grew nervous. At night his muscles twitched in his sleep, and in the daytime he could not relax and rest. He remained keyed up and his muscles continued to twitch. Also he grew sallow and his lint-cough grew worse. Then pneumonia laid hold of the feeble lungs within the contracted chest, and he lost his job in the glass-works.

Now he had returned to the jute mills where he had first begun with winding bobbins. But promotion was waiting for him. He was a good worker. He would next go on the starcher, and later he would go into the loom room. There was nothing after that except increased efficiency.

The machinery ran faster than when he had first gone to work, and his mind ran slower. He no longer dreamed at all, though his earlier years had been full of dreaming. Once he had been in love. It was when he first began guiding the cloth over the hot roller, and it was with the daughter of the superintendent. She was much older than he, a young woman, and he had seen her at a distance only a paltry half-dozen times. But that made no difference. On the surface of the cloth stream that poured past him, he pictured radiant futures wherein he performed prodigies of toil, invented miraculous machines, won to the mastership of the mills, and in the end took her in his arms and kissed her soberly on the brow.

But that was all in the long ago, before he had grown too old and tired to love. Also, she had married and gone away, and his mind had gone to sleep. Yet it had been a wonderful experience, and he used often to look back upon it as other men and women look back upon the time they believed in fairies. He had never believed in fairies nor Santa Claus; but he had believed implicitly in the smiling future his imagination had wrought into the steaming cloth stream.

He had become a man very early in life. At seven, when he drew his first wages, began his adolescence. A certain feeling of independence crept up in him, and the relationship between him and his mother changed. Somehow, as an earner and breadwinner, doing his own work in the world, he was more like an equal with her. Manhood, full-blown manhood, had come when he was eleven, at which time he had gone to work on the night shift for six months. No child works on the night shift and remains a child.

There had been several great events in his life. One of these had been when his mother bought some California prunes. Two others had been the two times when she cooked custard. Those had been events. He remembered them kindly. And at that time his mother had told him of a blissful dish she would sometime make—"floating island," she had called it, "better than custard." For years he had looked forward to the day when he would sit down to the table with floating island before him, until at last he had relegated the idea of it to the limbo of unattainable ideals.

Once he found a silver quarter lying on the sidewalk. That, also, was a great event in his life, withal a tragic one. He knew his duty on the instant the silver flashed on his eyes, before even he had picked it up. At home, as usual, there was not enough to eat, and home he should have taken it as he did his wages every Saturday night. Right conduct in this case was obvious; but he never had any spending of his money, and he was suffering from candy hunger. He was ravenous for the sweets that only on red-letter days he had ever tasted in his life.

He did not attempt to deceive himself. He knew it was sin, and deliberately he sinned when he went on a fifteen-cent candy debauch. Ten cents he saved for a future orgy; but not being accustomed to the carrying of money, he lost the ten cents. This occurred at the time when he was suffering all the torments of conscience, and it was to him an act of divine retribution. He had a frightened sense of the closeness of an awful and wrathful God. God had seen, and God had been swift to punish, denying him even the full wages of sin.

In memory he always looked back upon that event as the one

great criminal deed of his life, and at the recollection his conscience always awoke and gave him another twinge. It was the one skeleton in his closet. Also, being so made and circumstanced, he looked back upon the deed with regret. He was dissatisfied with the manner in which he had spent the quarter. He could have invested it better, and, out of his later knowledge of the quickness of God, he would have beaten God out by spending the whole quarter at one fell swoop. In retrospect he spent the quarter a thousand times, and each time to better advantage.

There was one other memory of the past, dim and faded, but stamped into his soul everlasting by the savage feet of his father. It was more like a nightmare than a remembered vision of a concrete thing—more like the race-memory of man that makes him fall in his sleep and that goes back to his arboreal ancestry.

This particular memory never came to Johnny in broad daylight when he was wide awake. It came at night, in bed, at the moment that his consciousness was sinking down and losing itself in sleep. It always aroused him to frightened wakefulness, and for the moment, in the first sickening start, it seemed to him that he lay crosswise on the foot of the bed. In the bed were the vague forms of his father and mother. He never saw what his father looked like. He had but one impression of his father, and that was that he had savage and pitiless feet.

His earlier memories lingered with him, but he had no late memories. All days were alike. Yesterday or last year were the same as a thousand years—or a minute. Nothing ever happened. There were no events to mark the march of time. Time did not march. It stood always still. It was only the whirling machines that moved, and they moved nowhere—in spite of the fact that they moved faster.

When he was fourteen, he went to work on the starcher. It was a colossal event. Something had at last happened that could be remembered beyond a night's sleep or a week's pay-day. It marked an era. It was a machine Olympiad, a thing to date from. "When I went to work on the starcher," or, "after," or "before I went to work on the starcher," were sentences often on his lips.

He celebrated his sixteenth birthday by going into the loom room and taking a loom. Here was an incentive again, for it was piece-work. And he excelled, because the clay of him had been moulded by the mills into the perfect machine. At the end of three months he was running two looms, and, later, three and four.

At the end of his second year at the looms he was turning out more yards than any other weaver, and more than twice as much as some of the less skilful ones. And at home things began to prosper as he approached the full stature of his earning power. Not, however, that his increased earnings were in excess of need. The children were growing up. They ate more. And they were going to school, and school-books cost money. And somehow, the faster he worked, the faster climbed the prices of things. Even the rent went up, though the house had fallen from bad to worse disrepair.

He had grown taller; but with his increased height he seemed leaner than ever. Also, he was more nervous. With the nervousness increased his peevishness and irritability. The children had learned by many bitter lessons to fight shy of him. His mother respected him for his earning power, but somehow her respect was tinctured with fear.

There was no joyousness in life for him. The procession of the days he never saw. The nights he slept away in twitching unconsciousness. The rest of the time he worked, and his consciousness was machine consciousness. Outside this his mind was a blank. He had no ideals, and but one illusion; namely, that he drank excellent coffee. He was a work-beast. He had no mental life whatever; yet deep down in the crypts of his mind, unknown to him, were being weighed and sifted every hour of his toil, every movement of his hands, every twitch of his muscles, and preparations were making for a future course of action that would amaze him and all his little world.

It was in the late spring that he came home from work one night aware of unusual tiredness. There was a keen expectancy in the air as he sat down to the table, but he did not notice. He went through the meal in moody silence, mechanically eating what was before him. The children um'd and ah'd and made smacking noises with their mouths. But he was deaf to them.

"D'ye know what you're eatin'?" his mother demanded at last, desperately.

He looked vacantly at the dish before him, and vacantly at her.

"Floatin' island," she announced triumphantly.

"Oh," he said.

"Floating island!" the children chorussed loudly.

"Oh," he said. And after two or three mouthfuls, he added, "I guess I ain't hungry to-night."

He dropped the spoon, shoved back his chair, and arose wearily from the table.

"An' I guess I'll go to bed."

His feet dragged more heavily than usual as he crossed the kitchen floor. Undressing was a Titan's task, a monstrous futility, and he wept weakly as he crawled into bed, one shoe still on. He was aware of a rising, swelling something inside his head that made his brain thick and fuzzy. His lean fingers felt as big as his wrist, while in the ends of them was a remoteness of sensation vague and fuzzy like his brain. The small of his back ached intolerably. All his bones ached. He ached everywhere. And in his head began the shrieking, pounding, crashing, roaring of a million looms. All space was filled with flying shuttles. They darted in and out, intricately, amongst the stars. He worked a thousand looms himself, and ever they speeded up, faster and faster, and his brain unwound, faster and faster, and became the thread that fed the thousand flying shuttles.

He did not go to work next morning. He was too busy weaving colossally on the thousand looms that ran inside his head. His mother went to work, but first she sent for the doctor. It was a severe attack of la grippe, he said. Jennie served as nurse and carried out his instructions.

It was a very severe attack, and it was a week before Johnny dressed and tottered feebly across the floor. Another week, the doctor said, and he would be fit to return to work. The foreman of the loom room visited him on Sunday afternoon, the first day of his convalescence. The best weaver in the room, the foreman told his mother. His job would be held for him. He could come back to work a week from Monday.

"Why don't you thank 'im, Johnny?" his mother asked anxiously.

"He's ben that sick he ain't himself yet," she explained apologetically to the visitor.

Johnny sat hunched up and gazing steadfastly at the floor. He sat in the same position long after the foreman had gone. It was warm outdoors, and he sat on the stoop in the afternoon. Sometimes his lips moved. He seemed lost in endless calculations.

Next morning, after the day grew warm, he took his seat on the stoop. He had pencil and paper this time with which to continue his calculations, and he calculated painfully and amazingly.

"What comes after millions?" he asked at noon, when Will came home from school. "An' how d'ye work 'em?"

That afternoon finished his task. Each day, but without paper and pencil, he returned to the stoop. He was greatly absorbed in the one tree that grew across the street. He studied it for hours at a time, and was unusually interested when the wind swayed its branches and fluttered its leaves. Throughout the week he seemed lost in a great communion with himself. On Sunday, sitting on the stoop, he laughed aloud, several times, to the perturbation of his mother, who had not heard him laugh in years.

Next morning, in the early darkness, she came to his bed to rouse him. He had had his fill of sleep all week, and awoke easily. He made no struggle, nor did he attempt to hold on to the bedding when she stripped it from him. He lay quietly, and spoke quietly.

"It ain't no use, ma."

"You'll be late," she said, under the impression that he was still stupid with sleep.

"I'm awake, ma, an' I tell you it ain't no use. You might as well lemme alone. I ain't goin' to git up."

"But you'll lose your job!" she cried.

"I ain't goin' to git up," he repeated in a strange, passionless voice.

She did not go to work herself that morning. This was sickness beyond any sickness she had ever known. Fever and delirium she could understand; but this was insanity. She pulled the bedding up over him and sent Jennie for the doctor.

When that person arrived, Johnny was sleeping gently, and gently he awoke and allowed his pulse to be taken.

"Nothing the matter with him," the doctor reported. "Badly debilitated, that's all. Not much meat on his bones."

"He's always been that way," his mother volunteered.

"Now go 'way, ma, an' let me finish my snooze."

Johnny spoke sweetly and placidly, and sweetly and placidly he rolled over on his side and went to sleep.

At ten o'clock he awoke and dressed himself. He walked out into the kitchen, where he found his mother with a frightened expression on her face.

"I'm goin' away, ma," he announced, "an' I jes' want to say good-by."

She threw her apron over her head and sat down suddenly and wept. He waited patiently.

"I might a-known it," she was sobbing.

"Where?" she finally asked, removing the apron from her head and gazing up at him with a stricken face in which there was little curiosity.

"I don't know—anywhere."

As he spoke, the tree across the street appeared with dazzling brightness on his inner vision. It seemed to lurk just under his eyelids, and he could see it whenever he wished.

"An' your job?" she quavered.

"I ain't never goin' to work again."

"My God, Johnny!" she wailed, "don't say that!"

What he had said was blasphemy to her. As a mother who hears her child deny God, was Johnny's mother shocked by his words.

"What's got into you, anyway?" she demanded, with a lame attempt at imperativeness.

"Figures," he answered. "Jes' figures. I've ben doin' a lot of figurin' this week, an' it's most surprisin'."

"I don't see what that's got to do with it," she sniffled.

Johnny smiled patiently, and his mother was aware of a distinct shock at the persistent absence of his peevishness and irritability.

"I'll show you," he said. "I'm plum' tired out. What makes me tired? Moves. I've ben movin' ever since I was born. I'm tired of movin', an' I ain't goin' to move any more. Remember when I worked in the glass-house? I used to do three hundred dozen a day. Now I reckon I made about ten different moves to each bottle. That's thirty-six thousan' moves a day. Ten days, three hundred an' sixty thousan' moves a day. One month, one million an' eighty thousan' moves. Chuck out the eighty thousan'—" he spoke with the complacent beneficence of a philanthropist—"chuck out the eighty thousan', that leaves a million moves a month—twelve million moves a year.

"At the looms I'm movin' twic'st as much. That makes twenty-five million moves a year, an' it seems to me I've ben a movin' that way 'most a million years.

"Now this week I ain't moved at all. I ain't made one move in hours an' hours. I tell you it was swell, jes' settin' there, hours an' hours, an' doin' nothin'. I ain't never ben happy before. I never had any time. I've ben movin' all the time. That ain't no way to be happy. An' I ain't goin' to do it any more. I'm jes' goin' to set, an' set, an' rest, an' rest, and then rest some more."

"But what's goin' to come of Will an' the children?" she asked despairingly.

"That's it, 'Will an' the children,'" he repeated.

But there was no bitterness in his voice. He had long known his mother's ambition for the younger boy, but the thought of it no longer rankled. Nothing mattered any more. Not even that.

"I know, ma, what you've ben plannin' for Will—keepin' him in school to make a bookkeeper out of him. But it ain't no use, I've quit. He's got to go to work."

"An' after I have brung you up the way I have," she wept, starting to cover her head with the apron and changing her mind.

"You never brung me up," he answered with sad kindliness. "I brung myself up, ma, an' I brung up Will. He's bigger'n me, an' heavier, an' taller. When I was a kid, I reckon I didn't git enough to eat. When he come along an' was a kid, I was workin' an' earnin' grub for him too. But that's done with. Will can go to work, same as me, or he can go to hell, I don't care which. I'm tired. I'm goin' now. Ain't you goin' to say good-by?"

She made no reply. The apron had gone over her head again, and she was crying. He paused a moment in the doorway.

"I'm sure I done the best I knew how," she was sobbing.

He passed out of the house and down the street. A wan delight came into his face at the sight of the lone tree. "Jes' ain't goin' to do nothin'," he said to himself, half aloud, in a crooning tone. He glanced wistfully up at the sky, but the bright sun dazzled and blinded him.

It was a long walk he took, and he did not walk fast. It took him past the jute-mill. The muffled roar of the loom room came to his ears, and he smiled. It was a gentle, placid smile. He hated no one, not even the pounding, shrieking machines. There was no bitterness in him, nothing but an inordinate hunger for rest.

The houses and factories thinned out and the open spaces increased as he approached the country. At last the city was behind him, and he was walking down a leafy lane beside the railroad track. He did not walk like a man. He did not look like a man. He was a travesty of the human. It was a twisted and stunted and nameless piece of life that shambled like a sickly ape, arms loose-hanging, stoop-shouldered, narrow-chested, grotesque and terrible.

He passed by a small railroad station and lay down in the grass under a tree. All afternoon he lay there. Sometimes he dozed, with muscles that twitched in his sleep. When awake, he lay without movement, watching the birds or looking up at the sky through the branches of the tree above him. Once or twice he laughed aloud, but without relevance to anything he had seen or felt.

After twilight had gone, in the first darkness of the night, a freight train rumbled into the station. When the engine was switching cars on to the side-track, Johnny crept along the side of the train. He pulled open the side-door of an empty box-car and awkwardly and laboriously climbed in. He closed the door. The engine whistled. Johnny was lying down, and in the darkness he smiled.

# TO BUILD A FIRE (1908)

DAY HAD BROKEN cold and gray, exceedingly cold and gray, when the man turned aside from the main Yukon trail and climbed the high earth-bank, where a dim and little-travelled trail led eastward through the fat spruce timberland. It was a steep bank, and he paused for breath at the top, excusing the act to himself by looking at his watch. It was nine o'clock. There was no sun nor hint of sun, though there was not a cloud in the sky. It was a clear day, and yet there seemed an intangible pall over the face of things, a subtle gloom that made the day dark, and that was due to the absence of sun. This fact did not worry the man. He was used to the lack of sun. It had been days since he had seen the sun, and he knew that a few more days must pass before that cheerful orb, due south, would just peep above the sky-line and dip immediately from view.

The man flung a look back along the way he had come. The Yukon lay a mile wide and hidden under three feet of ice. On top of this ice were as many feet of snow. It was all pure white, rolling in gentle undulations where the ice-jams of the freeze-up had formed. North and south, as far as his eye could see, it was unbroken white, save for a dark hair-line that curved and twisted from around the spruce-covered island to the south, and that curved and twisted away into the north, where it disappeared behind another spruce-covered island. This dark hair-line was the trail—the main trail—that led south five hundred miles to the Chilcoot Pass, Dyea, and salt water; and that led north seventy miles to Dawson, and still on to the north a thousand miles to Nulato, and finally to St. Michael on Bering Sea, a thousand miles and half a thousand more.

But all this—the mysterious, far-reaching hair-line trail, the absence of sun from the sky, the tremendous cold, and the strangeness and weirdness of it all—made no impression on the man. It was not because he was long used to it. He was a newcomer in the land, a *chechaquo*, and this was his first winter. The trouble with him was that he was without imagination. He was quick and alert in the things of life, but only in the things, and not in the significances. Fifty degrees below zero meant eighty-odd degrees of frost. Such fact impressed him as being cold and uncomfortable, and that was all. It did not lead him to meditate upon his frailty as a creature of temperature, and upon man's frailty in general, able only to live within certain narrow limits of heat and cold; and from there on it did not lead him to the conjectural field of immortality and man's place in the universe. Fifty degrees below zero stood for a bite of frost that hurt and that must be guarded against by the use of mittens, ear-flaps, warm moccasins, and thick socks. Fifty degrees below zero was to him just precisely fifty degrees below zero. That there should be anything more to it than that was a thought that never entered his head.

As he turned to go on, he spat speculatively. There was a sharp, explosive crackle that startled him. He spat again. And again, in the air, before it could fall to the snow, the spittle crackled. He knew that at fifty below spittle crackled on the snow, but this spittle had crackled in the air. Undoubtedly it was colder than fifty below—how much colder he did not know. But the temperature did not matter. He was bound for the old claim on the left fork of Henderson Creek, where the boys were already. They had come over across the divide from the Indian Creek country, while he had come the roundabout way to take a look at the possibilities of getting out logs in the spring from the islands in the Yukon. He would be in to camp by six o'clock; a bit after dark, it was true, but the boys would be there, a fire would be going, and a hot supper would be ready. As for lunch, he pressed his hand against the protruding bundle under his jacket. It was also under his shirt, wrapped up in a handkerchief and lying against the naked skin. It was the only way to keep the biscuits from freezing. He smiled agreeably to himself as he thought of those biscuits, each cut open and sopped in bacon grease, and each enclosing a generous slice of fried bacon.

He plunged in among the big spruce trees. The trail was faint. A foot of snow had fallen since the last sled had passed over, and he was glad he was without a sled, travelling light. In fact, he carried nothing but the lunch wrapped in the handkerchief. He was surprised, however, at the cold. It certainly was cold, he concluded, as he rubbed his numb nose and cheek-bones with his mittened hand. He was a warm-whiskered man, but the hair on his face did not protect the high cheek-bones and the eager nose that thrust itself aggressively into the frosty air.

At the man's heels trotted a dog, a big native husky, the proper wolf-dog, gray-coated and without any visible or temperamental difference from its brother, the wild wolf. The animal was depressed by the tremendous cold. It knew that it was no time for travelling. Its instinct told it a truer tale than was told to the man by the man's judgment. In reality, it was not merely colder than fifty below zero; it was colder than sixty below, than seventy below. It was seventy-five below zero. Since the freezing-point is thirty-two above zero, it meant that one hundred and seven degrees of frost obtained. The dog did not know anything about thermometers. Possibly in its brain there was no sharp consciousness of a condition of very cold such as was in the man's brain. But the brute had its instinct. It experienced a vague but menacing apprehension that subdued it and made it slink along at the man's heels, and that made it question eagerly every unwonted movement of the man as if expecting him to go into camp or to seek shelter somewhere and build a fire. The dog had learned fire, and it wanted fire, or else to burrow under the snow and cuddle its warmth away from the air.

The frozen moisture of its breathing had settled on its fur in a fine powder of frost, and especially were its jowls, muzzle, and eyelashes whitened by its crystalled breath. The man's red beard and mustache were likewise frosted, but more solidly, the deposit taking the form of ice and increasing with every warm, moist breath he exhaled. Also, the man was chewing tobacco, and the muzzle of ice held his lips so rigidly that he was unable to clear his chin when he expelled the juice. The result was that a crystal beard of the color and solidity of amber was increasing its length on his chin. If he fell down it would shatter itself, like glass, into brittle fragments. But he did not mind the appendage. It was the penalty all tobacco-chewers paid in that country, and he had been out before in two cold snaps. They had not been so cold as this, he knew, but by the spirit thermometer at Sixty Mile he knew they had been registered at fifty below and at fifty-five.

He held on through the level stretch of woods for several miles, crossed a wide flat of nigger-heads, and dropped down a bank to the frozen bed of a small stream. This was Henderson Creek, and he knew he was ten miles from the forks. He looked at his watch. It was ten o'clock. He was making four miles an hour, and he calculated that he would arrive at the forks at half-past twelve. He decided to celebrate that event by eating his lunch there.

The dog dropped in again at his heels, with a tail drooping discouragement, as the man swung along the creek-bed. The furrow of the old sled-trail was plainly visible, but a dozen inches of snow covered the marks of the last runners. In a month no man had come up or down that silent creek. The man held steadily on. He was not much given to thinking, and just then particularly he had nothing to think about save that he would eat lunch at the forks and that at six o'clock he would be in camp with the boys. There was nobody to talk to; and, had there been, speech would have been impossible because of the ice-muzzle on his mouth. So he continued monotonously to chew tobacco and to increase the length of his amber beard.

Once in a while the thought reiterated itself that it was very cold and that he had never experienced such cold. As he walked along he rubbed his cheek-bones and nose with the back of his mittened hand. He did this automatically, now and again changing hands. But rub as he would, the instant he stopped his cheek-bones went numb, and the following instant the end of his nose went numb. He was sure to frost his cheeks; he knew that, and experienced a pang of regret that he had not devised a nose-strap of the sort Bud wore in cold snaps. Such a strap passed across the cheeks, as well, and saved them. But it didn't matter much, after all. What were frosted cheeks? A bit painful, that was all; they were never serious.

Empty as the man's mind was of thoughts, he was keenly observant, and he noticed the changes in the creek, the curves and bends and timber-jams, and always he sharply noted where he placed his feet. Once, coming around a bend, he shied abruptly, like a startled horse, curved away from the place where he had been walking, and retreated several paces back along the trail. The creek he knew was frozen clear to the bottom,—no creek could contain water in that arctic winter,—but he knew also that there were springs that bubbled out from the hillsides and ran along under the snow and on top the ice of the creek. He knew that the coldest snaps never froze these springs, and he knew likewise their danger. They were traps. They hid pools of water under the snow that might be three inches deep, or three feet. Sometimes a skin of ice half an inch thick covered them, and in turn was covered by the snow. Sometimes there were alternate layers of water and ice-skin, so that when one broke through he kept on breaking through for a while, sometimes wetting himself to the waist.

That was why he had shied in such panic. He had felt the give under his feet and heard the crackle of a snow-hidden ice-skin. And to get his feet wet in such a temperature meant trouble and danger. At the very least it meant delay, for he would be forced to stop and build a fire, and under its protection to bare his feet while he dried his socks and moccasins. He stood and studied the creek-bed and its banks, and decided that the flow of water came from the right. He reflected awhile, rubbing his nose and cheeks, then skirted to the left, stepping gingerly and testing the footing for each step. Once clear of the danger, he took a fresh chew of tobacco and swung along at his four-mile gait.

In the course of the next two hours he came upon several similar traps. Usually the snow above the hidden pools had a sunken, candied appearance that advertised the danger. Once again, however, he had a close call; and once, suspecting danger, he compelled the dog to go on in front. The dog did not want to go. It hung back until the man shoved it forward, and then it went quickly across the white, unbroken surface. Suddenly it broke through, floundered to one side, and got away to firmer footing. It had wet its forefeet and legs, and almost immediately the water that clung to it turned to ice. It made quick efforts to lick the ice off its legs, then dropped down in the snow and began to bite out the ice that had formed between the toes. This was a matter of instinct. To permit the ice to remain would mean sore feet. It did not know this. It merely obeyed the mysterious prompting that arose from the deep crypts of its being. But the man knew, having achieved a judgment on the subject, and he removed the mitten from his right hand and helped tear out the ice-particles. He did not expose his fingers more than a minute, and was astonished at the swift numbness that smote them. It certainly was cold. He pulled on the mitten hastily, and beat the hand savagely across his chest.

At twelve o'clock the day was at its brightest. Yet the sun was too far south on its winter journey to clear the horizon. The bulge of the earth intervened between it and Henderson Creek, where the man walked under a clear sky at noon and cast no shadow. At half-past twelve, to the minute, he arrived at the forks of the creek. He was pleased at the speed he had made. If he kept it up, he would certainly be with the boys by six. He unbuttoned his jacket and shirt and drew forth his lunch. The action consumed no more than a quarter of a minute, yet in that brief moment the numbness laid hold of the exposed fingers. He did not put the mitten on, but, instead, struck the fingers a dozen sharp smashes against his leg. Then he sat down on a snow-covered log to eat. The sting that followed upon the striking of his fingers against his leg ceased so quickly that he was startled. He had had no chance to take a bite of biscuit. He struck the fingers repeatedly and returned them to the mitten, baring the other hand for the purpose of eating. He tried to take a mouthful, but the ice-muzzle prevented. He had forgotten to build a fire and thaw out. He chuckled at his foolishness, and as he chuckled he noted the numbness creeping into the exposed fingers. Also, he noted that the stinging which had first come to his toes when he sat down was already passing away. He wondered whether the toes were warm or numb. He moved them inside the moccasins and decided that they were numb.

He pulled the mitten on hurriedly and stood up. He was a bit frightened. He stamped up and down until the stinging returned into the feet. It certainly was cold, was his thought. That man from Sulphur Creek had spoken the truth when telling how cold it sometimes got in the country. And he had laughed at him at the time! That showed one must not be too sure of things. There was no mistake about it, it *was* cold. He strode up and down, stamping his feet and threshing his arms, until reassured by the returning warmth. Then he got out matches and proceeded to make a fire. From the undergrowth, where high water of the previous spring had lodged a supply of seasoned twigs, he got his fire-wood. Working carefully from a small beginning, he soon had a roaring fire, over which he thawed the ice from his face and in the protection of which he ate his biscuits. For the moment the cold of space was outwitted. The dog took satisfaction in the fire, stretching out close enough for warmth and far enough away to escape being singed.

When the man had finished, he filled his pipe and took his comfortable time over a smoke. Then he pulled on his mittens, settled the ear-flaps of his cap firmly about his ears, and took the creek trail up the left fork. The dog was disappointed and yearned back toward the fire. This man did not know cold. Possibly all the generations of his ancestry had been ignorant of cold, of real cold, of cold one hundred and seven degrees below freezing-point. But the dog knew; all its ancestry knew, and it had inherited the knowledge. And it knew that it was not good to walk abroad in such fearful cold. It was the time to lie snug in a hole in the snow and wait for a curtain of cloud to be drawn across the face of outer space whence this cold came. On the other hand, there was no keen intimacy between the dog and the man. The one was the toil-slave of the other, and the only caresses it had ever received were the caresses of the whip-lash and of harsh and menacing throat-sounds that threatened the whip-lash. So the dog made no effort to communicate its apprehension to the man. It was not concerned in the welfare of the man; it was for its own sake that it yearned back toward the fire. But the man whistled, and spoke to it with the sound of whip-lashes, and the dog swung in at the man's heels and followed after.

The man took a chew of tobacco and proceeded to start a new amber beard. Also, his moist breath quickly powdered with white his mustache, eyebrows, and lashes. There did not seem to be so many springs on the left fork of the Henderson, and for half an hour the man saw no signs of any. And then it happened. At a place where there were no signs, where the soft, unbroken snow seemed to advertise solidity beneath, the man broke through. It was not deep. He wet himself halfway to the knees before he floundered out to the firm crust.

He was angry, and cursed his luck aloud. He had hoped to get into camp with the boys at six o'clock, and this would delay him an hour, for he would have to build a fire and dry out his foot-gear. This was imperative at that low temperature—he knew that much; and he turned aside to the bank, which he climbed. On top, tangled in the underbrush about the trunks of several small spruce trees, was a high-water deposit of dry fire-wood—sticks and twigs, principally, but also larger portions of seasoned branches and fine, dry, last-year's grasses. He threw down several large pieces on top of the snow. This served for a foundation and prevented the young flame from drowning itself in the snow it otherwise would melt. The flame he got by touching a match to a small shred of birch-bark that he took from his pocket. This burned even more readily than paper. Placing it on the foundation, he fed the young flame with wisps of dry grass and with the tiniest dry twigs.

He worked slowly and carefully, keenly aware of his danger. Gradually, as the flame grew stronger, he increased the size of the twigs with which he fed it. He squatted in the snow, pulling the twigs out from their entanglement in the brush and feeding directly to the flame. He knew there must be no failure. When it is seventy-five below zero, a man must not fail in his first attempt to build a fire—that is, if his feet are wet. If his feet are dry, and he fails, he can run along the trail for half a mile and restore his circulation. But the circulation of wet and freezing feet cannot be restored by running when it is seventy-five below. No matter how fast he runs, the wet feet will freeze the harder.

All this the man knew. The old-timer on Sulphur Creek had told him about it the previous fall, and now he was appreciating the advice. Already all sensation had gone out of his feet. To build the fire he had been forced to remove his mittens, and the fingers had quickly gone numb. His pace of four miles an hour had kept his heart pumping blood to the surface of his body and to all the extremities. But the instant he stopped, the action of the pump eased down. The cold of space smote the unprotected tip of the planet, and he, being on that unprotected tip, received the full force of the blow. The blood of his body recoiled before it. The blood was alive, like the dog, and like the dog it wanted to hide away and cover itself up from the fearful cold. So long as he walked four miles an hour, he pumped that blood, willy-nilly, to the surface; but now it ebbed away and sank down into the recesses of his body. The extremities were the first to feel its absence. His wet feet froze the faster, and his exposed fingers numbed the faster, though they had not yet begun to freeze. Nose and cheeks were already freezing, while the skin of all his body chilled as it lost its blood.

But he was safe. Toes and nose and cheeks would be only touched by the frost, for the fire was beginning to burn with strength. He was feeding it with twigs the size of his finger. In another minute he would be able to feed it with branches the size of his wrist, and then he could remove his wet foot-gear, and, while it dried, he could keep his naked feet warm by the fire, rubbing them at first, of course, with snow. The fire was a success. He was safe. He remembered the advice of the old-timer on Sulphur Creek, and smiled. The old-timer had been very serious in laying down the law that no man must travel alone in the Klondike after fifty below. Well, here he was; he had had the accident; he was alone; and he had saved himself. Those old-timers were rather womanish, some of them, he thought. All a man had to do was to keep his head, and he was all right. Any man who was a man could travel alone. But it was surprising, the rapidity with which his cheeks and nose were freezing. And he had not thought his fingers could go lifeless in so short a time. Lifeless they were, for he could scarcely make them move together to grip a twig, and they seemed remote from his body and from him. When he touched a twig, he had to look and see whether or not he had hold of it. The wires were pretty well down between him and his finger-ends.

All of which counted for little. There was the fire, snapping and crackling and promising life with every dancing flame. He started to untie his moccasins. They were coated with ice; the thick German socks were like sheaths of iron halfway to the knees; and the moccasin strings were like rods of steel all twisted and knotted as by some conflagration. For a moment he tugged with his numb fingers, then, realizing the folly of it, he drew his sheath-knife.

But before he could cut the strings, it happened. It was his own fault or, rather, his mistake. He should not have built the fire under the spruce tree. He should have built it in the open. But it had been easier to pull the twigs from the brush and drop them directly on the fire. Now the tree under which he had done this carried a weight of snow on its boughs. No wind had blown for weeks, and each bough was fully freighted. Each time he had pulled a twig he had communicated a slight agitation to the tree—an imperceptible agitation, so far as he was concerned, but an agitation sufficient to bring about the disaster. High up in the tree one bough capsized its load of snow. This fell on the boughs beneath, capsizing them. This process continued, spreading out and involving the whole tree. It grew like an avalanche, and it descended without warning upon the man and the fire, and the fire was blotted out! Where it had burned was a mantle of fresh and disordered snow.

The man was shocked. It was as though he had just heard his own sentence of death. For a moment he sat and stared at the spot where the fire had been. Then he grew very calm. Perhaps the old-timer on Sulphur Creek was right. If he had only had a trail-mate he would have been in no danger now. The trail-mate could have built the fire. Well, it was up to him to build the fire over again, and this second time there must be no failure. Even if he succeeded, he would most likely lose some toes. His feet must be badly frozen by now, and there would be some time before the second fire was ready.

Such were his thoughts, but he did not sit and think them. He was busy all the time they were passing through his mind. He made a new foundation for a fire, this time in the open, where no treacherous tree could blot it out. Next, he gathered dry grasses and tiny twigs from the high-water flotsam. He could not bring his fingers together to pull them out, but he was able to gather them by the handful. In this way he got many rotten twigs and bits of green moss that were undesirable, but it was the best he could do. He worked methodically, even collecting an armful of the larger branches to be used later when the fire gathered strength. And all the while the dog sat and watched him, a certain yearning wistfulness in its eyes, for it looked upon him as the fire-provider, and the fire was slow in coming.

When all was ready, the man reached in his pocket for a second piece of birch-bark. He knew the bark was there, and, though he could not feel it with his fingers, he could hear its crisp rustling as he fumbled for it. Try as he would, he could not clutch hold of it. And all the time, in his consciousness, was the knowledge that each instant his feet were freezing. This thought tended to put him in a panic, but he fought against it and kept calm. He pulled on his mittens with his teeth, and threshed his arms back and forth, beating his hands with all his might against his sides. He did this sitting down, and he stood up to do it; and all the while the dog sat in the snow, its wolf-brush of a tail curled around warmly over its forefeet, its sharp wolf-ears pricked forward intently as it watched the man. And the man, as he beat and threshed with his arms and hands, felt a great surge of envy as he regarded the creature that was warm and secure in its natural covering.

After a time he was aware of the first far-away signals of sensation in his beaten fingers. The faint tingling grew stronger till it evolved into a stinging ache that was excruciating, but which the man hailed with satisfaction. He stripped the mitten from his right hand and fetched forth the birch-bark. The exposed fingers were quickly going numb again. Next he brought out his bunch of sulphur matches. But the tremendous cold had already driven the life out of his fingers. In his effort to separate one match from the others, the whole bunch fell in the snow. He tried to pick it out of the snow, but failed. The dead fingers could neither touch nor clutch. He was very careful. He drove the thought of his freezing feet, and nose, and cheeks, out of his mind, devoting his whole soul to the matches. He watched, using the sense of vision in place of that of touch, and when he saw his fingers on each side the bunch, he closed them—that is, he willed to close them, for the wires were down, and the fingers did not obey. He pulled the mitten on the right hand, and beat it fiercely against his knee. Then, with both mittened hands, he scooped the bunch of matches, along with much snow, into his lap. Yet he was no better off.

After some manipulation he managed to get the bunch between the heels of his mittened hands. In this fashion he carried it to his mouth. The ice crackled and snapped when by a violent effort he opened his mouth. He drew the lower jaw in, curled the upper lip out of the way, and scraped the bunch with his upper teeth in order to separate a match. He succeeded in getting one, which he dropped on his lap. He was no better off. He could not pick it up. Then he devised a way. He picked it up in his teeth and scratched it on his leg. Twenty times he scratched before he succeeded in lighting it. As it flamed he held it with his teeth to the birch-bark. But the burning brimstone went up his nostrils and into his lungs, causing him to cough spasmodically. The match fell into the snow and went out.

The old-timer on Sulphur Creek was right, he thought in the moment of controlled despair that ensued: after fifty below, a man should travel with a partner. He beat his hands, but failed in exciting any sensation. Suddenly he bared both hands, removing the mittens with his teeth. He caught the whole bunch between the heels of his hands. His arm-muscles not being frozen enabled him to press the hand-heels tightly against the matches. Then he scratched the bunch along his leg. It flared into flame, seventy sulphur matches at once! There was no wind to blow them out. He kept his head to one side to escape the strangling fumes, and held the blazing bunch to the birch-bark. As he so held it, he became aware of sensation in his hand. His flesh was burning. He could smell it. Deep down below the surface he could feel it. The sensation developed into pain that grew acute. And still he endured it, holding the flame of the matches clumsily to the bark that would not light readily because his own burning hands were in the way, absorbing most of the flame.

At last, when he could endure no more, he jerked his hands apart. The blazing matches fell sizzling into the snow, but the birch-bark was alight. He began laying dry grasses and the tiniest twigs on the flame. He could not pick and choose, for he had to lift the fuel between the heels of his hands. Small pieces of rotten wood and green moss clung to the twigs, and he bit them off as well as he could with his teeth. He cherished the flame carefully and awkwardly. It meant life, and it must not perish. The withdrawal of blood from the surface of his body now made him begin to shiver, and he grew more awkward. A large piece of green moss fell squarely on the little fire. He tried to poke it out with his fingers, but his shivering frame made him poke too far, and he disrupted the nucleus of the little fire, the burning grasses and tiny twigs separating and scattering. He tried to poke them together again, but in spite of the tenseness of the effort, his shivering got away with him, and the twigs were hopelessly scattered. Each twig gushed a puff of smoke and went out. The fire-provider had failed. As he looked apathetically about him, his eyes chanced on the dog, sitting across the ruins of the fire from him, in the snow, making restless, hunching movements, slightly lifting one forefoot and then the other, shifting its weight back and forth on them with wistful eagerness.

The sight of the dog put a wild idea into his head. He remembered the tale of the man, caught in a blizzard, who killed a steer and crawled inside the carcass, and so was saved. He would kill the dog and bury his hands in the warm body until the numbness went out of them. Then he could build another fire. He spoke to the dog, calling it to him; but in his voice was a strange note of fear that frightened the animal, who had never known the man to speak in such way before. Something was the matter, and its suspicious nature sensed danger— it knew not what danger, but somewhere, somehow, in its brain arose an apprehension of the man. It flattened its ears down at the sound of the man's voice, and its restless, hunching movements and the liftings and shiftings of its forefeet became more pronounced; but it would not come to the man. He got on his hands and knees and crawled toward the dog. This unusual posture again excited suspicion, and the animal sidled mincingly away.

The man sat up in the snow for a moment and struggled for calmness. Then he pulled on his mittens, by means of his teeth, and got upon his feet. He glanced down at first in order to assure himself that he was really standing up, for the absence of sensation in his feet left him unrelated to the earth. His erect position in itself started to drive the webs of suspicion from the dog's mind; and when he spoke peremptorily, with the sound of whip-lashes in his voice, the dog rendered its customary allegiance and came to him. As it came within reaching distance, the man lost his control. His arms flashed out to the dog, and he experienced genuine surprise when he discovered that his hands could not clutch, that there was neither bend nor feeling in the fingers. He had forgotten for the moment that they were frozen and that they were freezing more and more. All this happened quickly, and before the animal could get away, he encircled its body with his arms. He sat down in the snow, and in this fashion held the dog, while it snarled and whined and struggled.

But it was all he could do, hold its body encircled in his arms and sit there. He realized that he could not kill the dog. There was no way to do it. With his helpless hands he could neither draw nor hold his sheath-knife nor throttle the animal. He released it, and it plunged wildly away, with tail between its legs, and still snarling. It halted forty feet away and surveyed him curiously, with ears sharply pricked forward. The man looked down at his hands in order to locate them, and found them hanging on the ends of his arms. It struck him as curious that one should have to use his eyes in order to find out where his hands were. He began threshing his arms back and forth, beating the mittened hands against his sides. He did this for five minutes, violently, and his heart pumped enough blood up to the surface to put a stop to his shivering. But no sensation was aroused in the hands. He had an impression that they hung like weights on the ends of his arms, but when he tried to run the impression down, he could not find it.

A certain fear of death, dull and oppressive, came to him. This fear quickly became poignant as he realized that it was no longer a mere matter of freezing his fingers and toes, or of losing his hands and feet, but that it was a matter of life and death with the chances against him. This threw him into a panic, and he turned and ran up the creek-bed along the old, dim trail. The dog joined in behind and kept up with him. He ran blindly, without intention, in fear such as he had never known in his life. Slowly, as he ploughed and floundered through the snow, he began to see things again,—the banks of the creek, the old timber-jams, the leafless aspens, and the sky. The running made him feel better. He did not shiver. Maybe, if he ran on, his feet would thaw out; and, anyway, if he ran far enough, he would reach camp and the boys. Without doubt he would lose some fingers and toes and some of his face; but the boys would take care of him, and save the rest of him when he got there. And at the same time there was another thought in his mind that said he would never get to the camp and the boys; that it was too many miles away, that the freezing had too great a start on him, and that he would soon be stiff and dead. This thought he kept in the background and refused to consider. Sometimes it pushed itself forward and demanded to be heard, but he thrust it back and strove to think of other things.

It struck him as curious that he could run at all on feet so frozen that he could not feel them when they struck the earth and took the weight of his body. He seemed to himself to skim along above the surface, and to have no connection with the earth. Somewhere he had once seen a winged Mercury, and he wondered if Mercury felt as he felt when skimming over the earth.

His theory of running until he reached camp and the boys had one flaw in it: he lacked the endurance. Several times he stumbled, and finally he tottered, crumpled up, and fell. When he tried to rise, he failed. He must sit and rest, he decided, and next time he would merely walk and keep on going. As he sat and regained his breath, he noted that he was feeling quite warm and comfortable. He was not shivering, and it even seemed that a warm glow had come to his chest and trunk. And yet, when he touched his nose or cheeks, there was no sensation. Running would not thaw them out. Nor would it thaw out his hands and feet. Then the thought came to him that the frozen portions of his body must be extending. He tried to keep this thought down, to forget it, to think of something else; he was aware of the panicky feeling that it caused, and he was afraid of the panic. But the thought asserted itself, and persisted, until it produced a vision of his body totally frozen. This was too much, and he made another wild run along the trail. Once he slowed down to a walk, but the thought of the freezing extending itself made him run again.

And all the time the dog ran with him, at his heels. When he fell down a second time, it curled its tail over its forefeet and sat in front of him, facing him, curiously eager and intent. The warmth and security of the animal angered him, and he cursed it till it flattened down its ears appeasingly. This time the shivering came more quickly upon the man. He was losing in his battle with the frost. It was creeping into his body from all sides. The thought of it drove him on, but he ran no more than a hundred feet, when he staggered and pitched headlong. It was his last panic. When he had recovered his breath and control, he sat up and entertained in his mind the conception of meeting death with dignity. However, the conception did not come to him in such terms. His idea of it was that he had been making a fool of himself, running around like a chicken with its head cut off—such was the simile that occurred to him. Well, he was bound to freeze anyway, and he might as well take it decently. With this new-found peace of mind came the first glimmerings of drowsiness. A good idea, he thought, to sleep off to death. It was like taking an anæsthetic. Freezing was not so bad as people thought. There were lots worse ways to die.

He pictured the boys finding his body next day. Suddenly he found himself with them, coming along the trail and looking for himself. And, still with them, he came around a turn in the trail and found himself lying in the snow. He did not belong with himself any more, for even then he was out of himself, standing with the boys and looking at himself in the snow. It certainly was cold, was his thought. When he got back to the States he could tell the folks what real cold was. He drifted on from this to a vision of the old-timer on Sulphur Creek. He could see him quite clearly, warm and comfortable, and smoking a pipe.

"You were right, old hoss; you were right," the man mumbled to the old-timer of Sulphur Creek.

Then the man drowsed off into what seemed to him the most comfortable and satisfying sleep he had ever known. The dog sat facing him and waiting. The brief day drew to a close in a long, slow twilight. There were no signs of a fire to be made, and, besides, never in the dog's experience had it known a man to sit like that in the snow and make no fire. As the twilight drew on, its eager yearning for the fire mastered it, and with a great lifting and shifting of forefeet, it whined softly, then flattened its ears down in anticipation of being chidden by the man. But the man remained silent. Later, the dog whined loudly. And still later it crept close to the man and caught the scent of death. This made the animal bristle and back away. A little longer it delayed, howling under the stars that leaped and danced and shone brightly in the cold sky. Then it turned and trotted up the trail in the direction of the camp it knew, where were the other food-providers and fire-providers.

# THE CHINAGO

*"The coral waxes, the palm grows,
but man departs"*

—Tahitian proverb

AH CHO DID NOT understand French. He sat in the crowded court room, very weary and bored, listening to the unceasing, explosive French that now one official and now another uttered. It was just so much gabble to Ah Cho, and he marvelled at the stupidity of the Frenchmen who took so long to find out the murderer of Chung Ga, and who did not find him at all. The five hundred coolies on the plantation knew that Ah San had done the killing, and here was Ah San not even arrested. It was true that all the coolies had agreed secretly not to testify against one another; but then, it was so simple, the Frenchmen should have been able to discover that Ah San was the man. They were very stupid, these Frenchmen.

Ah Cho had done nothing of which to be afraid. He had had no hand in the killing. It was true he had been present at it, and Schemmer, the overseer on the plantation, had rushed into the barracks immediately afterward and caught him there, along with four or five others; but what of that? Chung Ga had been stabbed only twice. It stood to reason that five or six men could not inflict two stab wounds. At the most, if a man had struck but once, only two men could have done it.

So it was that Ah Cho reasoned, when he, along with his four companions, had lied and blocked and obfuscated in their statements to the court concerning what had taken place. They had heard the sounds of the killing, and, like Schemmer, they had run to the spot. They had got there before Schemmer—that was all. True, Schemmer had testified that, attracted by the sound of quarrelling as he chanced to pass by, he had stood for at least five minutes outside; that then, when he entered, he found the prisoners already inside; and that they had not entered just before, because he had been standing by the one door to the barracks. But what of that? Ah Cho and his four fellow-prisoners had testified that Schemmer was mistaken. In the end they would be let go. They were all confident of that. Five men could not have their heads cut off for two stab wounds. Besides, no foreign devil had seen the killing. But these Frenchmen were so stupid. In China, as Ah Cho well knew, the magistrate would order all of them to the torture and learn the truth. The truth was very easy to learn under torture. But these Frenchmen did not torture—bigger fools they! Therefore they would never find out who killed Chung Ga.

But Ah Cho did not understand everything. The English Company that owned the plantation had imported into Tahiti, at great expense, the five hundred coolies. The stockholders were clamoring for dividends, and the Company had not yet paid any; wherefore the Company did not want its costly contract laborers to start the practice of killing one another. Also, there were the French, eager and willing to impose upon the Chinagos the virtues and excellences of French law. There was nothing like setting an example once in a while; and, besides, of what use was New Caledonia except to send men to live out their days in misery and pain in payment of the penalty for being frail and human?

Ah Cho did not understand all this. He sat in the court room and waited for the baffled judgment that would set him and his comrades free to go back to the plantation and work out the terms of their contracts. This judgment would soon be rendered. Proceedings were drawing to a close. He could see that. There was no more testifying, no more gabble of tongues. The French devils were tired, too, and evidently waiting for the judgment. And as he waited he remembered back in his life to the time when he had signed the contract and set sail in the ship for Tahiti. Times had been hard in his seacoast village, and when he indentured himself to labor for five years in the South Seas at fifty cents Mexican a day, he had thought himself fortunate. There were men in his village who toiled a whole year for ten dollars Mexican, and there were women who made nets all the year round for five dollars, while in the houses of shopkeepers there were maid-servants who received four dollars for a year of service. And here he was to receive fifty cents a day; for one day, only one day, he was to receive that princely sum! What if the work were hard? At the end of the five years he would return home—that was in the contract—and he would never have to work again. He would be a rich man for life, with a house of his own, a wife, and children growing up to venerate him. Yes, and back of the house he would have a small garden, a place of meditation and repose, with goldfish in a tiny lakelet, and wind bells tinkling in the several trees, and there would be a high wall all around so that his meditation and repose should be undisturbed.

Well, he had worked out three of those five years. He was already a wealthy man (in his own country), through his earnings, and only two years more intervened between the cotton plantation on Tahiti and the meditation and repose that awaited him. But just now he was losing money because of the unfortunate accident of being present at the killing of Chung Ga. He had lain three weeks in prison, and for each day of those three weeks he had lost fifty cents. But now judgment would soon be given, and he would go back to work.

Ah Cho was twenty-two years old. He was happy and good-natured, and it was easy for him to smile. While his body was slim in the Asiatic way, his face was rotund. It was round, like the moon, and it irradiated a gentle complacence and a sweet kindliness of spirit that was unusual among his countrymen. Nor did his looks belie him. He never caused trouble, never took part in wrangling. He did not gamble. His soul was not harsh enough for the soul that must belong to a gambler. He was content with little things and simple pleasures. The hush and quiet in the cool of the day after the blazing toil in the cotton field was to him an infinite satisfaction. He could sit for hours gazing at a solitary flower and philosophizing about the mysteries and riddles of being. A blue heron on a tiny crescent of sandy beach, a silvery splatter of flying fish, or a sunset of pearl and rose across the lagoon, could entrance him to all forgetfulness of the procession of wearisome days and of the heavy lash of Schemmer.

Schemmer, Karl Schemmer, was a brute, a brutish brute. But he earned his salary. He got the last particle of strength out of the five hundred slaves; for slaves they were until their term of years was up. Schemmer worked hard to extract the strength from those five hundred sweating bodies and to transmute it into bales of fluffy cotton ready for export. His dominant, iron-clad, primeval brutishness was what enabled him to effect the transmutation. Also, he was assisted by a thick leather belt, three inches wide and a yard in length, with which he always rode and which, on occasion, could come down on the naked back of a stooping coolie with a report like a pistol-shot. These reports were frequent when Schemmer rode down the furrowed field.

Once, at the beginning of the first year of contract labor, he had killed a coolie with a single blow of his fist. He had not exactly crushed the man's head like an egg-shell, but the blow had been sufficient to addle what was inside, and, after being sick for a week, the man had died. But the Chinese had not complained to the French devils that ruled over Tahiti. It was their own lookout. Schemmer was their problem. They must avoid his wrath as they avoided the venom of the centipedes that lurked in the grass or crept into the sleeping quarters on rainy nights. The Chinagos—such they were called by the indolent, brown-skinned island folk—saw to it that they did not displease Schemmer too greatly. This was equivalent to rendering up to him a full measure of efficient toil. That blow of Schemmer's fist had been worth thousands of dollars to the Company, and no trouble ever came of it to Schemmer.

The French, with no instinct for colonization, futile in their childish playgame of developing the resources of the island, were only too glad to see the English Company succeed. What matter of Schemmer and his redoubtable fist? The Chinago that died? Well, he was only a Chinago. Besides, he died of sunstroke, as the doctor's certificate attested. True, in all the history of Tahiti no one had ever died of sunstroke. But it was that, precisely that, which made the death of this Chinago unique. The doctor said as much in his report. He was very candid. Dividends must be paid, or else one more failure would be added to the long history of failure in Tahiti.

There was no understanding these white devils. Ah Cho pondered their inscrutableness as he sat in the court room waiting the judgment. There was no telling what went on at the back of their minds. He had seen a few of the white devils. They were all alike—the officers and sailors on the ship, the French officials, the several white men on the plantation, including Schemmer. Their minds all moved in mysterious ways there was no getting at. They grew angry without apparent cause, and their anger was always dangerous. They were like wild beasts at such times. They worried about little things, and on occasion could out-toil even a Chinago. They were not temperate as Chinagos were temperate; they were gluttons, eating prodigiously and drinking more prodigiously. A Chinago never knew when an act would please them or arouse a storm of wrath. A Chinago could never tell. What pleased one time, the very next time might provoke an outburst of anger. There was a curtain behind the eyes of the white devils that screened the backs of their minds from the Chinago's gaze. And then, on top of it all, was that terrible efficiency of the white devils, that ability to do things, to make things go, to work results, to bend to their wills all creeping, crawling things, and the powers of the very elements themselves. Yes, the white men were strange and wonderful, and they were devils. Look at Schemmer.

Ah Cho wondered why the judgment was so long in forming. Not a man on trial had laid hand on Chung Ga. Ah San alone had killed him. Ah San had done it, bending Chung Ga's head back with one hand by a grip of his queue, and with the other hand, from behind, reaching over and driving the knife into his body. Twice had he driven it in. There in the court room, with closed eyes, Ah Cho saw the killing acted over again—the squabble, the vile words bandied back and forth, the filth and insult flung upon venerable ancestors, the curses laid upon unbegotten generations, the leap of Ah San, the grip on the queue of Chung Ga, the knife that sank twice into his flesh, the bursting open of the door, the irruption of Schemmer, the dash for the door, the escape of Ah San, the flying belt of Schemmer that drove the rest into the corner, and the firing of the revolver as a signal that brought help to Schemmer. Ah Cho shivered as he lived it over. One blow of the belt had bruised his cheek, taking off some of the skin. Schemmer had pointed to the bruises when, on the witness-stand, he had identified Ah Cho. It was only just now that the marks had become no longer visible. That had been a blow. Half an inch nearer the centre and it would have taken out his eye. Then Ah Cho forgot the whole happening in a vision he caught of the garden of meditation and repose that would be his when he returned to his own land.

He sat with impassive face, while the magistrate rendered the judgment. Likewise were the faces of his four companions impassive. And they remained impassive when the interpreter explained that the five of them had been found guilty of the murder of Chung Ga, and that Ah Chow should have his head cut off, Ah Cho serve twenty years in prison in New Caledonia, Wong Li twelve years, and Ah Tong ten years. There was no use in getting excited about it. Even Ah Chow remained expressionless as a mummy, though it was his head that was to be cut off. The magistrate added a few words, and the interpreter explained that Ah Chow's face having been most severely bruised by Schemmer's strap had made his identification so positive that, since one man must die, he might as well be that man. Also, the fact that Ah Cho's face likewise had been severely bruised, conclusively proving his presence at the murder and his undoubted participation, had merited him the twenty years of penal servitude. And down to the ten years of Ah Tong, the proportioned reason for each sentence was explained. Let the Chinagos take the lesson to heart, the Court said finally, for they must learn that the law would be fulfilled in Tahiti though the heavens fell.

The five Chinagos were taken back to jail. They were not shocked nor grieved. The sentences being unexpected was quite what they were accustomed to in their dealings with the white devils. From them a Chinago rarely expected more than the unexpected. The heavy punishment for a crime they had not committed was no stranger than the countless strange things that white devils did. In the weeks that followed, Ah Cho often contemplated Ah Chow with mild curiosity. His head was to be cut off by the guillotine that was being erected on the plantation. For him there would be no declining years, no gardens of tranquillity. Ah Cho philosophized and speculated about life and death. As for himself, he was not perturbed. Twenty years were merely twenty years. By that much was his garden removed from him—that was all. He was young, and the patience of Asia was in his bones. He could wait those twenty years, and by that time the heats of his blood would be assuaged and he would be better fitted for that garden of calm delight. He thought of a name for it; he would call it The Garden of the Morning Calm. He was made happy all day by the thought, and he was inspired to devise a moral maxim on the virtue of patience, which maxim proved a great comfort, especially to Wong Li and Ah Tong. Ah Chow, however, did not care for the maxim. His head was to be separated from his body in so short a time that he had no need for patience to wait for that event. He smoked well, ate well, slept well, and did not worry about the slow passage of time.

Cruchot was a gendarme. He had seen twenty years of service in the colonies, from Nigeria and Senegal to the South Seas, and those twenty years had not perceptibly brightened his dull mind. He was as slow-witted and stupid as in his peasant days in the south of France. He knew discipline and fear of authority, and from God down to the sergeant of gendarmes the only difference to him was the measure of slavish obedience which he rendered. In point of fact, the sergeant bulked bigger in his mind than God, except on Sundays when God's mouthpieces had their say. God was usually very remote, while the sergeant was ordinarily very close at hand.

Cruchot it was who received the order from the Chief Justice to the jailer commanding that functionary to deliver over to Cruchot the person of Ah Chow. Now, it happened that the Chief Justice had given a dinner the night before to the captain and officers of the French man-of-war. His hand was shaking when he wrote out the order, and his eyes were aching so dreadfully that he did not read over the order. It was only a Chinago's life he was signing away, anyway. So he did not notice that he had omitted the final letter in Ah Chow's name. The order read "Ah Cho," and, when Cruchot presented the order, the jailer turned over to him the person of Ah Cho. Cruchot took that person beside him on the seat of a wagon, behind two mules, and drove away.

Ah Cho was glad to be out in the sunshine. He sat beside the gendarme and beamed. He beamed more ardently than ever when he noted the mules headed south toward Atimaono. Undoubtedly Schemmer had sent for him to be brought back. Schemmer wanted him to work. Very well, he would work well. Schemmer would never have cause to complain. It was a hot day. There had been a stoppage of the trades. The mules sweated, Cruchot sweated, and Ah Cho sweated. But it was Ah Cho that bore the heat with the least concern. He had toiled three years under that sun on the plantation. He beamed and beamed with such genial good nature that even Cruchot's heavy mind was stirred to wonderment.

"You are very funny," he said at last.

Ah Cho nodded and beamed more ardently. Unlike the magistrate, Cruchot spoke to him in the Kanaka tongue, and this, like all Chinagos and all foreign devils, Ah Cho understood.

"You laugh too much," Cruchot chided. "One's heart should be full of tears on a day like this."

"I am glad to get out of the jail."

"Is that all?" The gendarme shrugged his shoulders.

"Is it not enough?" was the retort.

"Then you are not glad to have your head cut off?"

Ah Cho looked at him in abrupt perplexity and said:—

"Why, I am going back to Atimaono to work on the plantation for Schemmer. Are you not taking me to Atimaono?"

Cruchot stroked his long mustaches reflectively. "Well, well," he said finally, with a flick of the whip at the off mule, "so you don't know?"

"Know what?" Ah Cho was beginning to feel a vague alarm. "Won't Schemmer let me work for him any more?"

"Not after to-day." Cruchot laughed heartily. It was a good joke. "You see, you won't be able to work after to-day. A man with his head off can't work, eh?" He poked the Chinago in the ribs, and chuckled.

Ah Cho maintained silence while the mules trotted a hot mile. Then he spoke: "Is Schemmer going to cut off my head?"

Cruchot grinned as he nodded.

"It is a mistake," said Ah Cho, gravely. "I am not the Chinago that is to have his head cut off. I am Ah Cho. The honorable judge has determined that I am to stop twenty years in New Caledonia."

The gendarme laughed. It was a good joke, this funny Chinago trying to cheat the guillotine. The mules trotted through a cocoanut grove and for half a mile beside the sparkling sea before Ah Cho spoke again.

"I tell you I am not Ah Chow. The honorable judge did not say that my head was to go off."

"Don't be afraid," said Cruchot, with the philanthropic intention of making it easier for his prisoner. "It is not difficult to die that way." He snapped his fingers. "It is quick—like that. It is not like hanging on the end of a rope and kicking and making faces for five minutes. It is like killing a chicken with a hatchet. You cut its head off, that is all. And it is the same with a man. Pouf!—it is over. It doesn't hurt. You don't even think it hurts. You don't think. Your head is gone, so you cannot think. It is very good. That is the way I want to die— quick, ah, quick. You are lucky to die that way. You might get the leprosy and fall to pieces slowly, a finger at a time, and now and again a thumb, also the toes. I knew a man who was burned by hot water. It took him two days to die. You could hear him yelling a kilometre away. But you? Ah! so easy! Chck!—the knife cuts your neck like that. It is finished. The knife may even tickle. Who can say? Nobody who died that way ever came back to say."

He considered this last an excruciating joke, and permitted himself to be convulsed with laughter for half a minute. Part of his mirth was assumed, but he considered it his humane duty to cheer up the Chinago.

"But I tell you I am Ah Cho," the other persisted. "I don't want my head cut off."

Cruchot scowled. The Chinago was carrying the foolishness too far.

"I am not Ah Chow—" Ah Cho began.

"That will do," the gendarme interrupted. He puffed up his cheeks and strove to appear fierce.

"I tell you I am not—" Ah Cho began again.

"Shut up!" bawled Cruchot.

After that they rode along in silence. It was twenty miles from

Papeete to Atimaono, and over half the distance was covered by the time the Chinago again ventured into speech.

"I saw you in the court room, when the honorable judge sought after our guilt," he began. "Very good. And do you remember that Ah Chow, whose head is to be cut off—do you remember that he—Ah Chow—was a tall man? Look at me."

He stood up suddenly, and Cruchot saw that he was a short man. And just as suddenly Cruchot caught a glimpse of a memory picture of Ah Chow, and in that picture Ah Chow was tall. To the gendarme all Chinagos looked alike. One face was like another. But between tallness and shortness he could differentiate, and he knew that he had the wrong man beside him on the seat. He pulled up the mules abruptly, so that the pole shot ahead of them, elevating their collars.

"You see, it was a mistake," said Ah Cho, smiling pleasantly.

But Cruchot was thinking. Already he regretted that he had stopped the wagon. He was unaware of the error of the Chief Justice, and he had no way of working it out; but he did know that he had been given this Chinago to take to Atimaono and that it was his duty to take him to Atimaono. What if he was the wrong man and they cut his head off? It was only a Chinago when all was said, and what was a Chinago, anyway? Besides, it might not be a mistake. He did not know what went on in the minds of his superiors. They knew their business best. Who was he to do their thinking for them? Once, in the long ago, he had attempted to think for them, and the sergeant had said: "Cruchot, you are a fool! The quicker you know that, the better you will get on. You are not to think; you are to obey and leave thinking to your betters." He smarted under the recollection. Also, if he turned back to Papeete, he would delay the execution at Atimaono, and if he were wrong in turning back, he would get a reprimand from the sergeant who was waiting for the prisoner. And, furthermore, he would get a reprimand at Papeete as well.

He touched the mules with the whip and drove on. He looked at his watch. He would be half an hour late as it was, and the sergeant was bound to be angry. He put the mules into a faster trot. The more Ah Cho persisted in explaining the mistake, the more stubborn Cruchot became. The knowledge that he had the wrong man did not make his temper better. The knowledge that it was through no mistake of his confirmed him in the belief that the wrong he was doing was the right. And, rather than incur the displeasure of the sergeant, he would willingly have assisted a dozen wrong Chinagos to their doom.

As for Ah Cho, after the gendarme had struck him over the head with the butt of the whip and commanded him in a loud voice to shut up, there remained nothing for him to do but to shut up. The long ride continued in silence. Ah Cho pondered the strange ways of the foreign devils. There was no explaining them. What they were doing with him was of a piece with everything they did. First they found guilty five innocent men, and next they cut off the head of the man that even they, in their benighted ignorance, had deemed meritorious of no more than twenty years' imprisonment. And there was nothing he could do. He could only sit idly and take what these lords of life measured out to him. Once, he got in a panic, and the sweat upon his body turned cold; but he fought his way out of it. He endeavored to resign himself to his fate by remembering and repeating certain passages from the "Yin Chih Wen" ("The Tract of the Quiet Way"); but, instead, he kept seeing his dream-garden of meditation and repose. This bothered him, until he abandoned himself to the dream and sat in his garden listening to the tinkling of the wind-bells in the several trees. And lo! sitting thus, in the dream, he was able to remember and repeat the passages from "The Tract of the Quiet Way."

So the time passed nicely until Atimaono was reached and the mules trotted up to the foot of the scaffold, in the shade of which stood the impatient sergeant. Ah Cho was hurried up the ladder of the scaffold. Beneath him on one side he saw assembled all the coolies of the plantation. Schemmer had decided that the event would be a good object-lesson, and so had called in the coolies from the fields and compelled them to be present. As they caught sight of Ah Cho they gabbled among themselves in low voices. They saw the mistake; but they kept it to themselves. The inexplicable white devils had doubtlessly changed their minds. Instead of taking the life of one innocent man, they were taking the life of another innocent man. Ah Chow or Ah Cho—what did it matter which? They could never understand the white dogs any more than could the white dogs understand them. Ah Cho was going to have his head cut off, but they, when their two remaining years of servitude were up, were going back to China.

Schemmer had made the guillotine himself. He was a handy man, and though he had never seen a guillotine, the French officials had explained the principle to him. It was on his suggestion that they had ordered the execution to take place at Atimaono instead of at Papeete. The scene of the crime, Schemmer had argued, was the best possible place for the punishment, and, in addition, it would have a salutary influence upon the half-thousand Chinagos on the plantation. Schemmer had also volunteered to act as executioner, and in that capacity he was now on the scaffold, experimenting with the instrument he had made. A banana tree, of the size and consistency of a man's neck, lay under the guillotine. Ah Cho watched with fascinated eyes. The German, turning a small crank, hoisted the blade to the top of the little derrick he had rigged. A jerk on a stout piece of cord loosed the blade and it dropped with a flash, neatly severing the banana trunk.

"How does it work?" The sergeant, coming out on top the scaffold, had asked the question.

"Beautifully," was Schemmer's exultant answer. "Let me show you."

Again he turned the crank that hoisted the blade, jerked the cord, and sent the blade crashing down on the soft tree. But this time it went no more than two-thirds of the way through.

The sergeant scowled. "That will not serve," he said.

Schemmer wiped the sweat from his forehead. "What it needs is more weight," he announced. Walking up to the edge of the scaffold, he called his orders to the blacksmith for a twenty-five-pound piece of iron. As he stooped over to attach the iron to the broad top of the blade, Ah Cho glanced at the sergeant and saw his opportunity.

"The honorable judge said that Ah Chow was to have his head cut off," he began.

The sergeant nodded impatiently. He was thinking of the fifteen-mile ride before him that afternoon, to the windward side of the island, and of Berthe, the pretty half-caste daughter of Lafière, the pearl-trader, who was waiting for him at the end of it.

"Well, I am not Ah Chow. I am Ah Cho. The honorable jailer has made a mistake. Ah Chow is a tall man, and you see I am short."

The sergeant looked at him hastily and saw the mistake. "Schemmer!" he called, imperatively. "Come here."

The German grunted, but remained bent over his task till the chunk of iron was lashed to his satisfaction. "Is your Chinago ready?" he demanded.

"Look at him," was the answer. "Is he the Chinago?"

Schemmer was surprised. He swore tersely for a few seconds, and looked regretfully across at the thing he had made with his own hands and which he was eager to see work. "Look here," he said finally, "we can't postpone this affair. I've lost three hours' work already out of those five hundred Chinagos. I can't afford to lose it all over again for the right man. Let's put the performance through just the same. It is only a Chinago."

The sergeant remembered the long ride before him, and the pearl-trader's daughter, and debated with himself.

"They will blame it on Cruchot—if it is discovered," the German urged. "But there's little chance of its being discovered. Ah Chow won't give it away, at any rate."

"The blame won't lie with Cruchot, anyway," the sergeant said. "It must have been the jailer's mistake."

"Then let's go on with it. They can't blame us. Who can tell one Chinago from another? We can say that we merely carried out instructions with the Chinago that was turned over to us. Besides, I really can't take all those coolies a second time away from their labor."

They spoke in French, and Ah Cho, who did not understand a word of it, nevertheless knew that they were determining his destiny. He knew, also, that the decision rested with the sergeant, and he hung upon that official's lips.

"All right," announced the sergeant. "Go ahead with it. He is only a Chinago."

"I'm going to try it once more, just to make sure." Schemmer moved the banana trunk forward under the knife, which he had hoisted to the top of the derrick.

Ah Cho tried to remember maxims from "The Tract of the Quiet Way." "Live in concord," came to him; but it was not applicable. He was not going to live. He was about to die. No, that would not do. "Forgive malice"—yes, but there was no malice to forgive. Schemmer and the rest were doing this thing without malice. It was to them merely a piece of work that had to be done, just as clearing the jungle, ditching the water, and planting cotton were pieces of work that had to be done. Schemmer jerked the cord, and Ah Cho forgot "The Tract of the Quiet Way." The knife shot down with a thud, making a clean slice of the tree.

"Beautiful!" exclaimed the sergeant, pausing in the act of lighting a cigarette. "Beautiful, my friend."

Schemmer was pleased at the praise.

"Come on, Ah Chow," he said, in the Tahitian tongue.

"But I am not Ah Chow—" Ah Cho began.

"Shut up!" was the answer. "If you open your mouth again, I'll break your head."

The overseer threatened him with a clenched fist, and he remained silent. What was the good of protesting? Those foreign devils always had their way. He allowed himself to be lashed to the vertical board that was the size of his body. Schemmer drew the buckles tight—so tight that the straps cut into his flesh and hurt. But he did not complain. The hurt would not last long. He felt the board tilting over in the air toward the horizontal, and closed his eyes. And in that moment he caught a last glimpse of his garden of meditation and repose. It seemed to him that he sat in the garden. A cool wind was blowing, and the bells in the several trees were tinkling softly. Also, birds were making sleepy noises, and from beyond the high wall came the subdued sound of village life.

Then he was aware that the board had come to rest, and from muscular pressures and tensions he knew that he was lying on his back. He opened his eyes. Straight above him he saw the suspended knife blazing in the sunshine. He saw the weight which had been added, and noted that one of Schemmer's knots had slipped. Then he heard the sergeant's voice in sharp command. Ah Cho closed his eyes hastily. He did not want to see the knife descend. But he felt it—for one great fleeting instant. And in that instant he remembered Cruchot and what Cruchot had said. But Cruchot was wrong. The knife did not tickle. That much he knew before he ceased to know.

# KOOLAU THE LEPER

"BECAUSE WE ARE SICK they take away our liberty. We have obeyed the law. We have done no wrong. And yet they would put us in prison. Molokai is a prison. That you know. Niuli, there, his sister was sent to Molokai seven years ago. He has not seen her since. Nor will he ever see her. She must stay there until she dies. This is not her will. It is not Niuli's will. It is the will of the white men who rule the land. And who are these white men?

"We know. We have it from our fathers and our fathers' fathers. They came like lambs, speaking softly. Well might they speak softly, for we were many and strong, and all the islands were ours. As I say, they spoke softly. They were of two kinds. The one kind asked our permission, our gracious permission, to preach to us the word of God. The other kind asked our permission, our gracious permission, to trade with us. That was the beginning. To-day all the islands are theirs, all the land, all the cattle—everything is theirs. They that preached the word of God and they that preached the word of Rum have fore-gathered and become great chiefs. They live like kings in houses of many rooms, with multitudes of servants to care for them. They who had nothing have everything, and if you, or I, or any Kanaka be hungry, they sneer and say, 'Well, why don't you work? There are the plantations.' "

Koolau paused. He raised one hand, and with gnarled and twisted fingers lifted up the blazing wreath of hibiscus that crowned his black hair. The moon-light bathed the scene in silver. It was a night of peace, though those who sat about him and listened had all the seeming of

164

battle-wrecks. Their faces were leonine. Here a space yawned in a face where should have been a nose, and there an arm-stump showed where a hand had rotted off. They were men and women beyond the pale, the thirty of them, for upon them had been placed the mark of the beast.

They sat, flower-garlanded, in the perfumed, luminous night, and their lips made uncouth noises and their throats rasped approval of Koolau's speech. They were creatures who once had been men and women. But they were men and women no longer. They were monsters—in face and form grotesque caricatures of everything human. They were hideously maimed and distorted, and had the seeming of creatures that had been racked in millenniums of hell. Their hands, when they possessed them, were like harpy-claws. Their faces were the misfits and slips, crushed and bruised by some mad god at play in the machinery of life. Here and there were features which the mad god had smeared half away, and one woman wept scalding tears from twin pits of horror, where her eyes once had been. Some were in pain and groaned from their chests. Others coughed, making sounds like the tearing of tissue. Two were idiots, more like huge apes marred in the making, until even an ape were an angel. They mowed and gibbered in the moonlight, under crowns of drooping, golden blossoms. One, whose bloated ear-lobe flapped like a fan upon his shoulder, caught up a gorgeous flower of orange and scarlet and with it decorated the monstrous ear that flip-flapped with his every movement.

And over these things Koolau was king. And this was his kingdom,—a flower-throttled gorge, with beetling cliffs and crags, from which floated the blattings of wild goats. On three sides the grim walls rose, festooned in fantastic draperies of tropic vegetation and pierced by cave-entrances—the rocky lairs of Koolau's subjects. On the fourth side the earth fell away into a tremendous abyss, and, far below, could be seen the summits of lesser peaks and crags, at whose bases foamed and rumbled the Pacific surge. In fine weather a boat could land on the rocky beach that marked the entrance of Kalalau Valley, but the weather must be very fine. And a cool-headed mountaineer might climb from the beach to the head of Kalalau Valley, to this pocket among the peaks where Koolau ruled; but such a mountaineer must be very cool of head, and he must know the wild-goat trails as well. The marvel was that the mass of human wreckage that constituted Koolau's people should have been able to drag its helpless misery over the giddy goat-trails to this inaccessible spot.

"Brothers," Koolau began.

But one of the mowing, apelike travesties emitted a wild shriek of madness, and Koolau waited while the shrill cachination was tossed back and forth among the rocky walls and echoed distantly through the pulseless night.

"Brothers, is it not strange? Ours was the land, and behold, the land is not ours. What did these preachers of the word of God and the word of Rum give us for the land? Have you received one dollar, as much as one dollar, any one of you, for the land? Yet it is theirs, and in return they tell us we can go to work on the land, their land, and that what we produce by our toil shall be theirs. Yet in the old days we did not have to work. Also, when we are sick, they take away our freedom."

"Who brought the sickness, Koolau?" demanded Kiloliana, a lean and wiry man with a face so like a laughing faun's that one might expect to see the cloven hoofs under him. They were cloven, it was true, but the cleavages were great ulcers and livid putrefactions. Yet this was Kiloliana, the most daring climber of them all, the man who knew every goat-trail and who had led Koolau and his wretched followers into the recesses of Kalalau.

"Ay, well questioned," Koolau answered. "Because we would not work the miles of sugar-cane where once our horses pastured, they brought the Chinese slaves from over seas. And with them came the Chinese sickness—that which we suffer from and because of which they would imprison us on Molokai. We were born on Kauai. We have been to the other islands, some here and some there, to Oahu, to Maui, to Hawaii, to Honolulu. Yet always did we come back to Kauai. Why did we come back? There must be a reason. Because we love Kauai. We were born here. Here we have lived. And here shall we die—unless—unless—there be weak hearts amongst us. Such we do not want. They are fit for Molokai. And if there be such, let them not remain. To-morrow the soldiers land on the shore. Let the weak hearts go down to them. They will be sent swiftly to Molokai. As for us, we shall stay and fight. But know that we will not die. We have rifles. You know the narrow trails where men must creep, one by one. I, alone, Koolau, who was once a cowboy on Niihau, can hold the trail against a thousand men. Here is Kapalei, who was once a judge over men and a man with honor, but who is now a hunted rat, like you and me. Hear him. He is wise."

Kapalei arose. Once he had been a judge. He had gone to college at Punahou. He had sat at meat with lords and chiefs and the high representatives of alien powers who protected the interests of traders and missionaries. Such had been Kapalei. But now, as Koolau had said, he was a hunted rat, a creature outside the law, sunk so deep in the mire of human horror that he was above the law as well as beneath it. His face was featureless, save for gaping orifices and for the lidless eyes that burned under hairless brows.

"Let us not make trouble," he began. "We ask to be left alone. But if they do not leave us alone, then is the trouble theirs, and the penalty. My fingers are gone, as you see." He held up his stumps of hands that all might see. "Yet have I the joint of one thumb left, and it can pull a trigger as firmly as did its lost neighbor in the old days. We love Kauai. Let us live here, or die here, but do not let us go to the prison of Molokai. The sickness is not ours. We have not sinned. The men who preached the word of God and the word of Rum brought the sickness with the coolie slaves who work the stolen land. I have been a judge. I know the law and the justice, and I say to you it is unjust to steal a man's land, to make that man sick with the Chinese sickness, and then to put that man in prison for life."

"Life is short, and the days are filled with pain," said Koolau. "Let us drink and dance and be happy as we can."

From one of the rocky lairs calabashes were produced and passed around. The calabashes were filled with the fierce distillation of the root of the *ti*-plant; and as the liquid fire coursed through them and mounted to their brains, they forgot that they had once been men and women, for they were men and women once more. The woman who wept scalding tears from open eye-pits was indeed a woman apulse with life as she plucked the strings of an *ukulele* and lifted her voice in a barbaric love-call such as might have come from the dark forest-depths of the primeval world. The air tingled with her cry, softly imperious and seductive. Upon a mat, timing his rhythm to the woman's song, Kiloliana danced. It was unmistakable. Love danced in all his movements, and, next, dancing with him on the mat, was a woman whose heavy hips and generous breast gave the lie to her disease-corroded face. It was a dance of the living dead, for in their disintegrating bodies life still loved and longed. Ever the woman whose sightless eyes ran scalding tears chanted her love-cry, ever the dancers danced of love in the warm night, and ever the calabashes went around till in all their brains were maggots crawling of memory and desire. And with the woman on the mat danced a slender maid whose face was beautiful and unmarred, but whose twisted arms that rose and fell marked the disease's ravage. And the two idiots, gibbering and mouthing strange noises, danced apart, grotesque, fantastic, travestying love as they themselves had been travestied by life.

But the woman's love-cry broke midway, the calabashes were lowered, and the dancers ceased, as all gazed into the abyss above the sea, where a rocket flared like a wan phantom through the moonlit air.

"It is the soldiers," said Koolau. "Tomorrow there will be fighting. It is well to sleep and be prepared."

The lepers obeyed, crawling away to their lairs in the cliff, until only Koolau remained, sitting motionless in the moonlight, his rifle across his knees, as he gazed far down to the boats landing on the beach.

The far head of Kalalau Valley had been well chosen as a refuge. Except Kiloliana, who knew back-trails up the precipitous walls, no man could win to the gorge save by advancing across a knife-edged ridge. This passage was a hundred yards in length. At best, it was a scant twelve inches wide. On either side yawned the abyss. A slip, and to right or left the man would fall to his death. But once across he would find himself in an earthly paradise. A sea of vegetation laved the landscape, pouring its green billows from wall to wall, dripping from the cliff-lips in great vine-masses, and flinging a spray of ferns and air-plants into the multitudinous crevices. During the many months of Koolau's rule, he and his followers had fought with this vegetable sea. The choking jungle, with its riot of blossoms, had been driven back from the bananas, oranges, and mangoes that grew wild. In little clearings grew the wild arrowroot; on stone terraces, filled with soil scrapings, were the *taro* patches and the melons; and in every open space where the sunshine penetrated, were *papaia* trees burdened with their golden fruit.

Koolau had been driven to this refuge from the lower valley by the beach. And if he were driven from it in turn, he knew of gorges among the jumbled peaks of the inner fastnesses where he could lead his subjects and live. And now he lay with his rifle beside him, peering down through a tangled screen of foliage at the soldiers on the beach. He noted that they had large guns with them, from which the sunshine flashed as from mirrors. The knife-edged passage lay directly before him. Crawling upward along the trail that led to it he could see tiny specks of men. He knew they were not the soldiers, but the police. When they failed, then the soldiers would enter the game.

He affectionately rubbed a twisted hand along his rifle barrel and made sure that the sights were clean. He had learned to shoot as a wild-cattle hunter on Niihau, and on that island his skill as a marksman was unforgotten. As the toiling specks of men grew nearer and larger, he estimated the range, judged the deflection of the wind that swept at right angles across the line of fire, and calculated the chances of overshooting marks that were so far below his level. But he did not shoot. Not until they reached the beginning of the passage did he make his presence known. He did not disclose himself, but spoke from the thicket.

"What do you want?" he demanded.

"We want Koolau, the leper," answered the man who led the native police, himself a blue-eyed American.

"You must go back," Koolau said.

He knew the man, a deputy sheriff, for it was by him that he had been harried out of Niihau, across Kauai, to Kalalau Valley, and out of the valley to the gorge.

"Who are you?" the sheriff asked.

"I am Koolau, the leper," was the reply.

"Then come out. We want you. Dead or alive, there is a thousand dollars on your head. You cannot escape."

Koolau laughed aloud in the thicket.

"Come out!" the sheriff commanded, and was answered by silence.

He conferred with the police, and Koolau saw that they were preparing to rush him.

"Koolau," the sheriff called. "Koolau, I am coming across to get you."

"Then look first and well about you at the sun and sea and sky, for it will be the last time you behold them."

"That's all right, Koolau," the sheriff said soothingly. "I know you're a dead shot. But you won't shoot me. I have never done you any wrong."

Koolau grunted in the thicket.

"I say, you know, I've never done you any wrong, have I?" the sheriff persisted.

"You do me wrong when you try to put me in prison," was the reply. "And you do me wrong when you try for the thousand dollars on my head. If you will live, stay where you are."

"I've got to come across and get you. I'm sorry. But it is my duty."

"You will die before you get across."

The sheriff was no coward. Yet was he undecided. He gazed into the gulf on either side, and ran his eyes along the knife-edge he must travel. Then he made up his mind.

"Koolau," he called.

But the thicket remained silent.

"Koolau, don't shoot. I am coming."

The sheriff turned, gave some orders to the police, then started on his perilous way. He advanced slowly. It was like walking a tight rope. He had nothing to lean upon but the air. The lava rock crumbled under his feet, and on either side the dislodged fragments pitched downward through the depths. The sun blazed upon him, and his face was wet with sweat. Still he advanced, until the halfway point was reached.

"Stop!" Koolau commanded from the thicket. "One more step and I shoot."

The sheriff halted, swaying for balance as he stood poised above the void. His face was pale, but his eyes were determined. He licked his dry lips before he spoke.

"Koolau, you won't shoot me. I know you won't."

He started once more. The bullet whirled him half about. On his face was an expression of querulous surprise as he reeled to the fall. He tried to save himself by throwing his body across the knife-edge; but at that moment he knew death. The next moment the knife-edge was vacant. Then came the rush, five policemen, in single file, with superb steadiness, running along the knife-edge. At the same instant the rest of the posse opened fire on the thicket. It was madness. Five times Koolau pulled the trigger, so rapidly that his shots constituted a rattle. Changing his position and crouching low under the bullets that were biting and singing through the bushes, he peered out. Four of the police had followed the sheriff. The fifth lay across the knife-edge, still alive. On the farther side, no longer firing, were the surviving police. On the naked rock there was no hope for them. Before they could clamber down Koolau could have picked off the last man. But he did not fire, and, after a conference, one of them took off a white undershirt and waved it as a flag. Followed by another, he advanced along the knife-edge to their wounded comrade. Koolau gave no sign, but watched them slowly withdraw and become specks as they descended into the lower valley.

Two hours later, from another thicket, Koolau watched a body of police trying to make the ascent from the opposite side of the valley. He saw the wild goats flee before them as they climbed higher and higher, until he doubted his judgment and sent for Kiloliana who crawled in beside him.

"No, there is no way," said Kiloliana.

"The goats?" Koolau questioned.

"They come over from the next valley, but they cannot pass to this. There is no way. Those men are not wiser than goats. They may fall to their deaths. Let us watch."

"They are brave men," said Koolau. "Let us watch."

Side by side they lay among the morning-glories, with the yellow blossoms of the *hau* dropping upon them from overhead, watching the motes of men toil upward, till the thing happened, and three of them, slipping, rolling, sliding, dashed over a cliff-lip and fell sheer half a thousand feet.

Kiloliana chuckled.

"We will be bothered no more," he said.

"They have war guns," Koolau made answer. "The soldiers have not yet spoken."

In the drowsy afternoon, most of the lepers lay in their rock dens asleep. Koolau, his rifle on his knees, fresh-cleaned and ready, dozed in the entrance to his own den. The maid with the twisted arm lay below in the thicket and kept watch on the knife-edge passage. Suddenly Koolau was startled wide awake by the sound of an explosion on the beach. The next instant the atmosphere was incredibly rent asunder. The terrible sound frightened him. It was as if all the gods had caught the envelope of the sky in their hands and were ripping it apart as a woman rips apart a sheet of cotton cloth. But it was such an immense ripping, growing swiftly nearer. Koolau glanced up apprehensively, as if expecting to see the thing. Then high up on the cliff overhead the shell burst in a fountain of black smoke. The rock was shattered, the fragments falling to the foot of the cliff.

Koolau passed his hand across his sweaty brow. He was terribly shaken. He had had no experience with shell-fire, and this was more dreadful than anything he had imagined.

"One," said Kapahei, suddenly bethinking himself to keep count.

A second and a third shell flew screaming over the top of the wall, bursting beyond view. Kapahei methodically kept the count. The lepers crowded into the open space before the caves. At first they were frightened, but as the shells continued their flight overhead the leper folk became reassured and began to admire the spectacle. The two idiots shrieked with delight, prancing wild antics as each air-tormenting shell went by. Koolau began to recover his confidence. No damage was being done. Evidently they could not aim such large missiles at such long range with the precision of a rifle.

But a change came over the situation. The shells began to fall short. One burst below in the thicket by the knife-edge. Koolau remembered the maid who lay there on watch, and ran down to see. The smoke was still rising from the bushes when he crawled in. He was astounded. The branches were splintered and broken. Where the girl had lain was a hole in the ground. The girl herself was in shattered fragments. The shell had burst right on her.

First peering out to make sure no soldiers were attempting the passage, Koolau started back on the run for the caves. All the time the shells were moaning, whining, screaming by, and the valley was rumbling and reverberating with the explosions. As he came in sight of the caves, he saw the two idiots cavorting about, clutching each other's hands with their stumps of fingers. Even as he ran, Koolau saw a spout of black smoke rise from the ground, near to the idiots. They were flung apart bodily by the explosion. One lay motionless, but the other was dragging himself by his hands toward the cave. His legs trailed out helplessly behind him, while the blood was pouring from his body. He seemed bathed in blood, and as he crawled he cried like a little dog. The rest of the lepers, with the exception of Kapahei, had fled into the caves.

"Seventeen," said Kapahei. "Eighteen," he added.

This last shell had fairly entered into one of the caves. The explosion caused all the caves to empty. But from the particular cave no one emerged. Koolau crept in through the pungent, acrid smoke. Four bodies, frightfully mangled, lay about. One of them was the sightless woman whose tears till now had never ceased.

Outside, Koolau found his people in a panic and already beginning to climb the goat trail that led out of the gorge and on among the jumbled heights and chasms. The wounded idiot, whining feebly and dragging himself along on the ground by his hands, was trying to follow. But at the first pitch of the wall his helplessness overcame him and he fell back.

"It would be better to kill him," said Koolau to Kapahei, who still sat in the same place.

"Twenty-two," Kapahei answered. "Yes, it would be a wise thing to kill him. Twenty-three—twenty-four."

The idiot whined sharply when he saw the rifle leveled at him. Koolau hesitated, then lowered the gun.

"It is a hard thing to do," he said.

"You are a fool, twenty-six, twenty-seven," said Kapahei. "Let me show you."

He arose and, with a heavy fragment of rock in his hand, approached the wounded thing. As he lifted his arm to strike, a shell burst full upon him, relieving him of the necessity of the act and at the same time putting an end to his count.

Koolau was alone in the gorge. He watched the last of his people drag their crippled bodies over the brow of the height and disappear. Then he turned and went down to the thicket where the maid had been killed. The shell-fire still continued, but he remained; for far below he could see the soldiers climbing up. A shell burst twenty feet away. Flattening himself into the earth, he heard the rush of the fragments above his body. A shower of *hau* blossoms rained upon him. He lifted his head to peer down the trail, and sighed. He was very much afraid. Bullets from rifles would not have worried him, but this shell-fire was abominable. Each time a shell shrieked by he shivered and crouched; but each time he lifted his head again to watch the trail.

At last the shells ceased. This, he reasoned, was because the soldiers were drawing near. They crept along the trail in single file, and he tried to count them until he lost track. At any rate, there were a hundred or so of them—all come after Koolau the leper. He felt a fleeting prod of pride. With war guns and rifles, police and soldiers, they came for him, and he was only one man, a crippled wreck of a man at that. They offered a thousand dollars for him, dead or alive. In all his life he had never possessed that much money. The thought was a bitter one. Kapahei had been right. He, Koolau, had done no wrong. Because the *haoles* wanted labor with which to work the stolen land, they had brought in the Chinese coolies, and with them had come the sickness. And now, because he had caught the sickness, he was worth a thousand dollars—but not to himself. It was his worthless carcass, rotten with disease or dead from a bursting shell, that was worth all that money.

When the soldiers reached the knife-edged passage, he was prompted to warn them. But his gaze fell upon the body of the murdered maid, and he kept silent. When six had ventured on the knife-edge, he opened fire. Nor did he cease when the knife-edge was bare. He emptied his magazine, reloaded, and emptied it again. He kept on shooting. All his wrongs were blazing in his brain, and he was in a fury of vengeance. All down the goat trail the soldiers were firing, and though they lay flat and sought to shelter themselves in the shallow inequalities of the surface, they were exposed marks to him. Bullets whistled and thudded about him, and an occasional ricochet sang sharply through the air. One bullet ploughed a crease through his scalp, and a second burned across his shoulder-blade without breaking the skin.

It was a massacre, in which one man did the killing. The soldiers began to retreat, helping along their wounded. As Koolau picked them off he became aware of the smell of burnt meat. He glanced about him at first, and then discovered that it was his own hands. The heat of the rifle was doing it. The leprosy had destroyed most of the nerves in his hands. Though his flesh burned and he smelled it, there was no sensation.

He lay in the thicket, smiling, until he remembered the war guns. Without doubt they would open up on him again, and this time upon the very thicket from which he had inflicted the damage. Scarcely had he changed his position to a nook behind a small shoulder of the wall where he had noted that no shells fell, than the bombardment re-commenced. He counted the shells. Sixty more were thrown into the gorge before the war-guns ceased. The tiny area was pitted with their explosions, until it seemed impossible that any creature could have survived. So the soldiers thought, for, under the burning afternoon sun, they climbed the goat trail again. And again the knife-edged passage was disputed, and again they fell back to the beach.

For two days longer Koolau held the passage, though the soldiers contented themselves with flinging shells into his retreat. Then Pahau, a leper boy, came to the top of the wall at the back of the gorge and shouted down to him that Kiloliana, hunting goats that they might eat, had been killed by a fall, and that the women were frightened and knew not what to do. Koolau called the boy down and left him with a spare gun with which to guard the passage. Koolau found his people disheartened. The majority of them were too helpless to forage food for themselves under such forbidding circumstances, and all were starving. He selected two women and a man who were not too far gone with the disease, and sent them back to the gorge to bring up food and mats. The rest he cheered and consoled until even the weakest took a hand in building rough shelters for themselves.

But those he had dispatched for food did not return, and he started back for the gorge. As he came out on the brow of the wall, half a dozen rifles cracked. A bullet tore through the fleshy part of his shoulder, and his cheek was cut by a sliver of rock where a second bullet smashed against the cliff. In the moment that this happened, and he leaped back, he saw that the gorge was alive with soldiers. His own people had betrayed him. The shell-fire had been too terrible, and they had preferred the prison of Molokai.

Koolau dropped back and unslung one of his heavy cartridge-belts. Lying among the rocks, he allowed the head and shoulders of the first soldier to rise clearly into view before pulling trigger. Twice this happened, and then, after some delay, in place of a head and shoulders a white flag was thrust above the edge of the wall.

"What do you want?" he demanded.

"I want you, if you are Koolau the leper," came the answer.

Koolau forgot where he was, forgot everything, as he lay and marvelled at the strange persistence of these *haoles* who would have their will though the sky fell in. Aye, they would have their will over all men and all things, even though they died in getting it. He could not but admire them, too, what of that will in them that was stronger than life and that bent all things to their bidding. He was convinced of the hopelessness of his struggle. There was no gainsaying that terrible will of the *haoles*. Though he killed a thousand, yet would they rise like the sands of the sea and come upon him, ever more and more. They never knew when they were beaten. That was their fault and their virtue. It was where his own kind lacked. He could see, now, how the handful of the preachers of God and the preachers of Rum had conquered the land. It was because—

"Well, what have you got to say? Will you come with me?"

It was the voice of the invisible man under the white flag. There he was, like any *haole*, driving straight toward the end determined.

"Let us talk," said Koolau.

The man's head and shoulders arose, then his whole body. He was a smooth-faced, blue-eyed youngster of twenty-five, slender and natty in his captain's uniform. He advanced until halted, then seated himself a dozen feet away:—

"You are a brave man," said Koolau wonderingly. "I could kill you like a fly."

"No, you couldn't," was the answer.

"Why not?"

"Because you are a man, Koolau, though a bad one. I know your story. You kill fairly."

Koolau grunted, but was secretly pleased.

"What have you done with my people?" he demanded. "The boy, the two women, and the man?"

"They gave themselves up, as I have now come for you to do."

Koolau laughed incredulously.

"I am a free man," he announced. "I have done no wrong. All I ask is to be left alone. I have lived free, and I shall die free. I will never give myself up."

"Then your people are wiser than you," answered the young captain. "Look—they are coming now."

Koolau turned and watched the remnant of his band approach. Groaning and sighing, a ghastly procession, it dragged its wretchedness past. It was given to Koolau to taste a deeper bitterness, for they hurled imprecations and insults at him as they went by; and the panting hag who brought up the rear halted, and with skinny, harpy-claws extended, shaking her snarling death's head from side to side, she laid a curse upon him. One by one they dropped over the lip-edge and surrendered to the hiding soldiers.

"You can go now," said Koolau to the captain. "I will never give myself up. That is my last word. Good-by."

The captain slipped over the cliff to his soldiers. The next moment, and without a flag of truce, he hoisted his hat on his scabbard, and Koolau's bullet tore through it. That afternoon they shelled him out from the beach, and as he retreated into the high inaccessible pockets beyond, the soldiers followed him.

For six weeks they hunted him from pocket to pocket, over the volcanic peaks and along the goat trails. When he hid in the lantana jungle, they formed lines of beaters, and through lantana jungle and guava scrub they drove him like a rabbit. But ever he turned and doubled and eluded. There was no cornering him. When pressed too closely, his sure rifle held them back and they carried their wounded down the goat trails to the beach. There were times when they did the shooting as his brown body showed for a moment through the underbrush. Once, five of them caught him on an exposed goat trail between pockets. They emptied their rifles at him as he limped and climbed along his dizzy way. Afterward they found blood-stains and knew that he was wounded. At the end of six weeks they gave up. The soldiers and police returned to Honolulu, and Kalalau Valley was left to him for his own, though head-hunters ventured after him from time to time and to their own undoing.

Two years later, and for the last time, Koolau crawled unto a thicket and lay down among the *ti*-leaves and wild ginger blossoms. Free he had lived, and free he was dying. A slight drizzle of rain began to fall, and he drew a ragged blanket about the distorted wreck of his limbs. His body was covered with an oilskin coat. Across his chest he laid his Mauser rifle, lingering affectionately for a moment to wipe the dampness from the barrel. The hand with which he wiped had no fingers left upon it with which to pull the trigger.

He closed his eyes, for, from the weakness in his body and the fuzzy turmoil in his brain, he knew that his end was near. Like a wild animal he had crept into hiding to die. Half-conscious, aimless and wandering, he lived back in his life to his early manhood on Niihau. As life faded and the drip of the rain grew dim in his ears, it seemed to him that he was once more in the thick of the horse-breaking, with raw colts rearing and bucking under him, his stirrups tied together beneath, or charging madly about the breaking corral and driving the helping cowboys over the rails. The next instant, and with seeming naturalness, he found himself pursuing the wild bulls of the upland pastures, roping them and leading them down to the valleys. Again the sweat and dust of the branding pen stung his eyes and bit his nostrils.

All his lusty, whole-bodied youth was his, until the sharp pangs of impending dissolution brought him back. He lifted his monstrous hands and gazed at them in wonder. But how? Why? Why should the wholeness of that wild youth of his change to this? Then he remembered, and once again, and for a moment, he was Koolau, the leper. His eyelids fluttered wearily down and the drip of the rain ceased in his ears. A prolonged trembling set up in his body. This, too, ceased. He half-lifted his head, but it fell back. Then his eyes opened, and did not close. His last thought was of his Mauser, and he pressed it against his chest with his folded, fingerless hands.

# GOOD-BY, JACK

HAWAII IS A queer place. Everything socially is what I may call topsy-turvy. Not but what things are correct. They are almost too much so. But still things are sort of upside down. The most ultra-exclusive set there is the "Missionary Crowd." It comes with rather a shock to learn that in Hawaii the obscure, martyrdom-seeking missionary sits at the head of the table of the moneyed aristocracy. But it is true. The humble New Englanders who came out in the third decade of the nineteenth century, came for the lofty purpose of teaching the kanakas the true religion, the worship of the one only genuine and undeniable God. So well did they succeed in this, and also in civilizing the kanaka, that by the second or third generation he was practically extinct. This being the fruit of the seed of the Gospel, the fruit of the seed of the missionaries (the sons and the grandsons) was the possession of the islands themselves,—of the land, the ports, the town sites, and the sugar plantations. The missionary who came to give the bread of life remained to gobble up the whole heathen feast.

But that is not the Hawaiian queerness I started out to tell. Only one cannot speak of things Hawaiian without mentioning the missionaries. There is Jack Kersdale, the man I wanted to tell about; he came of missionary stock. That is, on his grandmother's side. His grandfather was old Benjamin Kersdale, a Yankee trader, who got his start for a million in the old days by selling cheap whiskey and square-face gin. There's another queer thing. The old missionaries and old traders were mortal enemies. You see, their interests conflicted. But their children made it up by intermarrying and dividing the islands between them.

Life in Hawaii is a song. That's the way Stoddard put it in his "Hawaii Noi":—

> *"Thy life is music—Fate the notes prolong!*
> *Each isle a stanza, and the whole a song."*

And he was right. Flesh is golden there. The native women are sun-ripe Junos, the native men bronzed Apollos. They sing, and dance, and all are flower-bejewelled and flower-crowned. And, outside the rigid "Missionary Crowd," the white men yield to the climate and the sun, and no matter how busy they may be, are prone to dance and sing and wear flowers behind their ears and in their hair. Jack Kersdale was one of these fellows. He was one of the busiest men I ever met. He was a several-times millionaire. He was a sugar king, a coffee planter, a rubber pioneer, a cattle rancher, and a promoter of three out of every four new enterprises launched in the islands. He was a society man, a club man, a yachtsman, a bachelor, and withal as handsome a man as was ever doted upon by mamas with marriageable daughters. Incidentally, he had finished his education at Yale, and his head was crammed fuller with vital statistics and scholarly information concerning Hawaii Nei than any other islander I ever encountered. He turned off an immense amount of work, and he sang and danced and put flowers in his hair as immensely as any of the idlers.

He had grit, and had fought two duels—both political—when he was no more than a raw youth essaying his first adventures in politics. In fact, he played a most creditable and courageous part in the last revolution, when the native dynasty was overthrown; and he could not have been over sixteen at the time. I am pointing out that he was no coward, in order that you may appreciate what happens later on. I've seen him in the breaking yard at the Haleakala Ranch, conquering a four-year-old brute that for two years had defied the pick of Von Tempsky's cow-boys. And I must tell of one other thing. It was down in Kona,—or up, rather, for the Kona people scorn to live at less than a thousand feet elevation. We were all on the *lanai* of Doctor Goodhue's bungalow. I was talking with Dottie Fairchild when it happened. A big centipede—it was seven inches, for we measured it afterward—fell from the rafters overhead squarely into her coiffure. I confess, the hideousness of it paralyzed me. I couldn't move. My mind refused to work. There, within two feet of me, the ugly venomous devil was writhing in her hair. It threatened at any moment to fall down upon her exposed shoulders—we had just come out from dinner.

"What is it?" she asked, starting to raise her hand to her head.

"Don't!" I cried. "Don't!"

"But what is it?" she insisted, growing frightened by the fright she read in my eyes and on my stammering lips.

My exclamation attracted Kersdale's attention. He glanced our way carelessly, but in that glance took in everything. He came over to us, but without haste.

"Please don't move, Dottie," he said quietly.

He never hesitated, nor did he hurry and make a bungle of it.

"Allow me," he said.

And with one hand he caught her scarf and drew it tightly around her shoulders so that the centipede could not fall inside her bodice. With the other hand—the right—he reached into her hair, caught the repulsive abomination as near as he was able by the nape of the neck, and held it tightly between thumb and forefinger as he withdrew it from her hair. It was as horrible and heroic a sight as man could wish to see. It made my flesh crawl. The centipede, seven inches of squirming legs, writhed and twisted and dashed itself about his hand, the body twining around the fingers and the legs digging into the skin and scratching as the beast endeavored to free itself. It bit him twice—I saw it—though he assured the ladies that he was not harmed as he dropped it upon the walk and stamped it into the gravel. But I saw him in the surgery five minutes afterward, with Doctor Goodhue scarifying the wounds and injecting permanganate of potash. The next morning Kersdale's arm was as big as a barrel, and it was three weeks before the swelling went down.

All of which has nothing to do with my story, but which I could not avoid giving in order to show that Jack Kersdale was anything but a coward. It was the cleanest exhibition of grit I have ever seen. He never turned a hair. The smile never left his lips. And he dived with thumb and forefinger into Dottie Fairchild's hair as gayly as if it had been a box of salted almonds. Yet that was the man I was destined to see stricken with fear a thousand times more hideous even than the fear that was mine when I saw that writhing abomination in Dottie Fairchild's hair, dangling over her eyes and the trap of her bodice.

I was interested in leprosy, and upon that, as upon every other island subject, Kersdale had encyclopedic knowledge. In fact, leprosy was one of his hobbies. He was an ardent defender of the settlement at Molokai, where all the island lepers were segregated. There was much talk and feeling among the natives, fanned by the demagogues, concerning the cruelties of Molokai, where men and women, not alone banished from friends and family, were compelled to live in perpetual imprisonment until they died. There were no reprieves, no commutations of sentences. "Abandon hope" was written over the portal of Molokai.

"I tell you they are happy there," Kersdale insisted. "And they are infinitely better off than their friends and relatives outside who have nothing the matter with them. The horrors of Molokai are all poppycock. I can take you through any hospital or any slum in any of the great cities of the world and show you a thousand times worse horrors. The living death! The creatures that once were men! Bosh! You ought to see those living deaths racing horses on the Fourth of July. Some of them own boats. One has a gasoline launch. They have nothing to do but have a good time. Food, shelter, clothes, medical attendance, everything, is theirs. They are the wards of the Territory. They have a much finer climate than Honolulu, and the scenery is magnificent. I shouldn't mind going down there myself for the rest of my days. It is a lovely spot."

So Kersdale on the joyous leper. He was not afraid of leprosy. He said so himself, and that there wasn't one chance in a million for him or any other white man to catch it, though he confessed afterward that one of his school chums, Alfred Starter, had contracted it, gone to Molokai, and there died.

"You know, in the old days," Kersdale explained, "there was no certain test for leprosy. Anything unusual or abnormal was sufficient to send a fellow to Molokai. The result was that dozens were sent there who were no more lepers than you or I. But they don't make that mistake now. The Board of Health tests are infallible. The funny thing is that when the test was discovered they immediately went down to Molokai and applied it, and they found a number who were not lepers. These were immediately deported. Happy to get away? They wailed harder at leaving the settlement than when they left Honolulu to go to it. Some refused to leave, and really had to be forced out. One of them even married a leper woman in the last stages and then wrote pathetic letters to the Board of Health, protesting against his expulsion on the ground that no one was so well able as he to take care of his poor old wife."

"What is this infallible test?" I demanded.

"The bacteriological test. There is no getting away from it. Doctor

Hervey—he's our expert, you know—was the first man to apply it here. He is a wizard. He knows more about leprosy than any living man, and if a cure is ever discovered, he'll be that discoverer. As for the test, it is very simple. They have succeeded in isolating the *bacillus leprae* and studying it. They know it now when they see it. All they do is to snip a bit of skin from the suspect and subject it to the bacteriological test. A man without any visible symptoms may be chock full of the leprosy bacilli."

"Then you or I, for all we know," I suggested, "may be full of it now."

Kersdale shrugged his shoulders and laughed.

"Who can say? It takes seven years for it to incubate. If you have any doubts go and see Doctor Hervey. He'll just snip out a piece of your skin and let you know in a jiffy."

Later on he introduced me to Dr. Hervey, who loaded me down with Board of Health reports and pamphlets on the subject, and took me out to Kalihi, the Honolulu receiving station, where suspects were examined and confirmed lepers were held for deportation to Molokai. These deportations occurred about once a month, when, the last goodbys said, the lepers were marched on board the little steamer, the *Noeau,* and carried down to the settlement.

One afternoon, writing letters at the club, Jack Kersdale dropped in on me.

"Just the man I want to see," was his greeting. "I'll show you the saddest aspect of the whole situation—the lepers wailing as they depart for Molokai. The *Noeau* will be taking them on board in a few minutes. But let me warn you not to let your feelings be harrowed. Real as their grief is, they'd wail a whole sight harder a year hence if the Board of Health tried to take them away from Molokai. We've just time for a whiskey and soda. I've a carriage outside. It won't take us five minutes to get down to the wharf."

To the wharf we drove. Some forty sad wretches, amid their mats, blankets, and luggage of various sorts, were squatting on the stringer piece. The *Noeau* had just arrived and was making fast to a lighter that lay between her and the wharf. A Mr. McVeigh, the superintendent of the settlement, was overseeing the embarkation, and to him I was introduced, also to Dr. Georges, one of the Board of Health physicians whom I had already met at Kalihi. The lepers were a woebegone lot. The faces of the majority were hideous—too horrible for me to describe. But here and there I noticed fairly good-looking persons, with no apparent signs of the fell disease upon them. One, I noticed, a little white girl, not more than twelve, with blue eyes and golden hair. One cheek, however, showed the leprous bloat. On my remarking upon the sadness of her alien situation among the brown-skinned afflicted ones, Doctor Georges replied:—

"Oh, I don't know. It's a happy day in her life. She comes from Kauai. Her father is a brute. And now that she has developed the disease she is going to join her mother at the settlement. Her mother was sent down three years ago—a very bad case."

"You can't always tell from appearances," Mr. McVeigh explained. "That man there, that big chap, who looks the pink of condition, with nothing the matter with him, I happen to know has a perforating ulcer in his foot and another in his shoulder blade. Then there are others—there, see that girl's hand, the one who is smoking the cigarette. See her twisted fingers. That's the anæsthetic form. It attacks the nerves. You could cut her fingers off with a dull knife, or rub them off on a nutmeg-grater, and she would not experience the slightest sensation."

"Yes, but that fine-looking woman, there," I persisted; "surely, surely, there can't be anything the matter with her. She is too glorious and gorgeous altogether."

"A sad case," Mr. McVeigh answered over his shoulder, already turning away to walk down the wharf with Kersdale.

She was a beautiful woman, and she was pure Polynesian. From my meagre knowledge of the race and its types I could not but conclude that she had descended from old chief stock. She could not have been more than twenty-three or four. Her lines and proportions were magnificent, and she was just beginning to show the amplitude of the women of her race.

"It was a blow to all of us," Dr. Georges volunteered. "She gave herself up voluntarily, too. No one suspected. But somehow she had contracted the disease. It broke us all up, I assure you. We've kept it out of the papers, though. Nobody but us and her family knows what has become of her. In fact, if you were to ask any man in Honolulu, he'd tell you it was his impression that she was somewhere in Europe. It was at her request that we've been so quiet about it. Poor girl, she has a lot of pride."

"But who is she?" I asked. "Certainly, from the way you talk about her, she must be somebody."

"Did you ever hear of Lucy Mokunui?" he asked.

"Lucy Mokunui?" I repeated, haunted by some familiar association. I shook my head. "It seems to me I've heard the name, but I've forgotten it."

"Never heard of Lucy Mokunui! The Hawaiian nightingale! I beg your pardon. Of course you are a *malahini,*[1] and could not be expected to know. Well, Lucy Mokunui was the best beloved of Honolulu—of all Hawaii, for that matter."

"You say *was,*" I interrupted.

"And I mean it. She is finished." He shrugged his shoulders pityingly. "A dozen *haoles*—I beg your pardon, white men—have lost their hearts to her at one time or another. And I'm not counting in the ruck. The dozen I refer to were *haoles* of position and prominence.

"She could have married the son of the Chief Justice if she'd wanted to. You think she's beautiful, eh? But you should hear her sing. Finest native woman singer in Hawaii Nei. Her throat is pure silver and melted sunshine. We adored her. She toured America first with the Royal Hawaiian Band. After that she made two more trips on her own—concert work."

"Oh!" I cried. "I remember now. I heard her two years ago at the Boston Symphony. So that is she. I recognize her now."

I was oppressed by a heavy sadness. Life was a futile thing at best. A short two years and this magnificent creature, at the summit of her magnificent success, was one of the leper squad awaiting deportation to Molokai. Henley's lines came into my mind:—

> *"The poor old tramp explains his poor old ulcers;*
> *Life is, I think, a blunder and a shame."*

I recoiled from my own future. If this awful fate fell to Lucy Mokunui, what might not my lot be?—or anybody's lot? I was thoroughly aware that in life we are in the midst of death—but to be in the midst of living death, to die and not be dead, to be one of that draft of creatures that once were men, aye, and women, like Lucy Mokunui, the epitome of all Polynesian charms, an artist as well, and well beloved of men—. I am afraid I must have betrayed my perturbation, for Doctor Georges hastened to assure me that they were very happy down in the settlement.

It was all too inconceivably monstrous. I could not bear to look

---

[1] *Malahini*—newcomer. [London's note]

at her. A short distance away, behind a stretched rope guarded by a policeman, were the lepers' relatives and friends. They were not allowed to come near. There were no last embraces, no kisses of farewell. They called back and forth to one another—last messages, last words of love, last reiterated instructions. And those behind the rope looked with terrible intensity. It was the last time they would behold the faces of their loved ones, for they were the living dead, being carted away in the funeral ship to the graveyard of Molokai.

Doctor Georges gave the command, and the unhappy wretches dragged themselves to their feet and under their burdens of luggage began to stagger across the lighter and aboard the steamer. It was the funeral procession. At once the wailing started from those behind the rope. It was blood-curdling; it was heart-rending. I never heard such woe, and I hope never to again. Kersdale and McVeigh were still at the other end of the wharf, talking earnestly—politics, of course, for both were head-over-heels in that particular game. When Lucy Mokunui passed me, I stole a look at her. She *was* beautiful. She was beautiful by our standards, as well—one of those rare blossoms that occur but once in generations. And she, of all women, was doomed to Molokai. She walked like a queen, across the lighter, straight on board, and aft on the open deck where the lepers huddled by the rail, wailing, now, to their dear ones on shore.

The lines were cast off, and the *Noeau* began to move away from the wharf. The wailing increased. Such grief and despair! I was just resolving that never again would I be a witness to the sailing of the *Noeau,* when McVeigh and Kersdale returned. The latter's eyes were sparkling, and his lips could not quite hide the smile of delight that was his. Evidently the politics they had talked had been satisfactory. The rope had been flung aside, and the lamenting relatives now crowded the stringer piece on either side of us.

"That's her mother," Doctor Georges whispered, indicating an old woman next to me, who was rocking back and forth and gazing at the steamer rail out of tear-blinded eyes. I noticed that Lucy Mokunui was also wailing. She stopped abruptly and gazed at Kersdale. Then she stretched forth her arms in that adorable, sensuous way that Olga Nethersole has of embracing an audience. And with arms outspread, she cried:

"Good-by, Jack! Good-by!"

He heard the cry, and looked. Never was a man overtaken by more crushing fear. He reeled on the stringer piece, his face went white to the roots of his hair, and he seemed to shrink and wither away inside his clothes. He threw up his hands and groaned, "My God! My God!" Then he controlled himself by a great effort.

"Good-by, Lucy! Good-by!" he called.

And he stood there on the wharf, waving his hands to her till the *Noeau* was clear away and the faces lining her after-rail were vague and indistinct.

"I thought you knew," said McVeigh, who had been regarding him curiously. "You, of all men, should have known. I thought that was why you were here."

"I know now," Kersdale answered with immense gravity. "Where's the carriage?"

He walked rapidly—half-ran—to it. I had to half-run myself to keep up with him.

"Drive to Doctor Hervey's," he told the driver. "Drive as fast as you can."

He sank down in the seat, panting and gasping. The pallor of his face had increased. His lips were compressed and the sweat was standing out on his forehead and upper lip. He seemed in some horrible agony.

"For God's sake, Martin, make those horses go!" he broke out suddenly. "Lay the whip into them!—do you hear?—lay the whip into them!"

"They'll break, sir," the driver remonstrated.

"Let them break," Kersdale answered. "I'll pay your fine and square you with the police. Put it to them. That's right. Faster! Faster!"

"And I never knew, I never knew," he muttered, sinking back in the seat and with trembling hands wiping the sweat away.

The carriage was bouncing, swaying and lurching around corners at such a wild pace as to make conversation impossible. Besides, there was nothing to say. But I could hear him muttering over and over, "And I never knew. I never knew."

# MAUKI

HE WEIGHED one hundred and ten pounds. His hair was kinky and negroid, and he was black. He was peculiarly black. He was neither blue-black nor purple-black, but plum-black. His name was Mauki, and he was the son of a chief. He had three *tambos*. *Tambo* is Melanesian for *taboo*, and is first cousin to that Polynesian word. Mauki's three *tambos* were as follows: first, he must never shake hands with a woman, nor have a woman's hand touch him or any of his personal belongings; secondly, he must never eat clams nor any food from a fire in which clams had been cooked; thirdly, he must never touch a crocodile, nor travel in a canoe that carried any part of a crocodile even if as large as a tooth.

Of a different black were his teeth, which were deep black, or, perhaps better, *lamp*-black. They had been made so in a single night, by his mother, who had compressed about them a powdered mineral which was dug from the landslide back of Port Adams. Port Adams is a salt-water village on Malaita, and Malaita is the most savage island in the Solomons—so savage that no traders nor planters have yet gained a foothold on it; while, from the time of the earliest bêche-de-mer fishers and sandalwood traders down to the latest labor recruiters equipped with automatic rifles and gasolene engines, scores of white adventurers have been passed out by tomahawks and soft-nosed Snider bullets. So Malaita remains to-day, in the twentieth century, the stamping ground of the labor recruiters, who farm its coasts for laborers who engage and contract themselves to toil on the plantations of the neighboring and more civilized islands for a wage of thirty dollars a year. The natives of those neighboring and more civilized islands have themselves become too civilized to work on plantations.

Mauki's ears were pierced, not in one place, nor two places, but in a couple of dozen places. In one of the smaller holes he carried a clay pipe. The larger holes were too large for such use. The bowl of the pipe would have fallen through. In fact, in the largest hole in each ear he habitually wore round wooden plugs that were an even four inches in diameter. Roughly speaking, the circumference of said holes was twelve and one-half inches. Mauki was catholic in his tastes. In the various smaller holes he carried such things as empty rifle cartridges, horseshoe nails, copper screws, pieces of string, braids of sennit, strips of green leaf, and, in the cool of the day, scarlet hibiscus flowers. From which it will be seen that pockets were not necessary to his well-being. Besides, pockets were impossible, for his only wearing apparel consisted of a piece of calico several inches wide. A pocket knife he wore in his hair, the blade snapped down on a kinky lock. His most prized possession was the handle of a china cup, which he suspended from a ring of turtle-shell, which, in turn, was passed through the partition-cartilage of his nose.

But in spite of embellishments, Mauki had a nice face. It was really a pretty face, viewed by any standard, and for a Melanesian it was a remarkably good-looking face. Its one fault was its lack of strength. It was softly effeminate, almost girlish. The features were small, regular, and delicate. The chin was weak, and the mouth was weak. There was no strength nor character in the jaws, forehead, and nose. In the eyes only could be caught any hint of the unknown quantities that were so large a part of his make-up and that other persons could not understand. These unknown quantities were pluck, pertinacity, fearlessness, imagination, and cunning; and when they found expression in some consistent and striking action, those about him were astounded.

Mauki's father was chief over the village at Port Adams, and thus, by birth a salt-water man, Mauki was half amphibian. He knew the way of the fishes and oysters, and the reef was an open book to him. Canoes, also, he knew. He learned to swim when he was a year old. At seven years he could hold his breath a full minute and swim straight down to bottom through thirty feet of water. And at seven years he was stolen by the bushmen, who cannot even swim and who are afraid of salt water. Thereafter Mauki saw the sea only from a distance, through rifts in the jungle and from open spaces on the high mountain sides. He became the slave of old Fanfoa, head chief over a score of scattered bush-villages on the range-lips of Malaita, the smoke of which, on calm mornings, is about the only evidence the seafaring white men have of the teeming interior population. For the whites do not penetrate Malaita. They tried it once, in the days when the search was on for gold, but they always left their heads behind to grin from the smoky rafters of the bushmen's huts.

When Mauki was a young man of seventeen, Fanfoa got out of tobacco. He got dreadfully out of tobacco. It was hard times in all his villages. He had been guilty of a mistake. Suo was a harbor so small that a large schooner could not swing at anchor in it. It was surrounded by mangroves that overhung the deep water. It was a trap, and into the trap sailed two white men in a small ketch. They were after recruits, and they possessed much tobacco and trade-goods, to say nothing of three rifles and plenty of ammunition. Now there were no salt-water men living at Suo, and it was there that the bushmen could come down to the sea. The ketch did a splendid traffic. It signed on twenty recruits the first day. Even old Fanfoa signed on. And that same day the score of new recruits chopped off the two white men's heads, killed the boat's crew, and burned the ketch. Thereafter, and for three months, there was tobacco and trade-goods in plenty and to spare in all the bush-villages. Then came the man-of-war that threw shells for miles into the hills, frightening the people out of their villages and into the deeper bush. Next the man-of-war sent landing parties ashore. The villages were all burned, along with the tobacco and trade-stuff. The cocoanuts and bananas were chopped down, the taro gardens uprooted, and the pigs and chickens killed.

It taught Fanfoa a lesson, but in the meantime he was out of tobacco. Also, his young men were too frightened to sign on with the recruiting vessels. That was why Fanfoa ordered his slave, Mauki, to be carried down and signed on for half a case of tobacco advance, along with knives, axes, calico, and beads, which he would pay for with his toil on the plantations. Mauki was sorely frightened when they brought him on board the schooner. He was a lamb led to the slaughter. White men were ferocious creatures. They had to be, or else they would not make a practice of venturing along the Malaita coast and into all harbors, two on a schooner, when each schooner carried from fifteen to twenty blacks as boat's crew, and often as high as sixty or seventy black recruits. In addition to this, there was always the danger of the shore population, the sudden attack and the cutting off of the schooner and all hands. Truly, white men must be terrible. Besides, they were possessed of such devil-devils—rifles that shot very rapidly many times, things of iron and brass that made the schooners go when there was no wind, and boxes that talked and laughed just as men talked and laughed. Ay, and he had heard of one white man whose particular devil-devil was so powerful that he could take out all his teeth and put them back at will.

Down into the cabin they took Mauki. On deck, the one white man kept guard with two revolvers in his belt. In the cabin the other white man sat with a book before him, in which he inscribed strange marks and lines. He looked at Mauki as though he had been a pig or a fowl, glanced under the hollows of his arms, and wrote in the book. Then he held out the writing stick and Mauki just barely touched it with his hand, in so doing pledging himself to toil for three years on the plantations of the Moongleam Soap Company. It was not explained to him that the will of the ferocious white men would be used to enforce the pledge, and that, behind all, for the same use, was all the power and all the warships of Great Britain.

Other blacks there were on board, from unheard-of far places, and when the white man spoke to them, they tore the long feather from Mauki's hair, cut that same hair short, and wrapped about his waist a lava-lava of bright yellow calico.

After many days on the schooner, and after beholding more land and islands than he had ever dreamed of, he was landed on New Georgia, and put to work in the field clearing jungle and cutting cane grass. For the first time he knew what work was. Even as a slave to Fanfoa he had not worked like this. And he did not like work. It was up at dawn and in at dark, on two meals a day. And the food was tiresome. For weeks at a time they were given nothing but sweet potatoes to eat, and for weeks at a time it would be nothing but rice. He cut out the cocoanut from the shells day after day; and for long days and weeks he fed the fires that smoked the copra, till his eyes got sore and he was set to felling trees. He was a good axe-man, and later he was put in the bridge-building gang. Once, he was punished by being put in the road-building gang. At times he served as boat's crew in the whale-boats, when they brought in copra from distant beaches or when the white men went out to dynamite fish.

Among other things he learned bêche-de-mer English, with which he could talk with all white men, and with all recruits who otherwise would have talked in a thousand different dialects. Also, he learned certain things about the white men, principally that they kept their word. If they told a boy he was going to receive a stick of tobacco, he got it. If they told a boy they would knock seven bells out of him if he did a certain thing, when he did that thing seven bells invariably were knocked out of him. Mauki did not know what seven bells were, but they occurred in bêche-de-mer, and he imagined them to be the blood and teeth that sometimes accompanied the process of knocking out seven bells. One other thing he learned: no boy was struck or punished unless he did wrong. Even when the white men were drunk, as they were frequently, they never struck unless a rule had been broken.

Mauki did not like the plantation. He hated work, and he was the son of a chief Furthermore, it was ten years since he had been stolen from Port Adams by Fanfoa, and he was homesick. He was even homesick for the slavery under Fanfoa. So he ran away. He struck back into the bush, with the idea of working southward to the beach and stealing a canoe in which to go home to Port Adams. But the fever got him, and he was captured and brought back more dead than alive.

A second time he ran away, in the company of two Malaita boys. They got down the coast twenty miles, and were hidden in the hut of a Malaita freeman, who dwelt in that village. But in the dead of night two white men came, who were not afraid of all the village people and who knocked seven bells out of the three runaways, tied them like pigs, and tossed them into the whale-boat. But the man in whose house they had hidden—seven times seven bells must have been knocked out of him from the way the hair, skin, and teeth flew, and he was discouraged for the rest of his natural life from harboring runaway laborers.

For a year Mauki toiled on. Then he was made a house-boy, and had good food and easy times, with light work in keeping the house clean and serving the white men with whiskey and beer at all hours of the day and most hours of the night. He liked it, but he liked Port Adams more. He had two years longer to serve, but two years were too long for him in the throes of homesickness. He had grown wiser with his year of service, and, being now a houseboy, he had opportunity. He had the cleaning of the rifles, and he knew where the key to the store-room was hung. He planned the escape, and one night ten Malaita boys and one boy from San Cristoval sneaked from the barracks and dragged one of the whale-boats down to the beach. It was Mauki who supplied the key that opened the padlock on the boat, and it was Mauki who equipped the boat with a dozen Winchesters, an immense amount of ammunition, a case of dynamite with detonators and fuse, and ten cases of tobacco.

The northwest monsoon was blowing, and they fled south in the night-time, hiding by day on detached and uninhabited islets, or dragging their whale-boat into the bush on the large islands. Thus they gained Guadalcanar, skirted halfway along it, and crossed the Indispensable Straits to Florida Island. It was here that they killed the San Cristoval boy, saving his head and cooking and eating the rest of him. The Malaita coast was only twenty miles away, but the last night a strong current and baffling winds prevented them from gaining across. Daylight found them still several miles from their goal. But daylight brought a cutter, in which were two white men, who were not afraid of eleven Malaita men armed with twelve rifles. Mauki and his companions were carried back to Tulagi, where lived the great white master of all the white men. And the great white master held a court, after which, one by one, the runaways were tied up and given twenty lashes each, and sentenced to a fine of fifteen dollars. Then they were sent back to New Georgia, where the white men knocked seven bells out of them all around and put them to work. But Mauki was no longer houseboy. He was put in the road-making gang. The fine of fifteen dollars had been paid by the white men from whom he had run away, and he was told that he would have to work it out, which meant six months' additional toil. Further, his share of the stolen tobacco earned him another year of toil.

Port Adams was now three years and a half away, so he stole a canoe one night, hid on the islets in Manning Straits, passed through the Straits, and began working along the eastern coast of Ysabel, only to be captured, two-thirds of the way along, by the white men on Meringe Lagoon. After a week, he escaped from them and took to the bush. There were no bush natives on Ysabel, only salt-water men, who were all Christians. The white men put up a reward of five hundred sticks of tobacco, and every time Mauki ventured down to the sea to steal a canoe he was chased by the salt-water men. Four months of this passed, when, the reward having been raised to a thousand sticks, he was caught and sent back to New Georgia and the road-building gang. Now a thousand sticks are worth fifty dollars, and Mauki had to pay the reward himself, which required a year and eight months' labor. So Port Adams was now five years away.

His homesickness was greater than ever, and it did not appeal to him to settle down and be good, work out his four years, and go home. The next time, he was caught in the very act of running away. His case was brought before Mr. Haveby, the island manager of the Moongleam Soap Company, who adjudged him an incorrigible. The Company had plantations on the Santa Cruz Islands, hundreds of miles across the sea, and there it sent its Solomon Islands' incorrigibles. And there Mauki was sent, though he never arrived. The schooner stopped at Santa Anna, and in the night Mauki swam ashore, where he stole two rifles and a case of tobacco from the trader and got away in a canoe to Cristoval. Malaita was now to the north, fifty or sixty miles away. But when he attempted the passage, he was caught by a light gale and driven back to Santa Anna, where the trader clapped him in irons and held him against the return of the schooner from Santa Cruz. The two rifles the trader recovered, but the case of tobacco was charged up to Mauki at the rate of another year. The sum of years he now owed the Company was six.

On the way back to New Georgia, the schooner dropped anchor in Marau Sound, which lies at the southeastern extremity of Guadalcanar. Mauki swam ashore with handcuffs on his wrists and got away to the bush. The schooner went on, but the Moongleam trader ashore offered a thousand sticks, and to him Mauki was brought by the bushmen with a year and eight months tacked on to his account. Again, and before the schooner called in, he got away, this time in a whaleboat accompanied by a case of the trader's tobacco. But a northwest gale wrecked him upon Ugi, where the Christian natives stole his tobacco and turned him over to the Moongleam trader who resided there. The tobacco the natives stole meant another year for him, and the tale was now eight years and a half.

"We'll send him to Lord Howe," said Mr. Haveby. "Bunster is there, and we'll let them settle it between them. It will be a case, I imagine, of Mauki getting Bunster, or Bunster getting Mauki, and good riddance in either event."

If one leaves Meringe Lagoon, on Ysabel, and steers a course due north, magnetic, at the end of one hundred and fifty miles he will lift the pounded coral beaches of Lord Howe above the sea. Lord Howe is a ring of land some one hundred and fifty miles in circumference, several hundred yards wide at its widest, and towering in places to a height of ten feet above sea-level. Inside this ring of sand is a mighty lagoon studded with coral patches. Lord Howe belongs to the Solomons neither geographically nor ethnologically. It is an atoll, while the Solomons are high islands; and its people and language are Polynesian, while the inhabitants of the Solomons are Melanesian. Lord Howe has been populated by the westward Polynesian drift which continues to this day, big outrigger canoes being washed upon its beaches by the southeast trade. That there has been a slight Melanesian drift in the period of the northwest monsoon, is also evident.

Nobody ever comes to Lord Howe, or Ontong-Java as it is sometimes called. Thomas Cook & Son do not sell tickets to it, and tourists do not dream of its existence. Not even a white missionary has landed on its shore. Its five thousand natives are as peaceable as they are primitive. Yet they were not always peaceable. The *Sailing Directions* speak of them as hostile and treacherous. But the men who compile the *Sailing Directions* have never heard of the change that was worked in the hearts of the inhabitants, who, not many years ago, cut off a big bark and killed all hands with the exception of the second mate. This survivor carried the news to his brothers. The captains of three trading schooners returned with him to Lord Howe. They sailed their vessels right into the lagoon and proceeded to preach the white man's gospel that only white men shall kill white men and that the lesser breeds must keep hands off. The schooners sailed up and down the lagoon, harrying and destroying. There was no escape from the narrow sand-circle, no bush to which to flee. The men were shot down at sight, and there was no avoiding being sighted. The villages were burned, the canoes smashed, the chickens and pigs killed, and the precious cocoanut-trees chopped down. For a month this continued, when the schooners sailed away; but the fear of the white man had been seared into the souls of the islanders and never again were they rash enough to harm one.

Max Bunster was the one white man on Lord Howe, trading in the pay of the ubiquitous Moongleam Soap Company. And the company billeted him on Lord Howe, because, next to getting rid of him, it was the most out-of-the-way place to be found. That the Company did not get rid of him was due to the difficulty of finding another man to take his place. He was a strapping big German, with something wrong in his brain. Semi-madness would be a charitable statement of his condition. He was a bully and a coward, and a thrice-bigger savage than any savage on the island. Being a coward, his brutality was of the cowardly order. When he first went into the Company's employ, he was stationed on Savo. When a consumptive colonial was sent to take his place, he beat him up with his fists and sent him off a wreck in the schooner that brought him.

Mr. Haveby next selected a young Yorkshire giant to relieve Bunster. The Yorkshire man had a reputation as a bruiser and preferred fighting to eating. But Bunster wouldn't fight. He was a regular little lamb—for ten days, at the end of which time the Yorkshire man was prostrated by a combined attack of dysentery and fever. Then Bunster went for him, among other things getting him down and jumping on him a score or so of times. Afraid of what would happen when his victim recovered, Bunster fled away in a cutter to Guvutu, where he signalized himself by beating up a young Englishman already crippled by a Boer bullet through both hips.

Then it was that Mr. Haveby sent Bunster to Lord Howe, the falling-off place. He celebrated his landing by mopping up half a case of gin and by thrashing the elderly and wheezy mate of the schooner which had brought him. When the schooner departed, he called the kanakas down to the beach and challenged them to throw him in a wrestling bout, promising a case of tobacco to the one who succeeded. Three kanakas he threw, but was promptly thrown by a fourth, who, instead of receiving the tobacco, got a bullet through his lungs.

And so began Bunster's reign on Lord Howe. Three thousand people lived in the principal village; but it was deserted, even in broad day, when he passed through. Men, women, and children fled before him. Even the dogs and pigs got out of the way, while the king was not above hiding under a mat. The two prime ministers lived in terror of Bunster, who never discussed any moot subject, but struck out with his fists instead.

And to Lord Howe came Mauki, to toil for Bunster for eight long years and a half. There was no escaping from Lord Howe. For better or worse, Bunster and he were tied together. Bunster weighed two hundred pounds. Mauki weighed one hundred and ten. Bunster was a degenerate brute. But Mauki was a primitive savage. While both had wills and ways of their own.

Mauki had no idea of the sort of master he was to work for. He had had no warnings, and he had concluded as a matter of course that Bunster would be like other white men, a drinker of much whiskey, a ruler and a lawgiver who always kept his word and who never struck a boy undeserved. Bunster had the advantage. He knew all about Mauki, and gloated over the coming into possession of him. The last cook was suffering from a broken arm and a dislocated shoulder, so Bunster made Mauki cook and general house-boy.

And Mauki soon learned that there were white men and white men. On the very day the schooner departed he was ordered to buy a chicken from Samisee, the native Tongan missionary. But Samisee had sailed across the lagoon and would not be back for three days. Mauki returned with the information. He climbed the steep stairway (the house stood on piles twelve feet above the sand), and entered the living-room to report. The trader demanded the chicken. Mauki opened his mouth to explain the missionary's absence. But Bunster did not care for explanations. He struck out with his fist. The blow caught Mauki on the mouth and lifted him into the air. Clear through the doorway he flew, across the narrow veranda, breaking the top railing, and down to the ground. His lips were a contused, shapeless mass, and his mouth was full of blood and broken teeth.

"That'll teach you that back talk don't go with me," the trader shouted, purple with rage, peering down at him over the broken railing.

Mauki had never met a white man like this, and he resolved to walk small and never offend. He saw the boat-boys knocked about, and one of them put in irons for three days with nothing to eat for the crime of breaking a rowlock while pulling. Then, too, he heard the gossip of the village and learned why Bunster had taken a third wife—by force, as was well known. The first and second wives lay in the graveyard, under the white coral sand, with slabs of coral rock at head and feet. They had died, it was said, from beatings he had given them. The third wife was certainly ill-used, as Mauki could see for himself.

But there was no way by which to avoid offending the white man, who seemed offended with life. When Mauki kept silent, he was struck and called a sullen brute. When he spoke, he was struck for giving back talk. When he was grave, Bunster accused him of plotting and gave him a thrashing in advance; and when he strove to be cheerful and to smile, he was charged with sneering at his lord and master and given a taste of stick. Bunster was a devil. The village would have done for him, had it not remembered the lesson of the three schooners. It might have done for him anyway, if there had been a bush to which to flee. As it was, the murder of the white men, of any white man, would bring a man-of-war that would kill the offenders and chop down the precious cocoanut-trees. Then there were the boat-boys, with minds fully made up to drown him by accident at the first opportunity to capsize the cutter. Only Bunster saw to it that the boat did not capsize.

Mauki was of a different breed, and, escape being impossible while Bunster lived, he was resolved to get the white man. The trouble was that he could never find a chance. Bunster was always on guard. Day and night his revolvers were ready to hand. He permitted nobody to pass behind his back, as Mauki learned after having been knocked down several times. Bunster knew that he had more to fear from the good-natured, even sweet-faced, Malaita boy than from the entire population of Lord Howe; and it gave added zest to the programme of torment he was carrying out. And Mauki walked small, accepted his punishments, and waited.

All other white men had respected his *tambos,* but not so Bunster. Mauki's weekly allowance of tobacco was two sticks. Bunster passed them to his woman and ordered Mauki to receive them from her hand. But this could not be, and Mauki went without his tobacco. In the same way he was made to miss many a meal, and to go hungry many a day. He was ordered to make chowder out of the big clams that grew in the lagoon. This he could not do, for clams were *tambo.* Six times in succession he refused to touch the clams, and six times he was knocked senseless. Bunster knew that the boy would die first, but called his refusal mutiny, and would have killed him had there been another cook to take his place.

One of the trader's favorite tricks was to catch Mauki's kinky locks and bat his head against the wall. Another trick was to catch Mauki unawares and thrust the live end of a cigar against his flesh. This Bunster called vaccination, and Mauki was vaccinated a number of times a week. Once, in a rage, Bunster ripped the cup handle from Mauki's nose, tearing the hole clear out of the cartilage.

"Oh, what a mug!" was his comment, when he surveyed the damage he had wrought.

The skin of a shark is like sandpaper, but the skin of a ray fish is like a rasp. In the South Seas the natives use it as a wood file in smoothing down canoes and paddles. Bunster had a mitten made of ray fish skin. The first time he tried it on Mauki, with one sweep of the hand it fetched the skin off his back from neck to armpit. Bunster was delighted. He gave his wife a taste of the mitten, and tried it out thoroughly on the boat-boys. The prime ministers came in for a stroke each, and they had to grin and take it for a joke.

"Laugh, damn you, laugh!" was the cue he gave.

Mauki came in for the largest share of the mitten. Never a day passed without a caress from it. There were times when the loss of so much cuticle kept him awake at night, and often the half-healed surface was raked raw afresh by the facetious Mr. Bunster. Mauki continued his patient wait, secure in the knowledge that sooner or later his time would come. And he knew just what he was going to do, down to the smallest detail, when the time did come.

One morning Bunster got up in a mood for knocking seven bells out of the universe. He began on Mauki, and wound up on Mauki, in the interval knocking down his wife and hammering all the boat-boys. At breakfast he called the coffee slops and threw the scalding contents of the cup into Mauki's face. By ten o'clock Bunster was shivering with ague, and half an hour later he was burning with fever. It was no ordinary attack. It quickly became pernicious, and developed into black-water fever. The days passed, and he grew weaker and weaker, never leaving his bed. Mauki waited and watched, the while his skin grew intact once more. He ordered the boys to beach the cutter, scrub her bottom, and give her a general overhauling. They thought the order emanated from Bunster, and they obeyed. But Bunster at the time was lying unconscious and giving no orders. This was Mauki's chance, but still he waited.

When the worst was past, and Bunster lay convalescent and conscious, but weak as a baby, Mauki packed his few trinkets, including the china cup handle, into his trade box. Then he went over to the village and interviewed the king and his two prime ministers.

"This fella Bunster, him good fella you like too much?" he asked.

They explained in one voice that they liked the trader not at all. The ministers poured forth a recital of all the indignities and wrongs that had been heaped upon them. The king broke down and wept. Mauki interrupted rudely.

"You savve me—me big fella marster my country. You no like 'm this fella white marster. Me no like 'm. Plenty good you put hundred cocoanut, two hundred cocoanut, three hundred cocoanut along cutter. Him finish, you go sleep 'm good fella. Altogether kanaka sleep 'm good fella. Bime by big fella noise along house, you no savve hear 'm that fella noise. You altogether sleep strong fella too much."

In like manner Mauki interviewed the boat-boys. Then he ordered Bunster's wife to return to her family house. Had she refused, he would have been in a quandary, for his *tamboo* would not have permitted him to lay hands on her.

The house deserted, he entered the sleeping-room, where the trader lay in a doze. Mauki first removed the revolvers, then placed the ray fish mitten on his hand. Bunster's first warning was a stroke of the mitten that removed the skin the full length of his nose.

"Good fella, eh?" Mauki grinned, between two strokes, one of which swept the forehead bare and the other of which cleaned off one side of his face. "Laugh, damn you, laugh."

Mauki did his work thoroughly, and the kanakas, hiding in their houses, heard the "big fella noise" that Bunster made and continued to make for an hour or more.

When Mauki was done, he carried the boat compass and all the rifles and ammunition down to the cutter, which he proceeded to ballast with cases of tobacco. It was while engaged in this that a hideous, skinless thing came out of the house and ran screaming down the beach till it fell in the sand and mowed and gibbered under the scorching sun. Mauki looked toward it and hesitated. Then he went over and removed the head, which he wrapped in a mat and stowed in the stern-locker of the cutter.

So soundly did the kanakas sleep through that long hot day that they did not see the cutter run out through the passage and head south, close-hauled on the southeast trade. Nor was the cutter ever sighted on that long tack to the shores of Ysabel, and during the tedious head-beat from there to Malaita. He landed at Port Adams with a wealth of rifles and tobacco such as no one man had ever possessed before. But he did not stop there. He had taken a white man's head, and only the bush could shelter him. So back he went to the bush-villages, where he shot old Fanfoa and half a dozen of the chief men, and made himself the chief over all the villages. When his father died, Mauki's brother ruled in Port Adams, and, joined together, salt-water men and bushmen, the resulting combination was the strongest of the ten score fighting tribes of Malaita.

More than his fear of the British government was Mauki's fear of the all-powerful Moongleam Soap Company; and one day a message came up to him in the bush, reminding him that he owed the Company eight and one-half years of labor. He sent back a favorable answer, and then appeared the inevitable white man, the captain of the schooner, the only white man during Mauki's reign who ventured the bush and came out alive. This man not only came out, but he brought with him seven hundred and fifty dollars in gold sovereigns—the money price of eight years and a half of labor plus the cost price of certain rifles and cases of tobacco.

Mauki no longer weighs one hundred and ten pounds. His stomach is three times its former girth, and he has four wives. He has many other things—rifles and revolvers, the handle of a china cup, and an excellent collection of bushmen's heads. But more precious than the entire collection is another head, perfectly dried and cured, with sandy hair and a yellowish beard, which is kept wrapped in the finest of fibre lava-lavas. When Mauki goes to war with villages beyond his realm, he invariably gets out this head, and, alone in his grass palace, contemplates it long and solemnly. At such times the hush of death falls on the village, and not even a pickaninny dares make a noise. The head is esteemed the most powerful devil-devil on Malaita, and to the possession of it is ascribed all of Mauki's greatness.

# THE STRENGTH OF THE STRONG

*Parables don't lie, but liars will parable.*

*—Lip-King*

OLD LONG BEARD paused in his narrative, licked his greasy fingers, and wiped them on his naked sides where his one piece of ragged bearskin failed to cover him. Crouched around him, on their hams, were three young men, his grandsons, Deer-Runner, Yellow-Head, and Afraid-of-the-Dark. In appearance they were much the same. Skins of wild animals partly covered them. They were lean and meager of build, narrow-hipped and crooked-legged, and at the same time deep-chested, with heavy arms and enormous hands. There was much hair on their chests and shoulders, and on the outsides of their arms and legs. Their heads were matted with uncut hair, long locks of which often strayed before their eyes, beady and black and glittering like the eyes of birds. They were narrow between the eyes and broad between the cheeks, while their lower jaws were projecting and massive.

It was a night of clear starlight, and below them, stretching away remotely, lay range on range of forest-covered hills. In the distance the heavens were red from the glow of a volcano. At their backs yawned the black mouth of a cave, out of which, from time to time, blew draughty gusts of wind. Immediately in front of them blazed a fire. At one side, partly devoured, lay the carcass of a bear, with about it, at a respectable distance, several large dogs, shaggy and wolf-like. Beside each man lay his bow and arrows and a huge club. In the cavemouth a number of rude spears leaned against the rock.

"So that was how we moved from the cave to the tree," old Long Beard spoke up.

They laughed boisterously, like big children, at recollection of a previous story his words called up. Long Beard laughed, too, the five-inch bodkin of bone, thrust midway through the cartilage of his nose, leaping and dancing and adding to his ferocious appearance. He did not exactly say the words recorded, but he made animal-like sounds with his mouth that meant the same thing.

"And that is the first I remember of the Sea Valley," Long Beard went on. "We were a very foolish crowd. We did not know the secret of strength. For, behold, each family lived by itself, and took care of itself. There were thirty families, but we got no strength from one another. We were in fear of each other all the time. No one ever paid visits. In the top of our tree we built a grass house, and on the platform outside was a pile of rocks, which were for the heads of any that might chance to try to visit us. Also, we had our spears and arrows. We never walked under the trees of the other families, either. My brother did, once, under old Boo-oogh's tree, and he got his head broken and that was the end of him.

Old Boo-oogh was very strong. It was said he could pull a grown man's head right off. I never heard of him doing it, because no man would give him a chance. Father wouldn't. One day, when father was down on the beach, Boo-oogh took after mother. She couldn't run fast, for the day before she had got her leg clawed by a bear when she was up on the mountain gathering berries. So Boo-oogh caught her and carried her up into his tree. Father never got her back. He was afraid. Old Boo-oogh made faces at him.

"But father did not mind. Strong-Arm was another strong man. He was one of the best fishermen. But one day, climbing after seagull eggs, he had a fall from the cliff. He was never strong after that. He coughed a great deal, and his shoulders drew near to each other. So father took Strong-Arm's wife. When he came around and coughed under our tree, father laughed at him and threw rocks at him. It was our way in those days. We did not know how to add strength together and become strong."

"Would a brother take a brother's wife?" Deer-Runner demanded.

"Yes, if he had gone to live in another tree by himself."

"But we do not do such things now," Afraid-of-the-Dark objected.

"It is because I have taught your fathers better." Long Beard thrust his hairy paw into the bear meat and drew out a handful of suet, which he sucked with a meditative air. Again he wiped his hands on his naked sides and went on. "What I am telling you happened in the long ago, before we knew any better."

"You must have been fools not to know better," was Deer-Runner's comment, Yellow-Head grunting approval.

"So we were, but we became bigger fools, as you shall see. Still, we did learn better, and this was the way of it. We Fish-Eaters had not learned to add our strength until our strength was the strength of all of us. But the Meat-Eaters, who lived across the divide in the Big Valley, stood together, hunted together, fished together, and fought together. One day they came into our valley. Each family of us got into its own cave and tree. There were only ten Meat-Eaters, but they fought together, and we fought each family by itself."

Long Beard counted long and perplexedly on his fingers.

"There were sixty men of us," was what he managed to say with fingers and lips combined. "And we were very strong, only we did not know it. So we watched the ten men attack Boo-oogh's tree. He made a good fight, but he had no chance. We looked on. When some of the Meat-Eaters tried to climb the tree, Boo-oogh had to show himself in order to drop stones on their heads, whereupon the other Meat-Eaters, who were waiting for that very thing, shot him full of arrows. And that was the end of Boo-oogh.

"Next, the Meat-Eaters got One-Eye and his family in his cave. They built a fire in the mouth and smoked him out, like we smoked out the bear there to-day. Then they went after Six-Fingers, up his tree, and, while they were killing him and his grown son, the rest of us ran away. They caught some of our women, and killed two old men who could not run fast and several children. The women they carried away with them to the Big Valley.

"After that the rest of us crept back, and, somehow, perhaps because we were in fear and felt the need for one another, we talked the thing over. It was our first council—our first real council. And in that council we formed our first tribe. For we had learned the lesson. Of the ten Meat-Eaters, each man had had the strength of ten, for the ten had fought as one man. They had added their strength together. But of the thirty families and the sixty men of us, we had had the strength of but one man, for each had fought alone.

"It was a great talk we had, and it was hard talk, for we did not have the words then as now with which to talk. The Bug made some of the words long afterward, and so did others of us make words from time to time. But in the end we agreed to add our strength together and to be as one man when the Meat-Eaters came over the divide to steal our women. And that was the tribe.

"We set two men on the divide, one for the day and one for the night, to watch if the Meat-Eaters came. These were the eyes of the tribe. Then, also, day and night, there were to be ten men awake with their clubs and spears and arrows in their hands, ready to fight. Before, when a man went after fish, or clams, or gull-eggs, he carried his weapons with him, and half the time he was getting food and half the time watching for fear some other man would get him. Now that was all changed. The men went out without their weapons and spent all their time getting food. Likewise, when the women went into the mountains after roots and berries, five of the ten men went with them to guard them. While all the time, day and night, the eyes of the tribe watched from the top of the divide.

"But troubles came. As usual, it was about the women. Men without wives wanted other men's wives, and there was much fighting between men, and now and again one got his head smashed or a spear through his body. While one of the watchers was on top the divide, another man stole his wife, and he came down to fight. Then the other watcher was in fear that someone would take his wife, and he came down likewise. Also, there was trouble among the ten men who carried always their weapons, and they fought five against five, till some ran away down the coast and the others ran after them.

"So it was that the tribe was left without eyes or guards. We had not the strength of sixty. We had no strength at all. So we held a council and made our first laws. I was but a cub at the time, but I remember. We said that, in order to be strong, we must not fight one another, and we made a law that when a man killed another him would the tribe kill. We made another law that whoso stole another man's wife him would the tribe kill. We said that whatever man had too great strength, and by that strength hurt his brothers in the tribe, him would we kill that his strength might hurt no more. For, if we let his strength hurt, the brothers would become afraid and the tribe would fall apart, and we would be as weak as when the Meat-Eaters first came upon us and killed Boo-oogh.

"Knuckle-Bone was a strong man, a very strong man, and he knew not law. He knew only his own strength, and in the fullness thereof he went forth and took the wife of Three-Clams. Three-Clams tried to fight, but Knuckle-Bone clubbed out his brains. Yet had Knuckle-Bone forgotten that all the men of us had added our strength to keep the law among us, and him we killed, at the foot of his tree, and hung his body on a branch as a warning that the law was stronger than any man. For we were the law, all of us, and no man was greater than the law.

"Then there were other troubles, for know, O Deer-Runner, and Yellow-Head, and Afraid-of-the-Dark, that it is not easy to make a tribe. There were many things, little things, that it was a great trouble to call all the men together to have a council about. We were having councils morning, noon, and night, and in the middle of the night. We could find little time to go out and get food, what of the councils, for there was always some little thing to be settled, such as naming two new watchers to take the place of the old ones on the hill, or naming how much food should fall to the share of the men who kept their weapons always in their hands and got no food for themselves.

"We stood in need of a chief man to do these things, who would be the voice of the council, and who would account to the council for the things he did. So we named Fith-Fith the chief man. He was a strong man, too, and very cunning, and when he was angry he made noises just like that, *fith-fith,* like a wildcat.

"The ten men who guarded the tribe were set to work making a wall of stones across the narrow part of the valley. The women and large children helped, as did other men, until the wall was strong. After that, all the families came down out of their caves and trees and built grass houses behind the shelter of the wall. These houses were large and much better than the caves and trees, and everybody had a better time of it because the men had added their strength together and become a tribe. Because of the wall and the guards and the watchers, there was more time to hunt and fish and pick roots and berries; there was more food, and better food, and no one went hungry. And Three-Legs, so named because his legs had been smashed when a boy and who walked with a stick—Three-Legs got the seed of the wild corn and planted it in the ground in the valley near his house. Also, he tried planting fat roots and other things he found in the mountain valleys.

"Because of the safety in the Sea Valley, which was because of the wall and the watchers and the guards, and because there was food in plenty for all without having to fight for it, many families came in from the coast valleys on both sides and from the high back mountains where they had lived more like wild animals than men. And it was not long before the Sea Valley filled up, and in it were countless families. But, before this happened, the land, which had been free to all and belonged to all, was divided up. Three-Legs began it when he planted corn. But most of us did not care about the land. We thought the marking of the boundaries with fences of stone was a foolishness. We had plenty to eat, and what more did we want? I remember that my father and I built stone fences for Three-Legs and were given corn in return.

"So only a few got all the land, and Three-Legs got most of it. Also, others that had taken land gave it to the few that held on, being paid in return with corn and fat roots, and bearskins, and fishes which the farmers got from the fishermen in exchange for corn. And, the first thing we knew, all the land was gone.

"It was about this time that Fith-Fith died and Dog-Tooth, his son, was made chief. He demanded to be made chief anyway, because his father had been chief before him. Also, he looked upon himself as a greater chief than his father. He was a good chief at first, and worked hard, so that the council had less and less to do. Then arose a new voice in the Sea Valley. It was Twisted-Lip. We had never thought much of him, until he began to talk with the spirits of the dead. Later we called him Big-Fat, because he ate over-much, and did no work, and grew round and large. One day Big-Fat told us that the secrets of the dead were his, and that he was the voice of God. He became great friends with Dog-Tooth, who commanded that we build Big-Fat a grass house. And Big-Fat put taboos all around this house and kept God inside.

"More and more Dog-Tooth became greater than the council, and when the council grumbled and said it would name a new chief, Big-Fat spoke with the voice of God and said no. Also, Three-Legs and the others who held the land stood behind Dog-Tooth. Moreover, the strongest man in the council was Sea-Lion, and him the land-owners gave land to secretly, along with many bearskins and baskets of corn. So Sea-Lion said that Big-Fat's voice was truly the voice of God and must be obeyed. And soon afterward Sea-Lion was named the voice of Dog-Tooth and did most of his talking for him.

"Then there was Little-Belly, a little man, so thin in the middle that he looked as if he had never had enough to eat. Inside the mouth of the river, after the sand-bar had combed the strength of the breakers, he built a big fish-trap. No man had ever seen or dreamed a fish-trap before. He worked weeks on it, with his son and his wife, while the rest of us laughed at their labors. But, when it was done, the first day he caught more fish in it than could the whole tribe in a week, whereat there was great rejoicing. There was only one other place in the river for a fish-trap, but, when my father and I and a dozen other men started to make a very large trap, the guards came from the big grass-house we had built for Dog-Tooth. And the guards poked us with their spears and told us begone, because Little-Belly was going to build a trap there himself on the word of Sea-Lion, who was the voice of Dog-Tooth.

"There was much grumbling, and my father called a council. But, when he rose to speak, him the Sea-Lion thrust through the throat with a spear and he died. And Dog-Tooth and Little-Belly, and Three-Legs and all that held land said it was good. And Big-Fat said it was the will of God. And after that all men were afraid to stand up in the council, and there was no more council.

"Another man, Pig-Jaw, began to keep goats. He had heard about it as among the Meat-Eaters, and it was not long before he had many flocks. Other men, who had no land and no fish-traps, and who else would have gone hungry, were glad to work for Pig-Jaw, caring for his goats, guarding them from wild dogs and tigers, and driving them to the feeding pastures in the mountains. In return, Pig-Jaw gave them goat-meat to eat and goat-skins to wear, and sometimes they traded the goat-meat for fish and corn and fat roots.

It was this time that money came to be. Sea-Lion was the man who first thought of it, and he talked it over with Dog-Tooth and Big-Fat. You see, these three were the ones that got a share of everything in the Sea Valley. One basket out of every three of corn was theirs, one fish out of every three, one goat out of every three. In return, they fed the guards and the watchers, and kept the rest for themselves. Sometimes, when a big haul of fish was made, they did not know what to do with all their share. So Sea-Lion set the women to making money out of shell—little round pieces, with a hole in each one, and all made smooth and fine. These were strung on strings, and the strings were called money.

"Each string was of the value of thirty fish, or forty fish, but the women, who made a string a day, were given two fish each. The fish came out of the shares of Dog-Tooth, Big-Fat, and Sea-Lion, which they three did not eat. So all the money belonged to them. Then they told Three-Legs and the other land owners that they would take their share of corn and roots in money, Little-Belly that they would take their share of fish in money, the Pig-Jaw that they would take their share of goats and cheese in money. Thus, a man who had nothing, worked for one who had, and was paid in money. With this money he bought corn, and fish, and meat, and cheese. And Three-Legs and all owners of things paid Dog-Tooth and Sea-Lion and Big-Fat their share in money. And they paid the guards and watchers in money, and the guards and watchers bought their food with the money. And, because money was cheap, Dog-Tooth made many more men into guards. And, because money was cheap to make, a number of men began to make money out of shell themselves. But the guards stuck spears in them and shot them full of arrows, because they were trying to break up the tribe. It was bad to break up the tribe, for then the Meat-Eaters would come over the divide and kill them all.

"Big-Fat was the voice of God, but he took Broken-Rib and made him into a priest, so that he became the voice of Big-Fat and did most of his talking for him. And both had other men to be servants to them. So, also, did Little-Belly and Three-Legs and Pig-Jaw have other men to lie in the sun about their grass houses and carry messages for them and give commands. And more and more were men taken away from work, so that those that were left worked harder than ever before. It seemed that men desired to do no work and strove to seek out other ways whereby men should work for them. Crooked-Eyes found such a way. He made the first fire-brew out of corn. And thereafter he worked no more, for he talked secretly with Dog-Tooth and Big-Fat and the other masters, and it was agreed that he should be the only one to make fire-brew. But Crooked-Eyes did no work himself. Men made the brew for him, and he paid them in money. Then he sold the fire-brew for money, and all men bought. And many strings of money did he give Dog-Tooth and Sea-Lion and all of them.

"Big-Fat and Broken-Rib stood by Dog-Tooth when he took his second wife, and his third wife. They said Dog-Tooth was different from other men and second only to God that Big-Fat kept in his taboo house, and Dog-Tooth said so, too, and wanted to know who were they to grumble about how many wives he took. Dog-Tooth had a big canoe made, and many more men he took from work, who did nothing and lay in the sun, save only when Dog-Tooth went in the canoe, when they paddled for him. And he made Tiger-Face head man over all the guards, so that Tiger-Face became his right arm, and when he did not like a man Tiger-Face killed that man for him. And Tiger-Face, also, made another man to be his right arm, and to give commands, and to kill for him.

"But this was the strange thing: as the days went by we who were left worked harder and harder, and yet did we get less and less to eat."

"But what of the goats and the corn and the fat roots and the fish-trap," spoke up Afraid-of-the-Dark, "what of all this? Was there not more food to be gained by man's work?"

"It is so," Long-Beard agreed. "Three men on the fish-trap got more fish than the whole tribe before there was a fish-trap. But have I not said we were fools? The more food we were able to get, the less food did we have to eat."

"But was it not plain that the many men who did not work ate it all up?" Yellow-Head demanded.

Long-Beard nodded his head sadly. "Dog-Tooth's dogs were stuffed with meat, and the men who lay in the sun and did no work were rolling in fat, and, at the same time, there were little children crying themselves to sleep with hunger biting them with every wail."

Deer-Runner was spurred by the recital of famine to tear out a chunk of bear-meat and broil it on a stick over the coals. This he devoured with smacking lips, while Long-Beard went on:

"When we grumbled Big-Fat arose, and with the voice of God said that God had chosen the wise men to own the land and the goats and the fish-trap and the fire-brew, and that without these wise men we would all be animals, as in the days when we lived in trees.

"And there arose one who became a singer of songs for the king. Him they called the Bug, because he was small and ungainly of face and limb and excelled not in work or deed. He loved the fattest marrow bones, the choicest fish, the milk warm from the goats, the first corn that was ripe, and the snug place by the fire. And thus, becoming singer of songs to the king, he found a way to do nothing and be fat. And when the people grumbled more and more, and some threw stones at the king's grass house, the Bug sang a song of how good it was to be a Fish-Eater. In his song he told that the Fish-Eaters were the chosen of God and the finest men God had made. He sang of the Meat-Eaters as pigs and crows, and sang how fine and good it was for the Fish-Eaters to fight and die doing God's work, which was the killing of Meat-Eaters. The words of his song were like fire in us, and we clamored to be led against the Meat-Eaters. And we forgot that we were hungry, and why we had grumbled, and were glad to be led by Tiger-Face over the divide, where we killed many Meat-Eaters and were content.

"But things were no better in the Sea Valley. The only way to get food was to work for Three-Legs or Little-Belly or Pig-Jaw; for there was no land that a man might plant with corn for himself. And often there were more men than Three-Legs and the others had work for. So these men went hungry, and so did their wives and children and their old mothers. Tiger-Face said they could become guards if they wanted to, and many of them did, and thereafter they did no work except to poke spears in the men who did work and who grumbled at feeding so many idlers.

"And when we grumbled, ever the Bug sang new songs. He said that Three-Legs and Pig-Jaw and the rest were strong men, and that that was why they had so much. He said that we should be glad to have strong men with us, else would we perish of our own worthlessness and the Meat-Eaters. Therefore, we should be glad to let such strong men have all they could lay hands on. And Big-Fat and Pig-Jaw and Tiger-Face and all the rest said it was true.

" 'All right,' said Long-Fang, 'then will I, too, be a strong man.' And he got himself corn and began to make fire-brew and sell it for strings of money. And, when Crooked-Eyes complained, Long-Fang said that he was himself a strong man, and that if Crooked-Eyes made any more noise he would bash his brains out for him. Whereat Crooked-Eyes was afraid and went and talked with Three-Legs and Pig-Jaw. And all three went and talked to Dog-Tooth. And Dog-Tooth spoke to Sea-Lion, and Sea-Lion sent a runner with a message to Tiger-Face. And Tiger-Face sent his guards, who burned Long-Fang's house along with the fire-brew he had made. Also, they killed him and all his family. And Big-Fat said it was good, and the Bug sang another song about how good it was to observe the law, and what a fine land the Sea Valley was, and how every man who loved the Sea Valley should go forth and kill the bad Meat-Eaters. And again his song was as fire to us, and we forgot to grumble.

"It was very strange. When Little-Belly caught too many fish, so that it took a great many to sell for a little money, he threw many of the fish back into the sea, so that more money would be paid for what was left. And Three-Legs often let many large fields lie idle so as to get more money for his corn. And the women, making so much money out of shell that much money was needed to buy with, Dog-Tooth stopped the making of money. And the women had no work, so they took the places of the men. I worked on the fish-trap, getting a string of money every five days. But my sister now did my work, getting a string of money for every ten days. The women worked cheaper, and there was less food, and Tiger-Face said for us to become guards. Only I could not become a guard because I was lame of one leg and Tiger-Face would not have me. And there were many like me. We were broken men and only fit to beg for work or to take care of the babies while the women worked."

Yellow-Head, too, was made hungry by the recital and broiled a piece of bear-meat on the coals.

"But why didn't you rise up, all of you, and kill Three-Legs and Pig-Jaw and Big-Fat and the rest and get enough to eat?" Afraid-in-the-Dark demanded.

"Because we could not understand," Long-Beard answered. "There was too much to think about, and, also, there were the guards sticking spears into us, and Big-Fat talking about God, and the Bug singing new songs. And when any man did think right, and said so, Tiger-Face and the guards got him, and he was tied out to the rocks at low tide so that the rising waters drowned him.

"It was a strange thing—the money. It was like the Bug's songs. It seemed all right, but it wasn't, and we were slow to understand. Dog-Tooth began to gather the money in. He put it in a big pile, in a grass house, with guards to watch it day and night. And the more money he piled in the house the dearer money became, so that a man worked a longer time for a string of money than before. Then, too, there was always talk of war with the Meat-Eaters, and Dog-Tooth and Tiger-Face filled many houses with corn, and dried fish, and smoked goat-meat, and cheese. And with the food piled there in mountains the people had not enough to eat. But what did it matter? Whenever the people grumbled too loudly the Bug sang a new song, and Big-Fat said it was God's word that we should kill Meat-Eaters, and Tiger-Face led us over the divide to kill and be killed. I was not good enough to be a guard and lie fat in the sun, but, when we made war, Tiger-Face was glad to take me along. And when we had eaten all the food stored in the houses we stopped fighting and went back to work to pile up more food."

"Then were you all crazy," commented Deer-Runner.

"Then were we indeed all crazy," Long-Beard agreed. "It was strange, all of it. There was Split-Nose. He said everything was wrong. He said it was true that we grew strong by adding our strength together. And he said that, when we first formed the tribe, it was right that the men whose strength hurt the tribe should be shorn of their strength—men who bashed their brothers' heads and stole their brothers' wives. And now, he said, the tribe was not getting stronger, but was getting weaker, because there were men with another kind of strength that were hurting the tribe—men who had the strength of the land, like Three-Legs; who had the strength of the fish-trap, like Little-Belly; who had the strength of all the goat meat, like Pig-Jaw. The thing to do, Split-Nose said, was to shear these men of their evil strength; to make them go to work, all of them, and to let no man eat who did not work.

"And the Bug sang another song about men like Split-Nose, who wanted to go back and live in trees.

"Yet Split-Nose said no; that he did not want to go back, but ahead; that they grew strong only as they added their strength together; and that, if the Fish-Eaters would add their strength to the Meat-Eaters, there would be no more fighting and no more watchers and no more guards, and that, with all men working, there would be so much food that each man would have to work not more than two hours a day.

"Then the Bug sang again, and he sang that Split-Nose was lazy, and he sang also the 'Song of the Bees.' It was a strange song, and those who listened were made mad, as from the drinking of strong fire-brew. The song was of a swarm of bees, and of a robber wasp who had come in to live with the bees and who was stealing all their honey. The wasp was lazy and told them there was no need to work; also, he told them to make friends with the bears, who were not honey-stealers but only very good friends. And the Bug sang in crooked words, so that those who listened knew that the swarm was the Sea Valley tribe, that the bears were the Meat-Eaters, and that the lazy wasp was Split-Nose. And, when the Bug sang that the bees listened to the wasp till the swarm was near to perishing, the people growled and snarled, and when the Bug sang that at last the good bees arose and stung the wasp to death, the people picked up stones from the ground and stoned Split-Nose to death till there was naught to be seen of him but the heap of stones they had flung on top of him. And there were many poor people who worked long and hard and had not enough to eat that helped throw the stones on Split-Nose.

"And, after the death of Split-Nose, there was but one other man that dared rise up and speak his mind, and that man was Hair-Face. 'Where is the strength of the strong?' he asked. 'We are the strong, all of us, and we are stronger than Dog-Tooth and Tiger-Face and Three-Legs and Pig-Jaw and all the rest who do nothing and eat much and weaken us by the hurt of their strength which is bad strength. Men who are slaves are not strong. If the man who first found the virtue and use of fire had used his strength we would have been his slaves, as we are the slaves to-day of Little-Belly, who found the virtue and use of the fish-trap; and of the men who found the virtue and use of the land, and the goats, and the fire-brew. Before, we lived in trees, my brothers, and no man was safe. But we fight no more with one another. We have added our strength together. Then let us fight no more with the Meat-Eaters. Let us add our strength and their strength together. Then will we be indeed strong. And then we will go out together, the Fish-Eaters and the Meat-Eaters, and we will kill the tigers and the lions and the wolves and the wild dogs, and we will pasture our goats on all the hillsides and plant our corn and fat roots in all the high mountain valleys. In that day we will be so strong that all the wild animals will flee before us and perish. And nothing will withstand us, for the strength of each man will be the strength of all men in the world.'

"So said Hair-Face, and they killed him, because, they said, he was a wild man and wanted to go back and live in a tree. It was very strange. Whenever a man arose and wanted to go forward all those that stood still said he went backward and should be killed. And the poor people helped stone him, and were fools. We were all fools, except those who were fat and did no work. The fools were called wise, and the wise were stoned. Men who worked did not get enough to eat, and the men who did not work ate too much.

"And the tribe went on losing strength. The children were weak and sickly. And, because we ate not enough, strange sicknesses came among us and we died like flies. And then the Meat-Eaters came upon us. We had followed Tiger-Face too often over the divide and killed them. And now they came to repay in blood. We were too weak and sick to man the big wall. And they killed us, all of us, except some of the women, which they took away with them. The Bug and I escaped, and I hid in the wildest places, and became a hunter of meat and went hungry no more. I stole a wife from the Meat-Eaters, and went to live in the caves of the high mountains where they could not find me. And we had three sons, and each son stole a wife from the Meat-Eaters. And the rest you know, for are you not the sons of my sons?"

"But the Bug?" queried Deer-Runner. "What became of him?"

"He went to live with the Meat-Eaters and to be a singer of songs to the king. He is an old man now, but he sings the same old songs; and, when a man rises up to go forward, he sings that that man is walking backward to live in a tree."

Long Beard dipped into the bear-carcass and sucked with toothless gums at a fist of suet.

"Some day," he said, wiping his hands on his sides, "all the fools will be dead and then all live men will go forward. The strength of the strong will be theirs, and they will add their strength together, so that, of all the men in the world, not one will fight with another. There will be no guards nor watchers on the walls. And all the hunting animals will be killed, and, as Hair-Face said, all the hillsides will be pastured with goats and all the high mountain valleys will be planted with corn and fat roots. And all men will be brothers, and no man will lie idle in the sun and be fed by his fellows. And all that will come to pass in the time when the fools are dead, and when there will be no more singers to stand still and sing the 'Song of the Bees.' Bees are not men."

# SAMUEL

MARGARET HENAN would have been a striking figure under any circumstances, but never more so than when I first chanced upon her, a sack of grain of fully a hundred-weight on her shoulder, as she walked with sure though tottering stride from the cart-tail to the stable, pausing for an instant to gather strength at the foot of the steep steps that led to the grain-bin. There were four of these steps, and she went up them, a step at a time, slowly, unwaveringly, and with so dogged a certitude that it never entered my mind that her strength could fail her and let that hundred-weight sack fall from the lean and withered frame that well-nigh doubled under it. For she was patently an old woman, and it was her age that made me linger by the cart and watch.

Six times she went between the cart and the stable, each time with a full sack on her back, and beyond passing the time of day with me she took no notice of my presence. Then, the cart empty, she fumbled for matches and lighted a short clay pipe, pressing down the burning surface of the tobacco with a calloused and apparently nerveless thumb. The hands were noteworthy. They were large-knuckled, sinewy and malformed by labor, rimed with callouses, the nails blunt and broken, and with here and there cuts and bruises, healed and healing, such as are common to the hands of hard-working men. On the back were huge, upstanding veins, eloquent of age and toil. Looking at them, it was hard to believe that they were the hands of the woman who had once been the belle of Island McGill. This last, of course, I learned later. At the time I knew neither her history nor her identity.

She wore heavy man's brogans. Her legs were stockingless, and I had noticed when she walked that her bare feet were thrust into the crinkly, iron-like shoes that sloshed about her lean ankles at every step. Her figure, shapeless and waistless, was garbed in a rough man's shirt and in a ragged flannel petticoat that had once been red. But it was her face, wrinkled, withered and weather-beaten, surrounded by an aureole of unkempt and straggling wisps of grayish hair, that caught and held me. Neither drifted hair nor serried wrinkles could hide the splendid dome of a forehead, high and broad without verging in the slightest on the abnormal.

The sunken cheeks and pinched nose told little of the quality of the life that flickered behind those clear blue eyes of hers. Despite the minutiæ of wrinkle-work that somehow failed to weazen them, her eyes were clear as a girl's—clear, out-looking, and far-seeing, and with an open and unblinking steadfastness of gaze that was disconcerting. The remarkable thing was the distance between them. It is a lucky man or woman who has the width of an eye between, but with Margaret Henan the width between her eyes was fully that of an eye and a half. Yet so symmetrically molded was her face that this remarkable feature produced no uncanny effect, and, for that matter, would have escaped the casual observer's notice. The mouth, shapeless and toothless, with down-turned corners and lips dry and parchment-like, nevertheless lacked the muscular slackness so usual with age. The lips might have been those of a mummy, save for that impression of rigid firmness they gave. Not that they were atrophied. On the contrary, they seemed tense and set with a muscular and spiritual determination. There, and in the eyes, was the secret of the certitude with which she carried the heavy sacks up the steep steps, with never a false step or over-balance, and emptied them in the grain-bin.

"You are an old woman to be working like this," I ventured.

She looked at me with that strange, unblinking gaze, and she thought and spoke with the slow deliberateness that characterized everything about her, as if well aware of an eternity that was hers and in which there was no need for haste. Again I was impressed by the enormous certitude of her. In this eternity that seemed so indubitably hers, there was time and to spare for safe-footing and stable equilibrium—for certitude, in short. No more in her spiritual life than in carrying the hundred-weights of grain, was there a possibility of a misstep or an overbalancing. The feeling produced in me was uncanny. Here was a human soul that, save for the most glimmering of contacts, was beyond the humanness of me. And the more I learned of Margaret Henan in the weeks that followed the more mysteriously remote she became. She was as alien as a far-journeyer from some other star, and no hint could she nor all the countryside give me of what norms of living, what heats of feeling, or rules of philosophic contemplation actuated her in all that she had been and was.

"I wull be suvunty-two come Guid Friday a fortnight," she said in reply to my question.

"But you are an old woman to be doing this man's work, and a strong man's work at that," I insisted.

Again she seemed to immerse herself in that atmosphere of contemplative eternity, and so strangely did it affect me that I should not have been surprised to have awaked a century or so later and found her just beginning to enunciate her reply:

"The work hoz tull be done, an' I am beholden tull no one."

"But have you no children, no family relations?"

"O, ay, a-plenty o' them, but they no see fut tull be helpun' me."

She drew out her pipe for a moment, then added, with a nod of her head toward the house, "I luv' wuth meself."

I glanced at the house, straw-thatched and commodious, at the large stable, and at the large array of fields I knew must belong with the place.

"It is a big bit of land for you to farm by yourself."

"O, ay, a bug but, suvunty acres. Ut kept me old mon buzzy, along wuth a son an' a hired mon, tull say naught o' extra honds un the harvest an' a maid-servant un the house."

She clambered into the cart, gathered the reins in her hands, and quizzed me with her keen, shrewd eyes.

"Belike ye hail from over the watter—Ameruky, I'm meanun'?"

"Yes, I'm a Yankee," I answered.

"Ye wull no be findun' mony Island McGill folk stoppun' un Ameruky?"

"No; I don't remember ever meeting one in the States."

She nodded her head.

"They are home-lovun' bodies, though I wull no be sayun' they are no fair-traveled. Yet they come home ot the last, them oz are no lost ot sea or kult by fevers an' such-like un foreign parts."

"Then your sons will have gone to sea and come home again?" I queried.

"O, ay, all savun' Samuel oz was drownded."

At the mention of Samuel I could have sworn to a strange light in her eyes, and it seemed to me, as by some telepathic flash, that I divined in her a tremendous wistfulness, an immense yearning. It seemed to me that here was the key to her inscrutableness, the clew that if followed properly would make all her strangeness plain. It came to me that here was a contact and that for the moment I was glimpsing into the soul of her. The question was tickling on my tongue, but she forestalled me.

She *tckh'd* to the horse, and with a "Guid day tull you, sir," drove off.

•   •   •

A simple, homely people, are the folk of Island McGill, and I doubt if a more sober, thrifty, and industrious folk is to be found in all the world. Meeting them abroad—and to meet them abroad one must meet them on the sea, for a hybrid seafaring and farmer breed are they—one would never take them to be Irish. Irish they claim to be, speaking of the North of Ireland with pride and sneering at their Scottish brothers; yet Scotch they undoubtedly are, transplanted Scotch of long ago, it is true, but none the less Scotch, with a thousand traits, to say nothing of their tricks of speech and woolly utterance, which nothing less than their Scotch clannishness could have preserved to this late day.

A narrow loch, scarcely half a mile wide, separates Island McGill from the mainland of Ireland; and, once across this loch, one finds himself in an entirely different country. The Scotch impression is strong, and the people, to commence with, are Presbyterians. When it is considered that there is no public house in all the island and that seven thousand souls dwell therein, some idea may be gained of the temperateness of the community. Wedded to old ways, public opinion and the ministers are powerful influences, while fathers and mothers are revered and obeyed as in few other places in this modern world. Courting lasts never later than ten at night, and no girl walks out with her young man without her parents' knowledge and consent.

The young men go down to the sea and sow their wild oats in the wicked ports, returning periodically, between voyages, to live the old intensive morality, to court till ten o'clock, to sit under the minister each Sunday, and to listen at home to the same stern precepts that the elders preached to them from the time they were laddies. Much they learned of women in the ends of the earth, these seafaring sons, yet a canny wisdom was theirs and they never brought wives home with them. The one solitary exception to this had been the schoolmaster, who had been guilty of bringing a wife from half a mile the other side of the loch. For this he had never been forgiven, and he rested under a cloud for the remainder of his days. At his death the wife went back across the loch to her own people, and the blot on the escutcheon of Island McGill was erased. In the end the sailor-men married girls of their own home land and settled down to become exemplars of all the virtues for which the island was noted.

Island McGill was without a history. She boasted none of the events that go to make history. There had never been any wearing of the green, any Fenian conspiracies, any land disturbances. There had been but one eviction, and that purely technical—a test case, and on advice of the tenant's lawyer. So Island McGill was without annals. History had passed her by. She paid her taxes, acknowledged her crowned rulers, and left the world alone; all she asked in return was that the world leave her alone. The world was composed of two parts—Island McGill and the rest of it. And whatever was not Island McGill was outlandish and barbarian; and well she knew, for did not her seafaring sons bring home report of that world and its ungodly ways?

•　　•　　•

It was from the skipper of a Glasgow tramp, as passenger from Colombo to Rangoon, that I had first learned of the existence of Island McGill; and it was from him that I had carried the letter that gave me entrance to the house of Mrs. Ross, widow of a master mariner, with a daughter living with her and with two sons, master mariners themselves and out upon the sea. Mrs. Ross did not take in boarders, and it was Captain Ross's letter alone that had enabled me to get from her bed and board. In the evening, after my encounter with Margaret Henan, I questioned Mrs. Ross, and I knew on the instant that I had in truth stumbled upon mystery.

Like all Island McGill folk, as I was soon to discover, Mrs. Ross was at first averse to discussing Margaret Henan at all. Yet it was from her I learned that evening that Margaret Henan had once been one of the island belles. Herself the daughter of a well-to-do farmer, she had married Thomas Henan, equally well-to-do. Beyond the usual housewife's tasks she had never been accustomed to work. Unlike many of the island women, she had never lent a hand in the fields.

"But what of her children?" I asked.

"Two o' the sons, Jamie an' Timothy uz married an' be goun' tull sea. Thot bug house close tull the post-office uz Jamie's. The daughters thot ha' no married be luvun' wuth them as dud marry. An' the rest be dead."

"The Samuels," Clara interpolated, with what I suspected was a giggle.

She was Mrs. Ross's daughter, a strapping young woman with handsome features and remarkably handsome black eyes.

" 'Tuz naught tull be smuckerun' ot," her mother reproved her.

"The Samuels?" I intervened. "I don't understand."

"Her four sons thot died."

"And were they all named Samuel?"

"Ay."

"Strange," I commented in the lagging silence.

"Very strange," Mrs. Ross affirmed, proceeding stolidly with the knitting of the woolen singlet on her knees—one of the countless undergarments that she interminably knitted for her skipper sons.

"And it was only the Samuels that died?" I queried, in further attempt.

"The others luv'd," was the answer. "A fine fomuly—no finer on the island. No better lods ever sailed out of Island McGill. The munuster held them up oz models tull pottern after. Nor was ever a whusper breathed again' the girls."

"But why is she left alone now in her old age?" I persisted. "Why don't her own flesh and blood look after her? Why does she live alone? Don't they ever go to see her or care for her?"

"Never a one un twenty years an' more now. She fetch't ut on tull herself. She drove them from the house just oz she drove old Tom Henan, thot was her husband, tull hus death."

"Drink?" I ventured.

Mrs. Ross shook her head scornfully, as if drink was a weakness beneath the weakest of Island McGill.

A long pause followed, during which Mrs. Ross knitted stolidly on, only nodding permission when Clara's young man, mate on one of the Shire Line sailing ships, came to walk out with her. I studied the half-dozen ostrich eggs, hanging in the corner against the wall like a cluster of some monstrous fruit. On each shell was painted precipitous and impossible seas through which full-rigged ships foamed with a lack of perspective only equaled by their sharp technical perfection. On the mantelpiece stood two large pearl shells, obviously a pair, intricately carved by the patient hands of New Caledonian convicts. In the center of the mantel was a stuffed bird of paradise, while about the room were scattered gorgeous shells from the southern seas, delicate sprays of coral sprouting from barnacled *pi-pi* shells and cased in glass, assegais from South Africa, stone-axes from New Guinea, huge Alaskan tobacco-pouches beaded with heraldic totem designs, a boomerang from Australia, divers ships in glass bottles, a cannibal *kai-kai* bowl from the Marquesas, and fragile cabinets from China and the Indies and inlaid with mother-of-pearl and precious woods.

I gazed at this varied trove brought home by sailor sons, and pondered the mystery of Margaret Henan, who had driven her husband to his death and been forsaken by all her kin. It was not the drink. Then what was it?—some shocking cruelty? some amazing infidelity? or some fearful, old-world peasant-crime?

I broached my theories, but to all Mrs. Ross shook her head.

"Ut was no thot," she said. "Margaret was a guid wife an' a guid mother, an' I doubt she would harm a fly. She brought up her fomuly God-fearin' an' decent-minded. Her trouble was thot she took lunatuc—turned eediot."

Mrs. Ross tapped significantly on her forehead to indicate a state of addlement.

"But I talked with her this afternoon," I objected, "and I found her a sensible woman—remarkably bright for one of her years."

"Ay, an' I'm grantun' all thot you say," she went on calmly. "But I am no referrun' tull thot. I am referrun' tull her wucked-headed an' vucious stubbornness. No more stubborn woman ever luv'd than Margaret Henan. Ut was all on account o' Samuel, which was the name o' her eldest an' they do say her favorut brother—hum oz died by hus own hond all through the munuster's mustake un no registerun' the new church ot Dublin. Ut was a lesson thot the name was musfortunate, but she would no take ut, an' there was talk when she called her first child Samuel—hum thot died o' the croup. An' wuth thot what does she do but call the next one Samuel, an' hum only three when he fell un tull the tub o' hot watter an' was plain cooked tull death. Ut all come, I tell you, o' her wucked-headed an' foolish stubbornness. For a Samuel she must hov; an' ut was the death of the four of her sons. After the first, dudna her own mother go down un the dirt tull her feet, a-beggun' an' pleadun' wuth her no tull name her next one Samuel? But she was no tull be turned from her purpose. Margaret Henan was always set un her ways, an' never more so thon on thot name Samuel.

"She was fair lunatuc on Samuel. Dudna her neighbors, an' all kuth an' kun savun' them thot luv'd un the house wuth her, get up an' walk out ot the christenun' of the second—hum thot was cooked?

Thot they dud, an' ot the very moment the munuster asked what would the bairn's name be. 'Samuel,' says she; an' wuth thot they got up an' walked out an' left the house. An' ot the door dudna her Aunt Fannie, her mother's suster, turn an' say loud for all tull hear: 'What for wull she be wantun' tull murder the wee thung?' The munuster heard fine, an' dudna like ut, but, oz he told my Larry afterward, what could he do? Ut was the woman's wush, an' there was no law again' a mother callun' her child accordun' tull her wush.

"An' then was there no' the third Samuel? An' when he was lost ot sea off the Cape, dudna she break all laws o' nature tull hov a fourth? She was forty-seven, I'm tellun' ye, an' she hod a child ot forty-seven. Thunk on ut! Ot forty-seven! Ut was fair scand'lous."

• • •

From Clara, next morning, I got the tale of Margaret Henan's favorite brother; and from here and there, in the week that followed, I pieced together the tragedy of Margaret Henan. Samuel Dundee had been the youngest of Margaret's four brothers, and, as Clara told me, she had well-nigh worshiped him. He was going to sea at the time, skipper of one of the sailing ships of the Bank Line, when he married Agnes Hewitt. She was described as a slender wisp of a girl, delicately featured and with a nervous organization of the supersensitive order. Theirs had been the first marriage in the "new" church, and after a two-weeks' honeymoon Samuel had kissed his bride good-bye and sailed in command of the *Loughbank,* a big four-masted bark.

And it was because of the "new" church that the minister's blunder occurred. Nor was it the blunder of the minister alone, as one of the elders later explained; for it was equally the blunder of the whole Presbytery of Coughleen, which included fifteen churches on Island McGill and the mainland. The old church, beyond repair, had been torn down and the new one built on the original foundation. Looking upon the foundation stones as similar to a ship's keel, it never entered the minister's nor the Presbytery's head that the new church was legally any other than the old church.

"An' three couples was married the first week un the new church," Clara said. "First of all, Samuel Dundee an' Agnes Hewitt; the next day Albert Mahan an' Minnie Duncan; an' by the week-end Eddie Troy and Flo Mackintosh—all sailor-men, an' un sux weeks' time the last of them back tull their ships an' awa', an' no one o' them dreamin' of the wuckedness they'd been ot."

The Imp of the Perverse must have chuckled at the situation. All things favored. The marriages had taken place in the first week of May, and it was not till three months later that the minister, as required by law, made his quarterly report to the civil authorities in Dublin. Promptly came back the announcement that his church had no legal existence, not being registered according to the law's demands. This was overcome by prompt registration; but the marriages were not to be so easily remedied. The three sailor-husbands were away, and their wives, in short, were not their wives.

"But the munuster was no for alarmin' the bodies," said Clara. "He kept hus council an' bided hus time, waitin' for the lods tull be back from sea. Oz luck would have ut, he was away across the island tull a christenun' when Albert Mahan arrives home onexpected, hus shup just docked ot Dublin. Ut's nine o'clock ot night when the munuster, un hus sluppers an' dressun' gown, gets the news. Up he jumps an' calls for horse an' saddle, an' then goes like the wund for Albert Mahan's. Albert uz just goun' tull bed an' hoz one shoe off when the munuster arrives.

" 'Come wuth me, the pair o' ye,' says he, breathless-like. 'What for, an' me dead weary an' goun' tull bed?' says Albert. 'Tull be lawful married,' says the munuster. Albert looks black an' says, 'Now munuster ye wull be jokin',' but tull humself, oz I've heard hum tell mony a time, he uz wonderun' thot the munuster should a-took tull whuskey ot hus time o' life.

" 'We be no married?' says Minnie. He shook his head. 'An' I om no Mussus Mahan?' 'No,' says he, 'ye are no Mussus Mahan. Ye are plain Muss Duncan.' 'But ye married us yoursel',' says she. 'I dud an' I dudna,' says he. An' wuth thot he tells them the whole upshot, an' Albert puts on hus shoe, an' they go with the munuster an' are married proper an' lawful, an' oz Albert Mahan says afterward mony's the time, ' 'Tus no every mon thot hoz two weddun' nights on Island McGill.' "

Six months later Eddie Troy came home and was promptly remarried. But Samuel Dundee was away on a three-years' voyage and his ship fell overdue. Further to complicate the situation, a baby boy, past two years old, was waiting for him in the arms of his wife. The months passed, and the wife grew thin with worrying. "Ut's no meself I'm thunkun' on," she is reported to have said many times, "but ut's the puir fatherless bairn. Uf aught happened tull Samuel where wull the bairn stond?"

Lloyds posted the *Loughbank* as missing, and the owners ceased the monthly remittance of Samuel's half-pay to his wife. It was the question of the child's legitimacy that preyed on her mind, and, when all hope of Samuel's return was abandoned, she drowned herself and the child in the loch. And here enters the greater tragedy. The *Lough-bank* was not lost. By a series of sea disasters and delays too interminable to relate, she had made one of those long, unsighted passages such as occur once or twice in half a century. How the Imp must have held both his sides! Back from the sea came Samuel, and when they broke the news to him something else broke somewhere in his heart or head. Next morning they found him where he had tried to kill himself across the grave of his wife and child. Never in the history of Island McGill was there so fearful a deathbed. He spat in the minister's face and reviled him, and died blaspheming so terribly that those that tended on him did so with averted gaze and trembling hands.

And, in the face of all this, Margaret Henan named her first child Samuel.

•   •   •

How account for the woman's stubbornness? Or was it a morbid obsession that demanded a child of hers should be named Samuel? Her third child was a girl, named after herself, and the fourth was a boy again. Despite the strokes of fate that had already bereft her, and despite the loss of friends and relatives, she persisted in her resolve to name the child after her brother. She was shunned at church by those who had grown up with her. Her mother, after a final appeal, left her house with the warning that if the child were so named she would never speak to her again. And though the old lady lived thirty-odd years longer she kept her word. The minister agreed to christen the child any name but Samuel, and every other minister on Island McGill refused to christen it by the name she had chosen. There was talk on the part of Margaret Henan of going to law at the time, but in the end she carried the child to Belfast and there had it christened Samuel.

And then nothing happened. The whole island was confuted. The boy grew and prospered. The schoolmaster never ceased averring that it was the brightest lad he had ever seen. Samuel had a splendid constitution, a tremendous grip on life. To everybody's amazement he escaped the usual run of childish afflictions. Measles, whooping-cough and mumps knew him not. He was armor-clad against germs, immune to all disease. Headaches and earaches were things unknown. "Never so much oz a boil or a pumple," as one of the old bodies told me, ever marred his healthy skin. He broke school records in scholarship and athletics, and whipped every boy of his size or years on Island McGill.

It was a triumph for Margaret Henan. This paragon was hers, and it bore the cherished name. With the one exception of her mother, friends and relatives drifted back and acknowledged that they had been mistaken; though there were old crones who still abided by their opinion and who shook their heads ominously over their cups of tea. The boy was too wonderful to last. There was no escaping the curse of the name his mother had wickedly laid upon him. The young generation joined Margaret Henan in laughing at them, but the old crones continued to shake their heads.

Other children followed. Margaret Henan's fifth was a boy, whom she called Jamie, and in rapid succession followed three girls, Alice, Sara, and Nora, the boy Timothy, and two more girls, Florence and Katie. Katie was the last and eleventh, and Margaret Henan, at thirty-five, ceased from her exertions. She had done well by Island McGill and the Queen. Nine healthy children were hers. All prospered. It seemed her ill luck had shot its bolt with the deaths of her first two. Nine lived, and one of them was named Samuel.

Jamie elected to follow the sea, though it was not so much a matter of election as compulsion, for the eldest sons on Island McGill remained on the land while all other sons went to the salt plowing. Timothy followed Jamie, and by the time the latter had got his first command, a steamer in the Bay trade out of Cardiff, Timothy was mate of a big sailing ship. Samuel, however, did not take kindly to the soil. The farmer's life had no attraction for him. His brothers went to sea, not out of desire, but because it was the only way for them to gain their bread; and he, who had no need to go, envied them when, returned from far voyages, they sat by the kitchen fire and told their bold tales of the wonderlands beyond the sea-rim.

Samuel became a teacher, much to his father's disgust, and even took extra certificates, going to Belfast for his examinations. When the old master retired, Samuel took over his school. Secretly, however, he studied navigation, and it was Margaret's delight when he sat by the kitchen fire, and, despite their master's tickets, tangled up his brothers in the theoretics of their profession. Tom Henan alone was outraged when Samuel, school teacher, gentleman, and heir to the Henan farm, shipped to sea before the mast. Margaret had an abiding faith in her son's star, and whatever he did she was sure was for the best. Like everything else connected with his glorious personality, there had never been known so swift a rise as in the case of Samuel. Barely with two years' sea experience before the mast, he was taken from the forecastle and made a provisional second mate. This occurred in a fever port on the West Coast, and the committee of skippers that examined him agreed that he knew more of the science of navigation than they had remembered or forgotten. Two years later he sailed from Liverpool, mate of the *Starry Grace,* with both master's and extra-master's tickets in his possession. And then it happened—the thing the old crones had been shaking their heads over for years.

It was told me by Gavin McNab, bosun of the *Starry Grace* at the time, himself an Island McGill man.

"Wull do I remember ut," he said. "We was runnin' our Eastun' down, an' makun' heavy weather of ut. Oz fine a sailor-mon oz ever walked was Samuel Henan. I remember the look of hum wull thot last marnun', a-watchun' them bug seas curlun' up astern, an' a-watchun' the old girl an' seeun' how she took them—the skupper down below an' drunkun' for days. Ut was ot seven thot Henan brought her up on tull the wund, not darun' tull run longer un thot fearful sea. Ot eight, after havun' breakfast, he turns un, an' a half hour after up comes the skupper, bleary-eyed an' shaky an' holdun' on tull the companion. Ut was fair smokun', I om tellun' ye, an' there he stood, blunkun' an' noddun' an' talkun' tull humsel'. 'Keep off,' says he ot last tull the mon ot the wheel. 'My God!' says the second mate, standun' beside hum. The skupper never looks tull hum ot all, but keeps on mutterun' an' jabberun' tull humsel'. All of a suddent-like he straightuns up an' throws hus head back, an' says: 'Put your wheel over, me mon—now, domn ye! Are ye deef thot ye'll no be hearun' me?'

"Ut was a drunken mon's luck, for the *Starry Grace* wore off afore thot God-Almighty gale wuthout shuppun' a bucket o' watter, the second mate shoutun' orders an' the crew jumpun' like mod. An' wuth thot the skupper nods contented-like tull humsel' an' goes below after more whuskey. Ut was plain murder o' the lives o' all of us, for ut was no the time for the buggest shup afloat tull be runnun'. Run? Never hov I seen the like! Ut was beyond all thunkun', an' me goun' tull sea, boy an' mon, for forty year. I tell you ut was fair awesome.

"The face o' the second mate was white oz death, an' he stood ut alone for half an hour, when ut was too much for hum an' he went below an' called Samuel an' the third. Ay, a fine sailor-mon thot Samuel, but ut was too much for hum. He looked an' studied, and looked an' studied, but he could no see hus way. He durst na heave tull. She would ha' been sweeput o' all honds an' stucks an' everythung afore

she could a-fetcht up. There was naught tull do but keep on runnun'.
An' uf ut worsened we were lost onyway, for soon or late thot over-
takun' sea was sure tull sweep us clear over poop an' all.

"Dud I say ut was a God-Almighty gale? Ut was worse nor thot.
The devil himself must ha' hod a hond un the brewun' o' ut, ut was
thot fearsome. I ha' looked on some sights, but I om no carun' tull
look on the like o' thot again. No mon dared tull be un hus bunk.
No, nor no mon on the decks. All honds of us stood on top the house
an' held on an' watched. The three mates was on the poop, with two
men ot the wheel, an' the only mon below was thot whuskey-blighted
captain snorun' drunk.

"An' then I see ut comun', a mile away, risun' above all the waves
like an island un the sea—the buggest wave ever I looked upon. The
three mates stood tulgether an' watched ut comun', a-prayun' like we
thot she would no break un passun' us. But ut was no tull be. Ot the
last, when she rose up like a mountain, curlun' above the stern an'
blottun' out the sky, the mates scottered, the second an' third runnun'
for the mizzen-shrouds an' climbun' up, but the first runnun' tull the
wheel tull lend a hond. He was a brave mon, thot Samuel Henan. He
run straight un tull the face o' thot father o' all waves, no thunkun'
on humself but thunkun' only o' the shup. The two men was lashed
tull the wheel, but he would be ready tull hond un the case they was
kult. An' then she took ut. We on the house could no see the poop
for the thousand tons o' watter thot hod hut ut. Thot wave cleaned
them out, took everythung along wuth ut—the two mates, climbun'
up the mizzen-ruggun', Samuel Henan runnun' tull the wheel, the two
men ot the wheel, ay, an' the wheel utself. We never saw aught o'
them, for she broached tull what o' the wheel goun', an' two men o'
us was drownded off the house, no tull mention the carpenter thot we
pucked up ot the break o' the poop wuth every bone o' hus body
broke tull he was like so much jelly."

·   ·   ·

And here enters the marvel of it, the miraculous wonder of that woman's heroic spirit. Margaret Henan was forty-seven when the news
came home of the loss of Samuel; and it was not long after that the
unbelievable rumor went around Island McGill. I say unbelievable.
Island McGill would not believe. Doctor Hall pooh-pooh'd it. Everybody laughed at it as a good joke. They traced back the gossip to Sara
Dack, servant to the Henans', and who alone lived with Margaret and

her husband. But Sara Dack persisted in her assertion and was called a low-mouthed liar. One or two dared question Tom Henan himself, but beyond black looks and curses for their presumption they elicited nothing from him.

The rumor died down, and the island fell to discussing in all its ramifications the loss of the *Grenoble* in the China Seas, with all her officers and half her crew born and married on Island McGill. But the rumor would not stay down. Sara Dack was louder in her assertions, the looks Tom Henan cast about him were blacker than ever, and Dr. Hall, after a visit to the Henan house, no longer pooh-pooh'd. Then Island McGill sat up, and there was a tremendous wagging of tongues. It was unnatural and ungodly. The like had never been heard. And when, as time passed, the truth of Sara Dack's utterances was manifest, the island folk decided, like the bosun of the *Starry Grace,* that only the devil could have had a hand in so untoward a happening. And the infatuated woman, so Sara Dack reported, insisted that it would be a boy. "Eleven bairns ha' I borne," she said; "sux o' them lossies an' five o' them loddies. An' sunce there be balance un all thungs, so wull there be balance wuth me. Sux o' one an' half a dozen o' the other— there uz the balance, an' oz sure oz the sun rises un the marnun', thot sure wull ut be a boy."

And boy it was, and a prodigy. Dr. Hall raved about its unblemished perfection and massive strength, and wrote a brochure on it for the Dublin Medical Society as the most interesting case of the sort in his long career. When Sara Dack gave the babe's unbelievable weight, Island McGill refused to believe and once again called her liar. But when Doctor Hall attested that he had himself weighed it and seen it tip that very notch, Island McGill held its breath and accepted whatever report Sara Dack made of the infant's progress or appetite. And once again Margaret Henan carried a babe to Belfast and had it christened Samuel.

•   •   •

"Oz good oz gold ut was," said Sara Dack to me.

Sara, at the time I met her, was a buxom, phlegmatic spinster of sixty, equipped with an experience so tragic and unusual that though her tongue ran on for decades its output would still be of imperishable interest to her cronies.

"Oz good oz gold," said Sara Dack. "Ut never fretted. Sut ut down un the sun by the hour an' never a sound ut would make oz long oz ut was no hungered. An' thot strong! The grup o' uts honds was like a mon's. I mind me, when ut was but hours old, ut grupped me so mighty thot I fetcht a scream I was thot frighted. Ut was the punk o' health. Ut slept an' ate, an' grew. Ut never bothered. Never a night's sleep ut lost tull no one, nor ever a munut's, an' thot wuth cuttin' uts teeth an' all. An' Margaret would dandle ut on her knee an' ask was there ever so fine a loddie un the three Kungdoms.

"The way ut grew! Ut was un keepun' wuth the way ut ate. Ot a year ut was the size o' a bairn of two. Ut was slow tull walk an' talk. Exceptun' for gurgly noises un uts throat an' for creepun' on all fours, ut dudna monage much un the walkun' an' talkun' line. But thot was tull be expected from the way ut grew. Ut all went tull growun' strong an' healthy. An' even old Tom Henan cheered up ot the might of ut an' said was there ever the like o' ut un the three Kungdoms. Ut was Doctor Hall thot first suspicioned, I mind me well, though ut was luttle I dreamt what he was up tull ot the time. I see hum holdun' thungs un front o' luttle Sammy's eyes, an' a-makun' noises, loud an' soft, an' far an' near, un luttle Sammy's ears. An' then I see Doctor Hall go away, wrunklun' hus eyebrows an' shakun' hus head like the bairn was ailun'. But he was no ailun', oz I could swear tull, me a-seeun' hum eat an' grow. But Doctor Hall no said a word tull Margaret an' I was no for guessun' the why he was sore-puzzled.

"I mind me when luttle Sammy first spoke. He was two years old an' the size of a child o' five, though he could no monage the walkun' yet but when around on all-fours, happy an' contented-like an' makun' no trouble oz long oz he was fed promptly, whuch was onusual often. I was hangun' the wash on the line ot the time when out he comes, on all-fours, hus bug head waggun' tull an' fro an' blunkun' un the sun. An' then, suddent, he talked. I was thot took a-back I near died o' fright, an' fine I knew ut then, the shakun' o' Doctor Hall's head. Talked? Never a bairn on Island McGill talked so loud an' tull such purpose. There was no mustakun' ut. I stood there all tremblun' an' shakun'. Little Sammy was brayun'. I tell you, sir, he was brayun' like an ass—just like thot, loud an' long an' cheerful tull ut seemed hus lungs ud crack.

"He was a eediot—a great, awful, monster eediot. Ut was after he talked thot Doctor Hall told Margaret, but she would no believe. Ut would all come right, she said. Ut was growun' too fast for aught else. Guv ut time, said she, an' we would see. But old Tom Henan knew, an' he never held up hus head again. He could no abide the thung, an' would no brung humsel' tull touch ut, though I om no

denyun' he was fair fascinated by ut. Mony the time I see hum wat-
chun' of ut aroun' a corner, lookun' ot ut tull hus eyes fair bulged
wuth the horror; an' when ut brayed old Tom ud stuck hus fungers
tull hus ears an' look thot miserable I could a-puttied hum.

"An' bray ut could! Ut was the only thung ut could do besides
eat an' grow. Whenever ut was hungry ut brayed, an' there was no
stoppun' ut save wuth food. An' always of a marnun', when first ut
crawled tull the kutchen-door an' blunked out ot the sun, ut brayed.
An' ut was brayun' that brought about uts end.

"I mind me well. Ut was three years old an' oz bug oz a lod o'
ten. Old Tom hed been goun' from bod tull worse, ploughun' up an'
down the fields an' talkun' an' mutterun' tull humself. On the marnun'
o' the day I mind me, he was suttun' on the bench outside the kutchen,
a-futtun' the handle tull a puck-axe. Unbeknown, the monster eediot
crawled tull the door an' brayed after hus fashion ot the sun. I see old
Tom start up an' look. An' there was the monster eediot, waggun' uts
bug head an' blunkun' an' brayun' like the great bug ass ut was. Ut
was too much for Tom. Somethin' went wrong wuth hum suddent-
like. He jumped tull hus feet an' fetcht the puck-handle down on the
monster eediot's head. An' he hut ut again an' again like ut was a mod
dog an' hum afeard o' ut. An' he went straight tull the stable an' hung
humsel' tull a rafter. An' I was no for stoppun' on after such-like, an'
I went tull stay along wuth me suster thot was married tull John Martin an' comfortable-off."

                              •   •   •

I sat on the bench by the kitchen door and regarded Margaret Henan,
while with her callous thumb she pressed down the live fire of her pipe
and gazed out across the twilight-sombered fields. It was the very
bench Tom Henan had sat upon that last sanguinary day of life. And
Margaret sat in the doorway where the monster, blinking at the sun,
had so often wagged its head and brayed. We had been talking for an
hour, she with that slow certitude of eternity that so befitted her; and,
for the life of me, I could lay no finger on the motives that ran through
the tangled warp and woof of her. Was she a martyr to Truth? Did
she have it in her to worship at so abstract a shrine? Had she conceived
Abstract Truth to be the one high goal of human endeavor on that
day of long ago when she named her first-born Samuel? Or was hers
the stubborn obstinacy of the ox? the fixity of purpose of the balky
horse? the stolidity of the self-willed peasant-mind? Was it whim or

fancy?—the one streak of lunacy in what was otherwise an eminently rational mind? Or, reverting, was hers the spirit of a Bruno? Was she convinced of the intellectual rightness of the stand she had taken? Was hers a steady, enlightened opposition to superstition? or—and a subtler thought—was she mastered by some vaster, profounder superstition, a fetish-worship of which the Alpha and the Omega was the cryptic *Samuel?*

"Wull ye be tellun' me," she said, "thot uf the second Samuel hod been named Larry thot he would no hov fell un the hot watter an' drownded? Atween you an' me, sir, an' ye are untellugent-lookun' tull the eye, would the name hov made ut onyways dufferent? Would the washun' no be done thot day uf he hod been Larry or Michael? Would hot watter no be hot, an' would hot watter no burn uf he hod hod ony other name but Samuel?"

I acknowledged the justice of her contention, and she went on.

"Do a wee but of a name change the plans o' God? Do the world run by hut or muss, an' be God a weak, shully-shallyun' creature thot ud alter the fate an' destiny o' thungs because the worm Margaret Henan seen fut tull name her bairn Samuel? There be my son Jamie. He wull no sign a Rooshan-Funn un hus crew because o' believun' thot Rooshan-Funns do be monajun' the wunds an' hov the makun' o' bod weather. Wull you be thunkun' so? Wull you be thunkun' thot God thot makes the wunds tull blow wull bend hus head from on high tull lussen tull the word o' a greasy Rooshan-Funn un some dirty shup's fo'c'sle?"

I said no, certainly not; but she was not to be set aside from pressing home the point of her argument.

"Then wull you be thunkun' thot God thot directs the stars un their courses, an' tull whose mighty foot the world uz but a footstool, wull you be thunkun' thot he wull take a spite again' Margaret Henan an' send a bug wave off the Cape tull wash her son un tull eternity, all because she was for namun' hum Samuel?"

"But why Samuel?" I asked.

"An' thot I dinna know. I wanted ut so."

"But *why* did you want it so?"

"An' uz ut me thot would be answerun' a such-like question? Be there ony mon luvun' or dead thot can answer? Who can tell the *why* o' like? My Jamie was fair daft on buttermilk; he would drunk ut tull, oz he said himself, hus back-teeth was awash. But my Tumothy could no abide buttermilk. I like tull lussen tull the thunder growlun' an' roarun', an' rampajun'. My Katie could no abide the noise of ut, but must scream an' flutter an' go runnun' for the mudmost o' a feather-bed. Never yet hov I heard the answer tull the *why* o' like. God alone hoz thot answer. You an' me be mortal an' we canna know. Enough for us tull know what we like an' what we duslike. *I like*—thot uz the first word an' the last. An' behind thot *like* no mon can go an' find the *why* o' ut. I *like* Samuel, an' I like ut wull. Ut uz a sweet name, an' there be a rollun' wonder un the sound o' ut thot passes onderstandun'."

The twilight deepened, and in the silence I gazed upon that splendid dome of a forehead which time could not mar, at the width between the eyes, and at the eyes themselves—clear, out-looking, and wide-seeing. She rose to her feet with an air of dismissing me, saying:

"Ut wull be a dark walk home, an' there wull be more thon a sprunkle o' wet un the sky."

"Have you any regrets, Margaret Henan?" I asked, suddenly and without forethought.

She studied me a moment.

"Ay, thot I no ha' borne another son."

"And you would . . . ?" I faltered.

"Ay, thot I would," she answered. "Ut would ha' been hus name."

I went down the dark road between the hawthorne hedges puzzling over the why of like, repeating *Samuel* to myself and aloud and listening to the rolling wonder in its sound that had charmed her soul and led her life in tragic places. *Samuel!* There was a rolling wonder in the sound. Ay, there was!

# A PIECE OF STEAK

WITH THE LAST MORSEL of bread Tom King wiped his plate clean of the last particle of flour gravy and chewed the resulting mouthful in a slow and meditative way. When he arose from the table, he was oppressed by the feeling that he was distinctly hungry. Yet he alone had eaten. The two children in the other room had been sent early to bed in order that in sleep they might forget they had gone supperless. His wife had touched nothing, and had sat silently and watched him with solicitous eyes. She was a thin, worn woman of the working-class, though signs of an earlier prettiness were not wanting in her face. The flour for the gravy she had borrowed from the neighbor across the hall. The last two ha'pennies had gone to buy the bread.

He sat down by the window on a rickety chair that protested under his weight, and quite mechanically he put his pipe in his mouth and dipped into the side pocket of his coat. The absence of any tobacco made him aware of his action, and, with a scowl for his forgetfulness, he put the pipe away. His movements were slow, almost hulking, as though he were burdened by the heavy weight of his muscles. He was a solid-bodied, stolid-looking man, and his appearance did not suffer from being overprepossessing. His rough clothes were old and slouchy. The uppers of his shoes were too weak to carry the heavy resoling that was itself of no recent date. And his cotton shirt, a cheap, two-shilling affair, showed a frayed collar and ineradicable paint stains.

But it was Tom King's face that advertised him unmistakably for what he was. It was the face of a typical prize-fighter; of one who had put in long years of service in the squared ring and, by that means, developed and emphasized all the marks of the fighting beast. It was distinctly a lowering countenance, and, that no feature of it might escape notice, it was clean-shaven. The lips were shapeless, and constituted a mouth harsh to excess, that was like a gash in his face. The jaw was aggressive, brutal, heavy. The eyes, slow of movement and heavy-lidded, were almost expressionless under the shaggy, indrawn brows. Sheer animal that he was, the eyes were the most animal-like feature about him. They were sleepy, lion-like—the eyes of a fighting animal. The forehead slanted quickly back to the hair, which, clipped close, showed every bump of a villainous-looking head. A nose, twice broken and moulded variously by countless blows, and a cauliflower ear, permanently swollen and distorted to twice its size, completed his adornment, while the beard, fresh-shaven as it was, sprouted in the skin and gave the face a blue-black stain.

All together, it was the face of a man to be afraid of in a dark alley or lonely place. And yet Tom King was not a criminal, nor had he ever done anything criminal. Outside of brawls, common to his walk in life, he had harmed no one. Nor had he ever been known to pick a quarrel. He was a professional, and all the fighting brutishness of him was reserved for his professional appearances. Outside the ring he was slow-going, easy-natured, and, in his younger days, when money was flush, too open-handed for his own good. He bore no grudges and had few enemies. Fighting was a business with him. In the ring he struck to hurt, struck to maim, struck to destroy; but there was no animus in it. It was a plain business proposition. Audiences assembled and paid for the spectacle of men knocking each other out. The winner took the big end of the purse. When Tom King faced the Woolloomooloo Gouger, twenty years before, he knew that the Gouger's jaw was only four months healed after having been broken in a Newcastle bout. And he had played for that jaw and broken it again in the ninth round, not because he bore the Gouger any ill-will, but because that was the surest way to put the Gouger out and win the big end of the purse. Nor had the Gouger borne him any ill-will for it. It was the game, and both knew the game and played it.

Tom King had never been a talker, and he sat by the window, morosely silent, staring at his hands. The veins stood out on the backs of the hands, large and swollen; and the knuckles, smashed and battered and malformed, testified to the use to which they had been put. He had never heard that a man's life was the life of his arteries, but well he knew the meaning of those big, upstanding veins. His heart had pumped too much blood through them at top pressure. They no longer did the work. He had stretched the elasticity out of them, and with their distention had passed his endurance. He tired easily now. No longer could he do a fast twenty rounds, hammer and tongs, fight, fight, fight, from gong to gong, with fierce rally on top of fierce rally, beaten to the ropes and in turn beating his opponent to the ropes, and rallying fiercest and fastest of all in that last, twentieth round, with the house on its feet and yelling, himself rushing, striking, ducking, raining showers of blows upon showers of blows and receiving showers of blows in return, and all the time the heart faithfully pumping the surging blood through the adequate veins. The veins, swollen at the time, had always shrunk down again, though not quite—each time, imperceptibly at first, remaining just a trifle larger than before. He stared at them and at his battered knuckles, and, for the moment, caught a vision of the youthful excellence of those hands before the first knuckle had been smashed on the head of Benny Jones, otherwise known as the Welsh Terror.

The impression of his hunger came back on him.

"Blimey, but couldn't I go a piece of steak!" he muttered aloud, clenching his huge fists and spitting out a smothered oath.

"I tried both Burke's an' Sawley's," his wife said half apologetically.

"An' they wouldn't?" he demanded.

"Not a ha'penny. Burke said—" She faltered.

"G'wan! Wot'd he say?"

"As how 'e was thinkin' Sandel ud do ye to-night, an' as how yer score was comfortable big as it was."

Tom King grunted, but did not reply. He was busy thinking of the bull terrier he had kept in his younger days to which he had fed steaks without end. Burke would have given him credit for a thousand steaks—then. But times had changed. Tom King was getting old; and old men, fighting before second-rate clubs, couldn't expect to run bills of any size with the tradesmen.

He had got up in the morning with a longing for a piece of steak, and the longing had not abated. He had not had a fair training for this fight. It was a drought year in Australia, times were hard, and even the most irregular work was difficult to find. He had had no sparring partner, and his food had not been of the best nor always sufficient. He had done a few days' navvy work when he could get it, and he had run around the Domain in the early mornings to get his legs in shape. But it was hard, training without a partner and with a wife and two kiddies that must be fed. Credit with the tradesmen had undergone very slight expansion when he was matched with Sandel. The secretary of the Gayety Club had advanced him three pounds— the loser's end of the purse—and beyond that had refused to go. Now and again he had managed to borrow a few shillings from old pals, who would have lent more only that it was a drought year and they were hard put themselves. No—and there was no use in disguising the fact—his training had not been satisfactory. He should have had better food and no worries. Besides, when a man is forty, it is harder to get into condition than when he is twenty.

"What time is it, Lizzie?" he asked.

His wife went across the hall to inquire, and came back.

"Quarter before eight."

"They'll be startin' the first bout in a few minutes," he said. "Only a try-out. Then there's a four-round spar 'tween Dealer Wells an' Gridley, an' a ten-round go 'tween Starlight an' some sailor bloke. I don't come on for over an hour."

At the end of another silent ten minutes, he rose to his feet.

"Truth is, Lizzie, I ain't had proper trainin'."

He reached for his hat and started for the door. He did not offer to kiss her—he never did on going out—but on this night she dared to kiss him, throwing her arms around him and compelling him to bend down to her face. She looked quite small against the massive bulk of the man.

"Good luck, Tom," she said. "You gotter do 'im."

"Ay, I gotter do 'im," he repeated. "That's all there is to it. I jus' gotter do 'im."

He laughed with an attempt at heartiness, while she pressed more closely against him. Across her shoulders he looked around the bare room. It was all he had in the world, with the rent overdue, and her and the kiddies. And he was leaving it to go out into the night to get meat for his mate and cubs—not like a modern working-man going to his machine grind, but in the old, primitive, royal, animal way, by fighting for it.

"I gotter do 'im," he repeated, this time a hint of desperation in his voice. "If it's a win, it's thirty quid—an' I can pay all that's owin', with a lump o' money left over. If it's a lose, I get naught—not even a penny for me to ride home on the tram. The secretary's give all that's comin' from a loser's end. Good-by, old woman. I'll come straight home if it's a win."

"An' I'll be waitin' up," she called to him along the hall.

It was full two miles to the Gayety, and as he walked along he remembered how in his palmy days—he had once been the heavy-weight champion of New South Wales—he would have ridden in a cab to the fight, and how, most likely, some heavy backer would have paid for the cab and ridden with him. There were Tommy Burns and that Yankee nigger, Jack Johnson—they rode about in motor-cars. And he walked! And, as any man knew, a hard two miles was not the best preliminary to a fight. He was an old un, and the world did not wag well with old uns. He was good for nothing now except navvy work, and his broken nose and swollen ear were against him even in that. He found himself wishing that he had learned a trade. It would have been better in the long run. But no one had told him, and he knew, deep down in his heart, that he would not have listened if they had. It had been so easy. Big money—sharp, glorious fights—periods of rest and loafing in between—a following of eager flatterers, the slaps on the back, the shakes of the hand, the toffs glad to buy him a drink for the privilege of five minutes' talk—and the glory of it, the yelling houses, the whirlwind finish, the referee's "King wins!" and his name in the sporting columns next day.

Those had been times! But he realized now, in his slow, ruminating way, that it was the old uns he had been putting away. He was Youth, rising; and they were Age, sinking. No wonder it had been easy—they with their swollen veins and battered knuckles and weary in the bones of them from the long battles they had already fought. He remembered the time he put out old Stowsher Bill, at Rush-Cutters Bay, in the eighteenth round, and how old Bill had cried afterward in the dressing-room like a baby. Perhaps old Bill's rent had been overdue. Perhaps he'd had at home a missus an' a couple of kiddies. And perhaps Bill, that very day of the fight, had had a hungering for a piece of steak. Bill had fought game and taken incredible punishment. He could see now, after he had gone through the mill himself, that Stowsher Bill had fought for a bigger stake, that night twenty years ago, than had young Tom King, who had fought for glory and easy money. No wonder Stowsher Bill had cried afterward in the dressing-room.

Well, a man had only so many fights in him, to begin with. It was the iron law of the game. One man might have a hundred hard fights in him, another man only twenty; each, according to the make of him and the quality of his fibre, had a definite number, and, when he had fought them, he was done. Yes, he had had more fights in him than most of them, and he had had far more than his share of the hard, gruelling fights—the kind that worked the heart and lungs to bursting, that took the elastic out of the arteries and made hard knots of muscle out of Youth's sleek suppleness, that wore out nerve and stamina and made brain and bones weary from excess of effort and endurance over-wrought. Yes, he had done better than all of them. There was none of his old fighting partners left. He was the last of the old guard. He had seen them all finished, and he had had a hand in finishing some of them.

They had tried him out against the old uns, and one after another he had put them away—laughing when, like old Stowsher Bill, they cried in the dressing-room. And now he was an old un, and they tried out the youngsters on him. There was that bloke, Sandel. He had come over from New Zealand with a record behind him. But nobody in Australia knew anything about him, so they put him up against old Tom King. If Sandel made a showing, he would be given better men to fight, with bigger purses to win; so it was to be depended upon that he would put up a fierce battle. He had everything to win by it—money and glory and career; and Tom King was the grizzled old chopping-block that guarded the highway to fame and fortune. And he had nothing to win except thirty quid, to pay to the landlord and the tradesmen. And, as Tom King thus ruminated, there came to his stolid vision the form of Youth, glorious Youth, rising exultant and invincible, supple of muscle and silken of skin, with heart and lungs that had never been tired and torn and that laughed at limitation of effort. Yes, Youth was the Nemesis. It destroyed the old uns and recked not that, in so doing, it destroyed itself. It enlarged its arteries and smashed its knuckles, and was in turn destroyed by Youth. For Youth was ever youthful. It was only Age that grew old.

At Castlereagh Street he turned to the left, and three blocks along came to the Gayety. A crowd of young larrikins hanging outside the door made respectful way for him, and he heard one say to another: "That's 'im! That's Tom King!"

Inside, on the way to his dressing-room, he encountered the sec-retary, a keen-eyed, shrewd-faced young man, who shook his hand.

"How are you feelin', Tom?" he asked.

"Fit as a fiddle," King answered, though he knew that he lied, and that if he had a quid, he would give it right there for a good piece of steak.

When he emerged from the dressing-room, his seconds behind him, and came down the aisle to the squared ring in the centre of the hall, a burst of greeting and applause went up from the waiting crowd. He acknowledged salutations right and left, though few of the faces did he know. Most of them were the faces of kiddies unborn when he was winning his first laurels in the squared ring. He leaped lightly to the raised platform and ducked through the ropes to his corner, where he sat down on a folding stool. Jack Ball, the referee, came over and shook his hand. Ball was a broken-down pugilist who for over ten years had not entered the ring as a principal. King was glad that he had him for referee. They were both old uns. If he should rough it with Sandel a bit beyond the rules, he knew Ball could be depended upon to pass it by.

Aspiring young heavyweights, one after another, were climbing into the ring and being presented to the audience by the referee. Also, he issued their challenges for them.

"Young Pronto," Bill announced, "from North Sydney, challenges the winner for fifty pounds side bet."

The audience applauded, and applauded again as Sandel himself sprang through the ropes and sat down in his corner. Tom King looked across the ring at him curiously, for in a few minutes they would be locked together in merciless combat, each trying with all the force of him to knock the other into unconsciousness. But little could he see, for Sandel, like himself, had trousers and sweater on over his ring costume. His face was strongly handsome, crowned with a curly mop of yellow hair, while his thick, muscular neck hinted at bodily magnificence.

Young Pronto went to one corner and then the other, shaking hands with the principals and dropping down out of the ring. The challenges went on. Ever Youth climbed through the ropes—Youth unknown, but insatiable—crying out to mankind that with strength and skill it would match issues with the winner. A few years before, in his own heyday of invincibleness, Tom King would have been amused and bored by these preliminaries. But now he sat fascinated, unable to shake the vision of Youth from his eyes. Always were these youngsters rising up in the boxing game, springing through the ropes and shouting their defiance; and always were the old uns going down before them. They climbed to success over the bodies of the old uns. And ever they came, more and more youngsters—Youth unquenchable and irresistible—and ever they put the old uns away, themselves becoming old uns and travelling the same downward path, while behind them, ever pressing on them, was Youth eternal—the new babies, grown lusty and dragging their elders down, with behind them more babies to the end of time—Youth that must have its will and that will never die.

King glanced over to the press box and nodded to Morgan, of the *Sportsman,* and Corbett, of the *Referee.* Then he held out his hands, while Sid Sullivan and Charley Bates, his seconds, slipped on his gloves and laced them tight, closely watched by one of Sandel's seconds, who first examined critically the tapes on King's knuckles. A second of his own was in Sandel's corner, performing a like office. Sandel's trousers were pulled off, and, as he stood up, his sweater was skinned off over his head. And Tom King, looking, saw Youth incarnate, deep-chested, heavy-thewed, with muscles that slipped and slid like live things under the white satin skin. The whole body was acrawl with life, and Tom King knew that it was a life that had never oozed its freshness out through the aching pores during the long fights wherein Youth paid its toll and departed not quite so young as when it entered.

The two men advanced to meet each other, and, as the gong sounded and the seconds clattered out of the ring with the folding stools, they shook hands and instantly took their fighting attitudes. And instantly, like a mechanism of steel and springs balanced on a hair trigger, Sandel was in and out and in again, landing a left to the eyes, a right to the ribs, ducking a counter, dancing lightly away and dancing menacingly back again. He was swift and clever. It was a dazzling exhibition. The house yelled its approbation. But King was not dazzled. He had fought too many fights and too many youngsters. He knew the blows for what they were—too quick and too deft to be dangerous. Evidently Sandel was going to rush things from the start. It was to be expected. It was the way of Youth, expending its splendor and excellence in wild insurgence and furious onslaught, overwhelming opposition with its own unlimited glory of strength and desire.

Sandel was in and out, here, there, and everywhere, light-footed and eager-hearted, a living wonder of white flesh and stinging muscle that wove itself into a dazzling fabric of attack, slipping and leaping like a flying shuttle from action to action through a thousand actions, all of them centred upon the destruction of Tom King, who stood between him and fortune. And Tom King patiently endured. He knew his business, and he knew Youth now that Youth was no longer his. There was nothing to do till the other lost some of his steam, was his thought, and he grinned to himself as he deliberately ducked so as to receive a heavy blow on the top of his head. It was a wicked thing to do, yet eminently fair according to the rules of the boxing game. A man was supposed to take care of his own knuckles, and, if he insisted on hitting an opponent on the top of the head, he did so at his own

peril. King could have ducked lower and let the blow whiz harmlessly
past, but he remembered his own early fights and how he smashed his
first knuckle on the head of the Welsh Terror. He was but playing the
game. That duck had accounted for one of Sandel's knuckles. Not that
Sandel would mind it now. He would go on, superbly regardless, hitting as hard as ever throughout the fight. But later on, when the long
ring battles had begun to tell, he would regret that knuckle and look
back and remember how he smashed it on Tom King's head.

The first round was all Sandel's, and he had the house yelling
with the rapidity of his whirlwind rushes. He overwhelmed King with
avalanches of punches, and King did nothing. He never struck once,
contenting himself with covering up, blocking and ducking and clinching to avoid punishment. He occasionally feinted, shook his head when
the weight of a punch landed, and moved stolidly about, never leaping
or springing or wasting an ounce of strength. Sandel must foam the
froth of Youth away before discreet Age could dare to retaliate. All
King's movements were slow and methodical, and his heavy-lidded,
slow-moving eyes gave him the appearance of being half asleep or
dazed. Yet they were eyes that saw everything, that had been trained
to see everything, that had been trained to see everything through all
his twenty years and odd in the ring. They were eyes that did not blink
or waver before an impending blow, but that coolly saw and measured
distance.

Seated in his corner for the minute's rest at the end of the round,
he lay back with outstretched legs, his arms resting on the right angle
of the ropes, his chest and abdomen heaving frankly and deeply as he
gulped down the air driven by the towels of his seconds. He listened
with closed eyes to the voices of the house, "Why don't yeh fight,
Tom?" many were crying. "Yeh ain't afraid of 'im, are yeh?"

"Muscle-bound," he heard a man on a front seat comment. "He
can't move quicker. Two to one on Sandel, in quids."

The gong struck and the two men advanced from their corners.
Sandel came forward fully three-quarters of the distance, eager to begin again; but King was content to advance the shorter distance. It
was in line with his policy of economy. He had not been well trained,
and he had not had enough to eat, and every step counted. Besides,
he had already walked two miles to the ringside. It was a repetition
of the first round, with Sandel attacking like a whirlwind and with the
audience indignantly demanding why King did not fight. Beyond feinting and several slowly delivered and ineffectual blows he did nothing
save block and stall and clinch. Sandel wanted to make the pace fast,

while King, out of his wisdom, refused to accommodate him. He grinned with a certain wistful pathos in his ring-battered countenance, and went on cherishing his strength with the jealousy of which only Age is capable. Sandel was Youth, and he threw his strength away with the munificent abandon of Youth. To King belonged the ring generalship, the wisdom bred of long, aching fights. He watched with cool eyes and head, moving slowly and waiting for Sandel's froth to foam away. To the majority of the onlookers it seemed as though King was hopelessly outclassed, and they voiced their opinion in offers of three to one on Sandel. But there were wise ones, a few, who knew King of old time, and who covered what they considered easy money.

The third round began as usual, one-sided, with Sandel doing all the leading and delivering all the punishment. A half-minute had passed when Sandel, overconfident, left an opening. King's eyes and right arm flashed in the same instant. It was his first real blow—a hook, with the twisted arch of the arm to make it rigid, and with all the weight of the half-pivoted body behind it. It was like a sleepy-seeming lion suddenly thrusting out a lightning paw. Sandel, caught on the side of the jaw, was felled like a bullock. The audience gasped and murmured awe-stricken applause. The man was not muscle-bound, after all, and he could drive a blow like a trip-hammer.

Sandel was shaken. He rolled over and attempted to rise, but the sharp yells from his seconds to take the count restrained him. He knelt on one knee, ready to rise, and waited, while the referee stood over him, counting the seconds loudly in his ear. At the ninth he rose in fighting attitude, and Tom King, facing him, knew regret that the blow had not been an inch nearer the point of the jaw. That would have been a knockout, and he could have carried the thirty quid home to the missus and the kiddies.

The round continued to the end of its three minutes, Sandel for the first time respectful of his opponent and King slow of movement and sleepy-eyed as ever. As the round neared its close, King, warned of the fact by sight of the seconds crouching outside ready for the spring in through the ropes, worked the fight around to his own corner. And when the gong struck, he sat down immediately on the waiting stool, while Sandel had to walk all the way across the diagonal of the square to his own corner. It was a little thing, but it was the sum of little things that counted. Sandel was compelled to walk that many more steps, to give up that much energy, and to lose a part of the precious minute of rest. At the beginning of every round King loafed slowly out from his corner, forcing his opponent to advance the greater distance. The end of every round found the fight manœuvred by King into his own corner so that he could immediately sit down.

Two more rounds went by, in which King was parsimonious of effort and Sandel prodigal. The latter's attempt to force a fast pace made King uncomfortable, for a fair percentage of the multitudinous blows showered upon him went home. Yet King persisted in his dogged slowness, despite the crying of the young hotheads for him to go in and fight. Again, in the sixth round, Sandel was careless, again Tom King's fearful right flashed out to the jaw, and again Sandel took the nine seconds count.

By the seventh round Sandel's pink of condition was gone, and he settled down to what he knew was to be the hardest fight in his experience. Tom King was an old un, but a better old un than he had ever encountered—an old un who never lost his head, who was remarkably able at defence, whose blows had the impact of a knotted club, and who had a knockout in either hand. Nevertheless, Tom King dared not hit often. He never forgot his battered knuckles, and knew that every hit must count if the knuckles were to last out the fight. As he sat in his corner, glancing across at his opponent, the thought came to him that the sum of his wisdom and Sandel's youth would constitute a world's champion heavyweight. But that was the trouble. Sandel would never become a world champion. He lacked the wisdom, and the only way for him to get it was to buy it with Youth; and when wisdom was his, Youth would have been spent in buying it.

King took every advantage he knew. He never missed an opportunity to clinch, and in effecting most of the clinches his shoulder drove stiffly into the other's ribs. In the philosophy of the ring a shoulder was as good as a punch so far as damage was concerned, and a great deal better so far as concerned expenditure of effort. Also, in the clinches King rested his weight on his opponent, and was loath to let go. This compelled the interference of the referee, who tore them apart, always assisted by Sandel, who had not yet learned to rest. He could not refrain from using those glorious flying arms and writhing muscles of his, and when the other rushed into a clinch, striking shoulder against ribs, and with head resting under Sandel's left arm, Sandel almost invariably swung his right behind his own back and into the projecting face. It was a clever stroke, much admired by the audience, but it was not dangerous, and was, therefore, just that much wasted strength. But Sandel was tireless and unaware of limitations, and King grinned and doggedly endured.

Sandel developed a fierce right to the body, which made it appear that King was taking an enormous amount of punishment, and it was only the old ringsters who appreciated the deft touch of King's left glove to the other's biceps just before the impact of the blow. It was true, the blow landed each time; but each time it was robbed of its power by that touch on the biceps. In the ninth round, three times inside a minute, King's right hooked its twisted arch to the jaw; and three times Sandel's body, heavy as it was, was levelled to the mat. Each time he took the nine seconds allowed him and rose to his feet, shaken and jarred, but still strong. He had lost much of his speed, and he wasted less effort. He was fighting grimly; but he continued to draw upon his chief asset, which was Youth. King's chief asset was experience. As his vitality had dimmed and his vigor abated, he had replaced them with cunning, with wisdom born of the long fights and with a careful shepherding of strength. Not alone had he learned never to make a superfluous movement, but he had learned how to seduce an opponent into throwing his strength away. Again and again, by feint of foot and hand and body he continued to inveigle Sandel into leaping back, ducking, or countering. King rested, but he never permitted Sandel to rest. It was the strategy of Age.

Early in the tenth round King began stopping the other's rushes with straight lefts to the face, and Sandel, grown wary, responded by drawing the left, then by ducking it and delivering his right in a swinging hook to the side of the head. It was too high up to be vitally effective; but when first it landed, King knew the old, familiar descent of the black veil of unconsciousness across his mind. For the instant, or for the slightest fraction of an instant, rather, he ceased. In the one moment he saw his opponent ducking out of his field of vision and the background of white, watching faces; in the next moment he again saw his opponent and the background of faces. It was as if he had slept for a time and just opened his eyes again, and yet the interval of unconsciousness was so microscopically short that there had been no time for him to fall. The audience saw him totter and his knees give, and then saw him recover and tuck his chin deeper into the shelter of his left shoulder.

Several times Sandel repeated the blow, keeping King partially dazed, and then the latter worked out his defence, which was also a counter. Feinting with his left he took a half-step backward, at the same time upper cutting with the whole strength of his right. So accurately was it timed that it landed squarely on Sandel's face in the full, downward sweep of the duck, and Sandel lifted in the air and curled backward, striking the mat on his head and shoulders. Twice

King achieved this, then turned loose and hammered his opponent to the ropes. He gave Sandel no chance to rest or to set himself, but smashed blow in upon blow till the house rose to its feet and the air was filled with an unbroken roar of applause. But Sandel's strength and endurance were superb, and he continued to stay on his feet. A knockout seemed certain, and a captain of police, appalled at the dreadful punishment, arose by the ringside to stop the fight. The gong struck for the end of the round and Sandel staggered to his corner, protesting to the captain that he was sound and strong. To prove it, he threw two back air-springs, and the police captain gave in.

Tom King, leaning back in his corner and breathing hard, was disappointed. If the fight had been stopped, the referee, perforce, would have rendered him the decision and the purse would have been his. Unlike Sandel, he was not fighting for glory or career, but for thirty quid. And now Sandel would recuperate in the minute of rest.

Youth will be served—this saying flashed into King's mind, and he remembered the first time he had heard it, the night when he had put away Stowsher Bill. The toff who had bought him a drink after the fight and patted him on the shoulder had used those words. Youth will be served! The toff was right. And on that night in the long ago he had been Youth. To-night Youth sat in the opposite corner. As for himself, he had been fighting for half an hour now, and he was an old man. Had he fought like Sandel, he would not have lasted fifteen minutes. But the point was that he did not recuperate. Those upstanding arteries and that sorely tried heart would not enable him to gather strength in the intervals between the rounds. And he had not had sufficient strength in him to begin with. His legs were heavy under him and beginning to cramp. He should not have walked those two miles to the fight. And there was the steak which he had got up longing for that morning. A great and terrible hatred rose up in him for the butchers who had refused him credit. It was hard for an old man to go into a fight without enough to eat. And a piece of steak was such a little thing, a few pennies at best; yet it meant thirty quid to him.

With the gong that opened the eleventh round, Sandel rushed, making a show of freshness which he did not really possess. King knew it for what it was—a bluff as old as the game itself. He clinched to save himself, then, going free, allowed Sandel to get set. This was what King desired. He feinted with his left, drew the answering duck and swinging upward hook, then made the half-step backward, delivered the upper cut full to the face and crumpled Sandel over to the mat. After that he never let him rest, receiving punishment himself, but inflicting far more, smashing Sandel to the ropes, hooking and driving all manner of blows into him, tearing away from his clinches or punching him out of attempted clinches, and ever when Sandel would have fallen, catching him with one uplifting hand and with the other immediately smashing him into the ropes where he could not fall.

The house by this time had gone mad, and it was his house, nearly every voice yelling: "Go it, Tom!" "Get 'im! Get 'im!" "You've got 'im, Tom! You've got 'im!" It was to be a whirlwind finish, and that was what a ringside audience paid to see.

And Tom King, who for half an hour had conserved his strength, now expended it prodigally in the one great effort he knew he had in him. It was his one chance—now or not at all. His strength was waning fast, and his hope was that before the last of it ebbed out of him he would have beaten his opponent down for the count. And as he continued to strike and force, coolly estimating the weight of his blows and the quality of the damage wrought, he realized how hard a man Sandel was to knock out. Stamina and endurance were his to an extreme degree, and they were the virgin stamina and endurance of Youth. Sandel was certainly a coming man. He had it in him. Only out of such rugged fibre were successful fighters fashioned.

Sandel was reeling and staggering, but Tom King's legs were cramping and his knuckles going back on him. Yet he steeled himself to strike the fierce blows, every one of which brought anguish to his tortured hands. Though now he was receiving practically no punishment, he was weakening as rapidly as the other. His blows went home, but there was no longer the weight behind them, and each blow was the result of a severe effort of will. His legs were like lead, and they dragged visibly under him; while Sandel's backers, cheered by this symptom, began calling encouragement to their man.

King was spurred to a burst of effort. He delivered two blows in succession—a left, a trifle too high, to the solar plexus, and a right cross to the jaw. They were not heavy blows, yet so weak and dazed was Sandel that he went down and lay quivering. The referee stood over him, shouting the count of the fatal seconds in his ear. If before the tenth second was called, he did not rise, the fight was lost. The house stood in hushed silence. King rested on trembling legs. A mortal dizziness was upon him, and before his eyes the sea of faces sagged and swayed, while to his ears, as from a remote distance, came the count of the referee. Yet he looked upon the fight as his. It was impossible that a man so punished could rise.

Only Youth could rise, and Sandel rose. At the fourth second he rolled over on his face and groped blindly for the ropes. By the seventh second he had dragged himself to his knee, where he rested, his head rolling groggily on his shoulders. As the referee cried "Nine!" Sandel stood upright, in proper stalling position, his left arm wrapped about his face, his right wrapped about his stomach. Thus were his vital points guarded, while he lurched forward toward King in the hope of effecting a clinch and gaining more time.

At the instant Sandel arose, King was at him, but the two blows he delivered were muffled on the stalled arms. The next moment Sandel was in the clinch and holding on desperately while the referee strove to drag the two men apart. King helped to force himself free. He knew the rapidity with which Youth recovered, and he knew that Sandel was his if he could prevent that recovery. One stiff punch would do it. Sandel was his, indubitably his. He had outgeneralled him, outfought him, outpointed him. Sandel reeled out of the clinch, balanced on the hair line between defeat or survival. One good blow would topple him over and down and out. And Tom King, in a flash of bitterness, remembered the piece of steak and wished that he had it then behind that necessary punch he must deliver. He nerved himself for the blow, but it was not heavy enough nor swift enough. Sandel swayed, but did not fall, staggering back to the ropes and holding on. King staggered after him, and, with a pang like that of dissolution, delivered another blow. But his body had deserted him. All that was left of him was a fighting intelligence that was dimmed and clouded from exhaustion. The blow that was aimed for the jaw struck no higher than the shoulder. He had willed the blow higher, but the tired muscles had not been able to obey. And, from the impact of the blow, Tom King himself reeled back and nearly fell. Once again he strove. This time his punch missed altogether, and, from absolute weakness, he fell against Sandel and clinched, holding on to him to save himself from sinking to the floor.

King did not attempt to free himself. He had shot his bolt. He was gone. And Youth had been served. Even in the clinch he could feel Sandel growing stronger against him. When the referee thrust them apart, there, before his eyes, he saw Youth recuperate. From instant to instant Sandel grew stronger. His punches, weak and futile at first, became stiff and accurate. Tom King's bleared eyes saw the gloved fist driving at his jaw, and he willed to guard it by interposing his arm. He saw the danger, willed the act; but the arm was too heavy. It seemed burdened with a hundredweight of lead. It would not lift itself, and he strove to lift it with his soul. Then the gloved fist landed home. He experienced a sharp snap that was like an electric spark, and, simultaneously, the veil of blackness enveloped him.

When he opened his eyes again he was in his corner, and he heard the yelling of the audience like the roar of the surf at Bondi Beach. A wet sponge was being pressed against the base of his brain, and Sid Sullivan was blowing cold water in a refreshing spray over his face and chest. His gloves had already been removed, and Sandel, bending over him, was shaking his hand. He bore no ill-will toward the man who had put him out, and he returned the grip with a heartiness that made his battered knuckles protest. Then Sandel stepped to the centre of the ring and the audience hushed its pandemonium to hear him accept young Pronto's challenge and offer to increase the side bet to one hundred pounds. King looked on apathetically while his seconds mopped the streaming water from him, dried his face, and prepared him to leave the ring. He felt hungry. It was not the ordinary, gnawing kind, but a great faintness, a palpitation at the pit of the stomach that communicated itself to all his body. He remembered back into the fight to the moment when he had Sandel swaying and tottering on the hair-line balance of defeat. Ah, that piece of steak would have done it! He had lacked just that for the decisive blow, and he had lost. It was all because of the piece of steak.

His seconds were half-supporting him as they helped him through the ropes. He tore free from them, ducked through the ropes unaided, and leaped heavily to the floor, following on their heels as they forced a passage for him down the crowded centre aisle. Leaving the dressing-room for the street, in the entrance to the hall, some young fellow spoke to him.

"W'y didn't yuh go in an' get 'im when yuh 'ad 'im?" the young fellow asked.

"Aw, go to hell!" said Tom King, and passed down the steps to the sidewalk.

The doors of the public house at the corner were swinging wide, and he saw the lights and the smiling barmaids, heard the many voices discussing the fight and the prosperous chink of money on the bar. Somebody called to him to have a drink. He hesitated perceptibly, then refused and went on his way.

He had not a copper in his pocket, and the two-mile walk home seemed very long. He was certainly getting old. Crossing the Domain, he sat down suddenly on a bench, unnerved by the thought of the missus sitting up for him, waiting to learn the outcome of the fight. That was harder than any knockout, and it seemed almost impossible to face.

He felt weak and sore, and the pain of his smashed knuckles warned him that, even if he could find a job at navvy work, it would be a week before he could grip a pick handle or a shovel. The hunger palpitation at the pit of the stomach was sickening. His wretchedness overwhelmed him, and into his eyes came an unwonted moisture. He covered his face with his hands, and, as he cried, he remembered Stowsher Bill and how he had served him that night in the long ago. Poor old Stowsher Bill! He could understand now why Bill had cried in the dressing-room.

# THE MADNESS OF
# JOHN HARNED

I TELL THIS for a fact. It happened in the bull-ring at Quito. I sat in the box with John Harned, and with Maria Valenzuela, and with Luis Cervallos. I saw it happen. I saw it all from first to last. I was on the steamer *Ecuadore* from Panama to Guayaquil. Maria Valenzuela is my cousin. I have known her always. She is very beautiful. I am a Spaniard—an Ecuadoriano, true, but I am descended from Pedro Patino, who was one of Pizarro's captains. They were brave men. They were heroes. Did not Pizarro lead three hundred and fifty Spanish cavaliers and four thousand Indians into the far Cordilleras in search of treasure? And did not all the four thousand Indians and three hundred of the brave cavaliers die on that vain quest? But Pedro Patino did not die. He it was that lived to found the family of the Patino. I am Ecuadoriano, true, but I am Spanish. I am Manuel de Jesus Patino. I own many haciendas, and ten thousand Indians are my slaves, though the law says they are free men who work by freedom of contract. The law is a funny thing. We Ecuadorianos laugh at it. It is our law. We make it for ourselves. I am Manuel de Jesus Patino. Remember that name. It will be written some day in history. There are revolutions in Ecuador. We call them elections. It is a good joke is it not?—what you call a pun?

John Harned was an American. I met him first at the Tivoli hotel in Panama. He had much money—this I have heard. He was going to Lima, but he met Maria Valenzuela in the Tivoli hotel. Maria Valenzuela is my cousin, and she is beautiful. It is true, she is the most beautiful woman in Ecuador. But also is she most beautiful in every country—in Paris, in Madrid, in New York, in Vienna. Always do all men look at her, and John Harned looked long at her at Panama. He loved her, that I know for a fact. She was Ecuadoriano, true—but she was of all countries; she was of all the world. She spoke many languages. She sang—ah! like an artiste. Her smile—wonderful, divine. Her eyes—ah! have I not seen men look in her eyes? They were what you English call amazing. They were promises of paradise. Men drowned themselves in her eyes.

Maria Valenzuela was rich—richer than I, who am accounted very rich in Ecuador. But John Harned did not care for her money. He had a heart—a funny heart. He was a fool. He did not go to Lima. He left the steamer at Guayaquil and followed her to Quito. She was coming home from Europe and other places. I do not see what she found in him, but she liked him. This I know for a fact, else he would not have followed her to Quito. She asked him to come. Well do I remember the occasion. She said:

"Come to Quito and I will show you the bull-fight—brave, clever, magnificent!"

But he said: "I go to Lima, not Quito. Such is my passage engaged on the steamer."

"You travel for pleasure—no?" said Maria Valenzuela; and she looked at him as only Maria Valenzuela could look, her eyes warm with the promise.

And he came. No; he did not come for the bull-fight. He came because of what he had seen in her eyes. Women like Maria Valenzuela are born once in a hundred years. They are of no country and no time. They are what you call universal. They are goddesses. Men fall down at their feet. They play with men and run them through their pretty fingers like sand. Cleopatra was such a woman they say; and so was Circe. She turned men into swine. Ha! ha! It is true—no?

It all came about because Maria Valenzuela said:

"You English people are—what shall I say?—savage—no? You prize-fight. Two men each hit the other with their fists till their eyes are blinded and their noses are broken. Hideous! And the other men who look on cry out loudly and are made glad. It is barbarous—no?"

"But they are men," said John Harned; "and they prize-fight out of desire. No one makes them prize-fight. They do it because they desire it more than anything else in the world."

Maria Valenzuela—there was scorn in her smile as she said:

"They kill each other often—is it not so? I have read it in the papers."

"But the bull," said John Harned. "The bull is killed many times in the bull-fight, and the bull does not come into the ring out of desire. It is not fair to the bull. He is compelled to fight. But the man in the prize-fight—no; he is not compelled."

"He is the more brute therefore," said Maria Valenzuela. "He is savage. He is primitive. He is animal. He strikes with his paws like a bear from a cave, and he is ferocious. But the bull-fight—ah! You have not seen the bull-fight—no? The toreador is clever. He must have skill. He is modern. He is romantic. He is only a man, soft and tender, and he faces the wild bull in conflict. And he kills with a sword, a slender sword, with one thrust, so, to the heart of the great beast. It is delicious. It makes the heart beat to behold—the small man, the great beast, the wide level sand, the thousands that look on without breath; the great beast rushes to the attack, the small man stands like a statue; he does not move, he is unafraid, and in his hand is the slender sword flashing like silver in the sun; nearer and nearer rushes the great beast with its sharp horns, the man does not move, and then—so—the sword flashes, the thrust is made, to the heart, to the hilt, the bull falls to the sand and is dead, and the man is unhurt. It is brave. It is magnificent! Ah!—I could love the toreador. But the man of the prize-fight—he is the brute, the human beast, the savage primitive, the maniac that receives many blows in his stupid face and rejoices. Come to Quito and I will show you the brave sport, the sport of men, the toreador and the bull."

But John Harned did not go to Quito for the bull-fight. He went because of Maria Valenzuela. He was a large man, more broad of shoulder than we Ecuadorianos, more tall, more heavy of limb and bone. True, he was larger even than most men of his own race. His eyes were blue, though I have seen them gray, and, sometimes, like cold steel. His features were large, too—not delicate like ours, and his jaw was very strong to look at. Also, his face was smooth-shaven like a priest's. Why should a man feel shame for the hair on his face? Did not God put it there? Yes, I believe in God. I am not a pagan like many of you English. God is good. He made me an Ecuadoriano with ten thousand slaves. And when I die I shall go to God. Yes, the priests are right.

But John Harned. He was a quiet man. He talked always in a low voice, and he never moved his hands when he talked. One would have thought his heart was a piece of ice; yet did he have a streak of warm in his blood, for he followed Maria Valenzuela to Quito. Also, and for all that he talked low without moving his hands, he was an animal, as you shall see—the beast primitive, the stupid, ferocious savage of the long ago that dressed in wild skins and lived in the caves along with the bears and wolves.

Luis Cervallos is my friend, the best of Ecuadorianos. He owns three cacao plantations at Naranjito and Chobo. At Milagro is his big sugar plantation. He has large haciendas at Ambato and Latacunga, and down the coast is he interested in oil-wells. Also has he spent much money in planting rubber along the Guayas. He is modern, like the Yankee; and, like the Yankee, full of business. He has much money, but it is in many ventures, and ever he needs more money for new ventures and for the old ones. He has been everywhere and seen everything. When he was a very young man he was in the Yankee military academy what you call West Point. There was trouble. He was made to resign. He does not like Americans. But he did like Maria Valenzuela, who was of his own country. Also, he needed her money for his ventures and for his gold mine in Eastern Ecuador where the painted Indians live. I was his friend. It was my desire that he should marry Maria Valenzuela. Further, much of my money had I invested in his ventures, more so in his gold mine which was very rich but which first required the expense of much money before it would yield forth its riches. If Luis Cervallos married Maria Valenzuela I should have more money very immediately.

But John Harned followed Maria Valenzuela to Quito, and it was quickly clear to us—to Luis Cervallos and me—that she looked upon John Harned with great kindness. It is said that a woman will have her will, but this is a case not in point, for Maria Valenzuela did not have her will—at least not with John Harned. Perhaps it would all have happened as it did, even if Luis Cervallos and I had not sat in the box that day at the bull-ring in Quito. But this I know: we *did* sit in the box that day. And I shall tell you what happened.

The four of us were in the one box, guests of Luis Cervallos. I was next to the Presidente's box. On the other side was the box of General José Eliceo Salazar. With him were Joaquin Endara and Urcisino Castillo, both generals, and Colonel Jacinto Fierro and Captain Baltazar de Echeverria. Only Luis Cervallos had the position and the influence to get that box next to the Presidente. I know for a fact that the Presidente himself expressed the desire to the management that Luis Cervallos should have that box.

The band finished playing the national hymn of Ecuador. The procession of the toreadors was over. The Presidente nodded to begin. The bugles blew, and the bull dashed in—you know the way, excited, bewildered, the darts in its shoulder burning like fire, itself seeking madly whatever enemy to destroy. The toreadors hid behind their shelters and waited. Suddenly they appeared forth, the capadors, five of them, from every side, their colored capes flinging wide. The bull paused at sight of such a generosity of enemies, unable in his own mind to know which to attack. Then advanced one of the capadores alone to meet the bull. The bull was very angry. With its fore-legs it pawed the sand of the arena till the dust rose all about it. Then it charged, with lowered head, straight for the lone capador.

It is always of interest, the first charge of the first bull. After a time it is natural that one should grow tired, a trifle, that the keenness should lose its edge. But that first charge of the first bull! John Harned was seeing it for the first time, and he could not escape the excitement—the sight of the man, armed only with a piece of cloth, and of the bull rushing upon him across the sand with sharp horns, widespreading.

"See!" cried Maria Valenzuela. "Is it not superb?"

John Harned nodded, but did not look at her. His eyes were sparkling, and they were only for the bull-ring. The capador stepped to the side, with a twirl of the cape eluding the bull and spreading the cape on his own shoulders.

"What do you think?" asked Maria Valenzuela. "Is it not a—what-you-call—sporting proposition—no?"

"It is certainly," said John Harned. "It is very clever."

She clapped her hands with delight. They were little hands. The audience applauded. The bull turned and came back. Again the capadore eluded him, throwing the cape on his shoulders, and again the audience applauded. Three times did this happen. The capadore was very excellent. Then he retired, and the other capadore played with the bull. After that they placed the banderillos in the bull, in the shoulders, on each side of the back-bone, two at a time. Then stepped forward Ordonez, the chief matador, with the long sword and the scarlet cape. The bugles blew for the death. He is not so good as Matestini. Still he is good, and with one thrust he drove the sword to the heart, and the bull doubled his legs under him and lay down and died. It was a pretty thrust, clean and sure; and there was much applause, and many of the common people threw their hats into the ring. Maria Valenzuela clapped her hands with the rest, and John Harned, whose cold heart was not touched by the event, looked at her with curiosity.

"You like it?" he asked.

"Always," she said, still clapping her hands.

"From a little girl," said Luis Cervallos. "I remember her first fight. She was four years old. She sat with her mother, and just like now she clapped her hands. She is a proper Spanish woman."

"You have seen it," said Maria Valenzuela to John Harned, as they fastened the mules to the dead bull and dragged it out. "You have seen the bull-fight and you like it—no? What do you think?"

"I think the bull had no chance," he said. "The bull was doomed from the first. The issue was not in doubt. Every one knew, before the bull entered the ring, that it was to die. To be a sporting proposition, the issue must be in doubt. It was one stupid bull who had never fought a man against five wise men who had fought many bulls. It would be possibly a little bit fair if it were one man against one bull."

"Or one man against five bulls," said Maria Valenzuela; and we all laughed, and Luis Cervallos laughed loudest.

"Yes," said John Harned, "against five bulls, and the man, like the bulls, never in the bull-ring before—a man like yourself, Senor Cervallos."

"Yet we Spanish like the bull-fight," said Luis Cervallos; and I swear the devil was whispering then in his ear, telling him to do that which I shall relate.

"Then must it be a cultivated taste," John Harned made answer. "We kill bulls by the thousand every day in Chicago, yet no one cares to pay admittance to see."

"That is butchery," said I; "but this—ah, this is an art. It is delicate. It is fine. It is rare."

"Not always," said Luis Cervallos. "I have seen clumsy matadors, and I tell you it is not nice."

He shuddered, and his face betrayed such what-you-call disgust, that I knew, then, that the devil was whispering and that he was beginning to play a part.

"Senor Harned may be right," said Luis Cervallos. "It may not be fair to the bull. For is it not known to all of us that for twenty-four hours the bull is given no water, and that immediately before the fight he is permitted to drink his fill?"

"And he comes into the ring heavy with water?" said John Harned quickly; and I saw that his eyes were very gray and very sharp and very cold.

"It is necessary for the sport," said Luis Cervallos. "Would you have the bull so strong that he would kill the toreadors?"

"I would that he had a fighting chance," said John Harned, facing the ring to see the second bull come in.

It was not a good bull. It was frightened. It ran around the ring in search of a way to get out. The capadors stepped forth and flared their capes, but he refused to charge upon them.

"It is a stupid bull," said Maria Valenzuela.

"I beg pardon," said John Harned; "but it would seem to me a wise bull. He knows he must not fight man. See! He smells death there in the ring."

True. The bull, pausing where the last one had died, was smelling the wet sand and snorting. Again he ran around the ring, with raised head, looking at the faces of the thousands that hissed him, that threw orange-peel at him and called him names. But the smell of blood decided him, and he charged a capador, so without warning that the man just escaped. He dropped his cape and dodged into the shelter. The bull struck the wall of the ring with a crash. And John Harned said, in a quiet voice, as though he talked to himself:

"I will give one thousand sucres to the lazar-house of Quito if a bull kills a man this day."

"You like bulls?" said Maria Valenzuela with a smile.

"I like such men less," said John Harned. "A toreador is not a brave man. He surely cannot be a brave man. See, the bull's tongue is already out. He is tired and he has not yet begun."

"It is the water," said Luis Cervallos.

"Yes, it is the water," said John Harned. "Would it not be safer to hamstring the bull before he comes on?"

Maria Valenzuela was made angry by this sneer in John Harned's words. But Luis Cervallos smiled so that only I could see him, and then it broke upon my mind surely the game he was playing. He and I were to be banderilleros. The big American bull was there in the box with us. We were to stick the darts in him till he became angry, and then there might be no marriage with Maria Valenzuela. It was a good sport. And the spirit of bull-fighters was in our blood.

The bull was now angry and excited. The capadors had great game with him. He was very quick, and sometimes he turned with such sharpness that his hind legs lost their footing and he plowed the sand with his quarter. But he charged always the flung capes and committed no harm.

"He has no chance," said John Harned. "He is fighting wind."

"He thinks the cape is his enemy," explained Maria Valenzuela. "See how cleverly the capador deceives him."

"It is his nature to be deceived," said John Harned. "Wherefore he is doomed to fight wind. The toreadors know it, the audience knows it, you know it, I know it—we all know from the first that he will fight wind. He only does not know it. It is his stupid beast-nature. He has no chance."

"It is very simple," said Luis Cervallos. "The bull shuts his eyes when he charges. Therefore—"

"The man steps out of the way and the bull rushes by," John Harned interrupted.

"Yes," said Luis Cervallos; "that is it. The bull shuts his eyes, and the man knows it."

"But cows do not shut their eyes," said John Harned. "I know a cow at home that is a Jersey and gives milk, that would whip the whole gang of them."

"But the toreadors do not fight cows," said I.

"They are afraid to fight cows," said John Harned.

"Yes," said Luis Cervallos; "they are afraid to fight cows. There would be no sport in killing toreadors."

"There would be some sport," said John Harned, "if a toreador were killed once in a while. When I become an old man, and mayhap a cripple, and should I need to make a living and be unable to do hard work, then would I become a bull-fighter. It is a light vocation for elderly gentlemen and pensioners."

"But see!" said Maria Valenzuela, as the bull charged bravely and the capador eluded it with a fling of his cape. "It requires skill so to avoid the beast."

"True," said John Harned. "But believe me, it requires a thousand times more skill to avoid the many and quick punches of a prize-fighter who keeps his eyes open and strikes with intelligence. Furthermore, this bull does not want to fight. Behold, he runs away."

It was not a good bull, for again it ran around the ring, seeking to find a way out.

"Yes these bulls are sometimes the most dangerous," said Luis Cervallos. "It can never be known what they will do next. They are wise. They are half cow. The bull-fighters never like them.—See! He has turned!"

Once again, baffled and made angry by the walls of the ring that would not let him out, the bull was attacking his enemies valiantly.

"His tongue is hanging out," said John Harned. "First, they fill him with water. Then they tire him out, one man and then another, persuading him to exhaust himself by fighting wind. While some tire him, others rest. But the bull they never let rest. Afterward, when he is quite tired and no longer quick, the matador sticks the sword into him."

The time had now come for the banderillos. Three times one of the fighters endeavored to place the darts, and three times did he fail. He but stung the bull and maddened it. The banderillos must go in, you know, two at a time, into the shoulders, on each side the backbone and close to it. If but one be placed, it is a failure. The crowd hissed and called for Ordonez. And then Ordonez did a great thing. Four times he stood forth, and four times, at the first attempt, he stuck in the banderillos, so that eight of them, well placed, stood out of the back of the bull at one time. The crowd went mad, and a rain of hats and money fell upon the sand of the ring.

And just then the bull charged unexpectedly one of the capadors. The man slipped and lost his head. The bull caught him—fortunately, between his wide horns. And while the audience watched, breathless and silent, John Harned stood up and yelled with gladness. Alone, in that hush of all of us, John Harned yelled. And he yelled for the bull. As you see yourself, John Harned wanted the man killed. His was a brutal heart. This bad conduct made those angry that sat in the box of General Salazar, and they cried out against John Harned. And Urcisino Castillo told him to his face that he was a dog of a Gringo and other things. Only it was in Spanish, and John Harned did not understand. He stood and yelled, perhaps for the time of ten seconds, when the bull was enticed into charging the other capadors and the man arose unhurt.

"The bull has no chance," John Harned said with sadness as he sat down. "The man was uninjured. They fooled the bull away from him." Then he turned to Maria Valenzuela and said: "I beg your pardon. I was excited."

She smiled and in reproof tapped his arm with her fan.

"It is your first bull-fight," she said. "After you have seen more you will not cry for the death of the man. You Americans, you see, are more brutal than we. It is because of your prize-fighting. We come only to see the bull killed."

"But I would the bull had some chance," he answered. "Doubtless, in time, I shall cease to be annoyed by the men who take advantage of the bull."

The bugles blew for the death. Ordonez stood forth with the sword and the scarlet cloth. But the bull had changed again, and did not want to fight. Ordonez stamped his foot in the sand, and cried out, and waved the scarlet cloth. Then the bull charged, but without heart. There was no weight to the charge. It was a poor thrust. The sword struck a bone and bent. Ordonez took a fresh sword. The bull, again stung to fight, charged once more. Five times Ordonez essayed the thrust, and each time the sword went but part way in or struck bone. The sixth time, the sword went in to the hilt. But it was a bad thrust. The sword missed the heart and stuck out half a yard through the ribs on the opposite side. The audience hissed the matador. I glanced at John Harned. He sat silent, without movement; but I could see his teeth were set, and his hands were clenched tight on the railing of the box.

All fight was now out of the bull, and, though it was no vital thrust, he trotted lamely what of the sword that stuck through him, in one side and out the other. He ran away from the matador and the capadors, and circled the edge of the ring, looking up at the many faces.

"He is saying: 'For God's sake let me out of this; I don't want to fight,' " said John Harned.

That was all. He said no more, but sat and watched, though sometimes he looked sideways at Maria Valenzuela to see how she took it. She was angry with the matador. He was awkward, and she had desired a clever exhibition.

The bull was now very tired, and weak from loss of blood, though far from dying. He walked slowly around the wall of the ring, seeking a way out. He would not charge. He had had enough. But he must be killed. There is a place, in the neck of a bull behind the horns, where the cord of the spine is unprotected and where a short stab will immediately kill. Ordonez stepped in front of the bull and lowered his scarlet cloth to the ground. The bull would not charge. He stood still and smelled the cloth, lowering his head to do so. Ordonez stabbed between the horns at the spot in the neck. The bull jerked his head up. The stab had missed. Then the bull watched the sword. When Ordonez moved the cloth on the ground, the bull forgot the sword and lowered his head to smell the cloth. Again Ordonez stabbed, and again he failed. He tried many times. It was stupid. And John Harned said nothing. At last a stab went home, and the bull fell to the sand, dead immediately, and the mules were made fast and he was dragged out.

"The Gringos say it is a cruel sport—no?" said Luis Cervallos. "That it is not humane. That it is bad for the bull. No?"

"No," said John Harned. "The bull does not count for much. It is bad for those that look on. It is degrading to those that look on. It teaches them to delight in animal suffering. It is cowardly for five men to fight one stupid bull. Therefore those that look on learn to be cowards. The bull dies, but those that look on live and the lesson is learned. The bravery of men is not nourished by scenes of cowardice."

Maria Valenzuela said nothing. Neither did she look at him. But she heard every word and her cheeks were white with anger. She looked out across the ring and fanned herself, but I saw that her hand trembled. Nor did John Harned look at her. He went on as though she were not there. He, too, was angry, coldly angry.

"It is the cowardly sport of a cowardly people," he said.

"Ah," said Luis Cervallos softly, "you think you understand us."

"I understand now the Spanish Inquisition," said John Harned. "It must have been more delightful than bull-fighting."

Luis Cervallos smiled but said nothing. He glanced at Maria Valenzuela, and knew that the bull-fight in the box was won. Never would she have further to do with the Gringo who spoke such words. But neither Luis Cervallos nor I was prepared for the outcome of the day. I fear we do not understand the Gringos. How were we to know that John Harned, who was so coldly angry, should go suddenly mad? But mad he did go, as you shall see. The bull did not count for much— he said so himself. Then why should the horse count for so much? That I cannot understand. The mind of John Harned lacked logic. That is the only explanation.

"It is not usual to have horses in the bull-ring at Quito," said Luis Cervallos, looking up from the program. "In Spain they always have them. But to-day, by special permission we shall have them. When the next bull comes on there will be horses and picadors—you know, the men who carry lances and ride the horses."

"The bull is doomed from the first," said John Harned. "Are the horses then likewise doomed?"

"They are blindfolded so that they may not see the bull," said Luis Cervallos. "I have seen many horses killed. It is a brave sight."

"I have seen the bull slaughtered," said John Harned. "I will now see the horse slaughtered, so that I may understand more fully the fine points of this noble sport."

"They are old horses," said Luis Cervallos, "that are not good for anything else."

"I see," said John Harned.

The third bull came on, and soon against it were both capadors and picadors. One picador took his stand directly below us. I agree, it was a thin and aged horse he rode, a bag of bones covered with mangy hide.

"It is a marvel that the poor brute can hold up the weight of the rider," said John Harned. "And now that the horse fights the bull, what weapons has it?"

"The horse does not fight the bull," said Luis Cervallos.

"Oh," said John Harned, "then is the horse there to be gored? That must be why it is blindfolded, so that it shall not see the bull coming to gore it."

"Not quite so," said I. "The lance of the picador is to keep the bull from goring the horse."

"Then are horses rarely gored?" asked John Harned.

"No," said Luis Cervallos. "I have seen, at Seville, eighteen horses killed in one day, and the people clamored for more horses."

"Were they blindfolded like this horse?" asked John Harned.

"Yes," said Luis Cervallos.

After that we talked no more, but watched the fight. And John Harned was going mad all the time, and we did not know. The bull refused to charge the horse. And the horse stood still, and because it could not see it did not know that the capadors were trying to make the bull charge upon it. The capadors teased the bull with their capes, and when it charged them they ran toward the horse and into their shelters. At last the bull was well angry, and it saw the horse before it.

"The horse does not know, the horse does not know," John Harned whispered like to himself, unaware that he voiced his thought aloud.

The bull charged, and of course the horse knew nothing till the picador failed and the horse found himself impaled on the bull's horns from beneath. The bull was magnificently strong. The sight of its strength was splendid to see. It lifted the horse clear into the air; and as the horse fell to its side on the ground the picador landed on his feet and escaped, while the capadors lured the bull away. The horse was emptied of its essential organs. Yet did it rise to its feet screaming. It was the scream of the horse that did it, that made John Harned completely mad; for he, too, started to rise to his feet. I heard him curse low and deep. He never took his eyes from the horse, which, still screaming, strove to run, but fell down instead and rolled on its back so that all its four legs were kicking in the air. Then the bull charged it and gored it again and again until it was dead.

John Harned was now on his feet. His eyes were no longer cold like steel. They were blue flames. He looked at Maria Valenzuela, and she looked at him, and in his face was a great loathing. The moment of his madness was upon him. Everybody was looking, now that the horse was dead; and John Harned was a large man and easy to be seen.

"Sit down," said Luis Cervallos, "or you will make a fool of yourself."

John Harned replied nothing. He struck out his fist. He smote Luis Cervallos in the face so that he fell like a dead man across the chairs and did not rise again. He saw nothing of what followed. But I saw much. Urcisino Castillo, leaning forward from the next box, with his cane struck John Harned full across the face. And John Harned smote him with his fist so that in falling he overthrew General Salazar. John Harned was now in what-you-call Berserker rage—no? The beast primitive in him was loose and roaring—the beast primitive of the holes and caves of the long ago.

"You came for a bull-fight," I heard him say, "and by God I'll show you a man-fight!"

It was a fight. The soldiers guarding the Presidente's box leaped across, but from one of them he took a rifle and beat them on their heads with it. From the other box Colonel Jacinto Fierro was shooting at him with a revolver. The first shot killed a soldier. This I know for a fact. I saw it. But the second shot struck John Harned in the side. Whereupon he swore, and with a lunge drove the bayonet of his rifle into Colonel Jacinto Fierro's body. It was horrible to behold. The Americans and the English are a brutal race. They sneer at our bull-fighting, yet do they delight in the shedding of blood. More men were killed that day because of John Harned than were ever killed in all the history of the bull-ring of Quito, yes, and of Guayaquil and all Ecuador.

It was the scream of the horse that did it. Yet why did not John Harned go mad when the bull was killed? A beast is a beast, be it bull or horse. John Harned was mad. There is no other explanation. He was blood-mad, a beast himself. I leave it to your judgment. Which is worse—the goring of the horse by the bull or the goring of Colonel Jacinto Fierro by the bayonet in the hands of John Harned? And John Harned gored others with that bayonet. He was full of devils. He fought with many bullets in him, and he was hard to kill. And Maria Valenzuela was a brave woman. Unlike the other women, she did not cry out nor faint. She sat still in her box, gazing out across the bull-ring. Her face was white and she fanned herself, but she never looked around.

From all sides came the soldiers and officers and the common people bravely to subdue the mad Gringo. It is true—the cry went up from the crowd to kill all the Gringos. It is an old cry in Latin-American countries, what of the dislike for the Gringos and their un-couth ways. It is true, the cry went up. But the brave Ecuadorianos killed only John Harned, and first he killed seven of them. Besides, there were many hurt. I have seen many bull-fights, but never have I seen anything so abominable as the scene in the boxes when the fight was over. It was like a field of battle. The dead lay around everywhere, while the wounded sobbed and groaned and some of them died. One man, whom John Harned had thrust through the belly with the bay-onet, clutched at himself with both his hands and screamed. I tell you for a fact it was more terrible than the screaming of a thousand horses.

No, Maria Valenzuela did not marry Luis Cervallos. I am sorry for that. He was my friend, and much of my money was invested in his ventures. It was five weeks before the surgeons took the bandages from his face. And there is a scar there to this day, on the cheek, under the eye. Yet John Harned struck him but once and struck him only with his naked fist. Maria Valenzuela is in Austria now. It is said she is to marry an Arch-Duke or some high nobleman. I do not know. I think she liked John Harned before he followed her to Quito to see the bull-fight. But why the horse? That is what I desire to know. Why should he watch the bull and say that it did not count, and then go immediately and most horribly mad because a horse screamed? There is no understanding the Gringos. They are barbarians.

# THE NIGHT-BORN

It was in the old Alta-Inyo Club—a warm night for San Francisco —and through the open windows, hushed and far, came the brawl of the streets. The talk had led on from the Graft Prosecution and the latest signs that the town was to be run wide open, down through all the grotesque sordidness and rottenness of man-hate and man-meanness, until the name of O'Brien was mentioned— O'Brien, the promising young pugilist who had been killed in the prize-ring the night before. At once the air had seemed to freshen. O'Brien had been a clean-living young man with ideals. He neither drank, smoked, nor swore, and his had been the body of a beautiful young god. He had even carried his prayer-book to the ringside. They found it in his coat pocket in the dressing-room . . . afterward.

Here was Youth, clean and wholesome, unsullied—the thing of glory and wonder for men to conjure with . . . after it has been lost to them and they have turned middle-aged. And so well did we conjure, that Romance came and for an hour led us far from the man-city and its snarling roar. Bardwell, in a way, started it by quoting from Thoreau; but it was old Trefethan, bald-headed and dewlapped, who took up the quotation and for the hour to come was Romance incarnate. At first we might have wondered how many Scotches he had consumed since dinner, but very soon all that was forgotten.

"It was in 1898—I was thirty-five then," he said. "Yes, I know

263

you are adding it up. You're right. I'm forty-seven* now; look ten years more; and the doctors say—damn the doctors anyway!"

He lifted the long glass to his lips and sipped it slowly to soothe away his irritation.

"But I was young . . . once. I was young twelve years ago, and I had hair on top of my head, and my stomach was lean as a runner's, and the longest day was none too long for me. I was a husky back there in '98. You remember me, Milner. You knew me then. Wasn't I a pretty good bit of all right?"

Milner nodded and agreed. Like Trefethan, he was another mining engineer who had cleaned up a fortune in the Klondike.

"You certainly were, old man," Milner said. "I'll never forget when you cleaned out those lumberjacks in the M. & M. that night that little newspaper man started the row. Slavin was in the country at the time,"—this to us—"and his manager wanted to get up a match with Trefethan."

"Well, look at me now," Trefethan commanded angrily. "That's what the Goldstead did to me—God knows how many millions, but nothing left in my soul . . . nor in my veins. The good red blood is gone. I am a jellyfish, a huge, gross mass of oscillating protoplasm, a—a . . ."

But language failed him, and he drew solace from the long glass.

"Women looked at me . . . then; and turned their heads to look a second time. Strange that I never married. But the girl. That's what I started to tell you about. I met her a thousand miles from anywhere, and then some. And she quoted to me those very words of Thoreau that Bardwell quoted a moment ago—the ones about the day-born gods and the night-born.

"It was after I had made my locations on Goldstead—and didn't know what a treasure-pot that creek was going to prove—that I made that trip east over the Rockies, angling across to the Great Slave. Up North there the Rockies are something more than a back-bone. They are a boundary, a dividing line, a wall impregnable and unscalable. There is no intercourse across them, though, on occasion, from the early days, wandering trappers have crossed them, though more were lost by the way than ever came through. And that was precisely why I tackled the job. It was a traverse any man would be proud to make. I am prouder of it right now than anything else I have ever done.

"It is an unknown land. Great stretches of it have never been

* Editor's note: The text of this first edition reads "forty-even."

explored. There are big valleys there where the white man has never set foot, and Indian tribes as primitive as ten thousand years . . . almost, for they have had some contact with the whites. Parties of them come out once in a while to trade, and that is all. Even the Hudson Bay Company failed to find them and farm them.

"And now the girl. I was coming up a stream—you'd call it a river in California—uncharted and unnamed. It was a noble valley, now shut in by high canyon walls, and again opening out into beautiful stretches, wide and long, with pasture shoulder-high in the bottoms, meadows dotted with flowers, and with clumps of timber—spruce—virgin and magnificent. The dogs were packing on their backs, and were sore-footed and played out; while I was looking for any bunch of Indians to get sleds and drivers from and go on with the first snow. It was late fall, but the way those flowers persisted surprised me. I was supposed to be in sub-arctic America, and high up among the buttresses of the Rockies, and yet there was that everlasting spread of flowers. Some day the white settlers will be in there and growing wheat down all that valley.

"And then I lifted a smoke, and heard the barking of the dogs—Indian dogs—and came into camp. There must have been five hundred of them, proper Indians at that, and I could see by the jerking-frames that the fall hunting had been good. And then I met her—Lucy. That was her name. Sign language—that was all we could talk with, till they led me to a big fly—you know, half a tent, open on the one side where a campfire burned. It was all of moose-skins, this fly—moose-skins, smoke-cured, hand-rubbed, and golden-brown. Under it everything was neat and orderly, as no Indian camp ever was. The bed was laid on fresh spruce boughs. There were furs galore, and on top of all was a robe of swan-skins—white swan-skins—I have never seen anything like that robe. And on top of it, sitting cross-legged, was Lucy. She was nut-brown. I have called her a girl. But she was not. She was a woman, a nut-brown woman, an Amazon, a full-blooded, full-bodied woman, and royal ripe. And her eyes were blue.

"That's what took me off my feet—her eyes—blue, not China blue, but deep blue, like the sea and sky all melted into one, and very wise. More than that, they had laughter in them—warm laughter, sun-warm and human, very human, and . . . shall I say feminine? They were. They were a woman's eyes, a proper woman's eyes. You know what that means. Can I say more? Also, in those blue eyes were, at the same time, a wild unrest, a wistful yearning, and a repose, an absolute repose, a sort of all-wise and philosophical calm."

Trefethan broke off abruptly.

"You fellows think I am screwed. I'm not. This is only my fifth since dinner. I am dead sober. I am solemn. I sit here now side by side with my sacred youth. It is not I—'old' Trefethan—that talks; it is my youth, and it is my youth that says those were the most wonderful eyes I have ever seen—so very calm, so very restless; so very wise, so very curious; so very old, so very young; so satisfied and yet yearning so wistfully. Boys, I can't describe them. When I have told you about her, you may know better for yourselves.

"She did not stand up. But she put out her hand.

" 'Stranger,' she said, 'I'm real glad to see you.'

"I leave it to you—that sharp, frontier, Western tang of speech. Picture my sensations. It was a woman, a white woman, but that tang! It was amazing that it should be a white woman, here, beyond the last boundary of the world—but the tang. I tell you, it hurt. It was like the stab of a flatted note. And yet, let me tell you, that woman was a poet. You shall see.

"She dismissed the Indians. And, by Jove, they went. They took her orders and followed her blind. She was *hi-yu skookum* chief. She told the bucks to make a camp for me and to take care of my dogs. And they did, too. And they knew enough not to get away with as much as a moccasin-lace of my outfit. She was a regular She-Who-Must-Be-Obeyed, and I want to tell you it chilled me to the marrow, sent those little thrills Marathoning up and down my spinal column, meeting a white woman out there at the head of a tribe of savages a thousand miles the other side of No Man's Land.

" 'Stranger,' she said, 'I reckon you're sure the first white that ever set foot in this valley. Set down an' talk a spell, and then we'll have a bite to eat. Which way might you be comin'?'

"There it was, that tang again. But from now to the end of the yarn I want you to forget it. I tell you I forgot it, sitting there on the edge of that swan-skin robe and listening and looking at the most wonderful woman that ever stepped out of the pages of Thoreau or of any other man's book.

"I stayed on there a week. It was on her invitation. She promised to fit me out with dogs and sleds and with Indians that would put me across the best pass of the Rockies in five hundred miles. Her fly was pitched apart from the others, on the high bank by the river, and a couple of Indian girls did her cooking for her and the camp work. And so we talked and talked, while the first snow fell and continued to fall and make a surface for my sleds. And this was her story.

"She was frontier-born, of poor settlers, and you know what that means—work, work, always work, work in plenty and without end.

" 'I never seen the glory of the world,' she said. 'I had no time. I knew it was right out there, anywhere, all around the cabin, but there was always the bread to set, the scrubbin' and the washin' and the work that was never done. I used to be plumb sick at times, jes' to get out into it all, especially in the spring when the songs of the birds drove me most clean crazy. I wanted to run out through the long pasture grass, wetting my legs with the dew of it, and to climb the rail fence, and keep on through the timber and up and up over the divide so as to get a look around. Oh, I had all kinds of hankerings—to follow up the canyon beds and slosh around from pool to pool, making friends with the water-dogs and the speckly trout; to peep on the sly and watch the squirrels and rabbits and small furry things and see what they was doing and learn the secrets of their ways. Seemed to me, if I had time, I could crawl among the flowers, and, if I was good and quiet, catch them whispering with themselves, telling all kinds of wise things that mere humans never know.' "

Trefethan paused to see that his glass had been refilled.

"Another time she said: 'I wanted to run nights like a wild thing, just to run through the moonshine and under the stars, to run white and naked in the darkness that I knew must feel like cool velvet, and to run and run and keep on running. One evening, plumb tuckered out—it had been a dreadful hard hot day, and the bread wouldn't raise and the churning had gone wrong, and I was all irritated and jerky—well, that evening I made mention to dad of this wanting to run of mine. He looked at me curious-some and a bit scared. And then he gave me two pills to take. Said to go to bed and get a good sleep and I'd be all hunky-dory in the morning. So I never mentioned my hankerings to him, or any one any more.'

"The mountain home broke up—starved out, I imagine—and the family came to Seattle to live. There she worked in a factory—long hours, you know, and all the rest, deadly work. And after a year of that she became waitress in a cheap restaurant—hash-slinger, she called it.

"She said to me once, 'Romance I guess was what I wanted. But there wan't no romance floating around in dishpans and washtubs, or in factories and hash-joints.'

"When she was eighteen she married—a man who was going up to Juneau to start a restaurant. He had a few dollars saved, and appeared prosperous. She didn't love him—she was emphatic about that;

but she was all tired out, and she wanted to get away from the unending drudgery. Besides, Juneau was in Alaska, and her yearning took the form of a desire to see that wonderland. But little she saw of it. He started the restaurant, a little cheap one, and she quickly learned what he had married her for . . . to save paying wages. She came pretty close to running the joint and doing all the work from waiting to dishwashing. She cooked most of the time as well. And she had four years of it.

"Can't you picture her, this wild woods creature, quick with every old primitive instinct, yearning for the free open, and mewed up in a vile little hash-joint and toiling and moiling for four mortal years?

" 'There was no meaning in anything,' she said. 'What was it all about? Why was I born? Was that all the meaning of life—just to work and work and be always tired?—to go to bed tired and to wake up tired, with every day like every other day unless it was harder?' She had heard talk of immortal life from the gospel sharps, she said, but she could not reckon that what she was doing was a likely preparation for her immortality.

"But she still had her dreams, though more rarely. She had read a few books—what, it is pretty hard to imagine, Seaside Library novels most likely; yet they had been food for fancy. 'Sometimes,' she said, 'when I was that dizzy from the heat of the cooking that if I didn't take a breath of fresh air I'd faint, I'd stick my head out of the kitchen window and close my eyes and see most wonderful things. All of a sudden I'd be traveling down a country road, and everything clean and quiet, no dust, no dirt; just streams ripplin' down sweet meadows, and lambs playing, breezes blowing the breath of flowers, and soft sunshine over everything; and lovely cows lazying knee-deep in quiet pools, and young girls bathing in a curve of stream all white and slim and natural—and I'd know I was in Arcady. I'd read about that country once, in a book. And maybe knights, all flashing in the sun, would come riding around a bend in the road, or a lady on a milk-white mare, and in the distance I could see the towers of a castle rising, or I just knew, on the next turn, that I'd come upon some palace, all white and airy and fairy-like, with fountains playing, and flowers all over everything, and peacocks on the lawn . . . and then I'd open my eyes, and the heat of the cooking range would strike on me, and I'd hear Jake sayin'—he was my husband—I'd hear Jake sayin', "Why ain't you served them beans? Think I can wait here all day!" Romance!—I reckon the nearest I ever come to it was when a drunken Armenian cook got the snakes and tried to cut my throat with a potato knife and I got my arm burned on the stove before I could lay him out with the potato stomper.

" 'I wanted easy ways, and lovely things, and Romance and all that; but it just seemed I had no luck nohow and was only and expressly born for cooking and dishwashing. There was a wild crowd in Juneau them days, but I looked at the other women, and their way of life didn't excite me. I reckon I wanted to be clean. I don't know why; I just wanted to, I guess; and I reckoned I might as well die dishwashing as die their way.' "

Trefethan halted in his tale for a moment, completing to himself some thread of thought.

"And this is the woman I met up there in the Arctic, running a tribe of wild Indians and a few thousand square miles of hunting territory. And it happened simply enough, though, for that matter, she might have lived and died among the pots and pans. But 'Came the whisper, came the vision.' That was all she needed, and she got it.

" 'I woke up one day,' she said. 'Just happened on it in a scrap of newspaper. I remember every word of it, and I can give it to you.' And then she quoted Thoreau's *Cry of the Human*:

" '*The young pines springing up in the corn field from year to year are to me a refreshing fact. We talk of civilizing the Indian, but that is not the name for his improvement. By the wary independence and aloofness of his dim forest life he preserves his intercourse with his native gods and is admitted from time to time to a rare and peculiar society with nature. He has glances of starry recognition, to which our saloons are strangers. The steady illumination of his genius, dim only because distant, is like the faint but satisfying light of the stars compared with the dazzling but ineffectual and shortlived blaze of candles. The Society Islanders had their day-born gods, but they were not supposed to be of equal antiquity with the . . . night-born gods.*'

"That's what she did, repeated it word for word, and I forgot the tang, for it was solemn, a declaration of religion—pagan, if you will; and clothed in the living garmenture of herself.

" 'And the rest of it was torn away,' she added, a great emptiness in her voice. 'It was only a scrap of newspaper. But that Thoreau was a wise man. I wish I knew more about him.' She stopped a moment, and I swear her face was ineffably holy as she said, 'I could have made him a good wife.'

"And then she went on. 'I knew right away, as soon as I read that, what was the matter with me. I was a night-born. I, who had lived all my life with the day-born, was a night-born. That was why I had never been satisfied with cooking and dishwashing; that was why I had hankered to run naked in the moonlight. And I knew that this dirty little Juneau hash-joint was no place for me. And right there and then I said, "I quit." I packed up my few rags of clothes, and started. Jake saw me and tried to stop me.

" ' "What you doing?" he says.

" ' "Divorcin' you and me," I says. "I'm headin' for tall timber and where I belong."

" ' "No you don't," he says, reaching for me to stop me. "The cookin' has got on your head. You listen to me talk before you up and do anything brash."

" 'But I pulled a gun—a little Colt's forty-four—and says, "This does my talkin' for me."

" 'And I left.' "

Trefethan emptied his glass and called for another.

"Boys, do you know what that girl did? She was twenty-two. She had spent her life over the dish-pan and she knew no more about the world than I do of the fourth dimension, or the fifth. All roads led to her desire. No; she didn't head for the dance-halls. On the Alaskan Pan-handle it is preferable to travel by water. She went down to the beach. An Indian canoe was starting for Dyea—you know the kind, carved out of a single tree, narrow and deep and sixty feet long. She gave them a couple of dollars and got on board.

" 'Romance?' she told me. 'It was Romance from the jump. There were three families altogether in that canoe, and that crowded there wasn't room to turn around, with dogs and Indian babies sprawling over everything, and everybody dipping a paddle and making that canoe go. And all around the great solemn mountains, and tangled drifts of clouds and sunshine. And oh, the silence! the great wonderful silence! And, once, the smoke of a hunter's camp, away off in the distance, trailing among the trees. It was like a picnic, a grand picnic, and I could see my dreams coming true, and I was ready for something to happen 'most any time. And it did.

" 'And that first camp, on the island! And the boys spearing fish in the mouth of the creek, and the big deer one of the bucks shot just around the point. And there were flowers everywhere, and in back from the beach the grass was thick and lush and neck-high. And some of the girls went through this with me, and we climbed the hillside behind and picked berries and roots that tasted sour and were good to eat. And we came upon a big bear in the berries making his supper, and he said "Oof!" and ran away as scared as we were. And then the camp, and the camp smoke, and the smell of fresh venison cooking. It was beautiful. I was with the night-born at last, and I knew that was where I belonged. And for the first time in my life, it seemed to me, I went to bed happy that night, looking out under a corner of the canvas at the stars cut off black by a big shoulder of mountain, and listening to the night-noises, and knowing that the same thing would go on next day and forever and ever, for I wasn't going back. And I never did go back.

" 'Romance! I got it next day. We had to cross a big arm of the ocean—twelve or fifteen miles, at least; and it came on to blow when we were in the middle. That night I was along on shore, with one wolf-dog, and I was the only one left alive.'

"Picture it yourself," Trefethan broke off to say. "The canoe was wrecked and lost, and everybody pounded to death on the rocks except her. She went ashore hanging on to a dog's tail, escaping the rocks and washing up on a tiny beach, the only one in miles.

" 'Lucky for me it was the mainland,' she said. 'So I headed right away back, through the woods and over the mountains and straight on anywhere. Seemed I was looking for something and knew I'd find it. I wasn't afraid. I was night-born, and the big timber couldn't kill me. And on the second day I found it. I came upon a small clearing and a tumbledown cabin. Nobody had been there for years and years. The roof had fallen in. Rotted blankets lay in the bunks, and pots and pans were on the stove. But that was not the most curious thing. Outside, along the edge of the trees, you can't guess what I found. The skeletons of eight horses, each tied to a tree. They had starved to death, I reckon, and left only little piles of bones scattered some here and there. And each horse had had a load on its back. There the loads lay, in among the bones—painted canvas sacks, and inside moosehide sacks, and inside the moosehide sacks—what do you think?'

"She stopped, reached under a corner of the bed among the spruce boughs, and pulled out a leather sack. She untied the mouth and ran out into my hand as pretty a stream of gold as I have ever seen—coarse gold, placer gold, some large dust, but mostly nuggets, and it was so fresh and rough that it scarcely showed signs of water-wash.

" 'You say you're a mining engineer,' she said, 'and you know this country. Can you name a pay-creek that has the color of that gold?'

"I couldn't. There wasn't a trace of silver. It was almost pure, and I told her so.

" 'You bet,' she said. 'I sell that for nineteen dollars an ounce.

You can't get over seventeen for Eldorado gold, and Minook gold don't fetch quite eighteen. Well, that was what I found among the bones—eight horse-loads of it, one hundred and fifty pounds to the load.'

" 'A quarter of a million dollars!' I cried out.

" 'That's what I reckoned it roughly,' she answered. 'Talk about Romance! And me a slaving the way I had all the years, when as soon as I ventured out, inside three days, this was what happened. And what became of the men that mined all that gold? Often and often I wonder about it. They left their horses, loaded and tied, and just disappeared off the face of the earth, leaving neither hide nor hair behind them. I never heard tell of them. Nobody knows anything about them. Well, being the night-born, I reckon I was their rightful heir.' "

Trefethan stopped to light a cigar.

"Do you know what that girl did? She cached the gold, saving out thirty pounds, which she carried back to the coast. Then she signaled a passing canoe, made her way to Pat Healy's trading post at Dyea, outfitted, and went over Chilcoot Pass. That was in '88—eight years before the Klondike strike, and the Yukon was a howling wilderness. She was afraid of the bucks, but she took two young squaws with her, crossed the lakes, and went down the river and to all the early camps on the Lower Yukon. She wandered several years over that country and then on in to where I met her. Liked the looks of it, she said, seeing, in her own words, 'a big bull caribou knee-deep in purple iris on the valley-bottom.' She hooked up with the Indians, doctored them, gained their confidence, and gradually took them in charge. She had only left that country once, and then, with a bunch of the young bucks, she went over Chilcoot, cleaned up her gold-cache, and brought it back with her.

" 'And here I be, stranger,' she concluded her yarn, 'and here's the most precious thing I own.'

"She pulled out a little pouch of buckskin, worn on her neck like a locket, and opened it. And inside, wrapped in oiled silk, yellowed with age and worn and thumbed, was the original scrap of newspaper containing the quotation from Thoreau.

" 'And are you happy? . . . satisfied?' I asked her. 'With a quarter of a million you wouldn't have to work down in the States. You must miss a lot.'

" 'Not much,' she answered. 'I wouldn't swop places with any woman down in the States. These are my people; this is where I belong. But there are times—' and in her eyes smoldered up that hungry yearning I've mentioned—'there are times when I wish most awful bad for that Thoreau man to happen along.'

" 'Why?' I asked.

" 'So as I could marry him. I do get mighty lonesome at spells. I'm just a woman—a real woman. I've heard tell of the other kind of women that gallivanted off like me and did queer things—the sort that become soldiers in armies and sailors on ships. But those women are queer themselves. They're more like men than women; they look like men and they don't have ordinary women's needs. They don't want love, nor little children in their arms and around their knees. I'm not that sort. I leave it to you, stranger. Do I look like a man?'

"She didn't. She was a woman, a beautiful, nut-brown woman, with a sturdy, health-rounded woman's body and with wonderful deep-blue woman's eyes.

" 'Ain't I woman?' she demanded. 'I am. I'm 'most all woman, and then some. And the funny thing is, though I'm night-born in everything else, I'm not when it comes to mating. I reckon that kind likes its own kind best. That's the way it is with me, anyway, and has been all these years.'

" 'You mean to tell me—' I began.

" 'Never,' she said, and her eyes looked into mine with the straightness of truth. 'I had one husband, only—him I call the Ox; and I reckon he's still down in Juneau running the hash-joint. Look him up, if you ever get back, and you'll find he's rightly named.'

"And look him up I did, two years afterward. He was all she said—solid and stolid, the Ox—shuffling around and waiting on the tables.

" 'You need a wife to help you,' I said.

" 'I had one once,' was his answer.

" 'Widower?'

" 'Yep. She went loco. She always said the heat of the cooking would get her, and it did. Pulled a gun on me one day and ran away with some Siwashes in a canoe. Caught a blow up the coast and all hands drowned.' "

Trefethan devoted himself to his glass and remained silent.

"But the girl?" Milner reminded him. "You left your story just as it was getting interesting, tender. Did it?"

"It did," Trefethan replied. "As she said herself, she was savage in everything except mating, and then she wanted her own kind. She was very nice about it, but she was straight to the point. She wanted to marry me.

" 'Stranger,' she said, 'I want you bad. You like this sort of life or you wouldn't be here trying to cross the Rockies in fall weather. It's a likely spot. You'll find few likelier. Why not settle down? I'll make you a good wife.'

"And then it was up to me. And she waited. I don't mind confessing that I was sorely tempted. I was half in love with her as it was. You know I have never married. And I don't mind adding, looking back over my life, that she is the only woman that ever affected me that way. But it was too preposterous, the whole thing, and I lied like a gentleman. I told her I was already married.

" 'Is your wife waiting for you?' she asked.

"I said yes.

" 'And she loves you?'

"I said yes.

"And that was all. She never pressed her point . . . except once, and then she showed a bit of fire.

" 'All I've got to do,' she said, 'is to give the word, and you don't get away from here. If I give the word, you stay on. . . . But I ain't going to give it. I wouldn't want you if you didn't want to be wanted . . . and if you didn't want me.'

"She went ahead and outfitted me and started me on my way.

" 'It's a darned shame, stranger,' she said, at parting. 'I like your looks, and I like you. If you ever change your mind, come back.'

"Now there was one thing I wanted to do, and that was to kiss her good-bye, but I didn't know how to go about it nor how she would take it.—I tell you I was half in love with her. But she settled it herself.

" 'Kiss me,' she said. 'Just something to go on and remember.'

"And we kissed, there in the snow, in that valley by the Rockies, and I left her standing by the trail and went on after my dogs. I was six weeks in crossing over the pass and coming down to the first post on Great Slave Lake."

The brawl of the streets came up to us like a distant surf. A steward, moving noiselessly, brought fresh siphons. And in the silence Trefethan's voice fell like a funeral bell:

"It would have been better had I stayed. Look at me."

We saw his grizzled mustache, the bald spot on his head, the puff-sacks under his eyes, the sagging cheeks, the heavy dewlap, the general tiredness and staleness and fatness, all the collapse and ruin of a man who had once been strong but who had lived too easily and too well.

"It's not too late, old man," Bardwell said, almost in a whisper.

"By God! I wish I weren't a coward!" was Trefethan's answering cry. "I could go back to her. She's there, now. I could shape up and live many a long year . . . with her . . . up there. To remain here is to commit suicide. But I am an old man—forty-seven—look at me. The trouble is," he lifted his glass and glanced at it, "the trouble is that suicide of this sort is so easy. I am soft and tender. The thought of the long day's travel with the dogs appals me; the thought of the keen frost in the morning and of the frozen sled-lashings frightens me—"

Automatically the glass was creeping toward his lips. With a swift surge of anger he made as if to crash it down upon the floor. Next came hesitancy and second thought. The glass moved upward to his lips and paused. He laughed harshly and bitterly, but his words were solemn: "Well, here's to the Night-Born. She *was* a wonder."

# WAR

## I

HE WAS A young man, not more than twenty-four or five, and he might have sat his horse with the careless grace of his youth had he not been so catlike and tense. His black eyes roved everywhere, catching the movements of twigs and branches where small birds hopped, questing ever onward through the changing vistas of trees and brush, and returning always to the clumps of undergrowth on either side. And as he watched, so did he listen, though he rode on in silence, save for the boom of heavy guns from far to the west. This had been sounding monotonously in his ears for hours, and only its cessation would have aroused his notice. For he had business closer to hand. Across his saddle-bow was balanced a carbine.

So tensely was he strung, that a bunch of quail, exploding into flight from under his horse's nose, startled him to such an extent that automatically, instantly, he had reined in and fetched the carbine half-way to his shoulder. He grinned sheepishly, recovered himself, and rode on. So tense was he, so bent upon the work he had to do, that the sweat stung his eyes unwiped, and unheeded rolled down his nose and spattered his saddle pommel. The band of his cavalryman's hat was fresh-stained with sweat. The roan horse under him was likewise wet. It was high noon of a breathless day of heat. Even the birds and squirrels did not dare the sun, but sheltered in shady hiding places among the trees.

Man and horse were littered with leaves and dusted with yellow pollen, for the open was ventured no more than was compulsory. They kept to the brush and trees, and invariably the man halted and peered out before crossing a dry glade or naked stretch of upland pasturage. He worked always to the north, though his way was devious, and it was from the north that he seemed most to apprehend that for which he was looking. He was no coward, but his courage was only that of the average civilized man, and he was looking to live, not die.

Up a small hillside he followed a cowpath through such dense scrub that he was forced to dismount and lead his horse. But when the path swung around to the west, he abandoned it and headed to the north again along the oak-covered top of the ridge.

The ridge ended in a steep descent—so steep that he zigzagged back and forth across the face of the slope, sliding and stumbling among the dead leaves and matted vines and keeping a watchful eye on the horse above that threatened to fall down upon him. The sweat ran from him, and the pollen-dust, settling pungently in mouth and nostrils, increased his thirst. Try as he would, nevertheless the descent was noisy, and frequently he stopped, panting in the dry heat and listening for any warning from beneath.

At the bottom he came out on a flat, so densely forested that he could not make out its extent. Here the character of the woods changed, and he was able to remount. Instead of the twisted hillside oaks, tall straight trees, big-trunked and prosperous, rose from the damp fat soil. Only here and there were thickets, easily avoided, while he encountered winding, park-like glades where the cattle had pastured in the days before war had run them off.

His progress was more rapid now, as he came down into the valley, and at the end of half an hour he halted at an ancient rail fence on the edge of a clearing. He did not like the openness of it, yet his path lay across to the fringe of trees that marked the banks of the stream. It was a mere quarter of a mile across that open, but the thought of venturing out in it was repugnant. A rifle, a score of them, a thousand, might lurk in that fringe by the stream.

Twice he essayed to start, and twice he paused. He was appalled by his own loneliness. The pulse of war that beat from the West suggested the companionship of battling thousands; here was naught but silence, and himself, and possible death-dealing bullets from a myriad ambushes. And yet his task was to find what he feared to find. He must go on, and on, till somewhere, some time, he encountered another man, or other men, from the other side, scouting, as he was scouting, to make report, as he must make report, of having come in touch.

Changing his mind, he skirted inside the woods for a distance, and again peeped forth. This time, in the middle of the clearing, he saw a small farmhouse. There were no signs of life. No smoke curled from the chimney, not a barnyard fowl clucked and strutted. The kitchen door stood open, and he gazed so long and hard into the black aperture that it seemed almost that a farmer's wife must emerge at any moment.

He licked the pollen and dust from his dry lips, stiffened himself, mind and body, and rode out into the blazing sunshine. Nothing stirred. He went on past the house, and approached the wall of trees and bushes by the river's bank. One thought persisted maddeningly. It was of the crash into his body of a high-velocity bullet. It made him feel very fragile and defenseless, and he crouched lower in the saddle.

Tethering his horse in the edge of the wood, he continued a hundred yards on foot till he came to the stream. Twenty feet wide it was, without perceptible current, cool and inviting, and he was very thirsty. But he waited inside his screen of leafage, his eyes fixed on the screen on the opposite side. To make the wait endurable, he sat down, his carbine resting on his knees. The minutes passed, and slowly his tenseness relaxed. At last he decided there was no danger; but just as he prepared to part the bushes and bend down to the water, a movement among the opposite bushes caught his eye.

It might be a bird. But he waited. Again there was an agitation of the bushes, and then, so suddenly that it almost startled a cry from him, the bushes parted and a face peered out. It was a face covered with several weeks' growth of ginger-colored beard. The eyes were blue and wide apart, with laughter-wrinkles in the corners that showed despite the tired and anxious expression of the whole face.

All this he could see with microscopic clearness, for the distance was no more than twenty feet. And all this he saw in such brief time, that he saw it as he lifted his carbine to his shoulder. He glanced along the sights, and knew that he was gazing upon a man who was as good as dead. It was impossible to miss at such point blank range.

But he did not shoot. Slowly he lowered the carbine and watched. A hand, clutching a water-bottle, became visible and the ginger beard bent downward to fill the bottle. He could hear the gurgle of the water. Then arm and bottle and ginger beard disappeared behind the closing bushes. A long time he waited, when, with thirst unslaked, he crept back to his horse, rode slowly across the sun-washed clearing, and passed into the shelter of the woods beyond.

## II

Another day, hot and breathless. A deserted farmhouse, large, with many outbuildings and an orchard, standing in a clearing. From the woods, on a roan horse, carbine across pommel, rode the young man with the quick black eyes. He breathed with relief as he gained the house. That a fight had taken place here earlier in the season was evident. Clips and empty cartridges, tarnished with verdigris, lay on the ground, which, while wet, had been torn up by the hoofs of horses. Hard by the kitchen garden were graves, tagged and numbered. From the oak tree by the kitchen door, in tattered, weatherbeaten garments, hung the bodies of two men. The faces, shriveled and defaced, bore no likeness to the faces of men. The roan horse snorted beneath them, and the rider caressed and soothed it and tied it farther away.

Entering the house, he found the interior a wreck. He trod on empty cartridges as he walked from room to room to reconnoiter from the windows. Men had camped and slept everywhere, and on the floor of one room he came upon stains unmistakable where the wounded had been laid down.

Again outside, he led the horse around behind the barn and invaded the orchard. A dozen trees were burdened with ripe apples. He filled his pockets, eating while he picked. Then a thought came to him, and he glanced at the sun, calculating the time of his return to camp. He pulled off his shirt, tying the sleeves and making a bag. This he proceeded to fill with apples.

As he was about to mount his horse, the animal suddenly pricked up its ears. The man, too, listened, and heard, faintly, the thud of hoofs on soft earth. He crept to the corner of the barn and peered out. A dozen mounted men, strung out loosely, approaching from the opposite side of the clearing, were only a matter of a hundred yards or so away. They rode on to the house. Some dismounted, while others remained in the saddle as an earnest that their stay would be short. They seemed to be holding a council, for he could hear them talking excitedly in the detested tongue of the alien invader. The time passed, but they seemed unable to reach a decision. He put the carbine away in its boot, mounted, and waited impatiently, balancing the shirt of apples on the pommel.

He heard footsteps approaching, and drove his spurs so fiercely into the roan as to force a surprised groan from the animal as it leaped forward. At the corner of the barn he saw the intruder, a mere boy of nineteen or twenty for all of his uniform, jump back to escape being run down. At the same moment the roan swerved, and its rider caught a glimpse of the aroused men by the house. Some were springing from their horses, and he could see the rifles going to their shoulders. He passed the kitchen door and the dried corpses swinging in the shade, compelling his foes to run around the front of the house. A rifle cracked, and a second, but he was going fast, leaning forward, low in the saddle, one hand clutching the shirt of apples, the other guiding the horse.

The top bar of the fence was four feet high, but he knew his roan and leaped it at full career to the accompaniment of several scattered shots. Eight hundred yards straight away were the woods, and the roan was covering the distance with mighty strides. Every man was now firing. They were pumping their guns so rapidly that he no longer heard individual shots. A bullet went through his hat, but he was unaware, though he did know when another tore through the apples on the pommel. And he winced and ducked even lower when a third bullet, fired low, struck a stone between his horse's legs and ricochetted off through the air, buzzing and humming like some incredible insect.

The shots died down as the magazines were emptied, until, quickly, there was no more shooting. The young man was elated. Through that astonishing fusillade he had come unscathed. He glanced back. Yes, they had emptied their magazines. He could see several reloading. Others were running back behind the house for their horses. As he looked, two already mounted, came back into view around the corner, riding hard. And at the same moment, he saw the man with the unmistakable ginger beard kneel down on the ground, level his gun, and coolly take his time for the long shot.

The young man threw his spurs into the horse, crouched very low, and swerved in his flight in order to distract the other's aim. And still the shot did not come. With each jump of the horse, the woods sprang nearer. They were only two hundred yards away, and still the shot was delayed.

And then he heard it, the last thing he was to hear, for he was dead ere he hit the ground in the long crashing fall from the saddle.

And they, watching at the house, saw him fall, saw his body bounce when it struck the earth, and saw the burst of red-cheeked apples that rolled about him. They laughed at the unexpected eruption of apples, and clapped their hands in applause of the long shot by the man with the ginger beard.

# TOLD IN THE
# DROOLING WARD

ME? I'M NOT A DROOLER. I'm the assistant. I don't know what Miss Jones or Miss Kelsey could do without me. There are fifty-five low-grade droolers in this ward, and how could they ever all be fed if I wasn't around? I like to feed droolers. They don't make trouble. They can't. Something's wrong with most of their legs and arms, and they can't talk. They're very low-grade. I can walk, and talk, and do things. You must be careful with the droolers and not feed them too fast. Then they choke. Miss Jones says I'm an expert. When a new nurse comes I show her how to do it. It's funny watching a new nurse try to feed them. She goes at it so slow and careful that supper time would be around before she finished shoving down their breakfast. Then I show her, because I'm an expert. Dr. Dalrymple says I am, and he ought to know. A drooler can eat twice as fast if you know how to make him.

My name's Tom. I'm twenty-eight years old. Everybody knows me in the institution. This is an institution, you know. It belongs to the State of California and is run by politics. I know. I've been here a long time. Everybody trusts me. I run errands all over the place, when I'm not busy with the droolers. I like droolers. It makes me think how lucky I am that I ain't a drooler.

I like it here in the Home. I don't like the outside. I know. I've been around a bit, and run away, and adopted. Me for the Home, and for the drooling ward best of all. I don't look like a drooler, do I? You can tell the difference soon as you look at me. I'm an assistant, expert

282

assistant. That's going some for a feeb. Feeb? Oh, that's feeble-minded. I thought you knew. We're all feebs in here.

But I'm a high-grade feeb. Dr. Dalrymple says I'm too smart to be in the Home, but I never let on. It's a pretty good place. And I don't throw fits like lots of the feebs. You see that house up there through the trees. The high-grade epilecs all live in it by themselves. They're stuck up because they ain't just ordinary feebs. They call it the club house, and they say they're just as good as anybody outside, only they're sick. I don't like them much. They laugh at me, when they ain't busy throwing fits. But I don't care. I never have to be scared about falling down and busting my head. Sometimes they run around in circles trying to find a place to sit down quick, only they don't. Low-grade epilecs are disgusting, and high-grade epilecs put on airs. I'm glad I ain't an epilec. There ain't anything to them. They just talk big, that's all.

Miss Kelsey says I talk too much. But I talk sense, and that's more than the other feebs do. Dr. Dalrymple says I have the gift of language. I know it. You ought to hear me talk when I'm by myself, or when I've got a drooler to listen. Sometimes I think I'd like to be a politician, only it's too much trouble. They're all great talkers; that's how they hold their jobs.

Nobody's crazy in this institution. They're just feeble in their minds. Let me tell you something funny. There's about a dozen high-grade girls that set the tables in the big dining room. Sometimes when they're done ahead of time, they all sit down in chairs in a circle and talk. I sneak up to the door and listen, and I nearly die to keep from laughing. Do you want to know what they talk? It's like this. They don't say a word for a long time. And then one says, "Thank God I'm not feeble-minded." And all the rest nod their heads and look pleased. And then nobody says anything for a time. After which the next girl in the circle says, "Thank God I'm not feeble-minded," and they nod their heads all over again. And it goes on around the circle, and they never say anything else. Now they're real feebs, ain't they? I leave it to you. I'm not that kind of a feeb, thank God.

Sometimes I don't think I'm a feeb at all. I play in the band and read music. We're all supposed to be feebs in the band except the leader. He's crazy. We know it, but we never talk about it except amongst ourselves. His job is politics, too, and we don't want him to lose it. I play the drum. They can't get along without me in this institution. I was sick once, so I know. It's a wonder the drooling ward didn't break down while I was in hospital.

I could get out of here if I wanted to. I'm not so feeble as some might think. But I don't let on. I have too good a time. Besides, everything would run down if I went away. I'm afraid some time they'll find out I'm not a feeb and send me out into the world to earn my own living. I know the world, and I don't like it. The Home is fine enough for me.

You see how I grin sometimes. I can't help that. But I can put it on a lot. I'm not bad, though. I look at myself in the glass. My mouth is funny, I know that, and it lops down, and my teeth are bad. You can tell a feeb anywhere by looking at his mouth and teeth. But that doesn't prove I'm a feeb. It's just because I'm lucky that I look like one.

I know a lot. If I told you all I know, you'd be surprised. But when I don't want to know, or when they want me to do something I don't want to do, I just let my mouth lop down and laugh and make foolish noises. I watch the foolish noises made by the low-grades, and I can fool anybody. And I know a lot of foolish noises. Miss Kelsey called me a fool the other day. She was very angry, and that was where I fooled her.

Miss Kelsey asked me once why I don't write a book about feebs. I was telling her what was the matter with little Albert. He's a drooler, you know, and I can always tell the way he twists his left eye what's the matter with him. So I was explaining it to Miss Kelsey, and, because she didn't know, it made her mad. But some day, mebbe, I'll write that book. Only it's so much trouble. Besides, I'd sooner talk.

Do you know what a micro is? It's the kind with the little heads no bigger than your fist. They're usually droolers, and they live a long time. The hydros don't drool. They have the big heads, and they're smarter. But they never grow up. They always die. I never look at one without thinking he's going to die. Sometimes, when I'm feeling lazy, or the nurse is mad at me, I wish I was a drooler with nothing to do and somebody to feed me. But I guess I'd sooner talk and be what I am.

Only yesterday Doctor Dalrymple said to me, "Tom," he said, "I just don't know what I'd do without you." And he ought to know, seeing as he's had the bossing of a thousand feebs for going on two years. Dr. Whatcomb was before him. They get appointed, you know. It's politics. I've seen a whole lot of doctors here in my time. I was here before any of them. I've been in this institution twenty-five years. No, I've got no complaints. The institution couldn't be run better.

It's a snap to be a high-grade feeb. Just look at Doctor Dalrymple.

He has troubles. He holds his job by politics. You bet we high-graders talk politics. We know all about it, and it's bad. An institution like this oughtn't to be run on politics. Look at Doctor Dalrymple. He's been here two years and learned a lot. Then politics will come along and throw him out and send a new doctor who don't know anything about feebs.

I've been acquainted with just thousands of nurses in my time. Some of them are nice. But they come and go. Most of the women get married. Sometimes I think I'd like to get married. I spoke to Dr. Whatcomb about it once, but he told me he was very sorry, because feebs ain't allowed to get married. I've been in love. She was a nurse. I won't tell you her name. She had blue eyes, and yellow hair, and a kind voice, and she liked me. She told me so. And she always told me to be a good boy. And I was, too, until afterward, and then I ran away. You see, she went off and got married, and she didn't tell me about it.

I guess being married ain't what it's cracked up to be. Dr. Anglin and his wife used to fight. I've seen them. And once I heard her call him a feeb. Now nobody has a right to call anybody a feeb that ain't. Dr. Anglin got awful mad when she called him that. But he didn't last long. Politics drove him out, and Doctor Mandeville came. He didn't have a wife. I heard him talking one time with the engineer. The engineer and his wife fought like cats and dogs, and that day Doctor Mandeville told him he was damn glad he wasn't tied to no petticoats. A petticoat is a skirt. I knew what he meant, if I was a feeb. But I never let on. You hear lots when you don't let on.

I've seen a lot in my time. Once I was adopted, and went away on the railroad over forty miles to live with a man named Peter Bopp and his wife. They had a ranch. Doctor Anglin said I was strong and bright, and I said I was, too. That was because I wanted to be adopted. And Peter Bopp said he'd give me a good home, and the lawyers fixed up the papers.

But I soon made up my mind that a ranch was no place for me. Mrs. Bopp was scared to death of me and wouldn't let me sleep in the house. They fixed up the woodshed and made me sleep there. I had to get up at four o'clock and feed the horses, and milk cows, and carry the milk to the neighbours. They called it chores, but it kept me going all day. I chopped wood, and cleaned chicken houses, and weeded vegetables, and did most everything on the place. I never had any fun. I hadn't no time.

Let me tell you one thing. I'd sooner feed mush and milk to feebs than milk cows with the frost on the ground. Mrs. Bopp was scared to let me play with her children. And I was scared, too. They used to make faces at me when nobody was looking, and call me "Looney." Everybody called me Looney Tom. And the other boys in the neighbourhood threw rocks at me. You never see anything like that in the Home here. The feebs are better behaved.

Mrs. Bopp used to pinch me and pull my hair when she thought I was too slow, and I only made foolish noises and went slower. She said I'd be the death of her some day. I left the boards off the old well in the pasture, and the pretty new calf fell in and got drowned. Then Peter Bopp said he was going to give me a licking. He did, too. He took a strap halter and went at me. It was awful. I'd never had a licking in my life. They don't do such things in the Home, which is why I say the Home is the place for me.

I know the law, and I knew he had no right to lick me with a strap halter. That was being cruel, and the guardianship papers said he mustn't be cruel. I didn't say anything. I just waited, which shows you what kind of a feeb I am. I waited a long time, and got slower, and made more foolish noises; but he wouldn't send me back to the Home, which was what I wanted. But one day, it was the first of the month, Mrs. Brown gave me three dollars, which was for her milk bill with Peter Bopp. That was in the morning. When I brought the milk in the evening I was to bring back the receipt. But I didn't. I just walked down to the station, bought a ticket like any one, and rode on the train back to the Home. That's the kind of a feeb I am.

Doctor Anglin was gone then, and Doctor Mandeville had his place. I walked right into his office. He didn't know me. "Hello," he said, "this ain't visiting day." "I ain't a visitor," I said. "I'm Tom. I belong here." Then he whistled and showed he was surprised. I told him all about it, and showed him the marks of the strap halter, and he got madder and madder all the time and said he'd attend to Mr. Peter Bopp's case.

And mebbe you think some of them little droolers weren't glad to see me.

I walked right into the ward. There was a new nurse feeding little Albert. "Hold on," I said. "That ain't the way. Don't you see how he's twisting that left eye? Let me show you." Mebbe she thought I was a new doctor, for she just gave me the spoon, and I guess I filled little Albert up with the most comfortable meal he'd had since I went away. Droolers ain't bad when you understand them. I heard Miss

Jones tell Miss Kelsey once that I had an amazing gift in handling droolers.

Some day, mebbe, I'm going to talk with Doctor Dalrymple and get him to give me a declaration that I ain't a feeb. Then I'll get him to make me a real assistant in the drooling ward, with forty dollars a month and my board. And then I'll marry Miss Jones and live right on here. And if she won't have me, I'll marry Miss Kelsey or some other nurse. There's lots of them that want to get married. And I won't care if my wife gets mad and calls me a feeb. What's the good? And I guess when one's learned to put up with droolers a wife won't be much worse.

I didn't tell you about when I ran away. I hadn't no idea of such a thing, and it was Charley and Joe who put me up to it. They're high-grade epilecs, you know. I'd been up to Doctor Wilson's office with a message, and was going back to the drooling ward, when I saw Charley and Joe hiding around the corner of the gymnasium and making motions to me. I went over to them.

"Hello," Joe said. "How's droolers?"

"Fine," I said. "Had any fits lately?"

That made them mad, and I was going on, when Joe said, "We're running away. Come on."

"What for?" I said.

"We're going up over the top of the mountain," Joe said.

"And find a gold mine," said Charley. "We don't have fits any more. We're cured."

"All right," I said. And we sneaked around back of the gymnasium and in among the trees. Mebbe we walked along about ten minutes, when I stopped.

"What's the matter?" said Joe.

"Wait," I said. "I got to go back."

"What for?" said Joe.

And I said, "To get little Albert."

And they said I couldn't, and got mad. But I didn't care. I knew they'd wait. You see, I've been here twenty-five years, and I know the back trails that lead up the mountain, and Charley and Joe didn't know those trails. That's why they wanted me to come.

So I went back and got little Albert. He can't walk, or talk, or do anything except drool, and I had to carry him in my arms. We went on past the last hayfield, which was as far as I'd ever gone. Then the woods and brush got so thick, and me not finding any more trail, we followed the cow-path down to a big creek and crawled through the fence which showed where the Home land stopped.

We climbed up the big hill on the other side of the creek. It was all big trees, and no brush, but it was so steep and slippery with dead leaves we could hardly walk. By and by we came to a real bad place. It was forty feet across, and if you slipped you'd fall a thousand feet, or mebbe a hundred. Anyway, you wouldn't fall—just slide. I went across first, carrying little Albert. Joe came next. But Charley got scared right in the middle and sat down.

"I'm going to have a fit," he said.

"No, you're not," said Joe. "Because if you was you wouldn't 'a' sat down. You take all your fits standing."

"This is a different kind of a fit," said Charley, beginning to cry.

He shook and shook, but just because he wanted to he couldn't scare up the least kind of a fit.

Joe got mad and used awful language. But that didn't help none. So I talked soft and kind to Charley. That's the way to handle feebs. If you get mad, they get worse. I know. I'm that way myself. That's why I was almost the death of Mrs. Bopp. She got mad.

It was getting along in the afternoon, and I knew we had to be on our way, so I said to Joe:

"Here, stop your cussing and hold Albert. I'll go back and get him."

And I did, too; but he was so scared and dizzy he crawled along on hands and knees while I helped him. When I got him across and took Albert back in my arms, I heard somebody laugh and looked down. And there was a man and woman on horseback looking up at us. He had a gun on his saddle, and it was her who was laughing.

"Who in hell's that?" said Joe, getting scared. "Somebody to catch us?"

"Shut up your cussing," I said to him. "That is the man who owns this ranch and writes books."

"How do you do, Mr. Endicott," I said down to him.

"Hello," he said. "What are you doing here?"

"We're running away," I said.

And he said, "Good luck. But be sure and get back before dark."

"But this is a real running away," I said.

And then both he and his wife laughed.

"All right," he said. "Good luck just the same. But watch out the bears and mountain lions don't get you when it gets dark."

Then they rode away laughing, pleasant like; but I wished he hadn't said that about the bears and mountain lions.

After we got around the hill, I found a trail, and we went much faster. Charley didn't have any more signs of fits, and began laughing and talking about gold mines. The trouble was with little Albert. He was almost as big as me. You see, all the time I'd been calling him little Albert, he'd been growing up. He was so heavy I couldn't keep up with Joe and Charley. I was all out of breath. So I told them they'd have to take turns in carrying him, which they said they wouldn't. Then I said I'd leave them and they'd get lost, and the mountain lions and bears would eat them. Charley looked like he was going to have a fit right there, and Joe said, "Give him to me." And after that we carried him in turn.

We kept right on up that mountain. I don't think there was any gold mine, but we might 'a' got to the top and found it, if we hadn't lost the trail, and if it hadn't got dark, and if little Albert hadn't tired us all out carrying him. Lots of feebs are scared of the dark, and Joe said he was going to have a fit right there. Only he didn't. I never saw such an unlucky boy. He never could throw a fit when he wanted to. Some of the feebs can throw fits as quick as a wink.

By and by it got real black, and we were hungry, and we didn't have no fire. You see, they don't let feebs carry matches, and all we could do was just shiver. And we'd never thought about being hungry. You see, feebs always have their food ready for them, and that's why it's better to be a feeb than earning your living in the world.

And worse than everything was the quiet. There was only one thing worse, and it was the noises. There was all kinds of noises every once in a while, with quiet spells in between. I reckon they were rabbits, but they made noises in the brush like wild animals—you know, rustle rustle, thump, bump, crackle crackle, just like that. First Charley got a fit, a real one, and Joe threw a terrible one. I don't mind fits in the Home with everybody around. But out in the woods on a dark night is different. You listen to me, and never go hunting gold mines with epilecs, even if they are high-grade.

I never had such an awful night. When Joe and Charley weren't throwing fits they were making believe, and in the darkness the shivers from the cold which I couldn't see seemed like fits, too. And I shivered so hard I thought I was getting fits myself. And little Albert, with nothing to eat, just drooled and drooled. I never seen him as bad as that before. Why, he twisted that left eye of his until it ought to have dropped out. I couldn't see it, but I could tell from the movements he made. And Joe just lay and cussed and cussed, and Charley cried and wished he was back in the Home.

We didn't die, and next morning we went right back the way we'd come. And little Albert got awful heavy. Doctor Wilson was mad as could be, and said I was the worst feeb in the institution, along with Joe and Charley. But Miss Striker, who was a nurse in the drooling ward then, just put her arms around me and cried, she was that happy I'd got back. I thought right there that mebbe I'd marry her. But only a month afterward she got married to the plumber that came up from the city to fix the gutter-pipes of the new hospital. And little Albert never twisted his eye for two days, it was that tired.

Next time I run away I'm going right over that mountain. But I ain't going to take epilecs along. They ain't never cured, and when they get scared or excited they throw fits to beat the band. But I'll take little Albert. Somehow I can't get along without him. And anyway, I ain't going to run away. The drooling ward's a better snap than gold mines, and I hear there's a new nurse coming. Besides, little Albert's bigger than I am now, and I could never carry him over a mountain. And he's growing bigger every day. It's astonishing.

# THE MEXICAN

## I

NOBODY KNEW his history—they of the Junta least of all. He was their "little mystery," their "big patriot," and in his way he worked as hard for the coming Mexican Revolution as did they. They were tardy in recognizing this, for not one of the Junta liked him. The day he first drifted into their crowded, busy rooms, they all suspected him of being a spy—one of the bought tools of the Diaz secret service. Too many of the comrades were in civil and military prisons scattered over the United States, and others of them, in irons, were even then being taken across the border to be lined up against adobe walls and shot.

At the first sight the boy did not impress them favorably. Boy he was, not more than eighteen and not over large for his years. He announced that he was Felipe Rivera, and that it was his wish to work for the Revolution. That was all—not a wasted word, no further explanation. He stood waiting. There was no smile on his lips, no geniality in his eyes. Big dashing Paulino Vera felt an inward shudder. Here was something forbidding, terrible, inscrutable. There was something venomous and snakelike in the boy's black eyes. They burned like cold fire, as with a vast, concentrated bitterness. He flashed them from the faces of the conspirators to the typewriter which little Mrs. Sethby was industriously operating. His eyes rested on hers but an instant—she had chanced to look up—and she, too, sensed the name-

291

less something that made her pause. She was compelled to read back in order to regain the swing of the letter she was writing.

Paulino Vera looked questioningly at Arrellano and Ramos, and questioningly they looked back and to each other. The indecision of doubt brooded in their eyes. This slender boy was the Unknown, vested with all the menace of the Unknown. He was unrecognizable, something quite beyond the ken of honest, ordinary revolutionists whose fiercest hatred for Diaz and his tyranny after all was only that of honest and ordinary patriots. Here was something else, they knew not what. But Vera, always the most impulsive, the quickest to act, stepped into the breach.

"Very well," he said coldly. "You say you want to work for the Revolution. Take off your coat. Hang it over there. I will show you —come—where are the buckets and cloths. The floor is dirty. You will begin by scrubbing it, and by scrubbing the floors of the other rooms. The spittoons need to be cleaned. Then there are the windows."

"Is it for the Revolution?" the boy asked.

"It is for the Revolution," Vera answered.

Rivera looked cold suspicion at all of them, then proceeded to take off his coat.

"It is well," he said.

And nothing more. Day after day he came to his work—sweeping, scrubbing, cleaning. He emptied the ashes from the stoves, brought up the coal and kindling, and lighted the fires before the most energetic one of them was at his desk.

"Can I sleep here?" he asked once.

Ah, ha! So that was it—the hand of Diaz showing through! To sleep in the rooms of the Junta meant access to their secrets, to the lists of names, to the addresses of comrades down on Mexican soil. The request was denied, and Rivera never spoke of it again. He slept they knew not where, and ate they knew not where nor how. Once, Arrellano offered him a couple of dollars. Rivera declined the money with a shake of the head. When Vera joined in and tried to press it upon him, he said:

"I am working for the Revolution."

It takes money to raise a modern revolution, and always the Junta was pressed. The members starved and toiled, and the longest day was none too long, and yet there were times when it appeared as if the Revolution stood or fell on no more than the matter of a few dollars. Once, the first time, when the rent of the house was two months behind and the landlord was threatening dispossession, it was Felipe Rivera, the scrub-boy in the poor, cheap clothes, worn and threadbare, who laid sixty dollars in gold on May Sethby's desk. There were other times. Three hundred letters, clicked out on the busy typewriters (appeals for assistance, for sanctions from the organized labor groups, requests for square news deals to the editors of newspapers, protests against the high-handed treatment of revolutionists by the United States courts), lay unmailed, awaiting postage. Vera's watch had disappeared—the old-fashioned gold repeater that had been his father's. Likewise had gone the plain gold band from May Sethby's third finger. Things were desperate. Ramos and Arrellano pulled their long mustaches in despair. The letters must go off, and the Post Office allowed no credit to purchasers of stamps. Then it was that Rivera put on his hat and went out. When he came back he laid a thousand two-cent stamps on May Sethby's desk.

"I wonder if it is the cursed gold of Diaz?" said Vera to the comrades.

They elevated their brows and could not decide. And Felipe Rivera, the scrubber for the Revolution, continued, as occasion arose, to lay down gold and silver for the Junta's use.

And still they could not bring themselves to like him. They did not know him. His ways were not theirs. He gave no confidences. He repelled all probing. Youth that he was, they could never nerve themselves to dare to question him.

"A great and lonely spirit, perhaps, I do not know, I do not know," Arrellano said helplessly.

"He is not human," said Ramos.

"His soul has been seared," said May Sethby. "Light and laughter have been burned out of him. He is like one dead, and yet he is fearfully alive."

"He has been through hell," said Vera. "No man could look like that who has not been through hell—and he is only a boy."

Yet they could not like him. He never talked, never inquired, never suggested. He would stand listening, expressionless, a thing dead, save for his eyes, coldly burning, while their talk of the Revolution ran high and warm. From face to face and speaker to speaker his eyes would turn, boring like gimlets of incandescent ice, disconcerting and perturbing.

"He is no spy," Vera confided to May Sethby. "He is a patriot—mark me, the greatest patriot of us all. I know it, I feel it, here in my heart and head I feel it. But him I know not at all."

"He has a bad temper," said May Sethby.

"I know," said Vera, with a shudder. "He has looked at me with those eyes of his. They do not love; they threaten; they are savage as a wild tiger's. I know, if I should prove unfaithful to the Cause, that he would kill me. He has no heart. He is pitiless as steel, keen and cold as frost. He is like moonshine in a winter night when a man freezes to death on some lonely mountain top. I am not afraid of Diaz and all his killers; but this boy, of him am I afraid. I tell you true. I am afraid. He is the breath of death."

Yet Vera it was who persuaded the others to give the first trust to Rivera. The line of communication between Los Angeles and Lower California had broken down. Three of the comrades had dug their own graves and been shot into them. Two more were United States prisoners in Los Angeles. Juan Alvarado, the Federal commander, was a monster. All their plans did he checkmate. They could no longer gain access to the active revolutionists, and the incipient ones, in Lower California.

Young Rivera was given his instructions and dispatched south. When he returned, the line of communication was reëstablished, and Juan Alvarado was dead. He had been found in bed, a knife hilt-deep in his breast. This had exceeded Rivera's instructions, but they of the Junta knew the times of his movements. They did not ask him. He said nothing. But they looked at one another and conjectured.

"I have told you," said Vera. "Diaz has more to fear from this youth than from any man. He is implacable. He is the hand of God."

The bad temper, mentioned by May Sethby, and sensed by them all, was evidenced by physical proofs. Now he appeared with a cut lip, a blackened cheek, or a swollen ear. It was patent that he brawled, somewhere in that outside world where he ate and slept, gained money, and moved in ways unknown to them. As the time passed, he had come to set type for the little revolutionary sheet they published weekly. There were occasions when he was unable to set type, when his knuckles were bruised and battered, when his thumbs were injured and helpless, when one arm or the other hung wearily at his side while his face was drawn with unspoken pain.

"A wastrel," said Arrellano.

"A frequenter of low places," said Ramos.

"But where does he get the money?" Vera demanded. "Only to-day, just now, have I learned that he paid the bill for white paper— one hundred and forty dollars."

"There are his absences," said May Sethby. "He never explains them."

"We should set a spy upon him," Ramos propounded.

"I should not care to be that spy," said Vera. "I fear you would never see me again, save to bury me. He has a terrible passion. Not even God would he permit to stand between him and the way of his passion."

"I feel like a child before him," Ramos confessed.

"To me he is power—he is the primitive, the wild wolf,—the striking rattlesnake, the stinging centipede," said Arrellano.

"He is the Revolution incarnate," said Vera. "He is the flame and the spirit of it, the insatiable cry for vengeance that makes no cry but that slays noiselessly. He is a destroying angel moving through the still watches of the night."

"I could weep over him," said May Sethby. "He knows nobody. He hates all people. Us he tolerates, for we are the way of his desire. He is alone . . . lonely." Her voice broke in a half sob and there was dimness in her eyes.

Rivera's ways and times were truly mysterious. There were periods when they did not see him for a week at a time. Once, he was away a month. These occasions were always capped by his return, when, without advertisement or speech, he laid gold coins on May Sethby's desk. Again, for days and weeks, he spent all his time with the Junta. And yet again, for irregular periods, he would disappear through the heart of each day, from early morning until late afternoon. At such times he came early and remained late. Arrellano had found him at midnight, setting type with fresh swollen knuckles, or mayhap it was his lip, new-split, that still bled.

## II

The time of the crisis approached. Whether or not the Revolution would be depended upon the Junta, and the Junta was hard-pressed. The need for money was greater than ever before, while money was harder to get. Patriots had given their last cent and now could give no more. Section gang laborers—fugitive peons from Mexico—were contributing half their scanty wages. But more than that was needed. The heart-breaking, conspiring, undermining toil of years approached fruition. The time was ripe. The Revolution hung on the balance. One shove more, one last heroic effort, and it would tremble across the scales to victory. They knew their Mexico. Once started, the Revolution would take care of itself. The whole Diaz machine would go down like a house of cards. The border was ready to rise. One Yankee, with a hundred I. W. W. men, waited the word to cross over the border and begin the conquest of Lower California. But he needed guns. And clear across to the Atlantic, the Junta in touch with them all and all of them needing guns, mere adventurers, soldiers of fortune, bandits, disgruntled American union men, socialists, anarchists, rough-necks, Mexican exiles, peons escaped from bondage, whipped miners from the bull-pens of Cœur d'Alene and Colorado who desired only the more vindictively to fight—all the flotsam and jetsam of wild spirits from the madly complicated modern world. And it was guns and ammunition, ammunition and guns—the unceasing and eternal cry.

Fling this heterogeneous, bankrupt, vindictive mass across the border, and the Revolution was on. The custom house, the northern ports of entry, would be captured. Diaz could not resist. He dared not throw the weight of his armies against them, for he must hold the south. And through the south the flame would spread despite. The people would rise. The defenses of city after city would crumple up. State after state would totter down. And at last, from every side, the victorious armies of the Revolution would close in on the City of Mexico itself, Diaz's last stronghold.

But the money. They had the men, impatient and urgent, who would use the guns. They knew the traders who would sell and deliver the guns. But to culture the Revolution thus far had exhausted the Junta. The last dollar had been spent, the last resource and the last starving patriot milked dry, and the great adventure still trembled on the scales. Guns and ammunition! The ragged battalions must be armed. But how? Ramos lamented his confiscated estates. Arrellano wailed the spendthriftness of his youth. May Sethby wondered if it would have been different had they of the Junta been more economical in the past.

"To think that the freedom of Mexico should stand or fall on a few paltry thousands of dollars," said Paulino Vera.

Despair was in all their faces. José Amarillo, their last hope, a recent convert, who had promised money, had been apprehended at his hacienda in Chihuahua and shot against his own stable wall. The news had just come through.

Rivera, on his knees, scrubbing, looked up, with suspended brush, his bare arms flecked with soapy, dirty water.

"Will five thousand do it?" he asked.

They looked their amazement. Vera nodded and swallowed. He could not speak, but he was on the instant invested with a vast faith.

"Order the guns," Rivera said, and thereupon was guilty of the longest flow of words they had ever heard him utter. "The time is short. In three weeks I shall bring you the five thousand. It is well. The weather will be warmer for those who fight. Also, it is the best I can do."

Vera fought his faith. It was incredible. Too many fond hopes had been shattered since he had begun to play the revolution game. He believed this threadbare scrubber of the Revolution, and yet he dared not believe.

"You are crazy," he said.

"In three weeks," said Rivera. "Order the guns."

He got up, rolled down his sleeves, and put on his coat.

"Order the guns," he said. "I am going now."

# III

After hurrying and scurrying, much telephoning and bad language, a night session was held in Kelly's office. Kelly was rushed with business; also, he was unlucky. He had brought Danny Ward out from New York, arranged the fight for him with Billy Carthey, the date was three weeks away, and for two days now, carefully concealed from the sporting writers, Carthey had been lying up, badly injured. There was no one to take his place. Kelly had been burning the wires East to every eligible lightweight, but they were tied up with dates and contracts. And now hope had revived, though faintly.

"You've got a hell of a nerve," Kelly addressed Rivera, after one look, as soon as they got together.

Hate that was malignant was in Rivera's eyes, but his face remained impassive.

"I can lick Ward," was all he said.

"How do you know? Ever see him fight?"

Rivera shook his head.

"He can beat you up with one hand and both eyes closed."

Rivera shrugged his shoulders.

"Haven't you got anything to say?" the fight promoter snarled.

"I can lick him."

"Who'd you ever fight, anyway?" Michael Kelly demanded. Michael was the promoter's brother, and ran the Yellowstone pool rooms where he made goodly sums on the fight game.

Rivera favored him with a bitter, unanswering stare.

The promoter's secretary, a distinctively sporty young man, sneered audibly.

"Well, you know Roberts," Kelly broke the hostile silence. "He ought to be here. I've sent for him. Sit down and wait, though from the looks of you, you haven't got a chance. I can't throw the public down with a bum fight. Ringside seats are selling at fifteen dollars, you know that."

When Roberts arrived, it was patent that he was mildly drunk. He was a tall, lean, slack-jointed individual, and his walk, like his talk, was a smooth and languid drawl.

Kelly went straight to the point.

"Look here, Roberts, you've been braggin' you discovered this little Mexican. You know Carthey's broke his arm. Well, this little yellow streak has the gall to blow in to-day and say he'll take Carthey's place. What about it?"

"It's all right, Kelly," came the slow response. "He can put up a fight."

"I suppose you'll be sayin' next that he can lick Ward," Kelly snapped.

Roberts considered judicially.

"No, I won't say that. Ward's a top-notcher and a ring general. But he can't hashhouse Rivera in short order. I know Rivera. Nobody can get his goat. He ain't got a goat that I could ever discover. And he's a two-handed fighter. He can throw in the sleep-makers from any position."

"Never mind that. What kind of a show can he put up? You've been conditioning and training fighters all your life. I take off my hat to your judgment. Can he give the public a run for its money?"

"He sure can, and he'll worry Ward a mighty heap on top of it. You don't know that boy. I do. I discovered him. He ain't got a goat. He's a devil. He's a wizzy-wooz if anybody should ask you. He'll make Ward sit up with a show of local talent that'll make the rest of you sit up. I won't say he'll lick Ward, but he'll put up such a show that you'll all know he's a comer."

"All right." Kelly turned to his secretary. "Ring up Ward. I warned him to show up if I thought it worth while. He's right across at the Yellowstone, throwin' chests and doing the popular." Kelly turned back to the conditioner. "Have a drink?"

Roberts sipped his highball and unburdened himself.

"Never told you how I discovered the little cuss. It was a couple of years ago he showed up out at the quarters. I was getting Prayne ready for his fight with Delaney. Prayne's wicked. He ain't got a tickle of mercy in his make-up. He'd chopped up his pardner's something cruel, and I couldn't find a willing boy that'd work with him. I'd noticed this little starved Mexican kid hanging around, and I was desperate. So I grabbed him, slammed on the gloves, and put him in. He was tougher'n rawhide, but weak. And he didn't know the first letter in the alphabet of boxing. Prayne chopped him to ribbons. But he hung on for two sickening rounds, when he fainted. Starvation, that was all. Battered? You couldn't have recognized him. I gave him half a dollar and a square meal. You oughta seen him wolf it down. He hadn't had a bite for a couple of days. That's the end of him, thinks I. But next day he showed up, stiff an' sore, ready for another half and a square meal. And he done better as time went by. Just a born fighter, and tough beyond belief. He hasn't a heart. He's a piece of ice. And he never talked eleven words in a string since I know him. He saws wood and does his work."

"I've seen 'm," the secretary said. "He's worked a lot for you."

"All the big little fellows has tried out on him," Roberts answered. "And he's learned from 'em. I've seen some of them he could lick. But his heart wasn't in it. I reckoned he never liked the game. He seemed to act that way."

"He's been fighting some before the little clubs the last few months," Kelly said.

"Sure. But I don't know what struck 'm. All of a sudden his heart got into it. He just went out like a streak and cleaned up all the little local fellows. Seemed to want the money, and he's won a bit, though his clothes don't look it. He's peculiar. Nobody knows his business. Nobody knows how he spends his time. Even when he's on the job, he plumb up and disappears most of each day soon as his work is done. Sometimes he just blows away for weeks at a time. But he don't take advice. There's a fortune in it for the fellow that gets the job of managin' him, only he won't consider it. And you watch him hold out for the cash money when you get down to terms."

It was at this stage that Danny Ward arrived. Quite a party it was. His manager and trainer were with him, and he breezed in like a gusty draught of geniality, good-nature, and all-conqueringness. Greetings flew about, a joke here, a retort there, a smile or a laugh for everybody. Yet it was his way, and only partly sincere. He was a good actor, and he had found geniality a most valuable asset in the game of getting on in the world. But down underneath he was the deliberate, cold-blooded fighter and business man. The rest was a mask. Those who knew him or trafficked with him said that when it came to brass tacks he was Danny-on-the-Spot. He was invariably present at all business discussions, and it was urged by some that his manager was a blind whose only function was to serve as Danny's mouth-piece.

Rivera's way was different. Indian blood, as well as Spanish, was in his veins, and he sat back in a corner, silent, immobile, only his black eyes passing from face to face and noting everything.

"So that's the guy," Danny said, running an appraising eye over his proposed antagonist. "How de do, old chap."

Rivera's eyes burned venomously, but he made no sign of acknowledgment. He disliked all Gringos, but this Gringo he hated with an immediacy that was unusual even in him.

"Gawd!" Danny protested facetiously to the promoter. "You ain't expectin' me to fight a deef mute." When the laughter subsided, he made another hit. "Los Angeles must be on the dink when this is the best you can scare up. What kindergarten did you get 'm from?"

"He's a good little boy, Danny, take it from me," Roberts defended. "Not as easy as he looks."

"And half the house is sold already," Kelly pleaded. "You'll have to take 'm on, Danny. It's the best we can do."

Danny ran another careless and unflattering glance over Rivera and sighed.

"I gotta be easy with 'm, I guess. If only he don't blow up."

Roberts snorted.

"You gotta be careful," Danny's manager warned. "No taking chances with a dub that's likely to sneak a lucky one across."

"Oh, I'll be careful all right, all right," Danny smiled. "I'll get 'm at the start an' nurse 'm along for the dear public's sake. What d' ye say to fifteen rounds, Kelly— An' then the hay for him?"

"That'll do," was the answer. "As long as you make it realistic."

"Then let's get down to biz." Danny paused and calculated. "Of course, sixty-five per cent. of gate receipts, same as with Carthey. But the split'll be different. Eighty will just about suit me." And to his manager, "That right?"

The manager nodded.

"Here, you, did you get that?" Kelly asked Rivera.

Rivera shook his head.

"Well, it's this way," Kelly exposited. "The purse'll be sixty-five per cent. of the gate receipts. You're a dub, and an unknown. You and Danny split, twenty per cent. goin' to you, an' eighty to Danny. That's fair, isn't it, Roberts?"

"Very fair, Rivera," Roberts agreed. "You see, you ain't got a reputation yet."

"What will sixty-five per cent. of the gate receipts be?" Rivera demanded.

"Oh, maybe five thousand, maybe as high as eight thousand," Danny broke in to explain. "Something like that. Your share'll come to something like a thousand or sixteen hundred. Pretty good for takin' a licking from a guy with my reputation. What d' ye say?"

Then Rivera took their breaths away.

"Winner takes all," he said with finality.

A dead silence prevailed.

"It's like candy from a baby," Danny's manager proclaimed.

Danny shook his head.

"I've been in the game too long," he explained. "I'm not casting reflections on the referee, or the present company. I'm not sayin' nothing about book-makers an' frame-ups that sometimes happen. But what I do say is that it's poor business for a fighter like me. I play safe. There's no tellin'. Mebbe I break my arm, eh? Or some guy slips me a bunch of dope?" He shook his head solemnly. "Win or lose, eighty is my split. What d' ye say, Mexican?"

Rivera shook his head.

Danny exploded. He was getting down to brass tacks now.

"Why, you dirty little greaser! I've a mind to knock your block off right now."

Roberts drawled his body to interposition between hostilities.

"Winner takes all," Rivera repeated sullenly.

"Why do you stand out that way?" Danny asked.

"I can lick you," was the straight answer.

Danny half started to take off his coat. But, as his manager knew, it was a grand stand play. The coat did not come off, and Danny allowed himself to be placated by the group. Everybody sympathized with him. Rivera stood alone.

"Look here, you little fool," Kelly took up the argument. "You're nobody. We know what you've been doing the last few months—putting away little local fighters. But Danny is class. His next fight after this will be for the championship. And you're unknown. Nobody ever heard of you out of Los Angeles."

"They will," Rivera answered with a shrug, "after this fight."

"You think for a second you can lick me?" Danny blurted in.

Rivera nodded.

"Oh, come; listen to reason," Kelly pleaded. "Think of the advertising."

"I want the money," was Rivera's answer.

"You couldn't win from me in a thousand years," Danny assured him.

"Then what are you holding out for?" Rivera countered. "If the money's that easy, why don't you go after it?"

"I will, so help me!" Danny cried with abrupt conviction. "I'll beat you to death in the ring, my boy—you monkeyin' with me this way. Make out the articles, Kelly. Winner take all. Play it up in the sportin' columns. Tell 'em it's a grudge fight. I'll show this fresh kid a few."

Kelly's secretary had begun to write, when Danny interrupted.

"Hold on!" He turned to Rivera. "Weights?"

"Ringside," came the answer.

"Not on your life, Fresh Kid. If winner takes all, we weigh in at ten A.M."

"And winner takes all?" Rivera queried.

Danny nodded. That settled it. He would enter the ring in his full ripeness of strength.

"Weigh in at ten," Rivera said.

The secretary's pen went on scratching.

"It means five pounds," Roberts complained to Rivera. "You've given too much away. You've thrown the fight right there. Danny'll be as strong as a bull. You're a fool. He'll lick you sure. You ain't got the chance of a dewdrop in hell."

Rivera's answer was a calculated look of hatred. Even this Gringo he despised, and him had he found the whitest Gringo of them all.

# IV

Barely noticed was Rivera as he entered the ring. Only a very slight and very scattering ripple of half-hearted hand-clapping greeted him. The house did not believe in him. He was the lamb led to slaughter at the hands of the great Danny. Besides, the house was disappointed. It had expected a rushing battle between Danny Ward and Billy Carthey, and here it must put up with this poor little tyro. Still further, it had manifested its disapproval of the change by betting two, and even three, to one on Danny. And where a betting audience's money is, there is its heart.

The Mexican boy sat down in his corner and waited. The slow minutes lagged by. Danny was making him wait. It was an old trick, but ever it worked on the young, new fighters. They grew frightened, sitting thus and facing their own apprehensions and a callous, tobacco-smoking audience. But for once the trick failed. Roberts was right. Rivera had no goat. He, who was more delicately coördinated, more finely nerved and strung than any of them, had no nerves of this sort. The atmosphere of foredoomed defeat in his own corner had no effect on him. His handlers were Gringos and strangers. Also they were scrubs—the dirty driftage of the fight game, without honor, without efficiency. And they were chilled, as well, with certitude that theirs was the losing corner.

"Now you gotta be careful," Spider Hagerty warned him. Spider was his chief second. "Make it last as long as you can—them's my instructions from Kelly. If you don't, the papers'll call it another bum fight and give the game a bigger black eye in Los Angeles."

All of which was not encouraging. But Rivera took no notice. He despised prize fighting. It was the hated game of the hated Gringo. He had taken up with it, as a chopping block for others in the training quarters, solely because he was starving. The fact that he was marvelously made for it, had meant nothing. He hated it. Not until he had come in to the Junta, had he fought for money, and he had found the money easy. Not first among the sons of men had he been to find himself successful at a despised vocation.

He did not analyze. He merely knew that he must win this fight. There could be no other outcome. For behind him, nerving him to this belief, were profounder forces than any the crowded house dreamed. Danny Ward fought for money, and for the easy ways of life that money would bring. But the things Rivera fought for burned in his brain—blazing and terrible visions, that, with eyes wide open, sitting lonely in the corner of the ring and waiting for his tricky antagonist, he saw as clearly as he had lived them.

He saw the white-walled, water-power factories of Rio Blanco. He saw the six thousand workers, starved and wan, and the little children, seven and eight years of age, who toiled long shifts for ten cents a day. He saw the perambulating corpses, the ghastly death's heads of men who labored in the dye-rooms. He remembered that he had heard his father call the dye-rooms the "suicide-holes," where a year was death. He saw the little patio, and his mother cooking and moiling at crude housekeeping and finding time to caress and love him. And his father he saw, large, big-moustached and deep-chested, kindly above all men, who loved all men and whose heart was so large that there was love to overflowing still left for the mother and the little muchacho playing in the corner of the patio. In those days his name had not been Felipe Rivera. It had been Fernandez, his father's and mother's name. Him had they called Juan. Later, he had changed it himself, for he had found the name of Fernandez hated by prefects of police, *jefes politicos,* and *rurales.*

Big, hearty Joaquin Fernandez! A large place he occupied in Rivera's visions. He had not understood at the time, but looking back he could understand. He could see him setting type in the little printery, or scribbling endless hasty, nervous lines on the much-cluttered desk. And he could see the strange evenings, when workmen, coming secretly in the dark like men who did ill deeds, met with his father and talked long hours where he, the muchacho, lay not always asleep in the corner.

As from a remote distance he could hear Spider Hagerty saying to him: "No layin' down at the start. Them's instructions. Take a beatin' an' earn your dough."

Ten minutes had passed, and he still sat in his corner. There were no signs of Danny, who was evidently playing the trick to the limit.

But more visions burned before the eye of Rivera's memory. The strike, or, rather, the lock-out, because the workers of Rio Blanco had helped their striking brothers of Puebla. The hunger, the expeditions in the hills for berries, the roots and herbs that all ate and that twisted and pained the stomachs of all of them. And then, the nightmare; the waste of ground before the company's store; the thousands of starving workers; General Rosalio Martinez and the soldiers of Porfirio Diaz; and the death-spitting rifles that seemed never to cease spitting, while the workers' wrongs were washed and washed again in their own blood. And that night! He saw the flat cars, piled high with the bodies of the slain, consigned to Vera Cruz, food for the sharks of the bay. Again he crawled over the grisly heaps, seeking and finding, stripped and mangled, his father and his mother. His mother he especially remembered—only her face projecting, her body burdened by the weight of dozens of bodies. Again the rifles of the soldiers of Porfirio Diaz cracked, and again he dropped to the ground and slunk away like some hunted coyote of the hills.

To his ears came a great roar, as of the sea, and he saw Danny Ward, leading his retinue of trainers and seconds, coming down the center aisle. The house was in wild uproar for the popular hero who was bound to win. Everybody proclaimed him. Everybody was for him. Even Rivera's own seconds warmed to something akin to cheerfulness when Danny ducked jauntily through the ropes and entered the ring. His face continually spread to an unending succession of smiles, and when Danny smiled he smiled in every feature, even to the laughter-wrinkles of the corners of the eyes and into the depths of the eyes themselves. Never was there so genial a fighter. His face was a running advertisement of good feeling, of good fellowship. He knew everybody. He joked, and laughed, and greeted his friends through the ropes. Those farther away, unable to suppress their admiration, cried loudly: "Oh, you Danny!" It was a joyous ovation of affection that lasted a full five minutes.

Rivera was disregarded. For all that the audience noticed, he did not exist. Spider Hagerty's bloated face bent down close to his.

"No gettin' scared," the Spider warned. "An' remember instructions. You gotta last. No layin' down. If you lay down, we got instructions to beat you up in the dressing rooms. Savve? You just gotta fight."

The house began to applaud. Danny was crossing the ring to him. Danny bent over, caught Rivera's right hand in both his own and shook it with impulsive heartiness. Danny's smile-wreathed face was close to his. The audience yelled its appreciation of Danny's display of sporting spirit. He was greeting his opponent with the fondness of a brother. Danny's lips moved, and the audience, interpreting the unheard words to be those of a kindly-natured sport, yelled again. Only Rivera heard the low words.

"You little Mexican rat," hissed from between Danny's gaily smiling lips, "I'll fetch the yellow outa you."

Rivera made no move. He did not rise. He merely hated with his eyes.

"Get up, you dog!" some man yelled through the ropes from behind.

The crowd began to hiss and boo him for his unsportsmanlike conduct, but he sat unmoved. Another great outburst of applause was Danny's as he walked back across the ring.

When Danny stripped, there was ohs! and ahs! of delight. His body was perfect, alive with easy suppleness and health and strength. The skin was white as a woman's, and as smooth. All grace, and resilience, and power resided therein. He had proved it in scores of battles. His photographs were in all the physical culture magazines.

A groan went up as Spider Hagerty peeled Rivera's sweater over his head. His body seemed leaner, because of the swarthiness of the skin. He had muscles, but they made no display like his opponent's. What the audience neglected to see was the deep chest. Nor could it guess the toughness of the fiber of the flesh, the instantaneousness of the cell explosions of the muscles, the fineness of the nerves that wired every part of him into a splendid fighting mechanism. All the audience saw was a brown-skinned boy of eighteen with what seemed the body of a boy. With Danny it was different. Danny was a man of twenty-four, and his body was a man's body. The contrast was still more striking as they stood together in the center of the ring receiving the referee's last instructions.

Rivera noticed Roberts sitting directly behind the newspaper men. He was drunker than usual, and his speech was correspondingly slower.

"Take it easy, Rivera," Roberts drawled. "He can't kill you, remember that. He'll rush you at the go-off, but don't get rattled. You just cover up, and stall, and clinch. He can't hurt you much. Just make believe to yourself that he's choppin' out on you at the trainin' quarters."

Rivera made no sign that he had heard.

"Sullen little devil," Roberts muttered to the man next to him. "He always was that way."

But Rivera forgot to look his usual hatred. A vision of countless rifles blinded his eyes. Every face in the audience, far as he could see, to the high dollar-seats, was transformed into a rifle. And he saw the long Mexican border arid and sun-washed and aching, and along it he saw the ragged bands that delayed only for the guns.

Back in his corner he waited, standing up. His seconds had crawled out through the ropes, taking the canvas stool with them. Diagonally across the squared ring, Danny faced him. The gong struck, and the battle was on. The audience howled its delight. Never had it seen a battle open more convincingly. The papers were right. It was a grudge fight. Three-quarters of the distance Danny covered in the rush to get together, his intention to eat up the Mexican lad plainly advertised. He assailed with not one blow, nor two, nor a dozen. He was a gyroscope of blows, a whirlwind of destruction. Rivera was nowhere. He was overwhelmed, buried beneath avalanches of punches delivered from every angle and position by a past master in the art. He was overborne, swept back against the ropes, separated by the referee, and swept back against the ropes again.

It was not a fight. It was a slaughter, a massacre. Any audience, save a prize fighting one, would have exhausted its emotions in that first minute. Danny was certainly showing what he could do—a splendid exhibition. Such was the certainty of the audience, as well as its excitement and favoritism, that it failed to take notice that the Mexican still stayed on his feet. It forgot Rivera. It rarely saw him, so closely was he enveloped in Danny's man-eating attack. A minute of this went by, and two minutes. Then, in a separation, it caught a clear glimpse of the Mexican. His lip was cut, his nose was bleeding. As he turned and staggered into a clinch, the welts of oozing blood, from his contacts with the ropes, showed in red bars across his back. But what the audience did not notice was that his chest was not heaving and that his eyes were coldly burning as ever. Too many aspiring champions, in the cruel welter of the training camps, had practiced this man-eating attack on him. He had learned to live through for a compensation of from half a dollar a go up to fifteen dollars a week —a hard school, and he was schooled hard.

Then happened the amazing thing. The whirling, blurring mix-up ceased suddenly. Rivera stood alone. Danny, the redoubtable Danny, lay on his back. His body quivered as consciousness strove to return to it. He had not staggered and sunk down, nor had he gone over in a long slumping fall. The right hook of Rivera had dropped him in midair with the abruptness of death. The referee shoved Rivera back with one hand, and stood over the fallen gladiator counting the seconds. It is the custom of prizefighting audiences to cheer a clean knockdown blow. But this audience did not cheer. The thing had been too unexpected. It watched the toll of the seconds in tense silence, and through this silence the voice of Roberts rose exultantly:

"I told you he was a two-handed fighter!"

By the fifth second, Danny was rolling over on his face, and when seven was counted, he rested on one knee, ready to rise after the count of nine and before the count of ten. If his knee still touched the floor at "ten," he was considered "down," and also "out." The instant his knee left the floor, he was considered "up," and in that instant it was Rivera's right to try and put him down again. Rivera took no chances. The moment that knee left the floor he would strike again. He circled around, but the referee circled in between, and Rivera knew that the seconds he counted were very slow. All Gringos were against him, even the referee.

At "nine" the referee gave Rivera a sharp thrust back. It was unfair, but it enabled Danny to rise, the smile back on his lips. Doubled partly over, with arms wrapped about face and abdomen, he cleverly stumbled into a clinch. By all the rules of the game the referee should have broken it, but he did not, and Danny clung on like a surf-battered barnacle and moment by moment recuperated. The last minute of the round was going fast. If he could live to the end, he would have a full minute in his corner to revive. And live to the end he did, smiling through all desperateness and extremity.

"The smile that won't come off!" somebody yelled, and the audience laughed loudly in its relief.

"The kick that Greaser's got is something God-awful," Danny gasped in his corner to his adviser while his handlers worked frantically over him.

The second and third rounds were tame. Danny, a tricky and consummate ring general, stalled and blocked and held on, devoting himself to recovering from that dazing first-round blow. In the fourth round he was himself again. Jarred and shaken, nevertheless his good condition had enabled him to regain his vigor. But he tried no man-eating tactics. The Mexican had proved a tartar. Instead, he brought to bear his best fighting powers. In tricks and skill and experience he was the master, and though he could land nothing vital, he proceeded scientifically to chop and wear down his opponent. He landed three blows to Rivera's one, but they were punishing blows only, and not deadly. It was the sum of many of them that constituted deadliness. He was respectful of this two-handed dub with the amazing short-arm kicks in both his fists.

In defense, Rivera developed a disconcerting straight-left. Again and again, attack after attack he straight-lefted away from him with accumulated damage to Danny's mouth and nose. But Danny was protean. That was why he was the coming champion. He could change from style to style of fighting at will. He now devoted himself to infighting. In this he was particularly wicked, and it enabled him to avoid the other's straight-left. Here he set the house wild repeatedly, capping it with a marvelous lock-break and lift of an inside upper-cut that raised the Mexican in the air and dropped him to the mat. Rivera rested on one knee, making the most of the count, and in the soul of him he knew the referee was counting short seconds on him.

Again, in the seventh, Danny achieved the diabolical inside uppercut. He succeeded only in staggering Rivera, but, in the ensuing moment of defenseless helplessness, he smashed him with another blow through the ropes. Rivera's body bounced on the heads of the newspaper men below, and they boosted him back to the edge of the platform outside the ropes. Here he rested on one knee, while the referee raced off the seconds. Inside the ropes, through which he must duck to enter the ring, Danny waited for him. Nor did the referee intervene or thrust Danny back.

The house was beside itself with delight.

"Kill 'm, Danny, kill 'm!" was the cry.

Scores of voices took it up until it was like a war-chant of wolves.

Danny did his best, but Rivera, at the count of eight, instead of nine, came unexpectedly through the ropes and safely into a clinch. Now the referee worked, tearing him away so that he could be hit, giving Danny every advantage that an unfair referee can give.

But Rivera lived, and the daze cleared from his brain. It was all of a piece. They were the hated Gringos and they were all unfair. And in the worst of it visions continued to flash and sparkle in his brain— long lines of railroad track that simmered across the desert; *rurales* and American constables; prisons and calabooses; tramps at water tanks—all the squalid and painful panorama of his odyssey after Rio Blanca and the strike. And, resplendent and glorious, he saw the great, red Revolution sweeping across his land. The guns were there before him. Every hated face was a gun. It was for the guns he fought. He was the guns. He was the Revolution. He fought for all Mexico.

The audience began to grow incensed with Rivera. Why didn't he take the licking that was appointed him? Of course he was going to be licked, but why should he be so obstinate about it? Very few were interested in him, and they were the certain, definite percentage of a gambling crowd that plays long shots. Believing Danny to be the winner, nevertheless they had put their money on the Mexican at four to ten and one to three. More than a trifle was up on the point of how many rounds Rivera could last. Wild money had appeared at the ringside proclaiming that he could not last seven rounds, or even six. The winners of this, now that their cash risk was happily settled, had joined in cheering on the favorite.

Rivera refused to be licked. Through the eighth round his opponent strove vainly to repeat the uppercut. In the ninth, Rivera stunned the house again. In the midst of a clinch he broke the lock with a quick, lithe movement, and in the narrow space between their bodies his right lifted from the waist. Danny went to the floor and took the safety of the count. The crowd was appalled. He was being bested at his own game. His famous right-uppercut had been worked back on him. Rivera made no attempt to catch him as he arose at "nine." The referee was openly blocking that play, though he stood clear when the situation was reversed and it was Rivera who desired to rise.

Twice in the tenth, Rivera put through the right-uppercut, lifted from waist to opponent's chin. Danny grew desperate. The smile never left his face, but he went back to his man-eating rushes. Whirlwind as he would, he could not damage Rivera, while Rivera, through the blur and whirl, dropped him to the mat three times in succession. Danny did not recuperate so quickly now, and by the eleventh round he was in a serious way. But from then till the fourteenth he put up the gamest exhibition of his career. He stalled and blocked, fought parsimoniously, and strove to gather strength. Also, he fought as foully as a successful fighter knows how. Every trick and device he employed, butting in the clinches with the seeming of accident, pinioning Rivera's glove between arm and body, heeling his glove on Rivera's mouth to clog his breathing. Often, in the clinches, through his cut and smiling lips he snarled insults unspeakable and vile in Rivera's ear. Everybody, from the referee to the house, was with Danny and was helping Danny. And they knew what he had in mind. Bested by this surprise-box of an unknown, he was pinning all on a single punch. He offered himself for punishment, fished, and feinted, and drew, for that one opening that would enable him to whip a blow through with all his strength and turn the tide. As another and greater fighter had done before him, he might do—a right and left, to solar plexus and across the jaw. He could do it, for he was noted for the strength of punch that remained in his arms as long as he could keep his feet.

Rivera's seconds were not half-caring for him in the intervals between rounds. Their towels made a showing, but drove little air into his panting lungs. Spider Hagerty talked advice to him, but Rivera knew it was wrong advice. Everybody was against him. He was surrounded by treachery. In the fourteenth round he put Danny down again, and himself stood resting, hands dropped at side, while the referee counted. In the other corner Rivera had been noting suspicious whisperings. He saw Michael Kelly make his way to Roberts and bend and whisper. Rivera's ears were a cat's, desert-trained, and he caught snatches of what was said. He wanted to hear more, and when his opponent arose he maneuvered the fight into a clinch over against the ropes.

"Got to," he could hear Michael, while Roberts nodded. "Danny's got to win—I stand to lose a mint—I've got a ton of money covered—my own—If he lasts the fifteenth I'm bust—The boy'll mind you. Put something across."

And thereafter Rivera saw no more visions. They were trying to job him. Once again he dropped Danny and stood resting, his hands at his side. Roberts stood up.

"That settled him," he said. "Go to your corner."

He spoke with authority, as he had often spoken to Rivera at the training quarters. But Rivera looked hatred at him and waited for Danny to rise. Back in his corner in the minute interval, Kelly, the promoter, came and talked to Rivera.

"Throw it, damn you," he rasped in a harsh low voice. "You gotta lay down, Rivera. Stick with me and I'll make your future. I'll let you lick Danny next time. But here's where you lay down."

Rivera showed with his eyes that he heard, but he made neither sign of assent nor dissent.

"Why don't you speak?" Kelly demanded angrily.

"You lose, anyway," Spider Hagerty supplemented. "The referee'll take it away from you. Listen to Kelly, and lay down."

"Lay down, kid," Kelly pleaded, "and I'll help you to the championship."

Rivera did not answer.

"I will, so help me, kid."

At the strike of the gong Rivera sensed something impending. The house did not. Whatever it was it was there inside the ring with him and very close. Danny's earlier surety seemed returned to him. The confidence of his advance frightened Rivera. Some trick was about to be worked. Danny rushed, but Rivera refused the encounter. He side-stepped away into safety. What the other wanted was a clinch. It was in some way necessary to the trick. Rivera backed and circled away, yet he knew, sooner or later, the clinch and the trick would come. Desperately he resolved to draw it. He made as if to effect the clinch with Danny's next rush. Instead, at the last instant, just as their bodies should have come together, Rivera darted nimbly back. And in the same instant Danny's corner raised a cry of foul. Rivera had fooled them. The referee paused irresolutely. The decision that trembled on his lips was never uttered, for a shrill, boy's voice from the gallery piped, "Raw work!"

Danny cursed Rivera openly, and forced him, while Rivera danced away. Also, Rivera made up his mind to strike no more blows at the body. In this he threw away half his chance of winning, but he knew if he was to win at all it was with the outfighting that remained to him. Given the least opportunity, they would lie a foul on him. Danny threw all caution to the winds. For two rounds he tore after and into the boy who dared not meet him at close quarters. Rivera was struck again and again; he took blows by the dozens to avoid the perilous clinch. During this supreme final rally of Danny's the audience rose to its feet and went mad. It did not understand. All it could see was that its favorite was winning after all.

"Why don't you fight?" it demanded wrathfully of Rivera. "You're yellow! You're yellow!" "Open up, you cur! Open up!" "Kill 'm, Danny! Kill 'm!" "You sure got 'm! Kill 'm!"

In all the house, bar none, Rivera was the only cold man. By temperament and blood he was the hottest-passioned there; but he had gone through such vastly greater heats that this collective passion of ten thousand throats, rising surge on surge, was to his brain no more than the velvet cool of a summer twilight.

Into the seventeenth round Danny carried his rally. Rivera, under a heavy blow, drooped and sagged. His hands dropped helplessly as he reeled backward. Danny thought it was his chance. The boy was at his mercy. Thus Rivera, feigning, caught him off his guard, lashing out a clean drive to the mouth. Danny went down. When he arose, Rivera felled him with a down-chop of the right on neck and jaw. Three times he repeated this. It was impossible for any referee to call these blows foul.

"Oh, Bill! Bill!" Kelly pleaded to the referee.

"I can't," that official lamented back. "He won't give me a chance."

Danny, battered and heroic, still kept coming up. Kelly and others near to the ring began to cry out to the police to stop it, though Danny's corner refused to throw in the towel. Rivera saw the fat police captain starting awkwardly to climb through the ropes, and was not sure what it meant. There were so many ways of cheating in this game of the Gringos. Danny, on his feet, tottered groggily and helplessly before him. The referee and the captain were both reaching for Rivera when he struck the last blow. There was no need to stop the fight, for Danny did not rise.

"Count!" Rivera cried hoarsely to the referee.

And when the count was finished, Danny's seconds gathered him up and carried him to his corner.

"Who wins?" Rivera demanded.

Reluctantly, the referee caught his gloved hand and held it aloft.

There were no congratulations for Rivera. He walked to his corner unattended, where his seconds had not yet placed his stool. He leaned backward on the ropes and looked his hatred at them, swept it on and about him till the whole ten thousand Gringos were included. His knees trembled under him, and he was sobbing from exhaustion. Before his eyes the hated faces swayed back and forth in the giddiness of nausea. Then he remembered they were the guns. The guns were his. The Revolution could go on.

# THE RED ONE

THERE IT WAS! The abrupt liberation of sound, as he timed it with his watch, Bassett likened to the trump of an archangel. Walls of cities, he meditated, might well fall down before so vast and compelling a summons. For the thousandth time vainly he tried to analyze the tone-quality of that enormous peal that dominated the land far into the strongholds of the surrounding tribes. The mountain gorge which was its source rang to the rising tide of it until it brimmed over and flooded earth and sky and air. With the wantonness of a sick man's fancy, he likened it to the mighty cry of some Titan of the Elder World vexed with misery or wrath. Higher and higher it arose, challenging and demanding in such profounds of volume that it seemed intended for ears beyond the narrow confines of the solar system. There was in it, too, the clamor of protest in that there were no ears to hear and comprehend its utterance.

—Such the sick man's fancy. Still he strove to analyze the sound. Sonorous as thunder was it, mellow as a golden bell, thin and sweet as a thrummed taut cord of silver—no; it was none of these, nor a blend of these. There were no words nor semblances in his vocabulary and experience with which to describe the totality of that sound.

Time passed. Minutes merged into quarters of hours, and quarters of hours into half hours, and still the sound persisted, ever changing from its initial vocal impulse yet never receiving fresh impulse—fading, dimming, dying as enormously as it had sprung into being. It became a confusion of troubled mutterings and babblings and colossal whisperings. Slowly it withdrew, sob by sob, into whatever great bosom had birthed it, until it whimpered deadly whispers of wrath and as equally seductive whispers of delight, striving still to be heard, to convey some cosmic secret, some understanding of infinite import and value. It dwindled to a ghost of sound that had lost its menace and promise, and became a thing that pulsed on in the sick man's consciousness for minutes after it had ceased. When he could hear it no longer, Bassett glanced at his watch. An hour had elapsed ere that archangel's trump had subsided into tonal nothingness.

Was this, then, *his* dark tower?—Bassett pondered, remembering his Browning and gazing at his skeleton-like and fever-wasted hands. And the fancy made him smile—of Childe Roland bearing a slug-horn to his lips with an arm as feeble as his was. Was it months, or years, he asked himself, since he first heard that mysterious call on the beach at Ringmanu? To save himself he could not tell. The long sickness had been most long. In conscious count of time he knew of months, many of them; but he had no way of estimating the long intervals of delirium and stupor. And how fared Captain Bateman of the blackbirder *Nari?* he wondered; and had Captain Bateman's drunken mate died of delirium tremens yet?

From which vain speculations, Bassett turned idly to review all that had occurred since that day on the beach of Ringmanu when he first heard the sound and plunged into the jungle after it. Sagawa had protested. He could see him yet, his queer little monkeyish face eloquent with fear, his back burdened with specimen cases, in his hands Bassett's butterfly net and naturalist's shotgun, as he quavered in Beche de mer English: "Me fella too much fright along bush. Bad fella boy too much stop'm along bush."

Bassett smiled sadly at the recollection. The little New Hanover boy had been frightened, but had proved faithful, following him without hesitancy into the bush in the quest after the source of the wonderful sound. No fire-hollowed tree-trunk, that, throbbing war through the jungle depths, had been Bassett's conclusion. Erroneous had been his next conclusion, namely, that the source or cause could not be more distant than an hour's walk and that he would easily be back by mid-afternoon to be picked up by the *Nari*'s whaleboat.

"That big fella noise no good, all the same devil-devil," Sagawa had adjudged. And Sagawa had been right. Had he not had his head hacked off within the day? Bassett shuddered. Without doubt Sagawa had been eaten as well by the bad fella boys too much that stopped along the bush. He could see him, as he had last seen him, stripped of the shotgun and all the naturalist's gear of his master, lying on the narrow trail where he had been decapitated barely the moment before. Yes, within a minute the thing had happened. Within a minute, looking back, Bassett had seen him trudging patiently along under his burdens. Then Bassett's own trouble had come upon him. He looked at the cruelly healed stumps of the first and second fingers of his left hand, then rubbed them softly into the indentation in the back of his skull. Quick as had been the flash of the long-handled tomahawk, he had been quick enough to duck away his head and partially to deflect the stroke with his up-flung hand. Two fingers and a nasty scalp-wound had been the price he paid for his life. With one barrel of his ten-gauge shotgun he had blown the life out of the bushman who had so nearly got him; with the other barrel he had peppered the bushmen bending over Sagawa, and had the pleasure of knowing that the major portion of the charge had gone into the one who leaped away with Sagawa's head. Everything had occurred in a flash. Only himself, the slain bushman, and what remained of Sagawa, were in the narrow, wild-pig run of a path. From the dark jungle on either side came no rustle of movement or sound of life. And he had suffered distinct and dreadful shock. For the first time in his life he had killed a human being, and he knew nausea as he contemplated the mess of his handiwork.

Then had begun the chase. He retreated up the pig-run before his hunters, who were between him and the beach. How many there were, he could not guess. There might have been one, or a hundred, for aught he saw of them. That some of them took to the trees and traveled along through the jungle roof he was certain; but at the most he never glimpsed more than an occasional flitting of shadows. No bow-strings twanged that he could hear; but every little while, whence discharged he knew not, tiny arrows whispered past him or struck tree-boles and fluttered to the ground beside him. They were bone-tipped and feather-shafted, and the feathers, torn from the breasts of humming-birds, iridesced like jewels.

Once—and now, after the long lapse of time, he chuckled gleefully at the recollection—he had detected a shadow above him that came to instant rest as he turned his gaze upward. He could make out nothing, but, deciding to chance it, had fired at it a heavy charge of number five shot. Squalling like an infuriated cat, the shadow crashed down through tree-ferns and orchids and thudded upon the earth at his feet, and, still squalling its rage and pain, had sunk its human teeth into the ankle of his stout tramping boot. He, on the other hand, was

not idle, and with his free foot had done what reduced the squalling
to silence. So inured to savagery had Bassett since become, that he
chuckled again with the glee of the recollection.

What a night had followed! Small wonder that he had accumulated such a virulence and variety of fevers, he thought, as he recalled
that sleepless night of torment, when the throb of his wounds was as
nothing compared with the myriad stings of the mosquitoes. There
had been no escaping them, and he had not dared to light a fire. They
had literally pumped his body full of poison, so that, with the coming
of day, eyes swollen almost shut, he had stumbled blindly on, not
caring much when his head should be hacked off and his carcass
started on the way of Sagawa's to the cooking fire. Twenty-four hours
had made a wreck of him—of mind as well as body. He had scarcely
retained his wits at all, so maddened was he by the tremendous in-
oculation of poison he had received. Several times he fired his shotgun
with effect into the shadows that dogged him. Stinging day insects and
gnats added to his torment, while his bloody wounds attracted hosts
of loathsome flies that clung sluggishly to his flesh and had to be
brushed off and crushed off.

Once, in that day, he heard again the wonderful sound, seemingly
more distant, but rising imperiously above the nearer war-drums in
the bush. Right there was where he had made his mistake. Thinking
that he had passed beyond it and that, therefore, it was between him
and the beach of Ringmanu, he had worked back toward it when in
reality he was penetrating deeper and deeper into the mysterious heart
of the unexplored island. That night, crawling in among the twisted
roots of a banyan tree, he had slept from exhaustion while the mosquitoes had had their will of him.

Followed days and nights that were vague as nightmares in his
memory. One clear vision he remembered was of suddenly finding
himself in the midst of a bush village and watching the old men and
children fleeing into the jungle. All had fled but one. From close at
hand and above him, a whimpering as of some animal in pain and
terror had startled him. And looking up he had seen her—a girl, or
young woman, rather, suspended by one arm in the cooking sun. Perhaps for days she had so hung. Her swollen, protruding tongue spoke
as much. Still alive, she gazed at him with eyes of terror. Past help, he
decided, as he noted the swellings of her legs which advertised that
the joints had been crushed and the great bones broken. He resolved
to shoot her, and there the vision terminated. He could not remember

whether he had or not, any more than could he remember how he chanced to be in that village or how he succeeded in getting away from it.

Many pictures, unrelated, came and went in Bassett's mind as he reviewed that period of his terrible wanderings. He remembered invading another village of a dozen houses and driving all before him with his shotgun save for one old man, too feeble to flee, who spat at him and whined and snarled as he dug open a ground-oven and from amid the hot stones dragged forth a roasted pig that steamed its essence deliciously through its green-leaf wrappings. It was at this place that a wantonness of savagery had seized upon him. Having feasted, ready to depart with a hind quarter of the pig in his hand, he deliberately fired the grass thatch of a house with his burning glass.

But seared deepest of all in Bassett's brain, was the dank and noisome jungle. It actually stank with evil, and it was always twilight. Rarely did a shaft of sunlight penetrate its matted roof a hundred feet overhead. And beneath that roof was an aërial ooze of vegetation, a monstrous, parasitic dripping of decadent life-forms that rooted in death and lived on death. And through all this he drifted, ever pursued by the flitting shadows of the anthropophagi, themselves ghosts of evil that dared not face him in battle but that knew, soon or late, that they would feed on him. Bassett remembered that at the time, in lucid moments, he had likened himself to a wounded bull pursued by plains' coyotes too cowardly to battle with him for the meat of him, yet certain of the inevitable end of him when they would be full gorged. As the bull's horns and stamping hoofs kept off the coyotes, so his shotgun kept off these Solomon Islanders, these twilight shades of bushmen of the island of Guadalcanal.

Came the day of the grass lands. Abruptly, as if cloven by the sword of God in the hand of God, the jungle terminated. The edge of it, perpendicular and as black as the infamy of it, was a hundred feet up and down. And, beginning at the edge of it, grew the grass—sweet, soft, tender, pasture grass that would have delighted the eyes and beasts of any husbandman and that extended, on and on, for leagues and leagues of velvet verdure, to the backbone of the great island, the towering mountain range flung up by some ancient earth-cataclysm, serrated and gullied but not yet erased by the erosive tropic rains. But the grass! He had crawled into it a dozen yards, buried his face in it, smelled it, and broken down in a fit of involuntary weeping.

And, while he wept, the wonderful sound had pealed forth—if by *peal*, he had often thought since, an adequate description could be given of the enunciation of so vast a sound so melting sweet. Sweet it was as no sound ever heard. Vast it was, of so mighty a resonance that it might have proceeded from some brazen-throated monster. And yet it called to him across that leagues-wide savannah, and was like a benediction to his long-suffering, pain-wracked spirit.

He remembered how he lay there in the grass, wet-cheeked but no longer sobbing, listening to the sound and wondering that he had been able to hear it on the beach of Ringmanu. Some freak of air pressures and air currents, he reflected, had made it possible for the sound to carry so far. Such conditions might not happen again in a thousand days or ten thousand days; but the one day it had happened had been the day he landed from the *Nari* for several hours' collecting. Especially had he been in quest of the famed jungle butterfly, a foot across from wing-tip to wing-tip, as velvet-dusky of lack of color as was the gloom of the roof, of such lofty arboreal habits that it resorted only to the jungle roof and could be brought down only by a dose of shot. It was for this purpose that Sagawa had carried the twenty-gauge shotgun.

Two days and nights he had spent crawling across that belt of grass land. He had suffered much, but pursuit had ceased at the jungle-edge. And he would have died of thirst had not a heavy thunderstorm revived him on the second day.

And then had come Balatta. In the first shade, where the savannah yielded to the dense mountain jungle, he had collapsed to die. At first she had squealed with delight at sight of his helplessness, and was for beating his brain out with a stout forest branch. Perhaps it was his very utter helplessness that had appealed to her, and perhaps it was her human curiosity that made her refrain. At any rate, she had re-frained, for he opened his eyes again under the impending blow, and saw her studying him intently. What especially struck her about him were his blue eyes and white skin. Coolly she had squatted on her hams, spat on his arm, and with her finger-tips scrubbed away the dirt of days and nights of muck and jungle that sullied the pristine white-ness of his skin.

And everything about her had struck him especially, although there was nothing conventional about her at all. He laughed weakly at the recollection, for she had been as innocent of garb as Eve before the fig-leaf adventure. Squat and lean at the same time, asymmetrically limbed, string-muscled as if with lengths of cordage, dirt-caked from infancy save for casual showers, she was as unbeautiful a prototype of woman as he, with a scientist's eye, had ever gazed upon. Her breasts advertised at the one time her maturity and youth; and, if by nothing else, her sex was advertised by the one article of finery with which she was adorned, namely a pig's tail, thrust through a hole in her left ear-lobe. So lately had the tail been severed, that its raw end still oozed blood that dried upon her shoulder like so much candle-droppings. And her face! A twisted and wizened complex of apish features, perforated by upturned, sky-open, Mongolian nostrils, by a mouth that sagged from a huge upper-lip and faded precipitately into a retreating chin, and by peering querulous eyes that blinked as blink the eyes of denizens of monkey-cages.

Not even the water she brought him in a forest-leaf, and the ancient and half-putrid chunk of roast pig, could redeem in the slightest the grotesque hideousness of her. When he had eaten weakly for a space, he closed his eyes in order not to see her, although again and again she poked them open to peer at the blue of them. Then had come the sound. Nearer, much nearer, he knew it to be; and he knew equally well, despite the weary way he had come, that it was still many hours distant. The effect of it on her had been startling. She cringed under it, with averted face, moaning and chattering with fear. But after it had lived its full life of an hour, he closed his eyes and fell asleep with Balatta brushing the flies from him.

When he awoke it was night, and she was gone. But he was aware of renewed strength, and, by then too thoroughly inoculated by the mosquito poison to suffer further inflammation, he closed his eyes and slept an unbroken stretch till sun-up. A little later Balatta had returned, bringing with her a half dozen women who, unbeautiful as they were, were patently not so unbeautiful as she. She evidenced by her conduct that she considered him her find, her property, and the pride she took in showing him off would have been ludicrous had his situation not been so desperate.

Later, after what had been to him a terrible journey of miles, when he collapsed in front of the devil-devil house in the shadow of the breadfruit tree, she had shown very lively ideas on the matter of retaining possession of him. Ngurn, whom Bassett was to know afterward as the devil-devil doctor, priest, or medicine man of the village, had wanted his head. Others of the grinning and chattering monkey-men, all as stark of clothes and bestial of appearance as Balatta, had wanted his body for the roasting oven. At that time he had not understood their language, if by *language* might be dignified the uncouth sounds they made to represent ideas. But Bassett had thoroughly understood the matter of debate, especially when the men pressed and prodded and felt of the flesh of him as if he were so much commodity in a butcher's stall.

Balatta had been losing the debate rapidly, when the accident happened. One of the men, curiously examining Bassett's shotgun, managed to cock and pull a trigger. The recoil of the butt into the pit of the man's stomach had not been the most sanguinary result, for the charge of shot, at a distance of a yard, had blown the head of one of the debaters into nothingness.

Even Balatta joined the others in flight, and, ere they returned, his senses already reeling from the oncoming fever-attack, Bassett had regained possession of the gun. Whereupon, although his teeth chattered with the ague and his swimming eyes could scarcely see, he held onto his fading consciousness until he could intimidate the bushmen with the simple magics of compass, watch, burning glass, and matches. At the last, with due emphasis of solemnity and awfulness, he had killed a young pig with his shotgun and promptly fainted.

Bassett flexed his arm-muscles in quest of what possible strength might reside in such weakness, and dragged himself slowly and totteringly to his feet. He was shockingly emaciated; yet, during the various convalescences of the many months of his long sickness, he had never regained quite the same degree of strength as this time. What he feared was another relapse such as he had already frequently experienced. Without drugs, without even quinine, he had managed so far to live through a combination of the most pernicious and most malignant of malarial and black-water fevers. But could he continue to endure? Such was his everlasting query. For, like the genuine scientist he was, he would not be content to die until he had solved the secret of the sound.

Supported by a staff, he staggered the few steps to the devil-devil house where death and Ngurn reigned in gloom. Almost as infamously dark and evil-stinking as the jungle was the devil-devil house—in Bassett's opinion. Yet therein was usually to be found his favorite crony and gossip, Ngurn, always willing for a yarn or a discussion, the while he sat in the ashes of death and in a slow smoke shrewdly revolved curing human heads suspended from the rafters. For, through the months' interval of consciousness of his long sickness, Bassett had mastered the psychological simplicities and lingual difficulties of the language of the tribe of Ngurn and Balatta, and Gngngn—the latter the addle-headed young chief who was ruled by Ngurn, and who, whispered intrigue had it, was the son of Ngurn.

"Will the Red One speak to-day?" Bassett asked, by this time so accustomed to the old man's gruesome occupation as to take even an interest in the progress of the smoke-curing.

With the eye of an expert Ngurn examined the particular head he was at work upon.

"It will be ten days before I can say 'finish,' " he said. "Never has any man fixed heads like these."

Bassett smiled inwardly at the old fellow's reluctance to talk with him of the Red One. It had always been so. Never, by any chance, had Ngurn or any other member of the weird tribe divulged the slightest hint of any physical characteristic of the Red One. Physical the Red One must be, to emit the wonderful sound, and though it was called the Red One, Bassett could not be sure that red represented the color of it. Red enough were the deeds and powers of it, from what abstract clews he had gleaned. Not alone, had Ngurn informed him, was the Red One more bestial powerful than the neighbor tribal gods, ever a-thirst for the red blood of living human sacrifices, but the neighbor gods themselves were sacrificed and tormented before him. He was the god of a dozen allied villages similar to this one, which was the central and commanding village of the federation. By virtue of the Red One many alien villages had been devastated and even wiped out, the prisoners sacrificed to the Red One. This was true to-day, and it extended back into old history carried down by word of mouth through the generations. When he, Ngurn, had been a young man, the tribes beyond the grass lands had made a war raid. In the counter raid, Ngurn and his fighting folk had made many prisoners. Of children alone over five score living had been bled white before the Red One, and many, many more men and women.

The Thunderer, was another of Ngurn's names for the mysterious deity. Also at times was he called The Loud Shouter, The God-Voiced, The Bird-Throated, The One with the Throat Sweet as the Throat of the Honey-Bird, The Sun Singer, and The Star-Born.

Why The Star-Born? In vain Bassett interrogated Ngurn. According to that old devil-devil doctor, the Red One had always been, just where he was at present, forever singing and thundering his will over men. But Ngurn's father, wrapped in decaying grass-matting and hanging even then over their heads among the smoky rafters of the devil-devil house, had held otherwise. That departed wise one had believed that the Red One came from out of the starry night, else why—so his argument had run—had the old and forgotten ones passed his name down as the Star-Born? Bassett could not but recognize something cogent in such argument. But Ngurn affirmed the long years of his long life, wherein he had gazed upon many starry nights, yet never had he found a star on grass land or in jungle depth—and he had looked for them. True, he had beheld shooting stars (this in reply to Bassett's contention); but likewise had he beheld the phosphorescence of fungoid growths and rotten meat and fireflies on dark nights, and the flames of wood-fires and of blazing candle-nuts; yet what were flame and blaze and glow when they had flamed, and blazed and glowed? Answer: memories, memories only, of things which had ceased to be, like memories of matings accomplished, of feasts forgotten, of desires that were the ghosts of desires, flaring, flaming, burning, yet unrealized in achievement of easement and satisfaction. Where was the appetite of yesterday? the roasted flesh of the wild pig the hunter's arrow failed to slay? the maid, unwed and dead, ere the young man knew her?

A memory was not a star, was Ngurn's contention. How could a memory be a star? Further, after all his long life he still observed the starry night-sky unaltered. Never had he noted the absence of a single star from its accustomed place. Besides, stars were fire, and the Red One was not fire—which last involuntary betrayal told Bassett nothing.

"Will the Red One speak to-morrow?" he queried.

Ngurn shrugged his shoulders as who should say.

"And the day after?—and the day after that?" Bassett persisted.

"I would like to have the curing of your head," Ngurn changed the subject. "It is different from any other head. No devil-devil has a head like it. Besides, I would cure it well. I would take months and months. The moons would come and the moons would go, and the smoke would be very slow, and I should myself gather the materials for the curing smoke. The skin would not wrinkle. It would be as smooth as your skin now."

He stood up, and from the dim rafters grimed with the smoking of countless heads, where day was no more than a gloom, took down a matting-wrapped parcel and began to open it.

"It is a head like yours," he said, "but it is poorly cured."

Bassett had pricked up his ears at the suggestion that it was a white man's head; for he had long since come to accept that these jungle-dwellers, in the midmost center of the great island, had never had intercourse with white men. Certainly he had found them without the almost universal Beche de mer English of the west South Pacific. Nor had they knowledge of tobacco, nor of gunpowder. Their few precious knives, made from lengths of hoop-iron, and their few and more precious tomahawks, made from cheap trade hatchets, he had surmised they had captured in war from the bushmen of the jungle beyond the grass lands, and that they, in turn, had similarly gained them from the salt water men who fringed the coral beaches of the shore and had contact with the occasional white men.

"The folk in the out beyond do not know how to cure heads," old Ngurn explained, as he drew forth from the filthy matting and placed in Bassett's hands an indubitable white man's head.

Ancient it was beyond question; white it was as the blond hair attested. He could have sworn it once belonged to an Englishman, and to an Englishman of long before by token of the heavy gold circlets still threaded in the withered earlobes.

"Now your head . . ." the devil-devil doctor began on his favorite topic.

"I'll tell you what," Bassett interrupted, struck by a new idea. "When I die I'll let you have my head to cure, if, first, you take me to look upon the Red One."

"I will have your head anyway when you are dead," Ngurn rejected the proposition. He added, with the brutal frankness of the savage: "Besides, you have not long to live. You are almost a dead man now. You will grow less strong. In not many months I shall have you here turning and turning in the smoke. It is pleasant, through the long afternoons, to turn the head of one you have known as well as I know you. And I shall talk to you and tell you the many secrets you want to know. Which will not matter, for you will be dead."

"Ngurn," Bassett threatened in sudden anger, "you know the Baby Thunder in the Iron that is mine." (This was in reference to his all-potent and all-awful shotgun.) "I can kill you any time, and then you will not get my head."

"Just the same, will Gngngn, or some one else of my folk get it," Ngurn complacently assured him. "And just the same will it turn and turn here in the devil-devil house in the smoke. The quicker you slay me with your Baby Thunder, the quicker will your head turn in the smoke."

And Bassett knew he was beaten in the discussion.

What was the Red One?—Bassett asked himself a thousand times in the succeeding week, while he seemed to grow stronger. What was the source of the wonderful sound? What was this Sun Singer, this Star-Born One, this mysterious deity, as bestial-conducted as the black and kinky-headed and monkey-like human beasts who worshiped it, and whose silver-sweet, bull-mouthed singing and commanding he had heard at the taboo distance for so long?

Ngurn had he failed to bribe with the inevitable curing of his head when he was dead. Gngngn, imbecile and chief that he was, was too imbecilic, too much under the sway of Ngurn, to be considered. Remained Balatta, who, from the time she found him and poked his blue eyes open to recrudescence of her grotesque, female hideousness, had continued his adorer. Woman she was, and he had long known that the only way to win from her treason to her tribe was through the woman's heart of her.

Bassett was a fastidious man. He had never recovered from the initial horror caused by Balatta's female awfulness. Back in England, even at best, the charm of woman, to him, had never been robust. Yet now, resolutely, as only a man can do who is capable of martyring himself for the cause of science, he proceeded to violate all the fineness and delicacy of his nature by making love to the unthinkably disgusting bushwoman.

He shuddered, but with averted face hid his grimaces and swallowed his gorge as he put his arm around her dirt-crusted shoulders and felt the contact of her rancid-oily and kinky hair with his neck and chin. But he nearly screamed when she succumbed to that caress so at the very first of the courtship and mowed and gibbered and squealed little, queer, pig-like gurgly noises of delight. It was too much. And the next he did in the singular courtship was to take her down to the stream and give her a vigorous scrubbing.

From then on he devoted himself to her like a true swain as frequently and for as long at a time as his will could override his repugnance. But marriage, which she ardently suggested, with due observance of tribal custom, he balked at. Fortunately, taboo rule was strong in the tribe. Thus, Ngurn could never touch bone, or flesh, or hide of crocodile. This had been ordained at his birth. Gngngn was denied ever the touch of woman. Such pollution, did it chance to occur, could be purged only by the death of the offending female. It had happened once, since Bassett's arrival, when a girl of nine, running in play, stumbled and fell against the sacred chief. And the girl-child was seen no more. In whispers, Balatta told Bassett that she had been three days and nights in dying before the Red One. As for Balatta, the breadfruit was taboo to her. For which Bassett was thankful. The taboo might have been water.

For himself, he fabricated a special taboo. Only could he marry, he explained, when the Southern Cross rode highest in the sky. Knowing his astronomy, he thus gained a reprieve of nearly nine months; and he was confident that within that time he would either be dead or escaped to the coast with full knowledge of the Red One and of the source of the Red One's wonderful voice. At first he had fancied the Red One to be some colossal statue, like Memnon, rendered vocal under certain temperature conditions of sunlight. But when, after a war raid, a batch of prisoners was brought in and the sacrifice made at night, in the midst of rain, when the sun could play no part, the Red One had been more vocal than usual, Bassett discarded that hypothesis.

In company with Balatta, sometimes with men and parties of women, the freedom of the jungle was his for three quadrants of the compass. But the fourth quadrant, which contained the Red One's abiding place, was taboo. He made more thorough love to Balatta—also saw to it that she scrubbed herself more frequently. Eternal female she was, capable of any treason for the sake of love. And, though the sight of her was provocative of nausea and the contact of her provocative of despair, although he could not escape her awfulness in his dream-haunted nightmares of her, he nevertheless was aware of the cosmic verity of sex that animated her and that made her own life of less value than the happiness of her lover with whom she hoped to mate. Juliet or Balatta? Where was the intrinsic difference? The soft and tender product of ultra-civilization, or her bestial prototype of a hundred thousand years before her?—there was no difference.

Bassett was a scientist first, a humanist afterward. In the jungle-heart of Guadalcanal he put the affair to the test, as in the laboratory he would have put to the test any chemical reaction. He increased his feigned ardor for the bushwoman, at the same time increasing the imperiousness of his will of desire over her to be led to look upon the Red One face to face. It was the old story, he recognized, that the woman must pay, and it occurred when the two of them, one day, were catching the unclassified and unnamed little black fish, an inch long, half-eel and half-scaled, rotund with salmon-golden roe, that frequented the fresh water and that were esteemed, raw and whole, fresh or putrid, a perfect delicacy. Prone in the muck of the decaying jungle-floor, Balatta threw herself, clutching his ankles with her hands, kissing his feet and making slubbery noises that chilled his backbone up and down again. She begged him to kill her rather than exact this ultimate love-payment. She told him of the penalty of breaking the taboo of the Red One—a week of torture, living, the details of which she yammered out from her face in the mire until he realized that he was yet a tyro in knowledge of the frightfulness the human was capable of wreaking on the human.

Yet did Bassett insist on having his man's will satisfied, at the woman's risk, that he might solve the mystery of the Red One's singing, though she should die long and horribly and screaming. And Balatta, being mere woman, yielded. She led him into the forbidden quadrant. An abrupt mountain, shouldering in from the north to meet a similar intrusion from the south, tormented the stream in which they had fished into a deep and gloomy gorge. After a mile along the gorge, the way plunged sharply upward until they crossed a saddle of raw limestone which attracted his geologist's eye. Still climbing, although he paused often from sheer physical weakness, they scaled forest-clad heights until they emerged on a naked mesa or tableland. Bassett recognized the stuff of its composition as black volcanic sand, and knew that a pocket magnet could have captured a full load of the sharply angular grains he trod upon.

And then, holding Balatta by the hand and leading her onward, he came to it—a tremendous pit, obviously artificial, in the heart of the plateau. Old history, the South Seas Sailing Directions, scores of remembered data and connotations swift and furious, surged through his brain. It was Mendana who had discovered the islands and named them Solomon's, believing that he had found that monarch's fabled mines. They had laughed at the old navigator's child-like credulity; and yet here stood himself, Bassett, on the rim of an excavation for all the world like the diamond pits of South Africa.

But no diamond this that he gazed down upon. Rather was it a pearl, with the depth of iridescence of a pearl; but of a size all pearls of earth and time welded into one, could not have totaled; and of a color undreamed of any pearl, or of anything else, for that matter, for it was the color of the Red One. And the Red One himself Bassett knew it to be on the instant. A perfect sphere, fully two hundred feet in diameter, the top of it was a hundred feet below the level of the rim. He likened the color quality of it to lacquer. Indeed, he took it to be some sort of lacquer, applied by man, but a lacquer too marvelously clever to have been manufactured by the bush-folk. Brighter than bright cherry-red, its richness of color was as if it were red builded upon red. It glowed and iridesced in the sunlight as if gleaming up from underlay under underlay of red.

In vain Balatta strove to dissuade him from descending. She threw herself in the dirt; but, when he continued down the trail that spiraled the pit-wall, she followed, cringing and whimpering her terror. That the red sphere had been dug out as a precious thing, was patent. Considering the paucity of members of the federated twelve villages and their primitive tools and methods, Bassett knew that the toil of a myriad generations could scarcely have made that enormous excavation.

He found the pit bottom carpeted with human bones, among which, battered and defaced, lay village gods of wood and stone. Some, covered with obscene totemic figures and designs, were carved from solid tree trunks forty or fifty feet in length. He noted the absence of the shark and turtle gods, so common among the shore villages, and was amazed at the constant recurrence of the helmet motive. What did these jungle savages of the dark heart of Guadalcanal know of helmets? Had Mendana's men-at-arms worn helmets and penetrated here centuries before? And if not, then whence had the bush-folk caught the motive?

Advancing over the litter of gods and bones, Balatta whimpering at his heels, Bassett entered the shadow of the Red One and passed on under its gigantic overhang until he touched it with his finger-tips. No lacquer that. Nor was the surface smooth as it should have been in the case of lacquer. On the contrary, it was corrugated and pitted, with here and there patches that showed signs of heat and fusing. Also, the substance of it was metal, though unlike any metal or combination of metals he had ever known. As for the color itself, he decided it to be no application. It was the intrinsic color of the metal itself.

He moved his finger-tips, which up to that had merely rested, along the surface, and felt the whole gigantic sphere quicken and live and respond. It was incredible! So light a touch on so vast a mass! Yet did it quiver under the fingertip caress in rhythmic vibrations that became whisperings and rustlings and mutterings of sound—but of sound so different; so elusive thin that it was shimmeringly sibilant; so mellow that it was maddening sweet, piping like an elfin horn, which last was just what Bassett decided would be like a peal from some bell of the gods reaching earthward from across space.

He looked to Balatta with swift questioning; but the voice of the Red One he had evoked had flung her face-downward and moaning among the bones. He returned to contemplation of the prodigy. Hollow it was, and of no metal known on earth, was his conclusion. It was right-named by the ones of old-time as the Star-Born. Only from the stars could it have come, and no thing of chance was it. It was a creation of artifice and mind. Such perfection of form, such hollowness that it certainly possessed, could not be the result of mere fortuitousness. A child of intelligences, remote and unguessable, working corporally in metals, it indubitably was. He stared at it in amaze, his brain a racing wild-fire of hypotheses to account for this far-journeyer who had adventured the night of space, threaded the stars, and now rose before him and above him, exhumed by patient anthropophagi, pitted and lacquered by its fiery bath in two atmospheres.

But was the color a lacquer of heat upon some familiar metal? Or was it an intrinsic quality of the metal itself? He thrust in the blade-point of his pocket-knife to test the constitution of the stuff. Instantly the entire sphere burst into a mighty whispering, sharp with protest, almost twanging goldenly if a whisper could possibly be considered to twang, rising higher, sinking deeper, the two extremes of the registry of sound threatening to complete the circle and coalesce into the bull-mouthed thundering he had so often heard beyond the taboo distance.

Forgetful of safety, of his own life itself, entranced by the wonder of the unthinkable and unguessable thing, he raised his knife to strike heavily from a long stroke, but was prevented by Balatta. She upreared on her own knees in an agony of terror, clasping his knees and supplicating him to desist. In the intensity of her desire to impress him, she put her forearm between her teeth and sank them to the bone.

He scarcely observed her act, although he yielded automatically to his gentler instincts and withheld the knife-hack. To him, human life had dwarfed to microscopic proportions before this colossal portent of higher life from within the distances of the sidereal universe. As had she been a dog, he kicked the ugly little bushwoman to her feet and compelled her to start with him on an encirclement of the base. Part way around, he encountered horrors. Even, among the others, did he recognize the sun-shriveled remnant of the nine-years girl who had accidentally broken Chief Gngngn's personality taboo. And, among what was left of these that had passed, he encountered what was left of one who had not yet passed. Truly had the bush-folk named themselves into the name of the Red One, seeing in him their own image which they strove to placate and please with such red offerings.

Farther around, always treading the bones and images of humans and gods that constituted the floor of this ancient charnel house of sacrifice, he came upon the device by which the Red One was made to send his call singing thunderingly across the jungle-belts and grass-lands to the far beach of Ringmanu. Simple and primitive was it as was the Red One's consummate artifice. A great king-post, half a hundred feet in length, seasoned by centuries of superstitious care, carven into dynasties of gods, each superimposed, each helmeted, each seated

in the open mouth of a crocodile, was slung by ropes, twisted of climbing vegetable parasites, from the apex of a tripod of three great forest
trunks, themselves carved into grinning and grotesque adumbrations
of man's modern concepts of art and god. From the striker king-post,
were suspended ropes of climbers to which men could apply their
strength and direction. Like a battering ram, this king-post could be
driven end-onward against the mighty, red-iridescent sphere.

Here was where Ngurn officiated and functioned religiously for
himself and the twelve tribes under him. Bassett laughed aloud, almost
with madness, at the thought of this wonderful messenger, winged
with intelligence across space, to fall into a bushman stronghold and
be worshiped by ape-like, man-eating and head-hunting savages. It was
as if God's Word had fallen into the muck mire of the abyss underlying
the bottom of hell; as if Jehovah's Commandments had been presented
on carved stone to the monkeys of the monkey cage at the Zoo; as if
the Sermon on the Mount had been preached in a roaring bedlam of
lunatics.

The slow weeks passed. The nights, by election, Bassett spent on the
ashen floor of the devil-devil house, beneath the ever-swinging, slow-
curing heads. His reason for this was that it was taboo to the lesser
sex of woman, and, therefore, a refuge for him from Balatta, who grew
more persecutingly and perilously loverly as the Southern Cross rode
higher in the sky and marked the imminence of her nuptials. His days
Bassett spent in a hammock swung under the shade of the great breadfruit tree before the devil-devil house. There were breaks in this program, when, in the comas of his devastating fever-attacks, he lay for
days and nights in the house of heads. Ever he struggled to combat
the fever, to live, to continue to live, to grow strong and stronger
against the day when he would be strong enough to dare the grass-
lands and the belted jungle beyond, and win to the beach, and to some
labor-recruiting, black-birding ketch or schooner, and on to civilization and the men of civilization, to whom he could give news of the
message from other worlds that lay, darkly worshiped by beast-men,
in the black heart of Guadalcanal's midmost center.

On other nights, lying late under the breadfruit tree, Bassett spent
long hours watching the slow setting of the western stars beyond the
black wall of jungle where it had been thrust back by the clearing for
the village. Possessed of more than a cursory knowledge of astronomy,
he took a sick man's pleasure in speculating as to the dwellers on the
unseen worlds of those incredibly remote suns, to haunt whose houses

of light, life came forth, a shy visitant, from the rayless crypts of matter. He could no more apprehend limits to time than bounds to space. No subversive radium speculations had shaken his steady scientific faith in the conservation of energy and the indestructibility of matter. Always and forever must there have been stars. And surely, in that cosmic ferment, all must be comparatively alike, comparatively of the same substance, or substances, save for the freaks of the ferment. All must obey, or compose, the same laws that ran without infraction through the entire experience of man. Therefore, he argued and agreed, must worlds and life be appanages to all the suns as they were appanages to the particular sun of his own solar system.

Even as he lay here, under the breadfruit tree, an intelligence that stared across the starry gulfs, so must all the universe be exposed to the ceaseless scrutiny of innumerable eyes, like his, though grantedly different, with behind them, by the same token, intelligences that questioned and sought the meaning and the construction of the whole. So reasoning, he felt his soul go forth in kinship with that august company, that multitude whose gaze was forever upon the arras of infinity.

Who were they, what were they, those far distant and superior ones who had bridged the sky with their gigantic, red-iridescent, heaven-singing message? Surely, and long since, had they, too, trod the path on which man had so recently, by the calendar of the cosmos, set his feet. And to be able to send such a message across the pit of space, surely they had reached those heights to which man, in tears and travail and bloody sweat, in darkness and confusion of many counsels, was so slowly struggling. And what were they on their heights? Had they won Brotherhood? Or had they learned that the law of love imposed the penalty of weakness and decay? Was strife, life? Was the rule of all the universe the pitiless rule of natural selection? And, and most immediately and poignantly, were their far conclusions, their long-won wisdoms, shut even then in the huge, metallic heart of the Red One, waiting for the first earth-man to read? Of one thing he was certain: No drop of red dew shaken from the lion-mane of some sun in torment, was the sounding sphere. It was of design, not chance, and it contained the speech and wisdom of the stars.

What engines and elements and mastered forces, what lore and mysteries and destiny-controls, might be there! Undoubtedly, since so much could be inclosed in so little a thing as the foundation stone of public building, this enormous sphere should contain vast histories, profounds of research achieved beyond man's wildest guesses, laws and formulæ that, easily mastered, would make man's life on earth, individual and collective, spring up from its present mire to inconceivable heights of purity and power. It was Time's greatest gift to blindfold, insatiable, and sky-aspiring man. And to him, Bassett, had been vouchsafed the lordly fortune to be the first to receive this message from man's interstellar kin!

No white man, much less no outland man of the other bush-tribes, had gazed upon the Red One and lived. Such the law expounded by Ngurn to Bassett. There was such a thing as blood brotherhood, Bassett, in return, had often argued in the past. But Ngurn had stated solemnly no. Even the blood brotherhood was outside the favor of the Red One. Only a man born within the tribe could look upon the Red One and live. But now, his guilty secret known only to Balatta, whose fear of immolation before the Red One fast-sealed her lips, the situation was different. What he had to do was to recover from the abominable fevers that weakened him and gain to civilization. Then would he lead an expedition back, and, although the entire population of Guadalcanal be destroyed, extract from the heart of the Red One the message of the world from other worlds.

But Bassett's relapses grew more frequent, his brief convalescences less and less vigorous, his periods of coma longer, until he came to know, beyond the last promptings of the optimism inherent in so tremendous a constitution as his own, that he would never live to cross the grass lands, perforate the perilous coast jungle, and reach the sea. He faded as the Southern Cross rose higher in the sky, till even Balatta knew that he would be dead ere the nuptial date determined by his taboo. Ngurn made pilgrimage personally and gathered the smoke materials for the curing of Bassett's head, and to him made proud announcement and exhibition of the artistic perfectness of his intention when Bassett should be dead. As for himself, Bassett was not shocked. Too long and too deeply had life ebbed down in him to bite him with fear of its impending extinction. He continued to persist, alternating periods of unconsciousness with periods of semi-consciousness, dreamy and unreal, in which he idly wondered whether he had ever truly beheld the Red One or whether it was a nightmare fancy of delirium.

Came the day when all mists and cobwebs dissolved, when he found his brain clear as a bell, and took just appraisement of his body's weakness. Neither hand nor foot could he lift. So little control of his body did he have, that he was scarcely aware of possessing one. Lightly indeed his flesh sat upon his soul, and his soul, in its briefness of clarity, knew by its very clarity, that the black of cessation was near.

He knew the end was close; knew that in all truth he had with his eyes beheld the Red One, the messenger between the worlds; knew that he would never live to carry that message to the world—that message, for aught to the contrary, which might already have waited man's hearing in the heart of Guadalcanal for ten thousand years. And Bassett stirred with resolve, calling Ngurn to him, out under the shade of the breadfruit tree, and with the old devil-devil doctor discussing the terms and arrangements of his last life effort, his final adventure in the quick of the flesh.

"I know the law, O Ngurn," he concluded the matter. "Whoso is not of the folk may not look upon the Red One and live. I shall not live anyway. Your young men shall carry me before the face of the Red One, and I shall look upon him, and hear his voice, and thereupon die, under your hand, O Ngurn. Thus will the three things be satisfied: the law, my desire, and your quicker possession of my head for which all your preparations wait."

To which Ngurn consented, adding:

"It is better so. A sick man who cannot get well is foolish to live on for so little a while. Also, is it better for the living that he should go. You have been much in the way of late. Not but what it was good for me to talk to such a wise one. But for moons of days we have held little talk. Instead, you have taken up room in the house of heads, making noises like a dying pig, or talking much and loudly in your own language which I do not understand. This has been a confusion to me, for I like to think on the great things of the light and dark as I turn the heads in the smoke. Your much noise has thus been a disturbance to the long-learning and hatching of the final wisdom that will be mine before I die. As for you, upon whom the dark has already brooded, it is well that you die now. And I promise you, in the long days to come when I turn your head in the smoke, no man of the tribe shall come in to disturb us. And I will tell you many secrets, for I am an old man and very wise, and I shall be adding wisdom to wisdom as I turn your head in the smoke."

So a litter was made, and, borne on the shoulders of half a dozen of the men, Bassett departed on the last little adventure that was to cap the total adventure, for him, of living. With a body of which he was scarcely aware, for even the pain had been exhausted out of it, and with a bright clear brain that accommodated him to a quiet ecstasy of sheer lucidness of thought, he lay back on the lurching litter and watched the fading of the passing world, beholding for the last time the breadfruit tree before the devil-devil house, the dim day be-

neath the matted jungle roof, the gloomy gorge between the shouldering mountains, the saddle of raw limestone, and the mesa of black,
volcanic sand.

Down the spiral path of the pit they bore him, encircling the
sheening, glowing Red One that seemed ever imminent to iridesce from
color and light into sweet singing and thunder. And over bones and
logs of immolated men and gods they bore him, past the horrors of
other immolated ones that yet lived, to the three-king-post tripod and
the huge king-post striker.

Here Bassett, helped by Ngurn and Balatta, weakly sat up, swaying weakly from the hips, and with clear, unfaltering, all-seeing eyes
gazed upon the Red One.

"Once, O Ngurn," he said, not taking his eyes from the sheening,
vibrating surface whereon and wherein all the shades of cherry-red
played unceasingly, ever a-quiver to change into sound, to become
silken rustlings, silvery whisperings, golden thrummings of cords, velvet pipings of elfland, mellow-distances of thunderings.

"I wait," Ngurn prompted after a long pause, the long-handled
tomahawk unassumingly ready in his hand.

"Once, O Ngurn," Bassett repeated, "let the Red One speak so
that I may see it speak as well as hear it. Then strike, thus, when I
raise my hand; for, when I raise my hand, I shall drop my head forward and make place for the stroke at the base of my neck. But, O
Ngurn, I, who am about to pass out of the light of day forever, would
like to pass with the wonder-voice of the Red One singing greatly in
my ears."

"And I promise you that never will a head be so well cured as
yours," Ngurn assured him, at the same time signaling the tribesmen
to man the propelling ropes suspended from the king-post striker.
"Your head shall be my greatest piece of work in the curing of heads."

Bassett smiled quietly to the old one's conceit, as the great carved
log, drawn back through two-score feet of space, was released. The
next moment he was lost in ecstasy at the abrupt and thunderous
liberation of sound. But such thunder! Mellow it was with precious-
ness of all sounding metals. Archangels spoke in it; it was magnificently beautiful before all other sounds; it was invested with the
intelligence of supermen of planets of other suns; it was the voice of
God, seducing and commanding to be heard. And—the everlasting
miracle of that interstellar metal! Bassett, with his own eyes, saw color
and colors transform into sound till the whole visible surface of the
vast sphere was a-crawl and titillant and vaporous with what he could

not tell was color or was sound. In that moment the interstices of matter were his, and the interfusings and intermating transfusings of matter and force.

Time passed. At the last Bassett was brought back from his ecstasy by an impatient movement of Ngurn. He had quite forgotten the old devil-devil one. A quick flash of fancy brought a husky chuckle into Bassett's throat. His shotgun lay beside him in the litter. All he had to do, muzzle to head, was press the trigger and blow his head into nothingness.

But why cheat him? was Bassett's next thought. Head-hunting, cannibal beast of a human that was as much ape as human, nevertheless Old Ngurn had, according to his lights, played squarer than square. Ngurn was in himself a fore-runner of ethics and contract, of consideration, and gentleness in man. No, Bassett decided; it would be a ghastly pity and an act of dishonor to cheat the old fellow at the last. His head was Ngurn's, and Ngurn's head to cure it would be.

And Bassett, raising his hand in signal, bending forward his head as agreed so as to expose cleanly the articulation to his taut spinal cord, forgot Balatta, who was merely a woman, a woman merely and only and undesired. He knew, without seeing, when the razor-edged hatchet rose in the air behind him. And for that instant, ere the end, there fell upon Bassett the shadow of the Unknown, a sense of impending marvel of the rending of walls before the imaginable. Almost, when he knew the blow had started and just ere the edge of steel bit the flesh and nerves, it seemed that he gazed upon the serene face of the Medusa, Truth—And, simultaneous with the bite of the steel on the onrush of the dark, in a flashing instant of fancy, he saw the vision of his head turning slowly, always turning, in the devil-devil house beside the breadfruit tree.

WAIKIKI, HONOLULU
*May 22, 1916*

# THE WATER BABY

I LENT A WEARY EAR to old Kohokumu's interminable chanting of the deeds and adventures of Maui, the Promethean demigod of Polynesia who fished up dry land from ocean depths with hooks made fast to heaven, who lifted up the sky where-under previously men had gone on all fours, not having space to stand erect, and who made the sun with its sixteen snared legs stand still and agree thereafter to traverse the sky more slowly—the sun being evidently a trade-unionist and believing in the six-hour day, while Maui stood for the open shop and the twelve-hour day.

"Now this," said Kohokumu, "is from Queen Liliuokalani's own family mele:

> " 'Maui became restless and fought the sun
> With a noose that he laid.
> And winter won the sun,
> And summer was won by Maui. . . .' "

Born in the Islands myself, I know the Hawaiian myths better than this old fisherman, although I possessed not his memorization that enabled him to recite them endless hours.

"And you believe all this?" I demanded in the sweet Hawaiian tongue.

"It was a long time ago," he pondered. "I never saw Maui with my own eyes. But all our old men from all the way back tell us these things, as I, an old man, tell them to my sons and grandsons, who will tell them to their sons and grandsons all the way ahead to come."

"You believe," I persisted, "that whopper of Maui roping the sun like a wild steer, and that other whopper of heaving up the sky from off the earth?"

"I am of little worth, and am not wise, O Lakana," my fisherman made answer. "Yet have I read the Hawaiian bible the missionaries translated to us, and there have I read that your Big Man of the Beginning made the earth and sky and sun and moon and stars, and all manner of animals from horses to cockroaches and from centipedes and mosquitoes to sea lice and jellyfish, and man and woman and everything, and all in six days. Why, Maui didn't do anything like that much. He didn't *make* anything. He just put things in order, that was all, and it took him a long, long time to make the improvements. And anyway, it is much easier and more reasonable to believe the little whopper than the big whopper."

And what could I reply? He had me on the matter of reasonableness. Besides, my head ached. And the funny thing, as I admitted to myself, was that evolution teaches in no uncertain voice that man did run on all fours ere he came to walk upright, that astronomy states flatly that the speed of the revolution of the earth on its axis has diminished steadily, thus increasing the length of day, and that the seismologists accept that all the islands of Hawaii were elevated from the ocean floor by volcanic action.

Fortunately, I saw a bamboo pole, floating on the surface several hundred feet away, suddenly up-end and start a very devil's dance. This was a diversion from the profitless discussion, and Kohokumu and I dipped our paddles and raced the little outrigger canoe to the dancing pole. Kohokumu caught the line that was fast to the butt of the pole and underhanded it in until a two-foot *ukikiki*, battling fiercely to the end, flashed its wet silver in the sun and began beating a tattoo on the inside bottom of the canoe. Kohokumu picked up a squirming, slimy squid, with his teeth bit a chunk of live bait out of it, attached the bait to the hook, and dropped line and sinker overside. The stick floated flat on the surface of the water, and the canoe drifted slowly away. With a survey of the crescent composed of a score of such sticks all lying flat, Kohokumu wiped his hands on his naked sides and lifted the wearisome and centuries-old chant of Kuali:

> " 'Oh, the great fishhook of Maui!
> Manai-i-ka-lani—"made fast to the heavens"!

*An earth-twisted cord ties the hook,*
*Engulfed from lofty Kauiki!*
*Its bait the red-billed Alae,*
*The bird to Hina sacred!*
*It sinks far down to Hawaii,*
*Struggling and in pain dying!*
*Caught is the land beneath the water,*
*Floated up, up to the surface,*
*But Hina hid a wing of the bird*
*And broke the land beneath the water!*
*Below was the bait snatched away*
*And eaten at once by the fishes,*
*The Ulua of the deep muddy places!'* "

His aged voice was hoarse and scratchy from the drinking of too much swipes at a funeral the night before, nothing of which contributed to make me less irritable. My head ached. The sun glare on the water made my eyes ache, while I was suffering more than half a touch of mal de mer from the antic conduct of the outrigger on the blobby sea. The air was stagnant. In the lee of Waihee, between the white beach and the reef, no whisper of breeze eased the still sultriness. I really think I was too miserable to summon the resolution to give up the fishing and go in to shore.

Lying back with closed eyes, I lost count of time. I even forgot that Kohokumu was chanting till reminded of it by his ceasing. An exclamation made me bare my eyes to the stab of the sun. He was gazing down through the water glass.

"It's a big one," he said, passing me the device and slipping overside feetfirst into the water.

He went under without splash and ripple, turned over, and swam down. I followed his progress through the water glass, which is merely an oblong box a couple of feet long, open at the top, the bottom sealed water-tight with a sheet of ordinary glass.

Now Kohokumu was a bore, and I was squeamishly out of sorts with him for his volubleness, but I could not help admiring him as I watched him go down. Past seventy years of age, lean as a spear, and shriveled like a mummy, he was doing what few young athletes of my race would do or could do. It was forty feet to bottom. There, partly exposed but mostly hidden under the bulge of a coral lump, I could discern his objective. His keen eyes had caught the projecting tentacle of a squid. Even as he swam, the tentacle was lazily withdrawn, so that there was no sign of the creature. But the brief exposure of the portion of one tentacle had advertised its owner as a squid of size.

The pressure at a depth of forty feet is no joke for a young man, yet it did not seem to inconvenience this oldster. I am certain it never crossed his mind to be inconvenienced. Unarmed, bare of body save for a brief *malo* or loin cloth, he was undeterred by the formidable creature that constituted his prey. I saw him steady himself with his right hand on the coral lump, and thrust his left arm into the hole to the shoulder. Half a minute elapsed, during which time he seemed to be groping and rooting around with his left hand. Then tentacle after tentacle, myriad-suckered and wildly waving, emerged. Laying hold of his arm, they writhed and coiled about his flesh like so many snakes. With a heave and a jerk appeared the entire squid, a proper devilfish or octopus.

But the old man was in no hurry for his natural element, the air above the water. There, forty feet beneath, wrapped about by an octopus that measured nine feet across from tentacle tip to tentacle tip and that could well drown the stoutest swimmer, he cooly and casually did the one thing that gave to him his empery over the monster. He shoved his lean, hawklike face into the very center of the slimy, squirming mass, and with his several ancient fangs bit into the heart and the life of the matter. This accomplished, he came upward slowly, as a swimmer should who is changing atmospheres from the depths. Alongside the canoe, still in the water and peeling off the grisly clinging thing, the incorrigible old sinner burst into the *pule* of triumph which had been chanted by countless squid-catching generations before him:

> " 'O Kanaloa of the taboo nights!
> *Stand upright on the solid floor!*
> *Stand upon the floor where lies the squid!*
> *Stand up to take the squid of the deep sea!*
>
> *Rise up, O Kanaloa!*
> *Stir up! Stir up! Let the squid awake!*
> *Let the squid that lies flat awake! Let the*
> *squid that lies spread out. . . .' "*

I closed my eyes and ears, not offering to lend him a hand, secure in the knowledge that he could climb back unaided into the unstable craft without the slightest risk of upsetting it.

"A very fine squid," he crooned. "It is a wahine squid. I shall now sing to you the song of the cowrie shell, the red cowrie shell that we used as a bait for the squid—"

"You were disgraceful last night at the funeral," I headed him off. "I heard all about it. You made much noise. You sang till everybody was deaf. You insulted the son of the widow. You drank swipes like a pig. Swipes are not good for your extreme age. Some day you will wake up dead. You ought to be a wreck to-day—"

"Ha!" he chuckled. "And you, who drank no swipes, who was a babe unborn when I was already an old man, who went to bed last night with the sun and the chickens—this day you are a wreck. Explain me that. My ears are as thirsty to listen as was my throat thirsty last night. And here to-day, behold, I am, as that Englishman who came here in his yacht used to say, I am in fine form, in devilish fine form."

"I give you up," I retorted, shrugging my shoulders. "Only one thing is clear, and that is that the devil doesn't want you. Report of your singing has gone before you."

"No," he pondered the idea carefully. "It is not that. The devil will be glad for my coming, for I have some very fine songs for him, and scandals and old gossips of the high aliis that will make him scratch his sides. So let me explain to you the secret of my birth. The Sea is my mother. I was born in a double canoe, during a Kona gale, in the channel of Kahoolawe. From her, the Sea, my mother, I received my strength. Whenever I return to her arms, as for a breast clasp, as I have returned this day, I grow strong again and immediately. She, to me, is the milk giver, the life source—"

"Shades of Antæus!" thought I.

"Some day," old Kohokumu rambled on, "when I am really old, I shall be reported of men as drowned in the sea. This will be an idle thought of men. In truth, I shall have returned into the arms of my mother, there to rest under the heart of her breast until the second birth of me, when I shall emerge into the sun a flashing youth of splendor like Maui himself when he was golden young."

"A queer religion," I commented.

"When I was younger I muddled my poor head over queerer religions," old Kohokumu retorted. "But listen, O Young Wise One, to my elderly wisdom. This I know: as I grow old I seek less for the truth from without me, and find more of the truth from within me. Why have I thought this thought of my return to my mother and of my rebirth from my mother into the sun? You do not know. I do not know, save that, without whisper of man's voice or printed word, without prompting from other-where, this thought has arisen from within me, from the deeps of me that are as deep as the sea. I am not a god. I do not make things. Therefore I have not made this thought. I do not know its father or its mother. It is of old time before me, and therefore it is true. Man does not make truth. Man, if he be not blind, only recognizes truth when he sees it. Is this thought that I have thought a dream?"

"Perhaps it is you that are a dream," I laughed. "And that I and sky and sea and the iron-hard land are dreams, all dreams."

"I have often thought that," he assured me soberly. "It may well be so. Last night I dreamed I was a lark bird, a beautiful singing lark of the sky like the larks on the upland pastures of Haleakala. And I flew up, up toward the sun, singing, singing, as old Kohokumu never sang. I tell you now that I dreamed I was a lark bird singing in the sky. But may not I, the real I, be the lark bird? And may not the telling of it be the dream that I, the lark bird, am dreaming now? Who are you to tell me aye or no? Dare you tell me I am not a lark bird asleep and dreaming that I am old Kohokumu?"

I shrugged my shoulders, and he continued triumphantly.

"And how do you know but what you are old Maui himself asleep and dreaming that you are John Lakana talking with me in a canoe? And may you not awake, old Maui yourself, and scratch your sides and say that you had a funny dream in which you dreamed you were a haole?"

"I don't know," I admitted. "Besides, you wouldn't believe me."

"There is much more in dreams than we know," he assured me with great solemnity. "Dreams go deep, all the way down, maybe to before the beginning. May not old Maui have only dreamed he pulled Hawaii up from the bottom of the sea? Then would this Hawaii land be a dream, and you and I and the squid there only parts of Maui's dream? And the lark bird, too?"

He sighed and let his head sink on his breast.

"And I worry my old head about the secrets undiscoverable," he resumed, "until I grow tired and want to forget, and so I drink swipes, and go fishing, and sing old songs, and dream I am a lark bird singing in the sky. I like that best of all, and often I dream it when I have drunk much swipes—"

In great dejection of mood he peered down into the lagoon through the water glass.

"There will be no more bites for a while," he announced. "The fish sharks are prowling around, and we shall have to wait until they are gone. And so that the time shall not be heavy, I will sing you the canoe-hauling song to Lono. You remember:

> " 'Give to me the trunk of the tree, O Lono!
> Give me the tree's main root, O Lono!
> Give me the ear of the tree, O Lono!—' "

"For the love of mercy, don't sing!" I cut him short. "I've got a headache, and your singing hurts. You may be in devilish fine form to-day, but your throat is rotten. I'd rather you talked about dreams, or told me whoppers."

"It is too bad that you are sick, and you so young," he conceded cheerily. "And I shall not sing any more. I shall tell you something you do not know and have never heard; something that is no dream and no whopper, but is what I know to have happened. Not very long ago there lived here, on the beach beside this very lagoon, a young boy whose name was Keikiwai, which, as you know, means Water Baby. He was truly a water baby. His gods were the sea and fish gods, and he was born with knowledge of the language of fishes, which the fishes did not know until the sharks found it out one day when they heard him talk it.

"It happened this way. The word had been brought, and the commands, by swift runners, that the king was making a progress around the island, and that on the next day a luau was to be served him by the dwellers here of Waihee. It was always a hardship, when the king made a progress, for the few dwellers in small places to fill his many stomachs with food. For he came always with his wife and her women, with his priests and sorcerers, his dancers and flute players and hula singers, and fighting men and servants, and his high chiefs with their wives, and sorcerers and fighting men and servants.

"Sometimes, in small places like Waihee, the path of his journey was marked afterward by leanness and famine. But a king must be fed, and it is not good to anger a king. So, like warning in advance of disaster, Waihee heard of his coming, and all food-getters of field and pond and mountain and sea were busied with getting food for the feast. And behold, everything was got, from the choicest of royal taro to sugar-cane joints for the roasting, from opihis to limu, from fowl to wild pig and poi-fed puppies—everything save one thing. The fishermen failed to get lobsters.

"Now be it known that the king's favorite food was lobster. He esteemed it above all *kao-kao* (food), and his runners had made special mention of it. And there were no lobsters, and it is not good to anger a king in the belly of him. Too many sharks had come inside the reef. That was the trouble. A young girl and an old man had been eaten by them. And of the young men who dared dive for lobsters, one was eaten, and one lost an arm, and another lost one hand and one foot.

"But there was Keikiwai, the Water Baby, only eleven years old, but half fish himself and talking the language of fishes. To his father the head men came, begging him to send the Water Baby to get lobsters to fill the king's belly and divert his anger.

"Now this, what happened, was known and observed. For the fishermen and their women, and the taro growers and the bird catchers, and the head men, and all Waihee, came down and stood back from the edge of the rock where the Water Baby stood and looked down at the lobsters far beneath on the bottom.

"And a shark, looking up with its cat's eyes, observed him, and sent out the shark call of 'fresh meat' to assemble all the sharks in the lagoon. For the sharks work thus together, which is why they are strong. And the sharks answered the call till there were forty of them, long ones and short ones and lean ones and round ones, forty of them by count; and they talked to one another, saying: 'Look at that titbit of a child, that morsel delicious of human-flesh sweetness without the salt of the sea in it, of which salt we have too much, savory and good to eat, melting to delight under our hearts as our bellies embrace it and extract from it its sweet.'

"Much more they said, saying: 'He has come for the lobsters. When he dives in he is for one of us. Not like the old man we ate yesterday, tough to dryness with age, nor like the young men whose members were too hard-muscled, but tender, so tender that he will melt in our gullets ere our bellies receive him. When he dives in, we will all rush for him, and the lucky one of us will get him, and, gulp, he will be gone, one bite and one swallow, into the belly of the luckiest one of us.'

"And Keikiwai, the Water Baby, heard the conspiracy, knowing the shark language; and he addressed a prayer, in the shark language, to the shark god Moku-halii, and the sharks heard and waved their tails to one another and winked their cat's eyes in token that they understood his talk. And then he said: 'I shall now dive for a lobster for the king. And no hurt shall befall me, because the shark with the shortest tail is my friend and will protect me.'

"And, so saying, he picked up a chunk of lava rock and tossed it into the water, with a big splash, twenty feet to one side. The forty sharks rushed for the splash, while he dived, and by the time they discovered they had missed him, he had gone to the bottom and come back and climbed out, within his hand a fat lobster, a wahine lobster, full of eggs, for the king.

" 'Ha!' said the sharks, very angry. 'There is among us a traitor. The titbit of a child, the morsel of sweetness, has spoken, and has exposed the one among us who has saved him. Let us now measure the length of our tails!'

"Which they did, in a long row, side by side, the shorter-tailed ones cheating and stretching to gain length on themselves, the longer-tailed ones cheating and stretching in order not to be out-cheated and out-stretched. They were very angry with the one with the shortest tail, and him they rushed upon from every side and devoured till nothing was left of him.

"Again they listened while they waited for the Water Baby to dive in. And again the Water Baby made his prayer in the shark language to Mokuhalii, and said: 'The shark with the shortest tail is my friend and will protect me.' And again the Water Baby tossed in a chunk of lava, this time twenty feet away off to the other side. The sharks rushed for the splash, and in their haste ran into one another, and splashed with their tails till the water was all foam and they could see nothing, each thinking some other was swallowing the titbit. And the Water Baby came up and climbed out with another fat lobster for the king.

"And the thirty-nine sharks measured tails, devouring the one with the shortest tail, so that there were only thirty-eight sharks. And the Water Baby continued to do what I have said, and the sharks to do what I have told you, while for each shark that was eaten by his brothers there was another fat lobster laid on the rock for the king. Of course, there was much quarreling and argument among the sharks when it came to measuring tails; but in the end it worked out in right-ness and justice, for, when only two sharks were left, they were the two biggest of the original forty.

"And the Water Baby again claimed the shark with the shortest tail was his friend, fooled the two sharks with another lava chunk, and brought up another lobster. The two sharks each claimed the other had the shorter tail, and each fought to eat the other, and the one with the longer tail won—"

"Hold, O Kohokumu!" I interrupted. "Remember that that shark had already—"

"I know just what you are going to say," he snatched his recital back from me. "And you are right. It took him so long to eat the thirty-ninth shark, for inside the thirty-ninth shark were already the nineteen other sharks he had eaten, and inside the fortieth shark were already the nineteen other sharks he had eaten, and he did not have the appetite he had started with. But do not forget he was a very big shark to begin with.

"It took him so long to eat the other shark, and the nineteen sharks inside the other shark, that he was still eating when darkness fell and the people of Waihee went away home with all the lobsters for the king. And didn't they find the last shark on the beach next morning dead and burst wide open with all he had eaten?"

Kohokumu fetched a full stop and held my eyes with his own shrewd ones.

"Hold, O Lakana!" he checked the speech that rushed to my tongue. "I know what next you would say. You would say that with my own eyes I did not see this, and therefore that I do not know what I have been telling you. But I do know, and I can prove it. My father's father knew the grandson of the Water Baby's father's uncle. Also, there, on the rocky point to which I point my finger now, is where the Water Baby stood and dived. I have dived for lobsters there myself. It is a great place for lobsters. Also, and often, have I seen sharks there. And there, on the bottom, as I should know, for I have seen and counted them, are the thirty-nine lava rocks thrown in by the Water Baby as I have described."

"But—" I began.

"Ha!" he baffled me. "Look! While we have talked the fish have begun again to bite."

He pointed to three of the bamboo poles erect and devil-dancing in token that fish were hooked and struggling on the lines beneath. As he bent to his paddle, he muttered, for my benefit:

"Of course I know. The thirty-nine lava rocks are still there. You can count them any day for yourself. Of course I know, and I know for a fact."

GLEN ELLEN
*October 2, 1916*

# The Call of the Wild

# I

## INTO THE PRIMITIVE

*"Old longings nomadic leap,*
*Chafing at custom's chain;*
*Again from its brumal sleep*
*Wakens the ferine strain."*

BUCK DID NOT READ the newspapers, or he would have known that trouble was brewing, not alone for himself, but for every tide-water dog, strong of muscle and with warm, long hair, from Puget Sound to San Diego. Because men, groping in the Arctic darkness, had found a yellow metal, and because steamship and transportation companies were booming the find, thousands of men were rushing into the Northland. These men wanted dogs, and the dogs they wanted were heavy dogs, with strong muscles by which to toil, and furry coats to protect them from the frost.

Buck lived at a big house in the sun-kissed Santa Clara Valley. Judge Miller's place, it was called. It stood back from the road, half hidden among the trees, through which glimpses could be caught of the wide cool veranda that ran around its four sides. The house was approached by gravelled driveways which wound about through wide-spreading lawns and under the interlacing boughs of tall poplars. At the rear things were on even a more spacious scale than at the front. There were great stables, where a dozen grooms and boys held forth, rows of vine-clad servants' cottages, an endless and orderly array of outhouses, long grape arbors, green pastures, orchards, and berry patches. Then there was the pumping plant for the artesian well, and the big cement tank where Judge Miller's boys took their morning plunge and kept cool in the hot afternoon.

And over this great demesne Buck ruled. Here he was born, and here he had lived the four years of his life. It was true, there were other dogs. There could not but be other dogs on so vast a place, but they did not count. They came and went, resided in the populous kennels, or lived obscurely in the recesses of the house after the fashion of Toots, the Japanese pug, or Ysabel, the Mexican hairless,—strange creatures that rarely put nose out of doors or set foot to ground. On the other hand, there were the fox terriers, a score of them at least, who yelped fearful promises at Toots and Ysabel looking out of the windows at them and protected by a legion of housemaids armed with brooms and mops.

But Buck was neither house-dog nor kennel-dog. The whole realm was his. He plunged into the swimming tank or went hunting with the Judge's sons; he escorted Mollie and Alice, the Judge's daughters, on long twilight or early morning rambles; on wintry nights he lay at the Judge's feet before the roaring library fire; he carried the Judge's grandsons on his back, or rolled them in the grass, and guarded their footsteps through wild adventures down to the fountain in the stable yard, and even beyond, where the paddocks were, and the berry patches. Among the terriers he stalked imperiously, and Toots and Ysabel he utterly ignored, for he was king,—king over all creeping, crawling, flying things of Judge Miller's place, humans included.

His father, Elmo, a huge St. Bernard, had been the Judge's inseparable companion, and Buck bid fair to follow in the way of his father. He was not so large,—he weighed only one hundred and forty pounds,—for his mother, Shep, had been a Scotch shepherd dog. Nevertheless, one hundred and forty pounds, to which was added the dignity that comes of good living and universal respect, enabled him to carry himself in right royal fashion. During the four years since his puppyhood he had lived the life of a sated aristocrat; he had a fine pride in himself; was even a trifle egotistical, as country gentlemen sometimes become because of their insular situation. But he had saved himself by not becoming a mere pampered house-dog. Hunting and kindred outdoor delights had kept down the fat and hardened his muscles; and to him, as to the cold-tubbing races, the love of water had been a tonic and a health preserver.

And this was the manner of dog Buck was in the fall of 1897, when the Klondike strike dragged men from all the world into the frozen North. But Buck did not read the newspapers, and he did not know that Manuel, one of the gardener's helpers, was an undesirable acquaintance. Manuel had one besetting sin. He loved to play Chinese lottery. Also, in his gambling, he had one besetting weakness—faith in a system; and this made his damnation certain. For to play a system requires money, while the wages of a gardener's helper do not lap over the needs of a wife and numerous progeny.

The Judge was at a meeting of the Raisin Growers Association, and the boys were busy organizing an athletic club, on the memorable night of Manuel's treachery. No one saw him and Buck go off through the orchard on what Buck imagined was merely a stroll. And with the exception of a solitary man, no one saw them arrive at the little flag station known as College Park. This man talked with Manuel, and money chinked between them.

"You might wrap up the goods before you deliver 'm," the stranger said gruffly, and Manuel doubled a piece of stout rope around Buck's neck under the collar.

"Twist it, an' you'll choke 'm plentee," said Manuel, and the stranger grunted a ready affirmative.

Buck had accepted the rope with quiet dignity. To be sure, it was an unwonted performance: but he had learned to trust in men he knew, and to give them credit for a wisdom that outreached his own. But when the ends of the rope were placed in the stranger's hands, he growled menacingly. He had merely intimated his displeasure, in his pride believing that to intimate was to command. But to his surprise the rope tightened around his neck, shutting off his breath. In quick rage he sprang at the man, who met him halfway, grappled him close by the throat, and with a deft twist threw him over on his back. Then the rope tightened mercilessly, while Buck struggled in a fury, his tongue lolling out of his mouth and his great chest panting futilely. Never in all his life had he been so vilely treated, and never in all his life had he been so angry. But his strength ebbed, his eyes glazed, and he knew nothing when the train was flagged and the two men threw him into the baggage car.

The next he knew, he was dimly aware that his tongue was hurting and that he was being jolted along in some kind of a conveyance.

The hoarse shriek of a locomotive whistling a crossing told him where he was. He had travelled too often with the Judge not to know the sensation of riding in a baggage car. He opened his eyes, and into them came the unbridled anger of a kidnapped king. The man sprang for his throat, but Buck was too quick for him. His jaws closed on the hand, nor did they relax till his senses were choked out of him once more.

"Yep, has fits," the man said, hiding his mangled hand from the baggageman, who had been attracted by the sounds of struggle. "I'm takin' 'm up for the boss to 'Frisco. A crack dog-doctor there thinks that he can cure 'm."

Concerning that night's ride, the man spoke most eloquently for himself, in a little shed back of a saloon on the San Francisco water front.

"All I get is fifty for it," he grumbled; "an' I wouldn't do it over for a thousand, cold cash."

His hand was wrapped in a bloody handkerchief, and the right trouser leg was ripped from knee to ankle.

"How much did the other mug get?" the saloon-keeper demanded.

"A hundred," was the reply. "Wouldn't take a sou less, so help me."

"That makes a hundred and fifty," the saloon-keeper calculated; "and he's worth it, or I'm a squarehead."

The kidnapper undid the bloody wrappings and looked at his lacerated hand. "If I don't get the hydrophoby—"

"It'll be because you was born to hang," laughed the saloon-keeper. "Here, lend me a hand before you pull your freight," he added.

Dazed, suffering intolerable pain from throat and tongue, with the life half throttled out of him, Buck attempted to face his tormentors. But he was thrown down and choked repeatedly, till they succeeded in filing the heavy brass collar from off his neck. Then the rope was removed, and he was flung into a cagelike crate.

There he lay for the remainder of the weary night, nursing his wrath and wounded pride. He could not understand what it all meant. What did they want with him, these strange men? Why were they keeping him pent up in this narrow crate? He did not know why, but he felt oppressed by the vague sense of impending calamity. Several times during the night he sprang to his feet when the shed door rattled open, expecting to see the Judge, or the boys at least. But each time it was the bulging face of the saloon-keeper that peered in at him by the sickly light of a tallow candle. And each time the joyful bark that trembled in Buck's throat was twisted into a savage growl.

But the saloon-keeper let him alone, and in the morning four men entered and picked up the crate. More tormentors, Buck decided, for they were evil-looking creatures, ragged and unkempt; and he stormed and raged at them through the bars. They only laughed and poked sticks at him, which he promptly assailed with his teeth till he realized that that was what they wanted. Whereupon he lay down sullenly and allowed the crate to be lifted into a wagon. Then he, and the crate in which he was imprisoned, began a passage through many hands. Clerks in the express office took charge of him; he was carted about in another wagon; a truck carried him, with an assortment of boxes and parcels, upon a ferry steamer; he was trucked off the steamer into a great railway depot, and finally he was deposited in an express car.

For two days and nights this express car was dragged along at the tail of shrieking locomotives; and for two days and nights Buck neither ate nor drank. In his anger he had met the first advances of the express messengers with growls, and they had retaliated by teasing him. When he flung himself against the bars, quivering and frothing, they laughed at him and taunted him. They growled and barked like detestable dogs, mewed, and flapped their arms and crowed. It was all very silly, he knew; but therefore the more outrage to his dignity, and his anger waxed and waxed. He did not mind the hunger so much, but the lack of water caused him severe suffering and fanned his wrath to fever-pitch. For that matter, high-strung and finely sensitive, the ill treatment had flung him into a fever, which was fed by the inflammation of his parched and swollen throat and tongue.

He was glad for one thing: the rope was off his neck. That had given them an unfair advantage; but now that it was off, he would show them. They would never get another rope around his neck. Upon that he was resolved. For two days and nights he neither ate nor drank, and during those two days and nights of torment, he accumulated a fund of wrath that boded ill for whoever first fell foul of him. His eyes turned blood-shot, and he was metamorphosed into a raging fiend. So changed was he that the Judge himself would not have recognized him; and the express messengers breathed with relief when they bundled him off the train at Seattle.

Four men gingerly carried the crate from the wagon into a small, high-walled back yard. A stout man, with a red sweater that sagged generously at the neck, came out and signed the book for the driver. That was the man, Buck divined, the next tormentor, and he hurled himself savagely against the bars. The man smiled grimly, and brought a hatchet and a club.

"You ain't going to take him out now?" the driver asked.

"Sure," the man replied, driving the hatchet into the crate for a pry.

There was an instantaneous scattering of the four men who had carried it in, and from safe perches on top the wall they prepared to watch the performance.

Buck rushed at the splintering wood, sinking his teeth into it, surging and wrestling with it. Wherever the hatchet fell on the outside, he was there on the inside, snarling and growling, as furiously anxious to get out as the man in the red sweater was calmly intent on getting him out.

"Now, you red-eyed devil," he said, when he had made an opening sufficient for the passage of Buck's body. At the same time he dropped the hatchet and shifted the club to his right hand.

And Buck was truly a red-eyed devil, as he drew himself together for the spring, hair bristling, mouth foaming, a mad glitter in his bloodshot eyes. Straight at the man he launched his one hundred and forty pounds of fury, surcharged with the pent passion of two days and nights. In mid air, just as his jaws were about to close on the man, he received a shock that checked his body and brought his teeth together with an agonizing clip. He whirled over, fetching the ground on his back and side. He had never been struck by a club in his life, and did not understand. With a snarl that was part bark and more scream he was again on his feet and launched into the air. And again the shock came and he was brought crushingly to the ground. This time he was aware that it was the club, but his madness knew no caution. A dozen times he charged, and as often the club broke the charge and smashed him down.

After a particularly fierce blow, he crawled to his feet, too dazed to rush. He staggered limply about, the blood flowing from nose and mouth and ears, his beautiful coat sprayed and flecked with bloody slaver. Then the man advanced and deliberately dealt him a frightful blow on the nose. All the pain he had endured was as nothing compared with the exquisite agony of this. With a roar that was almost lionlike in its ferocity, he again hurled himself at the man. But the man, shifting the club from right to left, coolly caught him by the under jaw, at the same time wrenching downward and backward. Buck described a complete circle in the air, and half of another, then crashed to the ground on his head and chest.

For the last time he rushed. The man struck the shrewd blow he had purposely withheld for so long, and Buck crumpled up and went down, knocked utterly senseless.

"He's no slouch at dog-breakin', that's wot I say," one of the men on the wall cried enthusiastically.

"Druther break cayuses any day, and twice on Sundays," was the reply of the driver, as he climbed on the wagon and started the horses.

Buck's senses came back to him, but not his strength. He lay where he had fallen, and from there he watched the man in the red sweater.

" 'Answers to the name of Buck,' " the man soliloquized, quoting from the saloon-keeper's letter which had announced the consignment of the crate and contents. "Well, Buck, my boy," he went on in a genial voice, "we've had our little ruction, and the best thing we can do is to let it go at that. You've learned your place, and I know mine. Be a good dog and all 'll go well and the goose hang high. Be a bad dog, and I'll whale the stuffin' outa you. Understand?"

As he spoke he fearlessly patted the head he had so mercilessly pounded, and though Buck's hair involuntarily bristled at touch of the hand, he endured it without protest. When the man brought him water he drank eagerly, and later bolted a generous meal of raw meat, chunk by chunk, from the man's hand.

He was beaten (he knew that); but he was not broken. He saw, once for all, that he stood no chance against a man with a club. He had learned the lesson, and in all his after life he never forgot it. That club was a revelation. It was his introduction to the reign of primitive law, and he met the introduction halfway. The facts of life took on a fiercer aspect; and while he faced that aspect uncowed, he faced it with all the latent cunning of his nature aroused. As the days went by, other dogs came, in crates and at the ends of ropes, some docilely, and some raging and roaring as he had come; and, one and all, he watched them pass under the dominion of the man in the red sweater. Again and again, as he looked at each brutal performance, the lesson was driven home to Buck: a man with a club was a lawgiver, a master to be obeyed, though not necessarily conciliated. Of this last Buck was never guilty, though he did see beaten dogs that fawned upon the man, and wagged their tails, and licked his hand. Also he saw one dog, that would neither conciliate nor obey, finally killed in the struggle for mastery.

Now and again men came, strangers, who talked excitedly, wheedlingly, and in all kinds of fashions to the man in the red sweater.

And at such times that money passed between them the strangers took one or more of the dogs away with them. Buck wondered where they went, for they never came back; but the fear of the future was strong upon him, and he was glad each time when he was not selected.

Yet his time came, in the end, in the form of a little weazened man who spat broken English and many strange and uncouth exclamations which Buck could not understand.

"Sacredam!" he cried, when his eyes lit upon Buck. "Dat one dam bully dog! Eh? How moch?"

"Three hundred, and a present at that," was the prompt reply of the man in the red sweater. "And seein' it's government money, you ain't got no kick coming, eh, Perrault?"

Perrault grinned. Considering that the price of dogs had been boomed skyward by the unwonted demand, it was not an unfair sum for so fine an animal. The Canadian Government would be no loser, nor would its despatches travel the slower. Perrault knew dogs, and when he looked at Buck he knew that he was one in a thousand—"One in ten t'ousand," he commented mentally.

Buck saw money pass between them, and was not surprised when Curly, a good-natured Newfoundland, and he were led away by the little weazened man. That was the last he saw of the man in the red sweater, and as Curly and he looked at receding Seattle from the deck of the *Narwhal,* it was the last he saw of the warm Southland. Curly and he were taken below by Perrault and turned over to a black-faced giant called François. Perrault was a French-Canadian, and swarthy; but François was a French-Canadian half-breed, and twice as swarthy. They were a new kind of men to Buck (of which he was destined to see many more), and while he developed no affection for them, he none the less grew honestly to respect them. He speedily learned that Perrault and François were fair men, calm and impartial in administering justice, and too wise in the way of dogs to be fooled by dogs.

In the 'tween-decks of the *Narwhal,* Buck and Curly joined two other dogs. One of them was a big, snow-white fellow from Spitzbergen who had been brought away by a whaling captain, and who had later accompanied a Geological Survey into the Barrens. He was friendly, in a treacherous sort of way, smiling into one's face the while he meditated some underhand trick, as, for instance, when he stole from Buck's food at the first meal. As Buck sprang to punish him, the lash of François's whip sang through the air, reaching the culprit first;

and nothing remained to Buck but to recover the bone. That was fair of François, he decided, and the half-breed began his rise in Buck's estimation.

The other dog made no advances, nor received any; also, he did not attempt to steal from the newcomers. He was a gloomy, morose fellow, and he showed Curly plainly that all he desired was to be left alone, and further, that there would be trouble if he were not left alone. "Dave" he was called, and he ate and slept, or yawned between times, and took interest in nothing, not even when the *Narwhal* crossed Queen Charlotte Sound and rolled and pitched and bucked like a thing possessed. When Buck and Curly grew excited, half wild with fear, he raised his head as though annoyed, favored them with an incurious glance, yawned, and went to sleep again.

Day and night the ship throbbed to the tireless pulse of the propeller, and though one day was very like another, it was apparent to Buck that the weather was steadily growing colder. At last, one morning, the propeller was quiet, and the *Narwhal* was pervaded with an atmosphere of excitement. He felt it, as did the other dogs, and knew that a change was at hand. François leashed them and brought them on deck. At the first step upon the cold surface, Buck's feet sank into a white mushy something very like mud. He sprang back with a snort. More of this white stuff was falling through the air. He shook himself, but more of it fell upon him. He sniffed it curiously, then licked some up on his tongue. It bit like fire, and the next instant was gone. This puzzled him. He tried it again, with the same result. The onlookers laughed uproariously, and he felt ashamed, he knew not why, for it was his first snow.

## II

### THE LAW OF CLUB AND FANG

Buck's first day on the Dyea beach was like a nightmare. Every hour was filled with shock and surprise. He had been suddenly jerked from the heart of civilization and flung into the heart of things primordial. No lazy, sun-kissed life was this, with nothing to do but loaf and be bored. Here was neither peace, nor rest, nor a moment's safety. All was confusion and action, and every moment life and limb were in peril. There was imperative need to be constantly alert; for these dogs and men were not town dogs and men. They were savages, all of them, who knew no law but the law of club and fang.

He had never seen dogs fight as these wolfish creatures fought, and his first experience taught him an unforgetable lesson. It is true, it was a vicarious experience, else he would not have lived to profit by it. Curly was the victim. They were camped near the log store, where she, in her friendly way, made advances to a husky dog the size of a full-grown wolf, though not half so large as she. There was no warning, only a leap in like a flash, a metallic clip of teeth, a leap out equally swift, and Curly's face was ripped open from eye to jaw.

It was the wolf manner of fighting, to strike and leap away; but there was more to it than this. Thirty or forty huskies ran to the spot and surrounded the combatants in an intent and silent circle. Buck did not comprehend that silent intentness, nor the eager way with which they were licking their chops. Curly rushed her antagonist, who struck again and leaped aside. He met her next rush with his chest, in a peculiar fashion that tumbled her off her feet. She never regained them. This was what the onlooking huskies had waited for. They closed in upon her, snarling and yelping, and she was buried, screaming with agony, beneath the bristling mass of bodies.

So sudden was it, and so unexpected, that Buck was taken aback. He saw Spitz run out his scarlet tongue in a way he had of laughing; and he saw François, swinging an axe, spring into the mess of dogs. Three men with clubs were helping him to scatter them. It did not take long. Two minutes from the time Curly went down, the last of her assailants were clubbed off. But she lay there limp and lifeless in the bloody, trampled snow, almost literally torn to pieces, the swart half-breed standing over her and cursing horribly. The scene often came back to Buck to trouble him in his sleep. So that was the way. No fair play. Once down, that was the end of you. Well, he would see to it that he never went down. Spitz ran out his tongue and laughed again, and from that moment Buck hated him with a bitter and deathless hatred.

Before he had recovered from the shock caused by the tragic passing of Curly, he received another shock. François fastened upon him an arrangement of straps and buckles. It was a harness, such as he had seen the grooms put on the horses at home. And as he had seen horses work, so he was set to work, hauling François on a sled to the forest that fringed the valley, and returning with a load of firewood.

Though his dignity was sorely hurt by thus being made a draught animal, he was too wise to rebel. He buckled down with a will and did his best, though it was all new and strange. François was stern, demanding instant obedience, and by virtue of his whip receiving instant obedience; while Dave, who was an experienced wheeler, nipped Buck's hind quarters whenever he was in error. Spitz was the leader, likewise experienced, and while he could not always get at Buck, he growled sharp reproof now and again, or cunningly threw his weight in the traces to jerk Buck into the way he should go. Buck learned easily, and under the combined tuition of his two mates and François made remarkable progress. Ere they returned to camp he knew enough to stop at "ho," to go ahead at "mush," to swing wide on the bends, and to keep clear of the wheeler when the loaded sled shot downhill at their heels.

"T'ree vair' good dogs," François told Perrault. "Dat Buck, heem pool lak hell. I tich heem queek as anyt'ing."

By afternoon, Perrault, who was in a hurry to be on the trail with his despatches, returned with two more dogs. "Billee" and "Joe" he called them, two brothers, and true huskies both. Sons of the one mother though they were, they were as different as day and night. Billee's one fault was his excessive good nature, while Joe was the very opposite, sour and introspective, with a perpetual snarl and a malignant eye. Buck received them in comradely fashion, Dave ignored them, while Spitz proceeded to thrash first one and then the other. Billee wagged his tail appeasingly, turned to run when he saw that appeasement was of no avail, and cried (still appeasingly) when Spitz's sharp teeth scored his flank. But no matter how Spitz circled, Joe whirled around on his heels to face him, mane bristling, ears laid back, lips writhing and snarling, jaws clipping together as fast as he could snap, and eyes diabolically gleaming—the incarnation of belligerent fear. So terrible was his appearance that Spitz was forced to forego disciplining him; but to cover his own discomfiture he turned upon the inoffensive and wailing Billee and drove him to the confines of the camp.

By evening Perrault secured another dog, an old husky, long and lean and gaunt, with a battle-scarred face and a single eye which flashed a warning of prowess that commanded respect. He was called Sol-leks, which means the Angry One. Like Dave, he asked nothing, gave nothing, expected nothing; and when he marched slowly and deliberately into their midst, even Spitz left him alone. He had one peculiarity which Buck was unlucky enough to discover. He did not like to be approached on his blind side. Of this offence Buck was unwittingly guilty, and the first knowledge he had of his indiscretion was when Sol-leks whirled upon him and slashed his shoulder to the bone for three inches up and down. Forever after Buck avoided his blind side, and to the last of their comradeship had no more trouble. His only apparent ambition, like Dave's, was to be left alone; though, as Buck was afterward to learn, each of them possessed one other and even more vital ambition.

That night Buck faced the great problem of sleeping. The tent, illumined by a candle, glowed warmly in the midst of the white plain; and when he, as a matter of course, entered it, both Perrault and François bombarded him with curses and cooking utensils, till he recovered from his consternation and fled ignominiously into the outer cold. A chill wind was blowing that nipped him sharply and bit with especial venom into his wounded shoulder. He lay down on the snow and attempted to sleep, but the frost soon drove him shivering to his feet. Miserable and disconsolate, he wandered about among the many tents, only to find that one place was as cold as another. Here and there savage dogs rushed upon him, but he bristled his neck-hair and snarled (for he was learning fast), and they let him go his way unmolested.

Finally an idea came to him. He would return and see how his own team-mates were making out. To his astonishment, they had disappeared. Again he wandered about through the great camp, looking for them, and again he returned. Were they in the tent? No, that could not be, else he would not have been driven out. Then where could they possibly be? With drooping tail and shivering body, very forlorn indeed, he aimlessly circled the tent. Suddenly the snow gave way beneath his fore legs and he sank down. Something wriggled under his feet. He sprang back, bristling and snarling, fearful of the unseen and unknown. But a friendly little yelp reassured him, and he went back to investigate. A whiff of warm air ascended to his nostrils, and there, curled up under the snow in a snug ball, lay Billee. He whined placatingly, squirmed and wriggled to show his good will and intentions, and even ventured, as a bribe for peace, to lick Buck's face with his warm wet tongue.

Another lesson. So that was the way they did it, eh? Buck confidently selected a spot, and with much fuss and waste effort proceeded to dig a hole for himself. In a trice the heat from his body filled the confined space and he was asleep. The day had been long and arduous, and he slept soundly and comfortably, though he growled and barked and wrestled with bad dreams.

Nor did he open his eyes till roused by the noises of the waking camp. At first he did not know where he was. It had snowed during the night and he was completely buried. The snow walls pressed him on every side, and a great surge of fear swept through him—the fear of the wild thing for the trap. It was a token that he was harking back through his own life to the lives of his forebears; for he was a civilized dog, an unduly civilized dog, and of his own experience knew no trap and so could not of himself fear it. The muscles of his whole body contracted spasmodically and instinctively, the hair on his neck and shoulders stood on end, and with a ferocious snarl he bounded straight up into the blinding day, the snow flying about him in a flashing cloud. Ere he landed on his feet, he saw the white camp spread out before him and knew where he was and remembered all that had passed from the time he went for a stroll with Manuel to the hole he had dug for himself the night before.

A shout from François hailed his appearance. "Wot I say?" the dog-driver cried to Perrault. "Dat Buck for sure learn queek as any-t'ing."

Perrault nodded gravely. As courier for the Canadian Government, bearing important despatches, he was anxious to secure the best dogs, and he was particularly gladdened by the possession of Buck.

Three more huskies were added to the team inside an hour, making a total of nine, and before another quarter of an hour had passed they were in harness and swinging up the trail toward the Dyea Cañon. Buck was glad to be gone, and though the work was hard he found he did not particularly despise it. He was surprised at the eagerness which animated the whole team and which was communicated to him; but still more surprising was the change wrought in Dave and Sol-leks. They were new dogs, utterly transformed by the harness. All passiveness and unconcern had dropped from them. They were alert and active, anxious that the work should go well, and fiercely irritable with whatever, by delay or confusion, retarded that work. The toil of the traces seemed the supreme expression of their being, and all that they lived for and the only thing in which they took delight.

Dave was wheeler or sled dog, pulling in front of him was Buck, then came Sol-leks; the rest of the team was strung out ahead, single file, to the leader, which position was filled by Spitz.

Buck had been purposely placed between Dave and Sol-leks so

that he might receive instruction. Apt scholar that he was, they were equally apt teachers, never allowing him to linger long in error, and enforcing their teaching with their sharp teeth. Dave was fair and very wise. He never nipped Buck without cause, and he never failed to nip him when he stood in need of it. As François's whip backed him up, Buck found it to be cheaper to mend his ways than to retaliate. Once, during a brief halt, when he got tangled in the traces and delayed the start, both Dave and Sol-leks flew at him and administered a sound trouncing. The resulting tangle was even worse, but Buck took good care to keep the traces clear thereafter; and ere the day was done, so well had he mastered his work, his mates about ceased nagging him. François's whip snapped less frequently, and Perrault even honored Buck by lifting up his feet and carefully examining them.

It was a hard day's run, up the Cañon, through Sheep Camp, past the Scales and the timber line, across glaciers and snowdrifts hundreds of feet deep, and over the great Chilcoot Divide, which stands between the salt water and the fresh and guards forbiddingly the sad and lonely North. They made good time down the chain of lakes which fills the craters of extinct volcanoes, and late that night pulled into the huge camp at the head of Lake Bennett, where thousands of gold-seekers were building boats against the break-up of the ice in the spring. Buck made his hole in the snow and slept the sleep of the exhausted just, but all too early was routed out in the cold darkness and harnessed with his mates to the sled.

That day they made forty miles, the trail being packed; but the next day, and for many days to follow, they broke their own trail, worked harder, and made poorer time. As a rule, Perrault travelled ahead of the team, packing the snow with webbed shoes to make it easier for them. François, guiding the sled at the gee-pole, sometimes exchanged places with him, but not often. Perrault was in a hurry, and he prided himself on his knowledge of ice, which knowledge was indispensable, for the fall ice was very thin, and where there was swift water, there was no ice at all.

Day after day, for days unending, Buck toiled in the traces. Always, they broke camp in the dark, and the first gray of dawn found them hitting the trail with fresh miles reeled off behind them. And always they pitched camp after dark, eating their bit of fish, and crawling to sleep into the snow. Buck was ravenous. The pound and a half of sun-dried salmon, which was his ration for each day, seemed to go nowhere. He never had enough, and suffered from perpetual hunger pangs. Yet the other dogs, because they weighed less and were born to the life, received a pound only of the fish and managed to keep in good condition.

He swiftly lost the fastidiousness which had characterized his old life. A dainty eater, he found that his mates, finishing first, robbed him of his unfinished ration. There was no defending it. While he was fighting off two or three, it was disappearing down the throats of the others. To remedy this, he ate as fast as they; and, so greatly did hunger compel him, he was not above taking what did not belong to him. He watched and learned. When he saw Pike, one of the new dogs, a clever malingerer and thief, slyly steal a slice of bacon when Perrault's back was turned, he duplicated the performance the following day, getting away with the whole chunk. A great uproar was raised, but he was unsuspected; while Dub, an awkward blunderer who was always getting caught, was punished for Buck's misdeed.

This first theft marked Buck as fit to survive in the hostile Northland environment. It marked his adaptability, his capacity to adjust himself to changing conditions, the lack of which would have meant swift and terrible death. It marked, further, the decay or going to pieces of his moral nature, a vain thing and a handicap in the ruthless struggle for existence. It was all well enough in the Southland, under the law of love and fellowship, to respect private property and personal feelings; but in the Northland, under the law of club and fang, whoso took such things into account was a fool, and in so far as he observed them he would fail to prosper.

Not that Buck reasoned it out. He was fit, that was all, and unconsciously he accommodated himself to the new mode of life. All his days, no matter what the odds, he had never run from a fight. But the club of the man in the red sweater had beaten into him a more fundamental and primitive code. Civilized, he could have died for a moral consideration, say the defence of Judge Miller's riding-whip; but the completeness of his decivilization was now evidenced by his ability to flee from the defence of a moral consideration and so save his hide. He did not steal for joy of it, but because of the clamor of his stomach. He did not rob openly, but stole secretly and cunningly, out of respect for club and fang. In short, the things he did were done because it was easier to do them than not to do them.

His development (or retrogression) was rapid. His muscles became hard as iron, and he grew callous to all ordinary pain. He achieved an internal as well as external economy. He could eat anything, no matter how loathsome or indigestible; and, once eaten, the juices of his stomach extracted the last least particle of nutriment; and his blood carried it to the farthest reaches of his body, building it into the toughest and stoutest of tissues. Sight and scent became remarkably keen, while his hearing developed such acuteness that in his sleep he heard the faintest sound and knew whether it heralded peace or peril. He learned to bite the ice out with his teeth when it collected between his toes; and when he was thirsty and there was a thick scum of ice over the water hole, he would break it by rearing and striking it with stiff fore legs. His most conspicuous trait was an ability to scent the wind and forecast it a night in advance. No matter how breathless the air when he dug his nest by tree or bank, the wind that later blew inevitably found him to leeward, sheltered and snug.

And not only did he learn by experience, but instincts long dead became alive again. The domesticated generations fell from him. In vague ways he remembered back to the youth of the breed, to the time the wild dogs ranged in packs through the primeval forest and killed their meat as they ran it down. It was no task for him to learn to fight with cut and slash and the quick wolf snap. In this manner had fought forgotten ancestors. They quickened the old life within him, and the old tricks which they had stamped into the heredity of the breed were his tricks. They came to him without effort or discovery, as though they had been his always. And when, on the still cold nights, he pointed his nose at a star and howled long and wolflike, it was his ancestors, dead and dust, pointing nose at star and howling down through the centuries and through him. And his cadences were their cadences, the cadences which voiced their woe and what to them was the meaning of the stillness, and the cold, and dark.

Thus, as token of what a puppet thing life is, the ancient song surged through him and he came into his own again; and he came because men had found a yellow metal in the North, and because Manuel was a gardener's helper whose wages did not lap over the needs of his wife and divers small copies of himself.

# III

## THE DOMINANT
## PRIMORDIAL BEAST

The dominant primordial beast was strong in Buck, and under the fierce conditions of trail life it grew and grew. Yet it was a secret growth. His newborn cunning gave him poise and control. He was too busy adjusting himself to the new life to feel at ease, and not only did he not pick fights, but he avoided them whenever possible. A certain deliberateness characterized his attitude. He was not prone to rashness and precipitate action; and in the bitter hatred between him and Spitz he betrayed no impatience, shunned all offensive acts.

On the other hand, possibly because he divined in Buck a dangerous rival, Spitz never lost an opportunity of showing his teeth. He even went out of his way to bully Buck, striving constantly to start the fight which could end only in the death of one or the other. Early in the trip this might have taken place had it not been for an unwonted accident. At the end of this day they made a bleak and miserable camp on the shore of Lake Le Barge. Driving snow, a wind that cut like a white-hot knife, and darkness had forced them to grope for a camping place. They could hardly have fared worse. At their backs rose a perpendicular wall of rock, and Perrault and François were compelled to make their fire and spread their sleeping robes on the ice of the lake itself. The tent they had discarded at Dyea in order to travel light. A few sticks of driftwood furnished them with a fire that thawed down through the ice and left them to eat supper in the dark.

Close in under the sheltering rock Buck made his nest. So snug and warm was it, that he was loath to leave it when François distributed the fish which he had first thawed over the fire. But when Buck finished his ration and returned, he found his nest occupied. A warning snarl told him that the trespasser was Spitz. Till now Buck had avoided trouble with his enemy, but this was too much. The beast in him roared. He sprang upon Spitz with a fury which surprised them both, and Spitz particularly, for his whole experience with Buck had gone to teach him that his rival was an unusually timid dog, who managed to hold his own only because of his great weight and size.

François was surprised, too, when they shot out in a tangle from the disrupted nest and he divined the cause of the trouble. "A-a-ah!"

he cried to Buck. "Gif it to heem, by Gar! Gif it to heem, the dirty t'eef!"

Spitz was equally willing. He was crying with sheer rage and eagerness as he circled back and forth for a chance to spring in. Buck was no less eager, and no less cautious, as he likewise circled back and forth for the advantage. But it was then that the unexpected happened, the thing which projected their struggle for supremacy far into the future, past many a weary mile of trail and toil.

An oath from Perrault, the resounding impact of a club upon a bony frame, and a shrill yelp of pain, heralded the breaking forth of pandemonium. The camp was suddenly discovered to be alive with skulking furry forms,—starving huskies, four or five score of them, who had scented the camp from some Indian village. They had crept in while Buck and Spitz were fighting, and when the two men sprang among them with stout clubs they showed their teeth and fought back. They were crazed by the smell of the food. Perrault found one with head buried in the grub-box. His club landed heavily on the gaunt ribs, and the grub-box was capsized on the ground. On the instant a score of the famished brutes were scrambling for the bread and bacon. The clubs fell upon them unheeded. They yelped and howled under the rain of blows, but struggled none the less madly till the last crumb had been devoured.

In the meantime the astonished team-dogs had burst out of their nests only to be set upon by the fierce invaders. Never had Buck seen such dogs. It seemed as though their bones would burst through their skins. They were mere skeletons, draped loosely in draggled hides, with blazing eyes and slavered fangs. But the hunger-madness made them terrifying, irresistible. There was no opposing them. The team-dogs were swept back against the cliff at the first onset. Buck was beset by three huskies, and in a trice his head and shoulders were ripped and slashed. The din was frightful. Billee was crying as usual. Dave and Sol-leks, dripping blood from a score of wounds, were fighting bravely side by side. Joe was snapping like a demon. Once, his teeth closed on the fore leg of a husky, and he crunched down through the bone. Pike, the malingerer, leaped upon the crippled animal, breaking its neck with a quick flash of teeth and a jerk. Buck got a frothing adversary by the throat, and was sprayed with blood when his teeth sank through the jugular. The warm taste of it in his mouth goaded him to greater fierceness. He flung himself upon another, and at the same time felt teeth sink into his own throat. It was Spitz, treacherously attacking from the side.

Perrault and François, having cleaned out their part of the camp, hurried to save their sled-dogs. The wild wave of famished beasts rolled back before them, and Buck shook himself free. But it was only for a moment. The two men were compelled to run back to save the grub, upon which the huskies returned to the attack on the team. Billee, terrified into bravery, sprang through the savage circle and fled away over the ice. Pike and Dub followed on his heels, with the rest of the team behind. As Buck drew himself together to spring after them, out of the tail of his eye he saw Spitz rush upon him with the evident intention of overthrowing him. Once off his feet and under that mass of huskies, there was no hope for him. But he braced himself to the shock of Spitz's charge, then joined the flight out on the lake.

Later, the nine team-dogs gathered together and sought shelter in the forest. Though unpursued, they were in a sorry plight. There was not one who was not wounded in four or five places, while some were wounded grievously. Dub was badly injured in a hind leg; Dolly, the last husky added to the team at Dyea, had a badly torn throat; Joe had lost an eye; while Billee, the good-natured, with an ear chewed and rent to ribbons, cried and whimpered throughout the night. At daybreak they limped warily back to camp, to find the marauders gone and the two men in bad tempers. Fully half their grub supply was gone. The huskies had chewed through the sled lashings and canvas coverings. In fact, nothing, no matter how remotely eatable, had escaped them. They had eaten a pair of Perrault's moose-hide moccasins, chunks out of the leather traces, and even two feet of lash from the end of François's whip. He broke from a mournful contemplation of it to look over his wounded dogs.

"Ah, my frien's," he said softly, "mebbe it mek you mad dog, dose many bites. Mebbe all mad dog, sacredam! Wot you t'ink, eh, Perrault?"

The courier shook his head dubiously. With four hundred miles of trail still between him and Dawson, he could ill afford to have madness break out among his dogs. Two hours of cursing and exertion got the harnesses into shape, and the wound-stiffened team was under way, struggling painfully over the hardest part of the trail they had yet encountered, and for that matter, the hardest between them and Dawson.

The Thirty Mile River was wide open. Its wild water defied the frost, and it was in the eddies only and in the quiet places that the ice held at all. Six days of exhausting toil were required to cover those thirty terrible miles. And terrible they were, for every foot of them was accomplished at the risk of life to dog and man. A dozen times, Perrault, nosing the way, broke through the ice bridges, being saved by the long pole he carried, which he so held that it fell each time across the hole made by his body. But a cold snap was on, the thermometer registering fifty below zero, and each time he broke through he was compelled for very life to build a fire and dry his garments.

Nothing daunted him. It was because nothing daunted him that he had been chosen for government courier. He took all manner of risks, resolutely thrusting his little weazened face into the frost and struggling on from dim dawn to dark. He skirted the frowning shores on rim ice that bent and crackled under foot and upon which they dared not halt. Once, the sled broke through, with Dave and Buck, and they were half-frozen and all but drowned by the time they were dragged out. The usual fire was necessary to save them. They were coated solidly with ice, and the two men kept them on the run around the fire, sweating and thawing, so close that they were singed by the flames.

At another time Spitz went through, dragging the whole team after him up to Buck, who strained backward with all his strength, his fore paws on the slippery edge and the ice quivering and snapping all around. But behind him was Dave, likewise straining backward, and behind the sled was François, pulling till his tendons cracked.

Again, the rim ice broke away before and behind, and there was no escape except up the cliff. Perrault scaled it by a miracle, while François prayed for just that miracle; and with every thong and sled lashing and the last bit of harness rove into a long rope, the dogs were hoisted, one by one, to the cliff crest. François came up last, after the sled and load. Then came the search for a place to descend, which descent was ultimately made by the aid of the rope, and night found them back on the river with a quarter of a mile to the day's credit.

By the time they made the Hootalinqua and good ice, Buck was played out. The rest of the dogs were in like condition; but Perrault, to make up lost time, pushed them late and early. The first day they covered thirty-five miles to the Big Salmon; the next day thirty-five more to the Little Salmon; the third day forty miles, which brought them well up toward the Five Fingers.

Buck's feet were not so compact and hard as the feet of the huskies. His had softened during the many generations since the day his last wild ancestor was tamed by a cave-dweller or river man. All day long he limped in agony, and camp once made, lay down like a dead dog. Hungry as he was, he would not move to receive his ration of fish, which François had to bring to him. Also, the dog-driver rubbed Buck's feet for half an hour each night after supper, and sacrificed the tops of his own moccasins to make four moccasins for Buck. This was a great relief, and Buck caused even the weazened face of Perrault to twist itself into a grin one morning, when François forgot the moccasins and Buck lay on his back, his four feet waving appealingly in the air, and refused to budge without them. Later his feet grew hard to the trail, and the worn-out foot-gear was thrown away.

At the Pelly one morning, as they were harnessing up, Dolly, who had never been conspicuous for anything, went suddenly mad. She announced her condition by a long, heartbreaking wolf howl that sent every dog bristling with fear, then sprang straight for Buck. He had never seen a dog go mad, nor did he have any reason to fear madness; yet he knew that here was horror, and fled away from it in a panic. Straight away he raced, with Dolly, panting and frothing, one leap behind; nor could she gain on him, so great was his terror, nor could he leave her, so great was her madness. He plunged through the wooded breast of the island, flew down to the lower end, crossed a back channel filled with rough ice to another island, gained a third island, curved back to the main river, and in desperation started to cross it. And all the time, though he did not look, he could hear her snarling just one leap behind. François called to him a quarter of a mile away and he doubled back, still one leap ahead, gasping painfully for air and putting all his faith in that François would save him. The dog-driver held the axe poised in his hand, and as Buck shot past him the axe crashed down upon mad Dolly's head.

Buck staggered over against the sled, exhausted, sobbing for breath, helpless. This was Spitz's opportunity. He sprang upon Buck, and twice his teeth sank into his unresisting foe and ripped and tore the flesh to the bone. Then François's lash descended, and Buck had the satisfaction of watching Spitz receive the worst whipping as yet administered to any of the teams.

"One devil, dat Spitz," remarked Perrault. "Some dam day heem keel dat Buck."

"Dat Buck two devils," was François's rejoinder. "All de tam I watch dat Buck I know for sure. Lissen: some dam fine day heem get mad lak hell an' den heem chew dat Spitz all up an' spit heem out on de snow. Sure. I know."

From then on it was war between them. Spitz, as lead-dog and acknowledged master of the team, felt his supremacy threatened by this strange Southland dog. And strange Buck was to him, for of the many Southland dogs he had known, not one had shown up worthily in camp and on trail. They were all too soft, dying under the toil, the frost, and starvation. Buck was the exception. He alone endured and prospered, matching the husky in strength, savagery, and cunning. Then he was a masterful dog, and what made him dangerous was the fact that the club of the man in the red sweater had knocked all blind pluck and rashness out of his desire for mastery. He was preëminently cunning, and could bide his time with a patience that was nothing less than primitive.

It was inevitable that the clash for leadership should come. Buck wanted it. He wanted it because it was his nature, because he had been gripped tight by that nameless, incomprehensible pride of the trail and trace—that pride which holds dogs in the toil to the last gasp, which lures them to die joyfully in the harness, and breaks their hearts if they are cut out of the harness. This was the pride of Dave as wheel-dog, of Sol-leks as he pulled with all his strength; the pride that laid hold of them at break of camp, transforming them from sour and sullen brutes into straining, eager, ambitious creatures; the pride that spurred them on all day and dropped them at pitch of camp at night, letting them fall back into gloomy unrest and uncontent. This was the pride that bore up Spitz and made him thrash the sled-dogs who blundered and shirked in the traces or hid away at harness-up time in the morning. Likewise it was this pride that made him fear Buck as a possible lead-dog. And this was Buck's pride, too.

He openly threatened the other's leadership. He came between him and the shirks he should have punished. And he did it deliberately. One night there was a heavy snowfall, and in the morning Pike, the malingerer, did not appear. He was securely hidden in his nest under a foot of snow. François called him and sought him in vain. Spitz was wild with wrath. He raged through the camp, smelling and digging in every likely place, snarling so frightfully that Pike heard and shivered in his hiding-place.

But when he was at last unearthed, and Spitz flew at him to punish him, Buck flew, with equal rage, in between. So unexpected was it, and so shrewdly managed, that Spitz was hurled backward and off his feet. Pike, who had been trembling abjectly, took heart at this open mutiny, and sprang upon his overthrown leader. Buck, to whom fair play was a forgotten code, likewise sprang upon Spitz. But François, chuckling at the incident while unswerving in the administration of justice, brought his lash down upon Buck with all his might. This failed to drive Buck from his prostrate rival, and the butt of the whip was brought into play. Half-stunned by the blow, Buck was knocked back-ward and the lash laid upon him again and again, while Spitz soundly punished the many times offending Pike.

In the days that followed, as Dawson grew closer and closer, Buck still continued to interfere between Spitz and the culprits; but he did it craftily, when François was not around. With the covert mutiny of Buck, a general insubordination sprang up and increased. Dave and Sol-leks were unaffected, but the rest of the team went from bad to worse. Things no longer went right. There was continual bickering and jangling. Trouble was always afoot, and at the bottom of it was Buck. He kept François busy, for the dog-driver was in constant ap-prehension of the life-and-death struggle between the two which he knew must take place sooner or later; and on more than one night the sounds of quarrelling and strife among the other dogs turned him out of his sleeping robe, fearful that Buck and Spitz were at it.

But the opportunity did not present itself, and they pulled into Dawson one dreary afternoon with the great fight still to come. Here were many men, and countless dogs, and Buck found them all at work. It seemed the ordained order of things that dogs should work. All day they swung up and down the main street in long teams, and in the night their jingling bells still went by. They hauled cabin logs and firewood, freighted up to the mines, and did all manner of work that horses did in the Santa Clara Valley. Here and there Buck met South-land dogs, but in the main they were the wild wolf husky breed. Every night, regularly, at nine, at twelve, at three, they lifted a nocturnal song, a weird and eerie chant, in which it was Buck's delight to join.

With the aurora borealis flaming coldly overhead, or the stars leaping in the frost dance, and the land numb and frozen under its pall of snow, this song of the huskies might have been the defiance of life, only it was pitched in minor key, with long-drawn wailings and half-sobs, and was more the pleading of life, the articulate travail of existence. It was an old song, old as the breed itself—one of the first songs of the younger world in a day when songs were sad. It was invested with the woe of unnumbered generations, this plaint by which Buck was so strangely stirred. When he moaned and sobbed, it was with the pain of living that was of old the pain of his wild fathers, and the fear and mystery of the cold and dark that was to them fear and mystery. And that he should be stirred by it marked the complete-ness with which he harked back through the ages of fire and roof to the raw beginnings of life in the howling ages.

Seven days from the time they pulled into Dawson, they dropped down the steep bank by the Barracks to the Yukon Trail, and pulled for Dyea and Salt Water. Perrault was carrying despatches if anything more urgent than those he had brought in; also, the travel pride had gripped him, and he purposed to make the record trip of the year. Several things favored him in this. The week's rest had recuperated the dogs and put them in thorough trim. The trail they had broken into the country was packed hard by later journeyers. And further, the police had arranged in two or three places deposits of grub for dog and man, and he was travelling light.

They made Sixty Mile, which is a fifty-mile run, on the first day; and the second day saw them booming up the Yukon well on their way to Pelly. But such splendid running was achieved not without great trouble and vexation on the part of François. The insidious revolt led by Buck had destroyed the solidarity of the team. It no longer was as one dog leaping in the traces. The encouragement Buck gave the rebels led them into all kinds of petty misdemeanors. No more was Spitz a leader greatly to be feared. The old awe departed, and they grew equal to challenging his authority. Pike robbed him of half a fish one night, and gulped it down under the protection of Buck. Another night Dub and Joe fought Spitz and made him forego the punishment they deserved. And even Billee, the good-natured, was less good-natured, and whined not half so placatingly as in former days. Buck never came near Spitz without snarling and bristling menacingly. In fact, his conduct approached that of a bully, and he was given to swaggering up and down before Spitz's very nose.

The breaking down of discipline likewise affected the dogs in their relations with one another. They quarrelled and bickered more than ever among themselves, till at times the camp was a howling bedlam. Dave and Sol-leks alone were unaltered, though they were made irritable by the unending squabbling. François swore strange barbarous oaths, and stamped the snow in futile rage, and tore his hair. His lash was always singing among the dogs, but it was of small avail. Directly his back was turned they were at it again. He backed up Spitz with his whip, while Buck backed up the remainder of the team. François knew he was behind all the trouble, and Buck knew he knew; but Buck was too clever ever again to be caught red-handed. He worked faithfully in the harness, for the toil had become a delight to him; yet it was a greater delight slyly to precipitate a fight amongst his mates and tangle the traces.

At the mouth of the Tahkeena, one night after supper, Dub turned up a snowshoe rabbit, blundered it, and missed. In a second the whole team was in full cry. A hundred yards away was a camp of the Northwest Police, with fifty dogs, huskies all, who joined the chase. The rabbit sped down the river, turned off into a small creek, up the frozen bed of which it held steadily. It ran lightly on the surface of the snow, while the dogs ploughed through by main strength. Buck led the pack, sixty strong, around bend after bend, but he could not gain. He lay down low to the race, whining eagerly, his splendid body flashing forward, leap by leap, in the wan white moonlight. And leap by leap, like some pale frost wraith, the snowshoe rabbit flashed on ahead.

All that stirring of old instincts which at stated periods drives men out from the sounding cities to forest and plain to kill things by chemically propelled leaden pellets, the blood lust, the joy to kill—all this was Buck's, only it was infinitely more intimate. He was ranging at the head of the pack, running the wild thing down, the living meat, to kill with his own teeth and wash his muzzle to the eyes in warm blood.

There is an ecstasy that marks the summit of life, and beyond which life cannot rise. And such is the paradox of living, this ecstasy comes when one is most alive, and it comes as a complete forgetfulness that one is alive. This ecstasy, this forgetfulness of living, comes to the artist, caught up and out of himself in a sheet of flame; it comes to the soldier, war-mad on a stricken field and refusing quarter; and it came to Buck, leading the pack, sounding the old wolf-cry, straining after the food that was alive and that fled swiftly before him through the moonlight. He was sounding the deeps of his nature, and of the parts of his nature that were deeper than he, going back into the womb of Time. He was mastered by the sheer surging of life, the tidal wave of being, the perfect joy of each separate muscle, joint, and sinew in that it was everything that was not death, that it was aglow and rampant, expressing itself in movement, flying exultantly under the stars and over the face of dead matter that did not move.

But Spitz, cold and calculating even in his supreme moods, left the pack and cut across a narrow neck of land where the creek made a long bend around. Buck did not know of this, and as he rounded the bend, the frost wraith of a rabbit still flitting before him, he saw another and larger frost wraith leap from the overhanging bank into the immediate path of the rabbit. It was Spitz. The rabbit could not turn, and as the white teeth broke its back in mid air it shrieked as loudly as a stricken man may shriek. At sound of this, the cry of Life plunging down from Life's apex in the grip of Death, the full pack at Buck's heels raised a hell's chorus of delight.

Buck did not cry out. He did not check himself, but drove in upon

Spitz, shoulder to shoulder, so hard that he missed the throat. They rolled over and over in the powdery snow. Spitz gained his feet almost as though he had not been overthrown, slashing Buck down the shoulder and leaping clear. Twice his teeth clipped together, like the steel jaws of a trap, as he backed away for better footing, with lean and lifting lips that writhed and snarled.

In a flash Buck knew it. The time had come. It was to the death. As they circled about, snarling, ears laid back, keenly watchful for the advantage, the scene came to Buck with a sense of familiarity. He seemed to remember it all,—the white woods, and earth, and moonlight, and the thrill of battle. Over the whiteness and silence brooded a ghostly calm. There was not the faintest whisper of air—nothing moved, not a leaf quivered, the visible breaths of the dogs rising slowly and lingering in the frosty air. They had made short work of the snowshoe rabbit, these dogs that were ill-tamed wolves; and they were now drawn up in an expectant circle. They, too, were silent, their eyes only gleaming and their breaths drifting slowly upward. To Buck it was nothing new or strange, this scene of old time. It was as though it had always been, the wonted way of things.

Spitz was a practised fighter. From Spitzbergen through the Arctic, and across Canada and the Barrens, he had held his own with all manner of dogs and achieved to mastery over them. Bitter rage was his, but never blind rage. In passion to rend and destroy, he never forgot that his enemy was in like passion to rend and destroy. He never rushed till he was prepared to receive a rush; never attacked till he had first defended that attack.

In vain Buck strove to sink his teeth in the neck of the big white dog. Wherever his fangs struck for the softer flesh, they were countered by the fangs of Spitz. Fang clashed fang, and lips were cut and bleeding, but Buck could not penetrate his enemy's guard. Then he warmed up and enveloped Spitz in a whirlwind of rushes. Time and time again he tried for the snow-white throat, where life bubbled near to the surface, and each time and every time Spitz slashed him and got away. Then Buck took to rushing, as though for the throat, when, suddenly drawing back his head and curving in from the side, he would drive his shoulder at the shoulder of Spitz, as a ram by which to overthrow him. But instead, Buck's shoulder was slashed down each time as Spitz leaped lightly away.

Spitz was untouched, while Buck was streaming with blood and panting hard. The fight was growing desperate. And all the while the silent and wolfish circle waited to finish off whichever dog went down.

As Buck grew winded, Spitz took to rushing, and he kept him staggering for footing. Once Buck went over, and the whole circle of sixty dogs started up; but he recovered himself, almost in mid air, and the circle sank down again and waited.

But Buck possessed a quality that made for greatness—imagination. He fought by instinct, but he could fight by head as well. He rushed, as though attempting the old shoulder trick, but at the last instant swept low to the snow and in. His teeth closed on Spitz's left fore leg. There was a crunch of breaking bone, and the white dog faced him on three legs. Thrice he tried to knock him over, then repeated the trick and broke the right fore leg. Despite the pain and helplessness, Spitz struggled madly to keep up. He saw the silent circle, with gleaming eyes, lolling tongues, and silvery breaths drifting upward, closing in upon him as he had seen similar circles close in upon beaten antagonists in the past. Only this time he was the one who was beaten.

There was no hope for him. Buck was inexorable. Mercy was a thing reserved for gentler climes. He manœuvred for the final rush. The circle had tightened till he could feel the breaths of the huskies on his flanks. He could see them, beyond Spitz and to either side, half crouching for the spring, their eyes fixed upon him. A pause seemed to fall. Every animal was motionless as though turned to stone. Only Spitz quivered and bristled as he staggered back and forth, snarling with horrible menace, as though to frighten off impending death. Then Buck sprang in and out; but while he was in, shoulder had at last squarely met shoulder. The dark circle became a dot on the moon-flooded snow as Spitz disappeared from view. Buck stood and looked on, the successful champion, the dominant primordial beast who had made his kill and found it good.

# IV

## WHO HAS WON TO MASTERSHIP

"Eh? Wot I say? I spik true w'en I say dat Buck two devils."

This was François's speech next morning when he discovered Spitz missing and Buck covered with wounds. He drew him to the fire and by its light pointed them out.

"Dat Spitz fight lak hell," said Perrault, as he surveyed the gaping rips and cuts.

"An' dat Buck fight lak two hells," was François's answer. "An' now we make good time. No more Spitz, no more trouble, sure."

While Perrault packed the camp outfit and loaded the sled, the dog-driver proceeded to harness the dogs. Buck trotted up to the place Spitz would have occupied as leader; but François, not noticing him, brought Sol-leks to the coveted position. In his judgment, Sol-leks was the best lead-dog left. Buck sprang upon Sol-leks in a fury, driving him back and standing in his place.

"Eh? eh?" François cried, slapping his thighs gleefully. "Look at dat Buck. Heem keel dat Spitz, heem t'ink to take de job."

"Go 'way, Chook!" he cried, but Buck refused to budge.

He took Buck by the scruff of the neck, and though the dog growled threateningly, dragged him to one side and replaced Sol-leks. The old dog did not like it, and showed plainly that he was afraid of Buck. François was obdurate, but when he turned his back Buck again displaced Sol-leks, who was not at all unwilling to go.

François was angry. "Now, by Gar, I feex you!" he cried, coming back with a heavy club in his hand.

Buck remembered the man in the red sweater, and retreated slowly; nor did he attempt to charge in when Sol-leks was once more brought forward. But he circled just beyond the range of the club, snarling with bitterness and rage; and while he circled he watched the club so as to dodge it if thrown by François, for he was become wise in the way of clubs.

The driver went about his work, and he called to Buck when he was ready to put him in his old place in front of Dave. Buck retreated two or three steps. François followed him up, whereupon he again retreated. After some time of this, François threw down the club, thinking that Buck feared a thrashing. But Buck was in open revolt. He wanted, not to escape a clubbing, but to have the leadership. It was his by right. He had earned it, and he would not be content with less.

Perrault took a hand. Between them they ran him about for the better part of an hour. They threw clubs at him. He dodged. They cursed him, and his fathers and mothers before him, and all his seed to come after him down to the remotest generation, and every hair on his body and drop of blood in his veins; and he answered curse with snarl and kept out of their reach. He did not try to run away, but retreated around and around the camp, advertising plainly that when his desire was met, he would come in and be good.

François sat down and scratched his head. Perrault looked at his watch and swore. Time was flying, and they should have been on the trail an hour gone. François scratched his head again. He shook it and grinned sheepishly at the courier, who shrugged his shoulders in sign that they were beaten. Then François went up to where Sol-leks stood and called to Buck. Buck laughed, as dogs laugh, yet kept his distance. François unfastened Sol-leks's traces and put him back in his old place. The team stood harnessed to the sled in an unbroken line, ready for the trail. There was no place for Buck save at the front. Once more François called, and once more Buck laughed and kept away.

"T'row down de club," Perrault commanded.

François complied, whereupon Buck trotted in, laughing triumphantly, and swung around into position at the head of the team. His traces were fastened, the sled broken out, and with both men running they dashed out on to the river trail.

Highly as the dog-driver had forevalued Buck, with his two devils, he found, while the day was yet young, that he had undervalued. At a bound Buck took up the duties of leadership; and where judgment was required, and quick thinking and quick acting, he showed himself the superior even of Spitz, of whom François had never seen an equal.

But it was in giving the law and making his mates live up to it, that Buck excelled. Dave and Sol-leks did not mind the change in leadership. It was none of their business. Their business was to toil, and toil mightily, in the traces. So long as that were not interfered with, they did not care what happened. Billee, the good-natured, could lead for all they cared, so long as he kept order. The rest of the team, however, had grown unruly during the last days of Spitz, and their surprise was great now that Buck proceeded to lick them into shape.

Pike, who pulled at Buck's heels, and who never put an ounce more of his weight against the breast-band than he was compelled to do, was swiftly and repeatedly shaken for loafing; and ere the first day was done he was pulling more than ever before in his life. The first night in camp, Joe, the sour one, was punished roundly—a thing that Spitz had never succeeded in doing. Buck simply smothered him by virtue of superior weight, and cut him up till he ceased snapping and began to whine for mercy.

The general tone of the team picked up immediately. It recovered its old-time solidarity, and once more the dogs leaped as one dog in the traces. At the Rink Rapids two native huskies, Teek and Koona, were added; and the celerity with which Buck broke them in took away François's breath.

"Nevaire such a dog as dat Buck!" he cried. "No, nevaire! Heem worth one t'ousan' dollair, by Gar! Eh? Wot you say, Perrault?"

And Perrault nodded. He was ahead of the record then, and gaining day by day. The trail was in excellent condition, well packed and hard, and there was no new-fallen snow with which to contend. It was not too cold. The temperature dropped to fifty below zero and remained there the whole trip. The men rode and ran by turn, and the dogs were kept on the jump, with but infrequent stoppages.

The Thirty Mile River was comparatively coated with ice, and they covered in one day going out what had taken them ten days coming in. In one run they made a sixty-mile dash from the foot of Lake Le Barge to the White Horse Rapids. Across Marsh, Tagish, and Bennett (seventy miles of lakes), they flew so fast that the man whose turn it was to run towed behind the sled at the end of a rope. And on the last night of the second week they topped White Pass and dropped down the sea slope with the lights of Skaguay and of the shipping at their feet.

It was a record run. Each day for fourteen days they had averaged forty miles. For three days Perrault and François threw chests up and down the main street of Skaguay and were deluged with invitations to drink, while the team was the constant centre of a worshipful crowd of dog-busters and mushers. Then three or four western bad men aspired to clean out the town, were riddled like pepper-boxes for their pains, and public interest turned to other idols. Next came official orders. François called Buck to him, threw his arms around him, wept over him. And that was the last of François and Perrault. Like other men, they passed out of Buck's life for good.

A Scotch half-breed took charge of him and his mates, and in company with a dozen other dog-teams he started back over the weary trail to Dawson. It was no light running now, nor record time, but heavy toil each day, with a heavy load behind; for this was the mail train, carrying word from the world to the men who sought gold under the shadow of the Pole.

Buck did not like it, but he bore up well to the work, taking pride in it after the manner of Dave and Sol-leks, and seeing that his mates, whether they prided in it or not, did their fair share. It was a monotonous life, operating with machine-like regularity. One day was very like another. At a certain time each morning the cooks turned out, fires were built, and breakfast was eaten. Then, while some broke camp, others harnessed the dogs, and they were under way an hour or so before the darkness fell which gave warning of dawn. At night, camp was made. Some pitched the flies, others cut firewood and pine boughs for the beds, and still others carried water or ice for the cooks. Also, the dogs were fed. To them, this was the one feature of the day, though it was good to loaf around, after the fish was eaten, for an hour or so with the other dogs, of which there were fivescore and odd. There were fierce fighters among them, but three battles with the fiercest brought Buck to mastery, so that when he bristled and showed his teeth they got out of his way.

Best of all, perhaps, he loved to lie near the fire, hind legs crouched under him, fore legs stretched out in front, head raised, and eyes blinking dreamily at the flames. Sometimes he thought of Judge Miller's big house in the sun-kissed Santa Clara Valley, and of the cement swimming-tank, and Ysabel, the Mexican hairless, and Toots, the Japanese pug; but oftener he remembered the man in the red sweater, the death of Curly, the great fight with Spitz, and the good things he had eaten or would like to eat. He was not homesick. The Sunland was very dim and distant, and such memories had no power over him. Far more potent were the memories of his heredity that gave things he had never seen before a seeming familiarity; the instincts (which were but the memories of his ancestors become habits) which had lapsed in later days, and still later, in him, quickened and become alive again.

Sometimes as he crouched there, blinking dreamily at the flames, it seemed that the flames were of another fire, and that as he crouched by this other fire he saw another and different man from the half-breed cook before him. This other man was shorter of leg and longer of arm, with muscles that were stringy and knotty rather than rounded and swelling. The hair of this man was long and matted, and his head slanted back under it from the eyes. He uttered strange sounds, and seemed very much afraid of the darkness, into which he peered continually, clutching in his hand, which hung midway between knee and foot, a stick with a heavy stone made fast to the end. He was all but naked, a ragged and fire-scorched skin hanging part way down his back, but on his body there was much hair. In some places, across the chest and shoulders and down the outside of the arms and thighs, it was matted into almost a thick fur. He did not stand erect, but with trunk inclined forward from the hips, on legs that bent at the knees. About his body there was a peculiar springiness, or resiliency, almost catlike, and a quick alertness as of one who lived in perpetual fear of things seen and unseen.

At other times this hairy man squatted by the fire with head between his legs and slept. On such occasions his elbows were on his knees, his hands clasped above his head as though to shed rain by the hairy arms. And beyond that fire, in the circling darkness, Buck could see many gleaming coals, two by two, always two by two, which he knew to be the eyes of great beasts of prey. And he could hear the crashing of their bodies through the undergrowth, and the noises they made in the night. And dreaming there by the Yukon bank, with lazy eyes blinking at the fire, these sounds and sights of another world would make the hair to rise along his back and stand on end across his shoulders and up his neck, till he whimpered low and suppressedly, or growled softly, and the half-breed cook shouted at him, "Hey, you Buck, wake up!" Whereupon the other world would vanish and the real world come into his eyes, and he would get up and yawn and stretch as though he had been asleep.

It was a hard trip, with the mail behind them, and the heavy work wore them down. They were short of weight and in poor condition when they made Dawson, and should have had a ten days' or a week's rest at least. But in two days' time they dropped down the Yukon bank from the Barracks, loaded with letters for the outside. The dogs were tired, the drivers grumbling, and to make matters worse, it snowed every day. This meant a soft trail, greater friction on the runners, and heavier pulling for the dogs; yet the drivers were fair through it all, and did their best for the animals.

Each night the dogs were attended to first. They ate before the drivers ate, and no man sought his sleeping-robe till he had seen to the feet of the dogs he drove. Still, their strength went down. Since the beginning of the winter they had travelled eighteen hundred miles, dragging sleds the whole weary distance; and eighteen hundred miles will tell upon life of the toughest. Buck stood it, keeping his mates up to their work and maintaining discipline, though he, too, was very tired. Billee cried and whimpered regularly in his sleep each night. Joe was sourer than ever, and Sol-leks was unapproachable, blind side or other side.

But it was Dave who suffered most of all. Something had gone wrong with him. He became more morose and irritable, and when camp was pitched at once made his nest, where his driver fed him. Once out of the harness and down, he did not get on his feet again till harness-up time in the morning. Sometimes, in the traces, when jerked by a sudden stoppage of the sled, or by straining to start it, he would cry out with pain. The driver examined him, but could find nothing. All the drivers became interested in his case. They talked it over at meal-time, and over their last pipes before going to bed, and one night they held a consultation. He was brought from his nest to the fire and was pressed and prodded till he cried out many times. Something was wrong inside, but they could locate no broken bones, could not make it out.

By the time Cassiar Bar was reached, he was so weak that he was falling repeatedly in the traces. The Scotch half-breed called a halt and took him out of the team, making the next dog, Sol-leks, fast to the sled. His intention was to rest Dave, letting him run free behind the sled. Sick as he was, Dave resented being taken out, grunting and growling while the traces were unfastened, and whimpering broken-heartedly when he saw Sol-leks in the position he had held and served so long. For the pride of trace and trail was his, and, sick unto death, he could not bear that another dog should do his work.

When the sled started, he floundered in the soft snow alongside the beaten trail, attacking Sol-leks with his teeth, rushing against him and trying to thrust him off into the soft snow on the other side, striving to leap inside his traces and get between him and the sled, and all the while whining and yelping and crying with grief and pain. The half-breed tried to drive him away with the whip; but he paid no heed to the stinging lash, and the man had not the heart to strike harder. Dave refused to run quietly on the trail behind the sled, where the going was easy, but continued to flounder alongside in the soft snow, where the going was most difficult, till exhausted. Then he fell, and lay where he fell, howling lugubriously as the long train of sleds churned by.

With the last remnant of his strength he managed to stagger along behind till the train made another stop, when he floundered past the sleds to his own, where he stood alongside Sol-leks. His driver lingered a moment to get a light for his pipe from the man behind. Then he returned and started his dogs. They swung out on the trail with re-markable lack of exertion, turned their heads uneasily, and stopped in surprise. The driver was surprised, too; the sled had not moved. He called his comrades to witness the sight. Dave had bitten through both of Sol-leks's traces, and was standing directly in front of the sled in his proper place.

He pleaded with his eyes to remain there. The driver was perplexed. His comrades talked of how a dog could break its heart through being denied the work that killed it, and recalled instances they had known, where dogs, too old for the toil, or injured, had died because they were cut out of the traces. Also, they held it a mercy, since Dave was to die anyway, that he should die in the traces, heart-easy and content. So he was harnessed in again, and proudly he pulled as of old, though more than once he cried out involuntarily from the bite of his inward hurt. Several times he fell down and was dragged in the traces, and once the sled ran upon him so that he limped thereafter in one of his hind legs.

But he held out till camp was reached, when his driver made a place for him by the fire. Morning found him too weak to travel. At harness-up time he tried to crawl to his driver. By convulsive efforts he got on his feet, staggered, and fell. Then he wormed his way forward slowly toward where the harnesses were being put on his mates. He would advance his fore legs and drag up his body with a sort of hitching movement, when he would advance his fore legs and hitch ahead again for a few more inches. His strength left him, and the last his mates saw of him he lay gasping in the snow and yearning toward them. But they could hear him mournfully howling till they passed out of sight behind a belt of river timber.

Here the train was halted. The Scotch half-breed slowly retraced his steps to the camp they had left. The men ceased talking. A revolver-shot rang out. The man came back hurriedly. The whips snapped, the bells tinkled merrily, the sleds churned along the trail; but Buck knew, and every dog knew, what had taken place behind the belt of river trees.

# V

## THE TOIL OF TRACE
## AND TRAIL

Thirty days from the time it left Dawson, the Salt Water Mail, with Buck and his mates at the fore, arrived at Skaguay. They were in a wretched state, worn out and worn down. Buck's one hundred and forty pounds had dwindled to one hundred and fifteen. The rest of his mates, though lighter dogs, had relatively lost more weight than he. Pike, the malingerer, who, in his lifetime of deceit, had often successfully feigned a hurt leg, was now limping in earnest. Sol-leks was limping, and Dub was suffering from a wrenched shoulderblade.

They were all terribly footsore. No spring or rebound was left in them. Their feet fell heavily on the trail, jarring their bodies and doubling the fatigue of a day's travel. There was nothing the matter with them except that they were dead tired. It was not the dead-tiredness that comes through brief and excessive effort, from which recovery is a matter of hours; but it was the dead-tiredness that comes through the slow and prolonged strength drainage of months of toil. There was no power of recuperation left, no reserve strength to call upon. It had been all used, the last least bit of it. Every muscle, every fibre, every cell, was tired, dead tired. And there was reason for it. In less than five months they had travelled twenty-five hundred miles, during the last eighteen hundred of which they had had but five days' rest. When they arrived at Skaguay they were apparently on their last legs. They could barely keep the traces taut, and on the down grades just managed to keep out of the way of the sled.

"Mush on, poor sore feets," the driver encouraged them as they tottered down the main street of Skaguay. "Dis is de las'. Den we get one long res'. Eh? For sure. One bully long res'."

The drivers confidently expected a long stopover. Themselves, they had covered twelve hundred miles with two days' rest, and in the nature of reason and common justice they deserved an interval of loafing. But so many were the men who had rushed into the Klondike, and so many were the sweethearts, wives, and kin that had not rushed in, that the congested mail was taking on Alpine proportions; also, there were official orders. Fresh batches of Hudson Bay dogs were to take the places of those worthless for the trail. The worthless ones were to be got rid of, and, since dogs count for little against dollars, they were to be sold.

Three days passed, by which time Buck and his mates found how really tired and weak they were. Then, on the morning of the fourth day, two men from the States came along and bought them, harness and all, for a song. The men addressed each other as "Hal" and "Charles." Charles was a middle-aged, lightish-colored man, with weak and watery eyes and a mustache that twisted fiercely and vigorously up, giving the lie to the limply drooping lip it concealed. Hal was a youngster of nineteen or twenty, with a big Colt's revolver and a hunting-knife strapped about him on a belt that fairly bristled with cartridges. This belt was the most salient thing about him. It advertised his callowness—a callowness sheer and unutterable. Both men were manifestly out of place, and why such as they should adventure the North is part of the mystery of things that passes understanding.

Buck heard the chaffering, saw the money pass between the man and the Government agent, and knew that the Scotch half-breed and the mail-train drivers were passing out of his life on the heels of Perrault and François and the others who had gone before. When driven with his mates to the new owners' camp, Buck saw a slipshod and slovenly affair, tent half stretched, dishes unwashed, everything in disorder; also, he saw a woman. "Mercedes" the men called her. She was Charles's wife and Hal's sister—a nice family party.

Buck watched them apprehensively as they proceeded to take down the tent and load the sled. There was a great deal of effort about their manner, but no businesslike method. The tent was rolled into an awkward bundle three times as large as it should have been. The tin dishes were packed away unwashed. Mercedes continually fluttered in the way of her men and kept up an unbroken chattering of remonstrance and advice. When they put a clothes-sack on the front of the sled, she suggested it should go on the back; and when they had put it on the back, and covered it over with a couple of other bundles, she discovered overlooked articles which could abide nowhere else but in that very sack, and they unloaded again.

Three men from a neighboring tent came out and looked on, grinning and winking at one another.

"You've got a right smart load as it is," said one of them; "and it's not me should tell you your business, but I wouldn't tote that tent along if I was you."

"Undreamed of!" cried Mercedes, throwing up her hands in dainty dismay. "However in the world could I manage without a tent?"

"It's springtime, and you won't get any more cold weather," the man replied.

She shook her head decidedly, and Charles and Hal put the last odds and ends on top the mountainous load.

"Think it'll ride?" one of the men asked.

"Why shouldn't it?" Charles demanded rather shortly.

"Oh, that's all right, that's all right," the man hastened meekly to say. "I was just a-wonderin', that is all. It seemed a mite top-heavy."

Charles turned his back and drew the lashings down as well as he could, which was not in the least well.

"An' of course the dogs can hike along all day with that contraption behind them," affirmed a second of the men.

"Certainly," said Hal, with freezing politeness, taking hold of the gee-pole with one hand and swinging his whip from the other. "Mush!" he shouted. "Mush on there!"

The dogs sprang against the breast-bands, strained hard for a few moments, then relaxed. They were unable to move the sled.

"The lazy brutes, I'll show them," he cried, preparing to lash out at them with the whip.

But Mercedes interfered, crying, "Oh, Hal, you mustn't," as she caught hold of the whip and wrenched it from him. "The poor dears! Now you must promise you won't be harsh with them for the rest of the trip, or I won't go a step."

"Precious lot you know about dogs," her brother sneered; "and I wish you'd leave me alone. They're lazy, I tell you, and you've got to whip them to get anything out of them. That's their way. You ask any one. Ask one of those men."

Mercedes looked at them imploringly, untold repugnance at sight of pain written in her pretty face.

"They're weak as water, if you want to know," came the reply from one of the men. "Plum tuckered out, that's what's the matter. They need a rest."

"Rest be blanked," said Hal, with his beardless lips; and Mercedes said, "Oh!" in pain and sorrow at the oath.

But she was a clannish creature, and rushed at once to the defence of her brother. "Never mind that man," she said pointedly. "You're driving our dogs, and you do what you think best with them."

Again Hal's whip fell upon the dogs. They threw themselves against the breast-bands, dug their feet into the packed snow, got down low to it, and put forth all their strength. The sled held as though it were an anchor. After two efforts, they stood still, panting. The whip was whistling savagely, when once more Mercedes interfered. She dropped on her knees before Buck, with tears in her eyes, and put her arms around his neck.

"You poor, poor dears," she cried sympathetically, "why don't you pull hard?—then you wouldn't be whipped." Buck did not like her, but he was feeling too miserable to resist her, taking it as part of the day's miserable work.

One of the onlookers, who had been clenching his teeth to suppress hot speech, now spoke up:—

"It's not that I care a whoop what becomes of you, but for the dogs' sakes I just want to tell you, you can help them a mighty lot by breaking out that sled. The runners are froze fast. Throw your weight against the gee-pole, right and left, and break it out."

A third time the attempt was made, but this time, following the advice, Hal broke out the runners which had been frozen to the snow. The overloaded and unwieldy sled forged ahead, Buck and his mates struggling frantically under the rain of blows. A hundred yards ahead the path turned and sloped steeply into the main street. It would have required an experienced man to keep the top-heavy sled upright, and Hal was not such a man. As they swung on the turn the sled went over, spilling half its load through the loose lashings. The dogs never stopped. The lightened sled bounded on its side behind them. They were angry because of the ill treatment they had received and the unjust load. Buck was raging. He broke into a run, the team following his lead. Hal cried "Whoa! whoa!" but they gave no heed. He tripped and was pulled off his feet. The capsized sled ground over him, and the dogs dashed on up the street, adding to the gayety of Skaguay as they scattered the remainder of the outfit along its chief thoroughfare.

Kind-hearted citizens caught the dogs and gathered up the scattered belongings. Also, they gave advice. Half the load and twice the dogs, if they ever expected to reach Dawson, was what was said. Hal and his sister and brother-in-law listened unwillingly, pitched tent, and overhauled the outfit. Canned goods were turned out that made men laugh, for canned goods on the Long Trail is a thing to dream about. "Blankets for a hotel," quoth one of the men who laughed and helped. "Half as many is too much; get rid of them. Throw away that tent, and all those dishes,—who's going to wash them, anyway? Good Lord, do you think you're travelling on a Pullman?"

And so it went, the inexorable elimination of the superfluous. Mercedes cried when her clothes-bags were dumped on the ground and article after article was thrown out. She cried in general, and she cried in particular over each discarded thing. She clasped hands about knees, rocking back and forth broken-heartedly. She averred she would not go an inch, not for a dozen Charleses. She appealed to everybody and to everything, finally wiping her eyes and proceeding to cast out even articles of apparel that were imperative necessaries. And in her zeal, when she had finished with her own, she attacked the belongings of her men and went through them like a tornado.

This accomplished, the outfit, though cut in half, was still a formidable bulk. Charles and Hal went out in the evening and bought six Outside dogs. These, added to the six of the original team, and Teek and Koona, the huskies obtained at the Rink Rapids on the record trip, brought the team up to fourteen. But the Outside dogs, though practically broken in since their landing, did not amount to much. Three were short-haired pointers, one was a Newfoundland, and the other two were mongrels of indeterminate breed. They did not seem to know anything, these newcomers. Buck and his comrades looked upon them with disgust, and though he speedily taught them their places and what not to do, he could not teach them what to do. They did not take kindly to trace and trail. With the exception of the two mongrels, they were bewildered and spirit-broken by the strange savage environment in which they found themselves and by the ill treatment they had received. The two mongrels were without spirit at all; bones were the only things breakable about them.

With the newcomers hopeless and forlorn, and the old team worn out by twenty-five hundred miles of continuous trail, the outlook was anything but bright. The two men, however, were quite cheerful. And they were proud, too. They were doing the thing in style, with fourteen dogs. They had seen other sleds depart over the Pass for Dawson, or come in from Dawson, but never had they seen a sled with so many as fourteen dogs. In the nature of Arctic travel there was a reason why fourteen dogs should not drag one sled, and that was that one sled could not carry the food for fourteen dogs. But Charles and Hal did not know this. They had worked the trip out with a pencil, so much to a dog, so many dogs, so many days, Q.E.D. Mercedes looked over their shoulders and nodded comprehensively, it was all so very simple.

Late next morning Buck led the long team up the street. There was nothing lively about it, no snap or go in him and his fellows. They were starting dead weary. Four times he had covered the distance between Salt Water and Dawson, and the knowledge that, jaded and tired, he was facing the same trail once more, made him bitter. His heart was not in the work, nor was the heart of any dog. The Outsides were timid and frightened, the Insides without confidence in their masters.

Buck felt vaguely that there was no depending upon these two men and the woman. They did not know how to do anything, and as the days went by it became apparent that they could not learn. They were slack in all things, without order or discipline. It took them half the night to pitch a slovenly camp, and half the morning to break that camp and get the sled loaded in fashion so slovenly that for the rest of the day they were occupied in stopping and rearranging the load. Some days they did not make ten miles. On other days they were unable to get started at all. And on no day did they succeed in making more than half the distance used by the men as a basis in their dog-food computation.

It was inevitable that they should go short on dog-food. But they hastened it by overfeeding, bringing the day nearer when underfeeding would commence. The Outside dogs, whose digestions had not been trained by chronic famine to make the most of little, had voracious appetites. And when, in addition to this, the worn-out huskies pulled weakly, Hal decided that the orthodox ration was too small. He doubled it. And to cap it all, when Mercedes; with tears in her pretty eyes and a quaver in her throat, could not cajole him into giving the dogs still more, she stole from the fish-sacks and fed them slyly. But it was not food that Buck and the huskies needed, but rest. And though they were making poor time, the heavy load they dragged sapped their strength severely.

Then came the underfeeding. Hal awoke one day to the fact that his dog-food was half gone and the distance only quarter covered; further, that for love or money no additional dog-food was to be obtained. So he cut down even the orthodox ration and tried to increase the day's travel. His sister and brother-in-law seconded him; but they were frustrated by their heavy outfit and their own incompetence. It was a simple matter to give the dogs less food; but it was impossible to make the dogs travel faster, while their own inability to get under way earlier in the morning prevented them from travelling longer hours. Not only did they not know how to work dogs, but they did not know how to work themselves.

The first to go was Dub. Poor blundering thief that he was, always getting caught and punished, he had none the less been a faithful worker. His wrenched shoulder-blade, untreated and unrested, went from bad to worse, till finally Hal shot him with the big Colt's revolver. It is a saying of the country that an Outside dog starves to death on the ration of the husky, so the six Outside dogs under Buck could do no less than die on half the ration of the husky. The Newfoundland went first, followed by the three short-haired pointers, the two mongrels hanging more grittily on to life, but going in the end.

By this time all the amenities and gentlenesses of the Southland had fallen away from the three people. Shorn of its glamour and romance, Arctic travel became to them a reality too harsh for their manhood and womanhood. Mercedes ceased weeping over the dogs, being too occupied with weeping over herself and with quarrelling with her husband and brother. To quarrel was the one thing they were never too weary to do. Their irritability arose out of their misery, increased with it, doubled upon it, outdistanced it. The wonderful patience of the trail which comes to men who toil hard and suffer sore, and remain sweet of speech and kindly, did not come to these two men and the woman. They had no inkling of such a patience. They were stiff and in pain; their muscles ached; their bones ached, their very hearts ached; and because of this they became sharp of speech, and hard words were first on their lips in the morning and last at night.

Charles and Hal wrangled whenever Mercedes gave them a chance. It was the cherished belief of each that he did more than his share of the work, and neither forbore to speak this belief at every opportunity. Sometimes Mercedes sided with her husband, sometimes with her brother. The result was a beautiful and unending family quarrel. Starting from a dispute as to which should chop a few sticks for the fire (a dispute which concerned only Charles and Hal), presently would be lugged in the rest of the family, fathers, mothers, uncles, cousins, people thousands of miles away, and some of them dead. That Hal's views on art, or the sort of society plays his mother's brother wrote, should have anything to do with the chopping of a few sticks of firewood, passes comprehension; nevertheless the quarrel was as likely to tend in that direction as in the direction of Charles's political prejudices. And that Charles's sister's tale-bearing tongue should be relevant to the building of a Yukon fire, was apparent only to Mercedes, who disburdened herself of copious opinions upon that topic, and incidentally upon a few other traits unpleasantly peculiar to her husband's family. In the meantime the fire remained unbuilt, the camp half pitched, and the dogs unfed.

Mercedes nursed a special grievance—the grievance of sex. She was pretty and soft, and had been chivalrously treated all her days. But the present treatment by her husband and brother was everything save chivalrous. It was her custom to be helpless. They complained. Upon which impeachment of what to her was her most essential sex-prerogative, she made their lives unendurable. She no longer considered the dogs, and because she was sore and tired, she persisted in riding on the sled. She was pretty and soft, but she weighed one hundred and twenty pounds—a lusty last straw to the load dragged by the weak and starving animals. She rode for days, till they fell in the traces and the sled stood still. Charles and Hal begged her to get off and walk, pleaded with her, entreated, the while she wept and importuned Heaven with a recital of their brutality.

On one occasion they took her off the sled by main strength. They never did it again. She let her legs go limp like a spoiled child, and sat down on the trail. They went on their way, but she did not move. After they had travelled three miles they unloaded the sled, came back for her, and by main strength put her on the sled again.

In the excess of their own misery they were callous to the suffering of their animals. Hal's theory, which he practised on others, was that one must get hardened. He had started out preaching it to his sister and brother-in-law. Failing there, he hammered it into the dogs with a club. At the Five Fingers the dog-food gave out, and a toothless old squaw offered to trade them a few pounds of frozen horse-hide for the Colt's revolver that kept the big hunting-knife company at Hal's hip. A poor substitute for food was this hide, just as it had been stripped from the starved horses of the cattlemen six months back. In its frozen state it was more like strips of galvanized iron, and when a dog wrestled it into his stomach it thawed into thin and innutritious leathery strings and into a mass of short hair, irritating and indigestible.

And through it all Buck staggered along at the head of the team as in a nightmare. He pulled when he could; when he could no longer pull, he fell down and remained down till blows from whip or club drove him to his feet again. All the stiffness and gloss had gone out of his beautiful furry coat. The hair hung down, limp and draggled, or matted with dried blood where Hal's club had bruised him. His muscles had wasted away to knotty strings, and the flesh pads had disappeared, so that each rib and every bone in his frame were outlined cleanly through the loose hide that was wrinkled in folds of emptiness. It was heartbreaking, only Buck's heart was unbreakable. The man in the red sweater had proved that.

As it was with Buck, so was it with his mates. They were perambulating skeletons. There were seven all together, including him. In their very great misery they had become insensible to the bite of the lash or the bruise of the club. The pain of the beating was dull and distant, just as the things their eyes saw and their ears heard seemed dull and distant. They were not half living, or quarter living. They were simply so many bags of bones in which sparks of life fluttered faintly. When a halt was made, they dropped down in the traces like dead dogs, and the spark dimmed and paled and seemed to go out. And when the club or whip fell upon them, the spark fluttered feebly up, and they tottered to their feet and staggered on.

There came a day when Billee, the good-natured, fell and could not rise. Hal had traded off his revolver, so he took the axe and knocked Billee on the head as he lay in the traces, then cut the carcass out of the harness and dragged it to one side. Buck saw, and his mates saw, and they knew that this thing was very close to them. On the next day Koona went, and but five of them remained: Joe, too far gone to be malignant; Pike, crippled and limping, only half conscious and not conscious enough longer to malinger; Sol-leks, the one-eyed, still faithful to the toil of trace and trail, and mournful in that he had so little strength with which to pull; Teek, who had not travelled so far that winter and who was now beaten more than the others because he was fresher; and Buck, still at the head of the team, but no longer enforcing discipline or striving to enforce it, blind with weakness half the time and keeping the trail by the loom of it and by the dim feel of his feet.

It was beautiful spring weather, but neither dogs nor humans were aware of it. Each day the sun rose earlier and set later. It was dawn by three in the morning, and twilight lingered till nine at night. The whole long day was a blaze of sunshine. The ghostly winter silence had given way to the great spring murmur of awakening life. This murmur arose from all the land, fraught with the joy of living. It came from the things that lived and moved again, things which had been as dead and which had not moved during the long months of frost. The sap was rising in the pines. The willows and aspens were bursting out in young buds. Shrubs and vines were putting on fresh garbs of green. Crickets sang in the nights, and in the days all manner of creeping, crawling things rustled forth into the sun. Partridges and woodpeckers were booming and knocking in the forest. Squirrels were chattering, birds singing, and overhead honked the wild-fowl driving up from the south in cunning wedges that split the air.

From every hill slope came the trickle of running water, the music of unseen fountains. All things were thawing, bending, snapping. The Yukon was straining to break loose the ice that bound it down. It ate away from beneath; the sun ate from above. Air-holes formed, fissures sprang and spread apart, while thin sections of ice fell through bodily into the river. And amid all this bursting, rending, throbbing of awakening life, under the blazing sun and through the soft-sighing breezes, like wayfarers to death, staggered the two men, the woman, and the huskies.

With the dogs falling, Mercedes weeping and riding, Hal swearing innocuously, and Charles's eyes wistfully watering, they staggered into John Thornton's camp at the mouth of White River. When they halted, the dogs dropped down as though they had all been struck dead. Mercedes dried her eyes and looked at John Thornton. Charles sat down on a log to rest. He sat down very slowly and painstakingly what of his great stiffness. Hal did the talking. John Thornton was whittling the last touches on an axe-handle he had made from a stick of birch. He whittled and listened, gave monosyllabic replies, and, when it was asked, terse advice. He knew the breed, and he gave his advice in the certainty that it would not be followed.

"They told us up above that the bottom was dropping out of the trail and that the best thing for us to do was to lay over," Hal said in response to Thornton's warning to take no more chances on the rotten ice. "They told us we couldn't make White River, and here we are." This last with a sneering ring of triumph in it.

"And they told you true," John Thornton answered. "The bottom's likely to drop out at any moment. Only fools, with the blind luck of fools, could have made it. I tell you straight, I wouldn't risk my carcass on that ice for all the gold in Alaska."

"That's because you're not a fool, I suppose," said Hal. "All the same, we'll go on to Dawson." He uncoiled his whip. "Get up there, Buck! Hi! Get up there! Mush on!"

Thornton went on whittling. It was idle, he knew, to get between a fool and his folly; while two or three fools more or less would not alter the scheme of things.

But the team did not get up at the command. It had long since passed into the stage where blows were required to rouse it. The whip flashed out, here and there, on its merciless errands. John Thornton compressed his lips. Sol-leks was the first to crawl to his feet. Teek followed. Joe came next, yelping with pain. Pike made painful efforts. Twice he fell over, when half up, and on the third attempt managed to rise. Buck made no effort. He lay quietly where he had fallen. The lash bit into him again and again, but he neither whined nor struggled. Several times Thornton started, as though to speak, but changed his mind. A moisture came into his eyes, and, as the whipping continued, he arose and walked irresolutely up and down.

This was the first time Buck had failed, in itself a sufficient reason to drive Hal into a rage. He exchanged the whip for the customary club. Buck refused to move under the rain of heavier blows which now fell upon him. Like his mates, he was barely able to get up, but, unlike them, he had made up his mind not to get up. He had a vague feeling of impending doom. This had been strong upon him when he pulled in to the bank, and it had not departed from him. What of the thin and rotten ice he had felt under his feet all day, it seemed that he sensed disaster close at hand, out there ahead on the ice where his master was trying to drive him. He refused to stir. So greatly had he suffered, and so far gone was he, that the blows did not hurt much. And as they continued to fall upon him, the spark of life within flickered and went down. It was nearly out. He felt strangely numb. As though from a great distance, he was aware that he was being beaten. The last sensations of pain left him. He no longer felt anything, though very faintly he could hear the impact of the club upon his body. But it was no longer his body, it seemed so far away.

And then, suddenly, without warning, uttering a cry that was inarticulate and more like the cry of an animal, John Thornton sprang upon the man who wielded the club. Hal was hurled backward, as though struck by a falling tree. Mercedes screamed. Charles looked on wistfully, wiped his watery eyes, but did not get up because of his stiffness.

John Thornton stood over Buck, struggling to control himself, too convulsed with rage to speak.

"If you strike that dog again, I'll kill you," he at last managed to say in a choking voice.

"It's my dog," Hal replied, wiping the blood from his mouth as he came back. "Get out of my way, or I'll fix you. I'm going to Dawson."

Thornton stood between him and Buck, and evinced no intention of getting out of the way. Hal drew his long hunting-knife. Mercedes screamed, cried, laughed, and manifested the chaotic abandonment of hysteria. Thornton rapped Hal's knuckles with the axe-handle, knocking the knife to the ground. He rapped his knuckles again as he tried to pick it up. Then he stooped, picked it up himself, and with two strokes cut Buck's traces.

Hal had no fight left in him. Besides, his hands were full with his sister, or his arms, rather; while Buck was too near dead to be of further use in hauling the sled. A few minutes later they pulled out from the bank and down the river. Buck heard them go and raised his head to see. Pike was leading, Sol-leks was at the wheel, and between were Joe and Teek. They were limping and staggering. Mercedes was riding the loaded sled. Hal guided at the gee-pole, and Charles stumbled along in the rear.

As Buck watched them, Thornton knelt beside him and with rough, kindly hands searched for broken bones. By the time his search had disclosed nothing more than many bruises and a state of terrible starvation, the sled was a quarter of a mile away. Dog and man watched it crawling along over the ice. Suddenly, they saw its back end drop down, as into a rut, and the gee-pole, with Hal clinging to it, jerk into the air. Mercedes's scream came to their ears. They saw Charles turn and make one step to run back, and then a whole section of ice give way and dogs and humans disappear. A yawning hole was all that was to be seen. The bottom had dropped out of the trail.

John Thornton and Buck looked at each other.

"You poor devil," said John Thornton, and Buck licked his hand.

# VI

## FOR THE LOVE OF
## A MAN

When John Thornton froze his feet in the previous December, his partners had made him comfortable and left him to get well, going on themselves up the river to get out a raft of saw-logs for Dawson. He was still limping slightly at the time he rescued Buck, but with the continued warm weather even the slight limp left him. And here, lying by the river bank through the long spring days, watching the running water, listening lazily to the songs of birds and the hum of nature, Buck slowly won back his strength.

A rest comes very good after one has travelled three thousand miles, and it must be confessed that Buck waxed lazy as his wounds healed, his muscles swelled out, and the flesh came back to cover his bones. For that matter, they were all loafing,—Buck, John Thornton, and Skeet and Nig,—waiting for the raft to come that was to carry them down to Dawson. Skeet was a little Irish setter who early made friends with Buck, who, in a dying condition, was unable to resent her first advances. She had the doctor trait which some dogs possess; and as a mother cat washes her kittens, so she washed and cleansed Buck's wounds. Regularly, each morning after he had finished his breakfast, she performed her self-appointed task, till he came to look for her ministrations as much as he did for Thornton's. Nig, equally friendly, though less demonstrative, was a huge black dog, half bloodhound and half deerhound, with eyes that laughed and a boundless good nature.

To Buck's surprise these dogs manifested no jealousy toward him. They seemed to share the kindliness and largeness of John Thornton.

As Buck grew stronger they enticed him into all sorts of ridiculous games, in which Thornton himself could not forbear to join; and in this fashion Buck romped through his convalescence and into a new existence. Love, genuine passionate love, was his for the first time. This he had never experienced at Judge Miller's down in the sun-kissed Santa Clara Valley. With the Judge's sons, hunting and tramping, it had been a working partnership; with the Judge's grandsons, a sort of pompous guardianship; and with the Judge himself, a stately and dignified friendship. But love that was feverish and burning, that was adoration, that was madness, it had taken John Thornton to arouse.

This man had saved his life, which was something; but, further, he was the ideal master. Other men saw to the welfare of their dogs from a sense of duty and business expediency; he saw to the welfare of his as if they were his own children, because he could not help it. And he saw further. He never forgot a kindly greeting or a cheering word, and to sit down for a long talk with them ("gas" he called it) was as much his delight as theirs. He had a way of taking Buck's head roughly between his hands, and resting his own head upon Buck's, of shaking him back and forth, the while calling him ill names that to Buck were love names. Buck knew no greater joy than that rough embrace and the sound of murmured oaths, and at each jerk back and forth it seemed that his heart would be shaken out of his body so great was its ecstasy. And when, released, he sprang to his feet, his mouth laughing, his eyes eloquent, his throat vibrant with unuttered sound, and in that fashion remained without movement, John Thornton would reverently exclaim, "God! you can all but speak!"

Buck had a trick of love expression that was akin to hurt. He would often seize Thornton's hand in his mouth and close so fiercely that the flesh bore the impress of his teeth for some time afterward. And as Buck understood the oaths to be love words, so the man understood this feigned bite for a caress.

For the most part, however, Buck's love was expressed in adoration. While he went wild with happiness when Thornton touched him or spoke to him, he did not seek these tokens. Unlike Skeet, who was wont to shove her nose under Thornton's hand and nudge and nudge till petted, or Nig, who would stalk up and rest his great head on Thornton's knee, Buck was content to adore at a distance. He would lie by the hour, eager, alert, at Thornton's feet, looking up into his face, dwelling upon it, studying it, following with keenest interest each fleeting expression, every movement or change of feature. Or, as chance might have it, he would lie farther away, to the side or rear, watching the outlines of the man and the occasional movements of his body. And often, such was the communion in which they lived, the strength of Buck's gaze would draw John Thornton's head around, and he would return the gaze, without speech, his heart shining out of his eyes as Buck's heart shone out.

For a long time after his rescue, Buck did not like Thornton to get out of his sight. From the moment he left the tent to when he entered it again, Buck would follow at his heels. His transient masters since he had come into the Northland had bred in him a fear that no master could be permanent. He was afraid that Thornton would pass out of his life as Perrault and François and the Scotch half-breed had passed out. Even in the night, in his dreams, he was haunted by this fear. At such times he would shake off sleep and creep through the chill to the flap of the tent, where he would stand and listen to the sound of his master's breathing.

But in spite of this great love he bore John Thornton, which seemed to bespeak the soft civilizing influence, the strain of the primitive, which the Northland had aroused in him, remained alive and active. Faithfulness and devotion, things born of fire and roof, were his; yet he retained his wildness and wiliness. He was a thing of the wild, come in from the wild to sit by John Thornton's fire, rather than a dog of the soft Southland stamped with the marks of generations of civilization. Because of his very great love, he could not steal from this man, but from any other man, in any other camp, he did not hesitate an instant; while the cunning with which he stole enabled him to escape detection.

His face and body were scored by the teeth of many dogs, and he fought as fiercely as ever and more shrewdly. Skeet and Nig were too good-natured for quarrelling,—besides, they belonged to John Thornton; but the strange dog, no matter what the breed or valor, swiftly acknowledged Buck's supremacy or found himself struggling for life with a terrible antagonist. And Buck was merciless. He had learned well the law of club and fang, and he never forewent an advantage or drew back from a foe he had started on the way to Death. He had lessoned from Spitz, and from the chief fighting dogs of the police and mail, and knew there was no middle course. He must master or be mastered; while to show mercy was a weakness. Mercy did not exist in the primordial life. It was misunderstood for fear, and such misunderstandings made for death. Kill or be killed, eat or be eaten, was the law; and this mandate, down out of the depths of Time, he obeyed.

He was older than the days he had seen and the breaths he had drawn. He linked the past with the present, and the eternity behind him throbbed through him in a mighty rhythm to which he swayed as the tides and seasons swayed. He sat by John Thornton's fire, a broad-breasted dog, white-fanged and long-furred; but behind him were the shades of all manner of dogs, half-wolves and wild wolves, urgent and prompting, tasting the savor of the meat he ate, thirsting for the water he drank, scenting the wind with him, listening with him and telling him the sounds made by the wild life in the forest, dictating his moods, directing his actions, lying down to sleep with him when he lay down, and dreaming with him and beyond him and becoming themselves the stuff of his dreams.

So peremptorily did these shades beckon him, that each day mankind and the claims of mankind slipped farther from him. Deep in the forest a call was sounding, and as often as he heard this call, mysteriously thrilling and luring, he felt compelled to turn his back upon the fire and the beaten earth around it, and to plunge into the forest, and on and on, he knew not where or why; nor did he wonder where or why, the call sounding imperiously, deep in the forest. But as often as he gained the soft unbroken earth and the green shade, the love for John Thornton drew him back to the fire again.

Thornton alone held him. The rest of mankind was as nothing. Chance travellers might praise or pet him; but he was cold under it all, and from a too demonstrative man he would get up and walk away. When Thornton's partners, Hans and Pete, arrived on the long-expected raft, Buck refused to notice them till he learned they were close to Thornton; after that he tolerated them in a passive sort of way, accepting favors from them as though he favored them by accepting. They were of the same large type as Thornton, living close to the earth, thinking simply and seeing clearly; and ere they swung the raft into the big eddy by the saw-mill at Dawson, they understood Buck and his ways, and did not insist upon an intimacy such as obtained with Skeet and Nig.

For Thornton, however, his love seemed to grow and grow. He, alone among men, could put a pack upon Buck's back in the summer travelling. Nothing was too great for Buck to do, when Thornton commanded. One day (they had grub-staked themselves from the proceeds of the raft and left Dawson for the head-waters of the Tanana) the men and dogs were sitting on the crest of a cliff which fell away, straight down, to naked bed-rock three hundred feet below. John Thornton was sitting near the edge, Buck at his shoulder. A thoughtless whim seized Thornton, and he drew the attention of Hans and Pete to the experiment he had in mind. "Jump, Buck!" he commanded, sweeping his arm out and over the chasm. The next instant he was grappling with Buck on the extreme edge, while Hans and Pete were dragging them back into safety.

"It's uncanny," Pete said, after it was over and they had caught their speech.

Thornton shook his head. "No, it is splendid, and it is terrible, too. Do you know, it sometimes makes me afraid."

"I'm not hankering to be the man that lays hands on you while he's around," Pete announced conclusively, nodding his head toward Buck.

"Py Jingo!" was Hans's contribution. "Not mineself either."

It was at Circle City, ere the year was out, that Pete's apprehensions were realized. "Black" Burton, a man evil-tempered and malicious, had been picking a quarrel with a tenderfoot at the bar, when Thornton stepped good-naturedly between. Buck, as was his custom, was lying in a corner, head on paws, watching his master's every action. Burton struck out, without warning, straight from the shoulder. Thornton was sent spinning, and saved himself from falling only by clutching the rail of the bar.

Those who were looking on heard what was neither bark nor yelp, but a something which is best described as a roar, and they saw Buck's body rise up in the air as he left the floor for Burton's throat. The man saved his life by instinctively throwing out his arm, but was hurled backward to the floor with Buck on top of him. Buck loosed his teeth from the flesh of the arm and drove in again for the throat. This time the man succeeded only in partly blocking, and his throat was torn open. Then the crowd was upon Buck, and he was driven off; but while a surgeon checked the bleeding, he prowled up and down, growling furiously, attempting to rush in, and being forced back by an array of hostile clubs. A "miners' meeting," called on the spot, decided that the dog had sufficient provocation, and Buck was discharged. But his reputation was made, and from that day his name spread through every camp in Alaska.

Later on, in the fall of the year, he saved John Thornton's life in quite another fashion. The three partners were lining a long and narrow poling-boat down a bad stretch of rapids on the Forty-Mile Creek. Hans and Pete moved along the bank, snubbing with a thin Manila rope from tree to tree, while Thornton remained in the boat, helping its descent by means of a pole, and shouting directions to the shore. Buck, on the bank, worried and anxious, kept abreast of the boat, his eyes never off his master.

At a particularly bad spot, where a ledge of barely submerged rocks jutted out into the river, Hans cast off the rope, and, while Thornton poled the boat out into the stream, ran down the bank with the end in his hand to snub the boat when it had cleared the ledge. This it did, and was flying down-stream in a current as swift as a mill-race, when Hans checked it with the rope and checked too suddenly. The boat flirted over and snubbed in to the bank bottom up, while Thornton, flung sheer out of it, was carried down-stream toward the worst part of the rapids, a stretch of wild water in which no swimmer could live.

Buck had sprung in on the instant; and at the end of three hundred yards, amid a mad swirl of water, he overhauled Thornton. When he felt him grasp his tail, Buck headed for the bank, swimming with all his splendid strength. But the progress shoreward was slow; the progress down-stream amazingly rapid. From below came the fatal roaring where the wild current went wilder and was rent in shreds and spray by the rocks which thrust through like the teeth of an enormous comb. The suck of the water as it took the beginning of the last steep pitch was frightful, and Thornton knew that the shore was impossible. He scraped furiously over a rock, bruised across a second, and struck a third with crushing force. He clutched its slipper top with both hands, releasing Buck, and above the roar of the churning water shouted: "Go, Buck! Go!"

Buck could not hold his own, and swept on down-stream, struggling desperately, but unable to win back. When he heard Thornton's command repeated, he partly reared out of the water, throwing his head high, as though for a last look, then turned obediently toward the bank. He swam powerfully and was dragged ashore by Pete and Hans at the very point where swimming ceased to be possible and destruction began.

They knew that the time a man could cling to a slippery rock in the face of that driving current was a matter of minutes, and they ran as fast as they could up the bank to a point far above where Thornton was hanging on. They attached the line with which they had been snubbing the boat to Buck's neck and shoulders, being careful that it should neither strangle him nor impede his swimming, and launched him into the stream. He struck out boldly, but not straight enough into the stream. He discovered the mistake too late, when Thornton was abreast of him and a bare half-dozen strokes away while he was being carried helplessly past.

Hans promptly snubbed with the rope, as though Buck were a boat. The rope thus tightening on him in the sweep of the current, he was jerked under the surface, and under the surface he remained till his body struck against the bank and he was hauled out. He was half drowned, and Hans and Pete threw themselves upon him, pounding the breath into him and the water out of him. He staggered to his feet and fell down. The faint sound of Thornton's voice came to them, and though they could not make out the words of it, they knew that he was in his extremity. His master's voice acted on Buck like an electric shock. He sprang to his feet and ran up the bank ahead of the men to the point of his previous departure.

Again the rope was attached and he was launched, and again he struck out, but this time straight into the stream. He had miscalculated once, but he would not be guilty of it a second time. Hans paid out the rope, permitting no slack, while Pete kept it clear of coils. Buck held on till he was on a line straight above Thornton; then he turned, and with the speed of an express train headed down upon him. Thornton saw him coming, and, as Buck struck him like a battering ram, with the whole force of the current behind him, he reached up and closed with both arms around the shaggy neck. Hans snubbed the rope around the tree, and Buck and Thornton were jerked under the water. Strangling, suffocating, sometimes one uppermost and sometimes the other, dragging over the jagged bottom, smashing against rocks and snags, they veered in to the bank.

Thornton came to, belly downward and being violently propelled back and forth across a drift log by Hans and Pete. His first glance was for Buck, over whose limp and apparently lifeless body Nig was setting up a howl, while Skeet was licking the wet face and closed eyes. Thornton was himself bruised and battered, and he went carefully over Buck's body, when he had been brought around, finding three broken ribs.

"That settles it," he announced. "We camp right here." And camp they did, till Buck's ribs knitted and he was able to travel.

That winter, at Dawson, Buck performed another exploit, not so heroic, perhaps, but one that put his name many notches higher on the totem-pole of Alaskan fame. This exploit was particularly gratifying to the three men; for they stood in need of the outfit which it furnished, and were enabled to make a long-desired trip into the virgin

East, where miners had not yet appeared. It was brought about by a conversation in the Eldorado Saloon, in which men waxed boastful of their favorite dogs. Buck, because of his record, was the target for these men, and Thornton was driven stoutly to defend him. At the end of half an hour one man stated that his dog could start a sled with five hundred pounds and walk off with it; a second bragged six hundred for his dog; and a third, seven hundred.

"Pooh! pooh!" said John Thornton; "Buck can start a thousand pounds."

"And break it out? and walk off with it for a hundred yards?" demanded Matthewson, a Bonanza King, he of the seven hundred vaunt.

"And break it out, and walk off with it for a hundred yards," John Thornton said coolly.

"Well," Matthewson said, slowly and deliberately, so that all could hear, "I've got a thousand dollars that says he can't. And there it is." So saying, he slammed a sack of gold dust of the size of a bologna sausage down upon the bar.

Nobody spoke. Thornton's bluff, if bluff it was, had been called. He could feel a flush of warm blood creeping up his face. His tongue had tricked him. He did not know whether Buck could start a thousand pounds. Half a ton! The enormousness of it appalled him. He had great faith in Buck's strength and had often thought him capable of starting such a load; but never, as now, had he faced the possibility of it, the eyes of a dozen men fixed upon him, silent and waiting. Further, he had no thousand dollars; nor had Hans or Pete.

"I've got a sled standing outside now, with twenty fifty-pound sacks of flour on it," Matthewson went on with brutal directness; "so don't let that hinder you."

Thornton did not reply. He did not know what to say. He glanced from face to face in the absent way of a man who has lost the power of thought and is seeking somewhere to find the thing that will start it going again. The face of Jim O'Brien, a Mastodon King and old-time comrade, caught his eyes. It was as a cue to him, seeming to rouse him to do what he would never have dreamed of doing.

"Can you lend me a thousand?" he asked, almost in a whisper.

"Sure," answered O'Brien, thumping down a plethoric sack by the side of Matthewson's. "Though it's little faith I'm having, John, that the beast can do the trick."

The Eldorado emptied its occupants into the street to see the test. The tables were deserted, and the dealers and gamekeepers came forth to see the outcome of the wager and to lay odds. Several hundred men, furred and mittened, banked around the sled within easy distance. Matthewson's sled, loaded with a thousand pounds of flour, had been standing for a couple of hours, and in the intense cold (it was sixty below zero) the runners had frozen fast to the hard-packed snow. Men offered odds of two to one that Buck could not budge the sled. A quibble arose concerning the phrase "break out." O'Brien contended it was Thornton's privilege to knock the runners loose, leaving Buck to "break it out" from a dead standstill. Matthewson insisted that the phrase included breaking the runners from the frozen grip of the snow. A majority of the men who had witnessed the making of the bet decided in his favor, whereat the odds went up to three to one against Buck.

There were no takers. Not a man believed him capable of the feat. Thornton had been hurried into the wager, heavy with doubt; and now that he looked at the sled itself, the concrete fact, with the regular team of ten dogs curled up in the snow before it, the more impossible the task appeared. Matthewson waxed jubilant.

"Three to one!" he proclaimed. "I'll lay you another thousand at that figure, Thornton. What d'ye say?"

Thornton's doubt was strong in his face, but his fighting spirit was aroused—the fighting spirit that soars above odds, fails to recognize the impossible, and is deaf to all save the clamor for battle. He called Hans and Pete to him. Their sacks were slim, and with his own the three partners could rake together only two hundred dollars. In the ebb of their fortunes, this sum was their total capital; yet they laid it unhesitatingly against Matthewson's six hundred.

The team of ten dogs was unhitched, and Buck, with his own harness, was put into the sled. He had caught the contagion of the excitement, and he felt that in some way he must do a great thing for John Thornton. Murmurs of admiration at his splendid appearance went up. He was in perfect condition, without an ounce of superfluous flesh, and the one hundred and fifty pounds that he weighed were so many pounds of grit and virility. His furry coat shone with the sheen of silk. Down the neck and across the shoulders, his mane, in repose as it was, half bristled and seemed to lift with every movement, as though excess of vigor made each particular hair alive and active. The great breast and heavy fore legs were no more than in proportion with the rest of the body, where the muscles showed in tight rolls underneath the skin. Men felt these muscles and proclaimed them hard as iron, and the odds went down to two to one.

"Gad, sir! Gad, sir!" stuttered a member of the latest dynasty, a king of the Skookum Benches. "I offer you eight hundred for him, sir, before the test, sir; eight hundred just as he stands."

Thornton shook his head and stepped to Buck's side.

"You must stand off from him," Matthewson protested. "Free play and plenty of room."

The crowd fell silent; only could be heard the voices of the gamblers vainly offering two to one. Everybody acknowledged Buck a magnificent animal, but twenty fifty-pound sacks of flour bulked too large in their eyes for them to loosen their pouch-strings.

Thornton knelt down by Buck's side. He took his head in his two hands and rested cheek on cheek. He did not playfully shake him, as was his wont, or murmur soft love curses; but he whispered in his ear. "As you love me, Buck. As you love me," was what he whispered. Buck whined with suppressed eagerness.

The crowd was watching curiously. The affair was growing mysterious. It seemed like a conjuration. As Thornton got to his feet, Buck seized his mittened hand between his jaws, pressing in with his teeth and releasing slowly, half-reluctantly. It was the answer, in terms, not of speech, but of love. Thornton stepped well back.

"Now, Buck," he said.

Buck tightened the traces, then slacked them for a matter of several inches. It was the way he had learned.

"Gee!" Thornton's voice rang out, sharp in the tense silence.

Buck swung to the right, ending the movement in a plunge that took up the slack and with a sudden jerk arrested his one hundred and fifty pounds. The load quivered, and from under the runners arose a crisp crackling.

"Haw!" Thornton commanded.

Buck duplicated the manœuvre, this time to the left. The crackling turned into a snapping, the sled pivoting and the runners slipping and grating several inches to the side. The sled was broken out. Men were holding their breaths, intensely unconscious of the fact.

"Now, MUSH!"

Thornton's command cracked out like a pistol-shot. Buck threw himself forward, tightening the traces with a jarring lunge. His whole body was gathered compactly together in the tremendous effort, the muscles writhing and knotting like live things under the silky fur. His great chest was low to the ground, his head forward and down, while his feet were flying like mad, the claws scarring the hard-packed snow in parallel grooves. The sled swayed and trembled, half-started forward. One of his feet slipped, and one man groaned aloud. Then the sled lurched ahead in what appeared a rapid succession of jerks, though it never really came to a dead stop again . . . half an inch . . . an inch . . . two inches. . . . The jerks perceptibly diminished; as the sled gained momentum, he caught them up, till it was moving steadily along.

Men gasped and began to breathe again, unaware that for a moment they had ceased to breathe. Thornton was running behind, encouraging Buck with short, cheery words. The distance had been measured off, and as he neared the pile of firewood which marked the end of the hundred yards, a cheer began to grow and grow, which burst into a roar as he passed the firewood and halted at command. Every man was tearing himself loose, even Matthewson. Hats and mittens were flying in the air. Men were shaking hands, it did not matter with whom, and bubbling over in a general incoherent babel.

But Thornton fell on his knees beside Buck. Head was against head, and he was shaking him back and forth. Those who hurried up heard him cursing Buck, and he cursed him long and fervently, and softly and lovingly.

"Gad, sir! Gad, sir!" spluttered the Skookum Bench king. "I'll give you a thousand for him, sir, a thousand, sir—twelve hundred, sir."

Thornton rose to his feet. His eyes were wet. The tears were streaming frankly down his cheeks. "Sir," he said to the Skookum Bench king, "no, sir. You can go to hell, sir. It's the best I can do for you, sir."

Buck seized Thornton's hand in his teeth. Thornton shook him back and forth. As though animated by a common impulse, the onlookers drew back to a respectful distance; nor were they again indiscreet enough to interrupt.

# VII

## THE SOUNDING OF
## THE CALL

When Buck earned sixteen hundred dollars in five minutes for John Thornton, he made it possible for his master to pay off certain debts and to journey with his partners into the East after a fabled lost mine, the history of which was as old as the history of the country. Many men had sought it; few had found it; and more than a few there were who had never returned from the quest. This lost mine was steeped in tragedy and shrouded in mystery. No one knew of the first man. The oldest tradition stopped before it got back to him. From the beginning there had been an ancient and ramshackle cabin. Dying men had sworn to it, and to the mine the site of which it marked, clinching their testimony with nuggets that were unlike any known grade of gold in the Northland.

But no living man had looted this treasure house, and the dead were dead; wherefore John Thornton and Pete and Hans, with Buck and half a dozen other dogs, faced into the East on an unknown trail to achieve where men and dogs as good as themselves had failed. They sledded seventy miles up the Yukon, swung to the left into the Stewart River, passed the Mayo and the McQuestion, and held on until the Stewart itself became a streamlet, threading the upstanding peaks which marked the backbone of the continent.

John Thornton asked little of man or nature. He was unafraid of the wild. With a handful of salt and a rifle he could plunge into the wilderness and fare wherever he pleased and as long as he pleased. Being in no haste, Indian fashion, he hunted his dinner in the course of the day's travel; and if he failed to find it, like the Indian, he kept on travelling, secure in the knowledge that sooner or later he would come to it. So, on this great journey into the East, straight meat was the bill of fare, ammunition and tools principally made up the load on the sled, and the time-card was drawn upon the limitless future.

To Buck it was boundless delight, this hunting, fishing, and indefinite wandering through strange places. For weeks at a time they would hold on steadily, day after day; and for weeks upon end they would camp, here and there, the dogs loafing and the men burning holes through frozen muck and gravel and washing countless pans of dirt by the heat of the fire. Sometimes they went hungry, sometimes they feasted riotously, all according to the abundance of game and the fortune of hunting. Summer arrived, and dogs and men packed on their backs, rafted across blue mountain lakes, and descended or ascended unknown rivers in slender boats whipsawed from the standing forest.

The months came and went, and back and forth they twisted through the uncharted vastness, where no men were and yet where men had been if the Lost Cabin were true. They went across divides in summer blizzards, shivered under the midnight sun on naked mountains between the timber line and the eternal snows, dropped into summer valleys amid swarming gnats and flies, and in the shadows of glaciers picked strawberries and flowers as ripe and fair as any the Southland could boast. In the fall of the year they penetrated a weird lake country, sad and silent, where wild-fowl had been, but where then there was no life nor sign of life—only the blowing of chill winds, the forming of ice in sheltered places, and the melancholy rippling of waves on lonely beaches.

And through another winter they wandered on the obliterated trails of men who had gone before. Once, they came upon a path blazed through the forest, an ancient path, and the Lost Cabin seemed very near. But the path began nowhere and ended nowhere, and it remained mystery, as the man who made it and the reason he made it remained mystery. Another time they chanced upon the time-graven wreckage of a hunting lodge, and amid the shreds of rotted blankets John Thornton found a long-barrelled flint-lock. He knew it for a Hudson Bay Company gun of the young days in the Northwest, when such a gun was worth its height in beaver skins packed flat. And that was all—no hint as to the man who in an early day had reared the lodge and left the gun among the blankets.

Spring came on once more, and at the end of all their wandering they found, not the Lost Cabin, but a shallow placer in a broad valley where the gold showed like yellow butter across the bottom of the washing-pan. They sought no farther. Each day they worked earned them thousands of dollars in clean dust and nuggets, and they worked every day. The gold was sacked in moose-hide bags, fifty pounds to the bag, and piled like so much firewood outside the spruce-bough lodge. Like giants they toiled, days flashing on the heels of days like dreams as they heaped the treasure up.

There was nothing for the dogs to do, save the hauling in of meat now and again that Thornton killed, and Buck spent long hours musing by the fire. The vision of the short-legged hairy man came to him more frequently, now that there was little work to be done; and often, blinking by the fire, Buck wandered with him in that other world which he remembered.

The salient thing of this other world seemed fear. When he watched the hairy man sleeping by the fire, head between his knees and hands clasped above, Buck saw that he slept restlessly, with many starts and awakenings, at which times he would peer fearfully into the darkness and fling more wood upon the fire. Did they walk by the beach of a sea, where the hairy man gathered shell-fish and ate them as he gathered, it was with eyes that roved everywhere for hidden danger and with legs prepared to run like the wind at its first appearance. Through the forest they crept noiselessly, Buck at the hairy man's heels; and they were alert and vigilant, the pair of them, ears twitching and moving and nostrils quivering, for the man heard and smelled as keenly as Buck. The hairy man could spring up into the trees and travel ahead as fast as on the ground, swinging by the arms from limb to limb, sometimes a dozen feet apart, letting go and catching, never falling, never missing his grip. In fact, he seemed as much at home among the trees as on the ground; and Buck had memories of nights of vigil spent beneath trees wherein the hairy man roosted, holding on tightly as he slept.

And closely akin to the visions of the hairy man was the call still sounding in the depths of the forest. It filled him with a great unrest and strange desires. It caused him to feel a vague, sweet gladness, and he was aware of wild yearnings and stirrings for he knew not what. Sometimes he pursued the call into the forest, looking for it as though it were a tangible thing, barking softly or defiantly, as the mood might dictate. He would thrust his nose into the cool wood moss, or into the black soil where long grasses grew, and snort with joy at the fat earth smells; or he would crouch for hours, as if in concealment, behind fungus-covered trunks of fallen trees, wide-eyed and wide-eared to all that moved and sounded about him. It might be, lying thus, that he hoped to surprise this call he could not understand. But he did not know why he did these various things. He was impelled to do them, and did not reason about them at all.

Irresistible impulses seized him. He would be lying in camp, dozing lazily in the heat of the day, when suddenly his head would lift and his ears cock up, intent and listening, and he would spring to his feet and dash away, and on and on, for hours, through the forest aisles and across the open spaces where the niggerheads bunched. He loved to run down dry watercourses, and to creep and spy upon the bird life in the woods. For a day at a time he would lie in the underbrush where he could watch the partridges drumming and strutting up and down. But especially he loved to run in the dim twilight of the summer midnights, listening to the subdued and sleepy murmurs of the forest, reading signs and sounds as man may read a book, and seeking for the mysterious something that called—called, waking or sleeping, at all times, for him to come.

One night he sprang from sleep with a start, eager-eyed, nostrils quivering and scenting, his mane bristling in recurrent waves. From the forest came the call (or one note of it, for the call was many noted), distinct and definite as never before,—a long-drawn howl, like, yet unlike, any noise made by husky dog. And he knew it, in the old familiar way, as a sound heard before. He sprang through the sleeping camp and in swift silence dashed through the woods. As he drew closer to the cry he went more slowly, with caution in every movement, till he came to an open place among the trees, and looking out saw, erect on haunches, with nose pointed to the sky, a long, lean, timber wolf.

He had made no noise, yet it ceased from its howling and tried to sense his presence. Buck stalked into the open, half crouching, body gathered compactly together, tail straight and stiff, feet falling with unwonted care. Every movement advertised commingled threatening and overture of friendliness. It was the menacing truce that marks the meeting of wild beasts that prey. But the wolf fled at sight of him. He followed, with wild leapings, in a frenzy to overtake. He ran him into a blind channel, in the bed of the creek, where a timber jam barred the way. The wolf whirled about, pivoting on his hind legs after the fashion of Joe and of all cornered husky dogs, snarling and bristling, clipping his teeth together in a continuous and rapid succession of snaps.

Buck did not attack, but circled him about and hedged him in with friendly advances. The wolf was suspicious and afraid; for Buck made three of him in weight, while his head barely reached Buck's shoulder. Watching his chance, he darted away, and the chase was resumed. Time and again he was cornered, and the thing repeated, though he was in poor condition, or Buck could not so easily have overtaken him. He would run till Buck's head was even with his flank, when he would whirl around at bay, only to dash away again at the first opportunity.

But in the end Buck's pertinacity was rewarded; for the wolf, finding that no harm was intended, finally sniffed noses with him. Then they became friendly, and played about in the nervous, half-coy way with which fierce beasts belie their fierceness. After some time of this the wolf started off at an easy lope in a manner that plainly showed he was going somewhere. He made it clear to Buck that he was to come, and they ran side by side through the sombre twilight, straight up the creek bed, into the gorge from which it issued, and across the bleak divide where it took its rise.

On the opposite slope of the watershed they came down into a level country where were great stretches of forest and many streams, and through these great stretches they ran steadily, hour after hour, the sun rising higher and the day growing warmer. Buck was wildly glad. He knew he was at last answering the call, running by the side of his wood brother toward the place from where the call surely came. Old memories were coming upon him fast, and he was stirring to them as of old he stirred to the realities of which they were the shadows. He had done this thing before, somewhere in that other and dimly remembered world, and he was doing it again, now, running free in the open, the unpacked earth underfoot, the wide sky overhead.

They stopped by a running stream to drink, and, stopping, Buck remembered John Thornton. He sat down. The wolf started on toward the place from where the call surely came, then returned to him, sniffing noses and making actions as though to encourage him. But Buck turned about and started slowly on the back track. For the better part of an hour the wild brother ran by his side, whining softly. Then he sat down, pointed his nose upward, and howled. It was a mournful howl, and as Buck held steadily on his way he heard it grow faint and fainter until it was lost in the distance.

John Thornton was eating dinner when Buck dashed into camp and sprang upon him in a frenzy of affection, overturning him, scrambling upon him, licking his face, biting his hand—"playing the general tom-fool," as John Thornton characterized it, the while he shook Buck back and forth and cursed him lovingly.

For two days and nights Buck never left camp, never let Thornton out of his sight. He followed him about at his work, watched him while he ate, saw him into his blankets at night and out of them in the morning. But after two days the call in the forest began to sound more imperiously than ever. Buck's restlessness came back on him, and he was haunted by recollections of the wild brother, and of the smiling land beyond the divide and the run side by side through the wide forest stretches. Once again he took to wandering in the woods, but the wild brother came no more; and though he listened through long vigils, the mournful howl was never raised.

He began to sleep out at night, staying away from camp for days at a time; and once he crossed the divide at the head of the creek and went down into the land of timber and streams. There he wandered for a week, seeking vainly for fresh sign of the wild brother, killing his meat as he travelled and travelling with the long, easy lope that seems never to tire. He fished for salmon in a broad stream that emptied somewhere into the sea, and by this stream he killed a large black bear, blinded by the mosquitoes while likewise fishing, and raging through the forest helpless and terrible. Even so, it was a hard fight, and it aroused the last latent remnants of Buck's ferocity. And two days later, when he returned to his kill and found a dozen wolverenes quarrelling over the spoil, he scattered them like chaff; and those that fled left two behind who would quarrel no more.

The blood-longing became stronger than ever before. He was a killer, a thing that preyed, living on the things that lived, unaided, alone, by virtue of his own strength and prowess, surviving triumphantly in a hostile environment where only the strong survived. Because of all this he became possessed of a great pride in himself, which communicated itself like a contagion to his physical being. It advertised itself in all his movements, was apparent in the play of every muscle, spoke plainly as speech in the way he carried himself, and made his glorious furry coat if anything more glorious. But for the stray brown on his muzzle and above his eyes, and for the splash of white hair that ran midmost down his chest, he might well have been mistaken for a gigantic wolf, larger than the largest of the breed. From his St. Bernard father he had inherited size and weight, but it was his shepherd mother who had given shape to that size and weight. His muzzle was the long wolf muzzle, save that it was larger than the muzzle of any wolf; and his head, somewhat broader, was the wolf head on a massive scale.

His cunning was wolf cunning, and wild cunning; his intelligence, shepherd intelligence and St. Bernard intelligence; and all this, plus an experience gained in the fiercest of schools, made him as formidable a creature as any that roamed the wild. A carnivorous animal, living on a straight meat diet, he was in full flower, at the high tide of his life, overspilling with vigor and virility. When Thornton passed a caressing hand along his back, a snapping and crackling followed the hand, each hair discharging its pent magnetism at the contact. Every part, brain and body, nerve tissue and fibre, was keyed to the most exquisite pitch; and between all the parts there was a perfect equilibrium or adjustment. To sights and sounds and events which required action, he responded with lightning-like rapidity. Quickly as a husky dog could leap to defend from attack or to attack, he could leap twice as quickly. He saw the movement, or heard sound, and responded in less time than another dog required to compass the mere seeing or hearing. He perceived and determined and responded in the same instant. In point of fact the three actions of perceiving, determining, and responding were sequential; but so infinitesimal were the intervals of time between them that they appeared simultaneous. His muscles were surcharged with vitality, and snapped into play sharply, like steel springs. Life streamed through him in splendid flood, glad and rampant, until it seemed that it would burst him asunder in sheer ecstasy and pour forth generously over the world.

"Never was there such a dog," said John Thornton one day, as the partners watched Buck marching out of camp.

"When he was made, the mould was broke," said Pete.

"Py jingo! I t'ink so mineself," Hans affirmed.

They saw him marching out of camp, but they did not see the instant and terrible transformation which took place as soon as he was within the secrecy of the forest. He no longer marched. At once he became a thing of the wild, stealing along softly, cat-footed, a passing shadow that appeared and disappeared among the shadows. He knew how to take advantage of every cover, to crawl on his belly like a snake, and like a snake to leap and strike. He could take a ptarmigan from its nest, kill a rabbit as it slept, and snap in mid air the little chipmunks fleeing a second too late for the trees. Fish, in open pools, were not too quick for him; nor were beaver, mending their dams, too wary. He killed to eat, not from wantonness; but he preferred to eat what he killed himself. So a lurking humor ran through his deeds, and it was his delight to steal upon the squirrels, and, when he all but had them, to let them go, chattering in mortal fear to the tree-tops.

As the fall of the year came on, the moose appeared in greater abundance, moving slowly down to meet the winter in the lower and less rigorous valleys. Buck had already dragged down a stray part-grown calf; but he wished strongly for larger and more formidable quarry, and he came upon it one day on the divide at the head of the creek. A band of twenty moose had crossed over from the land of streams and timber, and chief among them was a great bull. He was in a savage temper, and, standing over six feet from the ground, was as formidable an antagonist as even Buck could desire. Back and forth the bull tossed his great palmated antlers, branching to fourteen points and embracing seven feet within the tips. His small eyes burned with a vicious and bitter light, while he roared with fury at sight of Buck.

From the bull's side, just forward of the flank, protruded a feathered arrow-end, which accounted for his savageness. Guided by that instinct which came from the old hunting days of the primordial world, Buck proceeded to cut the bull out from the herd. It was no slight task. He would bark and dance about in front of the bull, just out of reach of the great antlers and of the terrible splay hoofs which could have stamped his life out with a single blow. Unable to turn his back on the fanged danger and go on, the bull would be driven into paroxysms of rage. At such moments he charged Buck, who retreated craftily, luring him on by a simulated inability to escape. But when he was thus separated from his fellows, two or three of the younger bulls would charge back upon Buck and enable the wounded bull to rejoin the herd.

There is a patience of the wild—dogged, tireless, persistent as life itself—that holds motionless for endless hours the spider in its web, the snake in its coils, the panther in its ambuscade; this patience belongs peculiarly to life when it hunts its living food; and it belonged to Buck as he clung to the flank of the herd, retarding its march, irritating the young bulls, worrying the cows with their half-grown calves, and driving the wounded bull mad with helpless rage. For half a day this continued. Buck multiplied himself, attacking from all sides, enveloping the herd in a whirlwind of menace, cutting out his victim as fast as it could rejoin its mates, wearing out the patience of creatures preyed upon, which is a lesser patience than that of creatures preying.

As the day wore along and the sun dropped to its bed in the northwest (the darkness had come back and the fall nights were six hours long), the young bulls retraced their steps more and more reluctantly to the aid of their beset leader. The down-coming winter was harrying them on to the lower levels, and it seemed they could never shake off this tireless creature that held them back. Besides, it was not the life of the herd, or of the young bulls, that was threatened. The life of only one member was demanded, which was a remoter interest than their lives, and in the end they were content to pay the toll.

As twilight fell the old bull stood with lowered head, watching his mates—the cows he had known, the calves he had fathered, the bulls he had mastered—as they shambled on at a rapid pace through the fading light. He could not follow, for before his nose leaped the merciless fanged terror that would not let him go. Three hundred-weight more than half a ton he weighed; he had lived a long, strong life, full of fight and struggle, and at the end he faced death at the teeth of a creature whose head did not reach beyond his great knuckled knees.

From then on, night and day, Buck never left his prey, never gave it a moment's rest, never permitted it to browse the leaves of trees or the shoots of young birch and willow. Nor did he give the wounded bull opportunity to slake his burning thirst in the slender trickling streams they crossed. Often, in desperation, he burst into long stretches of flight. At such times Buck did not attempt to stay him, but loped easily at his heels, satisfied with the way the game was played, lying down when the moose stood still, attacking him fiercely when he strove to eat or drink.

The great head drooped more and more under its tree of horns, and the shambling trot grew weak and weaker. He took to standing for long periods, with nose to the ground and dejected ears dropped limply; and Buck found more time in which to get water for himself and in which to rest. At such moments, panting with red lolling tongue and with eyes fixed upon the big bull, it appeared to Buck that a change was coming over the face of things. He could feel a new stir in the land. As the moose were coming into the land, other kinds of life were coming in. Forest and stream and air seemed palpitant with their presence. The news of it was borne in upon him, not by sight, or sound, or smell, but by some other and subtler sense. He heard nothing, saw nothing, yet knew that the land was somehow different; that through it strange things were afoot and ranging; and he resolved to investigate after he had finished the business in hand.

At last, at the end of the fourth day, he pulled the great moose down. For a day and a night he remained by the kill, eating and sleeping, turn and turn about. Then, rested, refreshed and strong, he turned his face toward camp and John Thornton. He broke into the long easy lope, and went on, hour after hour, never at loss for the tangled way, heading straight home through strange country with a certitude of direction that put man and his magnetic needle to shame.

As he held on he became more and more conscious of the new stir in the land. There was life abroad in it different from the life which had been there throughout the summer. No longer was this fact borne in upon him in some subtle, mysterious way. The birds talked of it, the squirrels chattered about it, the very breeze whispered of it. Several times he stopped and drew in the fresh morning air in great sniffs, reading a message which made him leap on with greater speed. He was oppressed with a sense of calamity happening, if it were not calamity already happened; and as he crossed the last watershed and dropped down into the valley toward camp, he proceeded with greater caution.

Three miles away he came upon a fresh trail that sent his neck hair rippling and bristling. It led straight toward camp and John Thornton. Buck hurried on, swiftly and stealthily, every nerve straining and tense, alert to the multitudinous details which told a story—all but the end. His nose gave him a varying description of the passage of the life on the heels of which he was travelling. He remarked the pregnant silence of the forest. The bird life had flitted. The squirrels were in hiding. One only he saw,—a sleek gray fellow, flattened against a gray dead limb so that he seemed a part of it, a woody excrescence upon the wood itself.

As Buck slid along with the obscureness of a gliding shadow, his nose was jerked suddenly to the side as though a positive force had gripped and pulled it. He followed the new scent into a thicket and found Nig. He was lying on his side, dead where he had dragged himself, an arrow protruding, head and feathers, from either side of his body.

A hundred yards farther on, Buck came upon one of the sled-dogs Thornton had bought in Dawson. This dog was thrashing about in a death-struggle, directly on the trail, and Buck passed around him without stopping. From the camp came the faint sound of many voices, rising and falling in a sing-song chant. Bellying forward to the edge of the clearing, he found Hans, lying on his face, feathered with arrows like a porcupine. At the same instant Buck peered out where the spruce-bough lodge had been and saw what made his hair leap straight up on his neck and shoulders. A gust of overpowering rage swept over him. He did not know that he growled, but he growled aloud with a terrible ferocity. For the last time in his life he allowed passion to usurp cunning and reason, and it was because of his great love for John Thornton that he lost his head.

The Yeehats were dancing about the wreckage of the spruce-bough lodge when they heard a fearful roaring and saw rushing upon them an animal the like of which they had never seen before. It was Buck, a live hurricane of fury, hurling himself upon them in a frenzy to destroy. He sprang at the foremost man (it was the chief of the Yeehats), ripping the throat wide open till the rent jugular spouted a fountain of blood. He did not pause to worry the victim, but ripped in passing, with the next bound tearing wide the throat of a second man. There was no withstanding him. He plunged about in their very midst, tearing, rending, destroying, in constant and terrific motion which defied the arrows they discharged at him. In fact, so inconceivably rapid were his movements, and so closely were the Indians tangled together, that they shot one another with the arrows; and one young hunter, hurling a spear at Buck in mid air, drove it through the chest of another hunter with such force that the point broke through the skin of the back and stood out beyond. Then a panic seized the Yeehats, and they fled in terror to the woods, proclaiming as they fled the advent of the Evil Spirit.

And truly Buck was the Fiend incarnate, raging at their heels and dragging them down like deer as they raced through the trees. It was a fateful day for the Yeehats. They scattered far and wide over the country, and it was not till a week later that the last of the survivors gathered together in a lower valley and counted their losses. As for Buck, wearying of the pursuit, he returned to the desolated camp. He found Pete where he had been killed in his blankets in the first moment of surprise. Thornton's desperate struggle was fresh-written on the earth, and Buck scented every detail of it down to the edge of a deep pool. By the edge, head and fore feet in the water, lay Skeet, faithful to the last. The pool itself, muddy and discolored from the sluice boxes, effectually hid what it contained, and it contained John Thornton; for Buck followed his trace into the water, from which no trace led away.

All day Buck brooded by the pool or roamed restlessly about the camp. Death, as a cessation of movement, as a passing out and away from the lives of the living, he knew, and he knew John Thornton was dead. It left a great void in him, somewhat akin to hunger, but a void which ached and ached, and which food could not fill. At times, when he paused to contemplate the carcasses of the Yeehats, he forgot the pain of it; and at such times he was aware of a great pride in himself,—a pride greater than any he had yet experienced. He had killed man, the noblest game of all, and he had killed in the face of the law of club and fang. He sniffed the bodies curiously. They had died so easily. It was harder to kill a husky dog than them. They were no match at all, were it not for their arrows and spears and clubs. Thenceforward he would be unafraid of them except when they bore in their hands their arrows, spears, and clubs.

Night came on, and a full moon rose high over the trees into the sky, lighting the land till it lay bathed in ghostly day. And with the coming of the night, brooding and mourning by the pool, Buck became alive to a stirring of the new life in the forest other than that which the Yeehats had made. He stood up, listening and scenting. From far away drifted a faint, sharp yelp, followed by a chorus of similar sharp yelps. As the moments passed the yelps grew closer and louder. Again Buck knew them as things heard in that other world which persisted in his memory. He walked to the centre of the open space and listened. It was the call, the many-noted call, sounding more luringly and compellingly than ever before. And as never before, he was ready to obey. John Thornton was dead. The last tie was broken. Man and the claims of man no longer bound him.

Hunting their living meat, as the Yeehats were hunting it, on the flanks of the migrating moose, the wolf pack had at last crossed over from the land of streams and timber and invaded Buck's valley. Into the clearing where the moonlight streamed, they poured in a silvery flood; and in the centre of the clearing stood Buck, motionless as a statue, waiting their coming. They were awed, so still and large he stood, and a moment's pause fell, till the boldest one leaped straight for him. Like a flash Buck struck, breaking the neck. Then he stood, without movement, as before, the stricken wolf rolling in agony behind him. Three others tried it in sharp succession; and one after the other they drew back, streaming blood from slashed throats or shoulders.

This was sufficient to fling the whole pack forward, pell-mell, crowded together, blocked and confused by its eagerness to pull down the prey. Buck's marvellous quickness and agility stood him in good stead. Pivoting on his hind legs, and snapping and gashing, he was everywhere at once, presenting a front which was apparently unbroken so swiftly did he whirl and guard from side to side. But to prevent them from getting behind him, he was forced back, down past the pool and into the creek bed, till he brought up against a high gravel bank. He worked along to a right angle in the bank which the men had made in the course of mining, and in this angle he came to bay, protected on three sides and with nothing to do but face the front.

And so well did he face it, that at the end of half an hour the wolves drew back discomfited. The tongues of all were out and lolling, the white fangs showing cruelly white in the moonlight. Some were lying down with heads raised and ears pricked forward; others stood on their feet, watching him; and still others were lapping water from the pool. One wolf, long and lean and gray, advanced cautiously, in a friendly manner, and Buck recognized the wild brother with whom he had run for a night and a day. He was whining softly, and, as Buck whined, they touched noses.

Then an old wolf, gaunt and battle-scarred, came forward. Buck writhed his lips into the preliminary of a snarl, but sniffed noses with him. Whereupon the old wolf sat down, pointed nose at the moon, and broke out the long wolf howl. The others sat down and howled. And now the call came to Buck in unmistakable accents. He, too, sat down and howled. This over, he came out of his angle and the pack crowded around him, sniffing in half-friendly, half-savage manner. The leaders lifted the yelp of the pack and sprang away into the woods.

The wolves swung in behind, yelping in chorus. And Buck ran with them, side by side with the wild brother, yelping as he ran.

And here may well end the story of Buck. The years were not many when the Yeehats noted a change in the breed of timber wolves; for some were seen with splashes of brown on head and muzzle, and with a rift of white centring down the chest. But more remarkable than this, the Yeehats tell of a Ghost Dog that runs at the head of the pack. They are afraid of this Ghost Dog, for it has cunning greater than they, stealing from their camps in fierce winters, robbing their traps, slaying their dogs, and defying their bravest hunters.

Nay, the tale grows worse. Hunters there are who fail to return to the camp, and hunters there have been whom their tribesmen found with throats slashed cruelly open and with wolf prints about them in the snow greater than the prints of any wolf. Each fall, when the Yeehats follow the movement of the moose, there is a certain valley which they never enter. And women there are who become sad when the word goes over the fire of how the Evil Spirit came to select that valley for an abiding-place.

In the summers there is one visitor, however, to that valley, of which the Yeehats do not know. It is a great, gloriously coated wolf, like, and yet unlike, all other wolves. He crosses alone from the smiling timber land and comes down into an open space among the trees. Here a yellow stream flows from rotted moose-hide sacks and sinks into the ground, with long grasses growing through it and vegetable mould overrunning it and hiding its yellow from the sun; and here he muses for a time, howling once, long and mournfully, ere he departs.

But he is not always alone. When the long winter nights come on and the wolves follow their meat into the lower valleys, he may be seen running at the head of the pack through the pale moonlight or glimmering borealis, leaping gigantic above his fellows, his great throat a-bellow as he sings a song of the younger world, which is the song of the pack.

# Selected Nonfiction

# TYPHOON OFF THE COAST
# OF JAPAN*

It WAS FOUR BELLS in the morning watch. We had just finished breakfast when the order came forward for the watch on deck to stand by
to heave her to and all hands stand by the boats.

"Port! hard *a* port!" cried our sailing-master. "Clew up the topsails! Let the flying jib run down! Back the jib over to windward and
run down the foresail!" And so was our schooner *Sophie Sutherland*
hove to off the Japan coast, near Cape Jerimo, on April 10, 1893.

Then came moments of bustle and confusion. There were eighteen
men to man the six boats. Some were hooking on the falls, others
casting off the lashings; boat-steerers appeared with boat-compasses
and water-breakers, and boat-pullers with the lunch boxes. Hunters
were staggering under two or three shotguns, a rifle and heavy ammunition box, all of which were soon stowed away with their oilskins
and mittens in the boats.

The sailing-master gave his last orders, and away we went, pulling
three pairs of oars to gain our positions. We were in the weather boat,
and so had a longer pull than the others. The first, second, and third
lee boats soon had all sail set and were running off to the southward
and westward with the wind beam, while the schooner was running
off to leeward of them, so that in case of accident the boats would
have fair wind home.

It was a glorious morning, but our boat-steerer shook his head

---

* From *Dutch Courage and Other Stories*; first published as "Story of a Typhoon
off Coast of Japan" in the San Francisco *Morning Call*, November 12, 1893.

ominously as he glanced at the rising sun and prophetically muttered: "Red sun in the morning, sailor take warning." The sun had an angry look, and a few light, fleecy "nigger-heads" in that quarter seemed abashed and frightened and soon disappeared.

Away off to the northward Cape Jerimo reared its black, forbidding head like some huge monster rising from the deep. The winter's snow, not yet entirely dissipated by the sun, covered it in patches of glistening white, over which the light wind swept on its way out to sea. Huge gulls rose slowly, fluttering their wings in the light breeze and striking their webbed feet on the surface of the water for over half a mile before they could leave it. Hardly had the patter, patter died away when a flock of sea quail rose, and with whistling wings flew away to windward, where members of a large band of whales were disporting themselves, their blowings sounding like the exhaust of steam engines. The harsh, discordant cries of a sea-parrot grated unpleasantly on the ear, and set half a dozen alert in a small band of seals that were ahead of us. Away they went, breaching and jumping entirely out of water. A sea-gull with slow, deliberate flight and long, majestic curves circled round us, and as a reminder of home a little English sparrow perched impudently on the fo'castle head, and, cocking his head on one side, chirped merrily. The boats were soon among the seals, and the bang! bang! of the guns could be heard from down to leeward.

The wind was slowly rising, and by three o'clock as, with a dozen seals in our boat, we were deliberating whether to go on or turn back, the recall flag was run up at the schooner's mizzen—a sure sign that with the rising wind the barometer was falling and that our sailing-master was getting anxious for the welfare of the boats.

Away we went before the wind with a single reef in our sail. With clenched teeth sat the boat-steerer, grasping the steering oar firmly with both hands, his restless eyes on the alert—a glance at the schooner ahead, as we rose on a sea, another at the mainsheet, and then one astern where the dark ripple of the wind on the water told him of a coming puff or a large white-cap that threatened to overwhelm us. The waves were holding high carnival, performing the strangest antics, as with wild glee they danced along in fierce pursuit—now up, now down, here, there, and everywhere, until some great sea of liquid green with its milk-white crest of foam rose from the ocean's throbbing bosom and drove the others from view. But only for a moment, for again under new forms they reappeared. In the sun's path they wandered, where every ripple, great or small, every little spit or spray looked like molten silver, where the water lost its dark green color and became a dazzling, silvery flood, only to vanish and become a wild waste of sullen turbulence, each dark foreboding sea rising and breaking, then rolling on again. The dash, the sparkle, the silvery light soon vanished with the sun, which became obscured by black clouds that were rolling swiftly in from the west, northwest; apt heralds of the coming storm.

We soon reached the schooner and found ourselves the last aboard. In a few minutes the seals were skinned, boats and decks washed, and we were down below by the roaring fo'castle fire, with a wash, change of clothes, and a hot, substantial supper before us. Sail had been put on the schooner, as we had a run of seventy-five miles to make to the southward before morning, so as to get in the midst of the seals, out of which we had strayed during the last two days' hunting.

We had the first watch from eight to midnight. The wind was soon blowing half a gale, and our sailing-master expected little sleep that night as he paced up and down the poop. The topsails were soon clewed up and made fast, then the flying jib run down and furled. Quite a sea was rolling by this time, occasionally breaking over the decks, flooding them and threatening to smash the boats. At six bells we were ordered to turn them over and put on storm lashings. This occupied us till eight bells, when we were relieved by the mid-watch. I was the last to go below, doing so just as the watch on deck was furling the spanker. Below all were asleep except our green hand, the "bricklayer," who was dying of consumption. The wildly dancing movements of the sea lamp cast a pale, flickering light through the fo'castle and turned to golden honey the drops of water on the yellow oilskins. In all the corners dark shadows seemed to come and go, while up in the eyes of her, beyond the pall bits, descending from deck to deck, where they seemed to lurk like some dragon at the cavern's mouth, it was dark as Erebus. Now and again, the light seemed to penetrate for a moment as the schooner rolled heavier than usual, only to recede, leaving it darker and blacker than before. The roar of the wind through the rigging came to the ear muffled like the distant rumble of a train crossing a trestle or the surf on the beach, while the loud crash of the seas on her weather bow seemed almost to rend the beams and planking asunder as it resounded through the fo'castle. The creaking and groaning of the timbers, stanchions, and bulkheads, as the strain the vessel was undergoing was felt, served to drown the groans of the dying man as he tossed uneasily in his bunk. The working of

the foremast against the deck beams caused a shower of flaky powder
to fall, and sent another sound mingling with the tumultous storm.
Small cascades of water streamed from the pall bits from the fo'castle
head above, and, joining issue with the streams from the wet oilskins,
ran along the floor and disappeared aft into the main hold.

At two bells in the middle watch—that is, in land parlance one
o'clock in the morning—the order was roared out on the fo'castle:
"All hands on deck and shorten sail!"

Then the sleepy sailors tumbled out of their bunk and into their
clothes, oil-skins, and seaboots and up on deck. 'Tis when that order
comes on cold, blustering nights that "Jack" grimly mutters: "Who
would not sell a farm and go to sea?"

It was on deck that the force of the wind could be fully appreciated, especially after leaving the stifling fo'castle. It seemed to stand
up against you like a wall, making it almost impossible to move on
the heaving decks or to breathe as the fierce gusts came dashing by.
The schooner was hove to under jib, foresail, and mainsail. We proceeded to lower the foresail and make it fast. The night was dark,
greatly impeding our labor. Still, though not a star or the moon could
pierce the black masses of storm clouds that obscured the sky as they
swept along before the gale, nature aided us in a measure. A soft light
emanated from the movement of the ocean. Each mighty sea, all phos-
phorescent and glowing with the tiny lights of myriads of animalculæ,
threatened to overwhelm us with a deluge of fire. Higher and higher,
thinner and thinner, the crest grew as it began to curve and overtop
preparatory to breaking, until with a roar it fell over the bulwarks, a
mass of soft glowing light and tons of water which sent the sailors
sprawling in all directions and left in each nook and cranny little
specks of light that glowed and trembled till the next sea washed them
away, depositing new ones in their places. Sometimes several seas following each other with great rapidity and thundering down on our
decks filled them full to the bulwarks, but soon they were discharged
through the lee scuppers.

To reef the mainsail we were forced to run off before the gale
under the single reefed jib. By the time we had finished the wind had
forced up such a tremendous sea that it was impossible to heave her
to. Away we flew on the wings of the storm through the muck and
flying spray. A wind sheer to starboard, then another to port as the
enormous seas struck the schooner astern and nearly broached her to.
As day broke we took in the jib, leaving not a sail unfurled. Since we
had begun scudding she had ceased to take the seas over her bow, but

amidships they broke fast and furious. It was a dry storm in the matter of rain, but the force of the wind filled the air with fine spray, which flew as high as the crosstrees and cut the face like a knife, making it impossible to see over a hundred yards ahead. The sea was a dark lead color as with long, slow, majestic roll it was heaped up by the wind into liquid mountains of foam. The wild antics of the schooner were sickening as she forged along. She would almost stop, as though climbing a mountain, then rapidly rolling to right and left as she gained the summit of a huge sea, she steadied herself and paused for a moment as though affrighted at the yawning precipice before her. Like an avalanche, she shot forward and down as the sea astern struck her with the force of a thousand battering rams, burying her bow to the catheads in the milky foam at the bottom that came on deck in all directions—forward, astern, to right and left, through the hawse-pipes and over the rail.

The wind began to drop, and by ten o'clock we were talking of heaving her to. We passed a ship, two schooners, and a four-masted barkentine under the smallest of canvas, and at eleven o'clock, running up the spanker and jib, we hove her to, and in another hour we were beating back again against the aftersea under full sail to regain the sealing ground away to the westward.

Below, a couple of men were sewing the "bricklayer's" body in canvas preparatory to the sea burial. And so with the storm passed away the "bricklayer's" soul.

# ON THE WRITER'S
# PHILOSOPHY OF LIFE*

THE LITERARY HACK, the one who is satisfied to turn out "pot boilers" for the rest of his or her life, will save time and vexation by passing this article by. It contains no hints as to the disposing of manuscript, the vagaries of the blue-pencil, the filing of material, nor the innate perversity of adjectives and adverbs. Petrified "Pen-trotters," pass on! This is for the writer—no matter how much hack-work he is turning out just now—who cherishes ambitions and ideals, and yearns for the time when agricultural newspapers and home magazines no more may occupy the major portion of his visiting list.

How are you, dear sir, madam, or miss, to achieve distinction in the field you have chosen? Genius? Oh, but you are no genius. If you were you would not be reading these lines. Genius is irresistible; it casts aside all shackles and restraints; it cannot be held down. Genius is a *rara avis,* not to be found fluttering in every grove as are you and I. But then you are talented? Yes, in an embryonic sort of way. The biceps of Hercules was a puny affair when he rolled about in swaddling-clothes. So with you—your talent is undeveloped. If it had received proper nutrition and were well matured, you would not be wasting your time over this. And if you think your talent really has attained its years of discretion, stop right here. If you think it has not, then by what methods do you think it will?

*By being original,* you at once suggest; then add, *and by constantly strengthening that originality.* Very good. But the question is

* *The Editor*, October 1899.

426

not merely being original—the veriest tyro knows that much—but now can you become original? How are you to cause the reading world to look eagerly for your work? to force the publishers to pant for it? You cannot expect to become original by following the blazed trail of another, by reflecting the radiations of some one else's originality. No one broke ground for Scott or Dickens, for Poe or Longfellow, for George Eliot or Mrs. Humphrey Ward, for Stevenson and Kipling, Anthony Hope, Stephen Crane, and many others of the lengthening list. Yet publishers and public have clamored for their ware. They conquered originality. And how? By not being silly weather-cocks, turning to every breeze that flows. They, with the countless failures, started even in the race; the world with its traditions was their common heritage. But in one thing they differed from the failures; they drew straight from the source, rejecting the material which filtered through other hands. They had no use for the conclusions and the conceits of others. They must put the stamp of "self" upon their work—a trade mark of far greater value than copyright. So, from the world and its traditions—which is another term for knowledge and culture—they drew at first hand, certain materials, which they builded into an individual philosophy of life.

Now this phrase, "a philosophy of life," will not permit of precise definition. In the first place it does not mean a philosophy on any one thing. It has no especial concern with any one of such questions as the past and future travail of the soul, the double and single standard of morals for the sexes, the economic independence of women, the possibility of acquired characters being inherited, spiritualism, reincarnation, temperance, etc. But it is concerned with all of them, in a way, and with all the other ruts and stumbling blocks which confront the man or woman who really lives. In short, it is an ordinary working philosophy of life.

Every permanently successful writer has possessed this philosophy. It was a view peculiarly his own. It was a yardstick by which he measured all things which came to his notice. By it he focused the characters he drew, the thoughts he uttered. Because of it his work was sane, normal, and fresh. It was something new, something the world wished to hear. It was his, and not a garbled mouthing of things the world had already heard.

But make no mistake. The possession of such a philosophy does not imply a yielding to the didactic impulse. Because one may have pronounced views on any question is no reason that he assault the public ear with a novel with a purpose, and for that matter, no reason that he should not. But it will be noticed, however, that this philosophy of the writer rarely manifests itself in a desire to sway the world to one side or the other of any problem. Some few great writers have been avowedly didactic, while some, like Robert Louis Stevenson, in a manner at once bold and delicate, have put themselves almost wholly into their work, and done so without once imparting the idea that they had something to teach.

And it must be understood that such a working philosophy enables the writer to put not only himself into his work, but to put that which is not himself but which is viewed and weighted by himself. Of none is this more true than of that triumvirate of intellectual giants—Shakespeare, Goethe, Balzac. Each was himself, and so much so, that there is no point of comparison. Each had drawn from this store his own working philosophy. And by this individual standard they accomplished their work. At birth they must have been very similar to all infants; but somehow, from the world and its traditions, they acquired something which their fellows did not. And this was neither more nor less than *something to say*.

Now you, young writer, have you something to say, or do you merely think you have something to say? If you have, there is nothing to prevent your saying it. If you are capable of thinking thoughts which the world would like to hear, the very form of the thinking is the expression. If you think clearly, you will write clearly; if your thoughts are worthy, so will your writing be worthy. But if your expression is poor, it is because your thought is poor, if narrow, because you are narrow. If your ideas are confused and jumbled, how can you expect a lucid utterance? If your knowledge is sparse or unsystematized, how can your words be broad or logical? And without the strong central thread of a working philosophy, how can you make order out of chaos? how can your foresight and insight be clear? how can you have a quantitive and qualitative perception of the relative importance of every scrap of knowledge you possess? And without all this how can you possibly be yourself? how can you have something fresh for the jaded ear of the world?

The only way of gaining this philosophy is by seeking it, by drawing the materials which go to compose it from the knowledge and culture of the world. What do you know of the world beneath its bubbling surface? What can you know of the bubbles unless you comprehend the forces at work in the depths of the cauldron? Can an artist paint an "Ecce Homo" without having a conception of the Hebrew myths and history, and all the varied traits which form collectively the character of the Jew, his beliefs and ideals, his passions and his pleasures, his hopes and fears! Can a musician compose a "Ride of the Valkyries" and know nothing of the great Teutonic epics? So with you—you must study. You must come to read the face of life with understanding. To comprehend the characters and phases of any movement, you must know the spirit which moves to action individuals and peoples, which gives birth and momentum to great ideas, which hangs a John Brown or crucifies a Savior. You must have your hand on the inner pulse of things. And the sum of all this will be your working philosophy, by which, in turn, you will measure, weigh, and balance, and interpret to the world. It is this stamp of personality of individual view, which is known as individuality.

What do you know of history, biology, evolution, ethics, and the thousand and one branches of knowledge? "But," you object, "I fail to see how such things can aid me in the writing of a romance or a poem." Ah, but they will. They broaden your thought, lengthen out your vistas, drive back the bounds of the field in which you work. They give you your philosophy, which is like unto no other man's philosophy, force you to original thought.

"But the task is stupendous," you protest; "I have no time." Others have not been deterred by its immensity. The years of your life are at your own disposal. Certainly you cannot expect to master it all, but in the proportion you do master it, just so will your efficiency increase, just so will you command the attention of your fellows. Time! When you speak of its lack you mean lack of economy in its use. Have you really learned *how* to read? How many insipid short stories and novels do you read in the course of a year, endeavoring either to master the art of storywriting or of exercising your critical faculty? How many magazines do you read clear through from beginning to end? There's time for you, time you have been wasting with a fool's prodigality— time which can never come again. Learn to discriminate in the selection of your reading and learn to skim judiciously. You laugh at the doddering graybeard who reads the daily paper, advertisements and all. But is it less pathetic, the spectacle you present in trying to breast the tide of current fiction? But don't shun it. Read the best, and the best only. Don't finish a tale simply because you have commenced it. Remember that you are a writer, first, last and always. Remember that these are the mouthings of others, and if you read them exclusively, that you may garble them; you will have nothing else to write about. Time! If you cannot find time, rest assured that the world will not find time to listen to you.

# FIRST AID TO
# RISING AUTHORS*

MANY ARE THE MOTIVES which drive men into setting foot on the thorny paths of literature; and among these impelling forces may be chiefly noted ambition.

Ambition is a very vague term. Let us get right down to the root of the matter, strip off all foolish fancies and cunning deceits and resolve the word into something more definite. Ambition for what? For fame? For notice? For an audience? For power? For a living? Indeed, for what?

Now, let it be remarked at this juncture that the discussion only appertains to individuals who really enter the arena and burden the mails in quest of a market. We have no concern with the true poet, who sings for the song's sake; who sings because force moves along the line of least resistance; who sings, in short, because he cannot help singing. Such a one does not send his songs between glued flaps to the uttermost ends of the earth, to harrow the souls of countless editors. At the best (or it may be the worst), after due persuasion, he gets out a private edition for gratuitous distribution among his nearest and dearest friends; but he does nothing more. Of course, should the note he strikes be pure and sweet and true, should it have the strong, deft, indefinable eternal touch, he cannot escape a constant increase in the number of his listeners. But it is they that bring him his market; for each warbles his songs to the other, and one to another, till at last all the world is divided 'twixt warbling and clamoring for warbles, and

* *The Junior Munsey Magazine*, December 1900.

wires and cables are hot with offers from anxious eyed publishers. In this case, it is the market which came to him; not he to the market.

But we are engaged in analyzing that ambition which leads men to make commodities of their written thoughts, and to send them forth, like turnips and cabbages, to be bought and sold. When a man does this thing, it is fair to ask why. Does he do it for fame? Let us see. In the first place, the question arises, does a man, solely impelled by a hungering for distinction or glory, ever become distinguished or glorious? It does not seem so. He may achieve notoriety, but never renown. The great men of the world become so because they had work to do in the world, and did it; because they worked busily and mightily, and lost themselves in their work, till they were surprised, one day, when honors fell thick upon them, and their names were on all men's lips. And, further, for the one who would sell his thoughts merely for the reward of sitting in the high places, is it not a ridiculous way to chase fame through publishers' offices and editorial sanctums, pestering a thousand busy coat tails, the owners of which he does not even know? Surely, laurels are not for such as he is!

Then, there are other men, ambitious just to see themselves in print. Just to have their friends say, "There's Soandso. Clever fellow, don't you know? Writes for the magazines." Such a man desires to have people speak of him; to sneak for a moment into the shilling gallery, and then walk proudly among those who know him as one who has sat among the writer people; to possess a caste distinction to which he was not born, and which, because of his innate asininity, he never can earn. There are such men—buttonhole the next editor you are introduced to, and ask him—petty, vain, and foolish creatures; but, while we weep for them, we cannot discuss as ambitious their misbegotten desires. Let us be charitable, lay the blame upon their ancestors, and pass on.

There are many others to be eliminated from the proposition; the specialists, for instance—doctors, lawyers, professors, historians, and scientists. These men write in their professional capacity, as men who have something to say. But their ambitions have been realized in the careers already chosen, and the literary work they do is only a modern phase of their careers. There are also the dabblers—people who are not abubble with some great word for the world, who are not swayed by vanity; who, by luck of birth or circumstance, have been removed from the struggle for existence, and their desire to be doing something; people who write for the same reason that they hunt, fish, travel, or attend the opera.

With all these, ambition, as a distinctive term, plays no part. To whom, then, does it apply? To two classes—those who have, or think they have, a message the world needs or would be glad to hear; and those whose lives have been cast on hard ground and in barren places, striving to make the belly need. The first is the smaller class. They are the heavenly, fire flashing, fire bringing creatures, so made that they must speak though ears be deaf and the heavens fall. History is full of them, and attests that they have spoken, whether on the graven tablets of Mount Sinai, in the warring pamphlets of a later period, or in the screaming Sunday newspaper of today. Their ambition is to teach, to help, to uplift. Self is no determining factor. They were not created primarily for their own good, but for the good of the world. Honor, glory, and power do not attract them. A crust of bread and a beggar's garb meet all their material desires. Existence is an episode; a means to an end. The world's comfort and happiness is their comfort and happiness. And, being helpers and advisers, they do not ask help or advice; nor will they take it if proffered them, for their courses are predestined, like the stars. And when all is said and done, who would have it otherwise?

But there yet remains the second class, and since it is the larger class, composed of clay born creatures like you and me, let us see the part played by ambition in rushing us into print. Ask the editors, the publishers, the booksellers, the reading public, and the answer will be, "Cash." Now, the idealist or the dreamer who has strayed thus far would better return. The question at issue is becoming brutal. Cash? Yes, cash! So put your head back among the clouds, and leave us alone. It's too bad, we know, that we are not to be satisfied with a crust of bread and a beggar's garb; but then, you see, we are only the clay born. Our sins be upon the heads of our progenitors, or whosoever had the shaping of us.

We are the ones who suffer from the belly need. We are joy loving, pleasure seeking, and we are ever hungry for the things which we deem the compensation of living. The world owes us something, and we intend dunning until we get it. True, most of the debts seem bad; wherefore, the more reason that we dun the harder. Some of us do not hold the bills to be very large, and will sign off for the most ridiculous sums. Others are more insistent; while not a few are sure they never can be paid enough for having been born. But we all consider ourselves creditors, and have early learned that we must do our own collecting.

We want good food, and plenty of it; meat as often as we feel inclined—not skirt steaks, but porterhouses; fruits; and, when the call is for cream, cream and not skim milk. We want nice houses, with sanitary plumbing and tight roofs, and we do not want to be cramped or stifled, either. We want high ceilings, big windows, and lots of sunshine; room outside for flowers to grow, and vines, and fig trees, and walks, wherein to wander in the cool of the day. And we want all kinds of nice things inside those houses—books, pictures, pianos, and couches with no end of cushions. We want good tobacco, and we want plenty of it, so that our friends may come and help us smoke it. And if their lips turn dry, we want to give them something better to drink than the ill tasting liquid for which we are so often mulcted by bloated corporations.

And we want to marry and multiply, and we want our multiplications to be pleasures, not worries. We want them to breathe good air, to eat things which befit an animal which walks upright, to see and hear things which give soul and right understanding. We want them to grow up fat and strong, with big muscles and large lungs and clear eyes. We want them to become men and women, strong of breed and big of heart, with a knowledge of things and a power of doing. We also want for ourselves saddle horses, bicycles, and automobiles; cameras, shot guns, and jointed rods; canoes, catboats, and yawls. We want railway tickets, tents, and camping outfits. We want to climb mountains, to walk barefoot on sandy shores, to plow the salt seas in whatever way most pleases us. We are tired of poring over illustrated atlases and guide books, and we want to go and see for ourselves. We are sick of weak photographs and worse copies of the masterpieces men have done. We want to see with our own eyes these paintings and sculptures, to hear with our own ears these singers and musicians. When India starves, or the town needs a library, or the poor man in our neighborhood loses his one horse and falls sick, we want to put our hands in our pockets and help. And to do all this, we want cash!

Because we want these things, and because we are going to rush into print to get them, it were perhaps well to know which kind of print to rush into in order to get most of them. We have chosen print because we thought we were better adapted for it; and, further, because we preferred it to pulling teeth, mending broken bones, adding up figures, or working with pick and shovel. Many men, paddling in the same boat with us, took up with literature for precisely similar reasons; but, unfortunately, they did not choose their particular field with due deliberation. So they suffered sore, and only learned of their mistake after the weary travail of years.

Grant Allen, who certainly achieved literary success, had such an experience. Returning from Jamaica to England in 1876, out of work, he decided to make his living with his pen. Prior to this, in spare moments, he had written a hundred or more magazine articles on philosophical and scientific subjects, not one of which had ever brought him in a penny. But he now devoted himself to writing a book, *Physiological Esthetics*, the publication of which cost him six hundred dollars. The reviews were favorable, and so good was it that it won him the friendship of men like Darwin and Spencer, and actually sold to the tune of nearly three hundred copies. When everything was cleaned up, he had lost, plus his time, a paltry hundred and fifty dollars. His next book was *The Color Sense*. This involved between five and six thousand references, required a year and a half to complete, and in the course of ten years netted him something like one hundred and fifty dollars. Does anybody ask why Grant Allen came to write fiction in his latter days?

So deeply did this mistake affect him, that he said, in 1893: "I had a ten years' struggle for bread, into the details of which I don't care to enter. It left me broken in health and spirit, with all the vitality and vivacity crushed out of me. If the object of this paper is to warn off ingenious and aspiring youth from the hardest worked and worst paid of all professions, I should say earnestly: 'Brain for brain, in no market can you sell your abilities to such poor advantage. Don't take to literature if you've capital enough to buy a good broom, and energy enough to annex a vacant crossing.' "

Whether this be so or not, is not the question at stake. The point is, that in the high tide of success Grant Allen was yet able to speak thus because of what he had suffered and undergone. As he saw it, no success under the sun could atone for the ten years' struggle. No monetary reward, no material comfort, no boundless demand for his wares, none of the satisfactions of life which were his, could compensate for what he had lost. The fact that a man should feel so when tasting the sweets of living, with the struggle all behind him, serves to show the bitterness of that struggle; and, further, to illustrate the enormity of the mistake.

So it were well that we, moved towards literature by belly need, should judiciously decide what part of us is the best to put on paper. Frankly, which pays the best—fiction, poetry, essay, history, philosophy, or science? The circulating library is an artery where one may feel the pulse of the market. That which is most read is most in demand, and was there ever a circulating library which did not put forth more fiction than all other forms of printed thought combined? The bookseller will tell the same story; likewise the publisher. Many an editor has advised a contributor to turn from the more serious fields to fiction; but rarely has the opposite advice been given. And why so? Surely not because the contributor was unfitted for the other and more serious fields. There are no end of fiction writers who could turn their hands to such, and turn them well. But they do not.

Dr. Weir Mitchell is undoubtedly capable of most important and well constructed medical tomes; but he prefers to write *The Adventures of François*. John Uri Lloyd was guilty of various works on chemistry; but now we are all reading his *Stringtown on the Pike*. Mr. Kipling could discourse profoundly on mechanical engineering and other technical subjects; yet we are pleasuring in *Captains Courageous* and *Stalky and Company*. And Grant Allen, aforementioned, who wrote the *Color Sense*, later wrote *The Tents of Shem* and *The Woman Who Did*. Not that we would infer that these gentlemen, and a myriad others, are sufferers from the belly need. No, no; no doubt it is simply inclination and temperament which lead them into paths where the primroses are more thickly sprinkled.

Let us, however, seek more concrete evidence, taking, for instance, the case of Herbert Spencer. Mr. Spencer's contribution to the world's knowledge is so great that we cannot really appreciate it. We lack perspective. Only future centuries may measure his work for what it is; and when a thousand generations of fiction writers have been laid away, one upon another, and forgotten, Spencer will be even better known than in this day. Yet he was forced to publish his philosophy at his own expense. By 1865, because of this, he owed fifty-five hundred dollars, and was driven into making the announcement that he would discontinue issuing his work. In America, Youmans raised seven thousand dollars, and in England, Huxley and Lubbock attempted to increase artificially the list of subscribers, by inducing people to take the work—not because they intended reading it, but in order to help support it. But the death of his father so increased Spencer's income that he declined to advantage by the kindness of his friends, and went on as before, bearing the loss himself.

A glance at the other side is quite apropos. Alphonse Daudet is said to have received two hundred thousand dollars for his *Sappho*. The *Pall Mall Gazette* paid Kipling seven hundred and fifty dollars for each of his "Barrack Room Ballads." For his short stories, he has received as high as a dollar per word. What scientist or philosopher ever achieved the like? Anthony Hope reserves the copyright, and receives four hundred and fifty dollars for a magazine article. Frank R. Stockton sells the shortest of his tales for something like five hundred dollars. The Harpers are said to have paid General Lew Wallace a hundred thousand dollars for his *Prince of India*. They also bought the American rights of *Trilby* for ten thousand dollars; but they afterwards, out of the largeness of their hearts, voluntarily sent Du Maurier forty thousand dollars more.

But, though fiction does pay best, it should go without saying that the same is not true of all fiction. The poorer class periodicals pay for stories anywhere from forty cents to a dollar per thousand words, and even then they sometimes pay under protest. Not infrequently, the major portion of such pittance is spent for stamps and stationery wherewith to dun for the remainder. There are publishers who never pay. And, so black is iniquity, some periodicals force the writer to subscribe ere they will publish his work without pay. But we who want the good things of the world will not be unwise enough to put our hands to this kind of work—unless we are incapable of better.

Then, again, there is another class of fiction to avoid, especially perilous to those of us who titubate between Grub Street and a country house flung about with twenty woodland acres. This consists of the inanely vapid sort which amuses the commonplace souls of the commonplace public, and the melodramatic messes which tickle the palates of the sensation mongers, who otherwise spend their time neurotically wandering through the yellow journals. Witness Charlotte M. Braeme and Laura Jean Libbey on the one hand, and Albert Ross and Archibald Clavering Gunter on the other. Of course it pays; but because we happen to be mercenarily inclined, there is no reason why we should lose our self respect. A man material enough of soul to work for his living is not, in consequence, so utterly bad as to be incapable of exercising choice. If scavenging be not to his liking, the more honor when he becomes a wood chopper. So with us. Though the dreamers and idealists scorn us because of our close contact with the earth, no disgrace need attach to that contact. The flesh may sit heavily upon us, yet may we stand erect and look one another in the eyes.

And in this connection we may well take a lesson from those same dreamers and idealists. Let us be fire bringers in a humble way. Let us have an eye to the ills of the world and its needs; and if we find messages, let us deliver them. Ah, pardon me, purely for materialistic reasons. We will weave about with our fictions, and make them beautiful, and sell them for goodly sums.

Of course there is a danger in this. It is liable to be catching. We may become possessed by our ideas, and be whisked away into the clouds. But we won't inoculate. Honor bright, we won't inoculate. And in the meantime, let us add to the list a few more of the good things we want.

# REVIEW OF FRANK NORRIS'S
## *THE OCTOPUS* *

> *"There it was, the Wheat, the Wheat! The little seed long planted, germinating in the deep, dark furrows of the soil, straining, swelling, suddenly in one night had burst upward to the light. The wheat had come up. It was before him, around him, everywhere, illimitable, immeasurable. The winter brownness of the ground was overlaid with a little shimmer of green. The promise of the sowing was being fulfilled. The earth, the loyal mother who never failed, who never disappointed, was keeping her faith again."*

VERY LONG AGO, we of the West heard it rumored that Frank Norris had it in mind to write the *Epic of the Wheat*. Nor can it be denied that many of us doubted—not the ability of Frank Norris merely, but the ability of the human of all humans. This great, incoherent, amorphous West! Who could grip the spirit and the essence of it, the luster and the wonder, and bind it all, definitely and sanely, within the covers of a printed book? Surely we of the West, who knew our West, may have been pardoned our lack of faith.

And now Frank Norris has done it; has, in a machine age, achieved what has been peculiarly the privilege of the man who lived in an heroic age; in short, has sung the *Epic of the Wheat*. "More power to his elbow," as Charles F. Lummis would say.

On first sight of the Valley of the San Joaquin, one can not help but call it "new and naked land." There is apparently little to be seen. A few isolated ranches in the midst of the vastness, no timber, a sparse population—that is all. And the men of the ranches, sweating in bitter toil, they must likewise be new and naked. So it would seem; but

---

* *Impressions*, June 1901.

Norris has given breadth to both, and depth. Not only has he gone down into the soil, into the womb of the passionate earth, yearning for motherhood, the sustenance of nations; but he has gone down into the heart of its people, simple, elemental, prone to the rude amenities of existence, growling, snarling with brute anger under cruel wrong. One needs must feel a sympathy for these men, workers and fighters, and for all of their weakness, a respect. And, after all, as Norris has well shown, their weakness is not inherent. It is the weakness of unorganization, the weakness of the force which they represent and of which they are a part, the agricultural force as opposed to the capitalistic force, the farmer against the financier, the tiller of the soil against the captain of industry.

No man, no large heart, lacking in spontaneous sympathy, incapable of great enthusiasms, could have written *The Octopus*. Presley, the poet, dreamer and singer, is a composite fellow. So far as mere surface incident goes, he is audaciously Edwin Markham; but down in the heart of him he is Frank Norris. Presley, groping vaguely in the silence of the burning night for the sigh of the land; Presley, with his great Song of the West forever leaping up in his imagination and forever eluding him; Presley, wrestling passionately for the swing of his "thundering progression of hexameters"—who is this Presley but Norris, grappling in keen travail with his problem of *The Octopus*, and doubting often, as we of the West have doubted?

Men obtain knowledge in two ways: by generalizing from experience; by gathering to themselves the generalizations of others. As regards Frank Norris, one can not avoid pausing speculation. It is patent that in this, his last and greatest effort, he has laid down uncompromisingly the materialistic conception of history, or, more politely, the economic interpretation of history. Now the question arises: Did Frank Norris acquire the economic interpretation of history from the printed records of the thoughts of other men, and thus equipped, approach his problem of *The Octopus*? or, rather, did he approach it, naive and innocent? and from direct contact with the great social forces was he not forced to so generalize for himself? It is a pretty question. Will he some day tell us?

Did Norris undergo the same evolution he has so strongly depicted in Presley? Presley's ultimate sociological concept came somewhat in this fashion: Shelgrim, the president and owner of the Pacific and Southwestern, laid "a thick, powerful forefinger on the table to emphasize his words. 'Try to believe this—to begin with—that railroads build themselves. Where there is a demand, sooner or later there will be a supply. Mr. Derrick, does he grow his wheat? The wheat grows itself. What does he count for? Does he supply the force? What do I count for? Do I build the railroad? You are dealing with forces, young man, when you speak of wheat and the railroads, not with men. There is the wheat, the supply. It must be carried to feed the people. There is the demand. The wheat is one force, the railroad another, and there is the law that governs them—supply and demand. Men have only little to do in the whole business. Complications may arise, conditions that bear hard on the individual—crush him, maybe—but the wheat will be carried to feed the people as inevitably as it will grow.' "

One feels disposed to quarrel with Norris for his inordinate realism. What does the world care whether Hooven's meat safe be square or oblong; whether it be lined with wire screen or mosquito netting; whether it be hung to the branches of the oak tree or to the ridge-pole of the barn; whether in fact, Hooven has a meat safe or not? "Feels disposed" is used advisedly. In truth, we can not quarrel with him. It is confession and capitulation. The facts are against us. He *has* produced results, Titanic results. Never mind the realism, the unimportant detail, minute description, Hooven's meat safe and the rest. Let it be stated flatly that by no other method could Frank Norris or anybody else have handled the vast Valley of the San Joaquin and the no less vast-tentacled *Octopus*. Results? It was the only way to paint the broad canvas he has painted, with the unflare in his brush.

But he gives us something more than realism. Listen to this:

"Once more the pendulum of the seasons swung in its mighty arcs."

.   .   .

"Then, faint and prolonged, across the levels of the ranch, he heard the engine whistling for Bonneville. Again and again, at rapid intervals in its flying course, it whistled for road crossings, for sharp curves, for trestles; ominous notes, hoarse, bellowing, ringing with accents of menace and defiance; and abruptly Presley saw again, in his imagination, the galloping monster, the terror of steel and steam, with its single eye, cyclopean, red, shooting from horizon to horizon; but saw it now as the symbol of a vast power, huge, terrible, flinging the echo of its thunder over all the reaches of the valley, leaving blood and destruction in its path; the leviathan, with tentacles of steel clutching into the soil, the soulless Force, the iron-hearted Power, the monster, the Colossus, the Octopus."

•   •   •

"The direct brutality of ten thousand acres of wheat, nothing but wheat as far as the eye could see, stunned her a little. There was something vaguely indecent in the sight, this food of the people, this elemental force, this basic energy, weltering here under the sun in all the unconscious nakedness of a sprawling, primordial Titan."

•   •   •

"Everywhere throughout the great San Joaquin, unseen and unheard, a thousand ploughs up-stirred the land, tens of thousands of shears clutched deep into the warm, moist soil. It was the long, stroking caress, vigorous, male, powerful, for which the Earth seemed panting. The heroic embrace of a multitude of iron hands, gripping down into the brown, warm flesh of the land that quivered responsive and passionate under this rude advance, so robust as to be almost an assault, so violent as to be veritably brutal. There, under the sun and under the speckless sheen of the sky, the wooing of the Titan began, the vast primal passion, the two world-forces, the elemental Male and Female, locked in a colossal embrace, at grapples in the throes of an infinite desire, at once terrible and divine, knowing no law, untamed, savage, natural sublime."

Many men, and women, too, pass through the pages of *The Octopus*, but one, greatest of all, we can not forbear mentioning in passing—Annixter. Annixter, rough almost to insolence, direct in speech, intolerant in his opinions, relying upon absolutely no one but himself; crusty of temper, bullying of disposition, a ferocious worker, and as widely trusted as he was widely hated; obstinate and contrary, cantankerous, and deliciously afraid of "female women"—this is Annixter. He is worth knowing. In such cunning fashion has Norris blown the breath of life into him, that his death comes with a shock which is seldom produced by deaths in fiction. Osterman, laying his head on his arms like a tired man going to rest, and Delaney, crawling instinctively out of the blood-welter to die in the growing wheat; but it is Annixter, instantly killed, falling without movement, for whom we first weep. A living man there died.

Well, the promise of *Moran* and *McTeague* has been realized. Can we ask more? Yet we have only the first of the trilogy. *The Epic of the Wheat* is no little thing. Content with *The Octopus*, we may look forward to *The Pit* and *The Wolf*. We shall not doubt this time.

# THE PEOPLE OF
# THE ABYSS

## CHAPTER I
### THE DESCENT

*Christ look upon us in this city,*
*And keep our sympathy and pity*
*Fresh, and our faces heavenward;*
*Lest we grow hard.*

*—Thomas Ashe*

"BUT YOU CAN'T DO IT, you know," friends said, to whom I applied for assistance in the matter of sinking myself down into the East End of London. "You had better see the police for a guide," they added, on second thought, painfully endeavoring to adjust themselves to the psychological processes of a madman who had come to them with better credentials than brains.

"But I don't want to see the police," I protested. "What I wish to do, is to go down into the East End and see things for myself. I wish to know how those people are living there, and why they are living there, and what they are living for. In short, I am going to live there myself."

"You don't want to *live* down there!" everybody said, with disapprobation writ large upon their faces. "Why, it is said there are places where a man's life isn't worth tu'pence."

"The very places I wish to see," I broke in.

"But you can't, you know," was the unfailing rejoinder.

"Which is not what I came to see you about," I answered brusquely, somewhat nettled by their incomprehension. "I am a stranger here, and I want you to tell me what you know of the East End, in order that I may have something to start on."

"But we know nothing of the East End. It is over there, somewhere." And they waved their hands vaguely in the direction where the sun on rare occasions may be seen to rise.

"Then I shall go to Cook's," I announced.

"Oh, yes," they said, with relief. "Cook's will be sure to know."

But O Cook, O Thomas Cook & Son, pathfinders and trail-clearers, living sign-posts to all the world and bestowers of first aid to bewildered travellers—unhesitatingly and instantly, with ease and celerity, could you send me to Darkest Africa or Innermost Thibet, but to the East End of London, barely a stone's throw distant from Ludgate Circus, you know not the way!

"You can't do it, you know," said the human emporium of routes and fares at Cook's Cheapside branch. "It is so—ahem—so unusual."

"Consult the police," he concluded authoritatively, when I persisted. "We are not accustomed to taking travellers to the East End; we receive no call to take them there, and we know nothing whatsoever about the place at all."

"Never mind that," I interposed, to save myself from being swept out of the office by his flood of negations. "Here's something you can do for me. I wish you to understand in advance what I intend doing, so that in case of trouble you may be able to identify me."

"Ah, I see; should you be murdered, we would be in position to identify the corpse."

He said it so cheerfully and cold-bloodedly that on the instant I saw my stark and mutilated cadaver stretched upon a slab where cool waters trickle ceaselessly, and him I saw bending over and sadly and patiently identifying it as the body of the insane American who *would* see the East End.

"No, no," I answered; "merely to identify me in case I get into a scrape with the 'bobbies.' " This last I said with a thrill; truly, I was gripping hold of the vernacular.

"That," he said, "is a matter for the consideration of the Chief Office."

"It is so unprecedented, you know," he added apologetically.

The man at the Chief Office hemmed and hawed. "We make it a

rule," he explained, "to give no information concerning our clients."

"But in this case," I urged, "it is the client who requests you to give the information concerning himself."

Again he hemmed and hawed.

"Of course," I hastily anticipated, "I know it is unprecedented, but—"

"As I was about to remark," he went on steadily, "it is unprecedented, and I don't think we can do anything for you."

However, I departed with the address of a detective who lived in the East End, and took my way to the American consul-general. And here, at last, I found a man with whom I could 'do business.' There was no hemming and hawing, no lifted brows, open incredulity, or blank amazement. In one minute I explained myself and my project, which he accepted as a matter of course. In the second minute he asked my age, height, and weight, and looked me over. And in the third minute, as we shook hands at parting, he said: "All right, Jack. I'll remember you and keep track."

I breathed a sigh of relief. Having built my ships behind me, I was now free to plunge into that human wilderness of which nobody seemed to know anything. But at once I encountered a new difficulty in the shape of my cabby, a gray-whiskered and eminently decorous personage, who had imperturbably driven me for several hours about the 'City.'

"Drive me down to the East End," I ordered, taking my seat.

"Where, sir?" he demanded with frank surprise.

"To the East End, anywhere. Go on."

The hansom pursued an aimless way for several minutes, then came to a puzzled stop. The aperture above my head was uncovered, and the cabman peered down perplexedly at me.

"I say," he said, "wot plyce yer wanter go?"

"East End," I repeated. "Nowhere in particular. Just drive me around, anywhere."

"But wot's the haddress, sir?"

"See here!" I thundered. "Drive me down to the East End, and at once!"

It was evident that he did not understand, but he withdrew his head and grumblingly started his horse.

Nowhere in the streets of London may one escape the sight of abject poverty, while five minutes' walk from almost any point will bring one to a slum; but the region my hansom was now penetrating was one unending slum. The streets were filled with a new and different race of people, short of stature, and of wretched or beer-sodden appearance. We rolled along through miles of bricks and squalor, and from each cross street and alley flashed long vistas of bricks and misery. Here and there lurched a drunken man or woman, and the air was obscene with sounds of jangling and squabbling. At a market, tottery old men and women were searching in the garbage thrown in the mud for rotten potatoes, beans, and vegetables, while little children clustered like flies around a festering mass of fruit, thrusting their arms to the shoulders into the liquid corruption, and drawing forth morsels, but partially decayed, which they devoured on the spot.

Not a hansom did I meet with in all my drive, while mine was like an apparition from another and better world, the way the children ran after it and alongside. And as far as I could see were the solid walls of brick, the slimy pavements, and the screaming streets; and for the first time in my life the fear of the crowd smote me. It was like the fear of the sea; and the miserable multitudes, street upon street, seemed so many waves of a vast and malodorous sea, lapping about me and threatening to well up and over me.

"Stepney, sir; Stepney Station," the cabby called down.

I looked about. It was really a railroad station, and he had driven desperately to it as the one familiar spot he had ever heard of in all that wilderness.

"Well?" I said.

He spluttered unintelligibly, shook his head, and looked very miserable. "I'm a strynger 'ere," he managed to articulate. "An' if yer don't want Stepney Station, I'm blessed if I know wotcher do want."

"I'll tell you what I want," I said. "You drive along and keep your eye out for a shop where old clothes are sold. Now, when you see such a shop, drive right on till you turn the corner, then stop and let me out."

I could see that he was growing dubious of his fare, but not long afterward he pulled up to the curb and informed me that an old clothes shop was to be found a bit of the way back.

"Won'tcher py me?" he pleaded. "There's seven an' six owin' me."

"Yes," I laughed, "and it would be the last I'd see of you."

"Lord lumme, but it'll be the last I see of you if yer don't py me," he retorted.

But a crowd of ragged onlookers had already gathered around the cab, and I laughed again and walked back to the old clothes shop.

Here the chief difficulty was in making the shopman understand that I really and truly wanted old clothes. But after fruitless attempts to press upon me new and impossible coats and trousers, he began to bring to light heaps of old ones, looking mysterious the while and hinting darkly. This he did with the palpable intention of letting me know that he had 'piped my lay,' in order to bulldose me, through fear of exposure, into paying heavily for my purchases. A man in trouble, or a high-class criminal from across the water, was what he took my measure for—in either case, a person anxious to avoid the police.

But I disputed with him over the outrageous difference between prices and values, till I quite disabused him of the notion, and he settled down to drive a hard bargain with a hard customer. In the end I selected a pair of stout though well-worn trousers, a frayed jacket with one remaining button, a pair of brogans which had plainly seen service where coal was shovelled, a thin leather belt, and a very dirty cloth cap. My underclothing and socks, however, were new and warm, but of the sort that any American waif, down in his luck, could acquire in the ordinary course of events.

"I must sy yer a sharp'un," he said, with counterfeit admiration, as I handed over the ten shillings finally agreed upon for the outfit. "Blimey, if you ain't ben up an' down Petticut Lane afore now. Yer trouseys is wuth five bob to hany man, an' a docker 'ud give two an' six for the shoes, to sy nothin' of the coat an' cap an' new stoker's singlet an' hother things."

"How much will you give me for them?" I demanded suddenly. "I paid you ten bob for the lot, and I'll sell them back to you, right now, for eight. Come, it's a go!"

But he grinned and shook his head, and though I had made a good bargain, I was unpleasantly aware that he had made a better one.

I found the cabby and a policeman with their heads together, but the latter, after looking me over sharply and particularly scrutinizing the bundle under my arm, turned away and left the cabby to wax mutinous by himself. And not a step would he budge till I paid him the seven shillings and sixpence owing him. Whereupon he was willing to drive me to the ends of the earth, apologizing profusely for his insistence, and explaining that one ran across queer customers in London Town.

But he drove me only to Highbury Vale, in North London, where my luggage was waiting for me. Here, next day, I took off my shoes (not without regret for their lightness and comfort), and my soft, gray travelling suit, and, in fact, all my clothing; and proceeded to array myself in the clothes of the other and unimaginable men, who must have been indeed unfortunate to have had to part with such rags for the pitiable sums obtainable from a dealer.

Inside my stoker's singlet, in the armpit, I sewed a gold sovereign (an emergency sum certainly of modest proportions); and inside my stoker's singlet I put myself. And then I sat down and moralized upon the fair years and fat, which had made my skin soft and brought the nerves close to the surface; for the singlet was rough and raspy as a hair shirt, and I am confident that the most rigorous of ascetics suffer no more than did I in the ensuing twenty-four hours.

The remainder of my costume was fairly easy to put on, though the brogans, or brogues, were quite a problem. As stiff and hard as if made of wood, it was only after a prolonged pounding of the uppers with my fists that I was able to get my feet into them at all. Then, with a few shillings, a knife, a handkerchief, and some brown papers and flake tobacco stowed away in my pockets, I thumped down the stairs and said good-by to my foreboding friends. As I passed out the door, the 'help,' a comely, middle-aged woman, could not conquer a grin that twisted her lips and separated them till the throat, out of involuntary sympathy, made the uncouth animal noises we are wont to designate as 'laughter.'

No sooner was I out on the streets than I was impressed by the difference in status effected by my clothes. All servility vanished from the demeanor of the common people with whom I came in contact. Presto! in the twinkling of an eye, so to say, I had become one of them. My frayed and out-at-elbows jacket was the badge and advertisement of my class, which was their class. It made me of like kind, and in place of the fawning and too-respectful attention I had hitherto received, I now shared with them a comradeship. The man in corduroy and dirty neckerchief no longer addressed me as 'sir' or 'governor.' It was 'mate,' now—and a fine and hearty word, with a tingle to it, and a warmth and gladness, which the other term does not possess. Governor! It smacks of mastery, and power, and high authority—the tribute of the man who is under to the man on top, delivered in the hope that he will let up a bit and ease his weight. Which is another way of saying that it is an appeal for alms.

This brings me to a delight I experienced in my rags and tatters which is denied the average American abroad. The European traveller from the States, who is not a Crœsus, speedily finds himself reduced to a chronic state of self-conscious sordidness by the hordes of cringing robbers who clutter his steps from dawn till dark, and deplete his pocketbook in a way that puts compound interest to the blush.

In my rags and tatters I escaped the pestilence of tipping, and encountered men on a basis of equality. Nay, before the day was out I turned the tables, and said, most gratefully, "Thank you, sir," to a gentleman whose horse I held, and who dropped a penny into my eager palm.

Other changes I discovered were wrought in my condition by my new garb. In crossing crowded thoroughfares I found I had to be, if anything, more lively in avoiding vehicles, and it was strikingly impressed upon me that my life had cheapened in direct ratio with my clothes. When before, I inquired the way of a policeman, I was usually asked, "Buss or 'ansom, sir?" But now the query became, "Walk or ride?" Also, at the railway stations it was the rule to be asked, "First or second, sir?" Now I was asked nothing, a third-class ticket being shoved out to me as a matter of course.

But there was compensation for it all. For the first time I met the English lower classes face to face, and knew them for what they were. When loungers and workmen, on street corners and in public houses, talked with me, they talked as one man to another, and they talked as natural men should talk, without the least idea of getting anything out of me for what they talked or the way they talked.

And when at last I made into the East End, I was gratified to find that the fear of the crowd no longer haunted me. I had become a part of it. The vast and malodorous sea had welled up and over me, or I had slipped gently into it, and there was nothing fearsome about it—with the one exception of the stoker's singlet.

## CHAPTER VI

### FRYING-PAN ALLEY AND A
### GLIMPSE OF INFERNO

*The beasts they hunger, and eat, and die,*
*And so do we, and the world's a sty.*
*"Swinehood hath no remedy,"*
*Say many men, and hasten by.*

—*Sidney Lanier*

Three of us walked down Mile End Road, and one was a hero. He was a slender lad of nineteen, so slight and frail, in fact, that, like Fra

Lippo Lippi, a puff of wind might double him up and turn him over. He was a burning young socialist, in the first throes of enthusiasm and ripe for martyrdom. As platform speaker or chairman he had taken an active and dangerous part in the many indoor and outdoor pro-Boer meetings which have vexed the serenity of Merry England these several years back. Little items he had been imparting to me as he walked along; of being mobbed in parks and on tram-cars; of climbing on the platform to lead the forlorn hope, when brother speaker after brother speaker had been dragged down by the angry crowd and cruelly beaten; of a siege in a church, where he and three others had taken sanctuary, and where, amid flying missiles and the crashing of stained glass, they had fought off the mob till rescued by platoons of constables; of pitched and giddy battles on stairways, galleries, and balconies; of smashed windows, collapsed stairways, wrecked lecture halls, and broken heads and bones—and then, with a regretful sigh, he looked at me and said: "How I envy you big, strong men! I'm such a little mite I can't do much when it comes to fighting."

And I, walking a head and shoulders above my two companions, remembered my own husky West and the stalwart men it had been my custom, in turn, to envy there. Also, as I looked at the mite of a youth with the heart of a lion, I thought, this is the type that on occasion rears barricades and shows the world that men have not forgotten how to die.

But up spoke my other companion, a man of twenty-eight who eked out a precarious existence in a sweating den.

"I'm a 'earty man, I am," he announced. "Not like the other chaps at my shop, I ain't. They consider me a fine specimen of manhood. W'y, d' ye know, I weigh one hundred and forty pounds!"

I was ashamed to tell him that I weighed one hundred and seventy, so I contented myself with taking his measure. Poor, misshapen little man! His skin an unhealthy color, body gnarled and twisted out of all decency, contracted chest, shoulders bent prodigiously from long hours of toil, and head hanging heavily forward and out of place! A " 'earty man," 'e was!

"How tall are you?"

"Five foot two," he answered proudly; "an' the chaps at the shop . . ."

"Let me see that shop," I said.

The shop was idle just then, but I still desired to see it. Passing Leman Street, we cut off to the left into Spitalfields, and dived into Frying-pan Alley. A spawn of children cluttered the slimy pavement, for all the world like tadpoles just turned frogs on the bottom of a dry pond. In a narrow doorway, so narrow that perforce we stepped over her, sat a woman with a young babe nursing at breasts grossly naked and libelling all the sacredness of motherhood. In the black and narrow hall behind her we waded through a mess of young life, and essayed an even narrower and fouler stairway. Up we went, three flights, each landing two feet by three in area, and heaped with filth and refuse.

There were seven rooms in this abomination called a house. In six of the rooms, twenty-odd people, of both sexes and all ages, cooked, ate, slept, and worked. In size the rooms averaged eight feet by eight, or possibly nine. The seventh room we entered. It was the den in which five men 'sweated.' It was seven feet wide by eight long, and the table at which the work was performed took up the major portion of the space. On this table were five lasts, and there was barely room for the men to stand to their work, for the rest of the space was heaped with cardboard, leather, bundles of shoe uppers, and a miscellaneous assortment of materials used in attaching the uppers of shoes to their soles.

In the adjoining room lived a woman and six children. In another vile hole lived a widow, with an only son of sixteen who was dying of consumption. The woman hawked sweetmeats on the street, I was told, and more often failed than not in supplying her son with the three quarts of milk he daily required. Further, this son, weak and dying, did not taste meat oftener than once a week; and the kind and quality of this meat cannot possibly be imagined by people who have never watched human swine eat.

"The w'y 'e coughs is somethin' terrible," volunteered my sweated friend, referring to the dying boy. "We 'ear 'im 'ere, w'ile we're workin', an' it's terrible, I say, terrible!"

And, what of the coughing and the sweetmeats, I found another menace added to the hostile environment of the children of the slum.

My sweated friend, when work was to be had, toiled with four other men in this eight-by-seven room. In winter a lamp burned nearly all the day and added its fumes to the overloaded air, which was breathed, and breathed, and breathed again.

In good times, when there was a rush of work, this man told me that he could earn as high as 'thirty bob a week.'—Thirty shillings! Seven dollars and a half!

"But it's only the best of us can do it," he qualified. "An' then we work twelve, thirteen, and fourteen hours a day, just as fast as we can. An' you should see us sweat! Just running from us! If you could see us, it'd dazzle your eyes—tacks flyin' out of mouth like from a machine. Look at my mouth."

I looked. The teeth were worn down by the constant friction of the metallic brads, while they were coal-black and rotten.

"I clean my teeth," he added, "else they'd be worse."

After he had told me that the workers had to furnish their own tools, brads, "grindery," cardboard, rent, light, and what not, it was plain that his thirty bob was a diminishing quantity.

"But how long does the rush season last, in which you receive this high wage of thirty bob?" I asked.

"Four months," was the answer; and for the rest of the year, he informed me, they average from 'half a quid' to a 'quid' a week, which is equivalent to from two dollars and a half to five dollars. The present week was half gone, and he had earned four bob, or one dollar. And yet I was given to understand that this was one of the better grades of sweating.

I looked out of the window, which should have commanded the back yards of the neighboring buildings. But there were no back yards, or, rather, they were covered with one-story hovels, cowsheds, in which people lived. The roofs of these hovels were covered with deposits of filth, in some places a couple of feet deep—the contributions from the back windows of the second and third stories. I could make out fish and meat bones, garbage, pestilential rags, old boots, broken earthenware, and all the general refuse of a human sty.

"This is the last year of this trade; they're getting machines to do away with us," said the sweated one mournfully, as we stepped over the woman with the breasts grossly naked and waded anew through the cheap young life.

We next visited the municipal dwellings erected by the London County Council on the site of the slums where lived Arthur Morrison's "Child of the Jago." While the buildings housed more people than before, it was much healthier. But the dwellings were inhabited by the better-class workmen and artisans. The slum people had simply drifted on to crowd other slums or to form new slums.

"An' now," said the sweated one, the 'earty man who worked so fast as to dazzle one's eyes, "I'll show you one of London's lungs. This is Spitalfields Garden." And he mouthed the word 'garden' with scorn.

The shadow of Christ's Church falls across Spitalfields Garden, and in the shadow of Christ's Church, at three o'clock in the afternoon, I saw a sight I never wish to see again. There are no flowers in this garden, which is smaller than my own rose garden at home. Grass only grows here, and it is surrounded by sharp-spiked iron fencing, as are all the parks of London Town, so that homeless men and women may not come in at night and sleep upon it.

As we entered the garden, an old woman, between fifty and sixty, passed us, striding with sturdy intention if somewhat rickety action, with two bulky bundles, covered with sacking, slung fore and aft upon her. She was a woman tramp, a houseless soul, too independent to drag her failing carcass through the workhouse door. Like the snail, she carried her home with her. In the two sacking-covered bundles were her household goods, her wardrobe, linen, and dear feminine possessions.

We went up the narrow gravelled walk. On the benches on either side was arrayed a mass of miserable and distorted humanity, the sight of which would have impelled Doré to more diabolical flights of fancy than he ever succeeded in achieving. It was a welter of rags and filth, of all manner of loathsome skin diseases, open sores, bruises, grossness, indecency, leering monstrosities, and bestial faces. A chill, raw wind was blowing, and these creatures huddled there in their rags, sleeping for the most part, or trying to sleep. Here were a dozen women, ranging in age from twenty years to seventy. Next a babe, possibly of nine months, lying asleep, flat on the hard bench, with neither pillow nor covering, nor with any one looking after it. Next, half a dozen men, sleeping bolt upright or leaning against one another in their sleep. In one place a family group, a child asleep in its sleeping mother's arms, and the husband (or male mate) clumsily mending a dilapidated shoe. On another bench a woman trimming the frayed strips of her rags with a knife, and another woman, with thread and needle, sewing up rents. Adjoining, a man holding a sleeping woman in his arms. Farther on, a man, his clothing caked with gutter mud, asleep with head in the lap of a woman, not more than twenty-five years old, and also asleep.

It was this sleeping that puzzled me. Why were nine out of ten of them asleep or trying to sleep? But it was not till afterward that I learned. *It is a law of the powers that be that the homeless shall not sleep by night.* On the pavement, by the portico of Christ's Church, where the stone pillars rise toward the sky in a stately row, were whole rows of men lying asleep or drowsing, and all too deep sunk in torpor to rouse or be made curious by our intrusion.

"A lung of London," I said; "nay, an abscess, a great putrescent sore."

"Oh, why did you bring me here?" demanded the burning young socialist, his delicate face white with sickness of soul and stomach sickness.

"Those women there," said our guide, "will sell themselves for thru'pence, or tu'pence, or a loaf of stale bread."

He said it with a cheerful sneer.

But what more he might have said I do not know, for the sick man cried, "For heaven's sake, let us get out of this."

# CHAPTER VIII

## THE CARTER AND THE CARPENTER

*It is not to die, nor even to die of hunger, that makes a man wretched. Many men have died; all men must die. But it is to live miserable, we know not why; to work sore, and yet gain nothing; to be heart-worn, weary, yet isolated, unrelated, girt in with a cold, universal Laissez-faire.*

*—Carlye*

The Carter, with his clean-cut face, chin beard, and shaved upper lip, I should have taken in the United States for anything from a master workman to a well-to-do farmer. The Carpenter—well, I should have taken him for a carpenter. He looked it, lean and wiry, with shrewd, observant eyes, and hands that had grown twisted to the handles of tools through forty-seven years' work at the trade. The chief difficulty with these men was that they were old, and that their children, instead of growing up to take care of them, had died. Their years had told on them, and they had been forced out of the whirl of industry by the younger and stronger competitors who had taken their places.

These two men, turned away from the casual ward of Whitechapel Workhouse, were bound with me for Poplar Workhouse. Not much of a show, they thought, but to chance it was all that remained to us. It was Poplar, or the streets and night. Both men were anxious for a bed, for they were 'about gone,' as they phrased it. The Carter, fifty-eight years of age, had spent the last three nights without shelter

454                                                            Selected Nonfiction

or sleep, while the Carpenter, sixty-five years of age, had been out five nights.

But, O dear, soft people, full of meat and blood, with white beds and airy rooms waiting you each night, how can I make you know what it is to suffer as you would suffer if you spent a weary night on London's streets? Believe me, you would think a thousand centuries had come and gone before the east paled into dawn; you would shiver till you were ready to cry aloud with the pain of each aching muscle; and you would marvel that you could endure so much and live. Should you rest upon a bench, and your tired eyes close, depend upon it the policeman would rouse you and gruffly order you to 'move on.' You may rest upon the bench, and benches are few and far between; but if rest means sleep, on you must go, dragging your tired body through the endless streets. Should you, in desperate slyness, seek some forlorn alley or dark passageway and lie down, the omnipresent policeman will rout you out just the same. It is his business to rout you out. It is a law of the powers that be that you shall be routed out.

But when the dawn came, the nightmare over, you would hale you home to refresh yourself, and until you died you would tell the story of your adventure to groups of admiring friends. It would grow into a mighty story. Your little eight-hour night would become an Odyssey and you a Homer.

Not so with these homeless ones who walked to Poplar Workhouse with me. And there are thirty-five thousand of them, men and women, in London Town this night. Please don't remember it as you go to bed; if you are as soft as you ought to be, you may not rest so well as usual. But for old men of sixty, seventy, and eighty, ill-fed, with neither meat nor blood, to greet the dawn unrefreshed, and to stagger through the day in mad search for crusts, with relentless night rushing down upon them again, and to do this five nights and days— O dear, soft people, full of meat and blood, how can you ever understand?

I walked up Mile End Road between the Carter and the Carpenter. Mile End Road is a wide thoroughfare, cutting the heart of East London, and there were tens of thousands of people abroad on it. I tell you this so that you may fully appreciate what I shall describe in the next paragraph. As I say, we walked along, and when they grew bitter and cursed the land, I cursed with them, cursed as an American waif would curse, stranded in a strange and terrible land. And, as I tried to lead them to believe, and succeeded in making them believe, they took me for a 'seafaring man,' who had spent his money in riotous living, lost his clothes (no unusual occurrence with seafaring men ashore), and was temporarily broke while looking for a ship. This accounted for my ignorance of English ways in general and casual wards in particular, and my curiosity concerning the same.

The Carter was hard put to keep the pace at which we walked (he told me that he had eaten nothing that day), but the Carpenter, lean and hungry, his gray and ragged overcoat flapping mournfully in the breeze, swung on in a long and tireless stride which reminded me strongly of the plains coyote. Both kept their eyes upon the pavement as they walked and talked, and every now and then one or the other would stoop and pick something up, never missing the stride the while. I thought it was cigar and cigarette stumps they were collecting, and for some time took no notice. Then I did notice.

*From the slimy sidewalk, they were picking up bits of orange peel, apple skin, and grape stems, and they were eating them. The pits of green gage plums they cracked between their teeth for the kernels inside. They picked up stray crumbs of bread the size of peas, apple cores so black and dirty one would not take them to be apple cores, and these things these two men took into their mouths, and chewed them, and swallowed them; and this, between six and seven o'clock in the evening of August 20, year of our Lord 1902, in the heart of the greatest, wealthiest, and most powerful empire the world has ever seen.*

# CHAPTER XXIII

## THE CHILDREN

*Where home is a hovel, and dull we grovel,*
*Forgetting the world is fair.*

There is one beautiful sight in the East End, and only one, and it is the children dancing in the street when the organ-grinder goes his round. It is fascinating to watch them, the new-born, the next generation, swaying and stepping, with pretty little mimicries and graceful inventions all their own, with muscles that move swiftly and easily, and bodies that leap airily, weaving rhythms never taught in dancing school.

I have talked with these children, here, there, and everywhere, and they struck me as being bright as other children, and in many ways even brighter. They have most active little imaginations. Their capacity for projecting themselves into the realm of romance and fantasy is remarkable. A joyous life is romping in their blood. They delight in music, and motion, and color, and very often they betray a startling beauty of face and form under their filth and rags.

But there is a Pied Piper of London Town who steals them all away. They disappear. One never sees them again, or anything that suggests them. You may look for them in vain amongst the generation of grown-ups. Here you will find stunted forms, ugly faces, and blunt and stolid minds. Grace, beauty, imagination, all the resiliency of mind and muscle, are gone. Sometimes, however, you may see a woman, not necessarily old, but twisted and deformed out of all womanhood, bloated and drunken, lift her draggled skirts and execute a few grotesque and lumbering steps upon the pavement. It is a hint that she was once one of those children who danced to the organ-grinder. Those grotesque and lumbering steps are all that is left of the promise of childhood. In the befogged recesses of her brain has arisen a fleeting memory that she was once a girl. The crowd closes in. Little girls are dancing beside her, about her, with all the pretty graces she dimly recollects, but can no more than parody with her body. Then she pants for breath, exhausted, and stumbles out through the circle. But the little girls dance on.

The children of the Ghetto possess all the qualities which make for noble manhood and womanhood; but the Ghetto itself, like an infuriated tigress turning on its young, turns upon and destroys all these qualities, blots out the light and laughter, and moulds those it does not kill into sodden and forlorn creatures, uncouth, degraded and wretched below the beasts of the field.

As to the manner in which this is done, I have in previous chapters described at length; here let Professor Huxley describe in brief: "Any one who is acquainted with the state of the population of all great industrial centres, whether in this or other countries, is aware that amidst a large and increasing body of that population there reigns supreme . . . that condition which the French call *la misère,* a word for which I do not think there is any exact English equivalent. It is a condition in which the food, warmth, and clothing which are necessary for the mere maintenance of the functions of the body in their normal state cannot be obtained; in which men, women, and children are forced to crowd into dens wherein decency is abolished, and the most ordinary conditions of healthful existence are impossible of attainment; in which the pleasures within reach are reduced to brutality and drunkenness; in which the pains accumulate at compound interest in the shape of starvation, disease, stunted development, and moral degradation; in which the prospect of even steady and honest industry is a life of unsuccessful battling with hunger, rounded by a pauper's grave."

In such conditions, the outlook for children is hopeless. They die like flies, and those that survive, survive because they possess excessive vitality and a capacity of adaptation to the degradation with which they are surrounded. They have no home life. In the dens and lairs in which they live they are exposed to all that is obscene and indecent. And as their minds are made rotten, so are their bodies made rotten by bad sanitation, overcrowding, and underfeeding. When a father and mother live with three or four children in a room where the children take turn about in sitting up to drive the rats away from the sleepers, when those children never have enough to eat and are preyed upon and made miserable and weak by swarming vermin, the sort of men and women the survivors will make can readily be imagined. . . .

# HOW I BECAME A
# SOCIALIST *

IT IS QUITE FAIR to say that I became a Socialist in a fashion somewhat similar to the way in which the Teutonic pagans became Christians— it was hammered into me. Not only was I not looking for Socialism at the time of my conversion, but I was fighting it. I was very young and callow, did not know much of anything, and though I had never even heard of a school called "Individualism," I sang the pæan of the strong with all my heart.

This was because I was strong myself. By strong I mean that I had good health and hard muscles, both of which possessions are easily accounted for. I had lived my childhood on California ranches, my boyhood hustling newspapers on the streets of a healthy Western city, and my youth on the ozone-laden waters of San Francisco Bay and the Pacific Ocean. I loved life in the open, and I toiled in the open, at the hardest kinds of work. Learning no trade, but drifting along from job to job, I looked on the world and called it good, every bit of it. Let me repeat, this optimism was because I was healthy and strong, bothered with neither aches nor weaknesses, never turned down by the boss because I did not look fit, able always to get a job at shovelling coal, sailorizing, or manual labor of some sort.

And because of all this, exulting in my young life, able to hold my own at work or fight, I was a rampant individualist. It was very natural. I was a winner. Wherefore I called the game, as I saw it played, or thought I saw it played, a very proper game for MEN. To

* From *War of the Classes*; first published in *The Comrade*, March 1903.

be a MAN was to write man in large capitals on my heart. To adventure like a man, and fight like a man, and do a man's work (even for a boy's pay)—these were things that reached right in and gripped hold of me as no other thing could. And I looked ahead into long vistas of a hazy and interminable future, into which, playing what I conceived to be MAN'S game, I should continue to travel with unfailing health, without accidents, and with muscles ever vigorous. As I say, this future was interminable. I could see myself only raging through life without end like one of Nietzsche's *blond beasts,* lustfully roving and conquering by sheer superiority and strength.

As for the unfortunates, the sick, and ailing, and old, and maimed, I must confess I hardly thought of them at all, save that I vaguely felt that they, barring accidents, could be as good as I if they wanted to real hard, and could work just as well. Accidents? Well, they represented FATE, also spelled out in capitals, and there was no getting around FATE. Napoleon had had an accident at Waterloo, but that did not dampen my desire to be another and later Napoleon. Further, the optimism bred of a stomach which could digest scrap iron and a body which flourished on hardships did not permit me to consider accidents as even remotely related to my glorious personality.

I hope I have made it clear that I was proud to be one of Nature's strong-armed noblemen. The dignity of labor was to me the most impressive thing in the world. Without having read Carlyle, or Kipling, I formulated a gospel of work which put theirs in the shade. Work was everything. It was sanctification and salvation. The pride I took in a hard day's work well done would be inconceivable to you. It is almost inconceivable to me as I look back upon it. I was as faithful a wage slave as ever capitalist exploited. To shirk or malinger on the man who paid me my wages was a sin, first, against myself, and second, against him. I considered it a crime second only to treason and just about as bad.

In short, my joyous individualism was dominated by the orthodox bourgeois ethics. I read the bourgeois papers, listened to the bourgeois preachers, and shouted at the sonorous platitudes of the bourgeois politicians. And I doubt not, if other events had not changed my career, that I should have evolved into a professional strike-breaker, (one of President Eliot's American heroes), and had my head and my earning power irrevocably smashed by a club in the hands of some militant trades-unionist.

Just about this time, returning from a seven months' voyage before the mast, and just turned eighteen, I took it into my head to go tramping. On rods and blind baggages I fought my way from the open West, where men bucked big and the job hunted the man, to the congested labor centres of the East, where men were small potatoes and hunted the job for all they were worth. And on this new *blond-beast* adventure I found myself looking upon life from a new and totally different angle. I had dropped down from the proletariat into what sociologists love to call the "submerged tenth," and I was startled to discover the way in which that submerged tenth was recruited.

I found there all sorts of men, many of whom had once been as good as myself and just as *blond-beastly;* sailor-men, soldier-men, labor-men, all wrenched and distorted and twisted out of shape by toil and hardship and accident, and cast adrift by their masters like so many old horses. I battered on the drag and slammed back gates with them, or shivered with them in box cars and city parks, listening the while to life-histories which began under auspices as fair as mine, with digestions and bodies equal to and better than mine, and which ended there before my eyes in the shambles at the bottom of the Social Pit.

And as I listened my brain began to work. The woman of the streets and the man of the gutter drew very close to me. I saw the picture of the Social Pit as vividly as though it were a concrete thing, and at the bottom of the Pit I saw them, myself above them, not far, and hanging on to the slippery wall by main strength and sweat. And I confess a terror seized me. What when my strength failed? when I should be unable to work shoulder to shoulder with the strong men who were as yet babes unborn? And there and then I swore a great oath. It ran something like this: *All my days I have worked hard with my body, and according to the number of days I have worked, by just that much am I nearer the bottom of the Pit. I shall climb out of the Pit, but not by the muscles of my body shall I climb out. I shall do no more hard work, and may God strike me dead if I do another day's hard work with my body more than I absolutely have to do.* And I have been busy ever since running away from hard work.

Incidentally, while tramping some ten thousand miles through the United States and Canada, I strayed into Niagara Falls, was nabbed by a fee-hunting constable, denied the right to plead guilty or not guilty, sentenced out of hand to thirty days' imprisonment for having no fixed abode and no visible means of support, handcuffed and chained to a bunch of men similarly circumstanced, carted down country to Buffalo, registered at the Erie County Penitentiary, had my head clipped and my budding mustache shaved, was dressed in convict stripes, compulsorily vaccinated by a medical student who practised on such as we, made to march the lock-step, and put to work under the eyes of guards armed with Winchester rifles—all for adventuring in *blond-beastly* fashion. Concerning further details deponent sayeth not, though he may hint that some of his plethoric national patriotism simmered down and leaked out of the bottom of his soul somewhere —at least, since that experience he finds that he cares more for men and women and little children than for imaginary geographical lines.

To return to my conversion. I think it is apparent that my rampant individualism was pretty effectively hammered out of me, and something else as effectively hammered in. But, just as I had been an individualist without knowing it, I was now a Socialist without knowing it, withal, an unscientific one. I had been reborn, but not renamed, and I was running around to find out what manner of thing I was. I ran back to California and opened the books. I do not remember which ones I opened first. It is an unimportant detail anyway. I was already It, whatever It was, and by aid of the books I discovered that It was a Socialist. Since that day I have opened many books, but no economic argument, no lucid demonstration of the logic and inevitableness of Socialism affects me as profoundly and convincingly as I was affected on the day when I first saw the walls of the Social Pit rise around me and felt myself slipping down, down, into the shambles at the bottom.

# GETTING INTO PRINT *

As SOON AS A fellow sells two or three things to the magazines, or successfully inveigles some publisher into bringing out a book, his friends all ask him how he managed to do it. So it is fair to conclude that the placing of books and of stories with the magazines is a highly interesting performance.

I know it was highly interesting to me; vitally interesting, I may say. I used to run through endless magazines and newspapers, wondering all the time how the writers of all that stuff managed to place it. To show that the possession of this knowledge was vitally important to me, let me state that I had many liabilities and no assets, no income, several mouths to feed, and for landlady a poor widow woman whose imperative necessities demanded that I should pay my rent with some degree of regularity. This was my economic situation when I buckled on the harness and went up against the magazines.

Further, and to the point, I knew positively nothing about it. I lived in California, far from the great publishing centers. I did not know what an editor looked like. I did not know a soul who had ever published anything; nor yet again, a soul, with the exception of my own, who had ever tried to write anything, much less tried to publish it. Still worse, and to show how badly off I really was, I did not know "500 Places to Sell Manuscripts," or THE EDITOR.

I had no one to give me tips, no one's experience to profit by. So

* *The Editor*, March 1903.

I sat down and wrote in order to get an experience of my own. I wrote everything—short stories, articles, anecdotes, jokes, essays, sonnets, ballads, vilanelles, triolets, songs, light plays in iambic tetrameter, and heavy tragedies in blank verse. These various creations I stuck into envelopes, enclosed return postage, and dropped into the mail. Oh, I was prolific. Day by day my manuscripts mounted up, till the problem of finding stamps for them became as great as that of making life livable for my widow landlady.

All my manuscripts came back. They continued to come back. The process seemed like the working of a soulless machine. I dropped the manuscript into the mail box. After the lapse of a certain approximate length of time, the manuscript was brought back to me by the postman. Accompanying it was a stereotyped rejection slip. A part of the machine, some cunning arrangement of cogs and cranks at the other end (it could not have been a living, breathing man with blood in his veins), had transferred the manuscript to another envelope, taken the stamps from the inside and pasted them outside, and added the rejection slip.

This went on for some months. I was still in the dark. I had not yet gained the smallest particle of experience. Concerning which was the more marketable, poetry or prose, jokes or sonnets, short stories or essays, I knew no more than when I began. I had vague ideas, however, dim and hazy ideas to the effect that a minimum rate of ten dollars a thousand words was paid; that if I only published two or three things the editors would clamor for my wares; that a manuscript held in some editor's hands for the small matter of four or five months did not necessarily mean a manuscript that was sold.

Concerning this minimum rate of ten dollars a thousand words, a thing in which I fondly believed, I must confess that I had gleaned it from some Sunday supplement. Likewise I must confess the beautiful and touching modesty with which I aspired. Let other men, thought I, receive the maximum rate, whatever marvelous sum it may be. As for myself, I shall always be content to receive the minimum rate. And, once I get started, I shall do no more than three thousand words a day, five days only in the week. This will give me plenty of recreation, while I shall be earning six hundred dollars a month without overstocking the market.

As I say, the machine worked for several months, and then, one morning, the postman brought me a letter, mark you a letter, not a long thick one but a short thin one, and from a magazine. My stamp problem and my landlady problem were pressing me cruelly, and this short thin letter from a magazine would of a certainty solve both problems in short order.

I could not open the letter right away. It seemed a sacred thing. It contained the written words of an editor. The magazine he represented I imagined ranked in the first class. I knew it held a four-thousand-word story of mine. What will it be? I asked. The minimum rate, I answered, modest as ever; forty dollars of course. Having thus guarded myself against any possible kind of disappointment, I opened the letter and read what I thought would be blazed in letters of fire on my memory for all time. Alas! the years are few, yet I have forgotten. But the gist of the letter was coldly to the effect that my story was available, that they would print it in the next number, and that they would pay me for it the sum of five dollars.

Five dollars! A dollar and a quarter a thousand! That I did not die right there and then convinces me that I am possessed of a singular ruggedness of soul which will permit me to survive and ultimately qualify for the oldest inhabitant.

Five dollars! When? The editor did not state. I didn't have even a stamp with which to convey my acceptance or rejection of his offer. Just then the landlady's little girl knocked at the back door. Both problems were clamoring more compellingly than ever for solution. It was plain there was no such thing as a minimum rate. Nothing remained but to get out and shovel coal. I had done it before and earned more money at it. I resolved to do it again; and I certainly should have, had it not been for the *Black Cat*.

Yes, the *Black Cat*. The postman brought me an offer from it of forty dollars for a four-thousand-word story, which same was more lengthy than strengthy, if I would grant permission to cut it down half. This was equivalent to a twenty-dollar rate. Grant permission? I told them they could cut it down two-halves if they'd only send the money along, which they did, by return mail. As for the five dollars previously mentioned, I finally received it, after publication and a great deal of embarrassment and trouble.

I forgot my coal shoveling resolution and continued to whang away at the typewriter—"to drip adjectives from the ends of my fingers," as some young woman has picturesquely phrased it. About this time, I do not remember how, I blundered upon THE EDITOR. The first number I read aroused in me a great regret for all my blind waste of energy. I may not tell a hundredth part of what I learned from THE

EDITOR, but I may say that it taught me how to solve the stamp and landlady problems by means of hackwork. It taught me the market for hackwork and the prices I might expect. So I was enabled to do a certain quantity of hack each month, enough to pay expenses, and devote the rest of my time to serious efforts, which are always hazardous financial undertakings.

In closing this brief narrative of experience, let me give a few painfully acquired generalizations. Don't quit your job in order to write unless there is none dependent upon you. Fiction pays best of all, and when it is of a fair quality is more easily sold. A good joke will sell quicker than a good poem, and, measured in sweat and blood, will bring better remuneration. Avoid the unhappy ending, the harsh, the brutal, the tragic, the horrible—if you care to see in print the things you write. (In this connection don't do as I do, but do as I say.)

Humor is the hardest to write, easiest to sell, and best rewarded. There are only a few who are able to do it. If you are able, do it by all means. You will find it a Klondike and a Rand rolled into one. Look as Mark Twain.

Don't dash off a six-thousand-word story before breakfast. Don't write too much. Concentrate your sweat on one story, rather than dissipate it over a dozen. Don't loaf and invite inspiration; light out after it with a club, and if you don't get it you will nonetheless get something that looks remarkably like it. Set yourself a "stint," and see that you do that "stint" each day; you will have more words to your credit at the end of the year.

Study the tricks of the writers who have arrived. They have mastered the tools with which you are cutting your fingers. They are doing things, and their work bears the internal evidence of how it is done. Don't wait for some good Samaritan to tell you, but dig it out for yourself.

See that your pores are open and your digestion is good. That is, I am confident, the most important rule of all. And don't fling Carlyle in my teeth, please.

Keep a notebook. Travel with it, eat with it, sleep with it. Slap into it every stray thought that flutters up into your brain. Cheap paper is less perishable than gray matter, and lead pencil markings endure longer than memory.

And work. Spell it in capital letters, WORK. Work all the time. Find out about this earth, this universe; this force and matter, and the spirit that glimmers up through force and matter from the maggot to

Godhead. And by all this I mean WORK for a philosophy of life. It does not hurt how wrong your philosophy of life may be, so long as you have one and have it well.

The three great things are: GOOD HEALTH; WORK; and a PHILOSOPHY OF LIFE. I may add, nay, must add, a fourth—SINCERITY. Without this, the other three are without avail; with it you may cleave to greatness and sit among the giants.

# THE TERRIBLE AND TRAGIC
# IN FICTION*

I am anxious that your firm should continue to be my publishers, and, if you would be willing to bring out the book, I
should be glad to accept the terms which you allowed me
before—that is, you receive all profits, and allow me twenty
copies for distribution to friends.

So wrote Edgar Allan Poe, on August 13, 1841, to the publishing
house of Lee & Blanchard. They replied:

We very much regret to say that the state of affairs is such
as to give little encouragement to new undertakings. . . . We
assure you that we regret this on your account as well as our
own, as it would give us great pleasure to promote your views
in relation to publication.

Five years later, in 1846, Poe wrote to Mr. E. H. Duyckinck:

For particular reasons I am anxious to have another volume
of my tales published before the first of March. Do you think
it possible to accomplish it for me? Would not Mr. Wiley
give me, say $50, in full for the copyright of the collection I
now send?

* From *Jack London Reports*; first published in *The Critic*, June 1903.

Measured by the earnings of contemporaneous writers, it is clear that Poe received little or nothing for the stories he wrote. In the autumn of 1900, one of the three extant copies of his "Tamerlane and Other Poems" sold for $2050—a sum greater, perhaps, than he received from the serial and book sales of all his stories and poems.*

On the one hand, he was more poorly rewarded than even the mediocre of his contemporaries; while, on the other hand, he produced a more powerful effect than the great majority of them and achieved a fame more brilliant and lasting.

Cooke, in a letter to Poe, says:

"The Valdemar Case" I read in a number of your *Broadway Journal* last winter—as I lay in a Turkey blind, muffled to the eyes in overcoats, &c., and pronounce it without hesitation the most damnable, vraisemblable, horrible, hairlifting, shocking, ingenious chapter of fiction that any brain ever conceived, or hands treated. That gelatinous, viscous sound of man's voice! there never was such an idea before. That story scared me in broad day, armed with a doublebarrel Tyron Turkey gun. What would it have done at midnight in some old ghostly countryhouse?

I have always found some one remarkable thing in your stories to haunt me long after reading them. The *teeth* of Berenice—the changing eyes of Morella—that red and glaring crack in the House of Usher—the pores of the deck in "The MS. Found in a Bottle"—the visible drops falling into the goblet in "Ligeia," &c.—there is always something of this sort to stick by the mind—by mine at least.

About this time Elizabeth Barrett Browning, then Miss Barrett, wrote to Poe:

Your "Raven" has produced a sensation, a "fit horror," here in England. . . . I hear of persons haunted by the "Nevermore," and one acquaintance of mine who has the misfortune of possessing a "bust of Pallas" never can bear to look at it in the twilight. . . . Then there is a tale of yours . . . which

---

* The manuscript of "The Bells" was sold at auction in Philadelphia on May 6th last for $2100. At the same sale the first edition of "Al Aaraaf, Tamerlane, and Minor Poems" was sold for $1815—Ed. *Critic*.

is going the round of the newspapers, about mesmerism, throwing us all into "most admired disorder," and dreadful doubts as to whether "it can be true," as the children say of ghost stories. The certain thing in the tale in question is the power of the writer, and the faculty he has of making horrible improbabilities seem near and familiar.

Though his stories threw people into "most admired disorders" and scared men in broad day in "Turkey blinds," and though his stories were read, one might say, universally, there seemed at the time a feeling against them which condemned them as a class of stories eminently repulsive and unreadable. The public read Poe's stories, but Poe was not in touch with that public. And when that public spoke to him through the mouths of the magazine editors, it spoke in no uncertain terms; and, rebelliously aspiring, he dreamed of a magazine of his own—no "namby-pamby" magazine, filled with "contemptible pictures, fashion-plates, music, and love-tales," but a magazine which uttered the thing for the thing's sake and told a story because it was a story rather than a hodge-podge which the public might claim it liked.

James E. Heath, writing to Poe concerning the "Fall of the House of Usher," said:

> He [White, editor of the *Southern Literary Messenger*] doubts whether the readers of the *Messenger* have much relish for tales of the German School, although written with great power and ability, and in this opinion, I confess to you frankly, I am strongly inclined to concur. I doubt very much whether tales of the wild, improbable, and terrible class can ever be permanently popular in this country. Charles Dickens it appears to me has given the final death-blow to writings of that description.

Nevertheless, the writer-men of that day, who wrote the popular stories and received readier sales and fatter checks, are dead and forgotten and their stories with them, while Poe and the stories of Poe live on. In a way, this side of Poe's history is a paradoxical tangle. Editors did not like to publish his stories nor people to read them, yet they were read universally and discussed and remembered, and went the round of the foreign newspapers. They earned him little money, yet they have since earned a great deal of money and to this day command a large and steady sale. It was the common belief at the time they appeared that they could never become popular in the United States, yet their steady sales, complete editions, and what-not, which continue to come out, attest a popularity that is, to say the least, enduring. The sombre and terrible "Fall of the House of Usher," "Ligeia," "Black Cat," "Cask of Amontillado," "Berenice," "Pit and the Pendulum," and "Masque of the Red Death" are read to-day with an eagerness as great as ever. And especially is this true of the younger generation which ofttimes places the seal of its approval on things the graybeards have read, approved, forgotten they have approved, and finally censured and condemned.

Yet the conditions which obtained in Poe's time obtain just as inexorably to-day. No self-respecting editor with an eye to the subscription-list can be bribed or bullied into admitting a terrible or tragic story into his magazine; while the reading public, when it does chance upon such stories in one way or another,—and it manages to chance upon them somehow,—says it does not care for them.

A person reads such a story, lays it down with a shudder, and says: "It makes my blood run cold. I never want to read anything like that again." Yet he or she will read something like that again, and again, and yet again, and return and read them over again. Talk with the average man or woman of the reading public and it will be found that they have read all, or nearly all, of the terrible and horrible tales which have been written. Also, they will shiver, express a dislike for such tales, and then proceed to discuss them with a keenness and understanding as remarkable as it is surprising.

When it is considered that so many condemns these tales and continue to read them (as is amply proved by heart-to-heart experience and by the book sales such as Poe's), the question arises: Are folk honest when they shudder and say they do not care for the terrible, the horrible, and the tragic? Do they really not like to be afraid? Or are they afraid that they do like to be afraid?

Deep down in the roots of the race is fear. It came first into the world, and it was the dominant emotion in the primitive world. To-day, for that matter, it remains the most firmly seated of the emotions. But in the primitive world people were uncomplex, not yet self-conscious, and they frankly delighted in terror-inspiring tales and religions. Is it true that the complex, self-conscious people of to-day do not delight in the things which inspire terror? or is it true that they are ashamed to make known their delight?

What is it that lures boys to haunted houses after dark, compelling

them to fling rocks and run away with their hearts going so thunder-
ously pit-a-pat as to drown the clatter of their flying feet? What is it
that grips a child, forcing it to listen to ghost stories which drive it
into ecstasies of fear, and yet forces it to beg for more and more? Is
it a baleful thing? a thing his instinct warns him as unhealthy and evil
the while his desire leaps out to it? Or, again, what is it that sends the
heart fluttering up and quickens the feet of the man or woman who
goes alone down a long, dark hall or up a winding stair? Is it a stirring
of the savage in them?—of the savage who has slept, but never died,
since the time the river-folk crouched over the fires of their squatting-
places, or the tree-folk bunched together and chattered in the dark?

Whatever the thing is, and whether it be good or evil, it is a thing
and it is real. It is a thing Poe rouses in us, scaring us in broad day
and throwing us into "admired disorders." It is rarely that the grown
person who is afraid of the dark will make confessions. It does not
seem to them proper to be afraid of the dark, and they are ashamed.
Perhaps people feel that it is not proper to delight in stories that arouse
fear and terror. They may feel instinctively that it is bad and injurious
to have such emotions aroused, and because of this are impelled to
say that they do not like such stories, while in actuality they do like
them.

The great emotion exploited by Dickens was fear, as Mr. Brooks
Adams has pointed out, just as courage was the great emotion exploited by Scott. The militant nobility seemed to possess an excess of
courage and to respond more readily to things courageous. On the
other hand, the rising bourgeoisie, the timid merchant-folk and city-
dwellers, fresh from the oppressions and robberies of their rough-
handed lords, seemed to possess an excess of fear, and to respond more
readily to things fearsome. For this reason they greedily devoured
Dickens's writings, for he was as peculiarly their spokesman as Scott
was the spokesman of the old and dying nobility.

But since Dickens's day, if we may judge by the editorial attitude
and by the dictum of the reading public, a change seems to have taken
place. In Dickens's day, the bourgeoisie, as a dominant class being but
newly risen, had fear still strong upon it, much as a negro mammy, a
couple of generations from Africa, stands in fear of the Voodoo. But
to-day it would seem that this same bourgeoisie, firmly seated and
triumphant, is ashamed of its old terror, which it remembers dimly,
as it might a bad nightmare. When fear was strong upon it, it loved
nothing better than fear-exciting things; but with fear far removed, no
longer menaced and harassed, it has become afraid of fear. By this is

meant that the bourgeoisie has become self-conscious, much in the same fashion that the black slave, freed and conscious of the stigma attached to "black," calls himself a colored gentleman, though in his heart of hearts he feels himself black nigger still. So the bourgeoisie may feel in a dim, mysterious way the stigma attached to the fear of its cowardly days, and, self-conscious, brands as improper all fear-exciting things, while deep down in its secret being it delights in them still.

All this, of course, is by the way,—a mere tentative attempt to account for a bit of contradictory psychology in the make-up of the reading public. But the facts of the case remain. The public is afraid of fear-exciting tales and hypocritically continues to enjoy them. W. W. Jacobs's recent collection of stories, "The Lady of the Barge," contains his usual inimitable humorous yarns intersprinkled with several terror-tales. It was asked of a dozen friends as to which story had affected them the most forcibly, and the unanimous answer was, "The Monkey's Paw." Now the "Monkey's Paw" is as perfect a terror-tale as any of its kind. Yet, without exception, after duly and properly shuddering and disclaiming all liking for such tales, they proceeded to discuss it with a warmth and knowledge which plainly advertised that, whatever strange sensations it had aroused, they were at any rate pleasurable sensations.

Long ago, Ambrose Bierce published his *Soldiers and Civilians*, a book crammed from cover to cover with unmitigated terror and horror. An editor who dared to publish one of these tales would be committing financial and professional suicide; and yet, year after year, people continue to talk about *Soldiers and Civilians*, while the innumerable sweet and wholesome, optimistic, and happy-ending books are forgotten as rapidly as they leave the press.

In the rashness of youth before he became converted to soberer ways, Mr. [W. C.] Morrow was guilty of *The Ape, the Idiot, and Other People*, wherein are to be found some of the most horrible horror-stories in the English language. It made his instant reputation, whereupon he conceived higher notions of his art, forswore the terrible and the horrible, and wrote other and totally different books. But these other books are not remembered as readily as is his first one by the people who in the same breath say they do not like stories such as may be found in *The Ape, the Idiot, and Other People*.

Of two collections of tales recently published, each of which contained one terror-story, nine out of ten reviewers, in each instance, selected the terror-story as worthy of most praise, and, after they had praised, five out of the nine of them proceeded to damn it. Rider Haggard's *She*, which is filled with gruesome terror, had a long and popular vogue, while the *Strange Case of Dr. Jekyll and Mr. Hyde* achieved, if anything, a greater success and brought [R. L.] Stevenson to the front.

Putting the horror-story outside the pale, can any story be really great, the theme of which is anything but tragic or terrible? Can the sweet commonplaces of life be made into anything else than sweetly commonplace stories?

It would not seem so. The great short stories in the world's literary treasure-house seem all to depend upon the tragic and terrible for their strength and greatness. Not half of them deal with love at all; and when they do, they derive their greatness, not from the love itself, but from the tragic and terrible with which the love is involved.

In this class may be ranked *Without Benefit of Clergy*, [R. Kipling] which is fairly typical. The love of John Holden and Ameera greatens because it is out of caste and precarious, and is made memorable by the tragic deaths of Tota and Ameera, the utter obliteration of the facts that they have lived, and the return of John Holden to his kind. Stress and strain are required to sound the deeps of human nature, and there is neither stress nor strain in sweet, optimistic, and placidly happy events. Great things can be done only under great provocation, and there is nothing greatly provoking in the sweet and placid round of existence. Romeo and Juliet are not remembered because things slipped smoothly along, nor are Abélard and Héloïse, Tristram and Iseult, Paolo and Francesca.

But the majority of the great short stories do not deal with love. "A Lodging for the Night" [R. L. Stevenson], for instance, one of the most rounded and perfect stories ever told, not only has no hint of love in it, but does not contain a hint of one character whom we would care to meet in life. Beginning with the murder of Thevenin, running through the fearful night in the streets and the robbing of the dead jade in the porch, and finishing with the old lord of Brisetout, who is not murdered because he possesses seven pieces of plate instead of ten, it contains nothing that is not terrible and repulsive. Yet it is the awfulness of it that makes it great. The play of words in the deserted house between Villon and the feeble lord of Brisetout, which is the story, would be no story at all were the stress and strain taken out of it and the two men placed *vis-à-vis* with a score of retainers at the old lord's back.

The "Fall of the House of Usher" depends upon all that is terrible for its greatness, and there is no more love in it than there is in Guy de Maupassant's "Necklace," or the "Piece of String," or in [R. Kipling] "The Man Who Was," and "Baa Baa, Black Sheep," which last is the most pitiful of all tragedies, a child's.

The editors of the magazines have very good reasons for refusing admission to the terrible and tragic. Their readers say they do not like the terrible and tragic, and that is enough, without going farther. But either their readers prevaricate most shamelessly or delude themselves into believing they tell the truth, or else the people who read the magazines are not the people who continue to buy, say, the works of Poe.

In the circumstances, there being a proved demand for the terrible and tragic, is there not room in the otherwise crowded field for a magazine devoted primarily to the terrible and tragic? A magazine such as Poe dreamed of, about which there shall be nothing namby-pamby, yellowish, or emasculated, and which will print stories that are bids for place and permanence rather than for the largest circulation?

On the face of it two things appear certain: That enough of that portion of the reading public which cares for the tragic and terrible would be sufficiently honest to subscribe; and that the writers of the land would be capable of supplying the stories. The only reason why such stories are not written to-day is that there is no magazine to buy them, and that the writer-folk are busy turning out the stuff, mainly ephemeral, which the magazines will buy. The pity of it is that the writer-folk are writing for bread first and glory after; and that their standard of living goes up as fast as their capacity for winning bread increases,—so that they never get around to glory,—the ephemeral flourishes, and the great stories remain unwritten.

# WHAT LIFE MEANS TO ME*

I WAS BORN IN THE working-class. Early I discovered enthusiasm, ambition, and ideals; and to satisfy these became the problem of my child-life. My environment was crude and rough and raw. I had no outlook, but an uplook rather. My place in society was at the bottom. Here life offered nothing but sordidness and wretchedness, both of the flesh and the spirit; for here flesh and spirit were alike starved and tormented.

Above me towered the colossal edifice of society, and to my mind the only way out was up. Into this edifice I early resolved to climb. Up above, men wore black clothes and boiled shirts, and women dressed in beautiful gowns. Also, there were good things to eat, and there was plenty to eat. This much for the flesh. Then there were the things of the spirit. Up above me, I knew, were unselfishnesses of the spirit, clean and noble thinking, keen intellectual living. I knew all this because I read "Seaside Library" novels, in which, with the exception of the villains and adventuresses, all men and women thought beautiful thoughts, spoke a beautiful tongue, and performed glorious deeds. In short, as I accepted the rising of the sun, I accepted that up above me was all that was fine and noble and gracious, all that gave decency and dignity to life, all that made life worth living and that remunerated one for his travail and misery.

But it is not particularly easy for one to climb up out of the working-class—especially if he is handicapped by the possession of

* From *Revolution and Other Essays*; first published in *Cosmopolitan Magazine*, March 1906.

ideals and illusions. I lived on a ranch in California, and I was hard put to find the ladder whereby to climb. I early inquired the rate of interest on invested money, and worried my child's brain into an understanding of the virtues and excellencies of that remarkable invention of man, compound interest. Further, I ascertained the current rates of wages for workers of all ages, and the cost of living. From all this data I concluded that if I began immediately and worked and saved until I was fifty years of age, I could then stop working and enter into participation in a fair portion of the delights and goodnesses that would then be open to me higher up in society. Of course, I resolutely determined not to marry, while I quite forgot to consider at all that great rock of disaster in the working-class world—sickness.

But the life that was in me demanded more than a meagre existence of scraping and scrimping. Also, at ten years of age, I became a newsboy on the streets of a city, and found myself with a changed uplook. All about me were still the same sordidness and wretchedness, and up above me was still the same paradise waiting to be gained; but the ladder whereby to climb was a different one. It was now the ladder of business. Why save my earnings and invest in government bonds, when, by buying two newspapers for five cents, with a turn of the wrist I could sell them for ten cents and double my capital? The business ladder was the ladder for me, and I had a vision of myself becoming a baldheaded and successful merchant prince.

Alas for visions! When I was sixteen I had already earned the title of "prince." But this title was given me by a gang of cut-throats and thieves, by whom I was called "The Prince of the Oyster Pirates." And at that time I had climbed the first rung of the business ladder. I was a capitalist. I owned a boat and a complete oyster-pirating outfit. I had begun to exploit my fellow-creatures. I had a crew of one man. As captain and owner I took two-thirds of the spoils, and gave the crew one-third, though the crew worked just as hard as I did and risked just as much his life and liberty.

This one rung was the height I climbed up the business ladder. One night I went on a raid amongst the Chinese fishermen. Ropes and nets were worth dollars and cents. It was robbery, I grant, but it was precisely the spirit of capitalism. The capitalist takes away the possessions of his fellow-creatures by means of a rebate, or of a betrayal of trust, or by the purchase of senators and supreme-court judges. I was merely crude. That was the only difference. I used a gun.

But my crew that night was one of those inefficients against whom the capitalist is wont to fulminate, because, forsooth, such inefficients increase expenses and reduce dividends. My crew did both. What of his carelessness he set fire to the big mainsail and totally destroyed it. There weren't any dividends that night, and the Chinese fishermen were richer by the nets and ropes we did not get. I was bankrupt, unable just then to pay sixty-five dollars for a new mainsail. I left my boat at anchor and went off on a bay-pirate boat on a raid up the Sacramento River. While away on this trip, another gang of bay pirates raided my boat. They stole everything, even the anchors; and later on, when I recovered the drifting hulk, I sold it for twenty dollars. I had slipped back the one rung I had climbed, and never again did I attempt the business ladder.

From then on I was mercilessly exploited by other capitalists. I had the muscle, and they made money out of it while I made but a very indifferent living out of it. I was a sailor before the mast, a long-shoreman, a roustabout; I worked in canneries, and factories, and laundries; I mowed lawns, and cleaned carpets, and washed windows. And I never got the full product of my toil. I looked at the daughter of the cannery owner, in her carriage, and knew that it was my muscle, in part, that helped drag along that carriage on its rubber tires. I looked at the son of the factory owner, going to college, and knew that it was my muscle that helped, in part, to pay for the wine and good fellowship he enjoyed.

But I did not resent this. It was all in the game. They were the strong. Very well, I was strong. I would carve my way to a place amongst them and make money out of the muscles of other men. I was not afraid of work. I loved hard work. I would pitch in and work harder than ever and eventually become a pillar of society.

And just then, as luck would have it, I found an employer that was of the same mind. I was willing to work, and he was more than willing that I should work. I thought I was learning a trade. In reality, I had displaced two men. I thought he was making an electrician out of me; as a matter of fact, he was making fifty dollars per month out of me. The two men I had displaced had received forty dollars each per month; I was doing the work of both for thirty dollars per month.

This employer worked me nearly to death. A man may love oysters, but too many oysters will disincline him toward that particular diet. And so with me. Too much work sickened me. I did not wish ever to see work again. I fled from work. I became a tramp, begging my way from door to door, wandering over the United States and sweating bloody sweats in slums and prisons.

I had been born in the working-class, and I was now, at the age of eighteen, beneath the point at which I had started. I was down in the cellar of society, down in the subterranean depths of misery about which it is neither nice nor proper to speak. I was in the pit, the abyss, the human cesspool, the shambles and the charnel-house of our civilization. This is the part of the edifice of society that society chooses to ignore. Lack of space compels me here to ignore it, and I shall say only that the things I there saw gave me a terrible scare.

I was scared into thinking. I saw the naked simplicities of the complicated civilization in which I lived. Life was a matter of food and shelter. In order to get food and shelter men sold things. The merchant sold shoes, the politician sold his manhood, and the representative of the people, with exceptions, of course, sold his trust; while nearly all sold their honor. Women, too, whether on the street or in the holy bond of wedlock, were prone to sell their flesh. All things were commodities, all people bought and sold. The one commodity that labor had to sell was muscle. The honor of labor had no price in the market-place. Labor had muscle, and muscle alone, to sell.

But there was a difference, a vital difference. Shoes and trust and honor had a way of renewing themselves. They were imperishable stocks. Muscle, on the other hand, did not renew. As the shoe merchant sold shoes, he continued to replenish his stock. But there was no way of replenishing the laborer's stock of muscle. The more he sold of his muscle, the less of it remained to him. It was his one commodity, and each day his stock of it diminished. In the end, if he did not die before, he sold out and put up his shutters. He was a muscle bankrupt, and nothing remained to him but to go down into the cellar of society and perish miserably.

I learned, further, that brain was likewise a commodity. It, too, was different from muscle. A brain seller was only at his prime when he was fifty or sixty years old, and his wares were fetching higher prices than ever. But a laborer was worked out or broken down at forty-five or fifty. I had been in the cellar of society, and I did not like the place as a habitation. The pipes and drains were unsanitary, and the air was bad to breathe. If I could not live on the parlor floor of society, I could, at any rate, have a try at the attic. It was true, the diet there was slim, but the air at least was pure. So I resolved to sell no more muscle, and to become a vender of brains.

Then began a frantic pursuit of knowledge. I returned to California and opened the books. While thus equipping myself to become a brain merchant, it was inevitable that I should delve into sociology. There I found, in a certain class of books, scientifically formulated, the simple sociological concepts I had already worked out for myself. Other and greater minds, before I was born, had worked out all that I had thought and a vast deal more. I discovered that I was a socialist.

The socialists were revolutionists, inasmuch as they struggled to overthrow the society of the present, and out of the material to build the society of the future. I, too, was a socialist and a revolutionist. I joined the groups of working-class and intellectual revolutionists, and for the first time came into intellectual living. Here I found keen-flashing intellects and brilliant wits; for here I met strong and alert-brained, withal horny-handed, members of the working-class; unfrocked preachers too wide in their Christianity for any congregation of Mammon-worshippers; professors broken on the wheel of university subservience to the ruling class and flung out because they were quick with knowledge which they strove to apply to the affairs of mankind.

Here I found, also, warm faith in the human, glowing idealism, sweetnesses of unselfishness, renunciation, and martyrdom—all the splendid, stinging things of the spirit. Here life was clean, noble, and alive. Here life rehabilitated itself, became wonderful and glorious; and I was glad to be alive. I was in touch with great souls who exalted flesh and spirit over dollars and cents, and to whom the thin wail of the starved slum child meant more than all the pomp and circumstance of commercial expansion and world empire. All about me were nobleness of purpose and heroism of effort, and my days and nights were sunshine and starshine, all fire and dew, with before my eyes, ever burning and blazing, the Holy Grail, Christ's own Grail, the warm human, long-suffering and maltreated, but to be rescued and saved at the last.

And I, poor foolish I, deemed all this to be a mere foretaste of the delights of living I should find higher above me in society. I had lost many illusions since the day I read "Seaside Library" novels on the California ranch. I was destined to lose many of the illusions I still retained.

As a brain merchant I was a success. Society opened its portals to me. I entered right in on the parlor floor, and my disillusionment proceeded rapidly. I sat down to dinner with the masters of society, and with the wives and daughters of the masters of society. The women were gowned beautifully, I admit; but to my naïve surprise I discovered that they were of the same clay as all the rest of the women I had known down below in the cellar. "The colonel's lady and Judy O'Grady were sisters under their skins"—and gowns.

It was not this, however, so much as their materialism, that shocked me. It is true, these beautifully gowned, beautiful women prattled sweet little ideals and dear little moralities; but in spite of their prattle the dominant key of the life they lived was materialistic. And they were so sentimentally selfish! They assisted in all kinds of sweet little charities, and informed one of the fact, while all the time the food they ate and the beautiful clothes they wore were bought out of dividends stained with the blood of child labor, and sweated labor, and of prostitution itself. When I mentioned such facts, expecting in my innocence that these sisters of Judy O'Grady would at once strip off their blood-dyed silks and jewels, they became excited and angry, and read me preachments about the lack of thrift, the drink, and the innate depravity that caused all the misery in society's cellar. When I mentioned that I couldn't quite see that it was the lack of thrift, the intemperance, and the depravity of a half-starved child of six that made it work twelve hours every night in a Southern cotton mill, these sisters of Judy O'Grady attacked my private life and called me an "agitator"—as though that, forsooth, settled the argument.

Nor did I fare better with the masters themselves. I had expected to find men who were clean, noble, and alive, whose ideals were clean, noble, and alive. I went about amongst the men who sat in the high places—the preachers, the politicians, the business men, the professors, and the editors. I ate meat with them, drank wine with them, automobiled with them, and studied them. It is true, I found many that were clean and noble; but with rare exceptions, they were not *alive*. I do verily believe I could count the exceptions on the fingers of my two hands. Where they were not alive with rottenness, quick with unclean life, they were merely the unburied dead—clean and noble, like well-preserved mummies, but not alive. In this connection I may especially mention the professors I met, the men who live up to that decadent university ideal, "the passionless pursuit of passionless intelligence."

I met men who invoked the name of the Prince of Peace in their diatribes against war, and who put rifles in the hands of Pinkertons with which to shoot down strikers in their own factories. I met men incoherent with indignation at the brutality of prize-fighting, and who, at the same time, were parties to the adulteration of food that killed each year more babies than even red-handed Herod had killed.

I talked in hotels and clubs and homes and Pullmans and steamer-chairs with captains of industry, and marvelled at how little travelled they were in the realm of intellect. On the other hand, I discovered that their intellect, in the business sense, was abnormally developed.

Also, I discovered that their morality, where business was concerned, was nil.

This delicate, aristocratic-featured gentleman, was a dummy director and a tool of corporations that secretly robbed widows and orphans. This gentleman, who collected fine editions and was an especial patron of literature, paid blackmail to a heavy-jowled, black-browed boss of a municipal machine. This editor, who published patent medicine advertisements and did not dare print the truth in his paper about said patent medicines for fear of losing the advertising, called me a scoundrelly demagogue because I told him that his political economy was antiquated and that his biology was contemporaneous with Pliny.

This senator was the tool and the slave, the little puppet of a gross, uneducated machine boss; so was this governor and this supreme court judge; and all three rode on railroad passes. This man, talking soberly and earnestly about the beauties of idealism and the goodness of God, had just betrayed his comrades in a business deal. This man, a pillar of the church and heavy contributor to foreign missions, worked his shop girls ten hours a day on a starvation wage and thereby directly encouraged prostitution. This man, who endowed chairs in universities, perjured himself in courts of law over a matter of dollars and cents. And this railroad magnate broke his word as a gentleman and a Christian when he granted a secret rebate to one of two captains of industry locked together in a struggle to the death.

It was the same everywhere, crime and betrayal, betrayal and crime—men who were alive, but who were neither clean nor noble, men who were clean and noble but who were not alive. Then there was a great, hopeless mass, neither noble nor alive, but merely clean. It did not sin positively nor deliberately; but it did sin passively and ignorantly by acquiescing in the current immorality and profiting by it. Had it been noble and alive it would not have been ignorant, and it would have refused to share in the profits of betrayal and crime.

I discovered that I did not like to live on the parlor floor of society. Intellectually I was bored. Morally and spiritually I was sickened. I remembered my intellectuals and idealists, my unfrocked preachers, broken professors, and clean-minded, class-conscious working men. I remembered my days and nights of sunshine and starshine, where life was all a wild sweet wonder, a spiritual paradise of unselfish adventure and ethical romance. And I saw before me, ever blazing and burning, the Holy Grail.

So I went back to the working-class, in which I had been born and where I belonged. I care no longer to climb. The imposing edifice of society above my head holds no delights for me. It is the foundation of the edifice that interests me. There I am content to labor, crowbar in hand, shoulder to shoulder, with intellectuals, idealists, and class-conscious workingmen, getting a solid pry now and again and setting the whole edifice rocking. Some day, when we get a few more hands and crowbars to work, we'll topple it over, along with all its rotten life and unburied dead, its monstrous selfishness and sodden materialism. Then we'll cleanse the cellar and build a new habitation for mankind, in which there will be no parlor floor, in which all the rooms will be bright and airy, and where the air that is breathed will be clean, noble, and alive.

Such is my outlook. I look forward to a time when man shall progress upon something worthier and higher than his stomach, when there will be a finer incentive to impel men to action than the incentive of to-day, which is the incentive of the stomach. I retain my belief in the nobility and excellence of the human. I believe that spiritual sweetness and unselfishness will conquer the gross gluttony of to-day. And last of all, my faith is in the working-class. As some Frenchman has said, "The stairway of time is ever echoing with the wooden shoe going up, the polished boot descending."

NEWTON, IOWA
*November, 1905*

# THINGS ALIVE*

I AM QUITE READY TO take Prof. Phelps' word for it that "there is probably no body of young men in the world more truly conservative than the students of Yale College;" or, if I could think of anything like an exception, it would be in favor of the student bodies of some of the smaller western colleges. It is undoubtedly true, in general, that American college life makes strongly for conservatism; that it disposes a man to take things as they are in preference to trying to make things as they should be; in short, that it tends to acceptivity rather than expressivity.

Modern American college life has in it a good many of the characteristics of old monasticism. The students shut themselves up, for a great part of the time, in their college walls, and find their mental pabulum principally in books and preachments. They have their daily round of duties; there are honors for those who perform these duties most conscientiously. They live largely in an atmosphere of book-congealed minds; minds, it is true, the noblest and greatest of all the times gone by. And they have the advantage of personal contact with many of the greatest and noblest minds of the present day.

From these sources they gain many and valuable theories of doing; but if suddenly forced to do, in a world, in place of a college, manner, most of them would find themselves very awkward about it. Just as a man, who had spent his time in reading and hearing about saws, might find himself considerably embarrassed if suddenly presented with a

* *Yale Monthly Magazine*, March 1906.

life-size copy of the real instrument, and told to go to work and saw something. This may explain, in some measure, the mental metamorphosis of the average college man who goes into business;—a metamorphosis probably more complete than any other outside of Ovid.

This state of affairs has its advantages, it is true, but it also has its disadvantages. That the world progresses by the activity of the people and circumstances which compose it, is acknowledged universally; and by the evolutionary definition of things good, the really "good" man is the man who helps along this process of development. Some sort of interest in things at first hand, an aliveness to the realities of present-day living, is a necessary component in the make-up of all good men. It is excellent to know the development of the Greek helot system, but perhaps it is just as important to know the political development, and the present trend of politics, in America.

It is the necessity of having this very aliveness,—this first-hand knowledge of things, and expression of himself in those things, that I should like, above all else, to impress upon the American college student. He does not seem to me to have a true mental grasp of present-day actualities. Sometimes I almost feel like hurling Bernard Shaw's bomb at his head,—that he hasn't a single thought later than Spencer. Now the world has done some little evolutioning since Spencer's time; and it is evolutioning now at about the customary rate;—some of us believe, at a good deal more than the customary rate. Men are dying and worms are eating them from a large variety of causes which did not exist in Shakespeare's time. There are hundreds of new things under the sun; something is always doing at the old stand of the human.

It is very possible to have a brain-understanding of these facts, and still totally disbelieve them; or at least, not really *know* them for truths. This may be the mental condition of the college student when he is told that about one-tenth of the men, women and children in these United States are starving in a very beastly manner. When he hears that the bodies of many working men in England are dried up for lack of proper nourishment until their skins hang loose upon their frames, he is likely to be amused at the grotesqueness of such a condition rather than shocked by its terribleness. Possibly this is because of the image of the common circus India-rubber man which the description conjures up in his mind; this freak being the only loose-skinned man with whom he is acquainted.

It astonished me considerably, and shocked me a little at first, when a hall full of Harvard men almost laughed me off my feet upon my telling them of some particularly harrowing experiences I have had with *les misérables* of our society. I think their amusement was caused by my relation of the incident of a couple of laborers eating filthy apple-cores, picked up from the gutters of a big city. If the same men had realized, had really appreciated, the meaning of such a diet, I don't think they would have laughed; at least, not so openly and whole-heartedly. They might have shrugged their shoulders, and said *laissez faire;* and a few of them might have snickered fastidiously,—but I don't think their laugh would have been one of such delighted amuse-ment. They were good fellows, clean fellows, noble fellows; but they simply couldn't appreciate what I was talking about. They had no real aliveness to the actuality of such conditions as I was trying to describe.

So it seems to me that one of the things America most needs to-day is the awakening, the vivifying of its college men. They should put out their hands, and feel the pulse of the world; and when they find that that pulse is beating in an unusually feverish and irregular manner,—which they must find, if they find the pulse at all,—much will have been accomplished toward inaugurating a healthier order of things.

# THE STORY OF AN
# EYE-WITNESS *

THE EARTHQUAKE SHOOK DOWN in San Francisco hundreds of thousands of dollars worth of walls and chimneys. But the conflagration that followed burned up hundreds of millions of dollars worth of property. There is no estimating within hundreds of millions the actual damage wrought.

Not in history has a modern imperial city been so completely destroyed. San Francisco is gone. Nothing remains of it but memories and fringe of dwelling houses on its outskirts. Its industrial section is wiped out. Its business section is wiped out. Its social and residential section is wiped out. The factories and warehouses, the great stores and newspaper buildings, the hotels and the palaces of the nabobs, are all gone. Remains only the fringe of dwelling houses on the outskirts of what was once San Francisco.

Within an hour after the earthquake shock, the smoke of San Francisco's burning was a lurid tower visible a hundred miles away. And for three days and nights this lurid tower swayed in the sky, reddening the sun, darkening the day, and filling the land with smoke.

On Wednesday morning at quarter past five came the earthquake. A minute later the flames were leaping upward. In a dozen different quarters south of Market Street, in the working class ghetto and in the factories, fires started. There was no opposing the flames. There was no organization, no communication. All the cunning adjustments of a twentieth century city had been smashed by the earthquake. The

* From *Jack London Reports*; first published in *Collier's Weekly*, May 5, 1906.

streets were humped into ridges and depressions, and piled with the debris of fallen walls. The steel rails were twisted into perpendicular and horizontal angles. The telephone and telegraph systems were disrupted. And the great water mains had burst. All the shrewd contrivances and safeguards of man had been thrown out of gear by thirty seconds' twitching of the earth-crust.

By Wednesday afternoon, inside of twelve hours, half the heart of the city was gone. At that time I watched the vast conflagration from out on the bay. It was dead calm. Not a flicker of wind stirred. Yet from every side wind was pouring in upon the city. East, west, north, and south, strong winds were blowing upon the doomed city. The heated air rising made an enormous suck. Thus did the fire of itself build its own colossal chimney through the atmosphere. Day and night this dead calm continued, and yet, near to the flames, the wind was often half a gale, so mighty was the suck.

Wednesday night saw the destruction of the very heart of the city. Dynamite was lavishly used, and many of San Francisco's proudest structures were crumbled by man himself into ruins, but there was no withstanding the onrush of the flames. Time and again successful stands were made by the firefighters, and every time the flames flanked around on either side, or came up from the rear, and turned to defeat the hard won victory.

An enumeration of the buildings destroyed would be a directory of San Francisco. An enumeration of the buildings undestroyed would be a line and several addresses. An enumeration of the deeds of heroism would stock a library and bankrupt the Carnegie medal fund. An enumeration of the dead—will never be made. All vestiges of them were destroyed by the flames. The number of the victims of the earthquake will never be known. South of Market Street, where the loss of life was particularly heavy, was the first to catch fire.

Remarkable as it may seem, Wednesday night, while the whole city crashed and roared into ruin, was a quiet night. There were no crowds. There was no shouting and yelling. There was no hysteria, no disorder. I passed Wednesday night in the path of the advancing flames, and in all those terrible hours I saw not one woman who wept, not one man who was excited, not one person who was in the slightest degree panic-stricken.

Before the flames, throughout the night, fled tens of thousands of homeless ones. Some were wrapped in blankets. Others carried bundles of bedding and dear household treasures. Sometimes a whole family was harnessed to a carriage or delivery wagon that was weighted down with their possessions. Baby-buggies, toy wagons and go-carts were used as trucks, while every other person was dragging a trunk. Yet everybody was gracious. The most perfect courtesy obtained. Never, in all San Francisco's history, were her people so kind and courteous as on this night of terror.

All night these tens of thousands fled before the flames. Many of them, the poor people from the labor ghetto, had fled all day as well. They had left their homes burdened with possessions. Now and again they lightened up, flinging out upon the street clothing and treasures they had dragged for miles.

They held on longest to their trunks, and over these trunks many a strong man broke his heart that night. The hills of San Francisco are steep, and up these hills, mile after mile, were the trunks dragged. Everywhere were trunks, with across them lying their exhausted owners, men and women. Before the march of the flames were flung picket-lines of soldiers. And a block at a time, as the flames advanced, these pickets retreated. One of their tasks was to keep the trunk-pullers moving. The exhausted creatures stirred on by the menace of bayonets, would arise and struggle up the steep pavements, pausing from weakness every five or ten feet.

Often, after surmounting a heart-breaking hill, they would find another wall of flame advancing upon them at right angles and be compelled to change anew the line of their retreat. In the end, completely played out, after toiling for a dozen hours like giants, thousands of them were compelled to abandon their trunks. Here the shopkeepers and soft members of the middle class were at a disadvantage. But the workingmen dug holes in vacant lots and backyards and buried their trunks.

At nine o'clock Wednesday evening, I walked down through the very heart of the city. I walked through miles and miles of magnificent buildings and towering skyscrapers. Here was no fire. All was in perfect order. The police patrolled the streets. Every building had its watchman at the door. And yet it was doomed, all of it. There was no water. The dynamite was giving out. And at right angles two different conflagrations were sweeping down upon it.

At one o'clock in the morning I walked down through the same section. Everything still stood intact. There was no fire. And yet there was a change. A rain of ashes was falling. The watchmen at the doors were gone. The police had been withdrawn. There were no firemen, no fire-engines, no men fighting with dynamite. The district had been absolutely abandoned.

I stood at the corner of Kearney and Market, in the very inner-most heart of San Francisco. Kearney Street was deserted. Half a dozen blocks away it was burning on both sides. The street was a wall of flame. And against this wall of flame, silhouetted sharply, were two United States cavalrymen sitting their horses, calmly watching. That was all. Not another person was in sight. In the intact heart of the city two troopers sat their horses and watched.

Surrender was complete. There was no water. The sewers had long since been pumped dry. There was no dynamite. Another fire had broken out farther up town, and now from three sides conflagrations were sweeping down. The fourth side had been burned earlier in the day. In that direction stood the tottering walls of the *Examiner* Building, the burned out *Call* Building, the smouldering ruins of the Grand Hotel, and the gutted, devastated, dynamited Palace Hotel.

The following will illustrate the sweep of the flames and the inability of men to calculate their spread. At eight o'clock Wednesday evening I passed through Union Square. It was packed with refugees. Thousands of them had gone to bed on the grass. Government tents had been set up, supper was being cooked, and the refugees were lining up for free meals.

At half-past one in the morning three sides of Union Square were in flames. The fourth side, where stood the great St. Francis Hotel, was still holding out. An hour later, ignited from top and sides, the St. Francis was flaming heavenward. Union Square, heaped high with mountains of trunks, was deserted. Troops, refugees, and all had retreated.

It was at Union Square that I saw a man offering a thousand dollars for a team of horses. He was in charge of a truck piled high with trunks from some hotel. It had been hauled here into what was considered safety and the horses had been taken out. The flames were on three sides of the Square, and there were no horses.

Also, at this time, standing beside the truck, I urged a man to seek safety in flight. He was all but hemmed in by several conflagrations. He was an old man and he was on crutches. Said he, "To-day is my birthday. Last night I was worth thirty thousand dollars. I bought five bottles of wine, some delicate fish, and other things for my birthday dinner. I have had no dinner, and all I own are these crutches."

I convinced him of his danger and started him limping on his way. An hour later, from a distance, I saw the truckload of trunks burning merrily in the middle of the street.

On Thursday morning, at quarter past five, just twenty-four hours after the earthquake, I sat on the steps of a small residence on Nob Hill. With me sat Japanese, Italians, Chinese, and Negroes—a bit of the cosmopolitan flotsam of the wreck of the city. All about were the palaces of the Nabob pioneers of forty-nine. To the east and south, at right angles, were advancing two mighty walls of flames.

I went inside with the owner of the house on the steps of which I sat. He was cool and cheerful and hospitable. "Yesterday morning," he said, "I was worth six hundred thousand dollars. This morning this house is all I have left. It will go in fifteen minutes." He pointed to a large cabinet. "That is my wife's collection of China. This rug upon which we stand is a present. It cost fifteen hundred dollars. Try that piano. Listen to its tone. There are few like it. There are no horses. The flames will be here in fifteen minutes."

Outside, the old Mark Hopkins residence, a palace, was just catching fire. The troops were falling back and driving the refugees before them. From every side came the roaring of flames, the crashing of walls, and the detonations of dynamite.

I passed out of the house. Day was trying to dawn through the smoke-pall. A sickly light was creeping over the face of things. Once only the sun broke through the smoke-pall, blood-red and showing quarter its usual size. The smoke-pall itself, viewed from beneath, was a rose-color that pulsed and fluttered with lavender shades. Then it turned to mauve and yellow and dun. There was no sun. And so dawned the second day on stricken San Francisco.

An hour later I was creeping past the shattered dome of the City Hall. Than it, there was no better exhibit of the destructive force of the earthquake. Most of the stone had been shaken from the great dome, leaving standing the naked frame-work of steel. Market Street was piled high with the wreckage, and across the wreckage, lay the overthrown pillars of the City Hall shattered into short crosswise sections.

This section of the city, with the exception of the Mint and the Post Office, was already a waste of smoking ruins. Here and there through the smoke, creeping warily under the shadows of tottering walls, emerged occasional men and women. It was like the meeting of the handful of survivors after the day of the end of the world.

On Mission Street lay a dozen steers, in a neat row stretching across the street, just as they had been struck down by the flying ruins of the earthquake. The fire had passed through afterward and roasted them. The human dead had been carried away before the fire came. At another place on Mission Street I saw a milk wagon. A steel telegraph pole had smashed down sheer through the driver's seat and crushed the front wheels. The milk cans lay scattered around.

All day Thursday and all Thursday night, all day Friday and Friday night, the flames still raged. Friday night saw the flames finally conquered, though not until Russian Hill and Telegraph Hill had been swept and three-quarters of a mile of wharves and docks had been licked up.

The great stand of the firefighters was made Thursday night on Van Ness Avenue. Had they failed here, the comparatively few remaining houses of the city would have been swept. Here were the magnificent residences of the second generation of San Francisco nabobs, and these, in a solid zone, were dynamited down across the path of the fire. Here and there, the flames leaped the zone, but these isolated fires were beaten out, principally by the use of wet blankets and rugs.

San Francisco, at the present time, is like the crater of a volcano, around which are camped tens of thousands of refugees. At the Presidio alone are at least twenty thousand. All the surrounding cities and towns are jammed with the homeless ones, where they are being cared for by the relief committees. The refugees were carried free by the railroads to any point they wished to go, and it is estimated that over one hundred thousand people have left the peninsula on which San Francisco stood. The government has the situation in hand, and, thanks to the immediate relief given by the whole United States, there is not the slightest possibility of a famine. The bankers and business men have already set about making preparations to rebuild San Francisco.

# REPORTS ON THE
## JAMES J. JEFFRIES-JACK JOHNSON
## CHAMPIONSHIP FIGHT

## JEFFRIES-JOHNSON NO. 9 *

RENO, NEV., JULY 1. —I am glad I'm here. There was never anything like this Reno at the present moment, with the great impending event only three days away. I should hate like poison if some Croesus should offer to pay me to stay away from the fight, telling me to fix my own price. Surely, there is a money price that would keep me away from the fight, but the attempt to calculate the amount would be very fatiguing. In lieu of the Croesus, all that I am afraid of now is that I'll be run over by a Reno electric car and miss the fight. However, when I consider the Reno street car I take heart of courage and think I shall have a fair chance.

Seriously, no man who loves the fighting game, has the price and is within striking distance of Reno should miss the fight. Viewed from every possible angle, there has never been anything like it in the history of the ring, and there is no chance for anything like it to occur in the future—at least within the lifetime of those alive today. Even if no more stringent legislation is passed against the game, even if every state threw itself wide open to prize-fighting, still there can be nothing like this fight for a generation to come.

* From *Jack London Reports*; first published in the New York *Herald*, July 2, 1910.

In the first place, never have two men like these ever faced each other in the ring. In all the contests of its long history, no two comparable giants have ever locked in combat. And in their own generation there is no third man who approaches them. It has taken not only a generation, but two races to produce them.

Johnson is a dusky wonder. For his size there has never been so clever a defensive boxer. Nor has there ever been a cooler-headed boxer. This coolness of his is one of his most remarkable attributes. So cool is he that his fighting at times seems lackadaisical, while at the same time it never has the seeming of brutality. In action there is very little hint of the fighting beast about him. There are hints of it, true, when sudden fierce moments come upon him and his face and force become tigerish. But it is not genuine. He simulates it. He is a play-actor deliberately playing a part. He is not mastered by this tigerishness. He is manufacturing it. Back in that cool brain of his he decides he needs this display of tigerishness in his business, and so he displays it.

Another of his remarkable attributes is an instinct for a blow that is positive genius. Locked in a clinch, body relaxed, his mind elsewhere, his gaze fixed on some one off to the side and outside the ring, himself talking to that outsider, say, about the disposition of the contents of a certain suit case—at such a moment his opponent starts a blow for his jaw, and he, without seeing or gauging or thinking, by some automatic divination, knows all about that blow, its force, sweep and direction. He merely rolls his head or pulls it back just far enough and not a fraction of an inch farther, and all the while, without a break, keeps up his conversation about the contents of that suit case. A wonderful fighter, indeed, is Johnson, utterly unlike any other fighter, a type by himself.

And against this man will stand Jeffries, an even more remarkable man, a grizzly giant, huge and rugged, of a type we are prone to believe was more common in other days when the world was young. And, despite his hugeness and ruggedness, he is so well proportioned from heel to head that the combination is startling. His is a perfection of symmetry that is the fruit of the highest organic development. And, if science tells aright, we are justified in believing that no such symmetry obtained among those giants of the younger world. The human in those days was in the process of becoming. It was muscular efficiency minus beauty of form and line. This big modern Jim Jeffries has both.

So far as the boxing game is concerned the contest next Monday is well named "the fight of the century." These two men, in a class by themselves so far as other fighters go, yet so radically different from each other as to have practically no salient characteristics in common, will fight a battle in a setting like unto nothing the ring has ever displayed. For the first time, two undefeated heavy-weight champions battle, and each goes up against the most dangerous and formidable man he has ever tackled. And they will fight in the presence of four other and earlier heavy-weight champions. Again are all the records broken, for next Monday, in the ring and the arena, will be six men who have held the honor of being world champion heavy-weights. Think of it—Sullivan, Corbett, Fitzsimmons, Burns, Jeffries and Johnson.

From the standpoint of the sporting world, there has never been so amazing a gathering. Almost every champion and ex-champion of every class will be at the ringside. There will be the famous trainers and conditioners of athletes, men like Muldoon and Murphy. There will be the athletes themselves, victors and leaders in all the games. And as for the noted and notorious sport followers, they will all be here. Every figure of sportdom, from Billy Jordan, the well beloved veteran announcer, down to the latest and youngest fight promoter, they will all be on the ground.

And they will watch these two strangely diverse heavy-weights battle, beside whom all other heavies look like middle-weights, Johnson, the fighting boxer, will go up against Jeffries, the boxing fighter. Both are cool, both are experienced, both are terrible. It will not be a short fight. It will be a great fight.

And so I say again to all you men who love the game, have the price, and are within striking distance of Reno—come. It is the fight of fights, the crowning fight of the whole ring, and perhaps the last great fight that will ever be held. Also, to you lovers of the game, who desire to see in flesh and blood the celebrities of the game, I say come. It would take years of traveling and fight following to see all the figures of sportdom that can be seen here in Reno in one day, and no admission charged. I, for one, hope for a toothless old age, when nothing is left but to mumble reminiscences, and in that time one of my greatest joys will be to maunder over all the wonderful details of the great fight at Reno—"yes, sir; in 1910, at Reno. I was there and sat by the ringside."

# JEFFRIES-JOHNSON FIGHT *

RENO, NEV., JULY 4. —Once again has Johnson sent down to defeat the chosen representative of the white race, and this time the greatest of them all. And, as of old, it was play for Johnson. From the opening to the closing round he never ceased his witty sallies, his exchanges of repartee with his opponent's seconds and with the spectators. And, for that matter, Johnson had a funny thing or two to say to Jeffries in every round. The golden smile was as much in evidence as ever, and neither did it freeze on his face nor did it vanish. It came and went throughout the fight spontaneously, naturally.

It was not a great battle, after all, save in its setting and its significance. Little Tommy Burns down in far-off Australia put up a faster, quicker, livelier battle than did Jeff. The fight today, and again I repeat, was great only in its significance. In itself it was not great. The issue, after the fiddling of the opening rounds, was never in doubt. In the fiddling of those first rounds the honors lay with Johnson, and for the rounds after the seventh or eighth it was more Johnson, while for the closing rounds it was all Johnson.

Johnson played, as usual. With his opponent not strong in the attack, Johnson, blocking and defending in masterly fashion, could afford to play. And he played and fought a white man in a white man's country, before a white man's crowd. And the crowd was a Jeffries crowd. When Jeffries sent in that awful rip of his the crowd would madly applaud, believing it had gone home to Johnson's stomach, and Johnson, deftly interposing his elbow, would smile in irony at the spectators, play-acting, making believe he thought the applause was for him—and never believing it at all.

The greatest battle of the century was a monologue delivered to twenty thousand spectators by a smiling negro who was never in doubt and who was never serious for more than a moment at a time.

As a fighter Johnson did not show himself a wonder. He did not have to. Never once was he extended. There was no need Jeff could not make him extend. Jeff never had him in trouble once. No blow Jeff ever landed hurt his dusky opponent. Johnson came out of the great fight practically undamaged. The blood on his lip was from a recent cut received in training which Jeff managed to reopen.

Jeff failed to lead and land. The quickness he brought into the

* From *Jack London Reports*; first published in the New York *Herald*, July 5, 1910.

fight quickly evaporated, and while Jeff was dead game to the end, he was not so badly punished. What he failed to bring into the ring with him was his stamina, which he lost somewhere in the last seven years. Jeff failed to come back. That is the whole story. His old-time vim and endurance were not there. Something has happened to him. He lost in retirement, outside of the ring, the stamina that the ring itself never robbed him of. As I have said, Jeff was not badly damaged. Every day boys take worse lacings in boxing bouts than Jeff took today.

Jeff today disposed of one question. He could not come back. Johnson in turn answered another question. He has not the yellow streak. But he only answered that question for to-day. The ferocity of the hairy-chested caveman and grizzly giant combined did not intimidate the cool-headed negro. Many thousands in the audience expected this intimidation and were correspondingly disappointed. Johnson was not scared, let it be said here and beyond the shadow of a doubt. Not for an instant did he show the flicker of fear that the Goliath against him might eat up.

But the question of the yellow streak is not answered for all time. Just as Johnson has never been extended, so has he never shown the yellow streak. Just as a man may rise up, heaven alone knows where, who will extend Johnson, just so may that man bring out the yellow streak, and then again, he may not. So far the burden of proof all rests on the conclusion that Johnson has no yellow streak.

And now to the battle and how it began. All praise to Tex Rickard, the gamest of sports, who pulled off the fight after countless difficulties, and who, cool, calm and quick with nervous aliveness, handled the vast crowd splendidly at the arena, and wound up by refereeing the fight.

Twenty thousand filled the great arena and waited patiently under the cloud-flecked wide Nevada sky. Of the many women present, some elected to sit in the screened boxes far back from the ring, for all the world like olden Spanish ladies at the theatre. But more, many more women, sat close to the ringside beside their husbands or brothers. They were the wiser far.

Merely to enumerate the celebrities at the ringside would be to write a sporting directory of America—at least a directory of the 400 of sportdom and of many more hundreds of near four hundreds. At 1:56, Billy Jordan cleared the ring amid cheers, and stood alone, the focal point of 20,000 pairs of eyes, until the great Muldoon climbed through the ropes to call tumultuous applause and ringing cheers from the 20,000 throats, for the State of Nevada, the people of Nevada and the Governor of Nevada.

Beginning with Tex Rickard, ovation after ovation was given to all the great ones, not forgetting Fitzsimmons, whom Billy Jordan introduced as "the greatest warrior of them all." And so they came, great one after great one, ceaselessly, endlessly, until they were swept away before the greatest of them all—the two men who were about to do battle.

It was 2:30 when Johnson entered. He came first, airy, happy and smiling, greeting friends and acquaintances here, there and everywhere in the audience, cool as ice, waving his hand in salute, smiling, smiling ever smiling, with eyes as well as lips, never missing a name nor a face, placid, plastic, nerveless, with never a signal flown of hesitancy nor timidity. Yet was he keyed up, keenly observant of all that was going on, even hearing much of the confused babble of tongues about him —hearing, ay, and understanding, too. There is nothing heavy nor primitive about this man Johnson. He is alive and quivering, every nerve fiber in his body and brain, withal that it is hidden, so artfully, or naturally, under that poise of facetious calm of his. He is a marvel of sensitiveness, sensibility and perceptibility. He has a perfect mechanism of mind and body. His mind works like chain lightning and his body obeys with equal swiftness.

But the great madness of applause went up when Jeffries entered the ring two minutes later. A quick superficial comparison between him and the negro would lead to a feeling of pity for the latter. For Jeff was all that has been said of him. When he stripped and his mighty body could be seen covered with mats of hair, all the primordial adjectives ever applied to him received their vindication. Nor did his face belie them. No facile emotion played on that face, no whims of the moment, no flutterings of a light-hearted temperament. Dark and somber and ominous was that face, solid and stolid and expressionless, with eyes that smouldered and looked savage.

The man of iron, grim with determination, sat down in his corner. And the care-free negro smiled and smiled. And that is the story of the fight. The man of iron, the grizzly giant was grim and serious. The man of summer temperament smiled and smiled. That is the story of the whole fight. It is the story of the fight by rounds.

At the opening of the first round they did not shake hands. Knowing the two men for what they are, it can be safely postulated that this neglect was due to Jeff or to the prompting of Jeff's corner. But it is not good that two boxers should not shake hands before a bout. I would suggest to these protagonists of a perishing game, if they wish to preserve the game, that they make the most of these little amenities that by custom grace their sport, and give it the veneer of civilization.

Both men went to work in that first round very easily, Johnson smiling, of course, and Jeff grim and determined. Johnson landed the first blow, a light one, and Jeff, in the clinches, gave a faint indication of his forthcoming tactics by roughing it, by crowding the negro around and by slightly bearing his weight upon him. It was a very easy round, with nothing of moment. Each was merely feeling the other out and both were exceedingly careful. At the conclusion of the round Johnson tapped Jeffries playfully on the shoulder, smiled good-naturedly and went to his corner. Jeff, in the first, showed flashes of cat-like quickness.

Second round, Jeff advanced with a momentary assumption of his famous crouch, to meet the broadly smiling. Jeff is really human and good-natured. He proved it right here. So friendly was that smile of Johnson, so irresistibly catching that Jeff, despite himself, smiled back. But Jeff's smiles were doomed to be very few in this fight.

And right here began a repetition of what took place down in Australia when Burns fought Johnson. Each time Burns said something harsh to Johnson, in the hope of making him lose his temper, Johnson responded by giving the white man a lacing. And so to-day, of course, Jeff did not talk to Johnson to amount to anything, but Corbett, in the corner, did it for Jeff. And each time Corbett cried out something particularly harsh, Johnson promptly administered a lacing to Jeff. It began in the second round. Corbett, in line with his plan of irritating the negro, called out loudly: "He wants to fight a little, Jim."

"You bet, I do," Johnson retorted, and with that he landed Jeff a stinging right uppercut.

Both men were tensely careful, Jeff trying to crowd and put his weight on in the clinches, Johnson striving more than the other to break out of the clinches. And at the end of the round, in his corner, Johnson was laughing gleefully. Certainly Jeff showed no signs of boring in, as had been promised by his enthusiastic supporters.

It was the same story in the third round, at the conclusion of which the irrepressible negro was guilty of waving his hands to friends in the audience.

In the fourth round Jeff showed up better, rushing and crowding and striking with more vim than hitherto shown. This seemed to have been caused by a sally of Johnson's and Jeff went at him in an angry sort of way. Promptly Jeff rushed, and even ere they came together, Johnson cried out:

"Don't rush me, Jim. You hear what I'm telling you?"

No sign there of being intimidated by Jeffries' first dynamic display of ferocity. All he managed to do was to reopen the training cut in Johnson's lip and to make Johnson playful. It was most anybody's round, and it was certainly more Jeff's than any preceding one.

Round five brought Jeff advancing with his crouch and showed that the blood from Johnson's lip had turned his smile to a gory one. But still he smiled and, to balance things off, he opened Jeff's lip until it bled more profusely than his own. From then until the end of the fight Jeff's face was never free from blood, a steady stream later flowing from his right nostril, added to by the opened cut on his left cheek. Corbett's running fire of irritation served but to make Johnson smile the merrier and to wink at him across Jeff's shoulder in the clinches.

So far no problems had been solved, no questions answered. The yellow streak had not appeared. Neither had Jeff bored in, ripped awfully, nor put it over Johnson in the clinches. Yet one thing had been shown. Jeff was not so fast as he had been. There was a shade of diminution in his speed.

Johnson signalized the opening of the sixth round by landing stinging blows to the face in one, two, three order. Johnson's quickness was startling. In response to an irritating remark from Corbett, Johnson replied suavely, "Too much on hand right now," and at the same instant he tore into Jeff. It was Johnson's first real, aggressive rush. It lasted but a second or two, but it was fierce and dandy, and at its conclusion it was manifest that Jeff's right eye was closing fast. The round ended with Johnson fighting and smiling strong, and with Jeff's nose, lip and cheek bleeding and his eye closed. Johnson's round by a smile all the way through.

The seventh round was a mild one, opening with Jeff grim and silent, and with Johnson leading and forcing. Both were careful, and nothing happened, save that once they exchanged blows right niftily. So far, Jeff's roughing, and crowding and bearing on of weight had amounted to nothing. Also, he was doing less and less of it.

"It only takes one or two, Jim," Corbett encouraged his principal in the eighth round. Promptly Johnson landed two stingers. After a pause he landed another. "See that?" he chirped sweetly to Corbett in the corner. Jeff showed signs perceptibly of slowing down in this round, rushing and crowding less and less. Johnson was working harder and his speed was as flash light as ever. Jeff's slowing down was not due to the punishment he had received, but to poorness of condition. He was flying the first signals of fatigue. He was advertising, faintly, it is true, that he had not come back.

The ninth round was introduced by a suggestion from Corbett, heroically carrying out the policy that was bringing his principle to destruction. "Make that big stiff fight," was Corbett's suggestion. "That's right; that's what they all say," was Johnson's answer, delivered with true Chesterfieldian grace across his adversary's shoulder. In the previous rounds Johnson had not wreaked much damage with the forecasted punch, the right uppercut. In this round he demonstrated indisputably that he could drive the left hand in a way that was surprising. Be it remembered that it had been long denied that he had any sort of a punch in that left of his. Incidentally, in this round he landed a blow near to Jeff's heart that must have been discouraging.

The tenth round showed Johnson, with his deft, unexpected left, as quick as ever, and Jeff's going slower and slower.

The conclusion of the first ten rounds may be summed up as follows: The fight was all in the favor of Johnson, who had shown no yellow, who had shown condition, who had shown undiminished speed, who had not used his right uppercut much, who had developed a savage left, who held his own in the clinches, who had not the best of the infighting and the outfighting, who was unhurt and who was smiling all the way. Jeff was in bad shape; he was tired, slower than ever, his few rushes had been futile, and the sports who had placed their money against him were jubilant. There were men who proclaimed they saw the end.

I refused to see this end, for I had picked Jeff to win, and I was hoping hugely—for what, I did not know; but for something to happen, for anything, that would turn the tide of battle. And yet I could not hide from myself the truth that Jeff had slowed down.

The eleventh round looked better for Jeff. Stung by a remark of Corbett's, Johnson rushed and provoked one grand rally from Jeff. It was faster fighting, and more continuous than at any time in the preceding ten rounds, culminating in a fierce rally, in which Jeff landed hard.

Round twelve found Johnson, if anything, quicker and more aggressive than ever.

"Thought you were going to have me wild?" Johnson queried sweetly of Corbett.

As usual, every remark of Corbett's brought more punishment to

Jeffries. And by the end of this round the second of two great questions was definitely answered. Jeff had not come back.

The thirteenth round was the beginning of the end. Beginning slowly enough, but stung by Corbett, Johnson put it all over him in the mouth fighting, and all over Jeff in the outfighting and infighting. From defense to attack, and back again, and back and forth, Johnson flashed like the amazing fighting mechanism he is. Jeff was silent and sick, while, as the round progressed, Corbett was noticeably silent.

A few entertained the fond hope that Jeff would recuperate. But it was futile. There was no come back to him. He was a fading, failing, heartsick, heartbroken man.

"Talk to him, Corbett," Jeff's friends appealed, in the fourteenth round. But Corbett could not talk. He had long since seen the end.

Yet through this round Johnson went in for one of his character-istic loafing spells. He took it easy, and played with the big gladiator, cool as a cucumber, smiling broadly as ever, yet as careful as ever.

"Right on the hip," he grinned once, as Jeff, in a desperate, dying flurry, managed to land a wild punch in that vicinity.

Corbett, likewise desperate, ventured a last sally. "Why don't you do something?" he cried to the loafing, laughing Johnson. "Too clever, too clever, like you," was the response.

Round fifteen, and the end. It was pitiful. There happened to Jeff the bitterness that he had so often made others taste, but which for the first time, perforce, he was made to taste himself. He who had never been knocked down was knocked down repeatedly. He who had never been knocked out was knocked out. Never mind the technical decision. Jeff was knocked out. That is all there is to it. An ignominy of ignominies, he was knocked out and through the ropes by the punch he never believed Johnson possessed—by the left, and not by the right.

As he lay across the lower rope while the seconds were told off, a cry that had in it tears and abject broken plea went up from many of the spectators.

"Don't let the negro knock him out, don't let the negro knock him out," was the oft-repeated cry.

There is little more to be said. Jeff did not come back. Johnson did not show the yellow streak, and it was Johnson's fight all the way through. Jeff was not old Jeff at all. Even so, it is to be doubted if the old Jeff could have put away this amazing negro from Texas, this black man with the unfailing smile, this king of fighters and monologists.

Corbett and Berger and the others were right. They wanted Jeff to do more boxing and fighting in his training. Nevertheless lacking the come back as he so potently did, this preliminary boxing and fight-ing would have profited him nothing. On the other hand, it would have saved his camp much of the money with which it backed him.

It was a slow fight. Faster, better fights may be seen every day of the year in any of the small clubs in the land. It is true these men were heavy-weights, yet for heavy-weights it was a slow fight. It must be granted that plucky Tommy Burns put up a much faster fight with Johnson a year and a half ago. Yet the American fight follower had to see this fight to-day in order to appreciate just what Burns did against this colored wonder.

Johnson is a wonder. No one understands him, this man who smiles. Well, the story of the fight is the story of a smile. If ever a man won by nothing more fatiguing than a smile, Johnson won to-day.

And where now is the champion who will make Johnson extend himself, who will glaze those bright eyes, remove that smile and silence that golden repartee?

# A CLASSIC OF THE SEA *

## INTRODUCTION TO "*TWO YEARS BEFORE THE MAST*"

ONCE IN A HUNDRED YEARS is a book written that lives not alone for its own century but which becomes a document for the future centuries. Such a book is Dana's. When Marryat's and Cooper's sea novels are gone to dust, stimulating and joyful as they have been to generations of men, still will remain "Two Years Before the Mast."

Paradoxical as it may seem, Dana's book is the classic of the sea, not because there was anything extraordinary about Dana, but for the precise contrary reason that he was just an ordinary, normal man, clear-seeing, hard-headed, controlled, fitted with adequate education to go about the work. He brought a trained mind to put down with untroubled vision what he saw of a certain phase of work-a-day life. There was nothing brilliant nor fly-away about him. He was not a genius. His heart never rode his head. He was neither overlorded by sentiment nor hag-ridden by imagination. Otherwise he might have been guilty of the beautiful exaggerations in Melville's "Typee" or the imaginative orgies in the latter's "Moby Dick." It was Dana's cool poise that saved him from being spread-eagled and flogged when two of his mates were so treated; it was his lack of abandon that prevented him from taking up permanently with the sea, that prevented him from seeing more than one poetical spot, and more than one romantic spot on all the coast of Old California. Yet these apparent defects were his

* From *The Human Drift*; first published in the *Independent*, December 14, 1911.

strength. They enabled him magnificently to write, and for all time, the picture of the sea-life of his time.

Written close to the middle of the last century, such has been the revolution worked in man's method of trafficking with the sea, that the life and conditions described in Dana's book have passed utterly away. Gone are the crack clippers, the driving captains, the hard-bitten but efficient foremast hands. Remain only crawling cargo tanks, dirty tramps, greyhound liners, and a sombre, sordid type of sailing ship. The only records broken to-day by sailing vessels are those for slowness. They are no longer built for speed, nor are they manned before the mast by as sturdy a sailor stock, nor aft the mast are they officered by sail-carrying captains and driving mates.

Speed is left to the liners, who run the silk, and tea, and spices. Admiralty courts, boards of trade, and underwriters frown upon driving and sail-carrying. No more are the free-and-easy, dare-devil days, when fortunes were made in fast runs and lucky ventures, not alone for owners, but for captains as well. Nothing is ventured now. The risks of swift passages cannot be abided. Freights are calculated to the last least fraction of per cent. The captains do no speculating, no bargain-making for the owners. The latter attend to all this, and by wire and cable rake the ports of the seven seas in quest of cargoes, and through their agents make all business arrangements.

It has been learned that small crews only, and large carriers only, can return a decent interest on the investment. The inevitable corollary is that speed and spirit are at a discount. There is no discussion of the fact that in the sailing merchant marine the seamen, as a class, have sadly deteriorated. Men no longer sell farms to go to sea. But the time of which Dana writes was the heyday of fortune-making and adventure on the sea—with the full connotation of hardship and peril always attendant.

It was Dana's fortune, for the sake of the picture that the *Pilgrim* was an average ship, with an average crew and officers, and managed with average discipline. Even the *hazing* that took place after the California coast was reached, was of the average sort. The *Pilgrim* savoured not in any way of a hell-ship. The captain, while not the sweetest-natured man in the world, was only an average down-east driver, neither brilliant nor slovenly in his seamanship, neither cruel nor sentimental in the treatment of his men. While, on the one hand, there were no extra liberty days, no delicacies added to the meagre forecastle fare, nor grog or hot coffee on double watches, on the other hand the crew was not chronically crippled by the continual play of knuckle-dusters and belaying pins. Once, and once only, were men flogged or ironed—a very fair average for the year 1834, for at that time flogging on board merchant vessels was already well on the decline.

The difference between the sea-life then and now can be no better epitomised than in Dana's description of the dress of the sailor of his day:

"The trousers tight around the hips, and thence hanging long and loose around the feet, a superabundance of checked shirt, a low-crowned, well-varnished black hat, worn on the back of the head, with half a fathom of black ribbon hanging over the left eye, and a peculiar tie to the black silk neckerchief."

Though Dana sailed from Boston only three-quarters of a century ago, much that is at present obsolete was then in full sway. For instance, the old word *larboard* was still in use. He was a member of the *larboard* watch. The vessel was on the *larboard* tack. It was only the other day, because of its similarity in sound to starboard, that *larboard* was changed to *port*. Try to imagine "All larboard bowlines on deck!" being shouted down into the forecastle of a present day ship. Yet that was the call used on the *Pilgrim* to fetch Dana and the rest of his watch on deck.

The chronometer, which is merely the least imperfect time-piece man has devised, makes possible the surest and easiest method by far of ascertaining longitude. Yet the *Pilgrim* sailed in a day when the chronometer was just coming into general use. So little was it depended upon that the *Pilgrim* carried only one, and that one, going wrong at the outset, was never used again. A navigator of the present would be aghast if asked to voyage for two years, from Boston, around the Horn to California, and back again, without a chronometer. In those days such a proceeding was a matter of course, for those were the days when dead reckoning was indeed something to reckon on, when running down the latitude was a common way of finding a place, and when lunar observations were direly necessary. It may be fairly asserted that very few merchant officers of to-day ever make a lunar observation, and that a large percentage are unable to do it.

"*Sept. 22nd.*, upon coming on deck at seven bells in the morning we found the other watch aloft throwing water upon the sails, and looking astern we saw a small, clipper-built brig with a black hull heading directly after us. We went to work immediately, and put all the canvas upon the brig which we could get upon her, rigging out oars for studding-sail yards; and continued wetting down the sails by buckets of water whipped up to the mast head. . . . She was armed, and full of men, and showed no colors."

The foregoing sounds like a paragraph from "Midshipman Easy" or the "Water Witch," rather than a paragraph from the soberest, faithfulest, and most literal chronicle of the sea ever written. And yet the chase by a pirate occurred, on board the brig *Pilgrim*, on September 22nd, 1834—something like only two generations ago.

Dana was the thorough-going type of man, not overbalanced and erratic, without quirk or quibble of temperament. He was efficient, but not brilliant. His was a general all-around efficiency. He was efficient at the law; he was efficient at college; he was efficient as a sailor; he was efficient in the matter of pride, when that pride was no more than the pride of a forecastle hand, at twelve dollars a month, in his seaman's task well done, in the smart sailing of his captain, in the cleanness and trimness of his ship.

There is no sailor whose cockles of the heart will not warm to Dana's description of the first time he sent down a royal yard. Once or twice he had seen it done. He got an old hand in the crew to coach him. And then, the first anchorage at Monterey, being pretty *thick* with the second mate, he got him to ask the mate to be sent up the first time the royal yards were struck. "Fortunately," as Dana describes it, "I got through without any word from the officer; and heard the 'well done' of the mate, when the yard reached the deck, with as much satisfaction as I ever felt at Cambridge on seeing a 'bene' at the foot of a Latin exercise."

"This was the first time I had taken a weather ear-ring, and I felt not a little proud to sit astride of the weather yard-arm, past the ear-ring, and sing out 'Haul out to leeward!' " He had been over a year at sea before he essayed this able seaman's task, but he did it, and he did it with pride. And with pride, he went down a four-hundred foot cliff, on a pair of top-gallant studding-sail halyards bent together, to dislodge several dollars worth of stranded bullock hides, though all the acclaim he got from his mates was: "What a d——d fool you were to risk your life for half a dozen hides!"

In brief, it was just this efficiency in pride, as well as work, that enabled Dana to set down, not merely the photograph detail of life before the mast and hide-droghing on the coast of California, but of the unvarnished, simple psychology and ethics of the forecastle hands who droghed the hides, stood at the wheel, made and took in sail, tarred down the rigging, holystoned the decks, turned in all-standing, grumbled as they cut about the kid, criticised the seamanship of their officers, and estimated the duration of their exile from the cubic space of the hide-house.

GLEN ELLEN, CALIFORNIA,
*August 13, 1911*

# INTRODUCTION TO
## *THE CRY FOR JUSTICE**

THIS ANTHOLOGY, I take it, is the first edition, the first gathering together of the body of the literature and art of the humanist thinkers of the world. As well done as it has been done, it will be better done in the future. There will be much adding, there will be a little subtracting, in the succeeding editions that are bound to come. The result will be a monument of the ages, and there will be none fairer.

Since reading of the Bible, the Koran, and the Talmud has enabled countless devout and earnest right-seeking souls to be stirred and uplifted to higher and finer planes of thought and action, then the reading of this humanist Holy Book cannot fail similarly to serve the needs of groping, yearning humans who seek to discern truth and justice amid the dazzle and murk of the thought-chaos of the present-day world.

No person, no matter how soft and secluded his own life has been, can read this Holy Book and not be aware that the world is filled with a vast mass of unfairness, cruelty, and suffering. He will find that it has been observed, during all the ages, by the thinkers, the seers, the poets, and the philosophers.

And such person will learn, possibly, that this fair world so brutally unfair, is not decreed by the will of God nor by any iron law of Nature. He will learn that the world can be fashioned a fair world indeed by the humans who inhabit it, by the very simple, and yet most difficult process of coming to an understanding of the world. Under-

* The Cry for Justice: An Anthology of the Literature of Social Protest, ed. Upton Sinclair (Philadelphia: John C. Winston, 1915).

standing, after all, is merely sympathy in its fine correct sense. And such sympathy, in its genuineness, makes toward unselfishness. Unselfishness inevitably connotes service. And service is the solution of the entire vexatious problem of man.

He, who by understanding becomes converted to the gospel of service, will serve truth to confute liars and make of them truth-tellers; will serve kindness so that brutality will perish; will serve beauty to the erasement of all that is not beautiful. And he who is strong will serve the weak that they may become strong. He will devote his strength, not to the debasement and defilement of his weaker fellows, but to the making of opportunity for them to make themselves into men rather than into slaves and beasts.

One has but to read the names of the men and women whose words burn in these pages, and to recall that by far more than average intelligence have they won to their place in the world's eye and in the world's brain long after the dust of them has vanished, to realize that due credence must be placed in their report of the world herein recorded. They were not tyrants and wastrels, hypocrites and liars, brewers and gamblers, market-riggers and stock-brokers. They were givers and servers, and seers and humanists. They were unselfish. They conceived of life, not in terms of profit, but of service.

Life tore at them with its heart-break. They could not escape the hurt of it by selfish refuge in the gluttonies of brain and body. They saw, and steeled themselves to see, clear-eyed and unafraid. Nor were they afflicted by some strange myopia. They all saw the same thing. They are all agreed upon what they saw. The totality of their evidence proves this with unswerving consistency. They have brought the report, these commissioners of humanity. It is here in these pages. It is a true report.

But not merely have they reported the human ills. They have proposed the remedy. And their remedy is of no part of all the jangling sects. It has nothing to do with the complicated metaphysical processes by which one may win to other worlds and imagined gains beyond the sky. It is a remedy for this world, since worlds must be taken one at a time. And yet, that not even the jangling sects should receive hurt by the making fairer of this world for this own world's sake, it is well, for all future worlds of them that need future worlds, that their splendor be not tarnished by the vileness and ugliness of this world.

It is so simple a remedy, merely service. Not one ignoble thought or act is demanded of any one of all men and women in the world to make fair the world. The call is for nobility of thinking, nobility of doing. The call is for service, and, such is the wholesomeness of it, he who serves all, best serves himself.

Times change, and men's minds with them. Down the past, civilizations have exposited themselves in terms of power, of world-power or of other-world power. No civilization has yet exposited itself in terms of love-of-man. The humanists have no quarrel with the previous civilizations. They were necessary in the development of man. But their purpose is fulfilled, and they may well pass, leaving man to build the new and higher civilization that will exposit itself in terms of love and service and brotherhood.

To see gathered here together this great body of human beauty and fineness and nobleness is to realize what glorious humans have already existed, do exist, and will continue increasingly to exist until all the world beautiful be made over in their image. We know how gods are made. Comes now the time to make a world.

HONOLULU
*March 6, 1915*

# EIGHT FACTORS OF
# LITERARY SUCCESS *

I WAS BORN IN San Francisco in 1876. Almost the first thing I realized were responsibilities. I have no recollection of being taught to read or write, though I could do both at the age of five. As a ranch boy, I worked hard from my eighth year.

"The adventure-lust was strong within me, and I left home. I joined the oyster pirates in the bay; shipped as sailor on a schooner; took a turn at salmon fishing; shipped before the mast and sailed for the Japanese coast on a seal-hunting expedition. After sealing for seven months I came back to California, and took odd jobs at coal shoveling and long-shoring, and also in a jute factory.

"Later, I tramped through the United States from California to Boston, and up and down, returning to the Pacific coast by way of Canada, where I served a term in jail for vagrancy. My tramping experience made me a Socialist. Previously, I had been impressed by the dignity of labor. Work was everything; it was sanctification and salvation. I had fought my way from the open West, where the job hunted the man, to the congested labor centers of the Eastern states, where men hunted the job for all they were worth. I saw the workers in the shambles of the Social Pit; and I found myself looking on life from a new and totally different, angle.

"In my nineteenth year I returned to Oakland and started at the High School. I remained a year, doing janitor work as a means of livelihood. After leaving the High School, in three months of 'cram-

* The Silhouette, February 1917.

ming' by myself I took the three years' work for that time and entered the University of California. I worked in a laundry, and with my pen to help me, kept on. The task was too much; when half way through my Freshman year, I had to quit.

"Three months later, having decided that I was a failure as a writer, I gave it up and left for the Klondike to prospect for gold. It was in the Klondike that I found myself. There nobody talks. Everybody thinks. You get your true perspective. I got mine.

"In answer to your question as to the greatest factors of my literary success, I will state that I consider them to be:

"Vast good luck. Good health; good brain; good mental and muscular correlation. Poverty. Reading Ouida's 'Signa' when I was eight years of age. The influence of Herbert Spencer's 'Philosophy of Style.' Because I got started twenty years before the fellows who are trying to start today.

"Because, of all the foregoing, I have been *real*, and did not cheat reality any step of the way, even in so microscopically small, and cosmically ludicrous, a detail as the wearing of a starched collar when it would have hurt my neck had I worn it.

"My health was good—in spite of every liberty I took with it—because I was born with a strong body, and lived an open-air life, rough, hard, exercising.

"I came of old American stock, of English and Welsh descent, but living in America for long before the French and Indian wars. Such accounts for my decent brain.

"Poverty made me hustle. My vast good luck prevented poverty from destroying me. Nearly all my oyster-pirate comrades are long since hanged, shot, drowned, killed by disease, or are spending their declining years in prison. Any one of all these things might have happened to me before I was seventeen—save for my vast good luck.

"Read Ouida's 'Signa.' I read it at the age of eight. The story begins: 'It was only a little lad.' The little lad was an Italian mountain peasant. He became an artist, with all Italy at his feet. When I read it, I was a little peasant on a poor California ranch. Reading the story, my narrow hill-horizon was pushed back, and all the world was made possible if I would dare it. I dared.

"Read 'Philosophy of Style.' It taught me the subtle and manifold operations necessary to transmute thought, beauty, sensation and emotion into black symbols on white paper; which symbols, through the reader's eye, were taken into his brain, and by his brain transmuted into thoughts, beauty, sensations and emotions that fairly corresponded with mine. Among other things, this taught me to *know* the brain of my reader, in order to select the symbols that would compel his brain to realize my thought, or vision, or emotion. Also, I learned that the right symbols were the ones that would require the expenditure of the minimum of my reader's brain energy, leaving the maximum of his brain energy to realize and enjoy the content of my mind, as conveyed to his mind.

"A word as to the writer of today:

"For one clever writer twenty years ago, there are, today, five hundred clever writers. Today, excellent writing is swamped in a sea of excellent writing. Or so it seems to me."

# A Selection of Letters

To the Editor, *San Francisco Bulletin*

Oakland, Calif.
Sept. 17, 1898

Dear Sir:

I have returned from a year's residence in the Clondyke, entering the country by way of Dyea and Chilcoot Pass. I left by way of St. Michaels, thus making altogether a journey of 2,500 miles on the Yukon in a small boat. I have sailed and traveled quite extensively in other parts of the world and have learned to seize upon that which is interesting, to grasp the true romance of things, and to understand the people I may be thrown amongst.

I have just completed an article of 4,000 words,[1] describing the trip from Dawson to St. Michaels in a rowboat. Kindly let me know if there would be any demand in your columns for it—of course, thoroughly understanding that the acceptance of the manuscript is to depend upon its literary and intrinsic value.

Yours very respectfully,
Jack London[2]

1. "From Dawson to the Sea," eventually published in the *Illustrated Buffalo Express*, June 4, 1899.
2. The editor answered in longhand on the bottom of JL's letter: "Interest in Alaska has subsided in an amazing degree. Then, again, so much has been written, that I do not think it would pay us to buy your story." Across the top, in CKL's hand, is written: "This is Jack's first letter to an editor."

## To Mabel Applegarth

962 East 16th. st.
Nov. 27, 1898

Dear Mabel:

Forgive my not writing, for I have been miserable and half sick. So nervous this morning that I could hardly shave myself. I knew by Thanksgiving that you were expecting me; but I delayed, hoping to start every day and everyday. And now, I receive a letter from Frank Atherton,[3] telling me that he will arrive either Monday night or Tuesday morning. So if things should come my way, I would be unable to go to College Park till he finishes his visit.

Everything seems to have gone wrong—why, I haven't received my twenty dollars for those essays yet.[4] Not a word as to how I stood in my Civil Service Exs.[5] Not a word from the *Youth's Companion*,[6] and it means to me what no one can possibly realize.

You seem to misunderstand. I thought I made it perfectly plain, that those squibs of poetry were merely diversions and experiments; yet you say—"But always the same theme." Theme had nothing to do with it; they were studies in structure and versification. Though it took me a long while, I have learned my lesson, and thanks to no one. I made ambitious efforts once. It makes me laugh to look back on them, though sometimes I am nearer to weeping. I was the greenest of tyros, dipping my brush into whitewash and coal-tar, and without the slightest knowledge of perspective, proportion or color, attempted masterpieces—without a soul to say "you are all wrong; herein you err; there is your mistake."[7]

Why, that poem on gold is one of the finest object-lessons in my possession—Ted has it now. I was ambitious in that. With no more comprehension of the aims and principles of poetry, than a crab, I proposed or rather, purposed to make something which would be something. I would strike out on new trails; I would improve upon

3. Frank Atherton, a classmate of JL at the Cole Grammar School in West Oakland and his closest boyhood friend. When Atherton married, JL was his best man. After JL had separated from Bessie, the Athertons shared his apartment at 1216 Telegraph Avenue in Oakland. For an account of Atherton's reminiscences, see his "Jack London in Boyhood Adventures" (MS: CSmH[Huntington Library]).

4. JL won two prizes for essays, worth ten dollars each, in the Oakland Fifth Ward Republican Club contest for campaign songs, essays, cartoons, and poems. Evidently he was never paid. See JL to M. Applegarth, ? December 31, 1898.

5. JL had taken the Civil Service Examination for mail carrier on October 1, 1898, at the Oakland Post Office. See JL to M. Applegarth, January 28, 1899.

the Spencerian Stanza; I would turn things upside down. So I tried what has been probably tried a thousand times and discarded because it was worthless; one Alexandrine at the end of the stanza was not enough; I added a second. I treated my theme as Dryden or Thompson[8] would have treated it. My elephantine diction was superb—I out-Johnsoned Johnson. I was a fool—and no one to tell me.

So you see, to-day, I am unlearning and learning anew, and is such things are merely principles, you can readily see why I don't care a snap for the theme. I have played Darius Green[9] once, and if my neck is broken a second time it will be my own fault. I shall not be ready for any flights till my flying machine is perfected, and to that perfection I am now applying myself. Until then, to the deuce with themes. I shall subordinate thought to technique till the latter is mastered; then I shall do vice a versa.

I do not know when I can be down—I may be digging sewers or shoveling coal next week. Am glad to hear you are better. Give my regards to every body.

Good bye,<br>Jack

## To Mabel Applegarth

962 East 16th. st.<br>Nov. 30, 1898

Dear Mabel:

Am replying at once. As to that medicine: since there is no certainty to my plans, I think it would be best to send up money to me and order to Owl Drug Co. Send at once, so Frank can take it back

---

6. JL's 21,000-word, 7-chapter serial "Where Boys Are Men" was sent on October 29, 1898, to the *Youth's Companion*, a juvenile and family weekly published in Boston from 1827 until 1929. Subsequently rejected by this magazine, it was accepted by *Youth and Age* on May 2, 1899, but was never published.
7. Possibly Robert Browning, "My Last Duchess" (1842), ll. 37–39: " 'Just this/Or that in you disgusts me; here you miss,/Or there exceed the mark.' "
8. James Thomson (1700–1748), Scottish poet, author of *The Seasons*.
9. In "Darius Green and His Flying Machine," a humorous poem by John Townsend Trowbridge collected in *The Vagabond and Other Poems* (1869), when Darius Green tests his contraption, instead of flying, he falls to earth, landing on his head.

with him. He does not go before Saturday, and the chances are that he will stay even longer.

I do appreciate your interest in my affairs, but—we have no common ground. In a general, vaguely general, way, you know my aspirations; but of the real Jack, his thoughts, feelings, etc., you are positively ignorant. Yet, little as you do know, you know more about me than any body else. I have fought and am fighting my battle alone.

You speak of going to my sister:[10] I know how well she loves me; do you know how? or why? I spent years in Oakland and we saw nothing of each other—perhaps once a year looked on each others face. If I had followed what she would have advised, had I sought her I would to-day be a clerk at forty dollars a month, a railroad man, or something similar. I would have winter clothes, would go to the theatre, have a nice circle of acquaintances, belong to some horrible little society like the W.R.C.,[11] talk as they talk, think as they think, do as they do—in short, I would have a full stomack, a warm body, no qualms of conscience, no bitterness of heart, no worrying ambition, no aim but to buy furniture on the installment plan and marry. I would be satisfied to live a puppet and die a puppet. Yes, and she would not have liked me half as well as she does. Because I felt that I was or wanted to be something more than a laborer, a dummy; because I showed that my brain was a little bit better than it should have been, considering my disadvantages and lack of advantages; because I was different from most fellows in my station; because of all this she took a liking to me. But all this was secondary; primarily, she was lonely, had no children, a husband who was no husband,[12] etc., she wanted someone to love. A great deal of this same feeling has been lavished upon the W.R.C. for the same reason.

If the world was at my feet to-morrow, none would be happier than she, and she would say she knew it would be so all the time. But until that time—well, she would advise to not think of it, to sink myself in two score years of oblivion with a full belly and no worry, to die as I had lived, an animal. Why should I so study that I may extract joy from reading some poem? She does not and does not miss

10. Eliza London Shepard (1867–1939), JL's stepsister and the wife of Capt. James H. Shepard.
11. The Woman's Relief Corps, an auxiliary to the Grand Army of the Republic. Eliza Shepard was later president of this organization.
12. Capt. James H. Shepard (1843–1917) was a middle-aged widower with three children when he met Eliza, who was sixteen. They married in 1884 and moved to Oakland.

anything; Tom Dick and Harry do not, and they are happy. Why should I develop my mind? It is not necessary for happiness. A babble of voices, petty scandals, and foolish nothings, should satisfy me. It does Tom Dick and Harry, and they are happy.

As long as my mother lives, I would not do this; but with her gone to-morrow, if I knew that my life would be such, that I was destined to live in Oakland, labor in Oakland at some steady occupation, and die in Oakland—then to-morrow I would cut my throat and call quits with the whole cursed business. You may call this the foolish effervescence of youthful ambition, and say that it will all tone down in time; but I have had my share of toning down.

Why, as you have laid down my duty in your letter, if I had followed it what would I have been to-day? I would be a laborer, and by that I mean I would be fitted for nothing else than labor. Do you know my childhood? When I was seven years old, at the country school of San Pedro,[13] this happened. Meat, I was that hungry for it I once opened a girl's basket and stole a piece of meat—a little piece the size of my two fingers. I ate it but I never repeated it. In those days, like Esau, I would have literally sold my birthright for a mess of pottage, a piece of meat. Great God! when those youngsters threw chunks of meat on the ground because of surfeit, I could have dragged it from the dirt and eaten it; but I did not. Just imagine the development of my mind, my soul, under such material conditions.

This meat incident is an epitome of my whole life.

I was eight years old when I put on my first undershirt made at or bought at a store. Duty—at ten years I was on the street selling newspapers. Every cent was turned over to my people, and I went to school in constant shame of the hats, shoes, clothes I wore. Duty—from then on, I had no childhood. Up at three o'clock in the morning to carry papers. When that was finished I did not go home but continued on to school. School out, my evening papers. Saturday I worked on an ice wagon. Sunday I went to a bowling alley and set up pins for drunken Dutchmen. Duty—I turned over every cent and went dressed like a scarecrow.

Was there any duty owing to me?

Fred[14] worked in the cannery for a short summer vacation—aye

13. JL's family had moved to the northwestern coastal area of San Mateo County, south of San Francisco, when he was seven. John London owned a potato farm there.
14. Fred Jacobs.

the reward was to be a term at college. I worked in the same cannery,[15] not for a vacation but for a year. For months at a time, during that year, I was up and at work at six in the morning. I took half an hour for dinner. I took half an hour for supper. I worked every night till ten, eleven and twelve o'clock. My wages were small, but I worked such long hours that I sometimes made as high as fifty dollars a month. Duty—I turned every cent over. Duty—I have worked in that hell hole for thirty-six straight hours, at a machine, and I was only a child. I remember how I was trying to save the money to buy a skiff—eight dollars. All that summer I saved and scraped. In the fall I had five dollars as a result of absolutely doing without all pleasure. My mother came to the machine where I worked and asked for it. I could have killed myself that night. After a year of hell to have that pitiful—to be robbed of that petty joy.

Duty—had I followed your conception of duty, I should never have gone to High School, never to the University,[16] never—I should have remained a laborer.

My body and soul were starved when I was a child, cannot they do without a few little luxuries for me at this stage of the game?

Aye, I at last kicked over the traces; but [not] even then, did I wholly run away from duty. Many a gold piece went into the family. When I returned from seven months at sea,[17] what did I do with my pay day? I bought a second hand hat, some forty cent shirts, two fifty-cent suits of underclothes, and a second hand coat and vest. I spent exactly seventy cents for drinks among the crowd I had known before I went to sea. The rest went to pay the debts of my father and to the family. When I was working in the jute mills,[18] I received forty dollars pay and at the same time twenty-five dollars from a prize in a literary contest.[19] I bought a ten dollar suit of clothes and got my watch out

---

15. In 1891 JL worked at a machine filling, closing, and soldering cans of fruits and vegetables for the R. Hickmott Canning Company, 625 Myrtle Street, Oakland.
16. JL entered the University of California in Berkeley in August 1896 but withdrew on February 4, 1897, because of his financial condition.
17. On January 20, 1893, JL signed on a three-masted sealing schooner, the *Sophia Sutherland*, bound for Japan. He returned home on August 26, 1893.
18. Probably the Pacific Jute Manufacturing Company, east of Lake Merritt, where JL worked at a machine winding the jute-twine from a bobbin in the fall of 1893.
19. "Story of a Typhoon off the Coast of Japan" won first prize in a descriptive-writing contest for writers under 22 sponsored by the *San Francisco Morning Call*. It was published in the *Morning Call*, November 12, 1893, and later included in *Dutch Courage and Other Stories* (New York: Macmillan, 1922).

of hock. That was all I spent. Two days afterward, I had to soak my watch to get money for tobacco.

How often, as I swept the rooms at High School,[20] has my father come to me at my work and got a half dollar, a dollar, or two dollars? And you know I had a place to put every bit of it myself. Aye, I have had my father come there, when I did not have a cent, and went to the *Ægis*[21] fellows and borrowed it—mortgaged my next month's wages.

Do you know what I suffered during that High School and University period? The imps of hell would have wept had they been with me. Does any one know? Can any one know? O the hours I have eaten out my heart in bitterness! Duty—I fought it off for two long years without cessation, and I am glad. You knew me before those two years—did they do me any good?

You say, "It is your duty, if you wish to hold the esteem of those whose approval or companionship is worth having." If I had followed that, would I have known you? If I had followed that, who would I now know whose companionship I would esteem? If I had followed that from childhood, whose companionship would I now be fitted to enjoy?—Tennyson's? or a bunch of brute hoodlums on a street corner?

I cannot lay bare, cannot put my heart on paper, but I have merely stated a few material facts of my life. These may be cues to my feelings. But unless you know the instrument on which they play, you will not know the music. Me—how I have felt and thought through all this struggle; how I feel and think now—you do not know. Hungry! Hungry! Hungry! From the time I stole the meat and knew no call above my belly, to now when the call is higher it has been hunger, nothing but hunger.

You cannot understand, nor never will.

Nor has anybody ever understood. The whole thing has been by itself. Duty said "do not go on; go to work." So said my sister, though she would not say it to my face. Every body looked askance; though they did not speak, I knew what they thought. Not a word of approval, but much of disapproval. If only some one had said, "I understand." From the hunger of my childhood, cold eyes have looked upon me, or

20. JL entered Oakland High School in the winter of 1895 and also worked as a janitor at the school. For another description of his growing up, see JL to Houghton, Mifflin & Co., January 31, 1900.
21. The *Ægis*, a high school student publication in which JL published a number of articles and stories.

questioned, or snickered and sneered. What hurt above all was that they were some my friends—not professed but real friends. I have calloused my exterior and receive the strokes as though they were not; as to how they hurt, no one knows but my own soul and me.

So be it. The end is not yet. If I die I shall die hard, fighting to the last, and hell shall receive no fitter inmate than myself. But for good or ill, it shall be as it has been—alone.

Mabel, remember this: the time is past when any John Halifax Gentleman ethics can go down with me.[22] I don't care if the whole present, all I possess, were swept away from me—I will build a new present; If I am left naked and hungry to-morrow—before I give in I will go on naked and hungry; if I were a woman I would prostitute myself to all men but that I would succeed—in short, I will.

Am sorry that I have devoted so much to myself, and glad that you are better. How I would like to come down, and I shall if things come my way.

Frank has been playing the violin and Johnny[23] the devil in the room while I have been writing this, so you will forgive its disconnectedness.

Tell Ted I shall write in a couple of days, and ask him to explain more fully what he meant about that hymn which was enclosed.

Yours,
Jack

To Anna Strunsky

962 East 16th. st.
Oakland, Calif.
Dec. 21, 1899

Dear Miss Strunsky:

Surely am I a barbarian, lacking in cunning of speech and deftness of touch. Perhaps I am only a Philistine. Mayhap the economic man incarnate. At least blundering and rough-shod, lacking even that ex-

22. In Dinah Mulock's novel *John Halifax, Gentleman* (1857), a poor orphan boy achieves success through hard work, honesty, and an innate nobility of character.
23. Johnny Miller (1892–1966), son of Ida London Miller. His father, Frank H. Miller, had deserted the family shortly after Johnny was born. While JL was in the Klondike, Johnny had moved in permanently with Flora London and became part of the extended household JL supported.

pression which should properly voice my thoughts. I call for a trial by jury. I throw myself on the mercy of the Court. Nay, after all is said and done, I plead not guilty.

"Somehow it is a new note to me, that of being seen as 'aimless, helpless, hopeless,' and I am uneasy under it all."

I rarely remember what I say in letters, sometimes retaining only vague recollections of what I do not say; but in the present case I am sure I said nothing like the above. I speculated on you as impartially as had you been a hod-carrier, a Hottentot, or a Christ. It was a first speculation; it dealt with but one portion of your being. And as I could not divorce Christ or the Hottentot from the rest of humanity as having nothing in common with it, so I could not divest you of the weaknesses which I know your fellows to suffer from. But such weaknesses are not to be classed under your three-fold caption, "aimless, helpless, hopeless." I granted aim. I then asked myself whether you had the qualities by which to realize it. I did not answer that question, for verily I did not nor do I know. I was even more generous. I granted the basic qualities, all-necessary for attainment, and only questioned the existence of the medium by which they could be made to meet with their proper end. And that question I did not answer (to myself) for I did not know, nor do I know.

This is my case. I call for your verdict.

Somehow I am like a fish out of water. I take to conventionality uneasily, rebelliously. I am used to saying what I think, neither more than less. Soft equivocation is no part of me. As had I spoken to a man who came out of nowhere, shared my bed and board for a night, and passed on, so did I speak to you. Life is very short. The melancholy of materialism can never be better expressed than by Fitzgerald's "O make haste!" One should have no time to dally. And further, should you know me, understand this: I, too, was a dreamer, on a farm, nay, a California ranch. But early, at only nine, the hard hand of the world was laid upon me. It has never relaxed. It has left me sentiment, but destroyed sentimentalism. It has made me practical, so that I am known as harsh, stern, uncompromising. It has taught me that reason is mightier than imagination; that the scientific man is superior to the emotional man. It has also given me a truer and a deeper romance of things, an idealism which is an inner sanctuary and which must be resolutely throttled in dealings with my kind, but which yet remains within the holy of holies, like an oracle, to be cherished always but to be made manifest or be consulted not on every occasion I go to market. To do this latter would bring upon me the ridicule of my fellows and make me a failure. To sum up, simply the eternal fitness of things.

All of which goes to show that people are prone to misunderstand me. May I have the privilege of not so classing you?

Nay, I did not walk down the street after Hamilton—I ran. And I had a heavy overcoat, and I was very warm and breathless. The emotional man in me had his will, and I was ridiculous.

I shall be over Saturday night. If you draw back upon yourself, what have I left? Take me this way: a stray guest, a bird of passage, splashing with salt-rimed wings through a brief moment of your life —a rude and blundering bird, used to large airs and great spaces, unaccustomed to the amenities of confined existence. An unwelcomed visitor, to be tolerated only because of the sacred law of food and blanket.

Very sincerely,
Jack London

## To Houghton, Mifflin & Co.

962 East 16th. st.
Oakland, Calif.
Jan. 31, 1900

Gentlemen:

In reply to yours of January 25th. requesting additional biographical data.[24] I see I shall have to piece out my previous narrative, which, in turn, will make this choppy.

My father was Pennsylvania-born, a soldier, scout, backwoodsman, trapper, and wanderer.[25] My mother was born in Ohio. Both came west independently, meeting and marrying in San Francisco, where I was born January 12, 1876. What little city life I then passed was in my babyhood. My life, from my fourth to my ninth years, was spent upon Californian ranches.[26] I learned to read and write about my

---

24. Houghton Mifflin had accepted *The Son of the Wolf* on November 1, 1899. Presumably the request for biographical data was for advertising purposes. For another description of JL's early life, see JL to M. Applegarth, November 30, 1898.
25. John London (1828–97), JL's stepfather. He was born in Clearfield County, Pennsylvania, fought in the Civil War, and lived in Iowa before coming to California with three of his nine children. He married Flora Wellman on September 7, 1876. See JL to M. Applegarth, November 16, 1898, n. I.
26. Actually dirt farms in Emeryville, Alameda, San Mateo County, and Livermore.

fifth year, though I do not remember anything about it. I always could read and write, and have no recollection antedating such a condition. Folks say I simply insisted upon being taught. Was an omniverous reader, principally because reading matter was scarce and I had to be grateful for whatever fell into my hands. Remember reading some of Trowbridge's works for boys[27] at six years of age. At seven I was reading Paul du Chaillu's *Travels*, Captain Cook's *Voyages*, and *Life of Garfield*.[28] And all through this Period I devoured what Seaside Library novels[29] I could borrow from the womenfolk and dime novels from the farm hands. At eight I was deep in Ouida[30] and Washington Irving. Also during this period read a great deal of American history. Also, life on a Californian ranch is not very nourishing to the imagination.

Somewhere around my ninth year we removed to Oakland, which, today, I believe, is a town of about eighty thousand, and is removed by thirty minutes from the heart of San Francisco. Here, most precious to me was a free library. Since that time Oakland has been my home seat. Here my father died,[31] and here I yet live with my mother. I have not married—the world is too large and its call too insistent.

However, from my ninth year, with the exception of the hours spent at school (and I earned them by hard labor), my life has been one of toil. It is worthless to give the long sordid list of occupations, none of them trades, all heavy manual labor. Of course I continued to read. Was never without a book. My education was popular, graduating from the grammar school[32] at about fourteen. Took a taste for the water. At fifteen left home and went upon a Bay life. San Francisco

27. John Townsend Trowbridge (1827–1916), popular writer of boys' stories and didactic narrative poems. He was a regular contributor to *Our Young Folks* and *Youth's Companion*. Among his best-known works are *Cudjo's Cave* (1864), the *Jack Hazard Series* (1871–75), and the *Silver Medal Series* (1877–82).
28. Probably either *Lost in the Jungle* (1870) or *Stories of the Gorilla Country* (1868), both subtitled "Narrated for Young Children," by Paul Belloni du Chaillu (1831–1903), French writer of romantic adventure stories; James Cook, *The Voyages of Captain James Cook* (1842); William M. Thayer, *From Log-Cabin to White House: The Story of President Garfield's Life* (1881).
29. The Seaside Library was a series of inexpensive reprints of more than two thousand popular romance and adventure novels, begun in 1877 by the publisher George Munro.
30. The pseudonym of Marie Louise de la Ramée (1839–1908), English novelist and writer of children's stories. Her novel *Signa* (1875) was one of JL's favorite books in his youth. See JL to Humble, December 11, 1914.
31. John London died on October 15, 1897.
32. Cole Grammar School, in West Oakland.

Bay is no mill pond by the way. I was a salmon fisher, an oyster pirate, a schooner sailor, a fish patrolman, a longshoresman, and a general sort of bay-faring adventurer—a boy in years and a man amongst men.[33] Always a book, and always reading when the rest were asleep; when they were awake I was one with them, for I was always a good comrade.

Within a week of my seventeenth birthday I shipped before the mast as sailor on a three top-mast sealing schooner. We went to Japan and hunted along the coast north to the Russian side of Bering Sea. This was my longest voyage; I could not again endure one of such length; not because it was tedious or long, but because life was so short. However, I have made short voyages, too brief to mention, and to-day am at home in any forecastle or stokehole—good comradeship, you know. I believe this comprises my travels; for I spoke at length in previous letter concerning my tramping and Klondiking. Have been all over Canada, Northwest Ty. Alaska, etc. etc, at different times, besides mining, prospecting and wandering through the Sierra Nevadas.

I have outlined my education. In the main I am self-educated; have had no mentor but myself. High school or college curriculums I simply selected from, finding it impossible to follow the rut—life and pocket book were both too short. I attended the first year of high school (Oakland), then stayed at home, without coaching, and crammed the next two years into three months and took the entrance examinations, and entered the University of California at Berkeley.[34] Was forced, much against my inclinations, to give this over just prior to the completion of my Freshman Year.

My father died while I was in the Klondike, and I returned home to take up the reins.

As to literary work: My first magazine article (I had done no newspaper work), was published in January, 1899; it is now the sixth story in the *Son of the Wolf*.[35] Since then I have done work for the

---

33. See JL to Johns, March 30, 1899, n. 7, and JL to the Corresponding Editor, *Youth's Companion*, March 9, 1903.

34. JL neglects to mention that both Bessie Maddern and Fred Jacobs tutored him for his college entrance examinations. See JL to E. Applegarth, September 13, 1898, n. 3, and November 14, 1898, n. I.

35. JL's first magazine article was actually "Two Gold Bricks," *Owl*, September 1897, published while he was in the Klondike; he evidently did not know about this publication. "To the Man on Trail," published in the *Overland Monthly*, January 1899, is the fifth, not the sixth, story in *The Son of the Wolf*.

*Overland Monthly*, the *Atlantic*, the *Wave*, the *Arena*, the *Youth's Companion*, the *Review of Reviews*, etc. etc., besides a host of lesser publications, and to say nothing of newspaper and syndicate work. Hackwork all, or nearly so, from a comic joke or triolet to pseudo-scientific disquisitions upon things about which I knew nothing. Hackwork for dollars, that's all, setting aside practically all ambitious efforts to some future period of less financial stringency. Thus, my literary life is just thirteen months old to-day.

Naturally, my reading early bred in me a desire to write, but my manner of life prevented me attempting it. I have had no literary help or advice of any kind—just been sort of hammering around in the dark till I knocked holes through here and there and caught glimpses of daylight. Common knowledge of magazine methods, etc., came to me as revelation. Not a soul to say here you err and there you mistake.

Of course, during my revolutionaire period I perpetrated my opinions upon the public through the medium of the local papers, gratis. But that was years ago when I went to high school and was more notorious than esteemed. Once, by the way, returned from my sealing voyage, I won a prize essay of twenty-five dollars from a San Francisco paper over the heads of Stanford and California Universities, both of which were represented by second and third place through their undergraduates.[36] This gave me hope for achieving something ultimately.

After my tramping trip I started to high school in 1895. I entered the University of California in 1896. Thus, had I continued, I would be just now preparing to take my sheepskin.

As to studies: I am always studying. The aim of the university is simply to prepare one for a whole future life of study. I have been denied this advantage, but am knocking along somehow. Never a night (whether I have gone out or not) but the last several hours are spent in bed with my books. All things interest me—the world is so very good. Principal studies are, scientific, sociological, and ethical—these, of course, including biology, economics, psychology, physiology, history, etc. etc. without end. And I strive, also, to not neglect literature.

Am healthy, love exercise, and take little. Shall pay the penalty some day.

There, I can't think of anything else. I know what data I have furnished is wretched, but autobiography is not entertaining to a narrator who is sick of it. Should you require further information, just

36. JL refers to "Story of a Typhoon off the Coast of Japan."

specify, and I shall be pleased to supply it. Also, I shall be grateful for the privilege of looking over the biographical note before it is printed.

Very truly yours,
Jack London

To Cloudesley Johns

1130 East 15th. st.
Oakland, Calif.
June 16, 1900

Dear Cloudesley:

To commence with, you do me wrong. When you asked if I thought you could do the "Philosophy of the Road," I had no idea of what it was to be, that is, how it was to be treated, and so, did not have the slightest idea concerning whether you could do it or not. Further, when I wrote you, I overlooked that query—that was all. Had I remembered I would have spoken as I have spoken at the head of this paragraph. I do take a little of it back. I did think at the time that by experience you certainly were fitted for it.

It is a fascinating subject. It has itched me for long, and it is often all I can do to keep away from writing on it. However, I have been and am still laying aside notes on it,[37] so that, some day, saturating myself with the life again, I will go ahead. But as you say, it is infinite.

But Cloudesley, do you think you are handling it just right? I don't forget that they were written for "Stories and Sketches of the Road," nor that you say they will have to be re-written; but still I ask, are you going about it right. You are treating it in much the manner Wyckoff treated the Workers East and West.[38] But he treated it scientifically, and empirically scientifically, if I may use the phrase. And for that matter, he dealt more with the workers than with the tramps;

37. Later used as the basis for The Road.
38. Walter Augustus Wyckoff (1865–1908), professor of sociology at Princeton; The Workers: An Experiment in Reality, in two vols., The East (1897) and The West (1898). To learn firsthand about the life of the unskilled worker, Wyckoff, posing as a common laborer, traveled from Connecticut to California between 1891 and 1893. The Workers, his account of his observations, was considered an important contribution to the sociological literature; its realistic reports of the conditions of workers' lives also increased public awareness of the need for more adequate welfare programs.

but the method of treatment still applies. As it seems to me, you are to dry. You are not, from your choice of subjects or topics, treating it as he treated it. Therefore your style should be different. You are handling stirring life, romance, things of human life and death, humor and pathos, etc. But God, man, handle them as they should be. Don't you tell the reader the philosophy of the road (except where you are actually there as participant in the first person). Don't you tell the reader. Don't. Don't. Don't. But HAVE YOUR CHARACTERS TELL IT BY THEIR DEEDS, ACTIONS, TALK, ETC. Then, and not until then, are you writing fiction and not a sociological paper upon a certain sub-stratum of society.

And get the atmosphere. Get the breadth and thickness to your stories, and not only the length (which is the mere narration). The reader, since it is fiction, doesn't want your dissertations on the subject, your observations, your knowledge as your knowledge, your thoughts about it, your ideas—BUT PUT ALL THOSE THINGS WHICH ARE YOURS INTO THE STORIES, INTO THE TALES, ELIMINATING YOURSELF (except when in the first person as participant). AND THIS WILL BE THE ATMOSPHERE. AND THIS ATMOSPHERE WILL BE YOU, DON'T YOU UNDERSTAND, YOU! YOU! YOU! And for this, and for this only, will the critics praise you, and the public appreciate you, and your work be art. In short, you will then be the artist; do not do it, and you will be the artisan. That's where all the difference comes in. Study your detestable Kipling; study your Beloved's[39] *Ebb Tide*. Study them and see how they eliminate themselves and create things that live, and breathe, and grip men, and cause reading lamps to burn overtime. Atmosphere stands always for the elimination of the artist, that is to say, the atmosphere is the artist; and when there is no atmosphere and the artist is yet there, it simply means that the machinery is creaking and that the reader hears it.

And get your good strong phrases, fresh, and vivid. And write intensively, not exhaustively or lengthily. Don't narrate—paint! draw! build!—CREATE! Better one thousand words which are builded, than a whole book of mediocre, spun-out, dashed-off stuff.

Think it over and see if you catch what I am driving at. Of course, if you intend what I have called a scientific paper, then don't do anything of these things I have suggested. They would be out of place. But if you intend fiction, then write fiction from the highest standpoint of fiction. Don't be so damnably specific, adding dry detail to dry

39. Robert Louis Stevenson.

detail. Put in life, and movement—and for God's sake no creaking. Damn you! Forget you! And then the world will remember you. But if you don't damn you, and don't forget you, then the world will close its ears to you. Pour all yourself into your work until your work becomes you, but no where let yourself be apparent. When, in the *Ebb Tide*, the schooner is at the pearl island, and the missionary pearler meets those three desperate men and puts his will against theirs for life or death, does the reader think of Stevenson? Does the reader have one thought of the writer? Nay, nay. Afterwards, when all is over, he recollects, and wonders, and loves Stevenson—but at the time? Not he.

Do the wheels in Shakespeare creak? When Hamlet soliloquizes, does the reader think at the time that it is Shakespeare? But afterwards, ah afterwards, and then he says, "Great is Shakespeare!"

Do you see what I mean? Now please don't fall upon what I have written in spirit other than with which it was written. I've hammered it out hastily, and not done it justice, I know, but it has all been sincere.

I can't speak of the good points in the Mss., for I have devoted my space to generalities. But you show a good grasp of psychology, which will or should be a wonderful aid when you get the right method. But I can't go into that. Haven't time. Have to get ready to go out and want to get this off first.

However, let me thank you for sending me the Mss.

I shall not answer the rest of your short letter, though I appreciated it all and would like to.

Jack London

To George P. Brett

Piedmont, Calif.<br>March 10/03

Dear Mr. Brett:

I am glad you like the *Call of the Wild*; but, unfortunately, I cannot accept your offer for all rights in it.[40] You see, the *Saturday Evening Post* bought the American serial rights of it, and already have

---

40. In his letter to JL of March 5, 1903 (CSmH), Brett offered to buy the entire copyright of *The Call of the Wild* for $2000 cash.

sent me over half of the proof-sheets; while Watt & Son are handling the English serial sale of it.

The whole history of this story has been very rapid. On my return from England I sat down to write it into a 4000 word yarn, but it got away from me & I was forced to expand it to its present length. I was working on it when you came to see me in January. At the time I had made up my mind to let you carry the uncompleted duplicate away with you; but somehow the conversation did not lead up to it & I became diffident. Then I sent a copy to the *Saturday Evening Post* and they at once accepted it.

They have paid me three cents a word for the American serial rights. This was the money I intended dividing between my debts and my South Sea trip. But when it arrived last week, my debts loomed so large & the South Seas loomed so expensive, that I compromised matters and bought a sloop-yacht for San Francisco Bay. It is now hauled out & being fitted up. I shall live on it a great deal, and on it I shall write the greater part of my sea-novel. The sloop is old, but it is roomy & fast. I can stand upright in the cabin which is quite large. I'll send you a picture of her some time.

I did not like the title, *The Call of the Wild*, and neither did the *Saturday Evening Post*. I racked my brains for a better title, & suggested *The Sleeping Wolf*. They, however, if in the meantime they do not hit upon a better title, are going to publish it in the *Post* under *The Wolf*. This I do not like so well as *The Sleeping Wolf*, which I do not like very much either. There is a good title somewhere, if we can only lay hold of it.[41]

The *Saturday Evening Post*, as first buyer, reserved the right of setting date for simultaneous serial publication in England & America, so they would be the ones to write to in this connection. Of course, they will illustrate it.

I should have been glad to close with your offer, both for the sake of the cash & of the experiment you mention;[42] but, as I have explained, the serial right has passed out of my hands. As a book, however, under the circumstances as they are, you may succeed in getting a fair sale out of it.

I shall shortly make a rough sketch of the map for frontispiece of

41. The novel was serialized as *The Call of the Wild*.
42. Brett wrote in his letter of March 5: "I would like to try an experiment with the story, i.e., publish it in a little different form to the ordinary run of stories and possibly this might help, not only the book itself, but the general reputation of your books as well."

*Fish Patrol Stories*. The difficulty with *Youth's Companion* is that they may not publish it serially for a good time to come.

Will you please send me five copies of *Children of the Frost* (if they have not already been sent), and also, One copy of *Guns, Ammunition, and Tackle*,[43] & charge to my account.

Sincerely yours,
Jack London

## To Charmian Kittredge

[Oakland]
Wednesday, Sept. 30, 1903

Yes, Mrs. Browning was very delicate physically, but Browning was a robust heavily-built man.

Do you know, I have always wanted to live clean all my life. And I have always felt, with rare exceptions, that I was living clean. And at the end of a watch of coal-shoveling, say, naked to the waist and black as an Ethiopian, I have felt that I was very clean.[44] Because of the very work I had just done. I felt clean—clean inside, and you know what I mean.

The most repulsive grossness to me, I think is a grossness of the tissues. I have watched club-men thus grow gross from high-living, from gluttony, in short, but, worst of all, this grossness seems never to stop there, but goes on into the face and seems to stamp the very soul.[45]

I love good living and I am afraid of it; so I leave it alone, save at rare intervals, when it is very delightful and all that, as it is for a child to play with fire. These days I feel not only virtuous but very glad each time I sit down to a simple meal prepared by Maggie.[46] I

---

43. Capt. A. W. Money, Horace Kephart, W. E. Carlin, A. L. A. Himmelwright, and John Harrington Keene, *Guns, Ammunition, & Tackle*, which, according to the *National Union Catalog*, was not published by Macmillan until 1904.
44. In 1894 JL had shoveled coal in the boiler room of the power plant of the Oakland, San Leandro & Haywards Electric Railway.
45 Ed. note: *cf*. London's characterization of Trefethan in "The Night-Born."
46. Maggie Atherton, Frank's wife.

know that it is for the good of my body and the good of my soul, and for the good of something more—for my love for you. Never so much as now, never so strongly as clean as you are clean, and you are very clean, my woman, clean inside!

I guess the watch'll have to keep till Friday. Friday—when I shall see you with the light again on your face and love you in the ways different from those of the woods!

And in different ways still I shall love you Thursday night in the good salt water. And in still other and different ways I shall love you forever and forever.

## To Frederick I. Bamford

Glen Ellen, Cal.<br>May 28—1905

Dear Mr. Bamford, dear friend:

We are glad to hear that you are getting along so well and are so happy. It's too bad that you can only get your country in the expensive doses of the Sanitarium. Of course the baths and treatments are all right, but after all, they are not the main thing. The main thing is the country itself, and the fact that you are out of the high pressure of city life. If you could only manage some less expensive way of taking the country, you would be able to lengthen the dose. A tent, ten miles from a railroad station or a mail box, an axe to chop your own wood with, a bucket to carry your own water with, a couple of pots and a frying-pan to cook your own food in, and all the rest of the time for simply loafing, without meeting people who ask you to outline the life of Caesar, would be the one very thing for you. This is just my suggestion. I may not know anything about it at all, and I give it for what it is worth.

The thing is, to cease being intellectual altogether. To take delight in little things, the bugs and crawling things, the birds, the leaves, etc., etc. The thing is to get so keenly interested in decently cooking a pot of rice, that you will forget that there ever was a socialist revolution, or a library, or high school children getting books for collateral reading, or anything else under the sun except the one end—a decently-cooked pot of rice. You see what I'm driving at. The idea is capable of untold enlargement.

I was very much taken with *De Profundis*, but I'm not going to make you think any thoughts by telling you what I thought about it.[47]

Everybody here sends you love, in which I join.

Oh, by the way, next time we ride over to Burke's I sincerely hope that I shall meet one less person than I did last time—that woman who lugged you and me in out of the hay and the sunshine to sit in a stuffy room and talk little nothings, for instance. I haven't anything against this particular woman, but against her kind. I didn't ride over to Burke's to see her, but to see you. I didn't come to Glen Ellen to see people, but to get away from people. All this à propos of a line in your letter saying that there were some people over there who would like to meet me, and for me to come to the ten o'clock breakfast. When I come over, I shall come over to see you, and though quite willing and glad to meet Doctor Burke, would want to cut out all the rest. I consider such people vampires and I haven't any life-blood to waste upon them.

> Frankly and sincerely yours,
> Jack London

## To Cloudesley Johns

> Glen Ellen, Calif.
> Sep 4 1905

Dear Cloudesley

So you're going to begin writing for money! Forgive me for rubbing it in. You've changed since several years ago when you placed *ART* first and dollars afterward.[48] You didn't quite sympathize with me in those days.

After all, there's nothing like life; and I, for one, have always stood, and shall always stand, for the exalting of the life that is in me over Art, or any other extraneous things.

> Wolf

47. Bamford had given JL a copy of Oscar Wilde, *De Profundis* (1905).
48. See JL to Johns, September 26, 1899, January 30 and February 10, 1900. "Art" was underlined twice.

## To "Dear Comrades"

[New York]
[? December 1905]

Dear Comrades:

Here it is at last! The book we have been waiting for these many years! The *Uncle Tom's Cabin* of wage slavery! Comrade Sinclair's book *The Jungle*! And what *Uncle Tom's Cabin* did for black slaves, *The Jungle* has a large chance to do for the wage slaves of to-day.

It is essentially a book of to-day. The beautiful theoretics of Bellamy's *Looking Backward* are all very good. They served a purpose and served it well. *Looking Backward* was a great book, but I dare to say that *The Jungle*, which has no beautiful theoretics, is even a greater book.

It is alive and warm. It is brutal with life. It is written of sweat and blood and groans and tears. It depicts, not what man ought to be, but what man is compelled to be in this our world in the twentieth century. It depicts, not what our country ought to be, or what it seems to be in the fancies of Fourth-of-July spell-binders, the home of liberty and equality, of opportunity—but it depicts what our country really is, the home of oppression and injustice, a nightmare of misery, an inferno of suffering, a human hell, a jungle of wild beasts.

And there you have the very essence of Upton Sinclair's book— *The Jungle*! And that is what he has named it. This book must go. And you, comrades, must make it go. It is a labor of love on the part of the man who wrote it. It must be a labor of love on your part to distribute it.

And take notice and remember, comrades, this book is straight proletarian. And straight proletarian it must be throughout. It is written by an intellectual proletarian. It is written for the proletariat. It is published by a proletarian publishing house. It is to be read by the proletariat. And depend upon it, if it is not circulated by the proletariat it will not be circulated at all. In short, it must be a supreme proletarian effort.

Remember, this book must go out in the face of the enemy. No capitalist publishing house would dare to publish it.[49] It will be laughed at—some; jeered at—some; abused—some; but most of all, worst of

49. *The Jungle* was published by Doubleday, Page & Co. in 1906. See also JL to Bamford, October 2, 1905, n. 4.

all, the most dangerous treatment it will receive is that of silence. For that is the way of capitalism.

Comrades, do not forget the conspiracy of silence. Silence is the deadliest danger this book has to face. The book stands on its own merits. You have read it and you know. All that it requires is a hearing. This hearing you must get for it. You must not permit this silence. You must shout out this book from the housetops, at all times, and at all places. You must talk about it, howl about it, do everything but keep quiet about it. Open your mouths and let out your lungs, raise such a clamor that those in the high places will wonder what all the row is about and perchance feel tottering under them the edifice of greed they have reared.

All you have to do is to give this book a start. You have read the book yourselves, and you will vouch for it. Once it gets its start it will run away from you. The printers will be worked to death getting out larger and larger editions. It will go out by the hundreds of thousands. It will be read by every workingman. It will open countless ears that have been deaf to Socialism. It will plough the soil for the seed of our propaganda. It will make thousands of converts to our cause. Comrades, it is up to you!

Send Sinclair that $1.20 to-day.

> Yours for the Revolution,
> Jack London

## To S. S. McClure

[Glen Ellen]
Apr 10 1906

Dear Mr. McClure:

In reply to yours of April 3.[50] Life is so short and people so silly, that from the very beginning of my career, when I first began to get newspaper notoriety because of my youthful socialism, I made it a

---

50. McClure wrote JL, April 3, 1906 (CSmH): "People are sending us questions based on this parallel from the *World*. Can't you give us something to quote back at them?" An article in the *New York World*, March 25, 1906, entitled "Singular Similarity of a Story Written by Jack London and One Printed Four Years Before a New Literary Puzzle," gave a lengthy discussion of the "similarity in thought and phraseology" between "Love of Life" and Augustus Bridle and J. K. MacDonald's "Lost in the Land of the Midnight Sun" (published in *McClure's*, December 1901).

point to deny nothing charged against me in the newspapers. On the other hand, I have made it a courtesy to deny such things when requested to do so by my friends. Wherefore, because of your request, I am now making this explanation of the similarity between my "Love of Life" and Augustus Bridle's and J. K. MacDonald's "Lost in the Land of the Midnight Sun."

It is a common practice of authors to draw material for their stories, from the newspapers. Here are facts of life reported in journalistic style, waiting to be made into literature. So common is this practice that often amusing consequences are caused by several writers utilizing the same material. Some years ago, while I was in England, a story of mine was published in the *San Francisco Argonaut*. In the *Century* of the same date was published a story by Frank Norris.[51] While these two stories were quite different in manner of treatment, they were patently the same in foundation and motive. At once the newspapers paralleled our stories. The explanation was simple: Norris and I had read the same newspaper account, and proceeded to exploit it. But the fun did not stop there. Somebody dug up a *Black Cat* published a year previous, in which was a similar story by another man who used the same foundation and motive.[52] Then Chicago hustled around and resurrected a story that had been published some months before the *Black Cat* story, and that was the same in foundation and motive. Of course, all these different writers had chanced upon the same newspaper article.

So common is this practice of authors, that it is recommended by all the instructors in the art of the short story, to read the newspapers and magazines in order to get material. Charles Reade swore by this practice.[53] I might name a lengthy list of the great writers who have advised this practice.

All the foregoing merely to show that this practice exists and is generally employed by story-writers. Now to the "Love of Life," which the New York *World* so generously paralleled with "Lost in the Land of the Midnight Sun." "Lost in the Land of the Midnight Sun" is not a story. It is a narrative of fact. It was published in *McClure's Mag-*

---

51. London's story was "Moon-Face." Norris's was "The Passing of Cock-eye Blacklock," *Century*, July 1902. See Franklin Walker, "Frank Norris and Jack London," *Mills College Magazine*, Spring 1966, pp. 15–23.
52. Charles Forrest McLean, "An Exploded Theory," *Black Cat*, November 1901.
53. Charles Reade (1814–84), English dramatist and novelist. Reade explained his methodology through the character Rolfe in the novel *A Terrible Temptation* (1871).

*azine.* It tells the actual sufferings of a man with a sprained ankle in the country of the Coppermine River. It is not fiction, and it is not literature. I took the facts of life contained in it, added to them many other facts of life gained from other sources, and made, or attempted to make, a piece of literature out of them. There was another narrative of suffering that I used quite as extensively as I did "Lost in the Land of the Midnight Sun." This other narrative was a newspaper account of a lost and wandering prospector near Nome, Alaska. On top of this, I drew upon all my own personal experience of hardship and suffering and starvation, and upon the whole fund of knowledge I had of the hardship and suffering and starvation of hundreds and thousands of other men.

If you will turn to the end of my "Love of Life," you will find that my rescued hero becomes suddenly fat. This abrupt obesity was caused by his stuffing under his shirt all the spare hardtack he could beg from the sailors. Now I did not invent this. It is a fact of life. You will find it in Lieutenant Greely's narrative of the Greely Polar Expedition.[54] I scarcely see how I could be charged with plagiarizing from Lieut. Greely; and yet if I plagiarized from Augustus Bridle and J. K. MacDonald for some of my material, I must have plagiarized from Lieut. Greely for some more of my material. And I must have plagiarized from the newspaper correspondent who described the wanderings of the Nome prospector, and I must have plagiarized from the experiences of scores and scores of Alaskan prospectors whose accounts I have heard from their own lips.

The *World,* however, did not charge me with plagiarism. It charged me with identity of time and situation. Certainly the *World* is right. I plead guilty, and I am glad that the *World* was intelligent enough not to charge me with identity of language.

But little remains to be said. It might be well to explain how that half-page of deadly parallel was published in the *World.* In the first place, SENSATION. Sensation is the goods demanded by a newspaper of its space-writers. The suggestion of plagiarism is always sensational. When a half-page of deadly parallel is run in a newspaper, plagiarism is certainly suggested. The loose meaning of words in the average mind would make ninety percent of the readers of such a parallel infer that plagiarism had been charged.

54. Adolphus W. Greely, *Three Years of Arctic Service: An Account of the Lady Franklin Bay Expedition of 1881–84 and the Attainment of the Farthest North* (1886). Several members of Greely's party died of starvation when relief supplies failed to reach them.

Secondly, the space-writer writes for a living. I hope for his own soul's sake that this particular space-writer also writes for his living. His newspaper wanted the goods of sensation, and by refusing to charge plagiarism, while leaving the inference of plagiarism to the reader, this space-writer sold half a page to the *World*.

In conclusion, I, in the course of making my living by turning journalism into literature, used material from various sources which had been collected and narrated by men who made their living by turning the facts of life into journalism. Along comes the space-writer on the *World* who makes his living by turning the doings of other men into sensation. Well, all three of us made our living; and who's got any kick coming?

Sincerely yours,
Jack London

P.S. Dear Mr. McClure: You are at liberty to use the whole foregoing letter any way you see fit. I should like to see it published in the *World*, incidentally. But I should not like to see it "revised."

## To George Sterling

Glen Ellen, Cal.
June 24, 1906

Dearest Greek!

If Hillquit and Hunter[55] didn't put it all over Bierce—I'll quit thinking at all.

Bierce's clever pessimism was nowhere against their science. He proved himself rudderless, compassless, and chartless. Bierce doesn't shine in a face to face battle with socialists. He's best at long range slinging ink. He was groggy at the drop of the hat and before they got done with him was looking anxiously around and wondering why the gong didn't ring.

All he did was to back and fill and potter around, dogmatize and contradict himself. When they cornered him, he went off on another tack, whereupon they'd overtake him and lambast him again.

Bierce, with biological and socialogical concepts that crystalized

55. Morris Hillquit (1869–1933), lawyer and Socialist Party candidate for mayor of New York in 1912, and Robert Hunter (1874–1942), author and candidate for governor of Connecticut on the Socialist Party ticket in 1910.

in the fervent heat of pessimism a generation ago, was—well, pathetic. And more pathetic still, he doesn't know it.

Wolf

## To the Editor of *Editor* Magazine

[Oakland]
[? April 1907]

1. I should advise the young story-writer to leave the old masters in literature alone, if he wishes to sell stories to the present-day magazines.[56] I should advise the young story-writer to study the stories in the current magazines; in this case, if he has anything in him he will succeed in selling stories to the modern editors. But I must append this warning: HE WILL SUCCEED WITH THE EDITORS OF TO-DAY; BUT IN THE CENTURIES TO COME HE WILL NOT HIMSELF BE ACCREDITED A MASTER IN LITERATURE.

2. No, the unknown writer has not an equal chance with the well-known author, even though his work is up to the standard of the latter. The unknown writer's work must be BETTER than the known author's work, in order for it to be accepted by the first-class magazines.

3. A well-told story with a weak plot is vastly more acceptable than a poorly-told story with a strong plot.

4. I consider the primary weakness in the average stories and verses of the younger writers to be lack of guts and plenitude of conventionality.

5. Observation, originality, imagination, sincerity, plus natural

56. For its article "The Royal Road to Authorship," the *Editor* requested a number of writers—including JL, Mark Twain, Gertrude Atherton, Owen Wister, and Mary E. Wilkins Freeman—to answer the following questions: "(1) Would you advise the young story writer to study the old masters in literature, or the stories in current magazines, in order to meet the demands of the modern editors? (2) Has the unknown writer an equal chance with the well-known author, provided his work is up to the standard of the latter's? (3) Which is the more acceptable—a well-told story with a weak plot, or a poorly-told story with a strong plot? (4) What do you consider the primary weakness in the average stories or verses of the younger writers? (5) What are the successful author's necessary qualifications in the matters of natural ability, education, life as he sees and lives it, technical training, etc.? (6) Do you care to offer any hints or suggestions, gleaned from your personal experiences in the climb to success, that may make easier the gaining of the heights for the beginner?"

ability, are the qualifications I consider necessary for the successful author. If he has the foregoing he is well educated. It won't take him long to learn grammar. Technical training will take time, and by technical training I mean mastery of form and expression. But if he have the foregoing qualifications, he'll master technical training.

6. The biggest hint I have to offer to the beginner is that he be not a slave to convention; that he build not as his fathers built; that he think for himself, and that he accept truth wherever he finds it, and not because it is garbed in fine linen and goes prancing around in an automobile or a church pulpit, a university-chair, or an editor's sanctum. In short, my hint is that the young writer who expects to become a great writer must think beyond the mass of his fellow-creatures, and that the mass of his fellow-creatures thinks along the same lines as think the preachers, the professors, and the editors.

Jack London

## To Becky London

Penduffry, Guadalcanar
Solomon Islands
Oct. 28, 1908

Dear Bess:

I am sending you in this letter two ear-rings which the savages wear here.

Joan tells me in her letter that you have a new tooth. Well, well, I am different from you. I get old teeth—from the savages. I pull them out. I pulled out one to-day for a big black cannibal. He groaned very much.[57]

Tell mama that I say that the pearls and rings and all the things I send you and Joan, are for you to have and use now. Never mind waiting until you are older.

When I was a little boy I liked candy. I never got any candy. By and by, they told me, when I was older I could eat all the candy I wanted. But when I was older my teeth were aching and I could not eat much candy.

Tell Joan I am writing a novel and that I have named the girl in

---

57. JL described his amateur dentistry in "The Amateur M.D."

it Joan.[58] When you are older I shall name a girl in one of my books after you. With a whole armful of love,

Daddy

## To Richard W. Gilder

Sydney, N.S.W., Australia
December 22, 1908

Dear Mr. Gilder:

I have been sick for many weeks now, am just out of hospital and pretty weak and wabbly, with a mass of correspondence piled up that almost gives me a collapse every time I look at it. Somewhere in that mountain of letters is a bunch of correspondence relating to "To Build a Fire." I cannot find it, and shall have to go on memory.

A long, long time ago I wrote a story for boys which I sold to the *Youth's Companion*. It was purely juvenile in treatment. Its motif was not only very strong, but was very true. Man after man in the Klondike has died alone after getting his feet wet, through failure to build a fire. As the years went by, I was worried by the inadequate treatment I had given that motif, and by the fact that I had treated it for boys merely. At last came the resolve to take the same motif and handle it for men. I had no access to the boys' version of it, and I wrote it just as though I had never used the motif before. I do not remember anything about the way I handled it for juveniles, but I do know, I am absolutely confident, that beyond the motif itself, there is no similarity of treatment whatever.[59]

I can only say that it never entered my head that there was anything ethically wrong in handling the same motif over again in the way I did, and I can only add that I am of the same opinion now, upon carefully considering the question. Please let me know how you feel about the matter.

Sincerely yours,
Jack London

58. The heroine of *Adventure* is named Joan Lackland.
59. Gilder was the Editor of *Century Magazine*, which published the 1908 version of London's story.

P.S.—My sickness is of so serious a nature that I am compelled to abandon the voyage of the *Snark* and to return to my own climate of California. The doctors in Australia can do nothing for me, because they do not know what is the matter with me. My trouble is nervous in origin; and all I can prescribe for myself is to return to an environment where I maintained a stable nervous equilibrium, in the hope of regaining that equilibrium.

## To William E. Walling

[Glen Ellen]
Nov 30 1909

My dear Walling:

In reply to yours of Nov. 24.[60] I am writing you immediately. Having been buried down in the South Seas for a couple of years, I am not now closely in touch with the socialist movement in the United States, so that everything in your letter has been news to me. I am forwarding your letter immediately to various socialists in California.

Depend upon me for one thing. I am a hopelessly non-compromising revolutionist, and I shall stand always for keeping the socialist party rigidly revolutionary. Any compromise such as an affiliation with the American Federation of Labor would be at this time suicidal.[61] Australia is a splendid example of this. They started a splendid socialist movement there, began to compromise in order to gain strength, and then became lost in the political organized labor movement, so that to-day, in my opinion, from the socialist viewpoint, Australia is more backward and far worse off than the United States. There is a little handful of struggling revolutionists down there and some pretty good fighting-men; but they are all too few. The labor-party swamps them out.

60. William English Walling (1877–1936), a founder of the Intercollegiate Socialist Society, the Women's Trade Union League, and the National Association for the Advancement of Colored People; married to Anna Strunsky in 1906. Walling wrote JL on November 24, 1909 (CSmH), that the Executive Committee of the Socialist Party was determined "to maintain themselves in office against all opposition, and . . . to form a labor party (more or less socialistic)."

61. Algie M. Simons, a founder of the American Socialist Party and former editor of the *International Socialist Review*, had written Walling to suggest that the Socialist Party affiliate with the American Federation of Labor, an organization which he felt more nearly represented the working class.

If the socialist movement in the United States goes in for opportunism, then it's Hurray for the Oligarchy and the Iron Heel, or, speaking seriously, it would mean a set-back of twenty years to the movement, at least, and heaven only knows how much more serious such a catastrophe would be.

Yours for the Revolution,
Jack London

## To the Editor, *Honolulu Advertiser*

[Glen Ellen]
Jan. 7, 1910

Dear sir:

Is the Territory of Hawaii to become part of the Twentieth Century world, or is it to remain provincial, like any backwoods settlement? I am prompted to make this query because of "The Bystander" who, on the staff of *The Advertiser,* has made some most provincial and untrue remarks about me.[62] I do not make reference to the letters of subscribers and readers, wherein I have been assailed, because a newspaper is supposed to publish communications from its subscribers and readers, even though they be lunatics or feeble-minded *cretins.*

But The Bystander is on the staff of *The Advertiser.* He sells his wit and *The Advertiser* buys, because it considers his wit is modern, worthwhile and up-to-date.

Here is some of the abuse which has been heaped upon me by The Bystander: I am a "sneak of the first water, a thoroughly untrustworthy man, and an ungrateful and untruthful bounder." Also, I am

---

62. "The Bystander" was the pseudonym of Lorrin A. Thurston (1858–1931), publisher of the *Honolulu Advertiser.* Thurston had befriended the Londons during their visit to Hawaii on the *Snark* cruise, and he and his wife accompanied them to the Haleakala Ranch on the island of Maui in July 1907. Later, however, Thurston came to feel that JL had maligned Hawaii. In "Jack London Takes His Pen in Hand—Novelist Writes and Receives Reply," *Honolulu Sunday Advertiser,* May 22, 1910, apparently repeating his comments from the earlier "Bystander" column, Thurston wrote: "Now, I look upon London as a sneak of the first water, a thoroughly untrustworthy man and an ungrateful and untruthful bounder. This is the result of his two latest Hawaiian stories, in both of which he has made the worst out of the leprosy situation here, distorted facts, invented others when the truth was not enough to suit his purpose and thoroughly misrepresented conditions."

a "dirty little sneak." Not only is the flavor of Bystander's vituperage essentially that of the backwoods, but so also are the untruths against me which he states and upon which he bases his vituperation.

Bystander accuses me of having been granted privileges by the authorities to visit the Leper Settlement at Molokai, and then of having abused those privileges by writing sensational and untrue short-stories about Molokai.

Now, here are the facts: by the consent of the authorities, I visited Molokai, and I wrote an article on Molokai that was so satisfactory to the authorities that the stamp of approval was given to it for publication to the world.[63]

Incidentally, I wrote a couple of short-stories dealing with leprosy, locating one on the Kona Coast of Hawaii, and the other on the Island of Niihau.[64] Both these stories were avowedly stories, things of fiction; and furthermore, they did not deal with Molokai, nor with any of the knowledge that I had gained while I was at Molokai. I have been interested in leper settlements for years, and have visited other leper settlements and lazar-houses before I ever came to Hawaii. Not only have my two short-stories nothing to do with the leper settlement on Molokai, but no data in those two short-stories was gathered on Molokai. And when Bystander says that I violated my promises to the authorities, made when I went to visit the leper settlement on Molokai, why said Bystander not only lies, but deliberately lies.

It is the perfect provincial note, to state absolute untruths concerning a stranger's visit to one's backwoods section, and upon this basis to rear an edifice of abuse. This is what Bystander has done, and has been countenanced in doing by the editor of the *Advertiser*.

And now, Mr. Editor, let me give you a few facts of my visit to Hawaii. I came to Hawaii on my own, subsidized by nobody; nor did Hawaii subsidize me, nor did I ask Hawaii to subsidize me. I paid my way on the steamer to Molokai, and I paid my way back on the steamer from Molokai. I spent a few thousands of dollars in Hawaii, and there is no man in Hawaii who can lift up his voice and say that I owe him one cent. On the other hand I can lift up my voice and say that the citizens of Hawaii owe me, and owe me a great many cents —that the dwellers of Hawaii, instead of subsidizing me, some of them, at any rate, played very deft and gentlemanly games of robbing me.

63. "The Lepers of Molokai."
64. "The Sheriff of Kona," *American Magazine*, August 1909, included in *The House of Pride*; and "Koolau the Leper."

On the other hand, I want to say that I was gloriously entertained by a number of persons in Hawaii; that I received a height of hospitality that cannot be excelled anywhere else on the earth; and that my heart goes out in love and appreciation to numerous friends that I made in Hawaii. But I wish to point out this weakness of Hawaii: namely, of elevating every chance visitor to its shores on a pedestal, seemingly for the purpose of casting potsherds at him. I had scarcely left the shores of Hawaii myself, when the papers let loose with an attack upon me charging me with having issued worthless checks. Bystander says that I was treated like a lion. All I can say is that it was a darned funny way to treat a lion. Again, I reiterate, this is the provincial note struck by Hawaii. And the sooner Hawaii gets over it the better. Of what use is a Promotion Committee, and of public broadminded citizens, when they allow a set of mediocre reporters to set their ethical newspaper pace for them and mould their opinions for them? So long as Hawaii is satisfied with the opinions of men of the caliber of Bystander, just that long is Hawaii contented to be provincial.

Sincerely yours,
Jack London

## To the "Comrades of the Mexican Revolution"

[Los Angeles]
[? February 4, 1911]

To the dear, brave comrades of the Mexican Revolution:[65]

We socialists, anarchists, hobos, chicken thieves, outlaws and undesirable citizens of the United States are with you heart and soul in your efforts to overthrow slavery and autocracy in Mexico. You will notice we are not respectable in these days of the reign of property. All the names you are being called, we have been called. And when graft and greed get up and begin to call names, honest men, brave

65. On February 5, 1911, socialists in Los Angeles held a rally at the Labor Temple to express support for Mexicans opposing the military dictatorship of Porfirio Diaz. JL had been invited to speak at the meeting. Unable to attend, he wrote instead this open letter. His support for the revolution was expressed in his story "The Mexican," *Saturday Evening Post*, August 19, 1911; included in *The Night-Born*.

men, patriotic men and martyrs can expect nothing else than to be
called chicken thieves and outlaws.

So be it. But I for one wish that there were more chicken thieves
and outlaws of the sort that formed the gallant band that took Mexicali,[66] of the sort that is heroically enduring the prison holes of Diaz,
of the sort that is fighting and dying and sacrificing in Mexico today.

I subscribe myself a chicken thief and a revolutionist,

Jack London.

To Ethan A. Cross

[Glen Ellen]
March 17, 1914

Dear Mr. Cross:

In reply to your letter of Jan. 31, 1914,[67] which I find was answered by Mrs. London in my absence, on Feb. 8, 1914. I am now
home again, and am hastening to write to you.

Go ahead and use "Samuel" in your book. Consider this letter
full permission. "Samuel" has not yet appeared in book form, but will
shortly appear in a collection of short stories published by The Macmillan Company.

I am convinced that the publication of "Samuel" in your book
will be of distinct advantage to me; and I hereby say go ahead and so
publish "Samuel," and impose upon you but one stipulation—that you
let me have several copies of the book when published.

Just a line of information upon our magazine policy in the United
States today. "Samuel" was hawked about by me to every big maga-

66. In February 1911, Mexican revolutionaries, along with members of the
International Workers of the World, seized Mexicali and set up the Socialist Republic of Lower California. Shortly thereafter the U.S. government had the leaders
arrested for violation of the neutrality laws between Mexico and the United States;
newspapers erroneously reported that JL was among those arrested.

67. Ethan A. Cross (1875–1962), professor of literature and English from 1906 to
1941 at Colorado State College of Education at Greeley. He first wrote JL on
December 19, 1911 (CSmH), for permission to use "The God of His Fathers" in
his forthcoming textbook, *The Short Story: A Technical and Literary Study* (1914).
When Doubleday refused permission to include that story, Cross, in his letter to
JL, January 31, 1914 (CSmH), asked to use "Samuel" instead. "Samuel" appeared
in the anthology, with the copyright information JL requested and a brief analysis
by Cross, who called the story "a true impression of life."

zine in the U.S., and was invariably refused. After years had passed, I let *The Bookman* have it, and, of course you know that for a high-pay short story writer like me, it meant, that with a magazine like *The Bookman*, that I was letting the story go for a song.

Personally, how can you account for the averseness of the American magazine editors regarding stories such as "Samuel"? I have always found this so with practically all of my best short stories—or what I deemed my best short stories; and I am frank to say that my best short stories, not by 99%, have been written because of this averseness of the American magazine editor to tackle a story that I, in my own judgment thought was a real story.

Sincerely yours,
Jack London

P.S. Referring again to your use of "Samuel," I must impress upon you particularly that you must be CERTAIN to publish, at bottom of first page, notice of my *Bookman* copyright, and also of my Macmillan copyright (date not yet arranged); otherwise I shall lose my copyright in "Samuel."

## To Joseph Conrad

Honolulu, T.H.
June 4, 1915

Dear Joseph Conrad:

The mynah birds are waking the hot dawn about me. The surf is thundering in my ears where it falls on the white sand of the beach, here at Waikiki, where the green grass at the roots of the coconut palms insists to the lip of the wave-wash. This night has been yours —and mine.

I had just begun to write when I read your first early work. I have merely madly appreciated you and communicated my appreciation to my friends through all these years. I never wrote you. I never dreamed to write you. But *Victory* has swept me off my feet, and I am inclosing herewith a carbon copy of a letter written to a friend at the end of this lost night's sleep.

Perhaps you will appreciate this lost night's sleep when I tell you that it was immediately preceded by a day's sail in a Japanese sampan of sixty miles from the Leper Settlement of Molokai (where Mrs. London and I had been revisiting old friends) to Honolulu.[68]

On your head be it.

Aloha (which is a sweet word of greeting, the Hawaiian greeting, meaning "my love be with you").[69]

Jack London

To Ethelda Hesser

Glen Ellen, California
September 21, 1915

Dear Ethelda Hesser:[70]

In belated reply to yours of August 9, 1915:

I have been away traveling, and have just returned home to wade into a mountain of correspondence. Hence, not only my belatedness, but, also, my asking you to forgive the brevity of this, my reply to your letter.

I am not sure that I agree with you that *The Little Lady of the Big House* is not good work. I am rather proud of that novel, myself.

68. The Londons sailed for Molokai on the *Likelike* on May 25. They visited the leper colony and Edward Goodhue on May 28 and 29 and returned to Honolulu on May 31.
69. Joseph Conrad responded in a letter to JL of September 10, 1915 (CSmH): "I am immensely touched by the kindness of your letter—that apart from intense satisfaction given me by the approval of an accomplished fellow-craftsman and a true brother in letters—of whose personality and art I have been intensely aware for many years. A few days before it reached me Percival Gibbon (a short-story writer and a most distinguished journalist and war corresp.) and I were talking you over endlessly, in the quiet hours of the night. Gibbon, who had just returned after 5 months on the Russian front, had been taking you in bulk, soaking himself in your prose. And we admired the vehemence of your strength and the delicacy of your perception with the greatest sympathy and respect. I haven't seen your latest yet. The reviews such as come my way are enthusiastic. The book is in my home but I wait to finish a thing (short) I am writing now before I sit down to read you. It'll be a reward for being a good industrious boy. For it is not easy to write here nowadays. At this very moment there is a heavy burst of gunfire in Dover. I can hear the quick firers and the big guns—and wonder what it is. The night before last a Zep passed over the house (not the first time) bound west on that raid on London of which you would have read already in your papers. Moreover I've just now a quonty wrist. This explains my clumsy handwriting. And so no more—this time. Keep me in your kind memory and accept a grateful and cordial handgrasp."
70. Ethelda Hesser, housewife and neophyte writer from Louisville, Kentucky.

Possibly you have been led astray in your judgment by the illustrations—as you suggested in your letter.[71]

I have two daughters going to high school at the present time and I assure you, in reply to your question, that after having come through all of the game of life, and of youth, at my present mature age of thirty-nine years I am firmly and solemnly convinced that the game is worth the candle.[72] I have had a very fortunate life, I have been luckier than many hundreds of millions of men in my generation have been lucky, and, while I have suffered much, I have lived much, seen much, and felt much that has been denied to the average man. Yes, indeed, the game is worth the candle. As a proof of it, my friends all tell me I am getting stout. That, in itself, is the advertisement of spiritual victory. Thanking you for your good letter,

Sincerely yours,
Jack London

## To John R. Lindmark

[Glen Ellen]
Sep. 21, 1915

Dear Lindmark:[73]

I am an idealist who believes in reality, and who, therefore, in all I write strive to be *real*, to keep both my own feet and the feet of my readers on the ground so that no matter how high we dream our dreams will be based on reality.

Jack London

71. Hesser wrote on August 9, 1915 (CSmH), to praise JL for *John Barleycorn, Martin Eden*, and *The Call of the Wild* and to express her disappointment in *The Little Lady of the Big House*, which she had been reading serially in *Cosmopolitan*. She felt that Howard Chandler Christy's "nincompoop pictures" may have spoiled the novel for her. See JL to Cotter, June 18, 1915.
72. Hesser, who had not placed any of her stories in magazines, asked JL if he thought "the [writing] game worth the candle." "It is a poor sport that is not worth the candle," George Herbert, *Jacula Prudentum* (1640).
73. John R. Lindmark, a bookseller in Poughkeepsie, New York. He wrote JL on August 26, 1915 (CSmH), asking for "a letter reinforcing in some strong and succinct way the motif of your muse," to be used in an advertising promotion to increase the sale of JL's books.

To Mary Austin

Glen Ellen, California<br>November 5, 1915

Dear Mary Austin:[74]

In reply to yours of October 26, 1915:

Your letter strikes me that you are serious. Now, why be serious with this bone-head world? Long ere this, I know that you have learned that the majority of the people who inhabit the planet Earth are bone-heads. Wherever the bone of their heads interferes there is no getting through.

I have read and enjoyed every bit of your "Jesus Christ" book as published serially in the *North American Review*. What if it does not get across?[75]

I have again and again written books that failed to get across. Long years ago, at the very beginning of my writing career, I attacked Nietzsche and his super-man idea. This was in *The Sea Wolf*. Lots of people read *The Sea Wolf*, no one discovered that it was an attack upon the superman philosophy. Later on, not mentioning my shorter efforts, I wrote another novel that was an attack upon the super-man idea, namely, my *Martin Eden*. Nobody discovered that this was such an attack. At another time I wrote an attack on ideas brought forth by Rudyard Kipling, and entitled my attack "The Strength of the Strong." No one was in the slightest way aware of the point of my story.

I am telling you all the foregoing merely to show that it is a very bone-head world indeed, and, also, that I never bother my head when my own books miss fire. And the point I am making to you is: why worry? Let the best effort of your heart and head miss fire. The best

74. Mary Austin (1868–1934), essayist, novelist, and playwright who was a founder of the artists and writers colony in Carmel. At this time, she was in New York and had turned from her earlier, more regional writing to issues of socialism, feminism, and religion.

75. In her letter of October 26, 1915 (CSmH), Austin complained that the point of her book *The Man Jesus; Being a Brief Account of the Life and Teaching of the Man of Nazareth* (1915) had been missed: "nobody seems to have discovered that I have said that Christian banking should be administered on behalf of those who serve rather than those who own. I thought that was a fairly suggestive conclusion—that a man could borrow money on his capacity to serve society rather than on his wife's diamonds." Austin's book appeared in *The North American Review* from June to November 1915.

effort of my heart and head has missed fire with you, as it has missed fire with practically everybody else in the world who reads, and I do not worry about it. I go ahead content to be admired for my red-blood brutality and for a number of other nice little things like that which are not true of my work at all.

Heavens, have *you* read *my* "Christ" story?[76] I doubt that anybody has read this "Christ" story of mine, though it has been published in book form on both sides of the Atlantic. Said book has been praised for its red-bloodedness and no mention has been made of my handling of the Christ situation in Jerusalem at all.

I tell you this, not because I am squealing, which I am not; but to show you that you are not alone in this miss-firing. Just be content with being called the "greatest American stylist."[77]

Those who sit alone must sit alone. They must continue to sit alone. As I remember it, the prophets and seers of all times have been compelled to sit alone except at such times when they were stoned or burned at the stake. The world is mostly bone-head and nearly all boob, and you have no complaint if the world calls you the "great stylist" and fails to recognize that your style is merely the very heart and soul of your brain. The world has an idea that style is something apart from heart and brain. Neither you nor I can un-convince the world of that idea.

I do not know what more I can say, except, that, had I you here with me for half an hour I could make my point more strongly, namely, that you are very lucky, and that you should be content to receive what the world gives you. The world will never give you due recognition for your "Christ" book. I, who never read serials, read your serial of the Christ and turned always to it first when my *North American Review* came in. I am not the world, you are not the world. The world feeds you, the world feeds me, but the world knows damn little of either of us.

Affectionately yours,
Jack London

76. *The Star Rover*, chap. 17.
77. In her letter of October 26 Austin wrote: "You don't know how tired I get of being called 'the greatest American stylist'—and there is H. G. Wells putting me on a lonely pedestal alongside Stephen Crane."

## To the Members of Local Glen Ellen, Socialist Labor Party

Honolulu
March 7, 1916

Dear Comrades:

I have just finished reading Comrade Edward B. Payne's resignation from the Local, of recent date, undated.

I am herewith tendering my own resignation from Local Glen Ellen, and for the diametrical opposite reason from the one instanced by Comrade Payne. I am resigning from the Socialist Party because of its lack of fire and fight, and its loss of emphasis on the class struggle.

I was originally a member of the old, revolutionary, up-on-its-hind-legs, fighting, Socialist Labor Party. Since then, and to the present time, I have been a fighting member of the Socialist party. My fighting record in the Cause is not, even at this late date, already entirely forgotten. Trained in the class struggle, as taught and practiced by the Socialist Labor Party, my own highest judgment concurring, I believed that the working class, by fighting, by never fusing, by never making terms with the enemy, could emancipate itself. Since the whole trend of socialism in the United States of recent years has been one of peaceableness and compromise, I find that my mind refuses further sanction of my remaining a party member. Hence my resignation.

Please include my comrade wife, Charmian K. London's, resignation with mine.

My final word is that liberty, freedom, and independence, are royal things that cannot be presented to, nor thrust upon, races or classes. If races and classes cannot rise up and by their own strength of brain and brawn wrest from the world liberty, freedom, and independence, they never, in time, can come to these royal possessions—and if such royal things are kindly presented to them by superior individuals, on silver platters, they will know not what to do with them, will fail to make use of them, and will be what they have always been in the past—inferior races and inferior classes.

Yours for the Revolution,
Jack London

To Leo B. Mihan

Glen Ellen, California
October 24, 1916

Dear Leo:[78]

I was down in bed, but the malady was not serious. It was merely damn painful, being, namely, rheumatism, of the acute kind. Charmian and I hope to see more of you up here on the ranch.

I have quite a few books on psychoanalysis, which you would have access to any time you are visiting us. Also, I have just recently subscribed to the *Psychoanalytic Review*,[79] which is a quarterly. Doctor Jung's book is a very remarkable book to me, and I do not hesitate to assert that you are no more excited about it than am I.[80] It is big stuff. I used to rave to Hamilton[81] about it when he was here.

I am leaving in a few days on my delayed trip to New York, but shall be back by the first of the year, and shall look forward to your seeing your way to come up and spend a real visit with us when there are not so many distracting persons around as there were last time.

Sincerely yours,
Jack London

78. Leo B. Mihan, a friend who lived in Berkeley.
79. Published in New York from 1913 to 1957.
80. On October 8, 1916 (CSmH), Mihan wrote: "I am now reading what to my mind is the greatest revelatory . . . book since Darwin's *Origin of Species*—Dr. Jung's *Psychology of the Unconscious*." For JL's notes and markings in Carl Jung's *Psychology of the Unconscious: A Study of the Transformations and Symbolisms of the Libido, a Contribution to the History of the Evolution of Thought* (1916), see David Mike Hamilton, *"The Tools of My Trade": The Annotated Books in Jack London's Library* (Seattle, 1986), pp. 175–76; see also James I. McClintock, "Jack London's Use of Carl Jung's *Psychology of the Unconscious*," *American Literature*, 42 (November 1970): 336–47.
81. Frank Strawn-Hamilton.

To Waldo Frank

Glen Ellen, California
November 5, 1916

My dear Mr. Frank:

In reply to your good letter of October 24, 1916—[82]

Two things prevent me from being kind to you in this matter of manuscripts of short stories which I have filed away on the shelf, and which have not been published.

First, there ain't no such short stories. Second, if there were, my contracts, which are exclusive, and blanket, would prevent me from permitting any one to publish such stories.

I am replying to your letter immediately, so that I have not yet had the pleasure of reading a copy of *The Seven Arts* which you mention having mailed to me.

I do not mind telling you that had the United States been as kindly toward the short story writer as France has always been kindly, from the beginning of my writing career I would have written many a score of short stories quite different from the ones I have written.

Sincerely yours,
Jack London

82. Waldo Frank (1889–1967), critic, novelist, and founder and editor of *The Seven Arts*, a monthly "little magazine" published in New York from November 1916 to October 1917. He wrote JL on October 24, 1916 (ULA), that he "had heard through several friends—Nina Wilcox Putnam and Theodore Dreiser among others" about "some short stories which are so good that you have been unable to sell them." Frank wanted one of them for *The Seven Arts*.

# SUGGESTIONS FOR
# FURTHER READING

THE REMARK that "more bad literature has been written about London ... than he wrote himself" is more pertinent today than when Harry Hartwick made it in 1934. No other American writer—not even Poe —has inspired so much misinformed biography and wrongheaded criticism. The canards about London's alleged pessimism, drug addiction, and suicide—as blatant examples—have persisted in the face of abundant evidence to the contrary, as have the half-truths about his alcoholism, racism, and sexism. To date, nearly three generations after his death, there is still no definitive biography. Until such work appears, the most useful sources of biographical information are London's own works—e.g., *The Tramp Diary*, *The Road*, *The Cruise of the Snark*, *John Barleycorn*, and *The Letters*—reinforced by Russ Kingman's *Pictorial Life* and *Definitive Chronology*.

Critical and interpretive studies of London's work have for the most part been superior to the biographical efforts. The past quarter-century has witnessed a dramatic improvement in both the quantity and the quality of critical commentary. It appears that Jack London criticism has, in fact, finally begun to come of age. Considerable credit for this improvement is due to Hensley Woodbridge's publication of the *Jack London Newsletter* (1967–88), which provided an invaluable forum for London scholars. Further credit should be given to Russ Kingman as executive director of the Jack London Foundation and, more recently, to Jeanne Campbell Reesman as executive coordinator of the Jack London Society. Both organizations have served to enhance the *esprit de corps* of London buffs and to stimulate the work of London scholars, not only through their newsletters but also through such activities as the Annual Jack London Banquet and Foundation Auction, the presentation of London sessions at the conferences of the American Literature Association and Modern Language Association, and the biennial Jack London International Symposia. In like spirit during the past decade have been the many commendable London sessions organized by Tony Williams and, most recently, by Susan Nuernberg at the annual conferences of the Popular Culture Association. Finally, credit is due to those university presses—Minnesota, North Carolina, Stanford, Washington, and Wisconsin, for example—whose editors have been open-minded enough to perceive the importance of London's contributions to American literary history.

The following reading list, while necessarily brief, indicates some of the most significant literature—good as well as bad—that has been written about Jack London.

# BIOGRAPHICAL AND
# CRITICAL STUDIES

Bamford, Georgia Loring. *The Mystery of Jack London: Some of His Friends, Also a Few Letters—A Reminiscence.* Oakland, CA: Georgia Loring Bamford—Piedmont, 1931. Valuable source of firsthand information about London's early years and his friendship with Frederick Irons Bamford, fellow Socialist and director of the Oakland Public Library.

Bender, Bert. *Sea-Brothers: The Tradition of American Sea Fiction from "Moby-Dick" to the Present.* Philadelphia: University of Pennsylvania, 1988. Ranks London alongside such other "great figures in our tradition of sea literature" as Cooper, Dana, Melville, and Hemingway.

Beauchamp, Gorman. *Jack London.* Starmont Reader's Guide 15. Mercer Island, WA: Starmont House, 1984. Biographically erratic but critically astute commentary on London's fantasy and science-fiction writings.

Feied, Frederick. *No Pie in the Sky: The Hobo as American Cultural Hero in the Works of Jack London, John Dos Passos, and Jack Kerouac.* "Jack London was the first American writer of any significance to speak of the tramp or hobo from intimate knowledge and understanding."

Foner, Philip S., ed. *Jack London, American Rebel: A Collection of His Social Writings Together with an Extensive Study of the Man and His Times.* New York: Citadel, 1947. Substantial introduction with strong socialistic bias.

Hedrick, Joan D. *Solitary Comrade: Jack London and His Work.* Chapel Hill: University of North Carolina, 1982. Psycho-biographical analysis of London's career from his early work through *Martin Eden,* with admittedly "scant attention to the [last] third of London's active career."

Hendricks, King. *Jack London: Master Craftsman of the Short Story.* Logan: The Faculty Association, Utah State University, 1966. Indicates three major characteristics of London's artistry: ability to weave a narrative, to create atmosphere, and to use irony effectively; discusses "To Build a Fire," "Love of Life," "The Law of Life," and "The Chinago."

Johnston, Carolyn. *Jack London—An American Radical?* Westport, CT: Greenwood, 1984. Well-researched study of London's socialism.

Kingman, Russ. *A Pictorial Life of Jack London.* New York: Crown, 1979. Sympathetic and reliable.

———. *Jack London: A Definitive Chronology.* Middletown, CA: Rejl, 1992. The most detailed resource on London's life available.

Labor, Earle. *Jack London.* New York: Twayne, 1974. Succinct critical introduction to London's life and works.

Lachtman, Howard. *Sporting Blood: Selections from Jack London's Greatest Sports Writing.* Novato, CA: Presidio, 1981. Includes cogent critical evaluations of London's fiction and nonfiction.

London, Charmian K. *The Book of Jack London.* 2 vols. New York: Century, 1921. Invaluable if biased source of information about London's life and personality.

London, Joan. *Jack London and His Times: An Unconventional Biography.* New York: Doubleday, Doran, 1939; rpt. Seattle: University of Washington Press, 1968, with a new introduction by the author. Remarkably objective study by London's daughter; complements the biography by his widow.

Lundquist, James. *Jack London: Adventures, Ideas, and Fiction.* New York: Ungar, 1987. Brief introduction, useful despite occasional factual errors.

Martin, Stoddard. *California Writers: Jack London, John Steinbeck, The Tough Guys.* New York: St. Martin's, 1983. Original and perceptive, especially in discussions of music, racism, and women in London's novels. Asserts that London "represents the beginning of serious California literature."

McClintock, James I. *White Logic: Jack London's Short Stories*. Grand Rapids, MI: Wolf House Books, 1975. Especially strong in discussions of Jung and Hawaiian stories.

Ownbey, Ray Wilson, ed. *Jack London: Essays in Criticism*. Santa Barbara, CA: Peregrine Smith, 1978. Contains ten essays on major themes in London's work.

Sinclair, Andrew. *Jack: A Biography of Jack London*. New York: Harper & Row, 1977. Facile, misleading account of London's life and personality, with obsessive emphasis upon his medical problems.

Stasz, Clarice. *American Dreamers: Charmian and Jack London*. New York: St. Martin's, 1988. Particularly valuable for its depiction of Charmian as a prototype for the New Woman.

Stone, Irving. *Sailor on Horseback: The Biography of Jack London*. Boston: Houghton Mifflin, 1938. Enthusiastic but unreliable "Biographical Novel," as it was subtitled after reviewers discovered numerous passages plagiarized from London's own writings.

Tavernier-Courbin, Jacqueline, ed. *Critical Essays on Jack London*. Boston: G.K. Hall, 1983. Comprehensive collection with twenty-three essays on London, including important selections by H. L. Mencken, Carl Sandburg, Oliver Madox Hueffer, Anatole France, and Katherine Mansfield, along with useful pieces by contemporary academic critics and a substantial introductory essay on London as a professional writer. Also contains a "bibliographical update" of Sherman's *Reference Guide*.

Walcutt, Charles Child. *Jack London*. University of Minnesota Pamphlets on American Writers. Minneapolis: University of Minnesota, 1966. Occasionally perceptive but hastily composed and uneven in critical judgments.

Walker, Dale L. *The Alien Worlds of Jack London*. Grand Rapids, MI: Wolf House Books, 1973. Pioneering treatment of London's "fantasy fiction."

———. *Curious Fragments: Jack London's Tales of Fantasy Fiction*. Port Washington, NY: Kennikat, 1975. Excellent introduction by Walker and foreword by Philip José Farmer.

Walker, Franklin. *Jack London and the Klondike*. San Marino, CA: Huntington Library, 1966. Articulate and definitive.

Watson, Charles N., Jr. *The Novels of Jack London: A Reappraisal*. Madison: University of Wisconsin, 1983. Impeccably researched and perceptive.

Wilcox, Earl J., ed. *The Call of the Wild by Jack London: A Casebook with Text, Background Sources, Reviews, Critical Essays, and Bibliography.* Comprehensive edition for scholars and teachers.

Williams, Tony. *Jack London—The Movies.* Middletown, CA: Rejl, 1992. First extensive study of its subject, covering film and television adaptations of London works from 1913 to the present.

Zamen, Mark E. *Standing Room Only: Jack London's Controversial Career as a Public Speaker.* New York: Peter Lang, 1990. Useful discussions of this neglected aspect of London's career.

## BIBLIOGRAPHIES

Sherman, Joan R. *Jack London: A Reference Guide.* Boston: G.K. Hall, 1977. Annotated guide to secondary writings.

Walker, Dale L., and James E. Sisson, III, eds. *The Fiction of Jack London: A Chronological Bibliography.* El Paso: Texas Western, 1972. Annotated, with photographs.

Woodbridge, Hensley C., John London, and George H. Tweney, comps. *Jack London: A Bibliography.* Georgetown, CA: Talisman, 1966; enlarged ed., Millwood, NY: Kraus, 1973. Comprehensive listing of both primary and secondary items.

## JOURNALS
### *Special Jack London Issues*

*American Book Collector* 17:3 (November 1966).
*American Literary Realism 1870–1910* 24:2 (Winter 1992).
*Modern Fiction Studies* 22:1 (Spring 1976).
*The Pacific Historian* 21:2 (Summer 1977) and 24:2 (Summer 1980).
*Thalia: Studies in Literary Humor* 12:1–2 (1992).
*Western American Literature* 11:2 (Summer 1976).

# FOR THE BEST IN PAPERBACKS, LOOK FOR THE

In every corner of the world, on every subject under the sun, Penguin represents quality and variety—the very best in publishing today.

For complete information about books available from Penguin—including Puffins, Penguin Classics, and Arkana—and how to order them, write to us at the appropriate address below. Please note that for copyright reasons the selection of books varies from country to country.

**In the United Kingdom:** Please write to *Dept. JC, Penguin Books Ltd, FREEPOST, West Drayton, Middlesex UB7 0BR.*

If you have any difficulty in obtaining a title, please send your order with the correct money, plus ten percent for postage and packaging, to *P.O. Box No. 11, West Drayton, Middlesex UB7 0BR*

**In the United States:** Please write to *Consumer Sales, Penguin USA, P.O. Box 999, Dept. 17109, Bergenfield, New Jersey 07621-0120.* VISA and MasterCard holders call 1-800-253-6476 to order all Penguin titles

**In Canada:** Please write to *Penguin Books Canada Ltd, 10 Alcorn Avenue, Suite 300, Toronto, Ontario M4V 3B2*

**In Australia:** Please write to *Penguin Books Australia Ltd, P.O. Box 257, Ringwood, Victoria 3134*

**In New Zealand:** Please write to *Penguin Books (NZ) Ltd, Private Bag 102902, North Shore Mail Centre, Auckland 10*

**In India:** Please write to *Penguin Books India Pvt Ltd, 706 Eros Apartments, 56 Nehru Place, New Delhi 110 019*

**In the Netherlands:** Please write to *Penguin Books Netherlands bv, Postbus 3507, NL-1001 AH Amsterdam*

**In Germany:** Please write to *Penguin Books Deutschland GmbH, Metzlerstrasse 26, 60594 Frankfurt am Main*

**In Spain:** Please write to *Penguin Books S. A., Bravo Murillo 19, 1° B, 28015 Madrid*

**In Italy:** Please write to *Penguin Italia s.r.l., Via Felice Casati 20, I-20124 Milano*

**In France:** Please write to *Penguin France S. A., 17 rue Lejeune, F–31000 Toulouse*

**In Japan:** Please write to *Penguin Books Japan, Ishikiribashi Building, 2–5–4, Suido, Bunkyo-ku, Tokyo 112*

**In Greece:** Please write to *Penguin Hellas Ltd, Dimocritou 3, GR–106 71 Athens*

**In South Africa:** Please write to *Longman Penguin Southern Africa (Pty) Ltd, Private Bag X08, Bertsham 2013*